- KPSV -

*The Editors*

MARY HENLEY RUBIO and ELIZABETH WATERSTON are both Professors Emeriti of the University of Guelph, Ontario, Canada. They are coeditors of *The Selected Journals of L. M. Montgomery, Volumes I* (1985), *II* (1987), *III* (1992), *IV* (1998), and *V* (2004). They are also coauthors of *Writing a Life: L. M. Montgomery* (1993), a short biography. Together in 1975 they founded and for over two decades served as editors of the academic journal *CCL: Canadian Children's Literature*. Their many other individual publications include Dr. Rubio's edition of *Harvesting Thistles: The Textual Garden of L. M. Montgomery* (1994) and Dr. Waterston's *Children's Literature in Canada* (1992), *Kindling Spirit: L. M. Montgomery's "Anne of Green Gables"* (1994), and *Rapt in Plaid: Canadian Literature and the Scottish Tradition* (2001). Dr. Rubio is completing an indepth biography of Montgomery to be published with Doubleday, and is working with the University of Guelph Library on a website called the "L. M. Montgomery Research Center."

A NORTON CRITICAL EDITION

# L. M. Montgomery
# ANNE OF GREEN GABLES

AUTHORITATIVE TEXT
BACKGROUNDS
CRITICISM

*Edited by*

MARY HENLEY RUBIO
UNIVERSITY OF GUELPH

*and*

ELIZABETH WATERSTON
UNIVERSITY OF GUELPH

W • W • NORTON & COMPANY • *New York* • *London*

W. W. Norton & Company has been independent since its founding in 1923, when William Warder Norton and Mary D. Herter Norton first published lectures delivered at the People's Institute, the adult education division of New York City's Cooper Union. The Nortons soon expanded their program beyond the Institute, publishing books by celebrated academics from America and abroad. By mid-century, the two major pillars of Norton's publishing program—trade books and college texts—were firmly established. In the 1950s, the Norton family trans-ferred control of the company to its employees, and today—with a staff of four hundred and a comparable number of trade, college, and professional titles pub-lished each year—W. W. Norton & Company stands as the largest and oldest publishing house owned wholly by its employees.

Every effort has been made to contact the copyright holders of each of the selections. Rights holders of any selections not credited should contact W. W. Norton & Company, Inc. for a correction to be made in the next printing of our work.

The text of this book is composed in Fairfield Medium
with the display set in Bernhard Modern.
Composition by Binghamton Valley Composition.
Series design by Antonina Krass.
Manufacturing by the Maple-Vail Book Group, Binghamton.
Production manager: Benjamin Reynolds.

Library of Congress Cataloging-in-Publication Data

Montgomery, L. M. (Lucy Maud), 1874–1942.
Anne of Green Gables : authoritative text, backgrounds, criticism /
L. M. Montgomery ; edited by Mary Henley Rubio and Elizabeth Waterston.
p. cm. — (A Norton critical edition)
Includes bibliographical references.

**ISBN-13: 978-0-393-92695-8 (pbk.)**
**ISBN-10: 0-393-92695-8 (pbk.)**

1. Montgomery, L. M. (Lucy Maud), 1874–1942. Anne of Green Gables.
2. Shirley, Anne (Fictitious character)—Fiction. 3. Girls—Fiction. 4. Orphans—
Fiction. 5. Friendship—Fiction. 6. Country life—Fiction. 7. Prince Edward
Island—Fiction. I. Rubio, Mary, 1939– II. Waterston, Elizabeth, 1922– III. Title.
PR9199.3.M6A75 2006
813'.52—dc22
2006047241

W. W. Norton & Company, Inc., 500 Fifth Avenue,
New York, N.Y. 10110-0017
www.wwnorton.com

W. W. Norton & Company Ltd., Castle House,
75/76 Wells Street, London W1T 3QT

1 2 3 4 5 6 7 8 9 0

# Contents

v

# Criticism

# Preface

In 1908, Lucy Maud Montgomery and her Boston publisher, L. C. Page, found to their surprise that *Anne of Green Gables* was an international best seller. Mark Twain wrote the unknown author, comparing her creation to "the immortal Alice"; Earl Grey, Governor General of Canada, insisted on meeting L. M. Montgomery; Swedish and Polish translators rushed to put the novel into the hands of foreign readers. The original audience of *Anne of Green Gables* was a mix of children and adults, men and women, simple readers and sophisticated ones.

Surprise has always been a keynote with *Anne of Green Gables*. The book itself begins with the surprise of a staid community when a red-headed orphan erupts into it. The thirty-four-year-old author who lived inconspicuously in a similar quiet village was jolted into a surprising new life of demands for sequels. Readers, including many would-be writers, were surprised by the book's affirmation of the values of imagination, friendship, and self-expression.

In the first decade after 1908, that rapturous readership persisted. Tourism to "Anne's Island" began to reflect the growing circle of "kindred spirits." In a world going awry with World War I, *Anne of Green Gables* offered consolation in the story of a happier, more manageable time. Then, during the 1920s and 30s, literary critics dimmed their approval of the book, deflected by modernism toward more abstruse novels like James Joyce's *Ulysses* and William Faulkner's *The Sound and the Fury*.

Nevertheless a world-wide circle of uncritical fans continued to grow. Translation into at least seventeen more languages expanded the numbers of readers, stirring up "Anne subcultures" in places as far away as Japan and Poland. Fan letters rolled in from an astonishing array of men and women, including two British Prime Ministers, Stanley Baldwin and Ramsay Macdonald. Soon films (first a "silent" one, and then a "talkie") further enlarged the audience for *Anne of Green Gables*.

In the 1980s, three-quarters of a century after Montgomery's book first appeared, there was to be another surprise. Readers were amazed to learn that for fifty-three years Lucy Maud Montgomery had secretly kept an unpredictably frank diary. Selections of these journals, published in five volumes beginning in 1985, chronicle the complex life of an often-frustrated creative woman. They suggest an unexpected disconnect between the funny, winsome character of "Anne" and the darker, driven woman who created her.

A new audience for *Anne of Green Gables* has now emerged. Montgomery's critical star began rising again with feminism, and with the growing interest in children's literature and popular culture. The novel has been co-opted by social historians, gender critics, and ecologists. Psychologists now note the angst and strain beneath Anne's vivacious surface. Literary critics debate the influence of British and American Romanticism on Montgomery, noting how closely she annotated her own copies of Byron, Scott, Whittier, Wordsworth, and Longfellow. Postcolonialists ponder the imperial overtones in Avonlea, theologians discuss the certitudes of a Presbyterian community and the Emersonian pantheism of Anne. A reader today can approach the novel with a new seriousness.

This Norton Critical Edition brings the book to a new audience. It opens with the annotated text of *Anne of Green Gables*, in its original April 1908 form, including original illustrations. A list of textual variations follows, plus a revelation of the additions made to the handwritten manuscript, showing the way the author reworked her novel. Selected passages quoted from the stories and poems that Montgomery read in her formative years, as well as from the writing of her contemporaries, illuminate her literary context. Her own journal entries about or related to *Anne of Green Gables* fill out the biographical and cultural background.

From the growing pile of books and articles about the novel, excerpts will reveal the many ways readers can approach and enjoy *Anne of Green Gables*. Contributors to this collection of modern views include critics from Australia, Canada, Sweden, and the Unites States; established scholars and younger critics; men and women; academics and "ordinary readers." Sociocultural studies turn to the world of books Montgomery moved through (Karr), the publishing market she worked in (Gerson), the local society she inhabited (Wood), or the cultural and religious background she inherited (Rubio). *Anne of Green Gables* can be read as a well-wrought romance, though an ambiguous one (Epperly); some of its ambiguities can be seen as concealing a resistance to heterosexual marriage (Gubar), while others are interpreted as revealing the valorization of motherhood (Devereux). One critic can extol Anne's power of imagination (Åhmansson) while another can emphasize her anxieties (Davey). One critic sets this novel into the American sequence of *Little Women* and *Rebecca of Sunnybrook Farm* (MacLulich), but a historian warns literary critics against this comparative method (Careless). On a particular such as Anne's red hair the book can be connected to a British literary chain, from Walter Scott to George Eliot (McMaster). The story can be seen as set within a landscape that is both objective and subjective (Johnston). As story, the novel can be admired for its careful structure (Waterston). Finally, one can approach this book by studying many readers' responses to it (Ross and Trillin), or can ponder the response of one particular reader (Atwood or Shields). These excerpts were selected—with difficulty—from an impressive body of excellent books and articles that we regretfully set aside in choosing a representative range of approaches. Readers may consult the Selected Bibliography for further biographical and critical materials.

At the close of this volume, a chronological table recalls those details of the author's life and region that passed through the alembic of her imagination to form this surprising novel. The arguments about its meanings go on, augmented by new presentations in film and television and on stage, and moving from the printed page to the Internet, where new networks of "Anne fans" and "Anne analysts" surface.

The critical superstructure is intriguing. In the end, however, one can return to the novel itself and find there the original enchantment.

Mary Henley Rubio
Elizabeth Waterston
UNIVERSITY OF GUELPH
GUELPH, ONTARIO, CANADA

# Acknowledgments

L. M. Montgomery's son, the late Dr. E. Stuart Macdonald, entrusted us with editing and publishing his mother's journals. This Norton text and our other Montgomery projects from 1980 to the present have been generously supported by grants from the Social Sciences and Humanities Research Council of Canada, with other assistance through the Office of Research at the University of Guelph and the Deans of Arts.

Librarians, archivists, and staff at the University of Guelph have been most helpful over the years, collecting and facilitating the use of the "L. M. Montgomery Collection" and the "Scottish Collection": Linda Amichand, Margaret Beckman, Lorne Bruce, Virginia Gillham, Bernard Katz, Ellen Morrison, Michael Ridley, Nancy Sadek, Helen Salmon, and Darlene Wiltsie. Thanks also go to the Interlibrary Loan staff at the University of Guelph, and to Miki Goral of the Education Library at the University of California at Los Angeles (UCLA).

Among our colleagues and friends in Prince Edward Island, we gratefully mention John and Jennie Macneill at Montgomery's Cavendish home, George and Maureen Campbell at Park Corner, Father Francis Bolger of Stanley Bridge, Dr. Angus Beck of Charlottetown, and Elizabeth DeBlois at the L. M. Montgomery Institute. We are especially indebted to Elizabeth Epperly for her assistance with manuscripts and for her wide-ranging in-depth scholarship on Montgomery; to Kevin Rice at the Confederation Centre in Charlottetown, who (with Judy Simpson) facilitated our access to the manuscript of *Anne of Green Gables* and to the handwritten additions to it; and to Simon Lloyd, archivist at the University of Prince Edward Island's Robertson Library, for making their collections of rare editions of *Anne of Green Gables* available to us.

Kindred spirits who have added to our understanding of Montgomery's influence abroad are Gabriella Åhmansson in Sweden, Yuko Izawa and Yoshiko Akamatsu in Japan, Jennifer H. Litster and Owen Dudley Edwards in Edinburgh, Margaret Anne Doody, Wendy Barry, and Beth Calvert in the United States, Barbara Wachowicz in Poland, Huifeng Hu in China and Kathy Jia (formerly of China), Bharati Parikh in India, and Mary McDonald-Rissanen in Finland.

In Canada, we are indebted to many other scholars, researchers, and editors like Paul and Hildi Froese Tiessen, Cecily Devereux, Irene Gammel, Laura Robinson, Marie C. Davis, Carolyn Strom Collins, Virginia Careless, Mary E. Doody Jones, Ben Lefebvre, and Yuka Kajihara, whose work on Montgomery has contributed to our knowledge. We also thank Judith Grant, author of a biography on Robertson Davies, and Marj Kohli for information on the Barnardo and other child relocation societies. Collectors Donna Jane Campbell of Ontario, who has donated her Montgomery collection to the L. M. Montgomery Institute at University of Prince Edward Island, and Ron I. Cohen of Ottawa, who has donated his Montgomery collection to the National Library of Canada, have greatly facilitated research on Montgomery's publishing history.

Especial thanks go to Bernard Katz, retired head of Archival and Special Collections, University of Guelph, a noted authority on Montgomery editions and publishing history, for his advice on editions and copyright law; to Evan W. Siddall for research into the Page Company in 1989–90; to the late Roger W. Straus and Robert Wohlforth of Farrar, Straus & Giroux who consented to interviews in 1991 about their acquisition of the L. C. Page Company; to the late W. Peter Coues, cousin and literary executor of L. C. Page, who kindly provided information in letters and interviews in the early 1990s.

The heirs of L. M. Montgomery—especially Ruth Macdonald, and also Kate Macdonald Butler and David Macdonald—have always supported our work. *Anne of Green Gables* and other indicia of "Anne" are trademarks and/or Canadian official marks of the Anne of Green Gables Licensing Authority Inc. *L. M. Montgomery, Emily of New Moon, The Story Girl,* and *The Blue Castle* and related indicia, characters, and names are also trademarks of the Heirs of L. M. Montgomery Inc.

Quotations from *The Selected Journals of L. M. Montgomery, Volumes I, II,* and *IV* (© 1985, 1987, 1998 University of Guelph), edited by Mary Rubio and Elizabeth Waterston and published by Oxford University Press, are reprinted with the permission of Oxford University Press Canada, with the consent of the editors and the University of Guelph, courtesy of the of L. M. Montgomery Collection, Archival and Special Collections, University of Guelph Library. The excerpt from Elizabeth Epperly's *The Fragrance of Sweet-Grass* (1992), and those from articles by Frank Davey, Carole Gerson, and Juliet McMaster in *Making Avonlea: L. M. Montgomery & Popular Culture,* ed. Irene Gammel (2002), are all reprinted by permission of the University of Toronto Press. Excerpts from Cecily Devereux and from Virginia Careless, from *Windows and Words: A Look at Canadian Children's Literature in English,* ed. Aïda Hudson and Susan-Ann Cooper (2003), are reprinted by permission of the University of Ottawa Press. The excerpt from Marah Gubar, from *The Lion and the Unicorn* 25.1, is reprinted with permission of the Johns Hopkins University Press. The excerpt from Elizabeth Waterston, *Kindling Spirit: L. M. Montgomery's "Anne of Green Gables"* (1993), is reprinted by permission of ECW Press. Selections from the work of Gabriella Åhmansson, Margaret Atwood, Rosemary Ross Johnston, Clarence Karr, Mary Henley Rubio, Catherine Sheldrick Ross, and Kate Wood are all reprinted by gracious consent of the authors, and the selection from T. D. MacLulich, by permission of his estate.

Our indispensable M.A. student research assistants were Angela Lombardi and Patrick Firth who helped compare copy-texts, update the Selected Bibliography, and scan articles. Katie Waterston deciphered and typed up LMM's manuscript additions and, with Tony Collins, Jennie Rubio, and Chris Lee, furnished valuable technical assistance and advice. We are deeply grateful to freelance editor Morgan Dennis for his extensive, wide-ranging, and invaluable editorial services on this and other Montgomery projects.

Jackie Kaiser of Westwood Creative Artists in Toronto facilitated this project. Carol Bemis, our editor at W. W. Norton, encouraged us from the outset; she and her assistant editor, Brian Baker, provided prompt, clear help throughout the process; copy-editor Katharine Nicholson Ings, who grew up in Prince Edward Island, cast a specially keen eye on the final manuscript.

Douglas Waterston and G. D. Killam put up with us when we were in editing mode. We are both fortunate in having wonderful, supportive families.

M. H. R.
E. W.

# Abbreviations

Throughout this volume the following abbreviations have been adopted:

AGG = *Anne of Green Gables*
LMM = L. M. Montgomery
SJ = *The Selected Journals of L. M. Montgomery*
PEI = Prince Edward Island
NCE = Norton Critical Edition
UP = University Press

# The Text of
# ANNE OF GREEN GABLES

# ANNE OF GREEN GABLES

By
L. M. MONTGOMERY

Illustrated by
M. A. and W. A. J. CLAUS

" The good stars met in your horoscope,
Made you of spirit and fire and dew."
— *Browning*.

BOSTON ❧ L. C. PAGE &
COMPANY ❧ MDCCCCVIII

Title page of the first edition (Boston: L. C. Page & Company, 1908).

TO THE MEMORY OF
## 𝔐𝔶 𝔉𝔞𝔱𝔥𝔢𝔯 𝔞𝔫𝔡 𝔐𝔬𝔱𝔥𝔢𝔯

# Illustrations

# Contents

---

* In the original L. C. Page edition, Mrs. Lynde's name is spelled as "RACHAEL" on the Contents page and as "RACHEL" throughout the text. This error was not corrected in subsequent printings of the first edition.

"THERE'S SOMETHING SO STYLISH ABOUT YOU, ANNE," SAID DIANA

# Anne of Green Gables

## Chapter I

### MRS. RACHEL LYNDE IS SURPRISED

MRS. RACHEL LYNDE lived just where the Avonlea[1] main road dipped down into a little hollow, fringed with alders and ladies' eardrops[2] and traversed by a brook that had its source away back in the woods of the old Cuthbert place; it was reputed to be an intricate, headlong brook in its earlier course through those woods, with dark secrets of pool and cascade; but by the time it reached Lynde's Hollow it was a quiet, well-conducted little stream, for not even a brook could run past Mrs. Rachel Lynde's door without due regard for decency and decorum; it probably was conscious that Mrs. Rachel was sitting at her window, keeping a sharp eye on everything that passed, from brooks and children up, and that if she noticed anything odd or out of place she would never rest until she had ferreted out the whys and wherefores thereof.

There are plenty of people, in Avonlea and out of it, who can attend closely to their neighbours' business by dint of neglecting their own; but Mrs. Rachel Lynde was one of those capable creatures who can manage their own concerns and those of other folks into the bargain. She was a notable housewife; her work was always done and well done; she "ran" the Sewing Circle, helped run the Sunday-school, and was the strongest prop of the Church Aid Society and Foreign Missions Auxiliary.[3] Yet with all this Mrs. Rachel found abundant time to sit for hours at her kitchen window, knitting "cot-

---

1. An imaginary rural village based on L. M. Montgomery's own Scottish-Canadian community of Cavendish, Prince Edward Island, Canada; the Cuthbert place and Lynde's Hollow are based on the houses of her Macneill relatives in Cavendish.
2. A small variety of *impatiens*, called "jewelweed" in the handwritten manuscript of *AGG*.
3. Mrs. Lynde dominates in women's groups serving the family (in the Circle where they sew and gossip), the children (in the Sunday classes where children learn Bible stories, sing hymns, and recite catechisms, as established one hundred years earlier in England to bring religion and literacy to slum children), the religion (in the Aid where they raise money to furnish the Church and assist needy families), and in the world community (where they helped support missionaries in Western Canada and abroad). LMM delighted to show the way such women interacted with the men who were nominally in power as husbands, managers, and ministers. Cf. LMM's 1903 story, "The Strike at Putney [Church]."

ton warp"[4] quilts—she had knitted sixteen of them, as Avonlea housekeepers were wont to tell in awed voices—and keeping a sharp eye on the main road that crossed the hollow and wound up the steep red hill beyond. Since Avonlea occupied a little triangular peninsula jutting out into the Gulf of St. Lawrence,[5] with water on two sides of it, anybody who went out of it or into it had to pass over that hill road and so run the unseen gauntlet of Mrs. Rachel's all-seeing eye.

She was sitting there one afternoon in early June. The sun was coming in at the window warm and bright; the orchard on the slope below the house was in a bridal flush of pinky-white bloom, hummed over by a myriad of bees. Thomas Lynde—a meek little man whom Avonlea people called "Rachel Lynde's husband"—was sowing his late turnip seed on the hill field beyond the barn; and Matthew Cuthbert ought to have been sowing his on the big red brook field away over by Green Gables.[6] Mrs. Rachel knew that he ought because she had heard him tell Peter Morrison the evening before in William J. Blair's store over at Carmody[7] that he meant to sow his turnip seed the next afternoon. Peter had asked him, of course, for Matthew Cuthbert had never been known to volunteer information about anything in his whole life.

And yet here was Matthew Cuthbert, at half-past three on the afternoon of a busy day, placidly driving over the hollow and up the hill; moreover, he wore a white collar and his best suit of clothes, which was plain proof that he was going out of Avonlea; and he had the buggy and the sorrel mare,[8] which betokened that he was going a considerable distance. Now, where was Matthew Cuthbert going and why was he going there?

Had it been any other man in Avonlea Mrs. Rachel, deftly putting this and that together, might have given a pretty good guess as to both questions. But Matthew so rarely went from home that it must be something pressing and unusual which was taking him; he was the shyest man alive and hated to have to go among strangers or to any place where he might have to talk. Matthew, dressed up with a white collar and driving in a buggy, was something that didn't happen

---

4. Made from thread normally used to set up weaving on a handloom.
5. PEI is a small island in this gulf, the largest estuary in the world; water from the Great Lakes flows through the St Lawrence River to the Atlantic Ocean through this gulf.
6. The Cuthbert house, so-named because the gables (the triangular upper section of the walls under the sloping part of the roof) were painted green for decoration. Many PEI people followed the British fashion of naming houses. (The "Green Gables" house is preserved in a national park in Cavendish, PEI.)
7. The nearest village with a seed store; perhaps based on Stanley Bridge, where Cavendish people bought supplies.
8. An open four-wheeled carriage, drawn by a reddish-brown mare, not by the heavier horses used for fieldwork.

often. Mrs. Rachel, ponder as she might, could make nothing of it and her afternoon's enjoyment was spoiled.

"I'll just step over to Green Gables after tea and find out from Marilla[9] where he's gone and why," the worthy woman finally concluded. "He doesn't generally go to town this time of year and he *never* visits; if he'd run out of turnip seed he wouldn't dress up and take the buggy to go for more; he wasn't driving fast enough to be going for a doctor. Yet something must have happened since last night to start him off. I'm clean puzzled, that's what, and I won't know a minute's peace of mind or conscience until I know what has taken Matthew Cuthbert out of Avonlea to-day."

Accordingly after tea Mrs. Rachel set out; she had not far to go; the big, rambling, orchard-embowered house where the Cuthberts lived was a scant quarter of a mile up the road from Lynde's Hollow. To be sure, the long lane made it a good deal further. Matthew Cuthbert's father, as shy and silent as his son after him, had got as far away as he possibly could from his fellow men without actually retreating into the woods when he founded his homestead.[1] Green Gables was built at the furthest edge of his cleared land and there it was to this day, barely visible from the main road along which all the other Avonlea houses were so sociably situated. Mrs. Rachel Lynde did not call living in such a place *living* at all.

"It's just *staying*, that's what," she said as she stepped along the deep-rutted, grassy lane bordered with wild rose bushes. "It's no wonder Matthew and Marilla are both a little odd, living away back here by themselves. Trees aren't much company, though dear knows if they were there'd be enough of them. I'd ruther look at people. To be sure, they seem contented enough; but then, I suppose, they're used to it. A body can get used to anything, even to being hanged, as the Irishman said."[2]

With this Mrs. Rachel stepped out of the lane into the backyard of Green Gables. Very green and neat and precise was that yard, set about on one side with great patriarchal willows and on the other with prim Lombardies.[3] Not a stray stick nor stone was to be seen, for Mrs. Rachel would have seen it if there had been. Privately she was of the opinion that Marilla Cuthbert swept that yard over as

---

9. This unusual name, Celtic in origin (meaning "shining sea"), is not a biblical name, like Matthew and Rachel; nor is it unique to *AGG*: for instance, Marilla Ricker (b.1840) became New Hampshire's first woman lawyer.
1. The property (with house and outbuildings) originally derived from a British crown grant in the 1790s.
2. A folk-saying that stereotypes the Irish as comical (and perhaps criminal), marking the bias of a Scottish community like Avonlea.
3. Tall thin poplar trees not common in PEI.

often as she swept her house. One could have eaten a meal off the ground without overbrimming the proverbial peck of dirt.[4]

Mrs. Rachel rapped smartly at the kitchen door and stepped in when bidden to do so. The kitchen at Green Gables was a cheerful apartment—or would have been cheerful if it had not been so painfully clean as to give it something of the appearance of an unused parlour. Its windows looked east and west; through the west one, looking out on the back yard, came a flood of mellow June sunlight; but the east one, whence you got a glimpse of the bloom white cherry-trees in the left orchard and nodding, slender birches down in the hollow by the brook, was greened over by a tangle of vines. Here sat Marilla Cuthbert, when she sat at all, always slightly distrustful of sunshine, which seemed to her too dancing and irresponsible a thing for a world which was meant to be taken seriously; and here she sat now, knitting, and the table behind her was laid for supper.

Mrs. Rachel, before she had fairly closed the door, had taken mental note of everything that was on that table. There were three plates laid, so that Marilla must be expecting some one home with Matthew to tea;[5] but the dishes were every-day dishes and there was only crab-apple preserves and one kind of cake, so that the expected company could not be any particular company. Yet what of Matthew's white collar and the sorrel mare? Mrs. Rachel was getting fairly dizzy with this unusual mystery about quiet, unmysterious Green Gables.

"Good evening, Rachel," Marilla said briskly. "This is a real fine evening, isn't it? Won't you sit down? How are all your folks?"

Something that for lack of any other name might be called friendship existed and always had existed between Marilla Cuthbert and Mrs. Rachel, in spite of—or perhaps because of—their dissimilarity.

Marilla was a tall, thin woman, with angles and without curves; her dark hair showed some gray streaks and was always twisted up in a hard little knot behind with two wire hairpins stuck aggressively through it. She looked like a woman of narrow experience and rigid conscience, which she was; but there was a saving something about her mouth which, if it had been ever so slightly developed, might have been considered indicative of a sense of humour.

"We're all pretty well," said Mrs. Rachel. "I was kind of afraid *you* weren't, though, when I saw Matthew starting off to-day. I thought maybe he was going to the doctor's."

Marilla's lips twitched understandingly. She had expected Mrs. Rachel up; she had known that the sight of Matthew jaunting off so unaccountably would be too much for her neighbour's curiosity.

4. The folk-saying "You have to eat a peck [eight quarts] of dirt in your lifetime" justifies careless housekeepers.
5. Light meal in late afternoon or evening.

"Oh, no, I'm quite well although I had a bad headache yesterday," she said. "Matthew went to Bright River. We're getting a little boy from an orphan asylum in Nova Scotia and he's coming on the train to-night."

If Marilla had said that Matthew had gone to Bright River[6] to meet a kangaroo from Australia Mrs. Rachel could not have been more astonished. She was actually stricken dumb for five seconds. It was unsupposable that Marilla was making fun of her, but Mrs. Rachel was almost forced to suppose it.

"Are you in earnest, Marilla?" she demanded when voice returned to her.

"Yes, of course," said Marilla, as if getting boys from orphan asylums[7] in Nova Scotia were part of the usual spring work on any well-regulated Avonlea farm instead of being an unheard of innovation.

Mrs. Rachel felt that she had received a severe mental jolt. She thought in exclamation points. A boy! Marilla and Matthew Cuthbert of all people adopting a boy! From an orphan asylum! Well, the world was certainly turning upside down! She would be surprised at nothing after this! Nothing!

"What on earth put such a notion into your head?" she demanded disapprovingly.

This had been done without her advice being asked, and must perforce be disapproved.

"Well, we've been thinking about it for some time—all winter in fact," returned Marilla. "Mrs. Alexander Spencer was up here one day before Christmas and she said she was going to get a little girl from the asylum over in Hopetown[8] in the spring. Her cousin lives there and Mrs. Spencer has visited her and knows all about it. So Matthew and I have talked it over off and on ever since. We thought we'd get a boy. Matthew is getting up in years, you know—he's sixty—and he isn't so spry as he once was. His heart troubles him a good deal. And you know how desperate hard it's got to be to get hired help. There's never anybody to be had but those stupid, half-grown little French boys;[9] and as soon as you do get one broke into your ways and taught something he's up and off to the lobster canneries or the States.[1] At first Matthew suggested getting a Barnardo

<hr>

6. Nearest town to the west of Avonlea with a train station, based on Hunter River, PEI.
7. Institutions housing the many children of indigent or dead parents. Commonly sent to foster families, orphans earned their keep on the farm or with housework. The first official orphanage in PEI was St Vincent's Orphanage which opened in 1910, operated by the Roman Catholic Diocese of Charlottetown. It closed in 1963. The first Protestant orphanage opened in 1922.
8. An imaginary town in Nova Scotia, Canada.
9. Marilla reflects Anglophone attitudes of condescension to the French, descendants of the first Europeans to settle in PEI. (Most of the French were expelled after the British occupation in 1763, as part of the Acadian clearance to Louisiana, then a French colony.)
1. A reflection of a general exodus to the United States of America or the Canadian West

boy.[2] But I said 'no' flat to that. 'They may be all right—I'm not saying they're not—but no London street Arabs[3] for me,' I said. 'Give me a native born at least. There'll be a risk, no matter who we get. But I'll feel easier in my mind and sleep sounder at nights if we get a born Canadian.' So in the end we decided to ask Mrs. Spencer to pick us out one when she went over to get her little girl. We heard last week she was going, so we sent her word by Richard Spencer's folks at Carmody to bring us a smart, likely boy of about ten or eleven. We decided that would be the best age—old enough to be of some use in doing chores right off and young enough to be trained up proper. We mean to give him a good home and schooling. We had a telegram from Mrs. Alexander Spencer to-day—the mail-man brought it from the station—saying they were coming on the five-thirty train to-night. So Matthew went to Bright River to meet him. Mrs. Spencer will drop him off there. Of course she goes on to White Sands[4] station herself."

Mrs. Rachel prided herself on always speaking her mind; she proceeded to speak it now, having adjusted her mental attitude to this amazing piece of news.

"Well, Marilla, I'll just tell you plain that I think you're doing a mighty foolish thing—a risky thing, that's what. You don't know what you're getting. You're bringing a strange child into your house and home and you don't know a single thing about him nor what his disposition is like nor what sort of parents he had nor how he's likely to turn out. Why, it was only last week I read in the paper[5] how a man and his wife up west of the Island took a boy out of an orphan asylum and he set fire to the house at night—set it *on purpose*, Marilla—and nearly burnt them to a crisp in their beds. And I know another case where an adopted boy used to suck the eggs—they couldn't break him of it. If you had asked my advice in the matter—which you didn't do, Marilla—I'd have said for mercy's sake not to think of such a thing, that's what."

This Job's comforting[6] seemed neither to offend nor alarm Marilla. She knitted steadily on.

---

during the late nineteenth and early twentieth century. Insufficient farming land or employment (e.g., in the lobster canneries) resulted in a net loss in the PEI population. The population of PEI peaked at 109,000 in 1891, then steadily declined for decades. It was 1971 before the population exceeded 109,000 again.

2. Children taken from British urban slums by Dr. Thomas Barnardo, an English philanthropist, and relocated to Canada or Australia, to provide cheap farm labor. The 1908 American edition misspelled this as "Barnado" and the 1925 British edition changed Barnardo to "Home."

3. Derogatory name for homeless children fending for themselves in the streets of nineteenth-century English cities.

4. Nearest town to the east of Avonlea with a train station, based on Rustico.

5. PEI newspapers in the late Victorian period carried comparable lurid stories.

6. Lugubrious suggestions offered by Job's friends when God tests his faith by inflicting many forms of suffering. *Holy Bible*, Job 4–31.

"I don't deny there's something in what you say, Rachel. I've had some qualms myself. But Matthew was terrible set on it. I could see that, so I gave in. It's so seldom Matthew sets his mind on anything that when he does I always feel it's my duty to give in. And as for the risk, there's risks in pretty near everything a body does in this world. There's risks in people's having children of their own if it comes to that—they don't always turn out well. And then Nova Scotia is right close to the Island. It isn't as if we were getting him from England or the States. He can't be much different from ourselves."

"Well, I hope it will turn out all right," said Mrs. Rachel in a tone that plainly indicated her painful doubts. "Only don't say I didn't warn you if he burns Green Gables down or puts strychnine[7] in the well—I heard of a case over in New Brunswick[8] where an orphan asylum child did that and the whole family died in fearful agonies. Only, it was a girl in that instance."

"Well, we're not getting a girl," said Marilla, as if poisoning wells were a purely feminine accomplishment and not to be dreaded in the case of a boy. "I'd never dream of taking a girl to bring up. I wonder at Mrs. Alexander Spencer for doing it. But there, *she* wouldn't shrink from adopting a whole orphan asylum if she took it into her head."

Mrs. Rachel would have liked to stay until Matthew came home with his imported orphan. But reflecting that it would be a good two hours at least before his arrival she concluded to go up the road to Robert Bell's and tell them the news. It would certainly make a sensation second to none, and Mrs. Rachel dearly loved to make a sensation. So she took herself away, somewhat to Marilla's relief, for the latter felt her doubts and fears reviving under the influence of Mrs. Rachel's pessimism.

"Well, of all things that ever were or will be!" ejaculated Mrs. Rachel when she was safely out in the lane. "It does really seem as if I must be dreaming. Well, I'm sorry for that poor young one and no mistake. Matthew and Marilla don't know anything about children and they'll expect him to be wiser and steadier than his own grandfather, if so be's he ever had a grandfather, which is doubtful. It seems uncanny to think of a child at Green Gables somehow; there's never been one there, for Matthew and Marilla were grown up when the new house was built—if they ever *were* children, which is hard to believe when one looks at them. I wouldn't be in that orphan's shoes for anything. My, but I pity him, that's what."

So said Mrs. Rachel to the wild rose bushes out of the fulness of her heart; but if she could have seen the child who was waiting

7. A highly poisonous alkaloid distilled from the plant Deadly Nightshade.
8. Like PEI, and Nova Scotia, a province in the Canadian "Maritimes," now (along with Newfoundland) called Atlantic Canada.

patiently at the Bright River station at that very moment her pity would have been still deeper and more profound.

## Chapter II

### MATTHEW CUTHBERT IS SURPRISED

Matthew Cuthbert and the sorrel mare jogged comfortably over the eight miles to Bright River. It was a pretty road, running along between snug farmsteads, with now and again a bit of balsamy fir wood to drive through or a hollow where wild plums hung out their filmy bloom. The air was sweet with the breath of many apple orchards and the meadows sloped away in the distance to horizon mists of pearl and purple; while

> "The little birds sang as if it were
> The one day of summer in all the year."[1]

Matthew enjoyed the drive after his own fashion, except during the moments when he met women and had to nod to them—for in Prince Edward Island you are supposed to nod to all and sundry you meet on the road whether you know them or not.

Matthew dreaded all women except Marilla and Mrs. Rachel; he had an uncomfortable feeling that the mysterious creatures were secretly laughing at him. He may have been quite right in thinking so, for he was an odd-looking personage, with an ungainly figure and long iron-gray hair that touched his stooping shoulders, and a full, soft brown beard which he had worn ever since he was twenty. In fact, he had looked at twenty very much as he looked at sixty, lacking a little of the grayness.

When he reached Bright River there was no sign of any train; he thought he was too early, so he tied his horse in the yard of the small Bright River hotel and went over to the station-house. The long platform was almost deserted; the only living creature in sight being a girl who was sitting on a pile of shingles[2] at the extreme end. Matthew, barely noting that it *was* a girl, sidled past her as quickly as possible without looking at her. Had he looked he could hardly have failed to notice the tense rigidity and expectation of her attitude and expression. She was sitting there waiting for something or somebody and, since sitting and waiting was the only thing to do just then, she sat and waited with all her might and main.

Matthew encountered the station-master locking up the ticket-

---

1. Slight variation from American James Russell Lowell, "The Vision of Sir Launfal" (1848) 1. 2.3–4.
2. Rectangular slips of wood ready for use in roofing or siding.

office preparatory to going home for supper, and asked him if the five-thirty train would soon be along.

"The five-thirty train has been in and gone half an hour ago," answered that brisk official. "But there was a passenger dropped off for you—a little girl. She's sitting out there on the shingles. I asked her to go into the ladies' waiting-room, but she informed me gravely that she preferred to stay outside. 'There was more scope for imagination,'[3] she said. She's a case,[4] I should say."

"I'm not expecting a girl," said Matthew blankly. "It's a boy I've come for. He should be here. Mrs. Alexander Spencer was to bring him over from Nova Scotia for me."

The station-master whistled.

"Guess there's some mistake," he said. "Mrs. Spencer came off the train with that girl and gave her into my charge. Said you and your sister were adopting her from an orphan asylum and that you would be along for her presently. That's all *I* know about it—and I haven't got any more orphans concealed hereabouts."

"I don't understand," said Matthew helplessly, wishing that Marilla was at hand to cope with the situation.

"Well, you'd better question the girl," said the station-master carelessly. "I dare say she'll be able to explain—she's got a tongue of her own, that's certain. Maybe they were out of boys of the brand you wanted."

He walked jauntily away, being hungry, and the unfortunate Matthew was left to do that which was harder for him than bearding a lion in its den[5]—walk up to a girl—a strange girl—an orphan girl—and demand of her why she wasn't a boy. Matthew groaned in spirit as he turned about and shuffled gently down the platform towards her.

She had been watching him ever since he had passed her and she had her eyes on him now. Matthew was not looking at her and would not have seen what she was really like if he had been, but an ordinary observer would have seen this:

A child of about eleven, garbed in a very short, very tight, very ugly dress of yellowish gray wincey.[6] She wore a faded brown sailor hat and beneath the hat, extending down her back, were two braids of very thick, decidedly red hair. Her face was small, white and thin,

---

3. In *AGG* there will be eleven more uses of this affected literary phrase which is derived from Lawrence Sterne's *A Sentimental Journey through France and Italy* (1768), chap. 42. The nature of the imagination was a much-debated concept in the eighteenth and nineteenth century.
4. A peculiar person (slang).
5. Bravely facing danger, like Daniel in the *Holy Bible* when thrown to the lions by King Nebuchadnezzar (Daniel 6.16–24). This phrase echoes a line in Walter Scott's *Marmion* (1808) 6.14.24.
6. Scotch word for a coarse fabric made of wool and linen or cotton. The name, derived from "linsey-woolsey," is used derisively six times in *AGG*.

also much freckled; her mouth was large and so were her eyes, that looked green in some lights and moods and gray in others.

So far, the ordinary observer; an extraordinary observer might have seen that the chin was very pointed and pronounced; that the big eyes were full of spirit and vivacity; that the mouth was sweet-lipped and expressive; that the forehead was broad and full; in short, our discerning extraordinary observer might have concluded that no commonplace soul inhabited the body of this stray woman-child of whom shy Matthew Cuthbert was so ludicrously afraid.

Matthew, however, was spared the ordeal of speaking first, for as soon as she concluded that he was coming to her she stood up, grasping with one thin brown hand the handle of a shabby, old-fashioned carpet-bag;[7] the other she held out to him.

"I suppose you are Mr. Matthew Cuthbert of Green Gables?" she said in a peculiarly clear, sweet voice. "I'm very glad to see you. I was beginning to be afraid you weren't coming for me and I was imagining all the things that might have happened to prevent you. I had made up my mind that if you didn't come for me to-night I'd go down the track to that big wild cherry-tree at the bend, and climb up into it to stay all night. I wouldn't be a bit afraid, and it would be lovely to sleep in a wild cherry-tree all white with bloom in the moon-shine, don't you think? You could imagine you were dwelling in marble halls,[8] couldn't you? And I was quite sure you would come for me in the morning, if you didn't to-night."

Matthew had taken the scrawny little hand awkwardly in his; then and there he decided what to do. He could not tell this child with the glowing eyes that there had been a mistake; he would take her home and let Marilla do that. She couldn't be left at Bright River anyhow, no matter what mistake had been made, so all questions and explanations might as well be deferred until he was safely back at Green Gables.

"I'm sorry I was late," he said shyly. "Come along. The horse is over in the yard. Give me your bag."

"Oh, I can carry it," the child responded cheerfully. "It isn't heavy. I've got all my worldly goods[9] in it, but it isn't heavy. And if it isn't carried in just a certain way the handle pulls out—so I'd better keep it because I know the exact knack of it.[1] It's an extremely old carpet-bag. Oh, I'm very glad you've come, even if it would have been nice

---

7. Traveling-bag, made of floor-covering material.
8. From Alfred Bunn's popular song "I dreamt I dwelt in marble halls," in the opera *The Bohemian Girl* (1843), which echoes one of LMM's favorite poems, Henry Wadsworth Longfellow's "Hymn to Night" (1839) line 2. LMM purchased Longfellow's complete poems in 1896, and her book is heavily underlined.
9. A phrase in a marriage ceremony, traditional since 1549. Cf. *Book of Common Prayer*: "With al my worldly goodes I thee endowe."
1. Skill in handling (colloquialism).

to sleep in a wild cherry-tree. We've got to drive a long piece,[2] haven't we? Mrs. Spencer said it was eight miles. I'm glad because I love driving. Oh, it seems so wonderful that I'm going to live with you and belong to you. I've never belonged to anybody—not really. But the asylum was the worst. I've only been in it four months, but that was enough. I don't suppose you ever were an orphan in an asylum, so you can't possibly understand what it is like. It's worse than anything you could imagine. Mrs. Spencer said it was wicked of me to talk like that, but I didn't mean to be wicked. It's so easy to be wicked without knowing it, isn't it? They were good, you know—the asylum people. But there is so little scope for the imagination in an asylum—only just in the other orphans. It *was* pretty interesting to imagine things about them—to imagine that perhaps the girl who sat next to you was really the daughter of a belted earl,[3] who had been stolen away from her parents in her infancy by a cruel nurse who died before she could confess. I used to lie awake at nights and imagine things like that, because I didn't have time in the day. I guess that's why I'm so thin—I *am* dreadful thin, ain't I? There isn't a pick[4] on my bones. I do love to imagine I'm nice and plump, with dimples in my elbows."

With this Matthew's companion stopped talking, partly because she was out of breath and partly because they had reached the buggy. Not another word did she say until they had left the village and were driving down a steep little hill, the road part of which had been cut so deeply into the soft soil that the banks, fringed with blooming wild cherry-trees and slim white birches, were several feet above their heads.

The child put out her hand and broke off a branch of wild plum that brushed against the side of the buggy.

"Isn't that beautiful? What did that tree, leaning out from the bank, all white and lacy, make you think of?" she asked.

"Well now, I dunno," said Matthew.

"Why, a bride, of course—a bride all in white with a lovely misty veil.[5] I've never seen one, but I can imagine what she would look like. I don't ever expect to be a bride myself. I'm so homely nobody will ever want to marry me—unless it might be a foreign missionary.[6] I suppose a foreign missionary mightn't be very particular. But I do

---

2. A long way (North American dialect).
3. Drawn from the ceremony where the monarch invests an earl with a sword and belt. Echoes "cook's son, duke's son, son of a belted earl," from "The Absent-Minded Beggar" (1899) by one of LMM's favorite poets, Rudyard Kipling, set to music by Arthur Sullivan.
4. A morsel of flesh (PEI colloquialism).
5. The tradition of bridal white was not universal: LMM's mother was married in green. Queen Victoria's 1840 wedding set the fashion of wearing a bridal veil.
6. A missionary to foreign parts, probably India or China, to convert the natives to Christianity.

hope that some day I shall have a white dress. That is my highest
ideal of earthly bliss. I just love pretty clothes. And I've never had a
pretty dress in my life that I can remember—but of course it's all
the more to look forward to, isn't it? And then I can imagine that I'm
dressed gorgeously. This morning when I left the asylum I felt so
ashamed because I had to wear this horrid old wincey dress. All the
orphans had to wear them, you know. A merchant in Hopetown last
winter donated three hundred yards of wincey to the asylum. Some
people said it was because he couldn't sell it, but I'd rather believe
that it was out of the kindness of his heart, wouldn't you? When we
got on the train I felt as if everybody must be looking at me and
pitying me. But I just went to work and imagined that I had on the
most beautiful pale blue silk dress—because when you *are* imagining
you might as well imagine something worth while—and a big hat all
flowers and nodding plumes, and a gold watch, and kid gloves and
boots.[7] I felt cheered up right away and I enjoyed my trip to the Island
with all my might. I wasn't a bit sick coming over in the boat.[8] Neither
was Mrs. Spencer, although she generally is. She said she hadn't
time to get sick, watching to see that I didn't fall overboard. She said
she never saw the beat of me[9] for prowling about. But if it kept her
from being seasick it's a mercy I did prowl, isn't it? And I wanted to
see everything that was to be seen on that boat, because I didn't
know whether I'd ever have another opportunity. Oh, there are a lot
more—cherry-trees all in bloom! This Island is the bloomiest place.
I just love it already, and I'm so glad I'm going to live here. I've always
heard that Prince Edward Island was the prettiest place in the world,
and I used to imagine I was living here, but I never really expected
I would. It's delightful when your imaginations come true, isn't it?
But those red roads are so funny. When we got into the train at
Charlottetown[1] and the red roads[2] began to flash past I asked Mrs.
Spencer what made them red and she said she didn't know and for
pity's sake not to ask her any more questions. She said I must have
asked her a thousand already. I suppose I had, too, but how are you
going to find out about things if you don't ask questions? And what
*does* make the roads red?"

"Well now, I dunno," said Matthew.

"Well, that is one of the things to find out sometime. Isn't it splen-

7. Ideas of fashion were spread by magazines like the elegant, popular *Godey's Lady's Book*,
   to which LMM's grandmother subscribed.
8. In 1908 the only way to reach PEI from the Canadian mainland was by ferry, over the
   choppy Northumberland Straits, but today there is a bridge from mainland Canada to the
   Island.
9. Anything to outdo me (colloquial, from the verb "beat," to win in a contest).
1. Capital of PEI; population in 1891 was 11,485.
2. Iron oxide, from iron-rich sedentary rock, combined with clay soil, presents the appearance
   of red soil in many areas of the world so that dirt roads appear reddish.

did to think of all the things there are to find out about? It just makes me feel glad to be alive—it's such an interesting world. It wouldn't be half so interesting if we knew all about everything, would it? There'd be no scope for imagination then, would there? But am I talking too much? People are always telling me I do. Would you rather I didn't talk? If you say so I'll stop. I *can* stop when I make up my mind to it, although it's difficult."

Matthew, much to his own surprise, was enjoying himself. Like most quiet folks he liked talkative people when they were willing to do the talking themselves and did not expect him to keep up his end of it. But he had never expected to enjoy the society of a little girl. Women were bad enough in all conscience, but little girls were worse. He detested the way they had of sidling past him timidly, with side-wise glances, as if they expected him to gobble them up at a mouthful if they ventured to say a word. This was the Avonlea type of well-bred little girl. But this freckled witch was very different, and although he found it rather difficult for his slower intelligence to keep up with her brisk mental processes he thought that he "kind of liked her chatter." So he said as shyly as usual:

"Oh, you can talk as much as you like. I don't mind."

"Oh, I'm so glad. I know you and I are going to get along together fine. It's such a relief to talk when one wants to and not be told that children should be seen and not heard. I've had that said to me a million times if I have once. And people laugh at me because I use big words. But if you have big ideas you have to use big words to express them, haven't you?"

"Well now, that seems reasonable," said Matthew.

"Mrs. Spencer said that my tongue must be hung in the middle.[3] But it isn't—it's firmly fastened at one end. Mrs. Spencer said your place was named Green Gables. I asked her all about it. And she said there were trees all around it. I was gladder than ever. I just love trees. And there weren't any at all about the asylum, only a few poor weeny-teeny things out in front with little whitewashed cagey things about them. They just looked like orphans themselves, those trees did. It used to make me want to cry to look at them. I used to say to them, 'Oh, you *poor* little things! If you were out in a great big woods with other trees all around you and little mosses and Junebells[4] grow-ing over your roots and a brook not far away and birds singing in your branches, you could grow, couldn't you? But you can't where you are. I know just exactly how you feel, little trees.' I felt sorry to leave them behind this morning. You do get so attached to things

3. Able to say twice as much as other people.
4. Wildflowers, named *linnaea borealis* for the Swedish botanist Linnaeus and the boreal northern region. Also called "twinflowers" because they have two pinkish-white bells which bloom in June and July in coniferous forests.

like that, don't you? Is there a brook anywhere near Green Gables? I forgot to ask Mrs. Spencer that."

"Well now, yes, there's one right below the house."

"Fancy! It's always been one of my dreams to live near a brook. I never expected I would, though. Dreams don't often come true, do they? Wouldn't it be nice if they did? But just now I feel pretty nearly perfectly happy. I can't feel exactly perfectly happy because—well, what colour would you call this?"

She twitched one of her long glossy braids over her thin shoulder and held it up before Matthew's eyes. Matthew was not used to deciding on the tints of ladies' tresses, but in this case there couldn't be much doubt.

"It's red, ain't it?" he said.

The girl let the braid drop back with a sigh that seemed to come from her very toes and to exhale forth all the sorrows of the ages.

"Yes, it's red," she said resignedly. "Now you see why I can't be perfectly happy. Nobody could who had red hair. I don't mind the other things so much—the freckles and the green eyes and my skinniness. I can imagine them away. I can imagine that I have a beautiful rose-leaf complexion and lovely starry violet eyes. But I *cannot* imagine that red hair away. I do my best. I think to myself, 'Now my hair is a glorious black, black as the raven's wing.' But all the time I *know* it is just plain red, and it breaks my heart. It will be my lifelong sorrow. I read of a girl once in a novel who had a lifelong sorrow, but it wasn't red hair. Her hair was pure gold rippling back from her alabaster brow.[5] What is an alabaster brow? I never could find out. Can you tell me?"

"Well now, I'm afraid I can't," said Matthew, who was getting a little dizzy. He felt as he had once felt in his rash youth when another boy had enticed him on the merry-go-round at a picnic.

"Well, whatever it was it must have been something nice because she was divinely beautiful. Have you ever imagined what it must feel like to be divinely beautiful?"

"Well now, no, I haven't," confessed Matthew ingenuously.

"I have, often. Which would you rather be if you had the choice— divinely beautiful or dazzlingly clever or angelically good?"

"Well now, I—I don't know exactly."

"Neither do I. I can never decide. But it doesn't make much real difference for it isn't likely I'll ever be either. It's certain I'll never be angelically good. Mrs. Spencer says—oh, Mr. Cuthbert! Oh, Mr. Cuthbert!! Oh, Mr. Cuthbert!!!"

That was not what Mrs. Spencer had said; neither had the child

---

5. A literary cliché: forehead like alabaster (pale, whitish, and translucent), appropriate to a high-born lady who protects her skin from sunshine. Alabaster is quarried in England and Italy and used in vases and statuary.

tumbled out of the buggy nor had Matthew done anything astonishing. They had simply rounded a curve in the road and found themselves in the "Avenue."

The "Avenue," so called by the Newbridge[6] people, was a stretch of road four or five hundred yards long, completely arched over with huge, wide-spreading apple-trees, planted years ago by an eccentric old farmer. Overhead was one long canopy of snowy fragrant bloom. Below the boughs the air was full of a purple twilight and far ahead a glimpse of painted sunset sky shone like a great rose window[7] at the end of a cathedral aisle.

Its beauty seemed to strike the child dumb. She leaned back in the buggy, her thin hands clasped before her, her face lifted rapturously to the white splendour above. Even when they had passed out and were driving down the long slope to Newbridge she never moved or spoke. Still with rapt face she gazed afar into the sunset west, with eyes that saw visions trooping splendidly across that glowing background. Through Newbridge, a bustling little village where dogs barked at them and small boys hooted and curious faces peered from the windows, they drove, still in silence. When three more miles had dropped away behind them the child had not spoken. She could keep silence, it was evident, as energetically as she could talk.

"I guess you're feeling pretty tired and hungry," Matthew ventured at last, accounting for her long visitation of dumbness[8] with the only reason he could think of. "But we haven't very far to go now—only another mile."

She came out of her reverie with a deep sigh and looked at him with the dreamy gaze of a soul that had been wandering afar, star-led.

"Oh, Mr. Cuthbert," she whispered, "that place we came through—that white place—what was it?"

"Well now, you must mean the Avenue," said Matthew after a few moments' profound reflection. "It is a kind of pretty place."

"Pretty? Oh, *pretty* doesn't seem the right word to use. Nor beautiful, either. They don't go far enough. Oh, it was wonderful—wonderful. It's the first thing I ever saw that couldn't be improved upon by imagination. It just satisfied me here"—she put one hand on her breast—"it made a queer funny ache and yet it was a pleasant ache. Did you ever have an ache like that, Mr. Cuthbert?"

"Well now, I just can't recollect that I ever had."

"I have it lots of times—whenever I see anything royally beautiful.

---

6. Perhaps New Glasgow: the road to Cavendish leads through this village.
7. Circular stained glass window, demarcated into petal shapes, as famously seen in Chartres Cathedral in France.
8. Struck silent by a divine force. In the *Holy Bible*, Zacharias is deprived of the power of speech by the Angel Gabriel. Luke 1.20.

But they shouldn't call that lovely place the Avenue. There is no meaning in a name like that. They should call it—let me see—the White Way of Delight.[9] Isn't that a nice imaginative name? When I don't like the name of a place or a person I always imagine a new one and always think of them so. There was a girl at the asylum whose name was Hepzibah[1] Jenkins, but I always imagined her as Rosalia DeVere.[2] Other people may call that place the Avenue, but I shall always call it the White Way of Delight. Have we really only another mile to go before we get home? I'm glad and I'm sorry. I'm sorry because this drive has been so pleasant and I'm always sorry when pleasant things end. Something still pleasanter may come after, but you can never be sure. And it's so often the case that it isn't pleasanter. That has been my experience anyhow. But I'm glad to think of getting home. You see, I've never had a real home since I can remember. It gives me that pleasant ache again just to think of coming to a really truly home. Oh, isn't that pretty!"

They had driven over the crest of a hill. Below them was a pond, looking almost like a river so long and winding was it. A bridge spanned it midway and from there to its lower end, where an amber-hued belt of sand-hills shut it in from the dark blue gulf beyond, the water was a glory of many shifting hues—the most spiritual shadings of crocus and rose and ethereal green, with other elusive tintings for which no name has ever been found. Above the bridge the pond ran up into fringing groves of fir and maple and lay all darkly translucent in their wavering shadows. Here and there a wild plum leaned out from the bank like a white-clad girl tip-toeing to her own reflection. From the marsh at the head of the pond came the clear, mournfully-sweet chorus of the frogs.[3] There was a little gray house peering around a white apple orchard on a slope beyond and, although it was not yet quite dark, a light was shining from one of its windows.

"That's Barry's pond," said Matthew.

"Oh, I don't like that name, either. I shall call it—let me see—the Lake of Shining Waters.[4] Yes, that is the right name for it. I know because of the thrill. When I hit on a name that suits exactly it gives me a thrill. Do things ever give you a thrill?"

Matthew ruminated.

"Well now, yes. It always kind of gives me a thrill to see them ugly

9. Blossoms of fruit trees in spring: PEI has many orchards.
1. Name of Isaiah's mother, spelled "Hephzibah" in the *Holy Bible*. It means "my delight is in her." Isaiah 62.4; also II Kings 21.1.
2. Another "deVere," in Alfred Tennyson's "Lady Clara Vere de Vere" (1842), is very nobly born, "The daughter of a hundred earls." l. 7.
3. Sounds resonating from the throat pouches of multitudes of male spring-peepers.
4. Based on the pond at Park Corner on the Campbell farm, with effects from William C. Macneill's Cavendish Pond.

white grubs[5] that spade up in the cucumber beds. I hate the look of them."

"Oh, I don't think that can be exactly the same kind of a thrill. Do you think it can? There doesn't seem to be much connection between grubs and lakes of shining waters, does there? But why do other people call it Barry's pond?"

"I reckon because Mr. Barry lives up there in that house. Orchard Slope's the name of his place. If it wasn't for that big bush[6] behind it you could see Green Gables from here. But we have to go over the bridge and round by the road, so it's near half a mile further."

"Has Mr. Barry any little girls? Well, not so very little either—about my size."

"He's got one about eleven. Her name is Diana."

"Oh!" with a long indrawing of breath. "What a perfectly lovely name!"

"Well now, I dunno. There's something dreadful heathenish[7] about it, seems to me. I'd ruther Jane or Mary or some sensible name like that. But when Diana was born there was a schoolmaster boarding there and they gave him the naming of her and he called her Diana."

"I wish there had been a schoolmaster like that around when *I* was born, then. Oh, here we are at the bridge. I'm going to shut my eyes tight. I'm always afraid going over bridges. I can't help imagining that perhaps, just as we get to the middle, they'll crumple up like a jack-knife and nip us.[8] So I shut my eyes. But I always have to open them for all when I think we're getting near the middle. Because, you see, if the bridge *did* crumple up I'd want to *see* it crumple. What a jolly rumble it makes! I always like the rumble part of it. Isn't it splendid there are so many things to like in this world? There, we're over. Now I'll look back. Good night, dear Lake of Shining Waters. I always say good night to the things I love, just as I would to people. I think they like it. That water looks as if it was smiling at me."

When they had driven up the further hill and around a corner Matthew said:

"We're pretty near home now. That's Green Gables over—"

"Oh, don't tell me," she interrupted breathlessly, catching at his partially raised arm and shutting her eyes that she might not see his gesture. "Let me guess. I'm sure I'll guess right."

She opened her eyes and looked about her. They were on the crest

---

5. Short fat wormlike larvae of an insect, usually a beetle.
6. "Bush" can refer to a single shrub, or to a forest (as in *Roughing it in the Bush*) in Canada.
7. The name of a Roman (heathen) goddess, therefore suspect to the orthodox Christian.
8. In her autobiographical essay *The Alpine Path* (1917), LMM revealed a lifelong fear of bridges.

of a hill. The sun had set some time since, but the landscape was still clear in the mellow afterlight. To the west a dark church spire rose up against a marigold sky. Below was a little valley and beyond a long, gently-rising slope with snug farmsteads scattered along it. From one to another the child's eyes darted, eager and wistful. At last they lingered on one away to the left, far back from the road, dimly white with blossoming trees in the twilight of the surrounding woods. Over it, in the stainless southwest sky, a great crystal-white star was shining like a lamp of guidance and promise.

"That's it, isn't it?" she said, pointing.

Matthew slapped the reins on the sorrel's back delightedly.

"Well now, you've guessed it! But I reckon Mrs. Spencer described it so's you could tell."

"No, she didn't—really she didn't. All she said might just as well have been about most of those other places. I hadn't any real idea what it looked like. But just as soon as I saw it I felt it was home. Oh, it seems as if I must be in a dream. Do you know, my arm must be black and blue from the elbow up, for I've pinched myself so many times to-day. Every little while a horrible sickening feeling would come over me and I'd be so afraid it was all a dream. Then I'd pinch myself to see if it was real—until suddenly I remembered that even supposing it was only a dream I'd better go on dreaming as long as I could; so I stopped pinching. But it *is* real and we're nearly home."

With a sigh of rapture she relapsed into silence. Matthew stirred uneasily. He felt glad that it would be Marilla and not he who would have to tell this waif[9] of the world that the home she longed for was not to be hers after all. They drove over Lynde's Hollow, where it was already quite dark, but not so dark that Mrs. Rachel could not see them from her window vantage, and up the hill and into the long lane of Green Gables. By the time they arrived at the house Matthew was shrinking from the approaching revelation with an energy he did not understand. It was not of Marilla or himself he was thinking or of the trouble this mistake was probably going to make for them, but of the child's disappointment. When he thought of that rapt light being quenched in her eyes he had an uncomfortable feeling that he was going to assist at murdering something—much the same feeling that came over him when he had to kill a lamb or calf or any other innocent little creature.

The yard was quite dark as they turned into it and the poplar leaves were rustling silkily all round it.

"Listen to the trees talking in their sleep," she whispered, as he lifted her to the ground. "What nice dreams they must have!"

9. Homeless, helpless child.

Then, holding tightly to the carpet-bag which contained "all her worldly goods," she followed him into the house.

# Chapter III

## MARILLA CUTHBERT IS SURPRISED

MARILLA came briskly forward as Matthew opened the door. But when her eyes fell on the odd little figure in the stiff, ugly dress, with the long braids of red hair and the eager, luminous eyes, she stopped short in amazement.

"Matthew Cuthbert, who's that?" she ejaculated. "Where is the boy?"

"There wasn't any boy," said Matthew wretchedly. "There was only *her*."

He nodded at the child, remembering that he had never even asked her name.

"No boy! But there *must* have been a boy," insisted Marilla. "We sent word to Mrs. Spencer to bring a boy."

"Well, she didn't. She brought *her*. I asked the station-master. And I had to bring her home. She couldn't be left there, no matter where the mistake had come in."

"Well, this is a pretty piece of business!" ejaculated Marilla.

During this dialogue the child had remained silent, her eyes roving from one to the other, all the animation fading out of her face. Suddenly she seemed to grasp the full meaning of what had been said. Dropping her precious carpet-bag she sprang forward a step and clasped her hands.

"You don't want me!" she cried. "You don't want me because I'm not a boy! I might have expected it. Nobody ever did want me. I might have known it was all too beautiful to last. I might have known nobody really did want me. Oh, what shall I do? I'm going to burst into tears!"

Burst into tears she did. Sitting down on a chair by the table, flinging her arms out upon it, and burying her face in them, she proceeded to cry stormily. Marilla and Matthew looked at each other deprecatingly across the stove. Neither of them knew what to say or do. Finally Marilla stepped lamely into the breach.[1]

"Well, well, there's no need to cry so about it."

"Yes, there *is* need!" The child raised her head quickly, revealing a tear-stained face and trembling lips. "*You* would cry, too, if

1. In military terms, finding a break in the line of soldiery.

"Matthew Cuthbert, who's that?" she ejaculated

you were an orphan and had come to a place you thought was going to be home and found that they didn't want you because you weren't a boy. Oh, this is the most *tragical* thing that ever happened to me!"

Something like a reluctant smile, rather rusty from long disuse, mellowed Marilla's grim expression.

"Well, don't cry any more. We're not going to turn you out-of-doors to-night. You'll have to stay here until we investigate this affair. What's your name?"

The child hesitated for a moment.

"Will you please call me Cordelia?"[2] she said eagerly.

"*Call* you Cordelia! Is that your name?"

"No-o-o, it's not exactly my name, but I would love to be called Cordelia. It's such a perfectly elegant name."

"I don't know what on earth you mean. If Cordelia isn't your name, what is?"

"Anne Shirley," reluctantly faltered forth the owner of that name, "but oh, please do call me Cordelia. It can't matter much to you what you call me if I'm only going to be here a little while, can it? And Anne is such an unromantic name."

"Unromantic fiddlesticks!"[3] said the unsympathetic Marilla. "Anne is a real good plain sensible name. You've no need to be ashamed of it."

"Oh, I'm not ashamed of it," explained Anne, "only I like Cordelia better. I've always imagined that my name was Cordelia—at least, I always have of late years. When I was young I used to imagine it was Geraldine, but I like Cordelia better now. But if you call me Anne please call me Anne spelled with an *e*."

"What difference does it make how it's spelled?" asked Marilla with another rusty smile as she picked up the teapot.

"Oh, it makes *such* a difference. It *looks* so much nicer. When you hear a name pronounced can't you always see it in your mind, just as if it was printed out? I can; and A-n-n looks dreadful, but A-n-n-e looks so much more distinguished.[4] If you'll only call me Anne spelled with an *e* I shall try to reconcile myself to not being called Cordelia."

"Very well, then, Anne spelled with an *e*, can you tell us how this mistake came to be made? We sent word to Mrs. Spencer to bring us a boy. Were there no boys at the asylum?"

"Oh, yes, there was an abundance of them. But Mrs. Spencer said *distinctly* that you wanted a girl about eleven years old. And the matron said she thought I would do. You don't know how delighted

---

2. Name of a beloved daughter in William Shakespeare's play, *King Lear* (1606).
3. Nonsense (colloquialism used since 1600).
4. Conversely, LMM was annoyed when people added an "e" to "Maud."

I was. I couldn't sleep all last night for joy. Oh," she added reproachfully, turning to Matthew, "why didn't you tell me at the station that
you didn't want me and leave me there? If I hadn't seen the White
Way of Delight and the Lake of Shining Waters it wouldn't be so
hard."

"What on earth does she mean?" demanded Marilla, staring at
Matthew.

"She—she's just referring to some conversation we had on the
road," said Matthew hastily. "I'm going out to put the mare in, Marilla. Have tea ready when I come back."

"Did Mrs. Spencer bring anybody over besides you?" continued
Marilla when Matthew had gone out.

"She brought Lily Jones for herself. Lily is only five years old and
she is very beautiful. She has nut-brown hair.[5] If I was very beautiful
and had nut-brown hair would you keep me?"

"No. We want a boy to help Matthew on the farm. A girl would
be of no use to us. Take off your hat. I'll lay it and your bag on the
hall table."

Anne took off her hat meekly. Matthew came back presently and
they sat down to supper. But Anne could not eat. In vain she nibbled
at the bread and butter and pecked at the crab-apple preserve out of
the little scalloped glass dish by her plate. She did not really make
any headway at all.

"You're not eating anything," said Marilla sharply, eying[6] her as if
it were a serious shortcoming.

Anne sighed.

"I can't. I'm in the depths of despair.[7] Can you eat when you are
in the depths of despair?"

"I've never been in the depths of despair, so I can't say," responded
Marilla.

"Weren't you? Well, did you ever try to *imagine* you were in the
depths of despair?"

"No, I didn't."

"Then I don't think you can understand what it's like. It's a very
uncomfortable feeling indeed. When you try to eat a lump comes
right up in your throat and you can't swallow anything, not even if
it was a chocolate caramel. I had one chocolate caramel once two
years ago and it was simply delicious. I've often dreamed since then
that I had a lot of chocolate caramels, but I always wake up just
when I'm going to eat them. I do hope you won't be offended because
I can't eat. Everything is extremely nice, but still I cannot eat."

5. "My nut-brown maiden" is an ancient Scottish highland love-song.
6. British variant spelling for "eyeing."
7. Echoes "Tears from the depth of some divine despair," from Alfred Tennyson, *The Princess*
(1847) 4.2.

"I guess she's tired," said Matthew, who hadn't spoken since his return from the barn. "Best put her to bed, Marilla."

Marilla had been wondering where Anne should be put to bed. She had prepared a couch in the kitchen chamber for the desired and expected boy. But, although it was neat and clean, it did not seem quite the thing to put a girl there somehow. But the spare room[8] was out of the question for such a stray waif, so there remained only the east gable room. Marilla lighted a candle and told Anne to follow her, which Anne spiritlessly did, taking her hat and carpet-bag from the hall table as she passed. The hall was fearsomely clean; the little gable chamber in which she presently found herself seemed still cleaner.

Marilla set the candle on a three-legged, three-cornered table and turned down the bedclothes.

"I suppose you have a nightgown?" she questioned.

Anne nodded.

"Yes, I have two. The matron of the asylum made them for me. They're fearfully skimpy. There is never enough to go around in an asylum, so things are always skimpy—at least in a poor asylum like ours. I hate skimpy night-dresses. But one can dream just as well in them as in lovely trailing ones, with frills around the neck, that's one consolation."

"Well, undress as quick as you can and go to bed. I'll come back in a few minutes for the candle. I daren't trust you to put it out yourself. You'd likely set the place on fire."

When Marilla had gone Anne looked around her wistfully. The whitewashed walls[9] were so painfully bare and staring that she thought they must ache over their own bareness. The floor was bare, too, except for a round braided mat[1] in the middle such as Anne had never seen before. In one corner was the bed, a high, old-fashioned one, with four dark, low-turned posts. In the other corner was the afore-said three-cornered table adorned with a fat, red velvet pincushion hard enough to turn the point of the most adventurous pin. Above it hung a little six by eight mirror. Midway between table and bed was the window, with an icy white muslin[2] frill over it, and opposite it was the wash-stand.[3] The whole apartment was of a rigidity not to be described in words, but which sent a shiver to the very

---

8. Bedroom reserved for guests. LMM remembered her childhood awe at the grandeur of the Macneill spare room. See *SJ2* 7.
9. An inexpensive coating of quicklime (calcium oxide), water, and sizing (e.g., starch) used upstairs here instead of the fancier wallpaper used downstairs.
1. Circular rug formed by sewing together braids of cotton or wool fabric.
2. Fine cotton cloth, named for Mosul in Iraq, where it originated.
3. A small free-standing cupboard. In the absence of indoor plumbing, bathroom facilities in each bedroom consisted of a jug of water, a basin, and a chamber pot stowed inside the cupboard.

marrow of Anne's bones. With a sob she hastily discarded her garments, put on the skimpy nightgown and sprang into bed where she
burrowed face downward into the pillow and pulled the clothes over
her head. When Marilla came up for the light various skimpy articles
of raiment scattered most untidily over the floor and a certain tem-
pestuous appearance of the bed were the only indications of any
presence save her own.

She deliberately picked up Anne's clothes, placed them neatly on
a prim yellow chair, and then, taking up the candle, went over to the
bed.

"Good night," she said, a little awkwardly, but not unkindly.

Anne's white face and big eyes appeared over the bedclothes with
a startling suddenness.

"How can you call it a *good* night when you know it must be the
very worst night I've ever had?" she said reproachfully.

Then she dived down into invisibility again.

Marilla went slowly down to the kitchen and proceeded to wash
the supper dishes. Matthew was smoking—a sure sign of perturba-
tion of mind. He seldom smoked, for Marilla set her face against it[4]
as a filthy habit; but at certain times and seasons he felt driven to it
and then Marilla winked at the practice, realizing that a mere man
must have some vent for his emotions.

"Well, this is a pretty kettle of fish,"[5] she said wrathfully. "This is
what comes of sending word instead of going ourselves. Robert Spencer's folks have twisted that message somehow. One of us will have
to drive over and see Mrs. Spencer to-morrow, that's certain. This
girl will have to be sent back to the asylum."

"Yes, I suppose so," said Matthew reluctantly.

"You *suppose* so! Don't you know it?"

"Well now, she's a real nice little thing, Marilla. It's kind of a pity
to send her back when she's so set on staying here."

"Matthew Cuthbert, you don't mean to say you think we ought to
keep her!"

Marilla's astonishment could not have been greater if Matthew
had expressed a predilection for standing on his head.

"Well now, no, I suppose not—not exactly," stammered Matthew,
uncomfortably driven into a corner for his precise meaning. "I suppose—we could hardly be expected to keep her."

"I should say not. What good would she be to us?"

"We might be some good to her," said Matthew suddenly and
unexpectedly.

---

4. Disparaged smoking. In the *Holy Bible*, "The Lord sets his face against wrongdoers."
Psalms 34.16.
5. A difficult situation (slang). Used by W. S. Gilbert in *Patience* (1881), Act 2, "Peers'
Chorus."

"Matthew Cuthbert, I believe that child has bewitched you![6] I can see as plain as plain that you want to keep her."

"Well now, she's a real interesting little thing," persisted Matthew. "You should have heard her talk coming from the station."

"Oh, she can talk fast enough. I saw that at once. It's nothing in her favour, either. I don't like children who have so much to say. I don't want an orphan girl and if I did she isn't the style I'd pick out. There's something I don't understand about her. No, she's got to be despatched[7] straightway back to where she came from."

"I could hire a French boy to help me," said Matthew, "and she'd be company for you."

"I'm not suffering for company," said Marilla shortly. "And I'm not going to keep her."

"Well now, it's just as you say, of course, Marilla," said Matthew rising and putting his pipe away. "I'm going to bed."

To bed went Matthew. And to bed, when she had put her dishes away, went Marilla, frowning most resolutely. And up-stairs, in the east gable, a lonely, heart-hungry, friendless child cried herself to sleep.

# Chapter IV

## MORNING AT GREEN GABLES

IT was broad daylight when Anne awoke and sat up in bed, staring confusedly at the window through which a flood of cheery sunshine was pouring and outside of which something white and feathery waved across glimpses of blue sky.

For a moment she could not remember where she was. First came a delightful thrill, as of something very pleasant; then a horrible remembrance. This was Green Gables and they didn't want her because she wasn't a boy!

But it was morning and, yes, it was a cherry-tree in full bloom outside of her window. With a bound she was out of bed and across the floor. She pushed up the sash—it went up stiffly and creakily, as if it hadn't been opened for a long time, which was the case; and it stuck so tight that nothing was needed to hold it up.

Anne dropped on her knees and gazed out into the June morning, her eyes glistening with delight. Oh, wasn't it beautiful? Wasn't it a lovely place? Suppose she wasn't really going to stay here! She would imagine she was. There was scope for imagination here.

6. Put a magical spell on you.
7. Sent off (British spelling). The North American spelling is "dispatched."

A huge cherry-tree grew outside, so close that its boughs tapped against the house, and it was so thick-set with blossoms that hardly a leaf was to be seen. On both sides of the house was a big orchard, one of apple-trees and one of cherry-trees, also showered over with blossoms; and their grass was all sprinkled with dandelions. In the garden below were lilac-trees purple with flowers, and their dizzily sweet fragrance drifted up to the window on the morning wind.

Below the garden a green field lush with clover sloped down to the hollow where the brook ran and where scores of white birches grew, upspringing airily out of an undergrowth suggestive of delightful possibilities in ferns and mosses and woodsy things generally. Beyond it was a hill, green and feathery with spruce and fir; there was a gap in it where the gray gable end of the little house she had seen from the other side of the Lake of Shining Waters was visible.

Off to the left were the big barns and beyond them, away down over green, low-sloping fields, was a sparkling blue glimpse of sea.

Anne's beauty-loving eyes lingered on it all, taking everything greedily in; she had looked on so many unlovely places in her life, poor child; but this was as lovely as anything she had ever dreamed.

She knelt there, lost to everything but the loveliness around her, until she was startled by a hand on her shoulder. Marilla had come in unheard by the small dreamer.

"It's time you were dressed," she said curtly.

Marilla really did not know how to talk to the child, and her uncomfortable ignorance made her crisp and curt when she did not mean to be.

Anne stood up and drew a long breath.

"Oh, isn't it wonderful?" she said, waving her hand comprehensively at the good world outside.

"It's a big tree," said Marilla, "and it blooms great, but the fruit don't amount to much never—small and wormy."

"Oh, I don't mean just the tree; of course it's lovely—yes, it's *radiantly* lovely—it blooms as if it meant it[1]—but I meant everything, the garden and the orchard and the brook and the woods, the whole big dear world. Don't you feel as if you just loved the world on a morning like this? And I can hear the brook laughing all the way up here. Have you ever noticed what cheerful things brooks are? They're always laughing. Even in winter-time I've heard them under the ice. I'm so glad there's a brook near Green Gables. Perhaps you think it doesn't make any difference to me when you're not going to keep me, but it does. I shall always like to remember that there is a brook

---

1. A quotation from the first entry in LMM's journal (*SJ1* 1) illustrating her dependence on her diary of ideas recorded in childhood.

at Green Gables even if I never see it again. If there wasn't a brook I'd be *haunted* by the uncomfortable feeling that there ought to be one. I'm not in the depths of despair this morning. I never can be in the morning. Isn't it a splendid thing that there are mornings? But I feel very sad. I've just been imagining that it was really me you wanted after all and that I was to stay here for ever and ever. It was a great comfort while it lasted. But the worst of imagining things is that the time comes when you have to stop and that hurts."

"You'd better get dressed and come down-stairs and never mind your imaginings," said Marilla as soon as she could get a word in edgewise. "Breakfast is waiting. Wash your face and comb your hair. Leave the window up and turn your bedclothes back over the foot of the bed. Be as smart as you can."

Anne could evidently be smart to some purpose for she was down-stairs in ten minutes' time, with her clothes neatly on, her hair brushed and braided, her face washed, and a comfortable conscious-ness pervading her soul that she had fulfilled all Marilla's require-ments. As a matter of fact, however, she had forgotten to turn back the bedclothes.

"I'm pretty hungry this morning," she announced, as she slipped into the chair Marilla placed for her. "The world doesn't seem such a howling wilderness[2] as it did last night. I'm so glad it's a sunshiny morning. But I like rainy mornings real well, too. All sorts of morn-ings are interesting, don't you think? You don't know what's going to happen through the day, and there's so much scope for imagination. But I'm glad it's not rainy to-day because it's easier to be cheerful and bear up under affliction on a sunshiny day. I feel that I have a good deal to bear up under. It's all very well to read about sorrows and imagine yourself living through them heroically, but it's not so nice when you really come to have them, is it?"

"For pity's sake hold your tongue," said Marilla. "You talk entirely too much for a little girl."

Thereupon Anne held her tongue so obediently and thoroughly that her continued silence made Marilla rather nervous, as if in the presence of something not exactly natural. Matthew also held his tongue,—but this at least was natural,—so that the meal was a very silent one.

As it progressed Anne became more and more abstracted, eating mechanically, with her big eyes fixed unswervingly and unseeingly on the sky outside the window. This made Marilla more nervous than ever; she had an uncomfortable feeling that while this odd child's

---

2. A barren place. In the *Holy Bible*, "He found him in a desert land, and in the waste howling wilderness." Deuteronomy 32.10.

body might be there at the table her spirit was far away in some remote airy cloudland, borne aloft on the wings of imagination. Who would want such a child about the place?

Yet Matthew wished to keep her, of all unaccountable things! Marilla felt that he wanted it just as much this morning as he had the night before, and that he would go on wanting it. That was Matthew's way—take a whim into his head and cling to it with the most amazing silent persistency—a persistency ten times more potent and effectual in its very silence than if he had talked it out.

When the meal was ended Anne came out of her reverie and offered to wash the dishes.

"Can you wash dishes right?" asked Marilla distrustfully.

"Pretty well. I'm better at looking after children, though. I've had so much experience at that. It's such a pity you haven't any here for me to look after."

"I don't feel as if I wanted any more children to look after than I've got at present. You're problem enough in all conscience. What's to be done with you I don't know. Matthew is a most ridiculous man."

"I think he's lovely," said Anne reproachfully. "He is so very sympathetic. He didn't mind how much I talked—he seemed to like it. I felt that he was a kindred spirit[3] as soon as ever I saw him."

"You're both queer enough, if that's what you mean by kindred spirits," said Marilla with a sniff. "Yes, you may wash the dishes. Take plenty of hot water, and be sure you dry them well. I've got enough to attend to this morning for I'll have to drive over to White Sands in the afternoon and see Mrs. Spencer. You'll come with me and we'll settle what's to be done with you. After you've finished the dishes go up-stairs and make your bed."

Anne washed the dishes deftly enough, as Marilla, who kept a sharp eye on the process, discerned. Later on she made her bed less successfully, for she had never learned the art of wrestling with a feather tick.[4] But it was done somehow and smoothed down; and then Marilla, to get rid of her, told her she might go out-of-doors and amuse herself until dinner-time.[5]

Anne flew to the door, face alight, eyes glowing. On the very threshold she stopped short, wheeled about, came back and sat down by the table, light and glow as effectually blotted out as if some one had clapped an extinguisher[6] on her.

3. Like-minded friend. From Thomas Gray, "Elegy Written in a Country Churchyard" (1750) l. 96. The phrase also appears in early feminist books, Elizabeth Schreiner's *Story of an African Farm* (1883), and Elizabeth von Arnin's *Elizabeth and her German Garden* (1898), both favorites of LMM.
4. A mattress (or sometimes comforter) made of striped cotton or linen ticking, filled with feathers.
5. The major meal, customarily served at mid-day on a farm.
6. A candle snuffer, conical shaped, with a long handle.

"What's the matter now?" demanded Marilla.

"I don't dare go out," said Anne, in the tone of a martyr relinquishing all earthly joys. "If I can't stay here there is no use in my loving Green Gables. And if I go out there and get acquainted with all those trees and flowers and the orchard and the brook I'll not be able to help loving it. It's hard enough now, so I won't make it any harder. I want to go out so much—everything seems to be calling to me, 'Anne, Anne, come out to us. Anne, Anne, we want a playmate'— but it's better not. There is no use in loving things if you have to be torn from them, is there? And it's *so* hard to keep from loving things, isn't it? That was why I was so glad when I thought I was going to live here. I thought I'd have so many things to love and nothing to hinder me. But that brief dream is over. I am resigned to my fate now, so I don't think I'll go out for fear I'll get unresigned again. What is the name of that geranium on the window-sill, please?"

"That's the apple-scented geranium."[7]

"Oh, I don't mean that sort of a name. I mean just a name you gave it yourself. Didn't you give it a name? May I give it one then? May I call it—let me see—Bonny[8] would do—may I call it Bonny while I'm here? Oh, do let me!"

"Goodness, I don't care. But where on earth is the sense of naming a geranium?"

"Oh, I like things to have handles[9] even if they are only geraniums. It makes them seem more like people. How do you know but that it hurts a geranium's feelings just to be called a geranium and nothing else? You wouldn't like to be called nothing but a woman all the time. Yes, I shall call it Bonny. I named that cherry-tree outside my bedroom window this morning. I called it Snow Queen[1] because it was so white. Of course, it won't always be in blossom, but one can imagine that it is, can't one?"

"I never in all my life saw or heard anything to equal her," muttered Marilla, beating a retreat down cellar after potatoes. "She *is* kind of interesting, as Matthew says. I can feel already that I'm wondering what on earth she'll say next. She'll be casting a spell over me, too. She's cast it over Matthew. That look he gave me when he went out said everything he said or hinted last night over again. I wish he was like other men and would talk things out. A body could answer back then and argue him into reason. But what's to be done with a man who just *looks*?"

---

7. Houseplant used as herb. *Pelargonium ororatissimum* releases a sweet smell when brushed, and its leaves are used in cooking jellies and salad-dressings.
8. Scottish dialect word for beautiful. This naming is another borrowing from LMM's childhood journal.
9. Names. Dictionaries define "handle" as a title (e.g., Sir) attached to a person's name. In *AGG*, "handle" is the name itself.
1. Echo of a story (1845) by Hans Christian Andersen, one of LMM's favorite authors.

Anne had relapsed into reverie, with her chin in her hands and her eyes on the sky, when Marilla returned from her cellar pilgrimage. There Marilla left her until the early dinner was on the table.

"I suppose I can have the mare and buggy this afternoon, Matthew?" said Marilla.

Matthew nodded and looked wistfully at Anne. Marilla intercepted the look and said grimly:

"I'm going to drive over to White Sands and settle this thing. I'll take Anne with me and Mrs. Spencer will probably make arrangements to send her back to Nova Scotia at once. I'll set your tea out for you and I'll be home in time to milk the cows."

Still Matthew said nothing and Marilla had a sense of having wasted words and breath. There is nothing more aggravating than a man who won't talk back—unless it is a woman who won't.

Matthew hitched the sorrel into the buggy in due time and Marilla and Anne set off. Matthew opened the yard gate for them, and as they drove slowly through, he said, to nobody in particular as it seemed:

"Little Jerry Buote[2] from the Creek was here this morning, and I told him I guessed I'd hire him for the summer."

Marilla made no reply, but she hit the unlucky sorrel such a vicious clip with the whip that the fat mare, unused to such treatment, whizzed indignantly down the lane at an alarming pace. Marilla looked back once as the buggy bounced along and saw that aggravating Matthew leaning over the gate, looking wistfully after them.

# Chapter V

### ANNE'S HISTORY

"Do you know," said Anne confidentially, "I've made up my mind to enjoy this drive. It's been my experience that you can nearly always enjoy things if you make up your mind firmly that you will. Of course, you must make it up *firmly*. I am not going to think about going back to the asylum while we're having our drive. I'm just going to think about the drive. Oh, look, there's one little early wild rose out! Isn't it lovely? Don't you think it must be glad to be a rose? Wouldn't it be nice if roses could talk? I'm sure they could tell us such lovely things. And isn't pink the most bewitching colour in the world? I love it, but I can't wear it. Red-headed people can't wear pink, not even

---

2. Named for a famous Acadian family. François Buote (born in Rustico) founded the first French-language school in PEI in 1815. Gilbert Buote founded PEI's first French publishing house.

in imagination. Did you ever know of anybody whose hair was red when she was young, but got to be another colour when she grew up?"

"No, I don't know as I ever did," said Marilla mercilessly, "and I shouldn't think it likely to happen in your case, either."

Anne sighed.

"Well, that is another hope gone. My life is a perfect graveyard of buried hopes.[1] That's a sentence I read in a book once, and I say it over to comfort myself whenever I'm disappointed in anything."

"I don't see where the comforting comes in myself," said Marilla.

"Why, because it sounds so nice and romantic, just as if I were a heroine in a book, you know. I am so fond of romantic things, and a graveyard full of buried hopes is about as romantic a thing as one can imagine, isn't it? I'm rather glad I have one. Are we going across the Lake of Shining Waters to-day?"

"We're not going over Barry's pond, if that's what you mean by your Lake of Shining Waters. We're going by the shore road."[2]

"Shore road sounds nice," said Anne dreamily. "Is it as nice as it sounds? Just when you said 'shore road' I saw it in a picture in my mind, as quick as that! And White Sands is a pretty name, too; but I don't like it as well as Avonlea. Avonlea is a lovely name. It just sounds like music. How far is it to White Sands?"

"It's five miles; and as you're evidently bent on talking you might as well talk to some purpose by telling me what you know about yourself."

"Oh, what I *know* about myself isn't really worth telling," said Anne eagerly. "If you'll only let me tell you what I *imagine* about myself you'll think it ever so much more interesting."

"No, I don't want any of your imaginings. Just you stick to bald facts. Begin at the beginning. Where were you born and how old are you?"

"I was eleven last March," said Anne, resigning herself to bald facts with a little sigh. "And I was born in Bolingbroke, Nova Scotia. My father's name was Walter Shirley, and he was a teacher in the Bolingbroke High School. My mother's name was Bertha Shirley.[3] Aren't Walter and Bertha lovely names? I'm so glad my parents had nice names. It would be a real disgrace to have a father named—well, say Jedediah,[4] wouldn't it?"

---

1. Echoes "If there be graveyards in the heart . . . Where linger buried hopes and dreams," from John Bennett's poem "God Bless You, Dear, Today!" which was published in a 1900 anthology of American poets.
2. Running parallel to the Gulf of St Lawrence on the North Shore of PEI.
3. In sequels to *AGG*, Anne names two of her sons Walter and Shirley, and one of her daughters Bertha Marilla. (Bertha, name of the heroine of Charles Dickens's *The Cricket on the Hearth* [1845], was popular in the Victorian period.)
4. Hebrew for "beloved of the Lord," the name the prophet Nathan gave to Solomon, son of

"I guess it doesn't matter what a person's name is as long as he behaves himself," said Marilla, feeling herself called upon to inculcate a good and useful moral.

"Well, I don't know." Anne looked thoughtful. "I read in a book once that a rose by any other name would smell as sweet,[5] but I've never been able to believe it. I don't believe a rose *would* be as nice if it was called a thistle or a skunk cabbage.[6] I suppose my father could have been a good man even if he had been called Jedediah; but I'm sure it would have been a cross.[7] Well, my mother was a teacher in the High School, too, but when she married father she gave up teaching, of course. A husband was enough responsibility. Mrs. Thomas said that they were a pair of babies and as poor as church mice. They went to live in a weeny-teeny little yellow house in Bolingbroke. I've never seen that house,[8] but I've imagined it thousands of times. I think it must have had honeysuckle over the parlour window and lilacs in the front yard and lilies of the valley just inside the gate. Yes, and muslin curtains in all the windows. Muslin curtains give a house such an air. I was born in that house. Mrs. Thomas said I was the homeliest baby she ever saw, I was so scrawny and tiny and nothing but eyes, but that mother thought I was perfectly beautiful. I should think a mother would be a better judge than a poor woman who came in to scrub, wouldn't you? I'm glad she was satisfied with me anyhow; I would feel so sad if I thought I was a disappointment to her—because she didn't live very long after that, you see. She died of fever when I was just three months old. I do wish she'd lived long enough for me to remember calling her mother. I think it would be so sweet to say 'mother,' don't you? And father died four days afterwards from fever, too. That left me an orphan and folks were at their wits' end, so Mrs. Thomas said, what to do with me. You see, nobody wanted me even then. It seems to be my fate. Father and mother had both come from places far away and it was well known they hadn't any relatives living. Finally Mrs. Thomas said she'd take me, though she was poor and had a drunken husband. She brought me up by hand. Do you know if there is anything in being brought up by hand[9] that ought to make people who are brought up that way better than other people? Because whenever I was naughty Mrs. Thomas would ask me how I could be

---

David and Bath-Sheba (II Samuel 12.25). LMM used the name again in "The Romance of Jedediah" (1912).

5. Echoes Juliet's speech, "What's in a name? That which we call a rose / By any other word would smell as sweet," from Shakespeare, *Romeo and Juliet* 2.2.43–44.

6. A plant whose hood-like leaves enclose a bud that has a fetid smell.

7. Something that must be borne, referring to Jesus carrying his cross on the way to the crucifixion. Luke 23.26.

8. Based on LMM's birthplace in Clifton, near Cavendish.

9. For Victorians, this meant being bottle-fed, not breast-fed. In Dickens' *Great Expectations*, Pip confuses this with the idea of corporal punishment.

such a bad girl when she had brought me up by hand—reproachful-like.

"Mr. and Mrs. Thomas moved away from Bolingbroke to Marys-ville,[1] and I lived with them until I was eight years old. I helped look after the Thomas children—there were four of them younger than me—and I can tell you they took a lot of looking after. Then Mr. Thomas was killed falling under a train and his mother offered to take Mrs. Thomas and the children, but she didn't want me. Mrs. Thomas was at *her* wits' end, so she said, what to do with me. Then Mrs. Hammond from up the river came down and said she'd take me, seeing I was handy with children, and I went up the river to live with her in a little clearing among the stumps.[2] It was a very lone-some place. I'm sure I could never have lived there if I hadn't had an imagination. Mr. Hammond worked a little saw-mill up there, and Mrs. Hammond had eight children. She had twins three times. I like babies in moderation, but twins three times in succession is *too much*. I told Mrs. Hammond so firmly, when the last pair came. I used to get so dreadfully tired carrying them about.

"I lived up river with Mrs. Hammond over two years, and then Mr. Hammond died and Mrs. Hammond broke up housekeeping. She divided her children among her relatives and went to the States. I had to go to the asylum at Hopetown, because nobody would take me. They didn't want me at the asylum, either; they said they were overcrowded as it was. But they had to take me and I was there four months until Mrs. Spencer came."

Anne finished up with another sigh, of relief this time. Evidently she did not like talking about her experiences in a world that had not wanted her.

"Did you ever go to school?" demanded Marilla, turning the sorrel mare down the shore road.

"Not a great deal. I went a little the last year I stayed with Mrs. Thomas. When I went up river we were so far from a school that I couldn't walk it in winter and there was vacation in summer, so I could only go in the spring and fall. But of course I went while I was at the asylum. I can read pretty well and I know ever so many pieces of poetry off by heart—'The Battle of Hohenlinden' and 'Edinburgh after Flodden,' and 'Bingen on the Rhine,' and lots of the 'Lady of the Lake' and most of 'The Seasons,' by James Thomson.[3] Don't you

1. A fictional place in Nova Scotia.
2. Trees cut to waist level and left to rot by shiftless farmers clearing a field.
3. Anne has studied poems about battles written half a century earlier by three Scottish men—Thomas Campbell's "Battle of Hohenlinden" (1803) about a French-Austrian war in 1800, William Aytoun's "Edinburgh after Flodden" (1849) about the defeat of Scots by the English in 1513, and Walter Scott's "The Lady of the Lake" (1810) about war in the Scottish Highlands—and by one more recent woman poet, Caroline Norton's "Bingen on the Rhine" (1867) about a dying German legionnaire in Algiers, as well as Scottish James

just love poetry that gives you a crinkly feeling up and down your back? There is a piece in the Fifth Reader[4]—'The Downfall of Poland'—that is just full of thrills. Of course, I wasn't in the Fifth Reader—I was only in the Fourth—but the big girls used to lend me theirs to read."

"Were those women—Mrs. Thomas and Mrs. Hammond—good to you?" asked Marilla, looking at Anne out of the corner of her eye.

"O-o-o-h." faltered Anne. Her sensitive little face suddenly flushed scarlet and embarrassment sat on her brow. "Oh, they *meant* to be—I know they meant to be just as good and kind as possible. And when people mean to be good to you, you don't mind very much when they're not quite—always. They had a good deal to worry them, you know. It's very trying to have a drunken husband, you see; and it must be very trying to have twins three times in succession, don't you think? But I feel sure they meant to be good to me."

Marilla asked no more questions. Anne gave herself up to a silent rapture over the shore road and Marilla guided the sorrel abstract-edly while she pondered deeply. Pity was suddenly stirring in her heart for the child. What a starved, unloved life she had had—a life of drudgery and poverty and neglect; for Marilla was shrewd enough to read between the lines of Anne's history and divine the truth. No wonder she had been so delighted at the prospect of a real home. It was a pity she had to be sent back. What if she, Marilla, should indulge Matthew's unaccountable whim and let her stay? He was set on it; and the child seemed a nice, teachable little thing.

"She's got too much to say," thought Marilla, "but she might be trained out of that. And there's nothing rude or slangy in what she does say. She's ladylike. It's likely her people were nice folks."

The shore road was "woodsy and wild and lonesome."[5] On the right hand, scrub firs, their spirits quite unbroken by long years of tussle with the gulf winds, grew thickly. On the left were the steep red sandstone cliffs, so near the track in places that a mare of less stead-iness than the sorrel might have tried the nerves of the people behind her. Down at the base of the cliffs were heaps of surf-worn rocks or little sandy coves inlaid with pebbles as with ocean jewels; beyond lay the sea, shimmering and blue, and over it soared the gulls, their pinions flashing silvery in the sunlight.

"Isn't the sea wonderful?" said Anne, rousing from a long, wide-eyed silence. "Once, when I lived in Marysville, Mr. Thomas hired

---

Thomson's nature poems, "The Seasons" (1730). LMM misspelled Thomson's name as Thompson, an error carried into the 1908 American edition. See NCE 254.

4. Anthology of poetry and prose prescribed in the 1880s for students for school use, pub-lished in London by Nelson between 1877 and 1898. "The Downfall of Poland" (1824) is also by Scottish Thomas Campbell.

5. A phrase from "Cobbler Keezar's Vision," a poem published 1861 by American poet John Greenleaf Whittier.

an express-wagon and took us all to spend the day at the shore ten miles away. I enjoyed every moment of that day, even if I had to look after the children all the time. I lived it over in happy dreams for years. But this shore is nicer than the Marysville shore. Aren't those gulls splendid? Would you like to be a gull? I think I would—that is, if I couldn't be a human girl. Don't you think it would be nice to wake up at sunrise and swoop down over the water and away out over that lovely blue all day; and then at night to fly back to one's nest? Oh, I can just imagine myself doing it. What big house is that just ahead, please?"

"That's the White Sands Hotel.[6] Mr. Kirke runs it, but the season hasn't begun yet. There are heaps of Americans come there for the summer. They think this shore is just about right."

"I was afraid it might be Mrs. Spencer's place," said Anne mournfully. "I don't want to get there. Somehow, it will seem like the end of everything."

## Chapter VI

### MARILLA MAKES UP HER MIND

GET there they did, however, in due season. Mrs. Spencer lived in a big yellow house at White Sands Cove, and she came to the door with surprise and welcome mingled on her benevolent face.

"Dear, dear," she exclaimed, "you're the last folks I was looking for to-day, but I'm real glad to see you. You'll put your horse in? And how are you, Anne?"

"I'm as well as can be expected, thank you," said Anne smilelessly. A blight seemed to have descended on her.

"I suppose we'll stay a little while to rest the mare," said Marilla, "but I promised Matthew I'd be home early. The fact is, Mrs. Spencer, there's been a queer mistake somewhere, and I've come over to see where it is. We sent word, Matthew and I, for you to bring us a boy from the asylum. We told your brother Robert to tell you we wanted a boy ten or eleven years old."

"Marilla Cuthbert, you don't say so!" said Mrs. Spencer in distress. "Why, Robert sent the word down by his daughter Nancy and she said you wanted a girl—didn't she, Flora Jane?" appealing to her daughter who had come out to the steps.

6. Based on a famous summer hotel in Rustico called "The Seaside Hotel," where the Prince of Wales (later King Edward VII) stayed when visiting PEI in the 1890s. It burned down at the turn of the century. (This hotel was not based on Dalvay, as in the 1985 television series.) American tourism had begun before the publication of *AGG*. In the summer of 1899 alone, 7,000 American visitors made the trek to PEI.

"She certainly did, Miss Cuthbert," corroborated Flora Jane earnestly.

"I'm dreadful sorry," said Mrs. Spencer. "It is too bad; but it certainly wasn't my fault, you see, Miss Cuthbert. I did the best I could and I thought I was following your instructions. Nancy is a terrible flighty thing. I've often had to scold her well for her heedlessness."

"It was our own fault," said Marilla resignedly. "We should have come to you ourselves and not left an important message to be passed along by word of mouth in that fashion. Anyhow, the mistake has been made and the only thing to do now is to set it right. Can we send the child back to the asylum? I suppose they'll take her back, won't they?"

"I suppose so," said Mrs. Spencer thoughtfully, "but I don't think it will be necessary to send her back. Mrs. Peter Blewett was up here yesterday, and she was saying to me how much she wished she'd sent by me for a little girl to help her. Mrs. Peter has a large family, you know, and she finds it hard to get help. Anne will be the very girl for her. I call it positively providential."

Marilla did not look as if she thought Providence[1] had much to do with the matter. Here was an unexpectedly good chance to get this unwelcome orphan off her hands, and she did not even feel grateful for it.

She knew Mrs. Peter Blewett only by sight as a small, shrewish-faced woman without an ounce of superfluous flesh on her bones. But she had heard of her. "A terrible worker and driver," Mrs. Peter was said to be; and discharged servant girls told fearsome tales of her temper and stinginess, and her family of pert, quarrelsome children. Marilla felt a qualm of conscience at the thought of handing Anne over to her tender mercies.[2]

"Well, I'll go in and we'll talk the matter over," she said.

"And if there isn't Mrs. Peter coming up the lane this blessed minute!" exclaimed Mrs. Spencer, bustling her guests through the hall into the parlour, where a deadly chill struck on them as if the air had been strained so long through dark green, closely drawn blinds that it had lost every particle of warmth it had ever possessed. "That is real lucky, for we can settle the matter right away. Take the armchair, Miss Cuthbert. Anne, you sit here on the ottoman and don't wriggle. Let me take your hats. Flora Jane, go out and put the kettle on. Good afternoon, Mrs. Blewett. We were just saying how fortunate it was you happened along. Let me introduce you two

---

1. Theological term for "divine goodness," but the word "Providence" appears only once in the *Holy Bible*, referring to the kindness of a Roman official, in Acts 24.2.
2. "The tender mercies of the wicked are cruel." Phrase used ironically in the *Holy Bible*, Proverbs 12.10.

ladies. Mrs. Blewett, Miss Cuthbert. Please excuse me for just a moment. I forgot to tell Flora Jane to take the buns out of the oven."

Mrs. Spencer whisked away, after pulling up the blinds. Anne, sitting mutely on the ottoman, with her hands clasped tightly in her lap, stared at Mrs. Blewett as one fascinated. Was she to be given into the keeping of this sharp-faced, sharp-eyed woman? She felt a lump coming up in her throat and her eyes smarted painfully. She was beginning to be afraid she couldn't keep the tears back when Mrs. Spencer returned, flushed and beaming, quite capable of taking any and every difficulty, physical, mental or spiritual, into consideration and settling it out of hand.

"It seems there's been a mistake about this little girl, Mrs. Blewett," she said. "I was under the impression that Mr. and Miss Cuthbert wanted a little girl to adopt. I was certainly told so. But it seems it was a boy they wanted. So if you're still of the same mind you were yesterday, I think she'll be just the thing for you."

Mrs. Blewett darted her eyes over Anne from head to foot.

"How old are you and what's your name?" she demanded.

"Anne Shirley," faltered the shrinking child, not daring to make any stipulations regarding the spelling thereof, "and I'm eleven years old."

"Humph! You don't look as if there was much to you. But you're wiry. I don't know but the wiry ones are the best after all. Well, if I take you you'll have to be a good girl, you know—good and smart and respectful. I'll expect you to earn your keep, and no mistake about that. Yes, I suppose I might as well take her off your hands, Miss Cuthbert. The baby's awful fractious,[3] and I'm clean worn out attending to him. If you like I can take her right home now."

Marilla looked at Anne and softened at sight of the child's pale face with its look of mute misery—the misery of a helpless little creature who finds itself once more caught in the trap from which it had escaped. Marilla felt an uncomfortable conviction that, if she denied the appeal of that look, it would haunt her to her dying day. Moreover, she did not fancy Mrs. Blewett. To hand a sensitive, "high-strung" child over to such a woman! No, she could not take the responsibility of doing that!

"Well, I don't know," she said slowly. "I didn't say that Matthew and I had absolutely decided that we wouldn't keep her. In fact, I may say that Matthew is disposed to keep her. I just came over to find out how the mistake had occurred. I think I'd better take her home again and talk it over with Matthew. I feel that I oughtn't to decide on anything without consulting him. If we make up our mind

3. Unruly, brawling.

not to keep her we'll bring or send her over to you to-morrow night. If we don't you may know that she is going to stay with us. Will that suit you, Mrs. Blewett?"

"I suppose it'll have to," said Mrs. Blewett ungraciously.

During Marilla's speech a sunrise had been dawning on Anne's face. First the look of despair faded out; then came a faint flush of hope; her eyes grew deep and bright as morning stars. The child was quite transfigured; and, a moment later, when Mrs. Spencer and Mrs. Blewett went out in quest of a recipe the latter had come to borrow, she sprang up and flew across the room to Marilla.

"Oh, Miss Cuthbert, did you really say that perhaps you would let me stay at Green Gables?" she said, in a breathless whisper, as if speaking aloud might shatter the glorious possibility. "Did you really say it? Or did I only imagine that you did?"

"I think you'd better learn to control that imagination of yours, Anne, if you can't distinguish between what is real and what isn't," said Marilla crossly. "Yes, you did hear me say just that and no more. It isn't decided yet and perhaps we will conclude to let Mrs. Blewett take you after all. She certainly needs you much more than I do."

"I'd rather go back to the asylum than go to live with her," said Anne passionately. "She looks exactly like a—like a gimlet."[4]

Marilla smothered a smile under the conviction that Anne must be reproved for such a speech.

"A little girl like you should be ashamed of talking so about a lady and a stranger," she said severely. "Go back and sit down quietly and hold your tongue and behave as a good girl should."

"I'll try to do and be anything you want me, if you'll only keep me," said Anne, returning meekly to her ottoman.

When they arrived back at Green Gables that evening Matthew met them in the lane. Marilla from afar had noted him prowling along it and guessed his motive. She was prepared for the relief she read in his face when he saw that she had at least brought Anne back with her. But she said nothing to him, relative to the affair, until they were both out in the yard behind the barn milking the cows. Then she briefly told him Anne's history and the result of the interview with Mrs. Spencer.

"I wouldn't give a dog I liked to that Blewett woman," said Matthew with unusual vim.

"I don't fancy her style myself," admitted Marilla, "but it's that or keeping her ourselves, Matthew. And, since you seem to want her, I suppose I'm willing—or have to be. I've been thinking over the idea until I've got kind of used to it. It seems a sort of duty. I've never

4. A small tool for boring holes.

brought up a child, especially a girl, and I dare say I'll make a terrible mess of it. But I'll do my best. So far as I'm concerned, Matthew, she may stay."

Matthew's shy face was a glow of delight.

"Well now, I reckoned you'd come to see it in that light, Marilla," he said. "She's such an interesting little thing."

"It'd be more to the point if you could say she was a useful little thing," retorted Marilla, "but I'll make it my business to see she's trained to be that. And mind, Matthew, you're not to go interfering with my methods. Perhaps an old maid doesn't know much about bringing up a child, but I guess she knows more than an old bachelor. So you just leave me to manage her. When I fail it'll be time enough to put your oar in."[5]

"There, there, Marilla, you can have your own way," said Matthew reassuringly. "Only be as good and kind to her as you can be without spoiling her. I kind of think she's one of the sort you can do anything with if you only get her to love you."

Marilla sniffed, to express her contempt for Matthew's opinions concerning anything feminine, and walked off to the dairy with the pails.

"I won't tell her to-night that she can stay," she reflected, as she strained the milk into the creamers. "She'd be so excited that she wouldn't sleep a wink. Marilla Cuthbert, you're fairly in for it. Did you ever suppose you'd see the day when you'd be adopting an orphan girl? It's surprising enough; but not so surprising as that Matthew should be at the bottom of it, him that always seemed to have such a mortal dread of little girls. Anyhow, we've decided on the experiment and goodness only knows what will come of it."

## Chapter VII

### ANNE SAYS HER PRAYERS

WHEN Marilla took Anne up to bed that night she said stiffly:

"Now, Anne, I noticed last night that you threw your clothes all about the floor when you took them off. That is a very untidy habit, and I can't allow it at all. As soon as you take off any article of clothing fold it neatly and place it on the chair. I haven't any use at all for little girls who aren't neat."

"I was so harrowed up in my mind last night that I didn't think about my clothes at all," said Anne. "I'll fold them nicely to-night.

5. Interfere (a colloquialism derived from nautical language).

They always made us do that at the asylum. Half the time, though,
I'd forget, I'd be in such a hurry to get into bed nice and quiet and
imagine things."

"You'll have to remember a little better if you stay here," admon-
ished Marilla. "There, that looks something like. Say your prayers
now and get into bed."[1]

"I never say any prayers," announced Anne.

Marilla looked horrified astonishment.

"Why, Anne, what do you mean? Were you never taught to say
your prayers? God always wants little girls to say their prayers. Don't
you know who God is, Anne?"

" 'God is a spirit, infinite, eternal and unchangeable, in His being,
wisdom, power, holiness, justice, goodness, and truth,' "[2] responded
Anne promptly and glibly.

Marilla looked rather relieved.

"So you do know something then, thank goodness! You're not quite
a heathen.[3] Where did you learn that?"

"Oh, at the asylum Sunday-school. They made us learn the whole
catechism.[4] I liked it pretty well. There's something splendid about
some of the words. 'Infinite, eternal and unchangeable.' Isn't that
grand? It has such a roll to it—just like a big organ playing. You
couldn't quite call it poetry, I suppose, but it sounds a lot like it,
doesn't it?"

"We're not talking about poetry, Anne—we are talking about saying your prayers. Don't you know it's a terrible wicked thing not to
say your prayers every night? I'm afraid you are a very bad little girl."

"You'd find it easier to be bad than good if you had red hair,"[5] said
Anne reproachfully. "People who haven't red hair don't know what
trouble is. Mrs. Thomas told me that God made my hair red *on
purpose*, and I've never cared about Him since. And anyhow I'd
always be too tired at night to bother saying prayers. People who
have to look after twins can't be expected to say their prayers. Now,
do you honestly think they can?"

Marilla decided that Anne's religious training must be begun at
once. Plainly there was no time to be lost.

"You must say your prayers while you are under my roof, Anne."

"Why, of course, if you want me to," assented Anne cheerfully.
"I'd do anything to oblige you. But you'll have to tell me what to say

1. Unquestioned routine in Protestant families in LMM's time: the child kneels by the bedside and prays.
2. Answer to the seventh question ("What is God?") in the Presbyterian Shorter Catechism.
3. From the Avonlea point of view, anyone not worshipping the God of Israel.
4. Set of questions and answers relating to religious beliefs. Presbyterian children learned
the Westminster Catechism, published in the 1640s.
5. Old wives' tale that red-headed people were bad-tempered, untrustworthy, and possibly
evil.

for this once. After I get into bed I'll imagine out a real nice prayer to say always. I believe that it will be quite interesting, now that I come to think of it."

"You must kneel down," said Marilla in embarrassment.

Anne knelt at Marilla's knee and looked up gravely.

"Why must people kneel down to pray? If I really wanted to pray I'll tell you what I'd do. I'd go out into a great big field all alone or into the deep, deep woods, and I'd look up into the sky—up—up—up—into that lovely blue sky that looks as if there was no end to its blueness. And then I'd just *feel* a prayer. Well, I'm ready. What am I to say?"

Marilla felt more embarrassed than ever. She had intended to teach Anne the childish classic, "Now I lay me down to sleep."[6] But she had, as I have told you, the glimmerings of a sense of humour—which is simply another name for a sense of the fitness of things; and it suddenly occurred to her that that simple little prayer, sacred to white-robed childhood lisping at motherly knees, was entirely unsuited to this freckled witch of a girl who knew and cared nothing about God's love, since she had never had it translated to her through the medium of human love.

"You're old enough to pray for yourself, Anne," she said finally. "Just thank God for your blessings and ask Him humbly for the things you want."

"Well, I'll do my best," promised Anne, burying her face in Marilla's lap. "Gracious heavenly Father—that's the way the ministers say it in church, so I suppose it's all right in a private prayer, isn't it?" she interjected, lifting her head for a moment. "Gracious heavenly Father, I thank Thee for the White Way of Delight and the Lake of Shining Waters and Bonny and the Snow Queen. I'm really extremely grateful for them. And that's all the blessings I can think of just now to thank Thee for. As for the things I want, they're so numerous that it would take a great deal of time to name them all, so I will only mention the two most important. Please let me stay at Green Gables; and please let me be good-looking when I grow up. I remain,

"Yours respectfully,
"ANNE SHIRLEY.

"There, did I do it all right?" she asked eagerly, getting up. "I could have made it much more flowery if I'd had a little more time to think it over."

Poor Marilla was only preserved from complete collapse by remembering that it was not irreverence, but simply spiritual igno-

---

6. Part of a very old prayer for children that begins "Matthew, Mark, Luke, and John, bless the bed that I lie on. Before I lay me down to sleep, I give my soul to Christ to keep" and ends "And if I die before I wake, I pray that Christ my soul will take."

rance on the part of Anne that was responsible for this extraordinary petition. She tucked the child up in bed, mentally vowing that she should be taught a prayer the very next day, and was leaving the room with the light when Anne called her back.

"I've just thought of it now. I should have said 'Amen' in place of 'yours respectfully,' shouldn't I?—the way the ministers do. I'd forgotten it, but I felt a prayer should be finished off in some way, so I put in the other. Do you suppose it will make any difference?"

"I—I don't suppose it will," said Marilla. "Go to sleep now like a good child. Good night."

"I can say good night to-night with a clear conscience," said Anne, cuddling luxuriously down among her pillows.

Marilla retreated to the kitchen, set the candle firmly on the table, and glared at Matthew.

"Matthew Cuthbert, it's about time somebody adopted that child and taught her something. She's next door to a perfect heathen. Will you believe that she never said a prayer in her life till to-night? I'll send to the manse[7] to-morrow and borrow the Peep of Day series,[8] that's what I'll do. And she shall go to Sunday-school just as soon as I can get some suitable clothes made for her. I foresee that I shall have my hands full. Well, well, we can't get through this world without our share of trouble. I've had a pretty easy life of it so far, but my time has come at last and I suppose I'll just have to make the best of it."

## Chapter VIII

### ANNE'S BRINGING-UP IS BEGUN

FOR reasons best known to herself, Marilla did not tell Anne that she was to stay at Green Gables until the next afternoon. During the forenoon she kept the child busy with various tasks and watched over her with a keen eye while she did them. By noon she had concluded that Anne was smart and obedient, willing to work and quick to learn; her most serious shortcoming seemed to be a tendency to fall into day-dreams in the middle of a task and forget all about it until such time as she was sharply recalled to earth by a reprimand or a catastrophe.

When Anne had finished washing the dinner dishes she suddenly confronted Marilla with the air and expression of one desperately

7. The house owned by the Presbyterian church, assigned as a home to the minister.
8. Best-selling Methodist Sunday School stories by Mrs. Favell Lee Bevan Mortimer, from Wales, published in Boston by the American Tract Society throughout the nineteenth century.

determined to learn the worst. Her thin little body trembled from head to foot; her face flushed and her eyes dilated until they were almost black; she clasped her hands tightly and said in an imploring voice:

"Oh, please, Miss Cuthbert, won't you tell me if you are going to send me away or not? I've tried to be patient all the morning, but I really feel that I cannot bear not knowing any longer. It's a dreadful feeling. Please tell me."

"You haven't scalded the dish-cloth[1] in clean hot water as I told you to do," said Marilla immovably. "Just go and do it before you ask any more questions, Anne."

Anne went and attended to the dish-cloth. Then she returned to Marilla and fastened imploring eyes on the latter's face.

"Well," said Marilla, unable to find any excuse for deferring her explanation longer, "I suppose I might as well tell you. Matthew and I have decided to keep you—that is, if you will try to be a good little girl and show yourself grateful. Why, child, whatever is the matter?"

"I'm crying," said Anne in a tone of bewilderment. "I can't think why. I'm glad as glad can be. Oh, *glad* doesn't seem the right word at all. I was glad about the White Way and the cherry blossoms— but this! Oh, it's something more than glad. I'm so happy. I'll try to be so good. It will be up-hill work, I expect, for Mrs. Thomas often told me I was desperately wicked.[2] However, I'll do my very best. But can you tell me why I'm crying?"

"I suppose it's because you're all excited and worked up," said Marilla disapprovingly. "Sit down on that chair and try to calm yourself. I'm afraid you both cry and laugh far too easily. Yes, you can stay here and we will try to do right by you. You must go to school; but it's only a fortnight till vacation so it isn't worth while for you to start before it opens again in September."

"What am I to call you?" asked Anne. "Shall I always say Miss Cuthbert? Can I call you Aunt Marilla?"

"No; you'll call me just plain Marilla. I'm not used to being called Miss Cuthbert and it would make me nervous."

"It sounds awfully disrespectful to say just Marilla," protested Anne.

"I guess there'll be nothing disrespectful in it if you're careful to speak respectfully. Everybody, young and old, in Avonlea calls me Marilla except the minister. He says Miss Cuthbert—when he thinks of it."

"I'd love to call you Aunt Marilla," said Anne wistfully. "I've never

---

1. Boiling the cloth used to wash dishes, a telling sign of good housewifery before disinfectants were available to destroy bacteria.
2. "The heart is deceitful above all things, and desperately wicked." *Holy Bible*, Jeremiah 17.9.

had an aunt or any relation at all—not even a grandmother. It would make me feel as if I really belonged to you. Can't I call you Aunt Marilla?"

"No. I'm not your aunt and I don't believe in calling people names that don't belong to them."

"But we could imagine you were my aunt."

"I couldn't," said Marilla grimly.

"Do you never imagine things different from what they really are?" asked Anne wide-eyed.

"No."

"Oh!" Anne drew a long breath. "Oh, Miss—Marilla, how much you miss!"

"I don't believe in imagining things different from what they really are," retorted Marilla. "When the Lord puts us in certain circumstances He doesn't mean for us to imagine them away. And that reminds me. Go into the sitting-room, Anne—be sure your feet are clean and don't let any flies in—and bring me out the illustrated card that's on the mantelpiece. The Lord's Prayer[3] is on it and you'll devote your spare time this afternoon to learning it off by heart. There's to be no more of such praying as I heard last night."

"I suppose I was very awkward," said Anne apologetically, "but then, you see, I'd never had any practice. You couldn't really expect a person to pray very well the first time she tried, could you? I thought out a splendid prayer after I went to bed, just as I promised you I would. It was nearly as long as a minister's and so poetical. But would you believe it? I couldn't remember one word when I woke up this morning. And I'm afraid I'll never be able to think out another one as good. Somehow, things never are so good when they're thought out a second time. Have you ever noticed that?"

"Here is something for you to notice, Anne. When I tell you to do a thing I want you to obey me at once and not stand stock-still and discourse about it. Just you go and do as I bid you."

Anne promptly departed for the sitting-room across the hall; she failed to return; after waiting ten minutes Marilla laid down her knitting and marched after her with a grim expression. She found Anne standing motionless before a picture hanging on the wall between the two windows, with her hands clasped behind her, her face uplifted, and her eyes astar with dreams. The white and green light strained through apple-trees and clustering vines outside fell over the rapt little figure with a half-unearthly radiance.

---

3. The prayer taught by Jesus which begins, "Our father which art in heaven." *Holy Bible*, Matthew 6.9–13.

"Anne, whatever are you thinking of?" demanded Marilla sharply. Anne came back to earth with a start.

"That," she said, pointing to the picture—a rather vivid chromo entitled, "Christ Blessing Little Children"[4]—"and I was just imagining I was one of them—that I was the little girl in the blue dress, standing off by herself in the corner as if she didn't belong to anybody, like me. She looks lonely and sad, don't you think? I guess she hadn't any father or mother of her own. But she wanted to be blessed, too, so she just crept shyly up on the outside of the crowd, hoping nobody would notice her—except Him. I'm sure I know just how she felt. Her heart must have beat and her hands must have got cold, like mine did when I asked you if I could stay. She was afraid He mightn't notice her. But it's likely He did, don't you think? I've been trying to imagine it all out—her edging a little nearer all the time until she was quite close to Him; and then He would look at her and put His hand on her hair and oh, such a thrill of joy as would run over her! But I wish the artist hadn't painted Him so sorrowful-looking. All His pictures are like that, if you've noticed. But I don't believe He could really have looked so sad or the children would have been afraid of Him."

"Anne," said Marilla, wondering why she had not broken into this speech long before, "you shouldn't talk that way. It's irreverent—positively irreverent."

Anne's eyes marvelled.

"Why, I felt just as reverent as could be. I'm sure I didn't mean to be irreverent."

"Well, I don't suppose you did—but it doesn't sound right to talk so familiarly about such things. And another thing, Anne, when I send you after something you're to bring it at once and not fall into mooning and imagining before pictures. Remember that. Take that card and come right to the kitchen. Now, sit down in the corner and learn that prayer off by heart."

Anne set the card up against the jugful of apple blossoms she had brought in to decorate the dinner-table—Marilla had eyed that decoration askance, but had said nothing—propped her chin on her hands, and fell to studying it intently for several silent minutes.

"I like this," she announced at length. "It's beautiful. I've heard it before—I heard the superintendent of the asylum Sunday-school say it over once. But I didn't like it then. He had such a cracked voice and he prayed it so mournfully. I really felt sure he thought praying was a disagreeable duty. This isn't poetry, but it makes me feel able just the same way poetry does. 'Our Father who art in heaven, hal-

---

4. A chromolithograph (a picture printed in colors with aniline dye) of a painting by Benjamin Roberts Haydon, commissioned in 1837 for a Liverpool chapel.

lowed be Thy name.' That is just like a line of music. Oh, I'm so glad you thought of making me learn this, Miss—Marilla."

"Well, learn it and hold your tongue," said Marilla shortly.

Anne tipped the vase of apple blossoms near enough to bestow a soft kiss on a pink-cupped bud, and then studied diligently for some moments longer.

"Marilla," she demanded presently, "do you think that I shall ever have a bosom friend[5] in Avonlea?"

"A—a what kind of a friend?"

"A bosom friend—an intimate friend, you know—a really kindred spirit to whom I can confide my inmost soul. I've dreamed of meeting her all my life. I never really supposed I would, but so many of my loveliest dreams have come true all at once that perhaps this one will, too. Do you think it's possible?"

"Diana Barry lives over at Orchard Slope and she's about your age. She's a very nice little girl, and perhaps she will be a playmate for you when she comes home. She's visiting her aunt over at Carmody just now. You'll have to be careful how you behave yourself, though. Mrs. Barry is a very particular woman. She won't let Diana play with any little girl who isn't nice and good."

Anne looked at Marilla through the apple blossoms, her eyes aglow with interest.

"What is Diana like? Her hair isn't red, is it? Oh, I hope not. It's bad enough to have red hair myself, but I positively couldn't endure it in a bosom friend."

"Diana is a very pretty little girl. She has black eyes and hair and rosy cheeks. And she is good and smart, which is better than being pretty."

Marilla was as fond of morals as the Duchess in Wonderland,[6] and was firmly convinced that one should be tacked on to every remark made to a child who was being brought up.

But Anne waved the moral inconsequently aside and seized only on the delightful possibilities before it.

"Oh, I'm so glad she's pretty. Next to being beautiful oneself—and that's impossible in my case—it would be best to have a beautiful bosom friend. When I lived with Mrs. Thomas she had a bookcase in her sitting-room with glass doors. There weren't any books in it; Mrs. Thomas kept her best china and her preserves there—when she had any preserves to keep. One of the doors was broken. Mr. Thomas smashed it one night when he was slightly intoxicated. But

---

5. Intimate friend: a term in use since the late sixteenth century. It appears, hyphenated, in John Keats's "To Autumn" (1820), l. 2: "Close bosom-friend of the maturing sun."
6. In Lewis Carroll's children's classic, *Alice in Wonderland* (1865), the Duchess' favorite phrase is, "And the moral of that is. . . ."

the other was whole and I used to pretend that my reflection in it was another little girl who lived in it. I called her Katie Maurice,[7] and we were very intimate. I used to talk to her by the hour, especially on Sunday, and tell her everything. Katie was the comfort and consolation of my life. We used to pretend that the bookcase was enchanted and that if I only knew the spell I could open the door and step right into the room where Katie Maurice lived, instead of into Mrs. Thomas' shelves of preserves and china. And then Katie Maurice would have taken me by the hand and led me out into a wonderful place, all flowers and sunshine and fairies, and we would have lived there happy for ever after. When I went to live with Mrs. Hammond it just broke my heart to leave Katie Maurice. She felt it dreadfully, too, I know she did, for she was crying when she kissed me good-bye through the bookcase door. There was no bookcase at Mrs. Hammond's. But just up the river a little way from the house there was a long green little valley, and the loveliest echo lived there. It echoed back every word you said, even if you didn't talk a bit loud. So I imagined that it was a little girl called Violetta and we were great friends and I loved her almost as well as I loved Katie Maurice—not quite, but almost, you know. The night before I went to the asylum I said good-bye to Violetta, and oh, her good-bye came back to me in such sad, sad tones. I had become so attached to her that I hadn't the heart to imagine a bosom friend at the asylum, even if there had been any scope for imagination there."

"I think it's just as well there wasn't," said Marilla drily. "I don't approve of such goings-on. You seem to half believe your own imaginations. It will be well for you to have a real live friend to put such nonsense out of your head. But don't let Mrs. Barry hear you talking about your Katie Maurices and your Violettas or she'll think you tell stories."

"Oh, I won't. I couldn't talk of them to everybody—their memories are too sacred for that. But I thought I'd like to have you know about them. Oh, look, here's a big bee just tumbled out of an apple blossom. Just think what a lovely place to live—in an apple blossom! Fancy going to sleep in it when the wind was rocking it. If I wasn't a human girl I think I'd like to be a bee and live among the flowers."

"Yesterday you wanted to be a sea-gull," sniffed Marilla. "I think you are very fickle-minded. I told you to learn that prayer and not talk. But it seems impossible for you to stop talking if you've got anybody that will listen to you. So go up to your room and learn it."

"Oh, I know it pretty nearly all now—all but just the last line."

---

7. LMM remembered having three imaginary friends, named Katie Maurice, Violetta, and Lucy Gray.

"Well, never mind, do as I tell you. Go to your room and finish learning it well, and stay there until I call you down to help me get tea."

"Can I take the apple blossoms with me for company?" pleaded Anne.

"No; you don't want your room cluttered up with flowers. You should have left them on the tree in the first place."

"I did feel a little that way, too," said Anne. "I kind of felt I shouldn't shorten their lovely lives by picking them—I wouldn't want to be picked if I were an apple blossom. But the temptation was *irresistible*. What do you do when you meet with an irresistible temptation?"

"Anne, did you hear me tell you to go to your room?"

Anne sighed, retreated to the east gable, and sat down in a chair by the window.

"There—I know this prayer. I learned that last sentence coming up-stairs. Now I'm going to imagine things into this room so that they'll always stay imagined. The floor is covered with a white velvet carpet with pink roses all over it and there are pink silk curtains at the windows. The walls are hung with gold and silver brocade tapestry. The furniture is mahogany.[8] I never saw any mahogany, but it does sound *so* luxurious. This is a couch all heaped with gorgeous silken cushions, pink and blue and crimson and gold, and I am reclining gracefully on it. I can see my reflection in that splendid big mirror hanging on the wall. I am tall and regal, clad in a gown of trailing white lace, with a pearl cross on my breast and pearls in my hair. My hair is of midnight darkness and my skin is a clear ivory pallor. My name is the Lady Cordelia Fitzgerald.[9] No, it isn't—I can't make *that* seem real."

She danced up to the little looking-glass and peered into it. Her pointed freckled face and solemn gray eyes peered back at her.

"You're only Anne of Green Gables," she said earnestly, "and I see you, just as you are looking now, whenever I try to imagine I'm the Lady Cordelia. But it's a million times nicer to be Anne of Green Gables than Anne of nowhere in particular, isn't it?"

She bent forward, kissed her reflection affectionately, and betook herself to the open window.

"Dear Snow Queen, good afternoon. And good afternoon, dear birches down in the hollow. And good afternoon, dear gray house up on the hill. I wonder if Diana is to be my bosom friend. I hope she will, and I shall love her very much. But I must never quite forget Katie Maurice and Violetta. They would feel so hurt if I did and I'd

8. Reddish-brown hardwood, imported from tropical countries for fine furniture.
9. The prefix "Fitz" (from French "*fils*") suggests a high-born person, as in James Fitz-James in *The Lady of the Lake*, or Fitzwilliam Darcy in Jane Austen's *Pride and Prejudice*.

hate to hurt anybody's feelings, even a little bookcase girl's or a little echo girl's. I must be careful to remember them and send them a kiss every day."

Anne blew a couple of airy kisses from her fingertips past the cherry blossoms and then, with her chin in her hands, drifted luxuriously out on a sea of day-dreams.

# Chapter IX

### MRS. RACHEL LYNDE IS PROPERLY HORRIFIED

ANNE had been a fortnight at Green Gables before Mrs. Lynde arrived to inspect her. Mrs. Rachel, to do her justice, was not to blame for this. A severe and unseasonable attack of grippe[1] had confined that good lady to her house ever since the occasion of her last visit to Green Gables. Mrs. Rachel was not often sick and had a well-defined contempt for people who were; but grippe, she asserted, was like no other illness on earth and could only be interpreted as one of the special visitations of Providence. As soon as her doctor allowed her to put her foot out-of-doors she hurried up to Green Gables, bursting with curiosity to see Matthew's and Marilla's orphan, concerning whom all sorts of stories and suppositions had gone abroad in Avonlea.

Anne had made good use of every waking moment of that fortnight. Already she was acquainted with every tree and shrub about the place. She had discovered that a lane opened out below the apple orchard and ran up through a belt of woodland; and she had explored it to its furthest end in all its delicious vagaries of brook and bridge, fir coppice[2] and wild cherry arch, corners thick with fern, and branching byways of maple and mountain ash.

She had made friends with the spring down in the hollow—that wonderful deep, clear icy-cold spring; it was set about with smooth red sandstones and rimmed in by great palm-like clumps of water fern; and beyond it was a log bridge over the brook.

That bridge led Anne's dancing feet up over a wooded hill beyond, where perpetual twilight reigned under the straight, thick-growing firs and spruces; the only flowers there were myriads of delicate "June bells," those shyest and sweetest of woodland blooms, and a few pale, aerial starflowers,[3] like the spirits of last year's blossoms.

---

1. French word for influenza.
2. A small area of evergreen trees, grown to be cut for kindling fires.
3. Wildflowers, *trientalis borealis*, four inches tall, hardy in the north, with seven leaves and seven-petalled white flowers.

Gossamers[4] glimmered like threads of silver among the trees and the fir boughs and tassels[5] seemed to utter friendly speech.

All these raptured voyages of exploration were made in the odd half-hours which she was allowed for play, and Anne talked Matthew and Marilla half-deaf over her discoveries. Not that Matthew complained, to be sure; he listened to it all with a wordless smile of enjoyment on his face; Marilla permitted the "chatter" until she found herself becoming too interested in it, whereupon she always promptly quenched Anne by a curt command to hold her tongue.

Anne was out in the orchard when Mrs. Rachel came, wandering at her own sweet will through the lush, tremulous grasses splashed with ruddy evening sunshine; so that good lady had an excellent chance to talk her illness fully over, describing every ache and pulse-beat with such evident enjoyment that Marilla thought even grippe must bring its compensations. When details were exhausted Mrs. Rachel introduced the real reason of her call.

"I've been hearing some surprising things about you and Matthew."

"I don't suppose you are any more surprised than I am myself," said Marilla. "I'm getting over my surprise now."

"It was too bad there was such a mistake," said Mrs. Rachel sympathetically. "Couldn't you have sent her back?"

"I suppose we could, but we decided not to. Matthew took a fancy to her. And I must say I like her myself—although I admit she has her faults. The house seems a different place already. She's a real bright little thing."

Marilla said more than she had intended to say when she began, for she read disapproval in Mrs. Rachel's expression.

"It's a great responsibility you've taken on yourself," said that lady gloomily, "especially when you've never had any experience with children. You don't know much about her or her real disposition, I suppose, and there's no guessing how a child like that will turn out. But I don't want to discourage you I'm sure, Marilla."

"I'm not feeling discouraged," was Marilla's dry response. "When I make up my mind to do a thing it stays made up. I suppose you'd like to see Anne. I'll call her in."

Anne came running in presently, her face sparkling with the delight of her orchard rovings; but, abashed at finding herself in the unexpected presence of a stranger, she halted confusedly inside the door. She certainly was an odd-looking little creature in the short tight wincey dress she had worn from the asylum, below which her thin legs seemed ungracefully long. Her freckles were more numer-

---

4. Light, filmy spider webs.
5. New growth on fir trees, hanging like tufts of loose threads.

ous and obtrusive than ever; the wind had ruffled her hatless hair into over-brilliant disorder; it had never looked redder than at that moment.

"Well, they didn't pick you for your looks, that's sure and certain," was Mrs. Rachel Lynde's emphatic comment. Mrs. Rachel was one of those delightful and popular people who pride themselves on speaking their mind without fear or favour.[6] "She's terrible skinny and homely, Marilla. Come here, child, and let me have a look at you. Lawful heart,[7] did any one ever see such freckles? And hair as red as carrots! Come here, child, I say."

Anne "came there," but not exactly as Mrs. Rachel expected. With one bound she crossed the kitchen floor and stood before Mrs. Rachel, her face scarlet with anger, her lips quivering, and her whole slender form trembling from head to foot.

"I hate you," she cried in a choked voice, stamping her foot on the floor. "I hate you—I hate you—I hate you—" a louder stamp with each assertion of hatred. "How dare you call me skinny and ugly? How dare you say I'm freckled and red-headed? You are a rude, impolite, unfeeling woman!"

"Anne!" exclaimed Marilla in consternation.

But Anne continued to face Mrs. Rachel undauntedly, head up, eyes blazing, hands clenched, passionate indignation exhaling from her like an atmosphere.

"How dare you say such things about me?" she repeated vehemently. "How would you like to have such things said about you? How would you like to be told that you are fat and clumsy and probably hadn't a spark of imagination in you? I don't care if I do hurt your feelings by saying so! I hope I hurt them. You have hurt mine worse than they were ever hurt before even by Mrs. Thomas' intoxicated husband. And I'll *never* forgive you for it, never, never!"

Stamp! Stamp!

"Did anybody ever see such a temper!" exclaimed the horrified Mrs. Rachel.

"Anne, go to your room and stay there until I come up," said Marilla, recovering her powers of speech with difficulty.

Anne, bursting into tears, rushed to the hall door, slammed it until the tins on the porch wall outside rattled in sympathy, and fled through the hall and up the stairs like a whirlwind. A subdued slam above told that the door of the east gable had been shut with equal vehemence.

"Well, I don't envy you your job bringing *that* up, Marilla," said Mrs. Rachel with unspeakable solemnity.

6. Legalism: without negative or positive bias.
7. Colloquialism, like "Good Gracious!" or "Mercy me!" which are substitutions to avoid taking a sacred name in vain.

"I HATE YOU," SHE CRIED IN A CHOKED VOICE, STAMPING HER FOOT ON THE FLOOR

Marilla opened her lips to say she knew not what of apology or deprecation. What she did say was a surprise to herself then and ever afterwards.

"You shouldn't have twitted[8] her about her looks, Rachel."

"Marilla Cuthbert, you don't mean to say that you are upholding her in such a terrible display of temper as we've just seen?" demanded Mrs. Rachel indignantly.

"No," said Marilla slowly, "I'm not trying to excuse her. She's been very naughty and I'll have to give her a talking to about it. But we must make allowances for her. She's never been taught what is right. And you *were* too hard on her, Rachel."

Marilla could not help tacking on that last sentence, although she was again surprised at herself for doing it. Mrs. Rachel got up with an air of offended dignity.

"Well, I see that I'll have to be very careful what I say after this, Marilla, since the fine feelings of orphans, brought from goodness knows where, have to be considered before anything else. Oh, no, I'm not vexed—don't worry yourself. I'm too sorry for you to leave any room for anger in my mind. You'll have your own troubles with that child. But if you'll take my advice—which I suppose you won't do, although I've brought up ten children and buried two—you'll do that 'talking to' you mention with a fair-sized birch switch.[9] I should think *that* would be the most effective language for that kind of a child. Her temper matches her hair I guess. Well, good evening, Marilla. I hope you'll come down to see me often as usual. But you can't expect me to visit here again in a hurry, if I'm liable to be flown at and insulted in such a fashion. It's something new in *my* experience."

Whereat Mrs. Rachel swept out and away—if a fat woman who always waddled *could* be said to sweep away—and Marilla with a very solemn face betook herself to the east gable.

On the way up-stairs she pondered uneasily as to what she ought to do. She felt no little dismay over the scene that had just been enacted. How unfortunate that Anne should have displayed such temper before Mrs. Rachel Lynde, of all people! Then Marilla suddenly became aware of an uncomfortable and rebuking consciousness that she felt more humiliation over this than sorrow over the discovery of such a serious defect in Anne's disposition. And how was she to punish her? The amiable suggestion of the birch switch— to the efficiency of which all of Mrs. Rachel's own children could have borne smarting testimony—did not appeal to Marilla. She did not believe she could whip a child. No, some other method of pun-

8. Teased or taunted.
9. Whip used to punish recalcitrant children: a branch from a birch tree, considered humane because flexible.

ishment must be found to bring Anne to a proper realization of the enormity of her offence.

Marilla found Anne face downward on her bed, crying bitterly, quite oblivious of muddy boots on a clean counterpane.[1]

"Anne," she said, not ungently.

No answer.

"Anne," with greater severity, "get off that bed this minute and listen to what I have to say to you."

Anne squirmed off the bed and sat rigidly on a chair beside it, her face swollen and tear-stained and her eyes fixed stubbornly on the floor.

"This is a nice way for you to behave, Anne! Aren't you ashamed of yourself?"

"She hadn't any right to call me ugly and red-headed," retorted Anne, evasive and defiant.

"You hadn't any right to fly into such a fury and talk the way you did to her, Anne. I was ashamed of you—thoroughly ashamed of you. I wanted you to behave nicely to Mrs. Lynde, and instead of that you have disgraced me. I'm sure I don't know why you should lose your temper like that just because Mrs. Lynde said you were red-haired and homely. You say it yourself often enough."

"Oh, but there's such a difference between saying a thing yourself and hearing other people say it," wailed Anne. "You may know a thing is so, but you can't help hoping other people don't quite think it is. I suppose you think I have an awful temper, but I couldn't help it. When she said those things something just rose right up in me and choked me. I *had* to fly out at her."

"Well, you made a fine exhibition of yourself I must say. Mrs. Lynde will have a nice story to tell about you everywhere—and she'll tell it, too. It was a dreadful thing for you to lose your temper like that, Anne."

"Just imagine how you would feel if somebody told you to your face that you were skinny and ugly," pleaded Anne tearfully.

An old remembrance suddenly rose up before Marilla. She had been a very small child when she had heard one aunt say of her to another, "What a pity she is such a dark, homely little thing." Marilla was every day of fifty before the sting had gone out of that memory.

"I don't say that I think Mrs. Lynde was exactly right in saying what she did to you, Anne," she admitted in a softer tone. "Rachel is too outspoken. But that is no excuse for such behaviour on your part. She was a stranger and an elderly person and my visitor—all three very good reasons why you should have been respectful to her.

1. Bedspread.

You were rude and saucy and"—Marilla had a saving inspiration of punishment—"you must go to her and tell her you are very sorry for your bad temper and ask her to forgive you."

"I can never do that," said Anne determinedly and darkly. "You can punish me in any way you like, Marilla. You can shut me up in a dark, damp dungeon inhabited by snakes and toads and feed me only on bread and water and I shall not complain. But I cannot ask Mrs. Lynde to forgive me."

"We're not in the habit of shutting people up in dark, damp dungeons," said Marilla drily, "especially as they're rather scarce in Avonlea. But apologize to Mrs. Lynde you must and shall and you'll stay here in your room until you can tell me you're willing to do it."

"I shall have to stay here for ever then," said Anne mournfully, "because I can't tell Mrs. Lynde I'm sorry I said those things to her. How can I? I'm *not* sorry. I'm sorry I've vexed you; but I'm *glad* I told her just what I did. It was a great satisfaction. I can't say I'm sorry when I'm not, can I? I can't even *imagine* I'm sorry."

"Perhaps your imagination will be in better working order by the morning," said Marilla, rising to depart. "You'll have the night to think over your conduct in and come to a better frame of mind. You said you would try to be a very good girl if we kept you at Green Gables, but I must say it hasn't seemed very much like it this evening."

Leaving this Parthian shaft[2] to rankle in Anne's stormy bosom, Marilla descended to the kitchen grievously troubled in mind and vexed in soul. She was as angry with herself as with Anne, because whenever she recalled Mrs. Rachel's dumfounded countenance her lips twitched with amusement and she felt a most reprehensible desire to laugh.

## Chapter X

### ANNE'S APOLOGY

MARILLA said nothing to Matthew about the affair that evening; but when Anne proved still refractory the next morning an explanation had to be made to account for her absence from the breakfast-table. Marilla told Matthew the whole story, taking pains to impress him with a due sense of the enormity of Anne's behaviour.

"It's a good thing Rachel Lynde got a calling down; she's a meddlesome old gossip," was Matthew's consolatory rejoinder.

---

2. A shot cast backward in leaving, in the manner of warriors of Parthia, ancient kingdom of West Asia.

"Matthew Cuthbert, I'm astonished at you. You know that Anne's behaviour was dreadful, and yet you take her part! I suppose you'll be saying next thing that she oughtn't to be punished at all."

"Well now—no—not exactly," said Matthew uneasily. "I reckon she ought to be punished a little. But don't be too hard on her, Marilla. Recollect she hasn't ever had any one to teach her right. You're—you're going to give her something to eat, aren't you?"

"When did you ever hear of me starving people into good behaviour?" demanded Marilla indignantly. "She'll have her meals regular, and I'll carry them up to her myself. But she'll stay up there until she's willing to apologize to Mrs. Lynde, and that's final, Matthew."

Breakfast, dinner, and supper were very silent meals—for Anne still remained obdurate. After each meal Marilla carried a well-filled tray to the east gable and brought it down later on not noticeably depleted. Matthew eyed its last descent with a troubled eye. Had Anne eaten anything at all?

When Marilla went out that evening to bring the cows from the back pasture, Matthew, who had been hanging about the barns and watching, slipped into the house with the air of a burglar and crept upstairs. As a general thing Matthew gravitated between the kitchen and the little bedroom off the hall where he slept; once in a while he ventured uncomfortably into the parlour or sitting-room when the minister came to tea. But he had never been upstairs in his own house since the spring he helped Marilla paper the spare bedroom, and that was four years ago.

He tiptoed along the hall and stood for several minutes outside the door of the east gable before he summoned courage to tap on it with his fingers and then open the door to peep in.

Anne was sitting on the yellow chair by the window, gazing mournfully out into the garden. Very small and unhappy she looked, and Matthew's heart smote him. He softly closed the door and tiptoed over to her.

"Anne," he whispered, as if afraid of being over heard, "how are you making it, Anne?"

Anne smiled wanly.

"Pretty well. I imagine a good deal, and that helps to pass the time. Of course, it's rather lonesome. But then, I may as well get used to that."

Anne smiled again, bravely facing the long years of solitary imprisonment before her.

Matthew recollected that he must say what he had come to say without loss of time, lest Marilla return prematurely.

"Well now, Anne, don't you think you'd better do it and have it over with?" he whispered. "It'll have to be done sooner or later, you

know, for Marilla's a dreadful determined woman—dreadful determined, Anne. Do it right off, I say, and have it over."

"Do you mean apologize to Mrs. Lynde?"

"Yes—apologize—that's the very word," said Matthew eagerly.
"Just smooth it over so to speak. That's what I was trying to get at."

"I suppose I could do it to oblige you," said Anne thoughtfully. "It
would be true enough to say I *am* sorry, because I am sorry now. I
wasn't a bit sorry last night. I was mad clear through, and I stayed
mad all night. I know I did because I woke up three times and I was
just furious every time. But this morning it was all over. I wasn't in
a temper any more—and it left a dreadful sort of goneness, too. I
felt so ashamed of myself. But I just couldn't think of going and
telling Mrs. Lynde so. It would be so humiliating. I made up my
mind I'd stay shut up here for ever rather than do that. But still—
I'd do anything for you—if you really want me to—"

"Well now, of course I do. It's terrible lonesome down-stairs without you. Just go and smooth it over—that's a good girl."

"Very well," said Anne resignedly. "I'll tell Marilla as soon as she
comes in that I've repented."

"That's right—that's right, Anne. But don't tell Marilla I said anything about it. She might think I was putting my oar in and I promised not to do that."

"Wild horses won't drag the secret from me,"[1] promised Anne solemnly. "How would wild horses drag a secret from a person anyhow?"

But Matthew was gone, scared at his own success. He fled hastily
to the remotest corner of the horse pasture lest Marilla should suspect what he had been up to. Marilla herself, upon her return to the
house, was agreeably surprised to hear a plaintive voice calling,
"Marilla," over the banisters.

"Well?" she said, going into the hall.

"I'm sorry I lost my temper and said rude things, and I'm willing
to go and tell Mrs. Lynde so."

"Very well." Marilla's crispness gave no sign of her relief. She had
been wondering what under the canopy[2] she should do if Anne did
not give in. "I'll take you down after milking."

Accordingly, after milking, behold Marilla and Anne walking down
the lane, the former erect and triumphant, the latter drooping and
dejected. But half-way down Anne's dejection vanished as if by
enchantment. She lifted her head and stepped lightly along, her eyes
fixed on the sunset sky and an air of subdued exhilaration about her.
Marilla beheld the change disapprovingly. This was no meek peni-

---

1. Old-time torture consisting of tying the victim hand and foot to four horses, driven apart.
2. Material suspended overhead—figuratively the sky.

tent[3] such as it behooved her to take into the presence of the offended Mrs. Lynde.

"What are you thinking of, Anne?" she asked sharply.

"I'm imagining out what I must say to Mrs. Lynde," answered Anne dreamily.

This was satisfactory—or should have been so. But Marilla could not rid herself of the notion that something in her scheme of punishment was going askew. Anne had no business to look so rapt and radiant.

Rapt and radiant Anne continued until they were in the very presence of Mrs. Lynde, who was sitting knitting by her kitchen window. Then the radiance vanished. Mournful penitence appeared on every feature. Before a word was spoken Anne suddenly went down on her knees before the astonished Mrs. Rachel and held out her hands beseechingly.

"Oh, Mrs. Lynde, I am so extremely sorry," she said with a quiver in her voice. "I could never express all my sorrow, no, not if I used up a whole dictionary. You must just imagine it. I behaved terribly to you—and I've disgraced the dear friends, Matthew and Marilla, who have let me stay at Green Gables although I'm not a boy. I'm a dreadfully wicked and ungrateful girl, and I deserve to be punished and cast out by respectable people for ever. It was very wicked of me to fly into a temper because you told me the truth. It *was* the truth; every word you said was true. My hair is red and I'm freckled and skinny and ugly. What I said to you was true, too, but I shouldn't have said it. Oh, Mrs. Lynde, please, please, forgive me. If you refuse it will be a lifelong sorrow to me. You wouldn't like to inflict a lifelong sorrow on a poor little orphan girl, would you, even if she had a dreadful temper? Oh, I am sure you wouldn't. Please say you forgive me, Mrs. Lynde."

Anne clasped her hands together, bowed her head, and waited for the word of judgment.

There was no mistaking her sincerity—it breathed in every tone of her voice. Both Marilla and Mrs. Lynde recognized its unmistakable ring. But the former understood in dismay that Anne was actually enjoying her valley of humiliation—was revelling in the thoroughness of her abasement. Where was the wholesome punishment upon which she, Marilla, had plumed herself?[4] Anne had turned it into a species of positive pleasure.

Good Mrs. Lynde, not being overburdened with perception, did not see this. She only perceived that Anne had made a very thorough

3. Someone who repents of sin.
4. Felt pride, as if decorated with feathers.

apology and all resentment vanished from her kindly, if somewhat officious, heart.

"There, there, get up, child," she said heartily, "Of course I forgive you. I guess I was a little too hard on you, anyway. But I'm such an outspoken person. You just mustn't mind me, that's what. It can't be denied your hair is terrible red; but I knew a girl once—went to school with her, in fact—whose hair was every mite as red as yours when she was young, but when she grew up it darkened to a real handsome auburn.[5] I wouldn't be a mite surprised if yours did, too—not a mite."

"Oh, Mrs. Lynde!" Anne drew a long breath as she rose to her feet. "You have given me a hope. I shall always feel that you are a bene-factor. Oh I could endure anything if I only thought my hair would be a handsome auburn when I grew up. It would be so much easier to be good if one's hair was a handsome auburn, don't you think? And now may I go out into your garden and sit on that bench under the apple-trees while you and Marilla are talking? There is so much more scope for imagination out there."

"Laws, yes, run along, child. And you can pick a bouquet of them white June lilies[6] over in the corner if you like."

As the door closed behind Anne Mrs. Lynde got briskly up to light a lamp.[7]

"She's a real odd little thing. Take this chair, Marilla; it's easier than the one you've got; I just keep that for the hired boy to sit on. Yes, she certainly is an odd child, but there is something kind of taking about her after all. I don't feel so surprised at you and Mat-thew keeping her as I did—nor so sorry for you, either. She may turn out all right. Of course, she has a queer way of expressing herself—a little too—well, too kind of forcible, you know; but she'll likely get over that now that she's come to live among civilized folks. And then, her temper's pretty quick, I guess; but there's one comfort, a child that has a quick temper, just blaze up and cool down, ain't never likely to be sly or deceitful. Preserve me from a sly child, that's what. On the whole, Marilla, I kind of like her."

When Marilla went home Anne came out of the fragrant twilight of the orchard with a sheaf of white narcissi in her hands.

"I apologized pretty well, didn't I?" she said proudly as they went down the lane. "I thought since I had to do it I might as well do it thoroughly."

---

5. "Golden-brown" in British dictionaries, "reddish-brown" in American ones.
6. Common name for narcissus blossoms, formed in daffodil-style like a white trumpet in a cup.
7. Oil lamp, in which a wick soaked in kerosene is turned up in a glass enclosure and ignited to give maximum light.

"You did it thoroughly, all right enough," was Marilla's comment. Marilla was dismayed at finding herself inclined to laugh over the recollection. She had also an uneasy feeling that she ought to scold Anne for apologizing so well but then that was ridiculous! She compromised with her conscience by saying severely:

"I hope you won't have occasion to make many more such apologies. I hope you'll try to control your temper now, Anne."

"That wouldn't be so hard if people wouldn't twit me about my looks," said Anne with a sigh. "I don't get cross about other things; but I'm *so* tired of being twitted about my hair and it just makes me boil right over. Do you suppose my hair will really be a handsome auburn when I grow up?"

"You shouldn't think so much about your looks, Anne. I'm afraid you are a very vain little girl."

"How can I be vain when I know I'm homely?" protested Anne. "I love pretty things; and I hate to look in the glass and see something that isn't pretty. It makes me feel so sorrowful—just as I feel when I look at any ugly thing. I pity it because it isn't beautiful."

"Handsome is as handsome does,"[8] quoted Marilla.

"I've had that said to me before, but I have my doubts about it," remarked sceptical Anne, sniffing at her narcissi. "Oh, aren't these flowers sweet! It was lovely of Mrs. Lynde to give them to me. I have no hard feelings against Mrs. Lynde now. It gives you a lovely, comfortable feeling to apologize and be forgiven, doesn't it? Aren't the stars bright to-night? If you could live in a star, which one would you pick? I'd like that lovely clear big one away over there above that dark hill."

"Anne, do hold your tongue,"[9] said Marilla, thoroughly worn out trying to follow the gyrations of Anne's thoughts.

Anne said no more until they turned into their own lane. A little gypsy wind came down it to meet them, laden with the spicy perfume of young dew-wet ferns. Far up in the shadows a cheerful light gleamed out through the trees from the kitchen at Green Gables. Anne suddenly came close to Marilla and slipped her hand into the older woman's hard palm.

"It's lovely to be going home and know it's home," she said. "I love Green Gables already, and I never loved any place before. No place ever seemed like home. Oh, Marilla, I'm so happy. I could pray right now and not find it a bit hard."

Something warm and pleasant welled up in Marilla's heart at touch of that thin little hand in her own—a throb of the maternity

8. A very common phrase, slightly altered from "Handsome is that handsome does," in Oliver Goldsmith's *The Vicar of Wakefield* (1766), chap. 1; also in *Rebecca of Sunnybrook Farm*. See NCE 303.
9. Be quiet (colloquial).

she had missed, perhaps. Its very unaccustomedness and sweetness disturbed her. She hastened to restore her sensations to their normal calm by inculcating a moral.

"If you'll be a good girl you'll always be happy, Anne. And you should never find it hard to say your prayers."

"Saying one's prayers isn't exactly the same thing as praying," said Anne meditatively. "But I'm going to imagine that I'm the wind that is blowing up there in those tree-tops. When I get tired of the trees I'll imagine I'm gently waving down here in the ferns—and then I'll fly over to Mrs. Lynde's garden and set the flowers dancing—and then I'll go with one great swoop over the clover field—and then I'll blow over the Lake of Shining Waters and ripple it all up into little sparkling waves. Oh, there's so much scope for imagination in a wind! So I'll not talk any more just now, Marilla."

"Thanks be to goodness for that," breathed Marilla in devout relief.

# Chapter XI

### ANNE'S IMPRESSIONS OF SUNDAY-SCHOOL

"Well, how do you like them?" said Marilla.

Anne was standing in the gable-room, looking solemnly at three new dresses spread out on the bed. One was of snuffy coloured ging-ham[1] which Marilla had been tempted to buy from a peddler the preceding summer because it looked so serviceable; one was of black-and-white checked sateen[2] which she had picked up at a bargain counter in the winter; and one was a stiff print of an ugly blue shade which she had purchased that week at a Carmody store.

She had made them up herself, and they were all made alike—plain skirts fulled tightly to plain fulled waists, with sleeves as plain as waist and skirt and tight as sleeves could be.

"I'll imagine that I like them," said Anne soberly.

"I don't want you to imagine it," said Marilla, offended. "Oh, I can see you don't like the dresses! What is the matter with them? Aren't they neat and clean and new?"

"Yes."

"Then why don't you like them?"

"They're—they're not—pretty," said Anne reluctantly.

"Pretty!" Marilla sniffed. "I didn't trouble my head about getting pretty dresses for you. I don't believe in pampering vanity, Anne, I'll tell you that right off. Those dresses are good, sensible, serviceable

---

1. Cotton cloth of dyed yarn, woven in plaids or stripes, used for housedresses or aprons. "Snuffy": dull brown, the color of snuff.
2. Glossy cotton cloth made to imitate satin.

dresses, without any frills or furbelows about them, and they're all you'll get this summer. The brown gingham and the blue print will do you for school when you begin to go. The sateen is for church and Sunday-school. I'll expect you to keep them neat and clean and not to tear them. I should think you'd be grateful to get most anything after those skimpy wincey things you've been wearing."

"Oh, I *am* grateful," protested Anne. "But I'd be ever so much gratefuller if—if you'd made just one of them with puffed sleeves.[3] Puffed sleeves are so fashionable now. It would give me such a thrill, Marilla, just to wear a dress with puffed sleeves."

"Well, you'll have to do without your thrill. I hadn't any material to waste on puffed sleeves. I think they are ridiculous-looking things anyhow. I prefer the plain, sensible ones."

"But I'd rather look ridiculous when everybody else does than plain and sensible all by myself," persisted Anne mournfully.

"Trust you for that! Well, hang those dresses carefully up in your closet, and then sit down and learn the Sunday-school lesson. I got a quarterly[4] from Mr. Bell for you and you'll go to Sunday-school to-morrow," said Marilla, disappearing downstairs in high dudgeon.[5]

Anne clasped her hands and looked at the dresses.

"I did hope there would be a white one with puffed sleeves," she whispered disconsolately. "I prayed for one, but I didn't much expect it on that account. I didn't suppose God would have time to bother about a little orphan girl's dress. I knew I'd just have to depend on Marilla for it. Well, fortunately I can imagine that one of them is of snow-white muslin with lovely lace frills and three-puffed sleeves."

The next morning warnings of a sick headache prevented Marilla from going to Sunday-school with Anne.

"You'll have to go down and call for Mrs. Lynde, Anne," she said. "She'll see that you get into the right class. Now, mind you behave yourself properly. Stay to preaching afterwards and ask Mrs. Lynde to show you our pew. Here's a cent for collection. Don't stare at people and don't fidget. I shall expect you to tell me the text when you come home."

Anne started off irreproachably, arrayed in the stiff black-and-white sateen, which, while decent as regards length and certainly not open to the charge of skimpiness, contrived to emphasize every corner and angle of her thin figure. Her hat was a little, flat, glossy, new sailor,[6] the extreme plainness of which had likewise much disap-

---

3. Gathered at top where the sleeve is attached to the bodice and again at the bottom where it is attached to a wrist-band or a tight lower-arm sleeve.
4. Bulletin with the season's Sunday School lessons.
5. Very angry or offended and ready for a dispute, from the French word for the hilt of a dagger.
6. A hat with a round crown surrounded by a turned-up brim, as worn by sailors.

pointed Anne, who had permitted herself secret visions of ribbon and flowers. The latter, however, were supplied before Anne reached the main road, for, being confronted half-way down the lane with a golden frenzy of wind-stirred buttercups[7] and a glory of wild roses, Anne promptly and liberally garlanded her hat with a heavy wreath of them. Whatever other people might have thought of the result it satisfied Anne, and she tripped gaily down the road, holding her ruddy head with its decoration of pink and yellow very proudly.

When she reached Mrs. Lynde's house she found that lady gone. Nothing daunted Anne proceeded onward to the church alone. In the porch she found a crowd of little girls, all more or less gaily attired in whites and blues and pinks, and all staring with curious eyes at this stranger in their midst, with her extraordinary head adornment. Avonlea little girls had already heard queer stories about Anne; Mrs. Lynde said she had an awful temper; Jerry Buote, the hired boy at Green Gables, said she talked all the time to herself or to the trees and flowers like a crazy girl. They looked at her and whispered to each other behind their quarterlies. Nobody made any friendly advances, then or later on when the opening exercises were over and Anne found herself in Miss Rogerson's class.

Miss Rogerson was a middle-aged lady who had taught a Sunday-school class for twenty years. Her method of teaching was to ask the printed questions from the quarterly and look sternly over its edge at the particular little girl she thought ought to answer the question.[8] She looked very often at Anne, and Anne, thanks to Marilla's drilling, answered promptly; but it may be questioned if she understood very much about either question or answer.

She did not think she liked Miss Rogerson, and she felt very miserable; every other little girl in the class had puffed sleeves. Anne felt that life was really not worth living without puffed sleeves.

"Well, how did you like Sunday-school?" Marilla wanted to know when Anne came home. Her wreath having faded, Anne had discarded it in the lane, so Marilla was spared the knowledge of that for a time.

"I didn't like it a bit. It was horrid."

"Anne Shirley!" said Marilla rebukingly.

Anne sat down on the rocker with a long sigh, kissed one of Bonny's leaves, and waved her hand to a blossoming fuchsia.[9]

"They might have been lonesome while I was away," she explained. "And now about the Sunday-school. I behaved well, just as you told me. Mrs. Lynde was gone, but I went right on myself. I went into

7. An echo from one of LMM's early poems, "Buttercups" (1899): "a golden frenzy flies / Through the light-hearted flowers."
8. LMM remembered the spinsters who were her Sunday School teachers. See NCE 286.
9. Plant with pendant flowers of purple, red, or white.

They looked at her and whispered to each other

the church, with a lot of other little girls, and I sat in the corner of a pew by the window while the opening exercises went on. Mr. Bell made an awfully long prayer. I would have been dreadfully tired before he got through if I hadn't been sitting by that window. But it looked right out on the Lake of Shining Waters, so I just gazed at that and imagined all sorts of splendid things."

"You shouldn't have done anything of the sort. You should have listened to Mr. Bell."

"But he wasn't talking to me," protested Anne. "He was talking to God and he didn't seem to be very much interested in it, either. I think he thought God was too far off to make it worth while. I said a little prayer myself, though. There was a long row of white birches hanging over the lake and the sunshine fell down through them, 'way,' way down, deep into the water. Oh, Marilla, it was like a beautiful dream! It gave me a thrill and I just said, 'Thank you for it, God,' two or three times."

"Not out loud, I hope," said Marilla anxiously.

"Oh, no, just under my breath. Well, Mr. Bell did get through at last and they told me to go into the class-room with Miss Rogerson's class. There were nine other girls in it. They all had puffed sleeves. I tried to imagine mine were puffed, too, but I couldn't. Why couldn't I? It was as easy as could be to imagine they were puffed when I was alone in the east gable, but it was awfully hard there among the others who had really truly puffs."

"You shouldn't have been thinking about your sleeves in Sunday-school. You should have been attending to the lesson. I hope you knew it."

"Oh, yes; and I answered a lot of questions. Miss Rogerson asked ever so many. I don't think it was fair for her to do all the asking. There were lots I wanted to ask her, but I didn't like to because I didn't think she was a kindred spirit. Then all the other little girls recited a paraphrase.[1] She asked me if I knew any. I told her I didn't, but I could recite, 'The Dog at His Master's Grave'[2] if she liked. That's in the Third Royal Reader. It isn't a really truly religious piece of poetry, but it's so sad and melancholy that it might as well be. She said it wouldn't do and she told me to learn the nineteenth paraphrase for next Sunday. I read it over in church afterwards and it's splendid. There are two lines in particular that just thrill me.

" 'Quick as the slaughtered squadrons fell
        In Midian's evil day.'[3]

1. In the Presbyterian *Hymnal*, the Psalms of David are rendered in rhymed metric form.
2. A gloomy poem in eight verses by Mrs. Lydia Sigourney, the "Sweet Singer of Connecticut," a sentimental poet of the 1840s.
3. Quoted from John Morrison, "The Race that Long in Darkness Pined," in *Scottish Para-*

I don't know what 'squadrons' means nor 'Midian,' either, but it sounds so tragical. I can hardly wait until next Sunday to recite it. I'll practise it all the week. After Sunday-school I asked Miss Roger-son—because Mrs. Lynde was too far away—to show me your pew. I sat just as still as I could and the text was Revelations, third chapter, second and third verses.[4] It was a very long text. If I was a minister I'd pick the short, snappy ones. The sermon was awfully long, too. I suppose the minister had to match it to the text. I didn't think he was a bit interesting. The trouble with him seems to be that he hasn't enough imagination. I didn't listen to him very much. I just let my thoughts run and I thought of the most surprising things."

Marilla felt helplessly that all this should be sternly reproved, but she was hampered by the undeniable fact that some of the things Anne had said, especially about the minister's sermons and Mr. Bell's prayers, were what she herself had really thought deep down in her heart for years, but had never given expression to. It almost seemed to her that those secret, unuttered, critical thoughts had suddenly taken visible and accusing shape and form in the person of this out-spoken morsel of neglected humanity.

# Chapter XII

### A SOLEMN VOW AND PROMISE

It was not until the next Friday that Marilla heard the story of the flower-wreathed hat. She came home from Mrs. Lynde's and called Anne to account.

"Anne, Mrs. Rachel says you went to church last Sunday with your hat rigged out ridiculous with roses and buttercups. What on earth put you up to such a caper? A pretty-looking object you must have been!"

"Oh, I know pink and yellow aren't becoming to me," began Anne.

"Becoming fiddlesticks! It was putting flowers on your hat at all, no matter what colour they were, that was ridiculous. You are the most aggravating child!"

"I don't see why it's any more ridiculous to wear flowers on your hat than on your dress," protested Anne. "Lots of little girls there had bouquets pinned on their dresses. What was the difference?"

Marilla was not to be drawn from the safe concrete into dubious paths of the abstract.

---

phrases (1781), based on several Old Testament passages, including: "Thus was Midian subdued before the children of Israel." Holy Bible, Judges 8.28. See NCE 290, 296.
4. A passage warning of imminent death. Sunday dinner conversation commonly consisted of rehashing the sermon.

"Don't answer me back like that, Anne.[1] It was very silly of you to do such a thing. Never let me catch you at such a trick again. Mrs. Rachel says she thought she would sink through the floor when she saw you come in all rigged out like that. She couldn't get near enough to tell you to take them off till it was too late. She says people talked about it something dreadful. Of course they would think I had no better sense than to let you go decked out like that."

"Oh, I'm so sorry," said Anne, tears welling into her eyes. "I never thought you'd mind. The roses and buttercups were so sweet and pretty I thought they'd look lovely on my hat. Lots of the little girls had artificial flowers on their hats. I'm afraid I'm going to be a dreadful trial to you. Maybe you'd better send me back to the asylum. That would be terrible; I don't think I could endure it; most likely I would go into consumption;[2] I'm so thin as it is, you see. But that would be better than being a trial to you."

"Nonsense," said Marilla, vexed at herself for having made the child cry. "I don't want to send you back to the asylum, I'm sure. All I want is that you should behave like other little girls and not make yourself ridiculous. Don't cry any more. I've got some news for you. Diana Barry came home this afternoon. I'm going up to see if I can borrow a skirt pattern from Mrs. Barry, and if you like you can come with me and get acquainted with Diana."

Anne rose to her feet, with clasped hands, the tears still glistening on her cheeks; the dish-towel she had been hemming slipped unheeded to the floor.

"Oh, Marilla, I'm frightened—now that it has come I'm actually frightened. What if she shouldn't like me! It would be the most tragical disappointment of my life."

"Now, don't get into a fluster. And I do wish you wouldn't use such long words. It sounds so funny in a little girl. I guess Diana'll like you well enough. It's her mother you've got to reckon with. If she doesn't like you it won't matter how much Diana does. If she has heard about your outburst to Mrs. Lynde and going to church with buttercups round your hat I don't know what she'll think of you. You must be polite and well-behaved, and don't make any of your startling speeches. For pity's sake, if the child isn't actually trembling!"

Anne *was* trembling. Her face was pale and tense.

"Oh, Marilla, you'd be excited, too, if you were going to meet a little girl you hoped to be your bosom friend and whose mother mightn't like you," she said as she hastened to get her hat.

1. Reflected in the dictum, "Children should be seen, not heard."
2. Tuberculosis, not only a major medical problem, but also a favorite ailment in romantic operas and women's novels. LMM's mother, Clara Macneill Montgomery, died of "galloping consumption" when LMM was a very small child.

They went over to Orchard Slope by the short cut across the brook and up the firry hill grove. Mrs. Barry came to the kitchen door in answer to Marilla's knock. She was a tall, black-eyed, black-haired woman, with a very resolute mouth. She had the reputation of being very strict with her children.

"How do you do, Marilla?" she said cordially. "Come in. And this is the little girl you have adopted, I suppose?"

"Yes, this is Anne Shirley," said Marilla.

"Spelled with an *e*," gasped Anne, who, tremulous and excited as she was, was determined there should be no misunderstanding on that important point.

Mrs. Barry, not hearing or not comprehending, merely shook hands and said kindly:

"How are you?"

"I am well in body although considerably rumpled up in spirit, thank you, ma'am," said Anne gravely. Then aside to Marilla in an audible whisper, "There wasn't anything startling in that, was there, Marilla?"

Diana was sitting on the sofa, reading a book which she dropped when the callers entered. She was a very pretty little girl, with her mother's black eyes and hair, and rosy cheeks, and the merry expression which was her inheritance from her father.

"This is my little girl, Diana," said Mrs. Barry. "Diana, you might take Anne out into the garden and show her your flowers. It will be better for you than straining your eyes over that book. She reads entirely too much—" this to Marilla as the little girls went out—"and I can't prevent her, for her father aids and abets her. She's always poring over a book. I'm glad she has the prospect of a playmate—perhaps it will take her more out-of-doors."

Outside in the garden, which was full of mellow sunset light streaming through the dark old firs to the west of it, stood Anne and Diana, gazing bashfully at one another over a clump of gorgeous tiger lilies.[3]

The Barry garden was a bowery wilderness of flowers which would have delighted Anne's heart at any time less fraught with destiny. It was encircled by huge old willows and tall firs, beneath which flourished flowers that loved the shade. Prim, right-angled paths, neatly bordered with clam-shells, intersected it like moist red ribbons and in the beds between old-fashioned flowers ran riot. There were rosy bleeding-hearts and great splendid crimson peonies; white, fragrant narcissi and thorny, sweet Scotch roses; pink and blue and white columbines and lilac-tinted Bouncing Bets; clumps of southern-

---

3. A country favorite: orange lilies, the symbols of Protestantism. Literary uses of this flower appear in Lewis Carroll's *Alice in Wonderland* (1865) and in J. M. Barrie's play *Peter Pan* (1904) as well as his novel by the same name (1911).

wood and ribbon grass and mint; purple Adam-and-Eve, daffodils, and masses of sweet clover white with its delicate, fragrant, feathery sprays; scarlet lightning that shot its fiery lances over prim white musk-flowers; a garden it was where sunshine lingered and bees hummed, and winds, beguiled into loitering, purred and rustled.[4]

"Oh, Diana," said Anne at last, clasping her hands and speaking almost in a whisper, "do you think—oh, do you think you can like me a little—enough to be my bosom friend?"

Diana laughed. Diana always laughed before she spoke.

"Why, I guess so," she said frankly. "I'm awfully glad you've come to live at Green Gables. It will be jolly to have somebody to play with. There isn't any other girl who lives near enough to play with, and I've no sisters big enough."

"Will you swear to be my friend for ever and ever?" demanded Anne eagerly.

Diana looked shocked.

"Why, it's dreadfully wicked to swear," she said rebukingly.

"Oh no, not my kind of swearing. There are two kinds, you know."

"I never heard of but one kind," said Diana doubtfully.

"There really is another. Oh, it isn't wicked at all. It just means vowing and promising solemnly."

"Well, I don't mind doing that," agreed Diana, relieved. "How do you do it?"

"We must join hands—so," said Anne gravely. "It ought to be over running water. We'll just imagine this path is running water. I'll repeat the oath first. I solemnly swear to be faithful to my bosom friend, Diana Barry, as long as the sun and moon shall endure. Now you say it and put my name in."

Diana repeated the "oath" with a laugh fore and aft. Then she said:

"You're a queer girl, Anne. I heard before that you were queer. But I believe I'm going to like you real well."

When Marilla and Anne went home Diana went with them as far as the log bridge. The two little girls walked with their arms about each other. At the brook they parted with many promises to spend the next afternoon together.

---

4. The least common flowers in the list are Bouncing Bets (fragrant pink flowers commonly called "soapwort"); southern-wood (aromatic shrub with soft gray-green foliage); Adam-and-Eve (a tiny native Canadian northern orchid, sometimes called "puttyroot"); scarlet lightning (bright clusters of four-petal flowers on a tall thin stalk, now commonly called "Maltese Cross" or "London Pride"); musk-flowers (probably musk-mallows, a hardy northern perennial with satiny, funnel-shaped flowers, mauve or white, resembling dwarfed hollyhocks). Flowers in this passage are reminiscent of LMM's description of her ideal garden: written in 1901, and interesting both for omissions and correspondences. See NCE 275–76.

"Well, did you find Diana a kindred spirit?" asked Marilla as they went up through the garden of Green Gables.

"Oh, yes," sighed Anne, blissfully unconscious of any sarcasm on Marilla's part. "Oh, Marilla, I'm the happiest girl on Prince Edward Island this very moment. I assure you I'll say my prayers with a right good-will to-night. Diana and I are going to build a playhouse in Mr. William Bell's birch grove to-morrow. Can I have those broken pieces of china that are out in the wood-shed? Diana's birthday is in February and mine is in March. Don't you think that is a very strange coincidence? Diana is going to lend me a book to read. She says it's perfectly splendid and tremenjusly[5] exciting. She's going to show me a place back in the woods where rice lilies[6] grow. Don't you think Diana has got very soulful eyes? I wish I had soulful eyes. Diana is going to teach me to sing a song called 'Nelly in the Hazel Dell.'[7] She's going to give me a picture to put up in my room; it's a perfectly beautiful picture, she says—a lovely lady in a pale blue silk dress. A sewing-machine agent[8] gave it to her. I wish I had something to give Diana. I'm an inch taller than Diana, but she is ever so much fatter; she says she'd like to be thin because it's so much more graceful, but I'm afraid she only said it to soothe my feelings. We're going to the shore some day to gather shells. We have agreed to call the spring down by the log bridge the Dryad's Bubble.[9] Isn't that a perfectly elegant name? I read a story once about a spring called that. A dryad is a sort of grown-up fairy, I think."

"Well, all I hope is you won't talk Diana to death," said Marilla. "But remember this in all your planning, Anne. You're not going to play all the time nor most of it. You'll have your work to do and it'll have to be done first."

Anne's cup of happiness was full, and Matthew caused it to over-flow. He had just got home from a trip to the store at Carmody, and he sheepishly produced a small parcel from his pocket and handed it to Anne, with a deprecatory look at Marilla.

"I heard you say you liked chocolate sweeties,[1] so I got you some," he said.

"Humph," sniffed Marilla. "It'll ruin her teeth and stomach. There,

---

5. Tremendously: a rare use of childish pronunciation. LMM usually assigns big words to Anne without specifying their pronunciation.

6. The tiny blossoms of wild lilies-of-the-valley (*maranthemum canadiense*) look like grains of rice.

7. Nelly is "lost and gone" in "The Hazel Dell," a popular song by G. F. Root of Boston (1853).

8. Aggressive salesmen touting the lock-stitch worked in rural districts throughout the United States and Canada in the 1880s. The Singer Sewing Machine Company, founded in 1851 in New York, patented from 1859 on, opened its first Canadian factory in Montreal in 1882.

9. A tree nymph of classic mythology which Anne links with the local spring of fresh water.

1. The British term for candies.

there, child, don't look so dismal. You can eat those, since Matthew has gone and got them. He'd better have brought you peppermints. They're wholesomer. Don't sicken yourself eating them all at once now."

"Oh, no, indeed, I won't," said Anne eagerly. "I'll just eat one to-night, Marilla. And I can give Diana half of them, can't I? The other half will taste twice as sweet to me if I give some to her. It's delightful to think I have something to give her."

"I will say it for the child," said Marilla when Anne had gone to her gable, "she isn't stingy. I'm glad, for of all faults I detest stinginess in a child. Dear me, it's only three weeks since she came, and it seems as if she'd been here always. I can't imagine the place without her. Now, don't be looking I-told-you-so, Matthew. That's bad enough in a woman, but it isn't to be endured in a man. I'm perfectly willing to own up that I'm glad I consented to keep the child and that I'm getting fond of her, but don't you rub it in, Matthew Cuthbert."

# Chapter XIII

### THE DELIGHTS OF ANTICIPATION

"It's time Anne was in to do her sewing," said Marilla, glancing at the clock and then out into the yellow August afternoon where everything drowsed in the heat. "She stayed playing with Diana more than half an hour more'n I gave her leave to; and now she's perched out there on the woodpile[1] talking to Matthew, nineteen to the dozen,[2] when she knows perfectly well that she ought to be at her work. And of course he's listening to her like a perfect ninny. I never saw such an infatuated man. The more she talks and the odder the things she says, the more he's delighted evidently. Anne Shirley, you come right in here this minute, do you hear me!"

A series of staccato taps on the west window brought Anne flying in from the yard, eyes shining, cheeks faintly flushed with pink, unbraided hair streaming behind her in a torrent of brightness.

"Oh, Marilla," she exclaimed breathlessly, "there's going to be a Sunday-school picnic next week—in Mr. Harmon Andrews' field, right near the Lake of Shining Waters. And Mrs. Superintendent Bell and Mrs. Rachel Lynde are going to make ice-cream[3]—think of it, Marilla—*ice-cream!* And oh, Marilla, can I go to it?"

1. Fire wood for the stoves, stacked outside the house.
2. Very quickly (an English colloquialism not in American dictionaries).
3. Made in a cylinder containing cream, sugar, and flavoring, placed in a case packed with ice and salt, and rotated with a hand-turned crank.

"Just look at the clock, if you please, Anne. What time did I tell you to come in?"

"Two o'clock—but isn't it splendid about the picnic, Marilla? Please can I go? Oh, I've never been to a picnic—I've dreamed of picnics, but I've never—"

"Yes, I told you to come at two o'clock. And it's a quarter to three. I'd like to know why you didn't obey me, Anne."

"Why, I meant to, Marilla, as much as could be. But you have no idea how fascinating Idlewild is. And then, of course, I had to tell Matthew about the picnic. Matthew is such a sympathetic listener. Please can I go?"

"You'll have to learn to resist the fascination of Idle-whatever-you-call-it. When I tell you to come in at a certain time I mean that time and not half an hour later. And you needn't stop to discourse with sympathetic listeners on your way, either. As for the picnic, of course you can go. You're a Sunday-school scholar, and it's not likely I'd refuse to let you go when all the other little girls are going."

"But—but," faltered Anne, "Diana says that everybody must take a basket of things to eat. I can't cook, as you know, Marilla, and— and—I don't mind going to a picnic without puffed sleeves so much, but I'd feel terribly humiliated if I had to go without a basket. It's been preying on my mind ever since Diana told me."

"Well, it needn't prey any longer. I'll bake you a basket."

"Oh, you dear good Marilla. Oh, you are so kind to me. Oh, I'm so much obliged to you."

Getting through with her "ohs" Anne cast herself into Marilla's arms and rapturously kissed her sallow cheek. It was the first time in her whole life that childish lips had voluntarily touched Marilla's face. Again that sudden sensation of startling sweetness thrilled her. She was secretly vastly pleased at Anne's impulsive caress, which was probably the reason why she said brusquely:

"There, there, never mind your kissing nonsense. I'd sooner see you doing strictly as you're told. As for cooking, I mean to begin giving you lessons in that some of these days. But you're so feather-brained, Anne, I've been waiting to see if you'd sober down a little and learn to be steady before I begin. You've got to keep your wits about you in cooking and not stop in the middle of things to let your thoughts rove over all creation. Now, get out your patchwork[4] and have your square done before tea-time."

"I do *not* like patchwork," said Anne dolefully, hunting out her workbasket and sitting down before a little heap of red and white diamonds with a sigh. "I think some kinds of sewing would be nice;

---

4. Cutting and sewing scraps of material into squares to make up a quilt or other item, a common task for little girls.

but there's no scope for imagination in patchwork. It's just one little seam after another and you never seem to be getting anywhere. But of course I'd rather be Anne of Green Gables sewing patchwork than Anne of any other place with nothing to do but play. I wish time went as quick sewing patches as it does when I'm playing with Diana, though. Oh, we do have such elegant times, Marilla. I have to furnish most of the imagination, but I'm well able to do that. Diana is simply perfect in every other way. You know that little piece of land across the brook that runs up between our farm and Mr. Barry's. It belongs to Mr. William Bell, and right in the corner there is a little ring of white birch trees—the most romantic spot, Marilla. Diana and I have our playhouse there. We call it Idlewild. Isn't that a poetical name? I assure you it took me some time to think it out. I stayed awake nearly a whole night before I invented it. Then, just as I was dropping off to sleep, it came like an inspiration. Diana was *enraptured* when she heard it. We have got our house fixed up elegantly. You must come and see it, Marilla—won't you? We have great big stones, all covered with moss, for seats, and boards from tree to tree for shelves. And we have all our dishes on them. Of course, they're all broken but it's the easiest thing in the world to imagine that they are whole. There's a piece of a plate with a spray of red and yellow ivy on it that is especially beautiful. We keep it in the parlour and we have the fairy glass[5] there, too. The fairy glass is as lovely as a dream. Diana found it out in the woods behind their chicken house. It's all full of rainbows—just little young rainbows that haven't grown big yet— and Diana's mother told her it was broken off a hanging lamp they once had. But it's nicer to imagine the fairies lost it one night when they had a ball, so we call it the fairy glass. Matthew is going to make us a table. Oh, we have named that little round pool over in Mr. Barry's field Willowmere.[6] I got that name out of the book Diana lent me. That was a thrilling book, Marilla. The heroine had five lovers. I'd be satisfied with one, wouldn't you? She was very handsome and she went through great tribulations. She could faint as easy as anything. I'd love to be able to faint, wouldn't you, Marilla? It's so romantic. But I'm really very healthy for all I'm so thin. I believe I'm getting fatter, though. Don't you think I am? I look at my elbows every morning when I get up to see if any dimples are coming. Diana is having a new dress made with elbow sleeves. She is going to wear it to the picnic. Oh, I do hope it will be fine next Wednesday. I don't feel that I could endure the disappointment if anything happened to prevent me from getting to the picnic. I suppose I'd live through it, but I'm certain it would be a lifelong sorrow. It wouldn't matter if I got to a

5. A crystal prism, of the kind used to decorate lamps.
6. "Mere" is a medieval word for a lake.

hundred picnics in after years; they wouldn't make up for missing this one. They're going to have boats on the Lake of Shining Waters—and ice-cream as I told you. I have never tasted ice-cream. Diana tried to explain what it was like, but I guess ice-cream is one of those things that are beyond imagination."

"Anne, you have talked even on for ten minutes by the clock," said Marilla. "Now, just for curiosity's sake, see if you can hold your tongue for the same length of time."

Anne held her tongue as desired. But for the rest of the week she talked picnic and thought picnic and dreamed picnic. On Saturday it rained and she worked herself up into such a frantic state lest it should keep on raining until and over Wednesday, that Marilla made her sew an extra patchwork square by way of steadying her nerves.

On Sunday Anne confided to Marilla on the way home from church that she grew actually cold all over with excitement when the minister announced the picnic from the pulpit.

"Such a thrill as went up and down my back, Marilla! I don't think I'd ever really believed until then that there was honestly going to be a picnic. I couldn't help fearing I'd only imagined it. But when a minister says a thing in the pulpit you just have to believe it."

"You set your heart too much on things, Anne," said Marilla with a sigh. "I'm afraid there'll be a great many disappointments in store for you through life."

"Oh, Marilla, looking forward to things is half the pleasure of them," exclaimed Anne. "You mayn't get the things themselves; but nothing can prevent you from having the fun of looking forward to them. Mrs. Lynde says, 'Blessed are they who expect nothing for they shall not be disappointed.'[7] But I think it would be worse to expect nothing than to be disappointed."

Marilla wore her amethyst brooch[8] to church that day as usual. Marilla always wore her amethyst brooch to church. She would have thought it rather sacrilegious to leave it off—as bad as forgetting her Bible or her collection dime.[9] That amethyst brooch was Marilla's most treasured possession. A sea-faring uncle had given it to her mother who in turn had bequeathed it to Marilla. It was an old-fashioned oval, containing a braid of her mother's hair, surrounded by a border of very fine amethysts. Marilla knew too little about precious stones to realize how fine the amethysts actually were; but she thought them very beautiful and was always pleasantly conscious

---

7. Called the ninth beatitude by Alexander Pope in "Letter to William Fortescue" (1725).
8. Violet or purple quartz semi-precious stones, set around a braid of hair make a traditional decoration.
9. Ten cents: an expected contribution from an adult to church finance and missions, to be placed in the collection plate when it is handed round.

of their violet shimmer at her throat, above her good brown satin dress, even although she could not see it.

Anne had been smitten with delighted admiration when she first saw that brooch.

"Oh, Marilla, it's a perfectly elegant brooch. I don't know how you can pay attention to the sermon or the prayers when you have it on. *I* couldn't, I know. I think amethysts are just sweet. They are what I used to think diamonds were like. Long ago, before I had ever seen a diamond, I read about them and I tried to imagine what they would be like. I thought they would be lovely glimmering purple stones.[1] When I saw a real diamond in a lady's ring one day I was so disappointed I cried. Of course, it was very lovely but it wasn't my idea of a diamond. Will you let me hold the brooch for one minute, Marilla? Do you think amethysts can be the souls of good violets?"

# Chapter XIV

## ANNE'S CONFESSION

ON the Monday evening before the picnic Marilla came down from her room with a troubled face.

"Anne," she said to that small personage, who was shelling peas by the spotless table and singing "Nelly of the Hazel Dell" with a vigour and expression that did credit to Diana's teaching, "did you see anything of my amethyst brooch? I thought I stuck it in my pincushion when I came home from church yesterday evening, but I can't find it anywhere."

"I—I saw it this afternoon when you were away at the Aid Society," said Anne, a little slowly. "I was passing your door when I saw it on the cushion, so I went in to look at it."

"Did you touch it?" said Marilla sternly.

"Y-e-e-s," admitted Anne, "I took it up and I pinned it on my breast just to see how it would look."

"You had no business to do anything of the sort. It's very wrong in a little girl to meddle. You shouldn't have gone into my room in the first place and you shouldn't have touched a brooch that didn't belong to you in the second. Where did you put it?"

"Oh, I put it back on the bureau.[1] I hadn't it on a minute. Truly, I didn't mean to meddle, Marilla. I didn't think about its being wrong to go in and try on the brooch; but I see now that it was and I'll never

1. An idea held by LMM as a child. See *SJ2* 42.
1. Chest of drawers in a bedroom. (In English usage, a writing desk with drawers.)

do it again. That's one good thing about me. I never do the same naughty thing twice."

"You didn't put it back," said Marilla. "That brooch isn't anywhere on the bureau. You've taken it out or something, Anne."

"I *did* put it back," said Anne quickly—pertly, Marilla thought. "I don't just remember whether I stuck it on the pincushion or laid it in the china tray. But I'm perfectly certain I put it back."

"I'll go and have another look," said Marilla, determining to be just. "If you put that brooch back it's there still. If it isn't I'll know you didn't, that's all!"

Marilla went to her room and made a thorough search, not only over the bureau but in every other place she thought the brooch might possibly be. It was not to be found and she returned to the kitchen.

"Anne, the brooch is gone. By your own admission you were the last person to handle it. Now, what have you done with it? Tell me the truth at once. Did you take it out and lose it?"

"No, I didn't," said Anne solemnly, meeting Marilla's angry gaze squarely. "I never took the brooch out of your room and that is the truth, if I was to be led to the block[2] for it—although I'm not very certain what a block is. So there, Marilla."

Anne's "so there" was only intended to emphasize her assertion, but Marilla took it as a display of defiance.

"I believe you are telling me a falsehood, Anne," she said sharply. "I know you are. There now, don't say anything more unless you are prepared to tell the whole truth. Go to your room and stay there until you are ready to confess."

"Will I take the peas with me?" said Anne meekly.

"No, I'll finish shelling them myself. Do as I bid you."

When Anne had gone Marilla went about her evening tasks in a very disturbed state of mind. She was worried about her valuable brooch. What if Anne had lost it? And how wicked of the child to deny having taken it, when anybody could see she must have! With such an innocent face, too!

"I don't know what I wouldn't sooner have had happen," thought Marilla, as she nervously shelled the peas. "Of course, I don't suppose she meant to steal it or anything like that. She's just taken it to play with or help along that imagination of hers. She must have taken it, that's clear, for there hasn't been a soul in that room since she was in it, by her own story, until I went up to-night. And the brooch is gone, there's nothing surer. I suppose she has lost it and is afraid

---

2. Reminiscent of the procession when royal personages such as Mary Queen of Scots went to the executioner's "block" to be beheaded.

to own up for fear she'll be punished. It's a dreadful thing to think she tells falsehoods. It's a far worse thing than her fit of temper. It's a fearful responsibility to have a child in your house you can't trust. Slyness and untruthfulness—that's what she has displayed. I declare I feel worse about that than about the brooch. If she'd only have told the truth about it I wouldn't mind so much."

Marilla went to her room at intervals all through the evening and searched for the brooch, without finding it. A bed-time visit to the east gable produced no result. Anne persisted in denying that she knew anything about the brooch but Marilla was only the more firmly convinced that she did.

She told Matthew the story the next morning. Matthew was confounded and puzzled; he could not so quickly lose faith in Anne but he had to admit that circumstances were against her.

"You're sure it hasn't fell down behind the bureau?" was the only suggestion he could offer.

"I've moved the bureau and I've taken out the drawers and I've looked in every crack and cranny,"[3] was Marilla's positive answer. "The brooch is gone and that child has taken it and lied about it. That's the plain, ugly truth, Matthew Cuthbert, and we might as well look it in the face."

"Well now, what are you going to do about it?" Matthew asked forlornly, feeling secretly thankful that Marilla and not he had to deal with the situation. He felt no desire to put his oar in this time.

"She'll stay in her room until she confesses," said Marilla grimly, remembering the success of this method in the former case. "Then we'll see. Perhaps we'll be able to find the brooch if she'll only tell where she took it; but in any case she'll have to be severely punished, Matthew."

"Well now, you'll have to punish her," said Matthew, reaching for his hat. "I've nothing to do with it, remember. You warned me off yourself."

Marilla felt deserted by every one. She could not even go to Mrs. Lynde for advice. She went up to the east gable with a very serious face and left it with a face more serious still. Anne steadfastly refused to confess. She persisted in asserting that she had not taken the brooch. The child had evidently been crying and Marilla felt a pang of pity which she sternly repressed. By night she was, as she expressed it, "beat out."

"You'll stay in this room until you confess, Anne. You can make up your mind to that," she said firmly.

"But the picnic is to-morrow, Marilla," cried Anne. "You won't

---

3. In every crevice and fissure.

keep me from going to that, will you? You'll just let me out for the afternoon, won't you? Then I'll stay here as long as you like afterwards *cheerfully*. But I *must* go to the picnic."

"You'll not go to picnics nor anywhere else until you've confessed, Anne."

"Oh, Marilla," gasped Anne.

But Marilla had gone out and shut the door.

Wednesday morning dawned as bright and fair as if expressly made to order for the picnic. Birds sang around Green Gables; the Madonna lilies[4] in the garden sent out whiffs of perfume that entered in on viewless winds[5] at every door and window, and wandered through halls and rooms like spirits of benediction. The birches in the hollow waved joyful hands as if watching for Anne's usual morning greeting from the east gable. But Anne was not at her window. When Marilla took her breakfast up to her she found the child sitting primly on her bed, pale and resolute, with tight-shut lips and gleaming eyes.

"Marilla, I'm ready to confess."

"Ah!" Marilla laid down her tray. Once again her method had succeeded; but her success was very bitter to her. "Let me hear what you have to say then, Anne."

"I took the amethyst brooch," said Anne, as if repeating a lesson she had learned. "I took it just as you said. I didn't mean to take it when I went in. But it did look so beautiful, Marilla, when I pinned it on my breast that I was overcome by an irresistible temptation. I imagined how perfectly thrilling it would be to take it to Idlewild and play I was the Lady Cordelia Fitzgerald. It would be so much easier to imagine I was the Lady Cordelia if I had a real amethyst brooch on. Diana and I made necklaces of roseberries[6] but what are roseberries compared to amethysts? So I took the brooch. I thought I could put it back before you came home. I went all the way around by the road to lengthen out the time. When I was going over the bridge across the Lake of Shining Waters I took the brooch off to have another look at it. Oh, how it did shine in the sunlight! And then, when I was leaning over the bridge, it just slipped through my fingers—so—and went down—down—down, all purply-sparkling, and sank forevermore beneath the Lake of Shining Waters. And that's the best I can do at confessing, Marilla."

Marilla felt hot anger surge up into her heart again. This child had

---

4. Pure-white, fragrant, long-stemmed flowers used as a symbol of the Virgin Mary in many paintings.
5. Movements of air. The phrase is used in a negative, frightening sense in Shakespeare's *Measure for Measure* 3.1.135.
6. Red rose hips, the seed pods that form on rose canes after blossom time.

taken and lost her treasured amethyst brooch and now sat there calmly reciting the details thereof without the least apparent compunction or repentance.

"Anne, this is terrible," she said, trying to speak calmly. "You are the very wickedest girl I ever heard of."

"Yes, I suppose I am," agreed Anne tranquilly. "And I know I'll have to be punished. It'll be your duty to punish me, Marilla. Won't you please get it over right off because I'd like to go to the picnic with nothing on my mind."

"Picnic, indeed! You'll go to no picnic to-day, Anne Shirley. That shall be your punishment. And it isn't half severe enough either for what you've done!"

"Not go to the picnic!" Anne sprang to her feet and clutched Marilla's hand. "But you *promised* me I might! Oh, Marilla, I must go to the picnic. That was why I confessed. Punish me any way you like but that. Oh, Marilla, please, please, let me go to the picnic. Think of the ice-cream! For anything you know I may never have a chance to taste ice-cream again."

Marilla disengaged Anne's clinging hands stonily.

"You needn't plead, Anne. You are not going to the picnic and that's final. No, not a word."

Anne realized that Marilla was not to be moved. She clasped her hands together, gave a piercing shriek, and then flung herself face downwards on the bed, crying and writhing in an utter abandonment of disappointment and despair.

"For the land's sake!" gasped Marilla, hastening from the room. "I believe the child is crazy. No child in her senses would behave as she does. If she isn't she's utterly bad. Oh dear, I'm afraid Rachel was right from the first. But I've put my hand to the plough[7] and I won't look back."

That was a dismal morning. Marilla worked fiercely and scrubbed the porch floor and the dairy shelves when she could find nothing else to do. Neither the shelves nor the porch needed it—but Marilla did. Then she went out and raked the yard.

When dinner was ready she went to the stairs and called Anne. A tear-stained face appeared, looking tragically over the banisters.

"Come down to your dinner, Anne."

"I don't want any dinner, Marilla," said Anne sobbingly. "I couldn't eat anything. My heart is broken. You'll feel remorse of conscience some day, I expect, for breaking it, Marilla, but I forgive you. Remember when the time comes that I forgive you. But please don't ask me

---

7. Undertake a task. As in the words of Jesus, "No man, having put his hand to the plough, and looking back, is for the kingdom of God." *Holy Bible*, Luke 9.62.

to eat anything, especially boiled pork and greens.[8] Boiled pork and greens are so unromantic when one is in affliction."

Exasperated Marilla returned to the kitchen and poured out her tale of woe to Matthew, who, between his sense of justice and his unlawful sympathy with Anne, was a miserable man.

"Well now, she shouldn't have taken the brooch, Marilla, or told stories about it," he admitted, mournfully surveying his plateful of unromantic pork and greens as if he, like Anne, thought it a food unsuited to crises of feeling, "but she's such a little thing—such an interesting little thing. Don't you think it's pretty rough not to let her go to the picnic when she's so set on it?"

"Matthew Cuthbert, I'm amazed at you. I think I've let her off entirely too easy. And she doesn't appear to realize how wicked she's been at all—that's what worries me most. If she'd really felt sorry it wouldn't be so bad. And you don't seem to realize it, neither; you're making excuses for her all the time to yourself—I can see that."

"Well now, she's such a little thing," feebly reiterated Matthew. "And there should be allowances made, Marilla. You know she's never had any bringing up."

"Well, she's having it now," retorted Marilla.

The retort silenced Matthew if it did not convince him. That dinner was a very dismal meal. The only cheerful thing about it was Jerry Buote, the hired boy, and Marilla resented his cheerfulness as a personal insult.

When her dishes were washed and her bread sponge set[9] and her hens fed Marilla remembered that she had noticed a small rent in her best black lace shawl when she had taken it off on Monday afternoon on returning from the Ladies' Aid. She would go and mend it.

The shawl was in a box in her trunk. As Marilla lifted it out, the sunlight, falling through the vines that clustered thickly about the window, struck upon something caught in the shawl—something that glittered and sparkled in facets of violet light. Marilla snatched at it with a gasp. It was the amethyst brooch, hanging to a thread of the lace by its catch!

"Dear life and heart," said Marilla blankly, "what does this mean? Here's my brooch safe and sound that I thought was at the bottom of Barry's pond. Whatever did that girl mean by saying she took it and lost it? I declare I believe Green Gables is bewitched. I remember now that when I took off my shawl Monday afternoon I laid it on the bureau for a minute. I suppose the brooch got caught in it somehow. Well!"

8. Pork ribs boiled to tenderize the meat; greens would normally include Swiss chard, beet, and turnip leaves.
9. Dough consisting of flour, water, and yeast, covered with a tea towel and set aside to rise in preparation for baking.

Marilla betook herself to the east gable, brooch in hand. Anne had cried herself out and was sitting dejectedly by the window.

"Anne Shirley," said Marilla solemnly, "I've just found my brooch hanging to my black lace shawl. Now I want to know what that rigmarole[1] you told me this morning meant."

"Why, you said you'd keep me here until I confessed," returned Anne wearily, "and so I decided to confess because I was bound to get to the picnic. I thought out a confession last night after I went to bed and made it as interesting as I could. And I said it over and over so that I wouldn't forget it. But you wouldn't let me go to the picnic after all, so all my trouble was wasted."

Marilla had to laugh in spite of herself. But her conscience pricked her.

"Anne, you do beat all! But I was wrong—I see that now. I shouldn't have doubted your word when I'd never known you to tell a story. Of course, it wasn't right for you to confess to a thing you hadn't done—it was very wrong to do so. But I drove you to it. So if you'll forgive me, Anne, I'll forgive you and we'll start square again. And now get yourself ready for the picnic."

Anne flew up like a rocket.[2]

"Oh, Marilla, isn't it too late?"

"No, it's only two o'clock. They won't be more than well gathered yet and it'll be an hour before they have tea. Wash your face and comb your hair and put on your gingham. I'll fill a basket for you. There's plenty of stuff baked in the house. And I'll get Jerry to hitch up the sorrel and drive you down to the picnic ground."

"Oh, Marilla," exclaimed Anne, flying to the wash stand. "Five minutes ago I was so miserable I was wishing I'd never been born and now I wouldn't change places with an angel!"

That night a thoroughly happy, completely tired out Anne returned to Green Gables in a state of beatification[3] impossible to describe.

"Oh, Marilla, I've had a perfectly scrumptious[4] time. Scrumptious is a new word I learned to-day. I heard Mary Alice Bell use it. Isn't it very expressive? Everything was lovely. We had a splendid tea and then Mr. Harmon Andrews took us all for a row on the Lake of Shining Waters—six of us at a time. And Jane Andrews nearly fell overboard. She was leaning out to pick water lilies and if Mr. Andrews hadn't caught her by her sash just in the nick of time she'd have fallen in and prob'ly[5] been drowned. I wish it had been me. It would have been such a romantic experience to have been nearly

1. Foolish, rambling statements (colloquialism, in use since 1736).
2. In fireworks, a display sent aloft on a stick; at sea, a signal launched into the night sky as a sign of distress.
3. The first step toward canonization as a saint.
4. First rate, glorious (colloquialism, in use since 1830s).
5. Probably (a regional mispronunciation).

drowned. It would be such a thrilling tale to tell. And we had the ice-cream. Words fail me to describe that ice-cream. Marilla, I assure you it was sublime."

That evening Marilla told the whole story to Matthew over her stocking basket.[6]

"I'm willing to own up that I made a mistake," she concluded candidly, "but I've learned a lesson. I have to laugh when I think of Anne's 'confession,' although I suppose I shouldn't for it really was a falsehood. But it doesn't seem as bad as the other would have been, somehow, and anyhow I'm responsible for it. That child is hard to understand in some respects. But I believe she'll turn out all right yet. And there's one thing certain, no house will ever be dull that she's in."

## Chapter XV

### A TEMPEST IN THE SCHOOL TEAPOT[1]

"WHAT a splendid day!" said Anne, drawing a long breath. "Isn't it good just to be alive on a day like this? I pity the people who aren't born yet for missing it. They may have good days, of course, but they can never have this one. And it's splendider still to have such a lovely way to go to school by, isn't it?"

"It's a lot nicer than going round by the road; that is so dusty and hot," said Diana practically, peeping into her dinner basket and mentally calculating if the three juicy, toothsome, raspberry tarts reposing there were divided among ten girls how many bites each girl would have.

The little girls of Avonlea school always pooled their lunches, and to eat three raspberry tarts all alone or even to share them only with one's best chum would have forever and ever branded as "awful mean" the girl who did it. And yet, when the tarts were divided among ten girls you just got enough to tantalize you.

The way Anne and Diana went to school *was* a pretty one. Anne thought those walks to and from school with Diana couldn't be improved upon even by imagination. Going around by the main road would have been so unromantic; but to go by Lovers' Lane and Willowmere and Violet Vale and the Birch Path was romantic, if ever anything was.[2]

Lovers' Lane opened out below the orchard at Green Gables and stretched far up into the woods to the end of the Cuthbert farm. It

---

6. Sewing basket full of socks to be mended.
1. Variation on a proverb used since classic times: "a tempest in a teapot."
2. In her journal LMM commented on these places, real or fictional. See *SJ2* 38–42.

was the way by which the cows were taken to the back pasture and the wood hauled home in winter. Anne had named it Lovers' Lane before she had been a month at Green Gables.

"Not that lovers ever really walk there," she explained to Marilla, "but Diana and I are reading a perfectly magnificent book and there's a Lovers' Lane in it. So we want to have one, too. And it's a very pretty name, don't you think? So romantic! We can imagine the lovers into it, you know. I like that lane because you can think out loud there without people calling you crazy."[3]

Anne, starting out alone in the morning, went down Lovers' Lane as far as the brook. Here Diana met her, and the two little girls went on up the lane under the leafy arch of maples—"maples are such sociable trees," said Anne; "they're always rustling and whispering to you,"—until they came to a rustic bridge. Then they left the lane and walked through Mr. Barry's back field and past Willowmere. Beyond Willowmere came Violet Vale—a little green dimple in the shadow of Mr. Andrew Bell's big woods. "Of course there are no violets there now," Anne told Marilla, "but Diana says there are millions of them in spring. Oh, Marilla, can't you just imagine you see them? It actually takes away my breath. I named it Violet Vale. Diana says she never saw the beat of me for hitting on fancy names for places. It's nice to be clever at something, isn't it? But Diana named the Birch Path. She wanted to, so I let her; but I'm sure I could have found something more poetical than plain Birch Path. Anybody can think of a name like that. But the Birch Path is one of the prettiest places in the world, Marilla."

It was. Other people besides Anne thought so when they stumbled on it. It was a little narrow, twisting path, winding down over a long hill straight through Mr. Bell's woods, where the light came down sifted through so many emerald screens that it was as flawless as the heart of a diamond. It was fringed in all its length with slim young birches, white-stemmed and lissom[4] boughed; ferns and starflowers and wild lilies-of-the-valley and scarlet tufts of pigeon berries[5] grew thickly along it; and always there was a delightful spiciness in the air and music of bird calls and the murmur and laugh of wood winds in the trees overhead. Now and then you might see a rabbit skipping across the road if you were quiet—which, with Anne and Diana, happened about once in a blue moon.[6] Down in the valley the path came out to the main road and then it was just up the spruce hill to the school.

3. LMM composed many of her stories while walking in the real "Lover's Lane" in Cavendish. [LMM spells this both Lover's Lane and Lovers' Lane. See SJ2 38–42.]
4. Flexible, supple, a contraction of "lithesome."
5. Blackish-red berries following the ripening of small white flowers on the long drooping branches of pokeweed, a tall perennial herb.
6. Proverbial phrase meaning very rarely.

The Avonlea school[7] was a whitewashed building, low in the eaves and wide in the windows, furnished inside with comfortable substantial old-fashioned desks that opened and shut, and were carved all over their lids with the initials and hieroglyphics of three generations of school-children. The schoolhouse was set back from the road and behind it was a dusky fir wood and a brook where all the children put their bottles of milk in the morning to keep cool and sweet until dinner hour.[8]

Marilla had seen Anne start off to school on the first day of September with many secret misgivings. Anne was such an odd girl. How would she get on with the other children? And how on earth would she ever manage to hold her tongue during school hours?

Things went better than Marilla feared, however. Anne came home that evening in high spirits.

"I think I'm going to like school here," she announced. "I don't think much of the master, though. He's all the time curling his moustache and making eyes at Prissy Andrews.[9] Prissy is grown-up, you know. She's sixteen and she's studying for the entrance examination into Queen's Academy at Charlottetown[1] next year. Tillie Boulter says the master is *dead gone* on her.[2] She's got a beautiful complexion and curly brown hair and she does it up so elegantly. She sits in the long seat at the back and he sits there, too, most of the time—to explain her lessons, he says. But Ruby Gillis says she saw him writing something on her slate[3] and when Prissy read it she blushed as red as a beet and giggled; and Ruby Gillis says she doesn't believe it had anything to do with the lesson."

"Anne Shirley, don't let me hear you talking about your teacher in that way again," said Marilla sharply. "You don't go to school to criticize the master. I guess he can teach *you* something and it's your business to learn. And I want you to understand right off that you are not to come home telling tales about him. That is something I won't encourage. I hope you were a good girl."

"Indeed I was," said Anne comfortably. "It wasn't so hard as you might imagine, either. I sit with Diana. Our seat is right by the win-

7. Based on the one-room schoolhouse LMM attended. Since 1835, land had been reserved for schools in PEI, and free non-sectarian public schools were available from 1852.
8. Based on LMM's own memory. See *SJ1* 377.
9. Perhaps based on LMM's experience in Saskatchewan where her teacher, Mr. Mustard, fell in love with her.
1. A post-secondary college based on Prince of Wales College in Charlottetown which had been established in 1835 as Central Academy and renamed in 1860. PWC provided teacher training and preparation for university. In 1879 (five years after LMM's birth), it became open to women. PWC is now absorbed in the University of Prince Edward Island.
2. Enamoured (slang). The manuscript read "sweet on her," another slang expression.
3. In place of paper and pen, junior schoolchildren each owned a wooden-framed book-sized piece of slate and a paper-wrapped slate pencil.

dow and we can look down to the Lake of Shining Waters. There are
a lot of nice girls in school and we had scrumptious fun playing at
dinner time. It's so nice to have a lot of little girls to play with. But
of course I like Diana best and always will. I *adore* Diana. I'm dreadfully far behind the others. They're all in the fifth book and I'm only
in the fourth. I feel that it's kind of a disgrace. But there's not one
of them has such an imagination as I have and I soon found that
out. We had reading and geography and Canadian History and dictation to-day. Mr. Phillips said my spelling was disgraceful and he
held up my slate so that everybody could see it, all marked over. I
felt so mortified, Marilla; he might have been politer to a stranger, I
think. Ruby Gillis gave me an apple and Sophia Sloane lent me a
lovely pink card with 'May I see you home?' on it. I'm to give it back
to her to-morrow. And Tillie Boulter let me wear her bead ring all
the afternoon. Can I have some of those pearl beads[4] off the old
pincushion in the garret[5] to make myself a ring? And oh, Marilla,
Jane Andrews told me that Minnie MacPherson told her that she
heard Prissy Andrews tell Sara Gillis that I had a very pretty nose.
Marilla, that is the first compliment I have ever had in my life and
you can't imagine what a strange feeling it gave me. Marilla, have I
really a pretty nose? I know you'll tell me the truth."

"Your nose is well enough," said Marilla shortly. Secretly she
thought Anne's nose was a remarkably pretty one; but she had no
intention of telling her so.

That was three weeks ago and all had gone smoothly so far. And
now, this crisp September morning, Anne and Diana were tripping
blithely down the Birch Path, two of the happiest little girls in Avonlea.

"I guess Gilbert Blythe will be in school to-day," said Diana. "He's
been visiting his cousins over in New Brunswick all summer and he
only came home Saturday night. He's *aw'fly* handsome, Anne. And
he teases the girls something terrible. He just torments our lives out."

Diana's voice indicated that she rather liked having her life tor-
mented out than not.

"Gilbert Blythe?" said Anne. "Isn't it his name that's written up on
the porch wall with Julia Bell's and a big 'Take Notice' over them?"

"Yes," said Diana, tossing her head, "but I'm sure he doesn't like
Julia Bell so very much. I've heard him say he studied the multiplication table by her freckles."

"Oh, don't speak about freckles to me," implored Anne. "It isn't
delicate when I've got so many. But I do think that writing take-

---

4. Not real pearls, but painted to have the sheen of pearls.
5. The attic, where out-of-use things were stored.

notices up on the wall about the boys and girls is the silliest ever. I should just like to see anybody dare to write my name up with a boy's. Not, of course," she hastened to add, "that anybody would."

Anne sighed. She didn't want her name written up. But it was a little humiliating to know that there was no danger of it.

"Nonsense," said Diana, whose black eyes and glossy tresses had played such havoc with the hearts of Avonlea schoolboys that her name figured on the porch walls in half a dozen take-notices. "It's only meant as a joke. And don't you be too sure your name won't ever be written up. Charlie Sloane is *dead gone* on you. He told his mother—his *mother*, mind you—that you were the smartest girl in school. That's better than being good-looking."

"No, it isn't," said Anne, feminine to the core. "I'd rather be pretty than clever. And I hate Charlie Sloane. I can't bear a boy with goggle eyes.[6] If any one wrote my name up with his I'd *never* get over it, Diana Barry. But it *is* nice to keep head of your class."

"You'll have Gilbert in your class after this," said Diana, "and he's used to being head of his class, I can tell you. He's only in the fourth book[7] although he's nearly fourteen. Four years ago his father was sick and had to go out to Alberta[8] for his health and Gilbert went with him. They were there three years and Gil didn't go to school hardly any until they came back. You won't find it so easy to keep head after this, Anne."

"I'm glad," said Anne quickly. "I couldn't really feel proud of keeping head of little boys and girls of just nine or ten. I got up yesterday spelling 'ebullition.' Josie Pye was head and, mind you, she peeped in her book. Mr. Phillips didn't see her—he was looking at Prissy Andrews—but I did. I just swept her a look of freezing scorn and she got as red as a beet and spelled it wrong after all."

"Those Pye girls are cheats all round," said Diana indignantly, as they climbed the fence of the main road. "Gertie Pye actually went and put her milk bottle in my place in the brook yesterday. Did you ever? I don't speak to her now."

When Mr. Phillips was in the back of the room hearing Prissy Andrews' Latin Diana whispered to Anne,

"That's Gilbert Blythe sitting right across the aisle from you, Anne. Just look at him and see if you don't think he's handsome."

Anne looked accordingly. She had a good chance to do so, for the said Gilbert Blythe was absorbed in stealthily pinning the long yellow

---

6. Protuberant, or with round glasses.
7. Children were organized into groups according to what level of reading they had mastered.
8. Canada's western area, near the Rockies, seemed a healthier place than sea-level PEI. Alberta joined Canadian Confederation in 1905; before that, schools were few. When LMM spent time in Saskatchewan, another western province, she attended school in a combination town center and dance hall.

braid of Ruby Gillis, who sat in front of him, to the back of her seat. He was a tall boy, with curly brown hair, roguish hazel eyes and a mouth twisted into a teasing smile. Presently Ruby Gillis started up to take a sum to the master; she fell back into her seat with a little shriek, believing that her hair was pulled out by the roots. Everybody looked at her and Mr. Phillips glared so sternly that Ruby began to cry. Gilbert had whisked the pin out of sight and was studying his history with the soberest face in the world; but when the commotion subsided he looked at Anne and winked with inexpressible drollery.

"I think your Gilbert Blythe *is* handsome," confided Anne to Diana, "but I think he's very bold. It isn't good manners to wink at a strange girl."

But it was not until the afternoon that things really began to happen.

Mr. Phillips was back in the corner explaining a problem in algebra to Prissy Andrews and the rest of the scholars were doing pretty much as they pleased, eating green apples, whispering, drawing pictures on their slates, and driving crickets, harnessed to strings,[9] up and down the aisle. Gilbert Blythe was trying to make Anne Shirley look at him and failing utterly, because Anne was at that moment totally oblivious, not only of the very existence of Gilbert Blythe, but of every other scholar in Avonlea school and of Avonlea school itself. With her chin propped on her hands and her eyes fixed on the blue glimpse of the Lake of Shining Waters that the west window afforded, she was far away in a gorgeous dreamland, hearing and seeing nothing save her own wonderful visions.

Gilbert Blythe wasn't used to putting himself out to make a girl look at him and meeting with failure. She *should* look at him, that red-haired Shirley girl with the little pointed chin and the big eyes that weren't like the eyes of any other girl in Avonlea school.

Gilbert reached across the aisle, picked up the end of Anne's long red braid, held it out at arm's length and said in a piercing whisper,

"Carrots! Carrots!"

Then Anne looked at him with a vengeance!

She did more than look. She sprang to her feet, her bright fancies fallen into cureless ruin. She flashed one indignant glance at Gilbert from eyes whose angry sparkle was swiftly quenched in equally angry tears.

"You mean, hateful boy!" she exclaimed passionately. "How dare you!"

And then—Thwack! Anne had brought her slate down on Gilbert's head and cracked it—slate, not head—clear across.

Avonlea school always enjoyed a scene. This was an especially

9. A schoolboy sport, appearing again when Anne becomes a teacher in *Anne of Avonlea*.

Thwack! Anne had brought her slate down on Gilbert's head

enjoyable one. Everybody said, "Oh" in horrified delight. Diana gasped. Ruby Gillis, who was inclined to be hysterical, began to cry. Tommy Sloane let his team of crickets escape him altogether while he stared open-mouthed at the tableau.

Mr. Phillips stalked down the aisle and laid his hand heavily on Anne's shoulder.

"Anne Shirley, what does this mean?" he said angrily.

Anne returned no answer. It was asking too much of flesh and blood to expect her to tell before the whole school that she had been called "carrots." Gilbert it was who spoke up stoutly.

"It was my fault, Mr. Phillips. I teased her."

Mr. Phillips paid no heed to Gilbert.

"I am sorry to see a pupil of mine displaying such a temper and such a vindictive spirit," he said in a solemn tone, as if the mere fact of being a pupil of his ought to root out all evil passions from the hearts of small imperfect mortals. "Anne, go and stand on the platform in front of the blackboard for the rest of the afternoon."

Anne would have infinitely preferred a whipping to this punishment, under which her sensitive spirit quivered as from a whiplash. With a white, set face she obeyed. Mr. Phillips took a chalk crayon and wrote on the blackboard above her head.

"Ann Shirley has a very bad temper. Ann Shirley must learn to control her temper," and then read it out loud so that even the primer class,[1] who couldn't read writing, should understand it.

Anne stood there the rest of the afternoon with that legend above her. She did not cry or hang her head. Anger was still too hot in her heart for that and it sustained her amid all her agony of humiliation. With resentful eyes and passion-red cheeks she confronted alike Diana's sympathetic gaze and Charlie Sloane's indignant nods and Josie Pye's malicious smiles. As for Gilbert Blythe, she would not even look at him. She would *never* look at him again! She would never speak to him!!

When school was dismissed Anne marched out with her red head held high. Gilbert Blythe tried to intercept her at the porch door.

"I'm awful sorry I made fun of your hair, Anne," he whispered contritely. "Honest I am. Don't be mad for keeps, now."

Anne swept by disdainfully, without look or sign of hearing. "Oh, how could you, Anne?" breathed Diana as they went down the road, half reproachfully, half admiringly. Diana felt that *she* could never have resisted Gilbert's plea.

"I shall never forgive Gilbert Blythe," said Anne firmly. "And Mr. Phillips spelled my name without an *e*, too. The iron has entered into my soul, Diana."[2]

1. Children in the first stage of schooling, who use a "primer" or first alphabet book.
2. Determined to resist. Biblical phrase as translated by Thomas Cranmer for the *Book of*

Diana hadn't the least idea what Anne meant but she understood it was something terrible.

"You mustn't mind Gilbert making fun of your hair," she said soothingly. "Why, he makes fun of all the girls. He laughs at mine because it's so black. He's called me a crow a dozen times; and I never heard him apologize for anything before, either."

"There's a great deal of difference between being called a crow and being called carrots," said Anne with dignity. "Gilbert Blythe has hurt my feelings *excruciatingly*,[3] Diana."

It is possible the matter might have blown over without more excruciation if nothing else had happened. But when things begin to happen they are apt to keep on.

Avonlea scholars often spent noon hour picking gum in Mr. Bell's spruce grove[4] over the hill and across his big pasture field. From there they could keep an eye on Eben Wright's house, where the master boarded.[5] When they saw Mr. Phillips emerging therefrom they ran for the schoolhouse; but the distance being about three times longer than Mr. Wright's lane they were very apt to arrive there, breathless and gasping, some three minutes too late.

On the following day Mr. Phillips was seized with one of his spasmodic fits of reform and announced, before going home to dinner, that he should expect to find all the scholars in their seats when he returned. Any one who came in late would be punished.

All the boys and some of the girls went to Mr. Bell's spruce grove as usual, fully intending to stay only long enough to "pick a chew." But spruce groves are seductive and yellow nuts of gum beguiling; they picked and loitered and strayed; and as usual the first thing that recalled them to a sense of the flight of time was Jimmy Glover shouting from the top of a patriarchal old spruce, "Master's coming."

The girls, who were on the ground, started first and managed to reach the schoolhouse in time but without a second to spare. The boys, who had to wriggle hastily down from the trees, were later; and Anne, who had not been picking gum at all but was wandering happily in the far end of the grove, waist deep among the bracken, singing softly to herself, with a wreath of rice lilies on her hair as if she were some wild divinity of the shadowy places, was latest of all. Anne could run like a deer, however; run she did with the impish result that she overtook the boys at the door and was swept into the school-

*Common Prayer* (1549/1552): "Whose feet they hurt in the stocks: the iron entered into his soul." Psalms 105.18.

3. As painfully as if crucified. An example of Anne's exaggerated and affected use of language.

4. Spruce trees exude a resin that can be softened and chewed like gum.

5. The teacher had no option but to board with one of the families in a small rural community. LMM boarded when she taught school in Bideford, Belmont, and Bedeque.

house among them just as Mr. Phillips was in the act of hanging up his hat.

Mr. Phillips' brief reforming energy was over; he didn't want the bother of punishing a dozen pupils; but it was necessary to do something to save his word, so he looked about for a scapegoat and found it in Anne, who had dropped into her seat, gasping for breath, with her forgotten lily wreath hanging askew over one ear and giving her a particularly rakish and dishevelled appearance.

"Anne Shirley, since you seem to be so fond of the boys' company we shall indulge your taste for it this afternoon," he said sarcastically. "Take those flowers out of your hair and sit with Gilbert Blythe."

The other boys snickered. Diana, turning pale with pity, plucked the wreath from Anne's hair and squeezed her hand. Anne stared at the master as if turned to stone.

"Did you hear what I said, Anne?" queried Mr. Phillips sternly.

"Yes, sir," said Anne slowly, "but I didn't suppose you really meant it."

"I assure you I did,"—still with the sarcastic inflection which all the children, and Anne especially, hated. It flicked on the raw. "Obey me at once."

For a moment Anne looked as if she meant to disobey. Then, realizing that there was no help for it, she rose haughtily, stepped across the aisle, sat down beside Gilbert Blythe, and buried her face in her arms on the desk. Ruby Gillis, who got a glimpse of it as it went down, told the others going home from school that she'd "acksually[6] never seen anything like it—it was so white, with awful little red spots in it."

To Anne, this was as the end of all things. It was bad enough to be singled out for punishment from among a dozen equally guilty ones; it was worse still to be sent to sit with a boy; but that that boy should be Gilbert Blythe was heaping insult on injury to a degree utterly unbearable. Anne felt that she could *not* bear it and it would be of no use to try. Her whole being seethed with shame and anger and humiliation.

At first the other scholars looked and whispered and giggled and nudged. But as Anne never lifted her head and as Gilbert worked fractions as if his whole soul was absorbed in them and them only, they soon returned to their own tasks and Anne was forgotten. When Mr. Phillips called the history class out Anne should have gone; but Anne did not move, and Mr. Phillips, who had been writing some verses "To Priscilla" before he called the class, was thinking about an obstinate rhyme still and never missed her. Once, when nobody

6. Actually. Another example of school child mispronunciation.

was looking, Gilbert took from his desk a little pink candy heart with a gold motto on it, "You are sweet," and slipped it under the curve of Anne's arm. Whereupon Anne arose, took the pink heart gingerly between the tips of her fingers, dropped it on the floor, ground it to powder beneath her heel, and resumed her position without deigning to bestow a glance on Gilbert.

When school went out Anne marched to her desk, ostentatiously took out everything therein, books and writing tablet, pen and ink, testament and arithmetic, and piled them neatly on her cracked slate.

"What are you taking all those things home for, Anne?" Diana wanted to know, as soon as they were out on the road. She had not dared to ask the question before.

"I am not coming back to school any more," said Anne.

Diana gasped and stared at Anne to see if she meant it.

"Will Marilla let you stay home?" she asked.

"She'll have to," said Anne. "I'll *never* go to school to that man again."

"Oh, Anne!" Diana looked as if she were ready to cry. "I do think you're mean. What shall I do? Mr. Phillips will make me sit with that horrid Gertie Pye—I know he will because she is sitting alone. Do come back, Anne."

"I'd do almost anything in the world for you, Diana," said Anne sadly. "I'd let myself be torn limb from limb if it would do you any good. But I can't do this, so please don't ask it. You harrow up my very soul."[7]

"Just think of all the fun you will miss," mourned Diana. "We are going to build the loveliest new house down by the brook; and we'll be playing ball next week and you've never played ball, Anne.[8] It's tremenjusly exciting. And we're going to learn a new song—Jane Andrews is practising it up now; and Alice Andrews is going to bring a new Pansy book[9] next week and we're all going to read it out loud, chapter about, down by the brook. And you know you are so fond of reading out loud, Anne."

Nothing moved Anne in the least. Her mind was made up. She would not go to school to Mr. Phillips again; she told Marilla so when she got home.

"Nonsense," said Marilla.

"It isn't nonsense at all," said Anne, gazing at Marilla with sol-

---

7. An agricultural image; harrowing the soil means breaking it up with an iron-toothed implement.
8. LMM gives directions for their form of ball in her later journal. See *SJ4* 424.
9. Isabella Macdonald Allen, writing as "Pansy," produced over a hundred moralistic books for young girls. LMM mocked the "Pansy" stories but she also picked up ideas from them (*SJ1* 253).

emn, reproachful eyes. "Don't you understand, Marilla? I've been insulted."

"Insulted fiddlesticks! You'll go to school tomorrow as usual."

"Oh, no." Anne shook her head gently. "I'm not going back, Marilla. I'll learn my lessons at home and I'll be as good as I can be and hold my tongue all the time if it's possible at all. But I will not go back to school I assure you."

Marilla saw something remarkably like unyielding stubbornness looking out of Anne's small face. She understood that she would have trouble in overcoming it; but she resolved wisely to say nothing more just then.

"I'll run down and see Rachel about it this evening," she thought. "There's no use reasoning with Anne now. She's too worked up and I've an idea she can be awful stubborn if she takes the notion. Far as I can make out from her story, Mr. Phillips has been carrying matters with a rather high hand. But it would never do to say so to her. I'll just talk it over with Rachel. She's sent ten children to school and she ought to know something about it. She'll have heard the whole story, too, by this time."

Marilla found Mrs. Lynde knitting quilts as industriously and cheerfully as usual.

"I suppose you know what I've come about," she said, a little shamefacedly.

Mrs. Rachel nodded.

"About Anne's fuss in school, I reckon," she said. "Tillie Boulter was in on her way home from school and told me about it."

"I don't know what to do with her," said Marilla. "She declares she won't go back to school. I never saw a child so worked up. I've been expecting trouble ever since she started to school. I knew things were going too smooth to last. She's so high-strung. What would you advise, Rachel?"

"Well, since you've asked my advice, Marilla," said Mrs. Lynde amiably—Mrs. Lynde dearly loved to be asked for advice—"I'd just humour her a little at first, that's what I'd do. It's my belief that Mr. Phillips was in the wrong. Of course, it doesn't do to say so to the children, you know. And of course he did right to punish her yesterday for giving way to temper. But to-day it was different. The others who were late should have been punished as well as Anne, that's what. And I don't believe in making the girls sit with the boys for punishment. It isn't modest. Tillie Boulter was real indignant.[1] She took Anne's part right through and said all the scholars did, too. Anne seems real popular among them, somehow. I never thought she'd take with them so well."

---

1. Mrs. Lynde's use of "real" as an adverb is colloquial and ungrammatical.

"Then you really think I'd better let her stay home," said Marilla in amazement.

"Yes. That is, I wouldn't say school to her again until she said it herself. Depend upon it, Marilla, she'll cool off in a week or so and be ready enough to go back of her own accord, that's what, while, if you were to make her go back right off, dear knows what freak or tantrum she'd take next and make more trouble than ever. The less fuss made the better, in my opinion. She won't miss much by not going to school, as far as *that* goes. Mr. Phillips isn't any good at all as a teacher. The order he keeps is scandalous, that's what, and he neglects the young fry[2] and puts all his time on those big scholars he's getting ready for Queen's. He'd never have got the school for another year if his uncle hadn't been a trustee—*the* trustee, for he just leads the other two around by the nose, that's what. I declare, I don't know what education in this Island is coming to."

Mrs. Rachel shook her head, as much as to say if she were only at the head of the education system of the Province things would be much better managed.

Marilla took Mrs. Rachel's advice and not another word was said to Anne about going back to school. She learned her lessons at home, did her chores, and played with Diana in the chilly purple autumn twilights; but when she met Gilbert Blythe on the road or encountered him in Sunday-school she passed him by with an icy contempt that was no whit thawed by his evident desire to appease her. Even Diana's efforts as a peacemaker were of no avail. Anne had evidently made up her mind to hate Gilbert Blythe to the end of life.

As much as she hated Gilbert, however, did she love Diana, with all the love of her passionate little heart, equally intense in its likes and dislikes. One evening Marilla, coming in from the orchard with a basket of apples, found Anne sitting alone by the east window in the twilight, crying bitterly.

"Whatever's the matter now, Anne?" she asked.

"It's about Diana," sobbed Anne luxuriously. "I love Diana so, Marilla. I cannot ever live without her. But I know very well when we grow up that Diana will get married and go away and leave me. And oh, what shall I do? I hate her husband—I just hate him furiously. I've been imagining it all out—the wedding and everything—Diana dressed in snowy garments,[3] with a veil, and looking as beautiful and regal as a queen; and me the bridesmaid, with a lovely dress, too, and puffed sleeves, but with a breaking heart hid beneath my smiling face. And then bidding Diana good-bye-e-e—" Here Anne broke down entirely and wept with increasing bitterness.

---

2. Literally small fish and by extension children.
3. A preview of a scene in *Anne of the Island*, when Anne helps Diana dress for her wedding.

Marilla turned quickly away to hide her twitching face; but it was no use; she collapsed on the nearest chair and burst into such a hearty and unusual peal of laughter that Matthew, crossing the yard outside, halted in amazement. When had he heard Marilla laugh like that before?

"Well, Anne Shirley," said Marilla as soon as she could speak, "if you must borrow trouble, for pity's sake borrow it handier home. I should think you had an imagination, sure enough."

# Chapter XVI

### DIANA IS INVITED TO TEA WITH TRAGIC RESULTS

OCTOBER was a beautiful month at Green Gables, when the birches in the hollow turned as golden as sunshine and the maples behind the orchard were royal crimson and the wild cherry-trees along the lane put on the loveliest shades of dark red and bronzy green, while the fields sunned themselves in aftermaths.

Anne revelled in the world of colour about her.

"Oh, Marilla," she exclaimed one Saturday morning coming dancing in with her arms full of gorgeous boughs, "I'm so glad I live in a world where there are Octobers. It would be terrible if we just skipped from September to November, wouldn't it? Look at these maple branches. Don't they give you a thrill—several thrills? I'm going to decorate my room with them."

"Messy things," said Marilla, whose aesthetic sense was not noticeably developed. "You clutter up your room entirely too much with out-of-doors stuff, Anne. Bedrooms were made to sleep in."

"Oh, and dream in too, Marilla. And you know one can dream so much better in a room where there are pretty things. I'm going to put these boughs in the old blue jug and set them on my table."

"Mind you don't drop leaves all over the stairs then. I'm going to a meeting of the Aid Society at Carmody this afternoon, Anne, and I won't likely be home before dark. You'll have to get Matthew and Jerry their supper, so mind you don't forget to put the tea to draw[1] until you sit down at the table as you did last time."

"It was dreadful of me to forget," said Anne apologetically, "but that was the afternoon I was trying to think of a name for Violet Vale and it crowded other things out. Matthew was so good. He never scolded a bit. He put the tea down himself and said we could wait awhile as well as not. And I told him a lovely fairy story while we were waiting, so he didn't find the time long at all. It was a beautiful

1. Make tea (British usage; the American equivalent is "to steep").

fairy story, Marilla. I forgot the end of it, so I made up an end for it myself and Matthew said he couldn't tell where the join came in."

"Matthew would think it all right, Anne, if you took a notion to get up and have dinner in the middle of the night. But you keep your wits about you this time. And—I don't really know if I'm doing right—it may make you more addle-pated[2] than ever—but you can ask Diana to come over and spend the afternoon with you and have tea here."

"Oh, Marilla!" Anne clasped her hands. "How perfectly lovely! You *are* able to imagine things after all or else you'd never have understood how I've longed for that very thing. It will seem so nice and grown-uppish. No fear of my forgetting to put the tea to draw when I have company. Oh, Marilla, can I use the rosebud spray tea-set?"

"No, indeed! The rosebud tea-set! Well, what next? You know I never use that except for the minister or the Aids. You'll put down the old brown tea-set. But you can open the little yellow crock[3] of cherry preserves. It's time it was being used anyhow—I believe it's beginning to work. And you can cut some fruit-cake and have some of the cookies and snaps."

"I can just imagine myself sitting down at the head of the table and pouring out the tea," said Anne, shutting her eyes ecstatically. "And asking Diana if she takes sugar! I know she doesn't but of course I'll ask her just as if I didn't know. And then pressing her to take another piece of fruit-cake and another helping of preserves. Oh, Marilla, it's a wonderful sensation just to think of it. Can I take her into the spare room to lay off her hat when she comes? And then into the parlour to sit?"

"No. The sitting-room will do for you and your company. But there's a bottle half full of raspberry cordial[4] that was left over from the church social the other night. It's on the second shelf of the sitting-room closet and you and Diana can have it if you like, and a cooky to eat with it along in the afternoon, for I daresay Matthew'll be late coming in to tea since he's hauling potatoes to the vessel."[5]

Anne flew down to the hollow, past the Dryad's Bubble and up the spruce path to Orchard Slope, to ask Diana to tea. As a result, just after Marilla had driven off to Carmody, Diana came over, dressed in her second best dress and looking exactly as it is proper to look when asked out to tea. At other times she was wont to run into the kitchen without knocking; but now she knocked primly at

2. Unsound in mind, like a rotten egg.
3. Earthenware pot holding preserves (whole fruit boiled with sugar) to prevent spoiling (or "working").
4. A non-alcoholic fruit drink in this community. In general English and North American usage, a cordial is an alcoholic drink that "stimulates" the heart.
5. Farm produce (principally potatoes, then as now a major PEI crop), commonly transported by boat from sea-shore villages.

the front door. And when Anne, dressed in *her* second best, as primly opened it, both little girls shook hands as gravely as if they had never met before. This unnatural solemnity lasted until after Diana had been taken to the east gable to lay off her hat and then had sat for ten minutes in the sitting-room, toes in position.

"How is your mother?" inquired Anne politely, just as if she had not seen Mrs. Barry picking apples that morning in excellent health and spirits.

"She is very well, thank you. I suppose Mr. Cuthbert is hauling potatoes to the *Lily Sands* this afternoon, is he?" said Diana, who had ridden down to Mr. Harmon Andrews' that morning in Matthew's cart.

"Yes. Our potato crop is very good this year. I hope your father's potato crop is good, too."

"It is fairly good, thank you. Have you picked many of your apples yet?"

"Oh, ever so many," said Anne, forgetting to be dignified and jumping up quickly. "Let's go out to the orchard and get some of the Red Sweetings,[6] Diana. Marilla says we can have all that are left on the tree. Marilla is a very generous woman. She said we could have fruitcake and cherry preserves for tea. But it isn't good manners to tell your company what you are going to give them to eat, so I won't tell you what she said we could have to drink. Only it begins with an *r* and a *c* and it's a bright red colour. I love bright red drinks, don't you? They taste twice as good as any other colour."

The orchard, with its great sweeping boughs that bent to the ground with fruit, proved so delightful that the little girls spent most of the afternoon in it, sitting in a grassy corner where the frost had spared the green and the mellow autumn sunshine lingered warmly, eating apples and talking as hard as they could. Diana had much to tell Anne of what went on in school. She had to sit with Gertie Pye and she hated it; Gertie squeaked her pencil all the time and it just made her—Diana's—blood run cold; Ruby Gillis had charmed all her warts away, true's you live, with a magic pebble that old Mary Joe from the Creek gave her. You had to rub the warts with the pebble and then throw it away over your left shoulder at the time of the new moon and the warts would all go.[7] Charlie Sloane's name was written up with Em White's on the porch wall and Em White was *awful mad* about it; Sam Boulter had "sassed" Mr. Phillips in class and Mr. Phillips whipped him and Sam's father came down to

---

6. An apple variety, one of many in the orchard-rich Island. Sweetings are mentioned in Roger Ascham's *The Scholemaster* (1570).

7. Skin growths caused by a readily transmitted virus. Folk-lore said warts came from touching frogs and that they could be cured by rubbing them with apples, potatoes, or in this case "magic pebbles."

the school and dared Mr. Phillips to lay a hand on one of his children again; and Mattie Andrews had a new red hood and a blue crossover[8] with tassels on it and the airs she put on about it were perfectly sickening; and Lizzie Wright didn't speak to Mamie Wilson because Mamie Wilson's grown-up sister had cut out Lizzie Wright's grown-up sister with her beau; and everybody missed Anne so and wished she'd come to school again; and Gilbert Blythe—

But Anne didn't want to hear about Gilbert Blythe. She jumped up hurriedly and said suppose they go in and have some raspberry cordial.

Anne looked on the second shelf of the room pantry but there was no bottle of raspberry cordial there. Search revealed it away back on the top shelf. Anne put it on a tray and set it on the table with a tumbler.

"Now, please help yourself, Diana," she said politely. "I don't believe I'll have any just now. I don't feel as if I wanted any after all those apples."

Diana poured herself out a tumblerful, looked at its bright red hue admiringly, and then sipped it daintily.

"That's awfully nice raspberry cordial, Anne," she said. "I didn't know raspberry cordial was so nice."

"I'm real glad you like it. Take as much as you want. I'm going to run out and stir the fire up. There are so many responsibilities on a person's mind when they're keeping house, isn't there?"

When Anne came back from the kitchen Diana was drinking her second glassful of cordial; and, being entreated thereto by Anne, she offered no particular objection to the drinking of a third. The tumblerfuls were generous ones and the raspberry cordial was certainly very nice.

"The nicest I ever drank," said Diana. "It's ever so much nicer than Mrs. Lynde's although she brags of hers so much. It doesn't taste a bit like hers."

"I should think Marilla's raspberry cordial would prob'ly be much nicer than Mrs. Lynde's," said Anne loyally. "Marilla is a famous cook. She is trying to teach me to cook but I assure you, Diana, it is uphill work. There's so little scope for imagination in cookery. You just have to go by rules. The last time I made a cake I forgot to put the flour in. I was thinking the loveliest story about you and me, Diana. I thought you were desperately ill with smallpox and everybody deserted you, but I went boldly to your bedside and nursed you back to life; and then I took the smallpox and died and I was buried under those poplar trees in the graveyard and you planted a rosebush

8. A shawl, fringed in this case. As a child under twelve, LMM wore a ribboned hood (*SJ3* 71).

by my grave and watered it with your tears; and you never, never forgot the friend of your youth who sacrificed her life for you. Oh, it was such a pathetic tale, Diana. The tears just rained down over my cheeks while I mixed the cake. But I forgot the flour and the cake was a dismal failure. Flour is so essential to cakes, you know. Marilla was very cross and I don't wonder. I'm a great trial to her. She was terribly mortified about the pudding sauce last week. We had a plum pudding for dinner on Tuesday and there was half the pudding and a pitcherful of sauce left over. Marilla said there was enough for another dinner and told me to set it on the pantry shelf and cover it. I meant to cover it just as much as could be, Diana, but when I carried it in I was imagining I was a nun—of course I'm a Protestant but I imagined I was a Catholic—taking the veil to bury a broken heart in cloistered seclusion; and I forgot all about covering the pudding sauce. I thought of it next morning and ran to the pantry. Diana, fancy if you can my extreme horror at finding a mouse drowned in that pudding sauce! I lifted the mouse out with a spoon and threw it out in the yard and then I washed the spoon in three waters. Marilla was out milking and I fully intended to ask her when she came in if I'd give the sauce to the pigs; but when she did come in I was imagining that I was a frost fairy[9] going through the woods turning the trees red and yellow, whichever they wanted to be, so I never thought about the pudding sauce again and Marilla sent me out to pick apples. Well, Mr. and Mrs. Chester Ross from Spencervale came here that morning. You know they are very stylish people, especially Mrs. Chester Ross. When Marilla called me in dinner was all ready and everybody was at the table. I tried to be as polite and dignified as I could be, for I wanted Mrs. Chester Ross to think I was a ladylike little girl even if I wasn't pretty. Everything went right until I saw Marilla coming with the plum pudding in one hand and the pitcher of pudding sauce, *warmed up*, in the other. Diana, that was a terrible moment. I remembered everything and I just stood up in my place and shrieked out, 'Marilla, you mustn't use that pudding sauce. There was a mouse drowned in it. I forgot to tell you before.' Oh, Diana, I shall never forget that awful moment if I live to be a hundred. Mrs. Chester Ross just *looked* at me and I thought I would sink through the floor with mortification. She is such a perfect house-keeper and fancy what she must have thought of us. Marilla turned red as fire but she never said a word—then. She just carried that sauce and pudding out and brought in some strawberry preserves. She even offered me some, but I couldn't swallow a mouthful. It was like heaping coals of fire on my head.[1] After Mrs. Chester

---

9. A variation on the legend of Jack Frost, who turns the world white with the first frost.
1. Countering an offense with kindness: "If thine enemy be hungry, give him bread to eat;

Ross went away Marilla gave me a dreadful scolding. Why, Diana, what is the matter?"

Diana had stood up very unsteadily; then she sat down again, putting her hands to her head.

"I'm—I'm awful sick," she said, a little thickly. "I—I—must go right home."

"Oh, you mustn't dream of going home without your tea," cried Anne in distress. "I'll get it right off—I'll go and put the tea down this very minute."

"I must go home," repeated Diana, stupidly but determinedly.

"Let me get you a lunch[2] anyhow," implored Anne. "Let me give you a bit of fruit-cake and some of the cherry preserves. Lie down on the sofa for a little while and you'll be better. Where do you feel bad?"

"I must go home," said Diana, and that was all she would say. In vain Anne pleaded.

"I never heard of company going home without tea," she mourned. "Oh, Diana, do you suppose that it's possible you're really taking the smallpox? If you are I'll go and nurse you, you can depend on that. I'll never forsake you. But I do wish you'd stay till after tea. Where do you feel bad?"

"I'm awful dizzy," said Diana.

And indeed, she walked very dizzily. Anne, with tears of disappointment in her eyes, got Diana's hat and went with her as far as the Barry yard fence. Then she wept all the way back to Green Gables, where she sorrowfully put the remainder of the raspberry cordial back into the pantry and got tea ready for Matthew and Jerry, with all the zest gone out of the performance.

The next day was Sunday and as the rain poured down in torrents from dawn till dusk Anne did not stir abroad from Green Gables. Monday afternoon Marilla sent her down to Mrs. Lynde's on an errand. In a very short space of time Anne came flying back up the lane, with tears rolling down her cheeks. Into the kitchen she dashed and flung herself face downward on the sofa in an agony.

"Whatever has gone wrong now, Anne?" queried Marilla in doubt and dismay. "I do hope you haven't gone and been saucy to Mrs. Lynde again."

No answer from Anne save more tears and stormier sobs!

"Anne Shirley, when I ask you a question I want to be answered. Sit right up this very minute and tell me what you are crying about."

Anne sat up, tragedy personified.

---

if he be thirsty, give him water to drink; for thou shalt heap coals of fire upon his head, and the Lord shall reward thee." *Holy Bible*, Proverbs 25.21–22.
2. Light refreshment between meals.

"Mrs. Lynde was up to see Mrs. Barry to-day and Mrs. Barry was in an awful state," she wailed. "She says that I set Diana *drunk* Saturday and sent her home in a disgraceful condition. And she says I must be a thoroughly bad, wicked little girl and she's never, never going to let Diana play with me again. Oh, Marilla, I'm just overcome with woe."

Marilla stared in blank amazement.

"Set Diana drunk!" she said when she found her voice. "Anne, are you or Mrs. Barry crazy? What on earth did you give her?"

"Not a thing but raspberry cordial," sobbed Anne. "I never thought raspberry cordial would set people drunk, Marilla,—not even if they drank three big tumblerfuls as Diana did. Oh, it sounds so—so— like Mrs. Thomas' husband! But I didn't mean to set her drunk."

"Drunk fiddlesticks!" said Marilla, marching to the sitting-room pantry. There on the shelf was a bottle which she at once recognized as one containing some of her three year old homemade currant wine[3] for which she was celebrated in Avonlea, although certain of the stricter sort, Mrs. Barry among them, disapproved strongly of it. And at the same time Marilla recollected that she had put the bottle of raspberry cordial down in the cellar instead of in the pantry as she had told Anne.

She went back to the kitchen with the wine bottle in her hand. Her face was twitching in spite of herself.

"Anne, you certainly have a genius for getting into trouble. You went and gave Diana currant wine instead of raspberry cordial. Didn't you know the difference yourself?"

"I never tasted it," said Anne. "I thought it was the cordial. I meant to be so—so—hospitable. Diana got awfully sick and had to go home. Mrs. Barry told Mrs. Lynde she was simply dead drunk. She just laughed silly like when her mother asked her what was the matter and went to sleep and slept for hours. Her mother smelled her breath and knew she was drunk. She had a fearful headache all day yesterday. Mrs. Barry is so indignant. She will never believe but what I did it on purpose."

"I should think she would better punish Diana for being so greedy as to drink three glassfuls of anything," said Marilla shortly. "Why, three of those big glasses would have made her sick even if it had only been cordial. Well, this story will be a nice handle for those folks who are so down on me for making currant wine, although I haven't made any for three years ever since I found out that the minister didn't approve. I just kept that bottle for sickness.[4] There,

---

3. Although PEI was officially a "dry" province, LMM's English-born grandmother was famous for her red currant wine (*SJ3* 105).
4. In a community devoted to "temperance" (i.e., prohibition of alcoholic drinks), brandy, rye whiskey, and wines were kept and used as remedies for many ailments.

there, child, don't cry. I can't see as you were to blame although I'm sorry it happened so."

"I must cry," said Anne. "My heart is broken. The stars in their courses fight against me, Marilla.[5] Diana and I are parted forever. Oh, Marilla, I little dreamed of this when first we swore our vows of friendship."

"Don't be foolish, Anne. Mrs. Barry will think better of it when she finds you're not really to blame. I suppose she thinks you've done it for a silly joke or something of that sort. You'd best go up this evening and tell her how it was."

"My courage fails me at the thought of facing Diana's injured mother," sighed Anne. "I wish you'd go, Marilla. You're so much more dignified than I am. Likely she'd listen to you quicker than to me."

"Well, I will," said Marilla, reflecting that it would probably be the wiser course. "Don't cry any more, Anne. It will be all right."

Marilla had changed her mind about its being all right by the time she got back from Orchard Slope. Anne was watching for her coming and flew to the porch door to meet her.

"Oh, Marilla, I know by your face that it's been no use," she said sorrowfully. "Mrs. Barry won't forgive me?"

"Mrs. Barry, indeed!" snapped Marilla. "Of all the unreasonable women I ever saw she's the worst. I told her it was all a mistake and you weren't to blame, but she just simply didn't believe me. And she rubbed it well in about my currant wine and how I'd always said it couldn't have the least effect on anybody. I just told her plainly that currant wine wasn't meant to be drunk three tumblerfuls at a time and that if a child I had to do with was so greedy I'd sober her up with a right good spanking."

Marilla whisked into the kitchen, grievously disturbed, leaving a very much distracted little soul in the porch behind her. Presently Anne stepped out bare-headed into the chill autumn dusk; very determinedly and steadily she took her way down through the sere clover field over the log bridge and up through the spruce grove, lighted by a pale little moon hanging low over the western woods. Mrs. Barry, coming to the door in answer to a timid knock, found a white-lipped, eager-eyed suppliant on the doorstep.

Her face hardened. Mrs. Barry was a woman of strong prejudices and dislikes, and her anger was of the cold, sullen sort which is always hardest to overcome. To do her justice, she really believed Anne had made Diana drunk out of sheer malice prepense,[6] and she

---

5. Doomed by fate: "The stars in their courses fought against Sisera." *Holy Bible*, Judges 5.20.
6. Spitefulness thought out in advance: this old-fashioned French legal phrase is used in one of LMM's favorite novels, Walter Scott's *Ivanhoe* (1819), chap. 1.

was honestly anxious to preserve her little daughter from the con-
tamination of further intimacy with such a child.

"What do you want?" she said stiffly.

Anne clasped her hands.

"Oh, Mrs. Barry, please forgive me. I did not mean to—to—
intoxicate Diana. How could I? Just imagine if you were a poor little
orphan girl that kind people had adopted and you had just one bosom
friend in all the world. Do you think you would intoxicate her on
purpose? I thought it was only raspberry cordial. I was firmly convinced it was raspberry cordial. Oh, please don't say that you won't
let Diana play with me any more. If you do you will cover my life
with a dark cloud of woe."

This speech, which would have softened good Mrs. Lynde's heart
in a twinkling, had no effect on Mrs. Barry except to irritate her still
more. She was suspicious of Anne's big words and dramatic gestures
and imagined that the child was making fun of her. So she said,
coldly and cruelly:

"I don't think you are a fit little girl for Diana to associate with.
You'd better go home and behave yourself."

Anne's lip quivered.

"Won't you let me see Diana just once to say farewell?" she
implored.

"Diana has gone over to Carmody with her father," said Mrs. Barry,
going in and shutting the door.

Anne went back to Green Gables calm with despair.

"My last hope is gone," she told Marilla. "I went up and saw Mrs.
Barry myself and she treated me very insultingly. Marilla, I do *not*
think she is a well-bred woman. There is nothing more to do except
to pray and I haven't much hope that that'll do much good because,
Marilla, I do not believe that God Himself can do very much with
such an obstinate person as Mrs. Barry."

"Anne, you shouldn't say such things," rebuked Marilla, striving
to overcome that unholy tendency to laughter which she was dismayed to find growing upon her. And indeed, when she told the
whole story to Matthew that night, she did laugh heartily over Anne's
tribulations.

But when she slipped into the east gable before going to bed and
found that Anne had cried herself to sleep an unaccustomed softness
crept into her face.

"Poor little soul," she murmured, lifting a loose curl of hair from
the child's tear-stained face. Then she bent down and kissed the
flushed cheek on the pillow.

# Chapter XVII

### A NEW INTEREST IN LIFE

THE next afternoon Anne, bending over her patchwork at the kitchen window, happened to glance out and beheld Diana down by the Dryad's Bubble beckoning mysteriously. In a trice Anne was out of the house and flying down to the hollow, astonishment and hope struggling in her expressive eyes. But the hope faded when she saw Diana's dejected countenance.

"Your mother hasn't relented?" she gasped.

Diana shook her head mournfully.

"No; and oh, Anne, she says I'm never to play with you again. I've cried and cried and I told her it wasn't your fault, but it wasn't any use. I had ever such a time coaxing her to let me come down and say good-bye to you. She said I was only to stay ten minutes and she's timing me by the clock."

"Ten minutes isn't very long to say an eternal farewell in," said Anne tearfully. "Oh, Diana, will you promise faithfully never to forget me, the friend of your youth, no matter what dearer friends may caress thee?"[1]

"Indeed I will," sobbed Diana, "and I'll never have another bosom friend—I don't want to have. I couldn't love anybody as I love you."

"Oh, Diana," cried Anne, clasping her hands, "do you *love* me?"

"Why, of course I do. Didn't you know that?"

"No." Anne drew a long breath. "I thought you *liked* me of course, but I never hoped you *loved* me. Why, Diana, I didn't think anybody could love me. Nobody ever has loved me since I can remember. Oh, this is wonderful! It's a ray of light which will forever shine on the darkness of a path severed from thee, Diana. Oh, just say it once again."

"I love you devotedly, Anne," said Diana stanchly,[2] "and I always will, you may be sure of that."

"And I will always love thee, Diana," said Anne, solemnly extending her hand. "In the years to come thy memory will shine like a star over my lonely life, as that last story we read together says. Diana, wilt thou give me a lock of thy jet-black tresses in parting to treasure forevermore?"

"Have you got anything to cut it with?" queried Diana, wiping away the tears which Anne's affecting accents had caused to flow afresh, and returning to practicalities.

"Yes. I've got my patchwork scissors in my apron pocket fortu-

---

1. Anne is using the second person singular (thou, thee, thy) for archaic poetic (and involuntarily comic) effect.
2. Firmly, with loyalty. Variant American spelling of preferred British "staunchly."

nately," said Anne. She solemnly clipped one of Diana's curls. "Fare thee well, my beloved friend. Henceforth we must be as strangers though living side by side. But my heart will ever be faithful to thee."

Anne stood and watched Diana out of sight, mournfully waving her hand to the latter whenever she turned to look back. Then she returned to the house, not a little consoled for the time being by this romantic parting.

"It is all over," she informed Marilla. "I shall never have another friend. I'm really worse off than ever before, for I haven't Katie Maurice and Violetta now. And even if I had it wouldn't be the same. Somehow, little dream girls are not satisfying after a real friend. Diana and I had such an affecting farewell down by the spring. It will be sacred in my memory forever. I used the most pathetic language[3] I could think of and said 'thou' and 'thee.' 'Thou' and 'thee' seem so much more romantic than 'you.' Diana gave me a lock of her hair and I'm going to sew it up in a little bag and wear it around my neck all my life. Please see that it is buried with me, for I don't believe I'll live very long. Perhaps when she sees me lying cold and dead before her Mrs. Barry may feel remorse for what she has done and will let Diana come to my funeral."

"I don't think there is much fear of your dying of grief as long as you can talk, Anne," said Marilla unsympathetically.

The following Monday Anne surprised Marilla by coming down from her room with her basket of books on her arm and her lips primmed up into a line of determination.

"I'm going back to school," she announced. "That is all there is left in life for me, now that my friend has been ruthlessly torn from me. In school I can look at her and muse over days departed."[4]

"You'd better muse over your lessons and sums," said Marilla, concealing her delight at this development of the situation. "If you're going back to school I hope we'll hear no more of breaking slates over people's heads and such carryings-on. Behave yourself and do just what your teacher tells you."

"I'll try to be a model pupil," agreed Anne dolefully. "There won't be much fun in it, I expect. Mr. Phillips said Minnie Andrews was a model pupil and there isn't a spark of imagination or life in her. She is just dull and poky and never seems to have a good time. But I feel so depressed that perhaps it will come easy to me now. I'm going round by the road. I couldn't bear to go by the Birch Path all alone. I should weep bitter tears if I did."

Anne was welcomed back to school with open arms. Her imagi-

---

3. Loaded with pathos or strong feeling.
4. In the past: "I mind me in the days departed, / How often underneath the sun / With childish bounds I used to run / To a garden long deserted." Elizabeth Barrett [Browning], "The Deserted Garden" (1838).

nation had been sorely missed in games, her voice in the singing, and her dramatic ability in the perusal aloud of books at dinner hour. Ruby Gillis smuggled three blue plums over to her during testament reading; Ella May MacPherson gave her an enormous yellow pansy cut from the covers of a floral catalogue[5]—a species of desk decoration much prized in Avonlea school. Sophia Sloane offered to teach her a perfectly elegant new pattern of knit lace,[6] *so* nice for trimming aprons. Katie Boulter gave her a perfume bottle to keep slate-water[7] in and Julia Bell copied carefully on a piece of pale pink paper, scalloped on the edges, the following effusion:

> "TO ANNE
> "When twilight drops her curtain down
> And pins it with a star
> Remember that you have a friend
> Though she may wander far."[8]

"It's so nice to be appreciated," sighed Anne rapturously to Marilla that night.

The girls were not the only scholars who "appreciated" her. When Anne went to her seat after dinner hour—she had been told by Mr. Phillips to sit with the model Minnie Andrews—she found on her desk a big luscious "strawberry apple."[9] Anne caught it up all ready to take a bite, when she remembered that the only place in Avonlea where strawberry apples grew was in the old Blythe orchard on the other side of the Lake of Shining Waters. Anne dropped the apple as if it were a redhot coal and ostentatiously wiped her fingers on her handkerchief. The apple lay untouched on her desk until the next morning, when little Timothy Andrews, who swept the school and kindled the fire, annexed it as one of his perquisites. Charlie Sloane's slate pencil, gorgeously bedizened[1] with striped red and yellow paper, costing two cents where ordinary pencils cost only one, which he sent up to her after dinner hour, met with a more favourable reception. Anne was graciously pleased to accept it and rewarded the donor with a smile which exalted that infatuated youth straightway into the seventh heaven of delight[2] and caused him to

5. Booklet published by a seed company to advertise flower seeds and bulbs.
6. Directions for creating an intricate edging for tablecloths or petticoats using very fine steel needles and thin cotton thread.
7. Slates were wiped clean with a wet rag.
8. Cliché for nightfall. Compare this popular verse for autograph albums with "Let us be glad the night drops her curtain" in William Dean Howells's *Their Wedding Journey* (1871), chap. 3.
9. An old-time favorite variety, crisp, sweet, and juicy.
1. Dressed gaudily.
2. Great joy, as in the Muslim and cabalist beliefs about the dwelling place of God and the angels.

make such fearful errors in his dictation that Mr. Phillips kept him
in after school to rewrite it.

But as,

> "The Caesar's pageant shorn of Brutus' bust
> Did but of Rome's best son remind her more,"[3]

so the marked absence of any tribute or recognition from Diana
Barry, who was sitting with Gertie Pye, embittered Anne's little triumph.

"Diana might just have smiled at me once, I think," she mourned
to Marilla that night. But the next morning a note, most fearfully
and wonderfully twisted and folded,[4] and a small parcel, were passed
across to Anne.

"Dear Anne," ran the former, "Mother says I'm not to play with
you or talk to you even in school. It isn't my fault and don't be cross
at me, because I love you as much as ever. I miss you awfully to tell
all my secrets to and I don't like Gertie Pye one bit. I made you one
of the new bookmarkers out of red tissue paper. They are awfully
fashionable now and only three girls in school know how to make
them. When you look at it remember

"Your true friend,
"DIANA BARRY."

Anne read the note, kissed the bookmark, and despatched a
prompt reply back to the other side of the school.

"MY OWN DARLING DIANA:—

"Of course I am not cross at you because you have to obey your
mother. Our spirits can comune. I shall keep your lovely present
forever. Minnie Andrews is a very nice little girl—although she has
no imagination—but after having been Diana's busum friend I cannot be Minnie's. Please excuse mistakes because my spelling isn't
very good yet, although much improoved.

"Yours until death us do part,[5]
"ANNE or CORDELIA SHIRLEY.

"P. S. I shall sleep with your letter under my pillow to-night.
"A. or C.S."

Marilla pessimistically expected more trouble since Anne had
again begun to go to school. But none developed. Perhaps Anne
caught something of the "model" spirit from Minnie Andrews; at
least she got on very well with Mr. Phillips thenceforth. She flung
herself into her studies heart and soul, determined not to be outdone
in any class by Gilbert Blythe. The rivalry between them was soon

---

3. Lord Byron's *Childe Harold's Pilgrimage* (1812) 4.59.
4. "I will praise thee, for I am fearfully and wonderfully made." *Holy Bible*, Psalms 139.14.
5. Phrase from the traditional Christian wedding ceremony.

apparent; it was entirely good-natured on Gilbert's side; but it is much to be feared that the same thing cannot be said of Anne, who had certainly an unpraiseworthy tenacity for holding grudges. She was as intense in her hatreds as in her loves. She would not stoop to admit that she meant to rival Gilbert in school work, because that would have been to acknowledge his existence which Anne persistently ignored; but the rivalry was there and honours fluctuated between them. Now Gilbert was head of the spelling class; now Anne, with a toss of her long red braids, spelled him down. One morning Gilbert had all his sums done correctly and had his name written on the blackboard on the roll of honour; the next morning Anne, having wrestled wildly with decimals the entire evening before, would be first. One awful day they were ties and their names were written up together. It was almost as bad as a "take-notice" and Anne's mortification was as evident as Gilbert's satisfaction. When the written examinations at the end of each month were held the suspense was terrible. The first month Gilbert came out three marks ahead. The second Anne beat him by five. But her triumph was marred by the fact that Gilbert congratulated her heartily before the whole school. It would have been ever so much sweeter to her if he had felt the sting of his defeat.

Mr. Phillips might not be a very good teacher; but a pupil so inflexibly determined on learning as Anne was could hardly escape making progress under any kind of a teacher. By the end of the term Anne and Gilbert were both promoted into the fifth class and allowed to begin studying the elements of "the branches"—by which Latin, geometry, French and algebra were meant. In geometry Anne met her Waterloo.[6]

"It's perfectly awful stuff, Marilla," she groaned. "I'm sure I'll never be able to make head or tail of it. There is no scope for imagination in it at all. Mr. Phillips says I'm the worst dunce he ever saw at it. And Gil—I mean some of the others are so smart at it. It is extremely mortifying, Marilla. Even Diana gets along better than I do. But I don't mind being beaten by Diana. Even although we meet as strangers now I still love her with an *inextinguishable* love. It makes me very sad at times to think about her. But really, Marilla, one can't stay sad very long in such an interesting world, can one?"

---

6. Total defeat, as in the battle of 1815 when British forces defeated the French army of Napoleon.

# Chapter XVIII

### ANNE TO THE RESCUE

ALL things great are wound up with all things little. At first glance it might not seem that the decision of a certain Canadian Premier[1] to include Prince Edward Island in a political tour could have much or anything to do with the fortunes of little Anne Shirley at Green Gables. But it had.

It was in January the Premier came, to address his loyal supporters and such of his non-supporters as chose to be present at the monster mass meeting[2] held in Charlottetown. Most of the Avonlea people were on the Premier's side of politics; hence, on the night of the meeting nearly all the men and a goodly proportion of the women had gone to town, thirty miles away. Mrs. Rachel Lynde had gone too. Mrs. Rachel Lynde was a red-hot politician and couldn't have believed that the political rally could be carried through without her, although she was on the opposite side of politics.[3] So she went to town and took her husband—Thomas would be useful in looking after the horse—and Marilla Cuthbert with her. Marilla had a sneaking interest in politics herself, and as she thought it might be her only chance to see a real live Premier, she promptly took it, leaving Anne and Matthew to keep house until her return the following day.

Hence, while Marilla and Mrs. Rachel were enjoying themselves hugely at the mass meeting, Anne and Matthew had the cheerful kitchen at Green Gables all to themselves. A bright fire was glowing in the old-fashioned Waterloo stove[4] and blue-white frost crystals were shining on the window-panes. Matthew nodded over a *Farmer's Advocate*[5] on the sofa and Anne at the table studied her lessons with grim determination, despite sundry wistful glances at the clock shelf, where lay a new book that Jane Andrews had lent her that day. Jane had assured her that it was warranted to produce any number of thrills, or words to that effect, and Anne's fingers tingled to reach out for it. But that would mean Gilbert Blythe's triumph on the morrow. Anne turned her back on the clock shelf and tried to imagine it wasn't there.

"Matthew, did you ever study geometry when you went to school?"

---

1. The Prime Minister of Canada between 1878 and 1891 (when LMM was young) was John A. Macdonald, leader of the Conservative party.
2. Journalistic phrase for huge political meeting.
3. The loyal opposition party at this time was Liberal, led by Macdonald's rival, Alexander Mackenzie.
4. Wrought-iron wood-burning stoves for heating and cooking, in common use in America from around 1820, the name reflecting memories of the Waterloo victory.
5. Agricultural and family paper, founded 1866 and published in London, Ontario, until 1965.

"Well now, no, I didn't," said Matthew, coming out of his doze with a start.

"I wish you had," sighed Anne, "because then you'd be able to sympathize with me. You can't sympathize properly if you've never studied it. It is casting a cloud over my whole life. I'm such a dunce at it, Matthew."

"Well now, I dunno," said Matthew soothingly. "I guess you're all right at anything. Mr. Phillips told me last week in Blair's store at Carmody that you was the smartest scholar in school and was making rapid progress. 'Rapid progress' was his very words. There's them as runs down Teddy Phillips and says he ain't much of a teacher; but I guess he's all right."

Matthew would have thought any one who praised Anne was "all right."

"I'm sure I'd get on better with geometry if only he wouldn't change the letters," complained Anne. "I learn the proposition off by heart, and then he draws it on the blackboard and puts different letters from what are in the book and I get all mixed up. I don't think a teacher should take such a mean advantage, do you? We're studying agriculture now and I've found out at last what makes the roads red. It's a great comfort. I wonder how Marilla and Mrs. Lynde are enjoying themselves. Mrs. Lynde says Canada is going to the dogs the way things are being run at Ottawa,[6] and that it's an awful warning to the electors. She says if women were allowed to vote[7] we would soon see a blessed change. What way do you vote, Matthew?"

"Conservative,"[8] said Matthew promptly. To vote Conservative was part of Matthew's religion.

"Then I'm Conservative too," said Anne decidedly. "I'm glad, because Gil—because some of the boys in school are Grits.[9] I guess Mr. Phillips is a Grit too, because Prissy Andrews' father is one, and Ruby Gillis says that when a man is courting he always has to agree with the girl's mother in religion and her father in politics. Is that true, Matthew?"

"Well now, I dunno," said Matthew.

"Did you ever go courting, Matthew?"

"Well now, no, I dunno's I ever did," said Matthew, who had certainly never thought of such a thing in his whole existence.

Anne reflected with her chin in her hands.

"It must be rather interesting, don't you think, Matthew? Ruby Gillis says when she grows up she's going to have ever so many beaus

6. The Canadian Parliament sits in Ottawa, Ontario, capital city of the Dominion of Canada.
7. When *AGG* was published, women did not have the vote, although suffragettes were agitating for it in Canada as well as in other countries. LMM was given the vote during WWI, as a Canadian woman with a son or husband or brother on active service.
8. In the 1880s, a political party in favor of protection for farm goods.
9. Slang term for the Liberal party, the party not in power at this time.

on the string and have them all crazy about her; but I think that would be too exciting. I'd rather have just one in his right mind. But Ruby Gillis knows a great deal about such matters because she has so many big sisters, and Mrs. Lynde says the Gillis girls have gone off like hot cakes. Mr. Phillips goes up to see Prissy Andrews nearly every evening. He says it is to help her with her lessons, but Miranda Sloane is studying for Queen's, too, and I should think she needed help a lot more than Prissy because she's ever so much stupider, but he never goes to help her in the evenings at all. There are a great many things in this world that I can't understand very well, Matthew."

"Well now, I dunno as I comprehend them all myself," acknowledged Matthew.

"Well, I suppose I must finish up my lessons. I won't allow myself to open that new book Jane lent me until I'm through. But it's a terrible temptation, Matthew. Even when I turn my back on it I can see it there just as plain. Jane said she cried herself sick over it. I love a book that makes me cry. But I think I'll carry that book into the sitting-room and lock it in the jam closet and give you the key. And you must *not* give it to me, Matthew, until my lessons are done, not even if I implore you on my bended knees. It's all very well to say resist temptation, but it's ever so much easier to resist it if you can't get the key. And then shall I run down the cellar and get some russets, Matthew? Wouldn't you like some russets?"[1]

"Well now, I dunno but what I would," said Matthew, who never ate russets but knew Anne's weakness for them.

Just as Anne emerged triumphantly from the cellar with her plateful of russets came the sound of flying footsteps on the icy board walk outside and the next moment the kitchen door was flung open and in rushed Diana Barry, white-faced and breathless, with a shawl wrapped hastily around her head. Anne promptly let go of her candle[2] and plate in her surprise, and plate, candle, and apples crashed together down the cellar ladder and were found at the bottom embedded in melted grease, the next day, by Marilla, who gathered them up and thanked mercy the house hadn't been set on fire.

"Whatever is the matter, Diana?" cried Anne. "Has your mother relented at last?"

"Oh, Anne, do come quick," implored Diana nervously. "Minnie May is awful sick—she's got croup,[3] Young Mary Joe[4] says—and

1. Another traditional English variety, a firm eating apple with yellow flesh and hard brownish skin, which stores well.
2. Hand-held candlestick, lighting the way down to the cold cellar where the apples are stored.
3. A childhood disease, potentially fatal, characterized by a loud cough that resembles the barking of a seal, difficult breathing, and a grunting noise or wheezing.
4. Presumably a French-Canadian, named Marie-Josephine.

father and mother are away to town and there's nobody to go for the doctor. Minnie May is awful bad and Young Mary Joe doesn't know what to do—and oh, Anne, I'm so scared!"

Matthew, without a word, reached out for cap and coat, slipped past Diana and away into the darkness of the yard.

"He's gone to harness the sorrel mare to go to Carmody for the doctor," said Anne, who was hurrying on hood and jacket. "I know it as well as if he'd said so. Matthew and I are such kindred spirits I can read his thoughts without words at all."

"I don't believe he'll find the doctor at Carmody," sobbed Diana. "I know that Doctor Blair went to town and I guess Doctor Spencer would go too, Young Mary Joe never saw anybody with croup and Mrs. Lynde is away. Oh, Anne!"

"Don't cry, Di," said Anne cheerily. "I know exactly what to do for croup. You forget that Mrs. Hammond had twins three times. When you look after three pairs of twins you naturally get a lot of experience. They all had croup regularly. Just wait till I get the ipecac[5] bottle—you mayn't have any at your house. Come on now."

The two little girls hastened out hand in hand and hurried through Lovers' Lane and across the crusted field beyond, for the snow was too deep to go by the shorter wood way. Anne, although sincerely sorry for Minnie May, was far from being insensible to the romance of the situation and to the sweetness of once more sharing that romance with a kindred spirit.

The night was clear and frosty, all ebony of shadow and silver of snowy slope; big stars were shining over the silent fields; here and there the dark pointed firs stood up with snow powdering their branches and the wind whistling through them. Anne thought it was truly delightful to go skimming through all this mystery and loveliness with your bosom friend who had been so long estranged.

Minnie May, aged three, was really very sick. She lay on the kitchen sofa, feverish and restless, while her hoarse breathing could be heard all over the house. Young Mary Joe, a buxom, broad-faced French girl from the Creek, whom Mrs. Barry had engaged to stay with the children during her absence, was helpless and bewildered, quite incapable of thinking what to do, or doing it if she thought of it.

Anne went to work with skill and promptness.

"Minnie May has croup all right; she's pretty bad, but I've seen them worse. First we must have lots of hot water.[6] I declare, Diana, there isn't more than a cupful in the kettle! There, I've filled it up, and, Mary Joe, you may put some wood in the stove. I don't want to

5. A preparation made from the dried roots and rhizomes of the shrub *cephaelis ipecacuanha*, used to induce vomiting so that the child with croup can get rid of phlegm.
6. To create steam to cut the phlegm.

hurt your feelings, but it seems to me you might have thought of this before if you'd any imagination. Now, I'll undress Minnie May and put her to bed, and you try to find some soft flannel cloths, Diana. I'm going to give her a dose of ipecac first of all."

Minnie May did not take kindly to the ipecac, but Anne had not brought up three pairs of twins for nothing. Down that ipecac went, not only once, but many times during the long, anxious night when the two little girls worked patiently over the suffering Minnie May, and Young Mary Joe, honestly anxious to do all she could, kept on a roaring fire and heated more water than would have been needed for a hospital of croupy babies.

It was three o'clock when Matthew came with the doctor, for he had been obliged to go all the way to Spencervale for one. But the pressing need for assistance was past. Minnie May was much better and was sleeping soundly.

"I was awfully near giving up in despair," explained Anne. "She got worse and worse until she was sicker than ever the Hammond twins were, even the last pair. I actually thought she was going to choke to death. I gave her every drop of ipecac in that bottle, and when the last dose went down I said to myself—not to Diana or Young Mary Joe, because I didn't want to worry them any more than they were worried, but I had to say it to myself just to relieve my feelings— 'This is the last lingering hope[7] and I fear 'tis a vain one.' But in about three minutes she coughed up the phlegm and began to get better right away. You must just imagine my relief, doctor, because I can't express it in words. You know there are some things that cannot be expressed in words."

"Yes, I know," nodded the doctor. He looked at Anne as if he were thinking some things about her that couldn't be expressed in words. Later on, however, he expressed them to Mr. and Mrs. Barry.

"That little red-headed girl they have over at Cuthbert's is as smart as they make 'em. I tell you she saved that baby's life, for it would have been too late by the time I got here. She seems to have a skill and presence of mind perfectly wonderful in a child of her age. I never saw anything like the eyes of her when she was explaining the case out to me."

Anne had gone home in the wonderful, white-frosted winter morning, heavy-eyed from loss of sleep, but still talking unweariedly to Matthew as they crossed the long white field and walked under the glittering fairy arch of the Lovers' Lane maples.

"Oh, Matthew, isn't it a wonderful morning? The world looks like something God had just imagined for His own pleasure, doesn't it?

---

7. "And my last lingering hope that thou / Shouldst win." Mrs. Hemans's "The Siege of Valencia" (1823) l. 185.

Those trees look as if I could blow them away with a breath—pouf! I'm so glad I live in a world where there are white frosts, aren't you? And I'm so glad Mrs. Hammond had three pairs of twins after all. If she hadn't I mightn't have known what to do for Minnie May. I'm real sorry I was ever cross with Mrs. Hammond for having twins. But, oh, Matthew, I'm so sleepy. I can't go to school. I just know I couldn't keep my eyes open and I'd be so stupid. But I hate to stay home for Gil—some of the others will get head of the class, and it's so hard to get up again—although of course the harder it is the more satisfaction you have when you do get up, haven't you?"

"Well now, I guess you'll manage all right," said Matthew, looking at Anne's white little face and the dark shadows under her eyes. "You just go right to bed and have a good sleep. I'll do all the chores."

Anne accordingly went to bed and slept so long and soundly that it was well on in the white and rosy winter afternoon when she awoke and descended to the kitchen where Marilla, who had arrived home in the meantime, was sitting knitting.

"Oh, did you see the Premier?" exclaimed Anne at once. "What did he look like, Marilla?"

"Well, he never got to be Premier on account of his looks," said Marilla. "Such a nose[8] as that man had! But he can speak. I was proud of being a Conservative. Rachel Lynde, of course, being a Liberal, had no use for him. Your dinner is in the oven, Anne; and you can get yourself some blue plum preserve out of the pantry. I guess you're hungry. Matthew has been telling me about last night. I must say it was fortunate you knew what to do. I wouldn't have had any idea myself, for I never saw a case of croup. There now, never mind talking till you've had your dinner. I can tell by the look of you that you're just full up with speeches, but they'll keep."

Marilla had something to tell Anne, but she did not tell it just then, for she knew if she did Anne's consequent excitement would lift her clear out of the region of such material matters as appetite or dinner. Not until Anne had finished her saucer of blue plums did Marilla say:

"Mrs. Barry was here this afternoon, Anne. She wanted to see you, but I wouldn't wake you up. She says you saved Minnie May's life, and she is very sorry she acted as she did in that affair of the currant wine. She says she knows now you didn't mean to set Diana drunk, and she hopes you'll forgive her and be good friends with Diana again. You're to go over this evening if you like, for Diana can't stir outside the door on account of a bad cold she caught last night. Now, Anne Shirley, for pity's sake don't fly clean up into the air."

---

8. John A. Macdonald did indeed have an out-sized nose. Contemporary cartoons characterized him: "A poor 'un for looks, but a rare 'un to go."

The warning seemed not unnecessary, so uplifted and aerial was Anne's expression and attitude as she sprang to her feet, her face irradiated with the flame of her spirit.

"Oh, Marilla, can I go right now—without washing my dishes? I'll wash them when I come back, but I cannot tie myself down to anything so unromantic as dish-washing at this thrilling moment."

"Yes, yes, run along," said Marilla indulgently. "Anne Shirley—are you crazy? Come back this instant and put something on you. I might as well call to the wind. She's gone without a cap or wrap. Look at her tearing through the orchard with her hair streaming. It'll be a mercy if she doesn't catch her death of cold."

Anne came dancing home in the purple winter twilight across the snowy places. Afar in the southwest was the great shimmering, pearl-like sparkle of an evening star in a sky that was pale golden and ethereal rose over gleaming white spaces and dark glens of spruce. The tinkles of sleigh-bells among the snowy hills came like elfin chimes through the frosty air, but their music was not sweeter than the song in Anne's heart and on her lips.

"You see before you a perfectly happy person, Marilla," she announced. "I'm perfectly happy—yes, in spite of my red hair. Just at present I have a soul above red hair. Mrs. Barry kissed me and cried and said she was so sorry and she could never repay me. I felt fearfully embarrassed, Marilla, but I just said as politely as I could, 'I have no hard feelings for you, Mrs. Barry. I assure you once for all that I did not mean to intoxicate Diana and henceforth I shall cover the past with the mantle of oblivion.'[9] That was a pretty dignified way of speaking, wasn't it, Marilla? I felt that I was heaping coals of fire on Mrs. Barry's head. And Diana and I had a lovely afternoon. Diana showed me a new fancy crochet stitch[1] her aunt over at Carmody taught her. Not a soul in Avonlea knows it but us, and we pledged a solemn vow never to reveal it to any one else. Diana gave me a beautiful card with a wreath of roses on it and a verse of poetry:

> " 'If you love me as I love you
> Nothing but death can part us two.'[2]

And that is true, Marilla. We're going to ask Mr. Phillips to let us sit together in school again, and Gertie Pye can go with Minnie Andrews. We had an elegant tea. Mrs. Barry had the very best china set out, Marilla, just as if I was real company. I can't tell you what a thrill it gave me. Nobody ever used their very best china on my account before. And we had fruit-cake and pound-cake and dough-

9. "Oblivion's mantle o'er the past." Mrs. Hemans's "Night Scene in Genoa" (1819) l. 83.
1. A new way to create a piece of edging or insertion for decorating household linens or personal garments.
2. Another verse commonly inscribed in autograph albums.

nuts and two kinds of preserves, Marilla. And Mrs. Barry asked me
if I took tea and said, 'Pa, why don't you pass the biscuits to Anne?'
It must be lovely to be grown up, Marilla, when just being treated
as if you were is so nice."

"I don't know about that," said Marilla with a brief sigh.

"Well, anyway, when I am grown up," said Anne decidedly, "I'm
always going to talk to little girls as if they were, too, and I'll never
laugh when they use big words. I know from sorrowful experience
how that hurts one's feelings. After tea Diana and I made taffy.[3] The
taffy wasn't very good, I suppose because neither Diana nor I had
ever made any before. Diana left me to stir it while she buttered the
plates and I forgot and let it burn; and then when we set it out on
the platform to cool the cat walked over one plate and that had to
be thrown away. But the making of it was splendid fun. Then when
I came home Mrs. Barry asked me to come over as often as I could
and Diana stood at the window and threw kisses to me all the way
down to Lovers' Lane. I assure you, Marilla, that I feel like praying
to-night and I'm going to think out a special brand-new prayer in
honour of the occasion."

# Chapter XIX

### A CONCERT, A CATASTROPHE, AND A CONFESSION

"MARILLA, can I go over to see Diana just for a minute?" asked
Anne, running breathlessly down from the east gable one February
evening.

"I don't see what you want to be traipsing about after dark for,"
said Marilla shortly. "You and Diana walked home from school
together and then stood down there in the snow for half an hour
more, your tongues going the whole blessed time, clickety-clack. So
I don't think you're very badly off to see her again."

"But she wants to see me," pleaded Anne. "She has something very
important to tell me."

"How do you know she has?"

"Because she just signalled to me from her window. We have
arranged a way to signal with our candles and cardboard. We set the
candle on the window-sill and make flashes by passing the cardboard
back and forth. So many flashes mean a certain thing. It was my
idea, Marilla."

"I'll warrant you it was," said Marilla emphatically. "And the next

3. A warm sticky mass of boiled sugar, butter, vinegar, and flavorings, stretched or pulled
   until cool and porous.

thing you'll be setting fire to the curtains with your signalling non-sense."

"Oh, we're very careful, Marilla. And it's so interesting. Two flashes mean, 'Are you there?' Three mean 'yes' and four 'no.' Five mean, 'Come over as soon as possible, because I have something important to reveal.' Diana has just signalled five flashes, and I'm really suffering to know what it is."

"Well, you needn't suffer any longer," said Marilla sarcastically. "You can go, but you're to be back here in just ten minutes, remember that."

Anne did remember it and was back in the stipulated time, although probably no mortal will ever know just what it cost her to confine the discussion of Diana's important communication within the limits of ten minutes. But at least she had made good use of them.

"Oh, Marilla, what do you think? You know to-morrow is Diana's birthday. Well, her mother told her she could ask me to go home with her from school and stay all night with her. And her cousins are coming over from Newbridge in a big pung sleigh[1] to go to the Debating Club concert at the hall to-morrow night. And they are going to take Diana and me to the concert—if you'll let me go, that is. You will, won't you, Marilla? Oh, I feel so excited."

"You can calm down then, because you're not going. You're better at home in your own bed, and as for that Club concert, it's all non-sense, and little girls should not be allowed to go out to such places at all."

"I'm sure the Debating Club is a most respectable affair," pleaded Anne.

"I'm not saying it isn't. But you're not going to begin gadding about[2] to concerts and staying out all hours of the night. Pretty doings for children. I'm surprised at Mrs. Barry's letting Diana go."

"But it's such a very special occasion," mourned Anne, on the verge of tears. "Diana has only one birthday in a year. It isn't as if birthdays were common things, Marilla. Prissy Andrews is going to recite 'Curfew Must Not Ring To-night.'[3] That is such a good moral piece, Marilla, I'm sure it would do me lots of good to hear it. And the choir are going to sing four lovely pathetic songs that are pretty near as good as hymns. And oh, Marilla, the minister is going to take part; yes, indeed, he is; he's going to give an address. That will be just about the same thing as a sermon. Please, mayn't I go, Marilla?"

1. A low horse-drawn sleigh with high sides, moving through the snow on runners.
2. Roaming in pursuit of pleasure.
3. American poem (1887) about a young English girl's heroic effort to save her lover from execution, by Rose Hartwick Thorpe, author of "Remember the Alamo."

"You heard what I said, Anne, didn't you? Take off your boots now and go to bed. It's past eight."

"There's just one more thing, Marilla," said Anne, with the air of producing the last shot in her locker.[4] "Mrs. Barry told Diana that we might sleep in the spare-room bed. Think of the honour of your little Anne being put in the spare-room bed."

"It's an honour you'll have to get along without. Go to bed, Anne, and don't let me hear another word out of you."

When Anne, with tears rolling over her cheeks, had gone sorrow-fully up-stairs, Matthew, who had been apparently sound asleep on the lounge[5] during the whole dialogue, opened his eyes and said decidedly:

"Well now, Marilla, I think you ought to let Anne go."

"I don't then," retorted Marilla. "Who's bringing this child up, Matthew, you or me?"

"Well now, you," admitted Matthew.

"Don't interfere then."

"Well now, I ain't interfering. It ain't interfering to have your own opinion. And my opinion is that you ought to let Anne go."

"You'd think I ought to let Anne go to the moon if she took the notion, I've no doubt," was Marilla's amiable rejoinder. "I might have let her spend the night with Diana, if that was all. But I don't approve of this concert plan. She'd go there and catch cold like as not, and have her head filled up with nonsense and excitement. It would unsettle her for a week. I understand that child's disposition and what's good for it better than you, Matthew."

"I think you ought to let Anne go," repeated Matthew firmly. Argument was not his strong point, but holding fast to his opinion certainly was. Marilla gave a gasp of helplessness and took refuge in silence. The next morning, when Anne was washing the breakfast dishes in the pantry, Matthew paused on his way out to the barn to say to Marilla again:

"I think you ought to let Anne go, Marilla."

For a moment Marilla looked things not lawful to be uttered. Then she yielded to the inevitable and said tartly:

"Very well, she can go, since nothing else'll please you."

Anne flew out of the pantry, dripping dish-cloth in hand.

"Oh, Marilla, Marilla, say those blessed words again."

"I guess once is enough to say them. This is Matthew's doings and I wash my hands of it. If you catch pneumonia sleeping in a strange bed or coming out of that hot hall in the middle of the night, don't

4. Ammunition in a sheet-metal chest, on board a warship.
5. Daybed kept in the kitchen, where the farmer rested during the daytime.

blame me, blame Matthew. Anne Shirley, you're dripping greasy water all over the floor. I never saw such a careless child."

"Oh, I know I'm a great trial to you, Marilla," said Anne repentantly. "I make so many mistakes. But then just think of all the mistakes I don't make, although I might. I'll get some sand[6] and scrub up the spots before I go to school. Oh, Marilla, my heart was just set on going to that concert. I never was to a concert in my life, and when the other girls talk about them in school I feel so out of it. You didn't know just how I felt about it, but you see Matthew did. Matthew understands me, and it's so nice to be understood, Marilla."

Anne was too excited to do herself justice as to lessons that morning in school. Gilbert Blythe spelled her down in class and left her clear out of sight in mental arithmetic. Anne's consequent humiliation was less than it might have been, however, in view of the concert and the spare-room bed. She and Diana talked so constantly about it all day that with a stricter teacher than Mr. Phillips dire disgrace must inevitably have been their portion.

Anne felt that she could not have borne it if she had not been going to the concert, for nothing else was discussed that day in school. The Avonlea Debating Club,[7] which met fortnightly all winter, had had several smaller free entertainments; but this was to be a big affair, admission ten cents, in aid of the library. The Avonlea young people had been practising for weeks, and all the scholars were especially interested in it by reason of older brothers and sisters who were going to take part. Everybody in school over nine years of age expected to go, except Carrie Sloane, whose father shared Marilla's opinions about small girls going out to night concerts. Carrie Sloane cried into her grammar all the afternoon and felt that life was not worth living.

For Anne the real excitement began with the dismissal of school and increased therefrom in crescendo until it reached to a crash of positive ecstasy in the concert itself. They had a "perfectly elegant tea;" and then came the delicious occupation of dressing in Diana's little room up-stairs. Diana did Anne's front hair in the new pompadour style[8] and Anne tied Diana's bows with the especial knack she possessed; and they experimented with at least half a dozen dif-

6. For scouring the floor. In *Emily Climbs* (1925) LMM describes a family tradition of sand-scouring the bare hardwood floor until it gleams.
7. Modeled on debates in the Cavendish Assembly Hall, in the tradition of late-Victorian literary and debating societies, a form of community entertainment before the invention of radio or television.
8. Hair pulled up from the forehead, high over a rolled pad or "rat" in the Gibson Girl style of the day, imitating that of Madame de Pompadour, mistress of King Louis XV of France in the eighteenth century. For young girls like Anne and Diana, hair would hang down the back to the waist.

ferent ways of arranging their back hair. At last they were ready, cheeks scarlet and eyes glowing with excitement.

True, Anne could not help a little pang when she contrasted her plain black tam[9] and shapeless, tight-sleeved, home-made gray cloth coat with Diana's jaunty fur cap and smart little jacket. But she remembered in time that she had an imagination and could use it.

Then Diana's cousins, the Murrays from Newbridge, came; they all crowded into the big pung sleigh, among straw and furry robes. Anne revelled in the drive to the hall, slipping along over the satin-smooth roads with the snow crisping under the runners. There was a magnificent sunset, and the snowy hills and deep blue water of the St. Lawrence Gulf seemed to rim in the splendour like a huge bowl of pearl and sapphire brimmed with wine and fire. Tinkles of sleigh-bells and distant laughter, that seemed like the mirth of wood elves, came from every quarter.

"Oh, Diana," breathed Anne, squeezing Diana's mittened hand under the fur robe, "isn't it all like a beautiful dream? Do I really look the same as usual? I feel so different that it seems to me it must show in my looks."

"You look awfully nice," said Diana, who having just received a compliment from one of her cousins, felt that she ought to pass it on. "You've got the loveliest colour."

The programme that night was a series of "thrills" for at least one listener in the audience, and, as Anne assured Diana, every suc-ceeding thrill was thrillier than the last. When Prissy Andrews, attired in a new pink silk waist[1] with a string of pearls about her smooth white throat and real carnations in her hair—rumour whis-pered that the master had sent all the way to town for them for her—"climbed the slimy ladder, dark without one ray of light,"[2] Anne shiv-ered in luxurious sympathy; when the choir sang "Far Above the Gentle Daisies"[3] Anne gazed at the ceiling as if it were frescoed with angels; when Sam Sloane proceeded to explain and illustrate "How Sockery Set a Hen"[4] Anne laughed until people sitting near her laughed too, more out of sympathy with her than with amusement at a selection that was rather threadbare even in Avonlea; and when Mr. Phillips gave Mark Antony's oration[5] over the dead body of Cae-sar in the most heart-stirring tones—looking at Prissy Andrews at

9. A big floppy beret like that worn in Robert Burns's poem, "Tam O'Shanter."
1. In American usage, a shirt-waist or blouse, a meaning not given in English dictionaries.
2. Prissy misquotes "climbed the dusty ladder on which fell no ray of light" from "The Curfew Must Not Ring Tonight," cited above.
3. Lyrics by American poet George Cooper (1869), set to music by Boston composer Harrison Millard.
4. Popular recitation piece, spoken in dialect by a Dutch character named Zachary.
5. In Shakespeare's play, Mark Antony's speech which begins "Friends, Romans, country-men . . ." culminates in the phrase ". . . put a tongue / In every wound of Caesar that should move / The stones of Rome to rise and mutiny." *Julius Caesar* 3.2.23–25.

the end of every sentence—Anne felt that she could rise and mutiny on the spot if but one Roman citizen led the way.

Only one number on the programme failed to interest her. When Gilbert Blythe recited "Bingen on the Rhine" Anne picked up Rhoda Murray's library book and read it until he had finished, when she sat rigidly stiff and motionless while Diana clapped her hands until they tingled.

It was eleven when they got home, sated with dissipation, but with the exceeding sweet pleasure of talking it all over still to come. Everybody seemed asleep and the house was dark and silent. Anne and Diana tiptoed into the parlour, a long narrow room out of which the spare room opened. It was pleasantly warm and dimly lighted by the embers of a fire in the grate.

"Let's undress here," said Diana. "It's so nice and warm."

"Hasn't it been a delightful time?" sighed Anne rapturously. "It must be splendid to get up and recite there. Do you suppose we will ever be asked to do it, Diana?"

"Yes, of course, some day. They're always wanting the big scholars to recite. Gilbert Blythe does often and he's only two years older than us. Oh, Anne, how could you pretend not to listen to him? When he came to the line,

" 'There's another, *not* a sister,'

he looked right down at you."[6]

"Diana," said Anne with dignity, "you are my bosom friend, but I cannot allow even you to speak to me of that person. Are you ready for bed? Let's run a race and see who'll get to the bed first."

The suggestion appealed to Diana. The two little white-clad figures flew down the long room, through the spare-room door, and bounded on the bed at the same moment. And then—something—moved beneath them, there was a gasp and a cry—and somebody said in muffled accents:

"Merciful goodness!"

Anne and Diana were never able to tell just how they got off that bed and out of the room. They only knew that after one frantic rush they found themselves tiptoeing shiveringly up-stairs.

"Oh, who was it—*what* was it?" whispered Anne, her teeth chattering with cold and fright.

"It was Aunt Josephine," said Diana, gasping with laughter. "Oh, Anne, it was Aunt Josephine, however she came to be there. Oh, and I know she will be furious. It's dreadful—it's really dreadful—but did you ever know anything so funny, Anne?"

"Who is your Aunt Josephine?"

---

6. In Chapter V, Anne learned this poem before coming to Green Gables.

"She's father's aunt and she lives in Charlottetown. She's awfully old—seventy anyhow—and I don't believe she was *ever* a little girl. We were expecting her out for a visit, but not so soon. She's awfully prim and proper and she'll scold dreadfully about this, I know. Well, we'll have to sleep with Minnie May—and you can't think how she kicks."

Miss Josephine Barry did not appear at the early breakfast the next morning. Mrs. Barry smiled kindly at the two little girls.

"Did you have a good time last night? I tried to stay awake until you came home, for I wanted to tell you Aunt Josephine had come and that you would have to go up-stairs after all, but I was so tired I fell asleep. I hope you didn't disturb your aunt, Diana."

Diana preserved a discreet silence, but she and Anne exchanged furtive smiles of guilty amusement across the table. Anne hurried home after breakfast and so remained in blissful ignorance of the disturbance which presently resulted in the Barry household until the late afternoon, when she went down to Mrs. Lynde's on an errand for Marilla.

"So you and Diana nearly frightened poor old Miss Barry to death last night?" said Mrs. Lynde severely, but with a twinkle in her eye. "Mrs. Barry was here a few minutes ago on her way to Carmody. She's feeling real worried over it. Old Miss Barry was in a terrible temper when she got up this morning—and Josephine Barry's temper is no joke, I can tell you that. She wouldn't speak to Diana at all."

"It wasn't Diana's fault," said Anne contritely. "It was mine. I suggested racing to see who would get into bed first."

"I knew it!" said Mrs. Lynde with the exultation of a correct guesser. "I knew that idea came out of your head. Well, it's made a nice lot of trouble, that's what. Old Miss Barry came out to stay for a month, but she declares she won't stay another day and is going right back to town to-morrow, Sunday and all as it is. She'd have gone to-day if they could have taken her. She had promised to pay for a quarter's music lessons for Diana, but now she is determined to do nothing at all for such a tomboy. Oh, I guess they had a lively time of it there this morning. The Barrys must feel cut up. Old Miss Barry is rich and they'd like to keep on the good side of her. Of course, Mrs. Barry didn't say just that to me, but I'm a pretty good judge of human nature, that's what."

"I'm such an unlucky girl," mourned Anne. "I'm always getting into scrapes[7] myself and getting my best friends—people I'd shed my heart's blood for—into them, too. Can you tell me why it is so, Mrs. Lynde?"

---

7. Awkward predicaments, usually resulting from an escapade. Listed in American but not in English dictionaries.

"It's because you're too heedless and impulsive, child, that's what. You never stop to think—whatever comes into your head to say or do you say or do it without a moment's reflection."

"Oh, but that's the best of it," protested Anne. "Something just flashes into your mind, so exciting, and you must out with it. If you stop to think it over you spoil it all. Haven't you never felt that yourself, Mrs. Lynde?"

No, Mrs. Lynde had not. She shook her head sagely.

"You must learn to think a little, Anne, that's what. The proverb you need to go by is 'Look before you leap'[8]—especially into spare-room beds."

Mrs. Lynde laughed comfortably over her mild joke, but Anne remained pensive. She saw nothing to laugh at in the situation, which to her eyes appeared very serious. When she left Mrs. Lynde's she took her way across the crusted fields to Orchard Slope. Diana met her at the kitchen door.

"Your Aunt Josephine was very cross about it, wasn't she?" whispered Anne.

"Yes," answered Diana, stifling a giggle with an apprehensive glance over her shoulder at the closed sitting-room door. "She was fairly dancing with rage, Anne. Oh, how she scolded. She said I was the worst-behaved girl she ever saw and that my parents ought to be ashamed of the way they had brought me up. She says she won't stay and I'm sure I don't care. But father and mother do."

"Why didn't you tell them it was my fault?" demanded Anne.

"It's likely I'd do such a thing, isn't it?" said Diana with just scorn. "I'm no telltale, Anne Shirley, and anyhow I was just as much to blame as you."

"Well, I'm going in to tell her myself," said Anne resolutely.

Diana stared.

"Anne Shirley, you'd never! why—she'll eat you alive!"

"Don't frighten me any more than I am frightened," implored Anne. "I'd rather walk up to a cannon's mouth. But I've got to do it, Diana. It was my fault and I've got to confess. I've had practice in confessing fortunately."

"Well, she's in the room," said Diana. "You can go in if you want to. I wouldn't dare. And I don't believe you'll do a bit of good."

With this encouragement Anne bearded the lion in its den—that is to say, walked resolutely up to the sitting-room door and knocked faintly. A sharp "Come in" followed.

Miss Josephine Barry, thin, prim and rigid, was knitting fiercely by the fire, her wrath quite unappeased and her eyes snapping through her gold-rimmed glasses. She wheeled around in her chair,

8. From the fable "The Fox and the Goat." *Fables of Aesop the Slave* (d. 560 B.C.E.).

expecting to see Diana, and beheld a white-faced girl whose great eyes were brimmed up with a mixture of desperate courage and shrinking terror.

"Who are you?" demanded Miss Josephine Barry without ceremony.

"I'm Anne of Green Gables," said the small visitor tremulously, clasping her hands with her characteristic gesture, "and I've come to confess, if you please."

"Confess what?"

"That it was all my fault about jumping into bed on you last night. I suggested it. Diana would never have thought of such a thing, I am sure. Diana is a very lady-like girl, Miss Barry. So you must see how unjust it is to blame her."

"Oh, I must, hey? I rather think Diana did her share of the jumping at least. Such carryings-on in a respectable house!"

"But we were only in fun," persisted Anne. "I think you ought to forgive us, Miss Barry, now that we've apologized. And anyhow, please forgive Diana and let her have her music lessons. Diana's heart is set on her music lessons, Miss Barry, and I know too well what it is to set your heart on a thing and not get it. If you must be cross with any one, be cross with me. I've been so used in my early days to having people cross at me that I can endure it much better than Diana can."

Much of the snap had gone out of the old lady's eyes by this time and was replaced by a twinkle of amused interest. But she still said severely:

"I don't think it is any excuse for you that you were only in fun. Little girls never indulged in that kind of fun when I was young. You don't know what it is to be awakened out of a sound sleep, after a long and arduous journey, by two great girls coming bounce down on you."

"I don't *know*, but I can *imagine*," said Anne eagerly. "I'm sure it must have been very disturbing. But then, there is our side of it too. Have you any imagination, Miss Barry? If you have, just put yourself in our place. We didn't know there was anybody in that bed and you nearly scared us to death. It was simply awful the way we felt. And then we couldn't sleep in the spare room after being promised. I suppose you are used to sleeping in spare rooms. But just imagine what you would feel like if you were a little orphan girl who had never had such an honour."

All the snap had gone by this time. Miss Barry actually laughed—a sound which caused Diana, waiting in speechless anxiety in the kitchen outside, to give a great gasp of relief.

"I'm afraid my imagination is a little rusty—it's so long since I used it," she said. "I dare say your claim to sympathy is just as strong as mine. It all depends on the way we look at it. Sit down here and tell me about yourself."

"I am very sorry I can't," said Anne firmly. "I would like to, because you seem like an interesting lady, and you might even be a kindred spirit although you don't look very much like it. But it is my duty to go home to Miss Marilla Cuthbert. Miss Marilla Cuthbert is a very kind lady who has taken me to bring up properly. She is doing her best, but it is very discouraging work. You must not blame her because I jumped on the bed. But before I go I do wish you would tell me if you will forgive Diana and stay just as long as you meant to in Avonlea."

"I think perhaps I will if you will come over and talk to me occasionally," said Miss Barry.

That evening Miss Barry gave Diana a silver bangle bracelet[9] and told the senior members of the household that she had unpacked her valise.

"I've made up my mind to stay simply for the sake of getting better acquainted with that Anne-girl," she said frankly. "She amuses me, and at my time of life an amusing person is a rarity."

Marilla's only comment when she heard the story was, "I told you so." This was for Matthew's benefit.

Miss Barry stayed her month out and over. She was a more agreeable guest than usual, for Anne kept her in good humour. They became firm friends.[1]

When Miss Barry went away she said:

"Remember, you Anne-girl, when you come to town you're to visit me and I'll put you in my very sparest spare-room bed to sleep."

"Miss Barry was a kindred spirit, after all," Anne confided to Marilla. "You wouldn't think so to look at her, but she is. You don't find it right out at first, as in Matthew's case, but after awhile you come to see it. Kindred spirits are not so scarce as I used to think. It's splendid to find out there are so many of them in the world."

## Chapter XX

### A GOOD IMAGINATION GONE WRONG

SPRING had come once more to Green Gables—the beautiful, capricious, reluctant Canadian spring, lingering along through April and May in a succession of sweet, fresh, chilly days, with pink sunsets and miracles of resurrection and growth. The maples in Lovers'

9. A wrist-ring, from Hindu word "*bangri.*"
1. LMM used comparable materials in an earlier story.

Lane were red-budded and little curly ferns pushed up around the Dryad's Bubble. Away up in the barrens,[1] behind Mr. Silas Sloane's place, the Mayflowers[2] blossomed out, pink and white stars of sweetness under their brown leaves. All the school girls and boys had one golden afternoon gathering them, coming home in the clear, echoing twilight with arms and baskets full of flowery spoil.

"I'm so sorry for people who live in lands where there are no Mayflowers," said Anne. "Diana says perhaps they have something better, but there couldn't be anything better than Mayflowers, could there, Marilla? And Diana says if they don't know what they are like they don't miss them. But I think that is the saddest thing of all. I think it would be *tragic*, Marilla, not to know what Mayflowers are like and *not* to miss them. Do you know what I think Mayflowers are, Marilla? I think they must be the souls of the flowers that died last summer and this is their heaven. But we had a splendid time to-day, Marilla. We had our lunch down in a big mossy hollow by an old well—such a *romantic* spot. Charlie Sloane dared Arty Gillis to jump over it, and Arty did because he wouldn't take a dare.[3] Nobody would in school. It is very *fashionable* to dare. Mr. Phillips gave all the Mayflowers he found to Prissy Andrews and I heard him say 'sweets to the sweet.'[4] He got that out of a book, I know; but it shows he has some imagination. I was offered some Mayflowers too, but I rejected them with scorn. I can't tell you the person's name because I have vowed never to let it cross my lips. We made wreaths of the Mayflowers and put them on our hats; and when the time came to go home we marched in procession down the road, two by two, with our bouquets and wreaths, singing 'My Home on the Hill.'[5] Oh, it was so thrilling, Marilla. All Mr. Silas Sloane's folks rushed out to see us and everybody we met on the road stopped and stared after us. We made a real sensation."

"Not much wonder! Such silly doings!" was Marilla's response.

After the Mayflowers came the violets, and Violet Vale was empurpled with them. Anne walked through it on her way to school with reverent steps and worshipping eyes, as if she trod on holy ground.[6]

"Somehow," she told Diana, "when I'm going through here I don't really care whether Gil—whether anybody gets ahead of me in class or not. But when I'm up in school it's all different and I care as much

---

1. Fields not suitable for crops.
2. Trailing arbutus, a low-growing plant, with leathery leaves and fragrant pink blossoms rising in spring clusters—one of LMM's favorite flowers.
3. Schoolyard challenge to do something dangerous.
4. Said by Queen Gertrude as she strews flowers on Ophelia's grave. Shakespeare, *Hamlet* 5.1.237.
5. A song (1866) by W. C. Baker, prolific American lyricist of the 1860s–70s.
6. Echoes Mrs. Hemans's "Ay, call it holy ground, / The land where first they trod!" from "The Landing of the Pilgrim Fathers" (1826), final stanza.

as ever. There's such a lot of different Annes in me. I sometimes think that is why I'm such a troublesome person. If I was just the one Anne it would be ever so much more comfortable, but then it wouldn't be half so interesting."

One June evening, when the orchards were pink-blossomed again, when the frogs were singing silverly sweet in the marshes about the head of the Lake of Shining Waters, and the air was full of the savour of clover fields and balsamic fir woods, Anne was sitting by her gable window. She had been studying her lessons, but it had grown too dark to see the book, so she had fallen into wide-eyed reverie, looking out past the boughs of the Snow Queen, once more be-starred with its tufts of blossom.

In all essential respects the little gable chamber was unchanged. The walls were as white, the pincushion as hard, the chairs as stiffly and yellowly upright as ever. Yet the whole character of the room was altered. It was full of a new vital, pulsing personality that seemed to pervade it and to be quite independent of schoolgirl books and dresses and ribbons, and even of the cracked blue jug full of apple blossoms on the table. It was as if all the dreams, sleeping and waking, of its vivid occupant had taken a visible although immaterial form and had tapestried the bare room with splendid filmy tissues of rainbow and moonshine. Presently Marilla came briskly in with some of Anne's freshly ironed school aprons.[7] She hung them over a chair and sat down with a short sigh. She had had one of her headaches that afternoon, and although the pain had gone she felt weak and "tuckered out," as she expressed it. Anne looked at her with eyes limpid with sympathy.

"I do truly wish I could have had the headache in your place, Marilla. I would have endured it joyfully for your sake."

"I guess you did your part in attending to the work and letting me rest," said Marilla. "You seem to have got on fairly well and made fewer mistakes than usual. Of course it wasn't exactly necessary to starch Matthew's handkerchiefs! And most people when they put a pie in the oven to warm up for dinner take it out and eat it when it gets hot instead of leaving it to be burned to a crisp. But that doesn't seem to be your way evidently."

Headaches always left Marilla somewhat sarcastic.

"Oh, I'm so sorry," said Anne penitently. "I never thought about that pie from the moment I put it in the oven till now, although I felt *instinctively* that there was something missing on the dinner table. I was firmly resolved, when you left me in charge this morning, not to imagine anything, but keep my thoughts on facts. I did pretty well until I put the pie in, and then an irresistible temptation came

---

7. Pinafores worn to cover and protect girls' dresses in school.

to me to imagine I was an enchanted princess shut up in a lonely tower with a handsome knight riding to my rescue on a coal-black steed. So that is how I came to forget the pie. I didn't know I starched the handkerchiefs. All the time I was ironing I was trying to think of a name for a new island Diana and I have discovered up the brook. It's the most ravishing spot, Marilla. There are two maple-trees on it and the brook flows right around it. At last it struck me that it would be splendid to call it Victoria Island because we found it on the Queen's birthday.[8] Both Diana and I are very loyal. But I'm very sorry about that pie and the handkerchiefs. I wanted to be extra good to-day because it's an anniversary. Do you remember what happened this day last year, Marilla?"

"No, I can't think of anything special."

"Oh, Marilla, it was the day I came to Green Gables. I shall never forget it. It was the turning-point in my life. Of course it wouldn't seem so important to you. I've been here for a year and I've been so happy. Of course, I've had my troubles, but one can live down troubles. Are you sorry you kept me, Marilla?"

"No, I can't say I'm sorry," said Marilla, who sometimes wondered how she could have lived before Anne came to Green Gables, "no, not exactly sorry. If you've finished your lessons, Anne, I want you to run over and ask Mrs. Barry if she'll lend me Diana's apron pattern."

"Oh—it's—it's too dark," cried Anne.

"Too dark? Why, it's only twilight. And goodness knows you've gone over often enough after dark."

"I'll go over early in the morning," said Anne eagerly. "I'll get up at sunrise and go over, Marilla."

"What has got into your head now, Anne Shirley? I want that pattern to cut out your new apron this evening. Go at once and be smart, too."

"I'll have to go around by the road, then," said Anne, taking up her hat reluctantly.

"Go by the road and waste half an hour! I'd like to catch you!"

"I can't go through the Haunted Wood,[9] Marilla," cried Anne desperately.

Marilla stared.

"The Haunted Wood! Are you crazy? What under the canopy is the Haunted Wood?"

"The spruce wood over the brook," said Anne in a whisper.

8. Queen Victoria had reigned over the British Empire since 1837; her birthday on May 24th was celebrated as "Victoria Day" or "The Queen's Birthday," as in the children's chant, "The 24th of May / Is the Queen's birthday; / If you don't give us a holiday / We'll all run away."
9. This bit of forest near LMM's home in Cavendish is now a tourist spot.

"Fiddlesticks! There is no such thing as a haunted wood anywhere. Who has been telling you such stuff?"

"Nobody," confessed Anne. "Diana and I just imagined the wood was haunted. All the places around here are so—so—*commonplace*. We just got this up for our own amusement. We began it in April. A haunted wood is so very romantic, Marilla. We chose the spruce grove because it's so gloomy. Oh, we have imagined the most harrowing things. There's a white lady walks along the brook just about this time of the night and wrings her hands and utters wailing cries. She appears when there is to be a death in the family. And the ghost of a little murdered child haunts the corner up by Idlewild; it creeps up behind you and lays its cold fingers on your hand—so. Oh, Marilla, it gives me a shudder to think of it. And there's a headless man stalks up and down the path and skeletons glower at you between the boughs. Oh, Marilla, I wouldn't go through the Haunted Wood after dark now for anything. I'd be sure that white things would reach out from behind the trees and grab me."

"Did ever any one hear the like!" ejaculated Marilla, who had listened in dumb amazement. "Anne Shirley, do you mean to tell me you believe all that wicked nonsense of your own imagination?"

"Not believe *exactly*," faltered Anne. "At least, I don't believe it in daylight. But after dark, Marilla, it's different. That is when ghosts walk."

"There are no such things as ghosts, Anne."

"Oh, but there are, Marilla," cried Anne eagerly. "I know people who have seen them. And they are respectable people. Charlie Sloane says that his grandmother saw his grandfather driving home the cows one night after he'd been buried for a year. You know Charlie Sloane's grandmother wouldn't tell a story for anything. She's a very religious woman. And Mrs. Thomas' father was pursued home one night by a lamb of fire with its head cut off hanging by a strip of skin. He said he knew it was the spirit of his brother and that it was a warning he would die within nine days. He didn't, but he died two years after, so you see it was really true. And Ruby Gillis says—"

"Anne Shirley," interrupted Marilla firmly, "I never want to hear you talking in this fashion again. I've had my doubts about that imagination of yours right along, and if this is going to be the outcome of it, I won't countenance any such doings. You'll go right over to Barry's, and you'll go through that spruce grove, just for a lesson and a warning to you. And never let me hear a word out of your head about haunted woods again."

Anne might plead and cry as she liked—and did, for her terror was very real. Her imagination had run away with her and she held the spruce grove in mortal dread after nightfall. But Marilla was inexorable. She marched the shrinking ghostseer down to the spring and ordered her to proceed straightway over the bridge and into the dusky retreats of wailing ladies and headless spectres beyond.

"Oh, Marilla, how can you be so cruel?" sobbed Anne. "What would you feel like if a white thing did snatch me up and carry me off?"

"I'll risk it," said Marilla unfeelingly. "You know I always mean what I say. I'll cure you of imagining ghosts into places. March, now."

Anne marched. That is, she stumbled over the bridge and went shuddering up the horrible dim path beyond. Anne never forgot that walk. Bitterly did she repent the license she had given to her imagination. The goblins of her fancy lurked in every shadow about her, reaching out their cold, fleshless hands to grasp the terrified small girl who had called them into being. A white strip of birch bark blowing up from the hollow over the brown floor of the grove made her heart stand still. The long-drawn wail of two old boughs rubbing against each other brought out the perspiration in beads on her forehead. The swoop of bats in the darkness over her was as the wings of unearthly creatures. When she reached Mr. William Bell's field she fled across it as if pursued by an army of white things, and arrived at the Barry kitchen door so out of breath that she could hardly gasp out her request for the apron pattern. Diana was away so that she had no excuse to linger. The dreadful return journey had to be faced. Anne went back over it with shut eyes, preferring to take the risk of dashing her brains out among the boughs to that of seeing a white thing. When she finally stumbled over the log bridge she drew one long shivering breath of relief.

"Well, so nothing caught you?" said Marilla unsympathetically.

"Oh, Mar—Marilla," chattered Anne, "I'll b-b-be cont-t-tented with c-c-commonplace places after this."

## Chapter XXI

### A NEW DEPARTURE IN FLAVOURINGS

"Dear me, there is nothing but meetings and partings in this world, as Mrs. Lynde says," remarked Anne plaintively, putting her slate and books down on the kitchen table on the last day of June and wiping her red eyes with a very damp handkerchief. "Wasn't it fortunate, Marilla, that I took an extra handkerchief to school to-day? I had a presentiment that it would be needed."

"I never thought you were so fond of Mr. Phillips that you'd require two handkerchiefs to dry your tears just because he was going away," said Marilla.

"I don't think I was crying because I was really so very fond of him," reflected Anne. "I just cried because all the others did. It was Ruby Gillis started it. Ruby Gillis has always declared she hated Mr. Phillips, but just as soon as he got up to make his farewell speech she burst into tears. Then all the girls began to cry, one after the other. I tried to hold out, Marilla. I tried to remember the time Mr. Phillips made me sit with Gil—with a boy; and the time he spelled my name without an *e* on the black-board; and how he said I was the worst dunce he ever saw at geometry and laughed at my spelling; and all the times he had been so horrid and sarcastic; but somehow I couldn't, Marilla, and I just had to cry too. Jane Andrews has been talking for a month about how glad she'd be when Mr. Phillips went away and she declared she'd never shed a tear. Well, she was worse than any of us and had to borrow a handkerchief from her brother— of course the boys didn't cry—because she hadn't brought one of her own, not expecting to need it. Oh, Marilla, it was heartrending. Mr. Phillips made such a beautiful farewell speech beginning, 'The time has come for us to part.' It was very affecting. And he had tears in his eyes too, Marilla. Oh, I felt dreadfully sorry and remorseful for all the times I'd talked in school and drawn pictures of him on my slate and made fun of him and Prissy. I can tell you I wished I'd been a model pupil like Minnie Andrews. *She* hadn't anything on her conscience. The girls cried all the way home from school. Carrie Sloane kept saying every few minutes, 'The time has come for us to part,' and that would start us off again whenever we were in any danger of cheering up. I do feel dreadfully sad, Marilla. But one can't feel quite in the depths of despair with two months vacation before them, can they, Marilla? And besides, we met the new minister and his wife coming from the station. For all I was feeling so bad about Mr. Phillips going away I couldn't help taking a little interest in a new minister, could I? His wife is very pretty. Not exactly regally lovely, of course—it wouldn't do, I suppose, for a minister to have a regally lovely wife, because it might set a bad example. Mrs. Lynde says the minister's wife over at Newbridge sets a very bad example because she dresses so fashionably. Our new minister's wife was dressed in blue muslin with lovely puffed sleeves and a hat trimmed with roses. Jane Andrews said she thought puffed sleeves were too worldly for a minister's wife, but I didn't make any such uncharitable remark, Marilla, because I know what it is to long for puffed sleeves. Besides, she's only been a minister's wife for a little while, so one should make allowances, shouldn't they? They are going to board with Mrs. Lynde until the manse is ready."

If Marilla, in going down to Mrs. Lynde's that evening, was actu- ated by any motive save her avowed one of returning the quilting-frames[1] she had borrowed the preceding winter, it was an amiable weakness[2] shared by most of the Avonlea people. Many a thing Mrs. Lynde had lent, sometimes never expecting to see it again, came home that night in charge of the borrowers thereof. A new minister,[3] and moreover a minister with a wife, was a lawful object of curiosity in a quiet little country settlement where sensations were few and far between.

Old Mr. Bentley, the minister whom Anne had found lacking in imagination, had been pastor of Avonlea for eighteen years. He was a widower when he came, and a widower he remained, despite the fact that gossip regularly married him to this, that or the other one, every year of his sojourn. In the preceding February he had resigned his charge and departed amid the regrets of his people, most of whom had the affection born of long intercourse for their good old minister in spite of his shortcomings as an orator. Since then the Avonlea church had enjoyed a variety of religious dissipation in listening to the many and various candidates and "supplies"[4] who came Sunday after Sunday to preach on trial. These stood or fell by the judgment of the fathers and mothers in Israel;[5] but a certain small, red-haired girl who sat meekly in the corner of the old Cuthbert pew also had her opinions about them and discussed the same in full with Matthew, Marilla always declining from principle to criticize ministers in any shape or form.

"I don't think Mr. Smith would have done, Matthew," was Anne's final summing up. "Mrs. Lynde says his delivery was so poor, but I think his worst fault was just like Mr. Bentley's—he had no imagination. And Mr. Terry had too much; he let it run away with him just as I did mine in the matter of the Haunted Wood. Besides, Mrs. Lynde says his theology wasn't sound. Mr. Gresham was a very good man and a very religious man, but he told too many funny stories and made the people laugh in church; he was undignified, and you must have some dignity about a minister, mustn't you, Matthew? I thought Mr. Marshall was decidedly attractive; but Mrs. Lynde says he isn't married, or even engaged, because she made special inquiries about him, and she says it would never do to have a young unmarried minister in Avonlea, because he might marry in the congregation

1. Big frames used by women at quilting bees consisted of 6' or 8' side boards; Marilla may have carried smaller frames used to sew individual squares.
2. Sheridan's *The School for Scandal* (1777) 5.1; also in Henry Fielding's *The History of Tom Jones* (1749) book. 10, chap. 8.
3. At the time she wrote *AGG*, LMM was being courted by a minister.
4. Since Presbyterianism left the choice of a local minister to the congregation rather than to a bishop, candidates for an empty pulpit would "preach for a call," while retired or neighboring ministers ("supplies") would conduct interim services.
5. Members of the congregation. These Presbyterians (and other nineteenth-century Protestants) focused on the Old Testament rather than the New Testament and identified themselves with the chosen people of Israel.

and that would make trouble.[6] Mrs. Lynde is a very far-seeing woman, isn't she, Matthew? I'm very glad they've called Mr. Allan. I liked him because his sermon was interesting and he prayed as if he meant it and not just as if he did it because he was in the habit of it. Mrs. Lynde says he isn't perfect, but she says she supposes we couldn't expect a perfect minister for seven hundred and fifty dollars a year,[7] and anyhow his theology is sound because she questioned him thoroughly on all the points of doctrine. And she knows his wife's people and they are most respectable and the women are all good housekeepers. Mrs. Lynde says that sound doctrine in the man and good housekeeping in the woman make an ideal combination for a minister's family."

The new minister and his wife were a young, pleasant-faced couple, still in their honeymoon, and full of all good and beautiful enthusiasms for their chosen life-work. Avonlea opened its heart to them from the start. Old and young liked the frank, cheerful young man with his high ideals, and the bright, gentle little lady who assumed the mistress-ship of the manse. With Mrs. Allan Anne fell promptly and whole-heartedly in love. She had discovered another kindred spirit.

"Mrs. Allan is perfectly lovely," she announced one Sunday afternoon. "She's taken our class and she's a splendid teacher. She said right away she didn't think it was fair for the teacher to ask all the questions, and you know, Marilla, that is exactly what I've always thought. She said we could ask her any question we liked, and I asked ever so many. I'm good at asking questions, Marilla."

"I believe you," was Marilla's emphatic comment.

"Nobody else asked any except Ruby Gillis, and she asked if there was to be a Sunday-school picnic this summer. I didn't think that was a very proper question to ask because it hadn't any connection with the lesson—the lesson was about Daniel in the lions' den[8]— but Mrs. Allan just smiled and said she thought there would be. Mrs. Allan has a lovely smile; she has such *exquisite* dimples in her cheeks.[9] I wish I had dimples in my cheeks, Marilla. I'm not half so skinny as I was when I came here, but I have no dimples yet. If I had perhaps I could influence people for good. Mrs. Allan said we ought always to try to influence other people for good. She talked so nice about everything. I never knew before that religion was such a cheerful thing. I always thought it was kind of melancholy, but Mrs.

6. At the time of writing *AGG*, LMM and other young women became rivals over the new minister, the Rev. Ewan Macdonald, a bachelor.

7. In 1903, the Rev. Ewan Macdonald was paid $670 for the dual charge of Cavendish and Stanley. The same year, the minister in Cardigan, PEI, received $775.

8. "The Lord saved Daniel in the midst of roaring lions because he was faithful." *Holy Bible*, Daniel 6. 16–23.

9. LMM presents an idealized picture of a minister's wife.

Allan's isn't, and I'd like to be a Christian if I could be one like her. I wouldn't want to be one like Mr. Superintendent Bell."

"It's very naughty of you to speak so about Mr. Bell," said Marilla severely. "Mr. Bell is a real good man."

"Oh, of course he's good," agreed Anne, "but he doesn't seem to get any comfort out of it. If I could be good I'd dance and sing all day because I was glad of it. I suppose Mrs. Allan is too old to dance and sing and of course it wouldn't be dignified in a minister's wife. But I can just feel she's glad she's a Christian and that she'd be one even if she could get to heaven without it."

"I suppose we must have Mr. and Mrs. Allan up to tea some day soon," said Marilla reflectively. "They've been most everywhere but here. Let me see. Next Wednesday would be a good time to have them. But don't say a word to Matthew about it, for if he knew they were coming he'd find some excuse to be away that day. He'd got so used to Mr. Bentley he didn't mind him, but he's going to find it hard to get acquainted with a new minister, and a new minister's wife will frighten him to death."

"I'll be as secret as the dead," assured Anne. "But oh, Marilla, will you let me make a cake for the occasion? I'd love to do something for Mrs. Allan, and you know I can make a pretty good cake by this time."

"You can make a layer cake," promised Marilla.

Monday and Tuesday great preparations went on at Green Gables. Having the minister and his wife to tea was a serious and important undertaking, and Marilla was determined not to be eclipsed by any of the Avonlea housekeepers. Anne was wild with excitement and delight. She talked it all over with Diana Tuesday night in the twilight, as they sat on the big red stones by the Dryad's Bubble and made rainbows in the water with little twigs dipped in fir balsam.[1]

"Everything is ready, Diana, except my cake which I'm to make in the morning, and the baking-powder biscuits which Marilla will make just before tea-time. I assure you, Diana, that Marilla and I have had a busy two days of it. It's such a responsibility having a minister's family to tea. I never went through such an experience before. You should just see our pantry. It's a sight to behold. We're going to have jellied chicken and cold tongue. We're to have two kinds of jelly, red and yellow, and whipped cream and lemon pie, and cherry pie, and three kinds of cookies, and fruit-cake, and Marilla's famous yellow plum preserves that she keeps especially for ministers, and pound cake and layer cake, and biscuits as aforesaid;[2] and new bread and old both, in case the minister is dyspeptic[3] and can't

1. The rainbow effect comes from the oil in the balsam.
2. A mock-legalistic phrase used for comic effect.
3. Suffering from indigestion.

eat new. Mrs. Lynde says ministers mostly are dyspeptic, but I don't think Mr. Allan has been a minister long enough for it to have had a bad effect on him. I just grow cold when I think of my layer cake. Oh, Diana, what if it shouldn't be good! I dreamed last night that I was chased all around by a fearful goblin with a big layer cake for a head."

"It'll be good, all right," assured Diana, who was a very comfortable sort of friend. "I'm sure that piece of the one you made that we had for lunch in Idlewild two weeks ago was perfectly elegant."

"Yes; but cakes have such a terrible habit of turning out bad just when you especially want them to be good," sighed Anne, setting a particularly well-balsamed twig afloat. "However, I suppose I shall just have to trust to Providence and be careful to put in the flour. Oh, look, Diana, what a lovely rainbow! Do you suppose the dryad will come out after we go away and take it for a scarf?"[4]

"You know there is no such thing as a dryad," said Diana. Diana's mother had found out about the Haunted Wood and had been decidedly angry over it. As a result Diana had abstained from any further imitative flights of imagination and did not think it prudent to cultivate a spirit of belief even in harmless dryads.

"But it's so easy to imagine there is," said Anne. "Every night, before I go to bed, I look out of my window and wonder if the dryad is really sitting here, combing her locks with the spring for a mirror. Sometimes I look for her footprints in the dew in the morning. Oh, Diana, don't give up your faith in the dryad!"

Wednesday morning came. Anne got up at sunrise because she was too excited to sleep. She had caught a severe cold in the head by reason of her dabbling in the spring on the preceding evening; but nothing short of absolute pneumonia could have quenched her interest in culinary matters that morning. After breakfast she proceeded to make her cake. When she finally shut the oven door upon it she drew a long breath.

"I'm sure I haven't forgotten anything this time, Marilla. But do you think it will rise? Just suppose perhaps the baking-powder isn't good? I used it out of the new can. And Mrs. Lynde says you can never be sure of getting good baking-powder nowadays when everything is so adulterated.[5] Mrs. Lynde says the Government ought to take the matter up, but she says we'll never see the day when a Tory[6] Government will do it. Marilla, what if that cake doesn't rise?"

---

4. Echoes a phrase from one of LMM's favorite novels: "One could cut a pretty enough scarf out of a rainbow." Charlotte Brontë, *Jane Eyre* (1847) chap. 24.
5. Pure food crusaders worked from the 1870s on to set the standards for commercial baking powder which had previously contained contaminating and inferior ingredients.
6. Slang for "Conservative," a major Canadian political party.

"We'll have plenty without it," was Marilla's unimpassioned way of looking at the subject.

The cake did rise, however, and came out of the oven as light and feathery as golden foam. Anne, flushed with delight, clapped it together with layers of ruby jelly and, in imagination, saw Mrs. Allan eating it and possibly asking for another piece!

"You'll be using the best tea-set, of course, Marilla," she said. "Can I fix up the table with ferns and wild roses?"

"I think that's all nonsense," sniffed Marilla. "In my opinion it's the eatables that matter and not flummery[7] decorations."

"Mrs. Barry had *her* table decorated," said Anne, who was not entirely guiltless of the wisdom of the serpent,[8] "and the minister paid her an elegant compliment. He said it was a feast for the eye as well as the palate."

"Well, do as you like," said Marilla, who was quite determined not to be surpassed by Mrs. Barry or anybody else. "Only mind you leave enough room for the dishes and the food."

Anne laid herself out to decorate in a manner and after a fashion that should leave Mrs. Barry's nowhere. Having abundance of roses and ferns and a very artistic taste of her own, she made that tea-table such a thing of beauty that when the minister and his wife sat down to it they exclaimed in chorus over its loveliness.

"It's Anne's doings," said Marilla, grimly just; and Anne felt that Mrs. Allan's approving smile was almost too much happiness for this world.

Matthew was there, having been inveigled into the party only goodness and Anne knew how. He had been in such a state of shyness and nervousness that Marilla had given him up in despair, but Anne took him in hand so successfully that he now sat at the table in his best clothes and white collar and talked to the minister not uninterestingly. He never said a word to Mrs. Allan, but that perhaps was not to be expected.

All went merry as a marriage bell[9] until Anne's layer cake was passed. Mrs. Allan, having already been helped to a bewildering variety, declined it. But Marilla, seeing the disappointment on Anne's face, said smilingly:

"Oh, you must take a piece of this, Mrs. Allan. Anne made it on purpose for you."

"In that case I must sample it," laughed Mrs. Allan, helping herself to a plump triangle, as did also the minister and Marilla.

Mrs. Allan took a mouthful of hers and a most peculiar expression

---

7. Flimsy and silly talk or flattery.
8. "Be ye therefore wise as serpents and harmless as doves." *Holy Bible*, Matthew 10.16.
9. "There was the sound of revelry by night . . . and all went merry as a marriage bell." Lord Byron, *Childe Harold's Pilgrimage* (1812) 3.21.8–9.

crossed her face; not a word did she say, however, but steadily ate away at it. Marilla saw the expression and hastened to taste the cake.

"Anne Shirley!" she exclaimed, "what on earth did you put into that cake?"

"Nothing but what the recipe said, Marilla," cried Anne with a look of anguish. "Oh, isn't it all right?"

"All right! It's simply horrible. Mrs. Allan, don't try to eat it. Anne, taste it yourself. What flavouring did you use?"

"Vanilla," said Anne, her face scarlet with mortification after tasting the cake. "Only vanilla. Oh, Marilla, it must have been the baking-powder. I had my suspicions of that bak—"

"Baking-powder fiddlesticks! Go and bring me the bottle of vanilla you used."

Anne fled to the pantry and returned with a small bottle partially filled with a brown liquid and labelled yellowly, "Best Vanilla."

Marilla took it, uncorked it, smelled it.

"Mercy on us, Anne, you've flavoured that cake with *anodyne liniment*.[1] I broke the liniment bottle last week and poured what was left into an old empty vanilla bottle. I suppose it's partly my fault— I should have warned you—but for pity's sake why couldn't you have smelled it?"

Anne dissolved into tears under this double disgrace.

"I couldn't—I had such a cold!" and with this she fairly fled to the gable chamber, where she cast herself on the bed and wept as one who refuses to be comforted.

Presently a light step sounded on the stairs and somebody entered the room.

"Oh, Marilla," sobbed Anne without looking up, "I'm disgraced for ever. I shall never be able to live this down. It will get out—things always do get out in Avonlea. Diana will ask me how my cake turned out and I shall have to tell her the truth. I shall always be pointed at as the girl who flavoured a cake with anodyne liniment. Gil—the boys in school will never get over laughing at it. Oh, Marilla, if you have a spark of Christian pity don't tell me that I must go down and wash the dishes after this. I'll wash them when the minister and his wife are gone, but I cannot ever look Mrs. Allan in the face again. Perhaps she'll think I tried to poison her. Mrs. Lynde says she knows an orphan girl who tried to poison her benefactor. But the liniment isn't poisonous. It's meant to be taken internally—although not in cakes. Won't you tell Mrs. Allan so, Marilla?"

"Suppose you jump up and tell her so yourself," said a merry voice.

1. Medicinal fluid used to relieve pain. Most patent liniments were composed of camphor, oil of peppermint, tincture of opium, water of ammonia, and turpentine oil. LMM used comparable material in "A New-Fashioned Flavoring" (1898), "Patty's Mistake" (1902), and "The Cake that Prissy Made" (1903). See *AGG*, ed. Devereux 344–64.

Anne flew up, to find Mrs. Allan standing by her bed, surveying her with laughing eyes.

"My dear little girl, you mustn't cry like this," she said, genuinely disturbed by Anne's tragic face. "Why, it's all just a funny mistake that anybody might make."

"Oh, no, it takes me to make such a mistake," said Anne forlornly. "And I wanted to have that cake so nice for you, Mrs. Allan."

"Yes, I know, dear. And I assure you I appreciate your kindness and thoughtfulness just as much as if it had turned out all right. Now, you mustn't cry any more, but come down with me and show me your flower garden. Miss Cuthbert tells me you have a little plot all your own. I want to see it, for I'm very much interested in flowers."

Anne permitted herself to be led down and comforted, reflecting that it was really providential that Mrs. Allan was a kindred spirit. Nothing more was said about the liniment cake, and when the guests went away Anne found that she had enjoyed the evening more than could have been expected, considering that terrible incident. Nevertheless she sighed deeply.

"Marilla, isn't it nice to think that to-morrow is a new day with no mistakes in it yet?"

"I'll warrant you'll make plenty in it," said Marilla. "I never saw your beat for making mistakes, Anne."

"Yes, and well I know it," admitted Anne mournfully. "But have you ever noticed one encouraging thing about me, Marilla? I never make the same mistake twice."

"I don't know as that's much benefit when you're always making new ones."

"Oh, don't you see, Marilla? There *must* be a limit to the mistakes one person can make, and when I get to the end of them, then I'll be through with them. That's a very comforting thought."

"Well, you'd better go and give that cake to the pigs," said Marilla. "It isn't fit for any human to eat, not even Jerry Buote."

# Chapter XXII

### ANNE IS INVITED OUT TO TEA

"AND what are your eyes popping out of your head about now?" asked Marilla, when Anne had just come in from a run to the post-office. "Have you discovered another kindred spirit?"

Excitement hung around Anne like a garment, shone in her eyes, kindled in every feature. She had come dancing up the lane, like a wind-blown sprite, through the mellow sunshine and lazy shadows of the August evening.

"No, Marilla, but oh, what do you think? I am invited to tea at the manse to-morrow afternoon! Mrs. Allan left the letter for me at the post-office. Just look at it, Marilla. 'Miss Anne Shirley, Green Gables.' That is the first time I was ever called 'Miss.' Such a thrill as it gave me! I shall cherish it for ever among my choicest treasures."

"Mrs. Allan told me she meant to have all the members of her Sunday-school class to tea in turn," said Marilla, regarding the wonderful event very coolly. "You needn't get in such a fever over it. Do learn to take things calmly, child."

For Anne to take things calmly would have been to change her nature. All "spirit and fire and dew,"[1] as she was, the pleasures and pains of life came to her with trebled intensity. Marilla felt this and was vaguely troubled over it, realizing that the ups and downs of existence would probably bear hardly on this impulsive soul and not sufficiently understanding that the equally great capacity for delight might more than compensate. Therefore Marilla conceived it to be her duty to drill Anne into a tranquil uniformity of disposition as impossible and alien to her as to a dancing sunbeam in one of the brook shallows. She did not make much headway, as she sorrowfully admitted to herself. The downfall of some dear hope or plan plunged Anne into "deeps of affliction." The fulfilment thereof exalted her to dizzy realms of delight. Marilla had almost begun to despair of ever fashioning this waif of the world into her model little girl of demure manners and prim deportment. Neither would she have believed that she really liked Anne much better as she was.

Anne went to bed that night speechless with misery because Matthew had said the wind was round northeast and he feared it would be a rainy day to-morrow. The rustle of the poplar leaves about the house worried her, it sounded so like pattering rain-drops, and the dull, faraway roar of the gulf, to which she listened delightedly at other times, loving its strange, sonorous, haunting rhythm, now seemed like a prophecy of storm and disaster to a small maiden who particularly wanted a fine day. Anne thought that the morning would never come.

But all things have an end, even nights before the day on which you are invited to take tea at the manse. The morning, in spite of Matthew's predictions, was fine and Anne's spirits soared to their highest.

"Oh, Marilla, there is something in me to-day that makes me just love everybody I see," she exclaimed as she washed the breakfast dishes. "You don't know how good I feel! Wouldn't it be nice if it

---

1. An epigraph on the title page of *AGG* reads, "The good stars met in your horoscope, / Made you of spirit and fire and dew."—Browning. In the original, Robert Browning's "Evelyn Hope" (1855) lines 19–20, the second line runs, "Made you of spirit, fire and dew—".

could last? I believe I could be a model child if I were just invited out to tea every day. But oh, Marilla, it's a solemn occasion, too. I feel so anxious. What if I shouldn't behave properly? You know I never had tea at a manse before, and I'm not sure that I know all the rules of etiquette, although I've been studying the rules given in the Etiquette Department of the *Family Herald*[2] ever since I came here. I'm so afraid I'll do something silly or forget to do something I should do. Would it be good manners to take a second helping of anything if you wanted to *very* much?"

"The trouble with you, Anne, is that you're thinking too much about yourself. You should just think of Mrs. Allan and what would be nicest and most agreeable for her," said Marilla, hitting for once in her life on a very sound and pithy piece of advice. Anne instantly realized this.

"You are right, Marilla. I'll try not to think about myself at all."

Anne evidently got through her visit without any serious breach of "etiquette" for she came home through the twilight, under a great, high-sprung sky gloried over with trails of saffron and rosy cloud, in a beatified state of mind and told Marilla all about it happily, sitting on the big red sandstone slab[3] at the kitchen door with her tired curly head in Marilla's gingham lap.

A cool wind was blowing down over the long harvest fields from the rims of firry western hills and whistling through the poplars. One clear star hung above the orchard and the fireflies were flitting over in Lovers' Lane, in and out among the ferns and rustling boughs. Anne watched them as she talked and somehow felt that wind and stars and fireflies were all tangled up together into something unutterably sweet and enchanting.

"Oh, Marilla, I've had a most *fascinating* time. I feel that I have not lived in vain and I shall always feel like that even if I should never be invited to tea at a manse again. When I got there Mrs. Allan met me at the door. She was dressed in the sweetest dress of pale pink organdy,[4] with dozens of frills and elbow sleeves, and she looked just like a seraph.[5] I really think I'd like to be a minister's wife when I grow up, Marilla. A minister mightn't mind my red hair because he wouldn't be thinking of such worldly things. But then of course one would have to be naturally good and I'll never be that, so I suppose there's no use in thinking about it. Some people are naturally good, you know, and others are not. I'm one of the others. Mrs. Lynde says

---

2. Major Canadian agricultural paper, published in Montreal since 1869 (to 1968). Family sections included hints on deportment as well as recipes and ideas for decorating the home. Many of LMM's short stories were published in this paper.
3. At the threshold of the house, the native PEI sandstone.
4. Delicate, sheer, stiff cotton (or sometimes silk) material.
5. A symbolic being (or angel) with six wings who waits attendance on the Lord and brings a vision to the prophet. *Holy Bible*, Isaiah 6.2; 6.6.

I'm full of original sin.[6] No matter how hard I try to be good I can never make such a success of it as those who are naturally good. It's a good deal like geometry, I expect. But don't you think the trying so hard ought to count for something? Mrs. Allan is one of the naturally good people. I love her passionately. You know there are some people, like Matthew and Mrs. Allan, that you can love right off without any trouble. And there are others, like Mrs. Lynde, that you have to try very hard to love. You know you *ought* to love them because they know so much and are such active workers in the church, but you have to keep reminding yourself of it all the time or else you forget. There was another little girl at the manse to tea, from the White Sands Sunday-school. Her name was Lauretta Bradley, and she was a very nice little girl. Not exactly a kindred spirit, you know, but still very nice. We had an elegant tea, and I think I kept all the rules of etiquette pretty well. After tea Mrs. Allan played and sang and she got Lauretta and me to sing, too. Mrs. Allan says I have a good voice and she says I must sing in the Sunday-school choir after this. You can't think how I was thrilled at the mere thought. I've longed so to sing in the Sunday-school choir, as Diana does, but I feared it was an honour I could never aspire to. Lauretta had to go home early because there is a big concert in the White Sands hotel to-night and her sister is to recite at it. Laurette says that the Americans at the hotel give a concert every fort-night in aid of the Charlottetown hospital, and they ask lots of the White Sands people to recite. Lauretta said she expected to be asked herself some day. I just gazed at her in awe. After she had gone Mrs. Allan and I had a heart to heart talk. I told her everything—about Mrs. Thomas and the twins and Katie Maurice and Violetta and coming to Green Gables and my troubles over geometry. And would you believe it, Marilla? Mrs. Allan told me she was a dunce at geometry, too. You don't know how that encouraged me. Mrs. Lynde came to the manse just before I left, and what do you think, Marilla? The trustees have hired a new teacher and it's a lady. Her name is Miss Muriel Stacy.[7] Isn't that a romantic name? Mrs. Lynde says they've never had a female teacher in Avonlea before and she thinks it is a dangerous innovation. But I think it will be splendid to have a lady teacher, and I really don't see how I'm going to live through the two weeks before school begins, I'm so impatient to see her."

---

6. Presbyterians, like most other Christians, held that every human is "born in sin" because of the primal fall of Adam and Eve.
7. Based on a favorite female teacher, Miss Hattie Gordon, who taught the young LMM. Female teachers were paid far less than men with the same qualifications.

# Chapter XXIII

### ANNE COMES TO GRIEF IN AN AFFAIR OF HONOUR

ANNE had to live through more than two weeks, as it happened. Almost a month having elapsed since the liniment cake episode, it was high time for her to get into fresh trouble of some sort, little mistakes, such as absent-mindedly emptying a pan of skim milk[1] into a basket of yarn balls in the pantry instead of into the pigs' bucket, and walking clean over the edge of the log bridge into the brook while wrapped in imaginative reverie, not really being worth counting.

A week after the tea at the manse Diana Barry gave a party.

"Small and select," Anne assured Marilla. "Just the girls in our class."

They had a very good time and nothing untoward happened until after tea, when they found themselves in the Barry garden, a little tired of all their games and ripe for any enticing form of mischief which might present itself. This presently took the form of "daring."

Daring was the fashionable amusement among the Avonlea small fry just then. It had begun among the boys, but soon spread to the girls, and all the silly things that were done in Avonlea that summer because the doers thereof were "dared" to do them would fill a book by themselves.

First of all Carrie Sloane dared Ruby Gillis to climb to a certain point in the huge old willow-tree before the front door; which Ruby Gillis, albeit in mortal dread of the fat green caterpillars with which said tree was infested and with the fear of her mother before her eyes if she should tear her new muslin dress, nimbly did, to the discomfiture of the aforesaid Carrie Sloane.

Then Josie Pye dared Jane Andrews to hop on her left leg around the garden without stopping once or putting her right foot to the ground; which Jane Andrews gamely tried to do, but gave out at the third corner and had to confess herself defeated.

Josie's triumph being rather more pronounced than good taste permitted, Anne Shirley dared her to walk along the top of the board fence which bounded the garden to the east. Now, to "walk" board fences requires more skill and steadiness of head and heel than one might suppose who has never tried it. But Josie Pye, if deficient in some qualities that make for popularity, had at least a natural and inborn gift, duly cultivated, for walking board fences. Josie walked the Barry fence with an airy unconcern which seemed to imply that a little thing like that wasn't worth a "dare." Reluctant admiration

---

1. Left over after skimming off cream or making butter, and sometimes added to household scraps fed to the pigs.

greeted her exploit, for most of the other girls could appreciate it, having suffered many things themselves in their efforts to walk fences. Josie descended from her perch, flushed with victory, and darted a defiant glance at Anne.

Anne tossed her red braids.

"I don't think it's such a very wonderful thing to walk a little, low, board fence," she said. "I knew a girl in Marysville who could walk the ridge-pole of a roof."[2]

"I don't believe it," said Josie flatly. "I don't believe anybody could walk a ridge-pole. *You* couldn't, anyhow."

"Couldn't I?" cried Anne rashly.

"Then I dare you to do it," said Josie defiantly. "I dare you to climb up there and walk the ridge-pole of Mr. Barry's kitchen roof."

Anne turned pale, but there was clearly only one thing to be done. She walked towards the house, where a ladder was leaning against the kitchen roof. All the fifth-class girls said, "Oh!" partly in excitement, partly in dismay.

"Don't you do it, Anne," entreated Diana. "You'll fall off and be killed. Never mind Josie Pye. It isn't fair to dare anybody to do anything so dangerous."

"I must do it. My honour is at stake," said Anne solemnly. "I shall walk that ridge-pole, Diana, or perish in the attempt. If I am killed you are to have my pearl bead ring."

Anne climbed the ladder amid breathless silence, gained the ridge-pole, balanced herself uprightly on that precarious footing, and started to walk along it, dizzily conscious that she was uncomfortably high up in the world and that walking ridge-poles was not a thing in which your imagination helped you out much. Nevertheless, she managed to take several steps before the catastrophe came. Then she swayed, lost her balance, stumbled, staggered and fell, sliding down over the sun-baked roof and crashing off it through the tangle of Virginia creeper[3] beneath—all before the dismayed circle below could give a simultaneous, terrified shriek.

If Anne had tumbled off the roof on the side up which she ascended Diana would probably have fallen heir to the pearl bead ring then and there. Fortunately she fell on the other side, where the roof extended down over the porch so nearly to the ground that a fall therefrom was a much less serious thing. Nevertheless, when Diana and the other girls had rushed frantically around the house— except Ruby Gillis, who remained as if rooted to the ground and went into hysterics—they found Anne lying all white and limp among the wreck and ruin of the Virginia creeper.

2. The strip of wood laid along the apex of the roof.
3. Quick-growing vine, used to cover unsightly walls.

BALANCED HERSELF UPRIGHTLY ON THAT PRECARIOUS FOOTING

"Anne, are you killed?" shrieked Diana, throwing herself on her knees beside her friend. "Oh, Anne, dear Anne, speak just one word to me and tell me if you're killed."

To the immense relief of all the girls, and especially of Josie Pye, who, in spite of lack of imagination, had been seized with horrible visions of a future branded as the girl who was the cause of Anne Shirley's early and tragic death, Anne sat dizzily up and answered uncertainly:

"No, Diana, I am not killed, but I think I am rendered unconscious."

"Where?" sobbed Carrie Sloane. "Oh, where, Anne?"

Before Anne could answer Mrs. Barry appeared on the scene. At sight of her Anne tried to scramble to her feet, but sank back again with a sharp little cry of pain.

"What's the matter? Where have you hurt yourself?" demanded Mrs. Barry.

"My ankle," gasped Anne. "Oh, Diana, please find your father and ask him to take me home. I know I can never walk there. And I'm sure I couldn't hop so far on one foot when Jane couldn't even hop around the garden."

Marilla was out in the orchard picking a panful of summer apples when she saw Mr. Barry coming over the log bridge and up the slope, with Mrs. Barry beside him and a whole procession of little girls trailing after him. In his arms he carried Anne, whose head lay limply against his shoulder.

At that moment Marilla had a revelation. In the sudden stab of fear that pierced to her very heart she realized what Anne had come to mean to her. She would have admitted that she liked Anne—nay, that she was very fond of Anne. But now she knew as she hurried wildly down the slope that Anne was dearer to her than anything on earth.

"Mr. Barry, what has happened to her?" she gasped, more white and shaken than the self-contained, sensible Marilla had been for many years.

Anne herself answered, lifting her head.

"Don't be very frightened, Marilla. I was walking the ridge-pole and I fell off. I expect I have sprained my ankle. But, Marilla, I might have broken my neck. Let us look on the bright side of things."

"I might have known you'd go and do something of the sort when I let you go to that party," said Marilla, sharp and shrewish in her very relief. "Bring her in here, Mr. Barry, and lay her on the sofa. Mercy me, the child has gone and fainted!"

It was quite true. Overcome by the pain of her injury, Anne had one more of her wishes granted to her. She had fainted dead away.

Matthew, hastily summoned from the harvest field, was straightway despatched for the doctor, who in due time came, to discover that the injury was more serious than they had supposed. Anne's ankle was broken.

That night, when Marilla went up to the east gable, where a white-faced girl was lying, a plaintive voice greeted her from the bed.

"Aren't you very sorry for me, Marilla?"

"It was your own fault," said Marilla, twitching down the blind and lighting a lamp.

"And that is just why you should be sorry for me," said Anne, "because the thought that it *is* all my own fault is what makes it so hard. If I could blame it on anybody I would feel so much better. But what would you have done, Marilla, if you had been dared to walk a ridge-pole?"

"I'd have stayed on good firm ground and let them dare away. Such absurdity!" said Marilla.

Anne sighed.

"But you have such strength of mind, Marilla. I haven't. I just felt that I couldn't bear Josie Pye's scorn. She would have crowed over me all my life. And I think I have been punished so much that you needn't be very cross with me, Marilla. It's not a bit nice to faint, after all. And the doctor hurt me dreadfully when he was setting my ankle. I won't be able to go around for six or seven weeks and I'll miss the new lady teacher. She won't be new any more by the time I'm able to go to school. And Gil—everybody will get ahead of me in class. Oh, I am an afflicted mortal. But I'll try to bear it all bravely if only you won't be cross with me, Marilla."

"There, there, I'm not cross," said Marilla. "You're an unlucky child, there's no doubt about that; but, as you say, you'll have the suffering of it. Here now, try and eat some supper."

"Isn't it fortunate I've got such an imagination?" said Anne. "It will help me through splendidly, I expect. What do people who haven't any imagination do when they break their bones, do you suppose, Marilla?"

Anne had good reason to bless her imagination many a time and oft during the tedious seven weeks that followed. But she was not solely dependent on it. She had many visitors and not a day passed without one or more of the schoolgirls dropping in to bring her flowers and books and tell her all the happenings in the juvenile world of Avonlea.

"Everybody has been so good and kind, Marilla," sighed Anne happily, on the day when she could first limp across the floor. "It isn't very pleasant to be laid up; but there *is* a bright side to it, Marilla. You find out how many friends you have. Why, even Superintendent Bell came to see me, and he's really a very fine man. Not a kindred spirit, of course; but still I like him and I'm awfully sorry I ever criticized his prayers. I believe now he really does mean them, only he has got into the habit of saying them as if he didn't. He could get over that if he'd take a little trouble. I gave him a good broad hint. I told him how hard I tried to make my own little private prayers interesting. He told me all about the time he broke his ankle when he was a boy. It does seem so strange to think of Superintendent Bell ever being a boy. Even my imagination has its limits for I can't imagine *that*. When I try to imagine him as a boy I see him with gray whiskers and spectacles, just as he looks in Sunday-school, only small. Now, it's so easy to imagine Mrs. Allan as a little girl. Mrs. Allan has been to see me fourteen times. Isn't that something to be proud of, Marilla? When a minister's wife has so many claims on her time! She is such a cheerful person to have visit you, too. She never tells you it's your own fault and she hopes you'll be a better girl on account of it. Mrs. Lynde always told me that when she came to see me; and she said it in a kind of way that made me feel she might hope I'd be a better girl, but didn't really believe I would. Even Josie Pye came to see me. I received her as politely as I could, because I think she was sorry she dared me to walk a ridge-pole. If I had been killed she would have had to carry a dark burden of remorse all her life. Diana has been a faithful friend. She's been over every day to cheer my lonely pillow. But oh, I shall be so glad when I can go to school for I've heard such exciting things about the new teacher. The girls all think she is perfectly sweet. Diana says she has the loveliest fair curly hair and such fascinating eyes. She dresses beautifully, and her sleeve puffs are bigger than anybody else's in Avonlea. Every other Friday afternoon she has recitations and everybody has to say a piece or take part in a dialogue. Oh, it's just glorious to think of it. Josie Pye says she hates it, but that is just because Josie has so little imagination. Diana and Ruby Gillis and Jane Andrews are preparing a dialogue, called 'A Morning Visit,'[4] for next Friday. And the Friday afternoons they don't have recitations Miss Stacy takes them all to the woods for a 'field' day and they study ferns and flowers and birds. And they have physical culture exercises[5] every morning and evening. Mrs. Lynde says she never heard of such goings-on and it all comes of having a lady teacher. But I think it must be splendid and I believe I shall find that Miss Stacy is a kindred spirit."

"There's one thing plain to be seen, Anne," said Marilla, "and that is that your fall off the Barry roof hasn't injured your tongue at all."

4. Perhaps a skit on ladies like the girls' mothers visiting each other. Other authors such as Anthony Trollope and Oliver Wendell Holmes have used the phrase.
5. Taking children outside the school, and directing marching and other exercises within the schoolroom. That a "sound mind" required a "sound body" had been advocated by educators from the classical age through John Locke's *On Education* (1692). See also Devereux 225–26n.

# Chapter XXIV

### MISS STACY AND HER PUPILS GET UP A CONCERT

IT was October again when Anne was ready to go back to school—a glorious October, all red and gold, with mellow mornings when the valleys were filled with delicate mists as if the spirit of autumn had poured them in for the sun to drain—amethyst, pearl, silver, rose, and smoke-blue.[1] The dews were so heavy that the fields glistened like cloth of silver and there were such heaps of rustling leaves in the hollows of many-stemmed woods to run crisply through. The Birch Path was a canopy of yellow and the ferns were sear and brown all along it. There was a tang in the very air that inspired the hearts of small maidens tripping, unlike snails, swiftly and willingly to school;[2] and it *was* jolly to be back again at the little brown desk beside Diana, with Ruby Gillis nodding across the aisle and Carrie Sloane sending up notes and Julia Bell passing a "chew" of gum down from the back seat. Anne drew a long breath of happiness as she sharpened her pencil and arranged her picture cards in her desk. Life was certainly very interesting.

In the new teacher she found another true and helpful friend. Miss Stacy was a bright, sympathetic young woman with the happy gift of winning and holding the affections of her pupils and bringing out the best that was in them mentally and morally. Anne expanded like a flower under this wholesome influence and carried home to the admiring Matthew and the critical Marilla glowing accounts of school work and aims.

"I love Miss Stacy with my whole heart, Marilla. She is so ladylike and she has such a sweet voice. When she pronounces my name I feel *instinctively* that she's spelling it with an *e*. We had recitations this afternoon. I just wish you could have been there to hear me recite 'Mary, Queen of Scots.'[3] I just put my whole soul into it. Ruby Gillis told me coming home that the way I said the line, 'Now for my father's arm, she said, my woman's heart farewell,' just made her blood run cold."

"Well now, you might recite it for me some of these days, out in the barn," suggested Matthew.

---

1. The colors in this passage are those favored in the art nouveau movement.
2. Adapting Jacques's speech on the ages of man: "And then the whining school-boy with his satchel / And shining morning face, creeping like snail, / Unwillingly to school." Shakespeare, *As You Like It* 2.7.
3. An 1830 poem by the Scottish poet Henry Glassford Bell glamorized the Stuart Queen who was put to death by order of Elizabeth I of England. Anne quoted lines 31–35 from this poem, which appeared in the *Fifth Royal Reader*. Its seventy-two lines place a burden on the student memorizing it. Like Anne, LMM could recite endless verses and entire long poems, such as Scott's *The Lady of the Lake*.

"Of course I will," said Anne meditatively, "but I won't be able to do it so well, I know. It won't be so exciting as it is when you have a whole schoolful before you hanging breathlessly on your words. I know I won't be able to make your blood run cold."

"Mrs. Lynde says it made *her* blood run cold to see the boys climbing to the very tops of those big trees on Bell's hill after crows' nests last Friday," said Marilla. "I wonder at Miss Stacy for encouraging it."

"But we wanted a crow's nest for nature study," explained Anne. "That was on our field afternoon. Field afternoons are splendid, Marilla. And Miss Stacy explains everything so beautifully. We have to write compositions on our field afternoons and I write the best ones."

"It's very vain of you to say so then. You'd better let your teacher say it."

"But she *did* say it, Marilla. And indeed I'm not vain about it. How can I be, when I'm such a dunce at geometry? Although I'm really beginning to see through it a little, too. Miss Stacy makes it so clear. Still, I'll never be good at it and I assure you it is a humbling reflection. But I love writing compositions. Mostly Miss Stacy lets us choose our own subjects; but next week we are to write a composition on some remarkable person. It's hard to choose among so many remarkable people who have lived. Mustn't it be splendid to be remarkable and have compositions written about you after you're dead? Oh, I would dearly love to be remarkable. I think when I grow up I'll be a trained nurse[4] and go with the Red Crosses[5] to the field of battle as a messenger of mercy. That is, if I don't go out as a foreign missionary. That would be very romantic, but one would have to be very good to be a missionary, and that would be a stumbling-block. We have physical culture exercises every day, too. They make you graceful and promote digestion."

"Promote fiddlesticks!" said Marilla, who honestly thought it was all nonsense.

But all the field afternoons and recitation Fridays and physical culture contortions paled before a project which Miss Stacy brought forward in November. This was that the scholars of Avonlea school should get up a concert and hold it in the hall on Christmas night, for the laudable purpose of helping to pay for a schoolhouse flag.[6]

---

4. Nursing had become a profession open to respectable young women in the 1880s, thanks partly to Florence Nightingale's work during the Crimean War (1854–56). Since 1873, training had been available in the United States, and the first nursing school in Canada opened in 1874.

5. In 1864 Henri Dunant in Switzerland instituted an international relief force, symbolized by the red cross of the Swiss flag.

6. The British Union Jack (not the Red Ensign) flew over the Cavendish (and Avonlea) school as the official Canadian flag; in 1965 Canada adopted its own maple leaf flag. After her first viewing of the 1919 *AGG* film by Realart, an incensed LMM wrote Feb. 22, 1920:

The pupils one and all taking graciously to this plan, the preparations for a programme were begun at once. And of all the excited performers-elect none was so excited as Anne Shirley, who threw herself into the undertaking heart and soul, hampered as she was by Marilla's disapproval. Marilla thought it all rank foolishness.

"It's just filling your heads up with nonsense and taking time that ought to be put on your lessons," she grumbled. "I don't approve of children's getting up concerts and racing about to practices. It makes them vain and forward and fond of gadding."

"But think of the worthy object," pleaded Anne. "A flag will cultivate a spirit of patriotism, Marilla."

"Fudge! There's precious little patriotism in the thoughts of any of you. All you want is a good time."

"Well, when you can combine patriotism and fun, isn't it all right? Of course it's real nice to be getting up a concert. We're going to have six choruses and Diana is to sing a solo. I'm in two dialogues— 'The Society for the Suppression of Gossip' and 'The Fairy Queen.'[7] The boys are going to have a dialogue, too. And I'm to have two recitations, Marilla. I just tremble when I think of it, but it's a nice thrilly kind of tremble. And we're to have a tableau at the last— 'Faith, Hope and Charity.'[8] Diana and Ruby and I are to be in it, all draped in white with flowing hair. I'm to be Hope, with my hands clasped—so—and my eyes uplifted. I'm going to practise my recitations in the garret. Don't be alarmed if you hear me groaning. I have to groan heartrendingly in one of them, and it's really hard to get up a good artistic groan, Marilla. Josie Pye is sulky because she didn't get the part she wanted in the dialogue. She wanted to be the fairy queen. That would have been ridiculous, for who ever heard of a fairy queen as fat as Josie? Fairy queens must be slender. Jane Andrews is to be the queen and I am to be one of her maids of honour. Josie says she thinks a red-haired fairy is just as ridiculous as a fat one, but I do not let myself mind what Josie says. I'm to have a wreath of white roses on my hair and Ruby Gillis is going to lend me her slippers[9] because I haven't any of my own. It's necessary for

"A skunk and an American flag were introduced—both equally unknown in P.E. Island. I could have shrieked with rage over the latter." *SJ2* 373.

7. The first is a farcical dialogue appearing in many school readers, making fun of women's meetings. LMM remembered appearing as "Miss Wise" in this piece at school. See *SJ2* 43. "The Fairy Queen" is based on a ballad collected by Bishop Percy in *Reliques of Ancient English Poetry* (1765). LMM remembered playing the queen in her schooldays. See NCE 290.

8. "And now abideth faith, hope, charity, these three: but the greatest of these is charity." *Holy Bible*, I Corinthians 13.13. Participants posed in postures appropriate for the topic, as if they were part of a picture. LMM wrote of a comparable concert in childhood. See NCE 290.

9. Shoes for indoors. Most children went to school barefoot in spring and summer, but wore boots in the winter. LMM complained that her grandmother made her wear shoes in the spring and summer: "I was never allowed to 'go barefoot' to school, and as all the other

fairies to have slippers, you know. You couldn't imagine a fairy wearing boots, could you? Especially with copper toes?[1] We are going to
decorate the hall with creeping spruce and fir mottoes[2] with pink
tissue-paper roses in them. And we are all to march in two by two
after the audience is seated, while Emma White plays a march on
the organ.[3] Oh, Marilla, I know you are not so enthusiastic about it
as I am, but don't you hope your little Anne will distinguish herself?"

"All I hope is that you'll behave yourself. I'll be heartily glad when
all this fuss is over and you'll be able to settle down. You are simply
good for nothing just now with your head stuffed full of dialogues
and groans and tableaus. As for your tongue, it's a marvel it's not
clean worn out."

Anne sighed and betook herself to the back yard, over which a
young new moon was shining through the leafless poplar boughs
from an apple-green western sky, and where Matthew was splitting
wood. Anne perched herself on a block and talked the concert over
with him, sure of an appreciative and sympathetic listener in this
instance at least.

"Well now, I reckon it's going to be a pretty good concert. And I
expect you'll do your part fine," he said, smiling down into her eager,
vivacious little face. Anne smiled back at him. Those two were the
best of friends and Matthew thanked his stars many a time and oft
that he had nothing to do with bringing her up. That was Marilla's
exclusive duty; if it had been his he would have been worried over
frequent conflicts between inclination and said duty. As it was, he
was free to "spoil Anne"—Marilla's phrasing—as much as he liked.
But it was not such a bad arrangement after all; a little "appreciation"
sometimes does quite as much good as all the conscientious "bringing up" in the world.

# Chapter XXV

## MATTHEW INSISTS ON PUFFED SLEEVES

MATTHEW was having a bad ten minutes of it. He had come into
the kitchen, in the twilight of a cold, gray December evening, and
had sat down in the wood-box corner[1] to take off his heavy boots,

---

children went so I felt keenly that this was a humiliating difference between them and
me. I wanted to be 'like the rest.' " *SJ1* 377 (January 7, 1910).
1. Reinforcement for sturdy boots.
2. Ground cover vines that can be twisted into wreaths and script.
3. A musical instrument worked by pumping foot pedals while playing on the keyboard. Small
organs were very popular in LMM's childhood, and she learned to play one.
1. In the kitchen, beyond the stove, to hold wood for the stove. The box would be big enough
to hide Matthew from view.

unconscious of the fact that Anne and a bevy of her schoolmates were having a practice of "The Fairy Queen" in the sitting-room. Presently they came trooping through the hall and out into the kitchen, laughing and chattering gaily. They did not see Matthew, who shrank bashfully back into the shadows beyond the wood-box with a boot in one hand and a bootjack[2] in the other, and he watched them shyly for the aforesaid ten minutes as they put on caps and jackets and talked about the dialogue and the concert. Anne stood among them, bright-eyed and animated as they; but Matthew suddenly became conscious that there was something about her different from her mates. And what worried Matthew was that the difference impressed him as being something that should not exist. Anne had a brighter face, and bigger, starrier eyes, and more delicate features than the others; even shy, unobservant Matthew had learned to take note of these things; but the difference that disturbed him did not consist in any of these respects. Then in what did it consist?

Matthew was haunted by this question long after the girls had gone, arm in arm, down the long, hard-frozen lane and Anne had betaken herself to her books. He could not refer it to Marilla, who, he felt, would be quite sure to sniff scornfully and remark that the only difference she saw between Anne and the other girls was that they sometimes kept their tongues quiet while Anne never did. This, Matthew felt, would be no great help.

He had recourse to his pipe that evening to help him study it out, much to Marilla's disgust. After two hours of smoking and hard reflection Matthew arrived at a solution of his problem. Anne was not dressed like the other girls!

The more Matthew thought about the matter the more he was convinced that Anne never had been dressed like the other girls—never since she had come to Green Gables. Marilla kept her clothed in plain, dark dresses, all made after the same unvarying pattern. If Matthew knew there was such a thing as fashion in dress it is as much as he did; but he was quite sure that Anne's sleeves did not look at all like the sleeves the other girls wore. He recalled the cluster of little girls he had seen around her that evening—all gay in waists of red and blue and pink and white—and he wondered why Marilla always kept her so plainly and soberly gowned.

Of course, it must be all right. Marilla knew best and Marilla was bringing her up. Probably some wise, inscrutable motive was to be served thereby. But surely it would do no harm to let the child have one pretty dress—something like Diana Barry always wore. Matthew decided that he would give her one; that surely could not be objected

2. A scoop-shaped tool for helping slide boots on and off.

to as an unwarranted putting in of his oar. Christmas was only a fortnight off. A nice new dress would be the very thing for a present. Matthew, with a sigh of satisfaction, put away his pipe and went to bed, while Marilla opened all the doors and aired the house.

The very next evening Matthew betook himself to Carmody to buy the dress, determined to get the worst over and have done with it. It would be, he felt assured, no trifling ordeal. There were some things Matthew could buy and prove himself no mean bargainer; but he knew he would be at the mercy of shopkeepers when it came to buying a girl's dress.

After much cogitation Matthew resolved to go to Samuel Lawson's store instead of William Blair's. To be sure, the Cuthberts always had gone to William Blair's; it was almost as much a matter of conscience with them as to attend the Presbyterian church and vote Conservative. But William Blair's two daughters frequently waited on customers there and Matthew held them in absolute dread. He could contrive to deal with them when he knew exactly what he wanted and could point it out; but in such a matter as this, requiring explanation and consultation, Matthew felt that he must be sure of a man behind the counter. So he would go to Lawson's, where Samuel or his son would wait on him.

Alas! Matthew did not know that Samuel, in the recent expansion of his business, had set up a lady clerk also; she was a niece of his wife's and a very dashing young person indeed, with a huge, drooping pompadour, big, rolling brown eyes, and a most extensive and bewildering smile. She was dressed with exceeding smartness and wore several bangle bracelets that glittered and rattled and tinkled with every movement of her hands. Matthew was covered with confusion at finding her there at all; and those bangles completely wrecked his wits at one fell swoop.

"What can I do for you this evening, Mr. Cuthbert?" Miss Lucilla Harris inquired, briskly and ingratiatingly, tapping the counter with both hands.

"Have you any—any—any—well now, say any garden rakes?" stammered Matthew.

Miss Harris looked somewhat surprised, as well she might, to hear a man inquiring for garden rakes in the middle of December.

"I believe we have one or two left over," she said, "but they're upstairs in the lumber-room. I'll go and see."

During her absence Matthew collected his scattered senses for another effort.

When Miss Harris returned with the rake and cheerfully inquired: "Anything else to-night, Mr. Cuthbert?" Matthew took his courage in both hands and replied: "Well now, since you suggest it, I might as well—take—that is—look at—buy some—some hayseed."

Miss Harris had heard Matthew Cuthbert called odd. She now concluded that he was entirely crazy.

"We only keep hayseed in the spring," she explained loftily. "We've none on hand just now."

"Oh, certainly—certainly—just as you say," stammered unhappy Matthew, seizing the rake and making for the door. At the threshold he recollected that he had not paid for it and he turned miserably back. While Miss Harris was counting out his change he rallied his powers for a final desperate attempt.

"Well now—if it isn't too much trouble—I might as well—that is—I'd like to look at—at—some sugar."

"White or brown?" queried Miss Harris patiently.

"Oh—well now—brown," said Matthew feebly.

"There's a barrel of it over there," said Miss Harris, shaking her bangles at it. "It's the only kind we have."

"I'll—I'll take twenty pounds of it," said Matthew, with beads of perspiration standing on his forehead.

Matthew had driven half-way home before he was his own man again. It had been a gruesome experience, but it served him right, he thought, for committing the heresy of going to a strange store. When he reached home he hid the rake in the tool-house, but the sugar he carried in to Marilla.

"Brown sugar!" exclaimed Marilla. "Whatever possessed you to get so much? You know I never use it except for the hired man's porridge or black fruit-cake.[3] Jerry's gone and I've made my cake long ago. It's not good sugar, either—it's coarse and dark—William Blair doesn't usually keep sugar like that."

"I—I thought it might come in handy sometime," said Matthew, making good his escape.

When Matthew came to think the matter over he decided that a woman was required to cope with the situation. Marilla was out of the question. Matthew felt sure she would throw cold water on his project at once. Remained only Mrs. Lynde; for of no other woman in Avonlea would Matthew have dared to ask advice. To Mrs. Lynde he went accordingly, and that good lady promptly took the matter out of the harassed man's hands.

"Pick out a dress[4] for you to give Anne? To be sure I will. I'm going to Carmody to-morrow and I'll attend to it. Have you something particular in mind? No? Well, I'll just go by my own judgment then. I believe a nice rich brown would just suit Anne, and William Blair

---

3. Cooked oatmeal; and cake dark because of the brown sugar and molasses.
4. That is, pick out dress material: ready-made dresses would not be available in the local store.

has some new gloria[5] in that's real pretty. Perhaps you'd like me to make it up for her, too, seeing that if Marilla was to make it Anne would probably get wind of it before the time and spoil the surprise? Well, I'll do it. No, it isn't a mite of trouble. I like sewing. I'll make it to fit my niece, Jenny Gillis, for she and Anne are as like as two peas as far as figure goes."

"Well now, I'm much obliged," said Matthew, "and—and—I dunno—but I'd like—I think they make the sleeves different nowadays to what they used to be. If it wouldn't be asking too much I—I'd like them made in the new way."

"Puffs? Of course. You needn't worry a speck more about it, Matthew. I'll make it up in the very latest fashion," said Mrs. Lynde. To herself she added when Matthew had gone:

"It'll be a real satisfaction to see that poor child wearing something decent for once. The way Marilla dresses her is positively ridiculous, that's what, and I've ached to tell her so plainly a dozen times. I've held my tongue though, for I can see Marilla doesn't want advice and she thinks she knows more about bringing children up than I do for all she's an old maid. But that's always the way. Folks that has brought up children know that there's no hard and fast method in the world that'll suit every child. But them as never have think it's all as plain and easy as Rule of Three—just set your three terms down so fashion,[6] and the sum'll work out correct. But flesh and blood don't come under the head of arithmetic and that's where Marilla Cuthbert makes her mistake. I suppose she's trying to cultivate a spirit of humility in Anne by dressing her as she does; but it's more likely to cultivate envy and discontent. I'm sure the child must feel the difference between her clothes and the other girls'. But to think of Matthew taking notice of it! That man is waking up after being asleep for over sixty years."

Marilla knew all the following fortnight that Matthew had something on his mind, but what it was she could not guess, until Christmas Eve, when Mrs. Lynde brought up the new dress. Marilla behaved pretty well on the whole, although it is very likely she distrusted Mrs. Lynde's diplomatic explanation that she had made the dress because Matthew was afraid Anne would find out about it too soon if Marilla made it.

"So this is what Matthew has been looking so mysterious over and grinning about to himself for two weeks, is it?" she said a little stiffly but tolerantly. "I knew he was up to some foolishness. Well, I must

---

5. A glossy, light but durable cloth, sometimes used for bridal gowns, and commonly used for parasols. The term "gloria" is still used in the umbrella trade.
6. In just such a way. "Rule of Three": a method of computation, involving three knowns from which an unknown quantity is found. In the formula, "A is to B as C is to X," the fourth element (X) is deducible from the pattern of the other three.

say I don't think Anne needed any more dresses. I made her three good, warm, serviceable ones this fall, and anything more is sheer extravagance. There's enough material in those sleeves alone to make a waist, I declare there is. You'll just pamper Anne's vanity, Matthew, and she's as vain as a peacock now. Well, I hope she'll be satisfied at last, for I know she's been hankering after those silly sleeves ever since they came in, although she never said a word after the first. The puffs have been getting bigger and more ridiculous right along; they're as big as balloons now. Next year anybody who wears them will have to go through a door sideways."

Christmas morning broke on a beautiful white world. It had been a very mild December and people had looked forward to a green Christmas; but just enough snow fell softly in the night to transfigure Avonlea. Anne peeped out from her frosted gable window with delighted eyes. The firs in the Haunted Wood were all feathery and wonderful; the birches and wild cherry-trees were outlined in pearl; the ploughed fields were stretches of snowy dimples; and there was a crisp tang in the air that was glorious. Anne ran down-stairs singing until her voice reechoed through Green Gables.

"Merry Christmas, Marilla! Merry Christmas, Matthew! Isn't it a lovely Christmas? I'm so glad it's white. Any other kind of Christmas doesn't seem real, does it? I don't like green Christmases. They're *not* green—they're just nasty faded browns and grays. What makes people call them green? Why—why—Matthew, is that for me? Oh, Matthew!"

Matthew had sheepishly unfolded the dress from its paper swathings and held it out with a deprecatory glance at Marilla, who feigned to be contemptuously filling the teapot, but nevertheless watched the scene out of the corner of her eye with a rather interested air.

Anne took the dress and looked at it in reverent silence. Oh, how pretty it was—a lovely soft brown gloria with all the gloss of silk; a skirt with dainty frills and shirrings; a waist elaborately pin-tucked in the most fashionable way, with a little ruffle of filmy lace at the neck.[7] But the sleeves—they were the crowning glory! Long elbow cuffs, and above them two beautiful puffs divided by rows of shirring and bows of brown silk ribbon.

"That's a Christmas present for you, Anne," said Matthew shyly. "Why—why—Anne, don't you like it? Well now—well now."

For Anne's eyes had suddenly filled with tears.

"*Like* it! Oh, Matthew!" Anne laid the dress over a chair and clasped her hands. "Matthew, it's perfectly exquisite. Oh, I can never

---

7. In Anne's dress the cloth is shirred by tightening threads run through it in parallel lines; pin-tucked by fine parallel pleats; and ruffled with frills of closely gathered trimming.

thank you enough. Look at those sleeves! Oh, it seems to me this must be a happy dream."

"Well, well, let us have breakfast," interrupted Marilla. "I must say, Anne, I don't think you needed the dress; but since Matthew has got it for you, see that you take good care of it. There's a hair ribbon Mrs. Lynde left for you. It's brown, to match the dress. Come now, sit in."

"I don't see how I'm going to eat breakfast," said Anne rapturously. "Breakfast seems so commonplace at such an exciting moment. I'd rather feast my eyes on that dress. I'm so glad that puffed sleeves are still fashionable. It did seem to me that I'd never get over it if they went out before I had a dress with them. I'd never have felt quite satisfied, you see. It was lovely of Mrs. Lynde to give me the ribbon, too. I feel that I ought to be a very good girl indeed. It's at times like this I'm sorry I'm not a model little girl; and I always resolve that I will be in future. But somehow it's hard to carry out your resolutions when irresistible temptations come. Still, I really will make an extra effort after this."

When the commonplace breakfast was over Diana appeared, crossing the white log bridge in the hollow, a gay little figure in her crimson ulster.[8] Anne flew down the slope to meet her.

"Merry Christmas, Diana! And oh, it's a wonderful Christmas. I've something splendid to show you. Matthew has given me the loveliest dress, with *such* sleeves. I couldn't even imagine any nicer."

"I've got something more for you," said Diana breathlessly. "Here—this box. Aunt Josephine sent us out a big box with ever so many things in it—and this is for you. I'd have brought it over last night, but it didn't come until after dark, and I never feel very comfortable coming through the Haunted Wood in the dark now."

Anne opened the box and peeped in. First a card with "For the Anne-girl and Merry Christmas," written on it; and then, a pair of the daintiest little kid slippers, with beaded toes and satin bows and glistening buckles.

"Oh," said Anne, "Diana, this is too much. I must be dreaming."

"*I* call it providential," said Diana. "You won't have to borrow Ruby's slippers now, and that's a blessing, for they're two sizes too big for you, and it would be awful to hear a fairy shuffling. Josie Pye would be delighted. Mind you, Rob Wright went home with Gertie Pye from the practice night before last. Did you ever hear anything equal to that?"

All the Avonlea scholars were in a fever of excitement that day, for the hall had to be decorated and a last grand rehearsal held.

The concert came off in the evening and was a pronounced suc-

8. Long waterproof coat named for a county in Ireland.

cess. The little hall was crowded; all the performers did excellently well, but Anne was the bright particular star[9] of the occasion, as even envy, in the shape of Josie Pye, dared not deny.

"Oh, hasn't it been a brilliant evening?" sighed Anne, when it was all over and she and Diana were walking home together under a dark, starry sky.

"Everything went off very well," said Diana practically. "I guess we must have made as much as ten dollars. Mind you, Mr. Allan is going to send an account of it to the Charlottetown papers."

"Oh, Diana, will we really see our names in print? It makes me thrill to think of it. Your solo was perfectly elegant, Diana. I felt prouder than you did when it was encored. I just said to myself, 'It is my dear bosom friend who is so honoured.' "

"Well, your recitations just brought down the house, Anne. That sad one was simply splendid."

"Oh, I was so nervous, Diana. When Mr. Allan called out my name I really cannot tell how I ever got up on that platform. I felt as if a million eyes were looking at me and through me, and for one dreadful moment I was sure I couldn't begin at all. Then I thought of my lovely puffed sleeves and took courage. I knew that I must live up to those sleeves, Diana. So I started in, and my voice seemed to be coming from ever so far away. I just felt like a parrot. It's providential that I practised those recitations so often up in the garret, or I'd never have been able to get through. Did I groan all right?"

"Yes, indeed, you groaned lovely," assured Diana.

"I saw old Mrs. Sloane wiping away tears when I sat down. It was splendid to think I had touched somebody's heart. It's so romantic to take part in a concert, isn't it? Oh, it's been a very memorable occasion indeed."

"Wasn't the boys' dialogue fine?" said Diana. "Gilbert Blythe was just splendid. Anne, I do think it's awful mean the way you treat Gil. Wait till I tell you. When you ran off the platform after the fairy dialogue one of your roses fell out of your hair. I saw Gil pick it up and put it in his breast-pocket.[1] There now. You're so romantic that I'm sure you ought to be pleased at that."

"It's nothing to me what that person does," said Anne loftily. "I simply never waste a thought on him, Diana."

That night Marilla and Matthew, who had been out to a concert for the first time in twenty years, sat for awhile by the kitchen fire after Anne had gone to bed.

---

9. Outstanding person. " 'Twere' all one / That I should love a bright particular star / And think to wed it, he is so above me." Shakespeare, *All's Well That Ends Well* 1.1.

1. Gilbert's jacket would be a Norfolk style, with two patch pockets, with another for his watch or wallet, higher up and likely inside.

"Well now, I guess our Anne did as well as any of them," said Matthew proudly.

"Yes, she did," admitted Marilla. "She's a bright child, Matthew. And she looked real nice, too. I've been kind of opposed to this concert scheme, but I suppose there's no real harm in it after all. Anyhow, I was proud of Anne to-night, although I'm not going to tell her so."

"Well now, I was proud of her and I did tell her so 'fore she went up-stairs," said Matthew. "We must see what we can do for her some of these days, Marilla. I guess she'll need something more than Avonlea school by and by."

"There's time enough to think of that," said Marilla. "She's only thirteen in March. Though to-night it struck me she was growing quite a big girl. Mrs. Lynde made that dress a mite too long, and it makes Anne look so tall. She's quick to learn and I guess the best thing we can do for her will be to send her to Queen's after a spell. But nothing need be said about that for a year or two yet."

"Well now, it'll do no harm to be thinking it over off and on," said Matthew. "Things like that are all the better for lots of thinking over."

# Chapter XXVI

### THE STORY CLUB IS FORMED

JUNIOR Avonlea found it hard to settle down to humdrum existence again. To Anne in particular things seemed fearfully flat, stale, and unprofitable[1] after the goblet of excitement she had been sipping for weeks. Could she go back to the former quiet pleasures of those far-away days before the concert? At first, as she told Diana, she did not really think she could.

"I'm positively certain, Diana, that life can never be quite the same again as it was in those olden days," she said mournfully, as if referring to a period of at least fifty years back. "Perhaps after awhile I'll get used to it, but I'm afraid concerts spoil people for every-day life. I suppose that is why Marilla disapproves of them. Marilla is such a sensible woman. It must be a great deal better to be sensible; but still, I don't believe I'd really want to be a sensible person, because they are so unromantic. Mrs. Lynde says there is no danger of my ever being one, but you can never tell. I feel just now that I may grow up to be sensible yet. But perhaps that is only because I'm tired.

---

1. Adapted from "How weary, stale, flat, and unprofitable / Seem to me all the uses of this world!" Shakespeare, *Hamlet* 1.2.

I simply couldn't sleep last night for ever so long. I just lay awake and imagined the concert over and over again. That's one splendid thing about such affairs—it's so lovely to look back to them."

Eventually, however, Avonlea school slipped back into its old groove and took up its old interests. To be sure, the concert left traces. Ruby Gillis and Emma White, who had quarrelled over a point of precedence in their platform seats, no longer sat at the same desk, and a promising friendship of three years was broken up. Josie Pye and Julia Bell did not "speak" for three months, because Josie Pye had told Bessie Wright that Julia Bell's bow when she got up to recite made her think of a chicken jerking its head, and Bessie told Julia. None of the Sloanes would have any dealings with the Bells, because the Bells had declared that the Sloanes had too much to do in the programme, and the Sloanes had retorted that the Bells were not capable of doing the little they had to do properly. Finally, Charlie Sloane fought Moody Spurgeon MacPherson, because Moody Spurgeon had said that Anne Shirley put on airs about her recitations, and Moody Spurgeon was "licked"; consequently Moody Spurgeon's sister, Ella May, would not "speak" to Anne Shirley all the rest of the winter. With the exception of these trifling frictions, work in Miss Stacy's little kingdom went on with regularity and smoothness.

The winter weeks slipped by. It was an unusually mild winter, with so little snow that Anne and Diana could go to school nearly every day by way of the Birch Path. On Anne's birthday they were tripping lightly down it, keeping eyes and ears alert amid all their chatter, for Miss Stacy had told them that they must soon write a composition on "A Winter's Walk in the Woods,"[2] and it behooved them to be observant.

"Just think, Diana, I'm thirteen years old to-day,"[3] remarked Anne in an awed voice. "I can scarcely realize that I'm in my teens. When I woke this morning it seemed to me that everything must be different. You've been thirteen for a month, so I suppose it doesn't seem such a novelty to you as it does to me. It makes life seem so much more interesting. In two more years I'll be really grown up. It's a great comfort to think that I'll be able to use big words then without being laughed at."

2. In 1911, LMM published a four-part study: "Spring in the Woods," "The Woods in Summer," "The Woods in Autumn," and "The Woods in Winter" in *Canadian Magazine*. In her copy of Whittier, purchased in 1896, passages on the woods and nature were heavily underlined.
3. Fans of LMM have offered theories about the year Anne was born, but there is disagreement. See Collins and Eriksson, *The Anne of Green Gables Treasury* (1991) and Careless, "The Highjacking of 'Anne,' " *CCL* 67 (1992): 48–56.

"Ruby Gillis says she means to have a beau[4] as soon as she's fifteen," said Diana.

"Ruby Gillis thinks of nothing but beaus," said Anne disdainfully. "She's actually delighted when any one writes her name up in a take-notice for all she pretends to be so mad. But I'm afraid that is an uncharitable speech. Mrs. Allan says we should never make uncharitable speeches; but they do slip out so often before you think, don't they? I simply can't talk about Josie Pye without making an uncharitable speech, so I never mention her at all. You may have noticed that. I'm trying to be as much like Mrs. Allan as I possibly can, for I think she's perfect. Mr. Allan thinks so too. Mrs. Lynde says he just worships the ground she treads on and she doesn't really think it right for a minister to set his affections so much on a mortal being. But then, Diana, even ministers are human and have their besetting sins just like everybody else. I had such an interesting talk with Mrs. Allan about besetting sins[5] last Sunday afternoon. There are just a few things it's proper to talk about on Sundays and that is one of them. My besetting sin is imagining too much and forgetting my duties. I'm striving very hard to overcome it and now that I'm really thirteen perhaps I'll get on better."

"In four more years we'll be able to put our hair up,"[6] said Diana. "Alice Bell is only sixteen and she is wearing hers up, but I think that's ridiculous. I shall wait until I'm seventeen."

"If I had Alice Bell's crooked nose," said Anne decidedly, "I wouldn't—but there! I won't say what I was going to because it was extremely uncharitable. Besides, I was comparing it with my own nose and that's vanity. I'm afraid I think too much about my nose ever since I heard that compliment about it long ago. It really is a great comfort to me. Oh, Diana, look, there's a rabbit. That's something to remember for our woods composition. I really think the woods are just as lovely in winter as in summer. They're so white and still, as if they were asleep and dreaming pretty dreams."

"I won't mind writing that composition when its time comes," sighed Diana. "I can manage to write about the woods, but the one we're to hand in Monday is terrible. The idea of Miss Stacy telling us to write a story out of our own heads!"

"Why, it's as easy as wink," said Anne.

"It's easy for you because you have an imagination," retorted Diana, "but what would you do if you had been born without one? I suppose you have your composition all done?"

4. A boyfriend (slang): from the French "*beau*," a handsome male.
5. "Let us lay aside every weight, and the sin which doth so easily beset us." *Holy Bible*, Hebrews 12.1.
6. Young women marked the time of maturation by changing from long unbound or pigtailed hair into a grownup hair style: hair swept up on the head or pulled back into the shape of a bun.

Anne nodded, trying hard not to look virtuously complacent and failing miserably.

"I wrote it last Monday evening. It's called 'The Jealous Rival; or, in Death Not Divided.'[7] I read it to Marilla and she said it was stuff and nonsense.[8] Then I read it to Matthew and he said it was fine. That is the kind of critic I like. It's a sad, sweet story. I just cried like a child while I was writing it. It's about two beautiful maidens called Cordelia Montmorency[9] and Geraldine Seymour who lived in the same village and were devotedly attached to each other. Cordelia was a regal brunette with a coronet of midnight hair and duskly flashing eyes. Geraldine was a queenly blonde with hair like spun gold and velvety purple eyes."[1]

"I never saw anybody with purple eyes," said Diana dubiously.

"Neither did I. I just imagined them. I wanted something out of the common. Geraldine had an alabaster brow, too. I've found out what an alabaster brow is. That is one of the advantages of being thirteen. You know so much more than you did when you were only twelve."

"Well, what became of Cordelia and Geraldine?" asked Diana, who was beginning to feel rather interested in their fate.

"They grew in beauty side by side until they were sixteen. Then Bertram DeVere came to their native village and fell in love with the fair Geraldine.[2] He saved her life when her horse ran away with her in a carriage, and she fainted in his arms and he carried her home three miles; because, you understand, the carriage was all smashed up. I found it rather hard to imagine the proposal because I had no experience to go by. I asked Ruby Gillis if she knew anything about how men proposed because I thought she'd likely be an authority on the subject, having so many sisters married. Ruby told me she was hid in the hall pantry when Malcolm Andrews proposed to her sister Susan. She said Malcolm told Susan that his dad had given him the farm in his own name and then said, 'What do you say, darling pet, if we get hitched this fall?' And Susan said, 'Yes—no—I don't know— let me see,'—and there they were, engaged as quick as that. But I didn't think that sort of a proposal was a very romantic one, so in the end I had to imagine it out as well as I could. I made it very flowery and poetical and Bertram went on his knees, although Ruby

7. "Saul and Jonathan were lovely and pleasant in their lives, and in death they were not divided." *Holy Bible*, II Samuel 1.23.

8. Valueless matter (idiom).

9. In Canadian history, Montmorency suggests Henri II, Duc de Montmorency, Viceroy of New France, 1620–25, for whom Montmorency Falls near Quebec are named.

1. "Velvety purple" is a cliché used often in seed catalogues for "eyes" of flowers such as iris or daylilies.

2. The names Bertram and Geraldine echo Elizabeth Barrett Browning's "Lady Geraldine's Courtship" (1844), the poem that attracted Robert Browning to the author.

Gillis says it isn't done nowadays. Geraldine accepted him in a speech a page long. I can tell you I took a lot of trouble with that speech. I rewrote it five times and I look upon it as my masterpiece. Bertram gave her a diamond ring and a ruby necklace and told her they would go to Europe for a wedding tour, for he was immensely wealthy. But then, alas, shadows began to darken over their path. Cordelia was secretly in love with Bertram herself and when Geraldine told her about the engagement she was simply furious, especially when she saw the necklace and the diamond ring. All her affection for Geraldine turned to bitter hate and she vowed that she should never marry Bertram. But she pretended to be Geraldine's friend the same as ever. One evening they were standing on the bridge over a rushing turbulent stream and Cordelia, thinking they were alone, pushed Geraldine over the brink with a wild, mocking, 'Ha, ha, ha.' But Bertram saw it all and he at once plunged into the current, exclaiming, 'I will save thee, my peerless Geraldine.' But alas, he had forgotten he couldn't swim, and they were both drowned, clasped in each other's arms. Their bodies were washed ashore soon afterwards. They were buried in the one grave and their funeral was most imposing, Diana. It's so much more romantic to end a story up with a funeral than a wedding. As for Cordelia, she went insane with remorse and was shut up in a lunatic asylum. I thought that was a poetical retribution for her crime."

"How perfectly lovely!" sighed Diana, who belonged to Matthew's school of critics. "I don't see how you can make up such thrilling things out of your own head, Anne. I wish my imagination was as good as yours."

"It would be if you'd only cultivate it," said Anne cheeringly. "I've just thought of a plan, Diana. Let you and I have a story club[3] all our own and write stories for practice. I'll help you along until you can do them by yourself. You ought to cultivate your imagination, you know. Miss Stacy says so. Only we must take the right way. I told her about the Haunted Wood, but she said we went the wrong way about it in that."

This was how the story club came into existence. It was limited to Diana and Anne at first, but soon it was extended to include Jane Andrews and Ruby Gillis and one or two others who felt that their imaginations needed cultivating. No boys were allowed in it— although Ruby Gillis opined that their admission would make it more exciting—and each member had to produce one story a week.

"It's extremely interesting," Anne told Marilla. "Each girl has to read her story out loud and then we talk it over. We are going to keep them all sacredly and have them to read to our descendants.

---

3. LMM's journal reports the source of the Story Club. See *SJ2* 43.

We each write under a nom-de-plume.[4] Mine is Rosamond Mont-morency. All the girls do pretty well. Ruby Gillis is rather sentimen-tal. She puts too much love-making into her stories and you know too much is worse than too little. Jane never puts any because she says it makes her feel so silly when she has to read it out loud. Jane's stories are extremely sensible. Then Diana puts too many murders into hers. She says most of the time she doesn't know what to do with the people so she kills them off to get rid of them. I mostly always have to tell them what to write about, but that isn't hard for I've millions of ideas."

"I think this story-writing business is the foolishest yet," scoffed Marilla. "You'll get a pack of nonsense into your heads and waste time that should be put on your lessons. Reading stories is bad enough but writing them is worse."[5]

"But we're so careful to put a moral into them all, Marilla," explained Anne. "I insist upon that. All the good people are rewarded and all the bad ones are suitably punished. I'm sure that must have a wholesome effect. The moral is the great thing. Mr. Allan says so. I read one of my stories to him and Mrs. Allan and they both agreed that the moral was excellent. Only they laughed in the wrong places. I like it better when people cry. Jane and Ruby almost always cry when I come to the pathetic parts. Diana wrote her Aunt Josephine about our club and her Aunt Josephine wrote back that we were to send her some of our stories. So we copied out four of our very best and sent them. Miss Josephine Barry wrote back that she had never read anything so amusing in her life. That kind of puzzled us because the stories were all very pathetic and almost everybody died. But I'm glad Miss Barry liked them. It shows our club is doing some good in the world.[6] Mrs. Allan says that ought to be our object in everything. I do really try to make it my object but I forget so often when I'm having fun. I hope I shall be a little like Mrs. Allan when I grow up. Do you think there is any prospect of it, Marilla?"

"I shouldn't say there was a great deal," was Marilla's encouraging answer. "I'm sure Mrs. Allan was never such a silly, forgetful little girl as you are."

"No; but she wasn't always so good as she is now either," said Anne seriously. "She told me so herself—that is, she said she was a dread-ful mischief when she was a girl and was always getting into scrapes. I felt so encouraged when I heard that. Is it very wicked of me, Marilla, to feel encouraged when I hear that other people have been bad and mischievous? Mrs. Lynde says it is. Mrs. Lynde says she always feels shocked when she hears of any one ever having been

4. Writer's pseudonym.
5. The Puritan view of fiction as lies, useless, and a usurpation of the Creator's function.
6. Anne justifies writing on moral grounds.

naughty, no matter how small they were. Mrs. Lynde says she once heard a minister confess that when he was a boy he stole a strawberry tart out of his aunt's pantry and she never had any respect for that minister again. Now, I wouldn't have felt that way. I'd have thought that it was real noble of him to confess it, and I'd have thought what an encouraging thing it would be for small boys nowadays who do naughty things and are sorry for them to know that perhaps they may grow up to be ministers in spite of it. That's how I'd feel, Marilla."

"The way I feel at present, Anne," said Marilla, "is that it's high time you had those dishes washed. You've taken half an hour longer than you should with all your chattering. Learn to work first and talk afterwards."

# Chapter XXVII

## VANITY AND VEXATION OF SPIRIT[1]

MARILLA, walking home one late April evening from an Aid meeting, realized that the winter was over and gone with the thrill of delight that spring never fails to bring to the oldest and saddest as well as to the youngest and merriest. Marilla was not given to subjective analysis of her thoughts and feelings. She probably imagined that she was thinking about the Aids and their missionary box and the new carpet for the vestry-room,[2] but under these reflections was a harmonious consciousness of red fields smoking into pale-purply mists in the declining sun, of long, sharp-pointed fir shadows falling over the meadow beyond the brook, of still, crimson-budded maples around a mirror-like wood-pool, of a wakening in the world and a stir of hidden pulses under the gray sod. The spring was abroad in the land and Marilla's sober, middle-aged step was lighter and swifter because of its deep, primal gladness.

Her eyes dwelt affectionately on Green Gables, peering through its network of trees and reflecting the sunlight back from its windows in several little coruscations[3] of glory. Marilla, as she picked her steps along the damp lane, thought that it was really a satisfaction to know that she was going home to a briskly snapping wood fire and a table nicely spread for tea, instead of to the cold comfort of old Aid meeting evenings before Anne had come to Green Gables.

Consequently, when Marilla entered her kitchen and found the

1. "I have seen all the works that are done under the sun; and, behold, all is vanity and vexation of spirit." *Holy Bible*, Ecclesiastes 1.14.
2. Area of the church where vestments (church garments) are kept, where the minister dons his robes, and where some church session meetings are held.
3. Sparklings, flashings.

fire black out, with no sign of Anne anywhere, she felt justly disappointed and irritated. She had told Anne to be sure and have tea ready at five o'clock, but now she must hurry to take off her second-best dress and prepare the meal herself against Matthew's return from ploughing.

"I'll settle Miss Anne when she comes home," said Marilla grimly, as she shaved up kindlings with a carving knife and more vim[4] than was strictly necessary. Matthew had come in and was waiting patiently for his tea in his corner. "She's gadding off somewhere with Diana, writing stories or practising dialogues or some such tomfoolery, and never thinking once about the time or her duties. She's just got to be pulled up short and sudden on this sort of thing. I don't care if Mrs. Allan does say she's the brightest and sweetest child she ever knew. She may be bright and sweet enough, but her head is full of nonsense and there's never any knowing what shape it'll break out in next. Just as soon as she grows out of one freak she takes up with another. But there! Here I am saying the very thing I was so riled with Rachel Lynde for saying at the Aid to-day. I was real glad when Mrs. Allan spoke up for Anne, for if she hadn't I know I'd have said something too sharp to Rachel before everybody. Anne's got plenty of faults, goodness knows, and far be it from me to deny it. But I'm bringing her up and not Rachel Lynde, who'd pick faults in the Angel Gabriel[5] himself if he lived in Avonlea. Just the same, Anne has no business to leave the house like this when I told her she was to stay home this afternoon and look after things. I must say, with all her faults, I never found her disobedient or untrustworthy before and I'm real sorry to find her so now."

"Well now, I dunno," said Matthew, who, being patient and wise and, above all, hungry, had deemed it best to let Marilla talk her wrath out unhindered, having learned by experience that she got through with whatever work was on hand much quicker if not delayed by untimely argument. "Perhaps you're judging her too hasty, Marilla. Don't call her untrustworthy until you're sure she has disobeyed you. Mebbe[6] it can all be explained—Anne's a great hand at explaining."

"She's not here when I told her to stay," retorted Marilla. "I reckon she'll find it hard to explain *that* to my satisfaction. Of course I knew you'd take her part, Matthew. But I'm bringing her up, not you."

It was dark when supper was ready, and still no sign of Anne,

4. Energy (considered a colloquialism in England, though not in the United States).
5. The Archangel who serves as God's messenger (*Holy Bible*, Daniel 8.16 and 9.21). In the New Testament, Gabriel appears as messenger to Zacharias (Luke 1.19) and to Mary (Luke 1.26), foretelling the birth of John and of Jesus. In John Milton's *Paradise Lost* (1607), Gabriel defeats Satan and stands guard over Paradise.
6. "Maybe"; "dunno": "don't know." Matthew uses a more colloquial pronunciation than Marilla.

coming hurriedly over the log bridge or up Lovers' Lane, breathless and repentant with a sense of neglected duties. Marilla washed and put away the dishes grimly. Then, wanting a candle to light her down cellar, she went up to the east gable for the one that generally stood on Anne's table. Lighting it, she turned around to see Anne herself lying on the bed, face downward among the pillows.

"Mercy on us," said astonished Marilla, "have you been asleep, Anne?"

"No," was the muffled reply.

"Are you sick then?" demanded Marilla anxiously, going over to the bed.

Anne cowered deeper into her pillows as if desirous of hiding herself for ever from mortal eyes.

"No. But please, Marilla, go away and don't look at me. I'm in the depths of despair and I don't care who gets head in class or writes the best composition or sings in the Sunday-school choir any more. Little things like that are of no importance now because I don't suppose I'll ever be able to go anywhere again. My career is closed. Please, Marilla, go away and don't look at me."

"Did any one ever hear the like?" the mystified Marilla wanted to know. "Anne Shirley, whatever is the matter with you? What have you done? Get right up this minute and tell me. This minute, I say. There now, what is it?"

Anne had slid to the floor in despairing obedience.

"Look at my hair, Marilla," she whispered.

Accordingly, Marilla lifted her candle and looked scrutinizingly at Anne's hair, flowing in heavy masses down her back. It certainly had a very strange appearance.

"Anne Shirley, what have you done to your hair? Why, it's *green*!"[7]

Green it might be called, if it were any earthly colour—a queer, dull, bronzy green, with streaks here and there of the original red to heighten the ghastly effect. Never in all her life had Marilla seen anything so grotesque as Anne's hair at that moment.

"Yes, it's green," moaned Anne. "I thought nothing could be as bad as red hair. But now I know it's ten times worse to have green hair. Oh, Marilla, you little know how utterly wretched I am."

"I little know how you got into this fix, but I mean to find out," said Marilla. "Come right down to the kitchen—it's too cold up here—and tell me just what you've done. I've been expecting something queer for some time. You haven't got into any scrape for over two months, and I was sure another one was due. Now, then, what did you do to your hair?"

---

7. Perhaps Anne's red hair takes dye in a peculiar way, or there may be traces of copper in Avonlea water (copper turns green in reaction to air), or the dye may be adulterated.

"I dyed it."

"Dyed it! Dyed your hair! Anne Shirley, didn't you know it was a wicked[8] thing to do?"

"Yes, I knew it was a little wicked," admitted Anne. "But I thought it was worth while to be a little wicked to get rid of red hair. I counted the cost, Marilla. Besides, I meant to be extra good in other ways to make up for it."

"Well," said Marilla sarcastically, "if I'd decided it was worth while to dye my hair I'd have dyed it a decent colour at least. I wouldn't have dyed it green."

"But I didn't mean to dye it green, Marilla," protested Anne deject-edly. "If I was wicked I meant to be wicked to some purpose. He said it would turn my hair a beautiful raven black—he positively assured me that it would. How could I doubt his word, Marilla? I know what it feels like to have your word doubted. And Mrs. Allan says we should never suspect any one of not telling us the truth unless we have proof that they're not. I have proof now—green hair is proof enough for anybody. But I hadn't then and I believed every word he said *implicitly*."

"Who said? Who are you talking about?"

"The pedlar that was here this afternoon. I bought the dye from him."

"Anne Shirley, how often have I told you never to let one of those Italians[9] in the house! I don't believe in encouraging them to come around at all."

"Oh, I didn't let him in the house. I remembered what you told me, and I went out, carefully shut the door, and looked at his things on the step. Besides, he wasn't an Italian—he was a German Jew.[1] He had a big box full of very interesting things and he told me he was working hard to make enough money to bring his wife and chil-dren out from Germany. He spoke so feelingly about them that it touched my heart. I wanted to buy something from him to help him in such a worthy object. Then all at once I saw the bottle of hair dye. The pedlar[2] said it was warranted to dye any hair a beautiful raven black and wouldn't wash off. In a trice I saw myself with beautiful raven black hair and the temptation was irresistible. But the price of the bottle was seventy-five cents[3] and I had only fifty cents left out

---

8. In the sense that religious dogma held that alteration (or ornamentation) of one's person is vain and deceitful, especially in a child.
9. For Marilla this can be a generic term for suspect dark-skinned people or foreigners.
1. European pogroms drove Jews into a wandering life.
2. In his pack this itinerant merchant would bring spools of thread, buttons, ribbons, spices. (American spelling: "peddler.")
3. One cent being a *child's* weekly expected church collection money, 75 cents was a con-siderable sum.

of my chicken money.[4] I think the pedlar had a very kind heart, for he said that, seeing it was me, he'd sell it for fifty cents and that was just giving it away. So I bought it, and as soon as he had gone I came up here and applied it with an old hair-brush as the directions said. I used up the whole bottle, and oh, Marilla, when I saw the dreadful colour it turned my hair I repented of being wicked, I can tell you. And I've been repenting ever since."

"Well, I hope you'll repent to good purpose," said Marilla severely, "and that you've got your eyes opened to where your vanity has led you, Anne. Goodness knows what's to be done. I suppose the first thing is to give your hair a good washing and see if that will do any good."

Accordingly, Anne washed her hair, scrubbing it vigorously with soap and water, but for all the difference it made she might as well have been scouring its original red. The pedlar had certainly spoken the truth when he declared that the dye wouldn't wash off, however his veracity might be impeached in other respects.

"Oh, Marilla, what shall I do?" questioned Anne in tears. "I can never live this down. People have pretty well forgotten my other mistakes—the liniment cake and setting Diana drunk and flying into a temper with Mrs. Lynde. But they'll never forget this. They will think I am not respectable. Oh, Marilla, 'what a tangled web we weave when first we practise to deceive.'[5] That is poetry, but it is true. And oh, how Josie Pye will laugh! Marilla, I *cannot* face Josie Pye. I am the unhappiest girl in Prince Edward Island."

Anne's unhappiness continued for a week. During that time she went nowhere and shampooed her hair every day. Diana alone of outsiders knew the fatal secret, but she promised solemnly never to tell, and it may be stated here and now that she kept her word. At the end of the week Marilla said decidedly:

"It's no use, Anne. That is fast dye if ever there was any. Your hair must be cut off; there is no other way. You can't go out with it looking like that."

Anne's lips quivered, but she realized the bitter truth of Marilla's remarks. With a dismal sigh she went for the scissors.

"Please cut it off at once, Marilla, and have it over. Oh, I feel that my heart is broken. This is such an unromantic affliction. The girls in books[6] lose their hair in fevers or sell it to get money for some

---

4. Farm women and girls augmented family funds by keeping chickens and collecting and selling eggs.
5. "O, what a tangled web we weave / When first we practice to deceive!" Walter Scott, *Marmion* (1808) 6.17. LMM later uses this phrase as the title for her 1931 novel.
6. In *Little Women* (1868), Jo March sells her long hair to help family finances. LMM later uses the motif of hair loss (because of fever) in *Pat of Silver Bush* (1933) chap. 26.

good deed, and I'm sure I wouldn't mind losing my hair in some such fashion half so much. But there is nothing comforting in having your hair cut off because you've dyed it a dreadful colour, is there? I'm going to weep all the time you're cutting it off, if it won't interfere. It seems such a tragic thing."

Anne wept then, but later on, when she went upstairs and looked in the glass, she was calm with despair. Marilla had done her work thoroughly and it had been necessary to shingle the hair as closely as possible. The result was not becoming, to state the case as mildly as may be. Anne promptly turned her glass to the wall.

"I'll never, never look at myself again until my hair grows," she exclaimed passionately.

Then she suddenly righted the glass.

"Yes, I will, too. I'd do penance for being wicked that way. I'll look at myself every time I come to my room and see how ugly I am. And I won't try to imagine it away, either. I never thought I was vain about my hair, of all things, but now I know I was, in spite of its being red, because it was so long and thick and curly. I expect something will happen to my nose next."

Anne's clipped head made a sensation in school on the following Monday, but to her relief nobody guessed the real reason for it, not even Josie Pye, who, however, did not fail to inform Anne that she looked like a perfect scarecrow.

"I didn't say anything when Josie said that to me," Anne confided that evening to Marilla, who was lying on the sofa after one of her headaches, "because I thought it was part of my punishment and I ought to bear it patiently. It's hard to be told you look like a scarecrow and I wanted to say something back. But I didn't. I just swept her one scornful look and then I forgave her. It makes you feel very virtuous when you forgive people, doesn't it? I mean to devote all my energies to being good after this and I shall never try to be beautiful again. Of course it's better to be good. I know it is, but it's sometimes so hard to believe a thing even when you know it. I do really want to be good, Marilla, like you and Mrs. Allan and Miss Stacy, and grow up to be a credit to you. Diana says when my hair begins to grow to tie a black velvet ribbon around my head with a bow at one side. She says she thinks it will be very becoming. I will call it a snood[7]—that sounds so romantic. But am I talking too much, Marilla? Does it hurt your head?"

"My head is better now. It was terrible bad this afternoon, though. These headaches of mine are getting worse and worse. I'll have to

---

7. A net to confine the hair. In Walter Scott's *The Lady of the Lake* Ellen wears a silken snood.

see a doctor about them. As for your chatter, I don't know that I mind it—I've got so used to it."

Which was Marilla's way of saying that she liked to hear it.

## Chapter XXVIII

### AN UNFORTUNATE LILY MAID[1]

"OF course you must be Elaine,[2] Anne," said Diana. "I could never have the courage to float down there."

"Nor I," said Ruby Gillis with a shiver. "I don't mind floating down when there's two or three of us in the flat[3] and we can sit up. It's fun then. But to lie down and pretend I was dead—I just couldn't. I'd die really of fright."

"Of course it would be romantic," conceded Jane Andrews. "But I know I couldn't keep still. I'd be popping up every minute or so to see where I was and if I wasn't drifting too far out. And you know, Anne, that would spoil the effect."

"But it's so ridiculous to have a red-headed Elaine," mourned Anne. "I'm not afraid to float down and I'd *love* to be Elaine. But it's ridiculous just the same. Ruby ought to be Elaine because she is so fair and has such lovely long golden hair—Elaine had 'all her bright hair streaming down,' you know. And Elaine was the lily maid. Now, a red-haired person cannot be a lily maid."

"Your complexion is just as fair as Ruby's," said Diana earnestly, "and your hair is ever so much darker than it used to be before you cut it."

"Oh, do you really think so?" exclaimed Anne, flushing sensitively with delight. "I've sometimes thought it was myself—but I never dared to ask any one for fear she would tell me it wasn't. Do you think it could be called auburn now, Diana?"

"Yes, and I think it is real pretty," said Diana, looking admiringly at the short, silky curls that clustered over Anne's head and were held in place by a very jaunty black velvet ribbon and bow.

They were standing on the bank of the pond, below Orchard Slope, where a little headland fringed with birches ran out from the bank; at its tip was a small wooden platform built out into the water for

---

1. Elaine "the fair, Elaine the loveable / Elaine, the lily maid of Astolat" is the heroine of Alfred Tennyson's "Lancelot and Elaine," *Idylls of the King* (1859). Her story is enacted in parody in this chapter. See NCE 301–02.
2. As in Malory's *Morte d'Arthur* (1485), Tennyson's heroine dies for love of Sir Lancelot, and arranges her own funeral cortège, by barge down river to Camelot.
3. Flat-bottomed boat.

the convenience of fishermen and duck hunters. Ruby and Jane were spending the midsummer afternoon with Diana, and Anne had come over to play with them.

Anne and Diana had spent most of their playtime that summer on and about the pond. Idlewild was a thing of the past, Mr. Bell having ruthlessly cut down the little circle of trees in his back pasture in the spring. Anne had sat among the stumps and wept, not without an eye to the romance of it; but she was speedily consoled, for, after all, as she and Diana said, big girls of thirteen, going on fourteen, were too old for such childish amusements as playhouses, and there were more fascinating sports to be found about the pond. It was splendid to fish for trout over the bridge and the two girls learned to row themselves about in the little flat-bottomed dory[4] Mr. Barry kept for duck shooting.

It was Anne's idea that they dramatize Elaine. They had studied Tennyson's poem in school the preceding winter, the Superintendent of Education having prescribed it in the English course for the Prince Edward Island schools.[5] They had analyzed and parsed[6] it and torn it to pieces in general until it was a wonder there was any meaning at all left in it for them, but at least the fair lily maid and Lancelot and Guinevere and King Arthur had become very real people to them, and Anne was devoured by secret regret that she had not been born in Camelot.[7] Those days, she said, were so much more romantic than the present.

Anne's plan was hailed with enthusiasm. The girls had discovered that if the flat were pushed off from the landing-place it would drift down with the current under the bridge and finally strand itself on another headland lower down which ran out at a curve in the pond. They had often gone down like this and nothing could be more convenient for playing Elaine.

"Well, I'll be Elaine," said Anne, yielding reluctantly, for, although she would have been delighted to play the principal character, yet her artistic sense demanded fitness for it and this, she felt, her limitations made impossible. "Ruby, you must be King Arthur and Jane will be Guinevere and Diana must be Lancelot. But first you must be the brothers and the father. We can't have the old dumb servitor[8] because there isn't room for two in the flat when one is lying down. We must pall the barge[9] all its length in

---

4. Flat-bottomed rowboat with high sides and a sharp prow.
5. The English curriculum, set to guarantee uniformity throughout the Province.
6. Analyzed its parts of speech. The English course involved teaching composition and rhetoric as well as literature.
7. Legendary capitol of King Arthur's kingdom and site of the Round Table.
8. In the poem, an old manservant who is a mute accompanies the "lily maid."
9. To cover with a funeral cloth (pall). The 1908 American edition mistakenly read "pail the barge."

blackest samite.[1] That old black shawl of your mother's will be just the thing, Diana."

The black shawl having been procured, Anne spread it over the flat and then lay down on the bottom, with closed eyes and hands folded over her breast.

"Oh, she does look really dead," whispered Ruby Gillis nervously, watching the still, white little face under the flickering shadows of the birches. "It makes me feel frightened, girls. Do you suppose it's really right to act like this? Mrs. Lynde says that all play-acting is abominably wicked."[2]

"Ruby, you shouldn't talk about Mrs. Lynde," said Anne severely. "It spoils the effect because this is hundreds of years before Mrs. Lynde was born. Jane, you arrange this. It's silly for Elaine to be talking when she's dead."

Jane rose to the occasion. Cloth of gold for coverlet there was none,[3] but an old piano scarf of yellow Japanese crêpe was an excellent substitute.[4] A white lily was not obtainable just then, but the effect of a tall blue iris placed in one of Anne's folded hands was all that could be desired.

"Now, she's all ready," said Jane. "We must kiss her quiet brows and, Diana, you say, 'Sister, farewell for ever,' and Ruby, you say, 'Farewell, sweet sister,' both of you as sorrowfully as you possibly can. Anne, for goodness sake smile a little. You know Elaine 'lay as though she smiled.' That's better. Now push the flat off."

The flat was accordingly pushed off, scraping roughly over an old embedded stake[5] in the process. Diana and Jane and Ruby only waited long enough to see it caught in the current and headed for the bridge before scampering up through the woods, across the road, and down to the lower headland where, as Lancelot and Guinevere and the King, they were to be in readiness to receive the lily maid.

For a few minutes Anne, drifting slowly down, enjoyed the romance of her situation to the full. Then something happened not at all romantic. The flat began to leak. In a very few moments it was necessary for Elaine to scramble to her feet, pick up her cloth of gold coverlet and pall of blackest samite and gaze blankly at a big crack in the bottom of her barge through which the water was literally pouring. That sharp stake at the landing had torn off the strip of batting[6] nailed on the flat. Anne did not know this, but it did not

---

1. A heavy silk fabric, often interwoven with gold or silver, worn in the Middle Ages.
2. Puritans held that playing a part was a form of lying, and this added to the legendary belief that theatre people were wicked.
3. Inversion for poetic effect.
4. Draping fancy material on a piano was fashionable, and in the 1880s all things Japanese were very much in vogue, witness Gilbert and Sullivan's *Mikado* (1885). Or perhaps this exotic artifact is a trace of a PEI-based missionary.
5. Perhaps a pile, part of an old pier.
6. Although boat seams were sometimes corked with candlewick batting (soft cotton) pressed

take her long to realize that she was in a dangerous plight. At this rate the flat would fill and sink long before it could drift to the lower headland. Where were the oars? Left behind at the landing!

Anne gave one gasping little scream which nobody ever heard; she was white to the lips, but she did not lose her self-possession. There was one chance—just one.

"I was horribly frightened," she told Mrs. Allan the next day, "and it seemed like years while the flat was drifting down to the bridge and the water rising in it every moment. I prayed, Mrs. Allan, most earnestly, but I didn't shut my eyes to pray, for I knew the only way God could save me was to let the flat float close enough to one of the bridge piles[7] for me to climb up on it. You know the piles are just old tree trunks and there are lots of knots and old branch stubs on them. It was proper to pray, but I had to do my part by watching out and right well I knew it. I just said, 'Dear God, please take the flat close to a pile and I'll do the rest,' over and over again. Under such circumstances you don't think much about making a flowery prayer. But mine was answered, for the flat bumped right into a pile for a minute and I flung the scarf and the shawl over my shoulder and scrambled up on a big providential stub. And there I was, Mrs. Allan, clinging to that slippery old pile with no way of getting up or down. It was a very unromantic position, but I didn't think about that at the time. You don't think much about romance when you have just escaped from a watery grave. I said a grateful prayer at once and then I gave all my attention to holding on tight, for I knew I should probably have to depend on human aid to get back to dry land."

The flat drifted under the bridge and then promptly sank in midstream. Ruby, Jane, and Diana, already awaiting it on the lower headland, saw it disappear before their very eyes and had not a doubt but that Anne had gone down with it. For a moment they stood still, white as sheets, frozen with horror at the tragedy; then, shrieking at the tops of their voices, they started on a frantic run up through the woods, never pausing as they crossed the main road to glance the way of the bridge. Anne, clinging desperately to her precarious foothold, saw their flying forms and heard their shrieks. Help would soon come, but meanwhile her position was a very uncomfortable one.

The minutes passed by, each seeming an hour to the unfortunate lily maid. Why didn't somebody come? Where had the girls gone? Suppose they had fainted, one and all! Suppose nobody ever came! Suppose she grew so tired and cramped that she could hold on no longer! Anne looked at the wicked green depths below her, wavering

---

in with a sharp piece of steel, "batten" is a nautical term for a strip of wood nailed on to secure seams or to reinforce the storage hatches on a boat, as in "batten down the hatches." LMM's handwritten manuscript clearly says "batting."

7. Heavy lumber used as uprights in mooring and supporting the bridge.

with long, oily shadows, and shivered. Her imagination began to suggest all manner of gruesome possibilities to her.

Then, just as she thought she really could not endure the ache in her arms and wrists another moment, Gilbert Blythe came rowing under the bridge in Harmon Andrews' dory!

Gilbert glanced up and, much to his amazement, beheld a little white scornful face looking down upon him with big, frightened but also scornful gray eyes.

"Anne Shirley! How on earth did you get there?" he exclaimed.

Without waiting for an answer he pulled close to the pile and extended his hand. There was no help for it; Anne, clinging to Gilbert Blythe's hand, scrambled down into the dory, where she sat, drabbled and furious, in the stern with her arms full of dripping shawl and wet crêpe. It was certainly extremely difficult to be dignified under the circumstances!

"What has happened, Anne?" asked Gilbert, taking up his oars.

"We were playing Elaine," explained Anne frigidly, without even looking at her rescuer, "and I had to drift down to Camelot in the barge—I mean the flat. The flat began to leak and I climbed out on the pile. The girls went for help. Will you be kind enough to row me to the landing?"

Gilbert obligingly rowed to the landing and Anne, disdaining assistance, sprang nimbly on shore.

"I'm very much obliged to you," she said haughtily as she turned away. But Gilbert had also sprung from the boat and now laid a detaining hand on her arm.

"Anne," he said hurriedly, "look here. Can't we be good friends? I'm awfully sorry I made fun of your hair that time. I didn't mean to vex you and I only meant it for a joke. Besides, it's so long ago. I think your hair is awfully pretty now—honest I do. Let's be friends."

For a moment Anne hesitated. She had an odd, newly awakened consciousness under all her outraged dignity that the half-shy, half-eager expression in Gilbert's hazel eyes was something that was very good to see. Her heart gave a quick, queer little beat. But the bitterness of her old grievance promptly stiffened up her wavering determination. That scene of two years before flashed back into her recollection as vividly as if it had taken place yesterday. Gilbert had called her "carrots" and had brought about her disgrace before the whole school. Her resentment, which to other and older people might be as laughable as its cause, was in no whit allayed and softened by time seemingly. She hated Gilbert Blythe! She would never forgive him!

"No," she said coldly, "I shall never be friends with you, Gilbert Blythe; and I don't want to be!"

"All right!" Gilbert sprang into his skiff with an angry colour in his

He pulled close to the pile and extended his hand

cheeks. "I'll never ask you to be friends again, Anne Shirley. And I don't care either!"

He pulled away with swift defiant strokes, and Anne went up the steep, ferny little path under the maples. She held her head very high, but she was conscious of an odd feeling of regret. She almost wished she had answered Gilbert differently. Of course, he had insulted her terribly, but still—! Altogether, Anne rather thought it would be a relief to sit down and have a good cry. She was really quite unstrung, for the reaction from her fright and cramped clinging was making itself felt.

Half-way up the path she met Jane and Diana rushing back to the pond in a state narrowly removed from positive frenzy. They had found nobody at Orchard Slope, both Mr. and Mrs. Barry being away. Here Ruby Gillis had succumbed to hysterics, and was left to recover from them as best she might, while Jane and Diana flew through the Haunted Wood and across the brook to Green Gables. There they had found nobody either, for Marilla had gone to Carmody and Matthew was making hay in the back field.

"Oh, Anne," gasped Diana, fairly falling on the former's neck and weeping with relief and delight, "Oh, Anne—we thought—you were—drowned—and we felt like murderers—because we had made—you be—Elaine. And Ruby is in hysterics—oh, Anne, how did you escape?"

"I climbed up on one of the piles," explained Anne wearily, "and Gilbert Blythe came along in Mr. Andrews' dory and brought me to land."

"Oh, Anne, how splendid of him! Why, it's so romantic!" said Jane, finding breath enough for utterance at last. "Of course you'll speak to him after this."

"Of course I won't," flashed Anne with a momentary return of her old spirit. "And I don't want ever to hear the word romantic again, Jane Andrews. I'm awfully sorry you were so frightened, girls. It is all my fault. I feel sure I was born under an unlucky star.[8] Everything I do gets me or my dearest friends into a scrape. We've gone and lost your father's flat, Diana, and I have a presentiment that we'll not be allowed to row on the pond any more."

Anne's presentiment[9] proved more trustworthy than presentiments are apt to do. Great was the consternation in the Barry and Cuthbert households when the events of the afternoon became known.

"Will you *ever* have any sense, Anne?" groaned Marilla.

"Oh, yes, I think I will, Marilla," returned Anne optimistically. A

---

8. Astrology presumes that human fate is determined according to the stars predominating at a birth.
9. Premonition, a feeling about what the future will be.

good cry, indulged in the grateful solitude of the east gable, had soothed her nerves and restored her to her wonted cheerfulness. "I think my prospects of becoming sensible are brighter now than ever."

"I don't see how," said Marilla.

"Well," explained Anne, "I've learned a new and valuable lesson to-day. Ever since I came to Green Gables I've been making mistakes, and each mistake has helped to cure me of some great shortcoming. The affair of the amethyst brooch cured me of meddling with things that didn't belong to me. The Haunted Wood mistake cured me of letting my imagination run away with me. The liniment cake mistake cured me of carelessness in cooking. Dyeing my hair cured me of vanity. I never think about my hair and nose now—at least, very seldom. And to-day's mistake is going to cure me of being too romantic. I have come to the conclusion that it is no use trying to be romantic in Avonlea. It was probably easy enough in towered Camelot[1] hundreds of years ago, but romance is not appreciated now. I feel quite sure that you will soon see a great improvement in me in this respect, Marilla."

"I'm sure I hope so," said Marilla skeptically.

But Matthew, who had been sitting mutely in his corner, laid a hand on Anne's shoulder when Marilla had gone out.

"Don't give up all your romance, Anne," he whispered shyly, "a little of it is a good thing—not too much, of course—but keep a little of it, Anne, keep a little of it."

## Chapter XXIX

### AN EPOCH IN ANNE'S LIFE

ANNE was bringing the cows home from the back pasture by way of Lovers' Lane. It was a September evening and all the gaps and clearings in the woods were brimmed up with ruby sunset light. Here and there the lane was splashed with it, but for the most part it was already quite shadowy beneath the maples, and the spaces under the firs were filled with a clear violet dusk like airy wine. The winds were out in their tops, and there is no sweeter music on earth than that which the wind makes in the fir-trees at evening.

The cows swung placidly down the lane, and Anne followed them dreamily, repeating aloud the battle canto from "Marmion"[2]—which

1. "Tower'd Camelot" is used repeatedly in Tennyson's poem, "The Lady of Shalott" (1833/ 1842).
2. The sixth canto of Walter Scott's epic poem describes the disastrous battle of Flodden, where Scottish power was broken by the English. See NCE 296–97.

had also been part of their English course the preceding winter and which Miss Stacy had made them learn off by heart—and exulting in its rushing lines and the clash of spears in its imagery. When she came to the lines:

> "The stubborn spearsmen still made good
> Their dark impenetrable wood,"

she stopped in ecstasy to shut her eyes that she might the better fancy herself one of that heroic ring. When she opened them again it was to behold Diana coming through the gate that led into the Barry field and looking so important that Anne instantly divined there was news to be told. But betray too eager curiosity she would not.

"Isn't this evening just like a purple dream, Diana? It makes me so glad to be alive. In the mornings I always think the mornings are best; but when evening comes I think it's lovelier still."

"It's a very fine evening," said Diana, "but oh, I have such news, Anne. Guess. You can have three guesses."

"Charlotte Gillis is going to be married in the church[3] after all and Mrs. Allan wants us to decorate it," cried Anne.

"No. Charlotte's beau won't agree to that, because nobody ever has been married in the church yet, and he thinks it would seem too much like a funeral. It's too mean, because it would be such fun. Guess again."

"Jane's mother is going to let her have a birthday party?"

Diana shook her head, her black eyes dancing with merriment.

"I can't think what it can be," said Anne in despair, "unless it's that Moody Spurgeon MacPherson saw you home from prayer-meeting last night. Did he?"

"I should think not," exclaimed Diana indignantly. "I wouldn't be likely to boast of it if he did, the horrid creature! I knew you couldn't guess it. Mother had a letter from Aunt Josephine to-day, and Aunt Josephine wants you and me to go to town next Tuesday and stop with her for the Exhibition.[4] There!"

"Oh, Diana," whispered Anne, finding it necessary to lean up against a maple-tree for support, "do you really mean it? But I'm afraid Marilla won't let me go. She will say that she can't encourage gadding about. That was what she said last week when Jane invited me to go with them in their double-seated buggy to the American concert at the White Sands Hotel. I wanted to go, but Marilla said

---

3. Most Presbyterian marriages took place in the home, unlike traditional Roman Catholic and Anglican ceremonies. LMM married the Rev. Ewan Macdonald in her Aunt Annie Campbell's home in Park Corner, PEI.

4. Founded in 1879, the annual Charlottetown Fair hosted province-wide competitions in livestock, farm produce, and household arts.

I'd be better at home learning my lessons and so would Jane. I was bitterly disappointed, Diana. I felt so heart-broken that I wouldn't say my prayers when I went to bed. But I repented of that and got up in the middle of the night and said them."

"I'll tell you," said Diana, "we'll get mother to ask Marilla. She'll be more likely to let you go then; and if she does we'll have the time of our lives, Anne. I've never been to an Exhibition, and it's so aggravating to hear the other girls talking about their trips. Jane and Ruby have been twice, and they're going this year again."

"I'm not going to think about it at all until I know whether I can go or not," said Anne resolutely. "If I did and then was disappointed, it would be more than I could bear. But in case I do go I'm very glad my new coat will be ready by that time. Marilla didn't think I needed a new coat. She said my old one would do very well for another winter and that I ought to be satisfied with having a new dress. The dress is very pretty, Diana—navy blue and made so fashionably. Marilla always makes my dresses fashionably now, because she says she doesn't intend to have Matthew going to Mrs. Lynde to make them. I'm so glad. It is ever so much easier to be good if your clothes are fashionable. At least, it is easier for me. I suppose it doesn't make such a difference to naturally good people. But Matthew said I must have a new coat, so Marilla bought a lovely piece of blue broadcloth,[5] and it's being made by a real dressmaker over at Carmody. It's to be done Saturday night, and I'm trying not to imagine myself walking up the church aisle on Sunday in my new suit and cap, because I'm afraid it isn't right to imagine such things. But it just slips into my mind in spite of me. My cap is so pretty. Matthew bought it for me the day we were over at Carmody. It is one of those little blue velvet ones that are all the rage, with gold cord and tassels. Your new hat is elegant, Diana, and so becoming. When I saw you come into church last Sunday my heart swelled with pride to think you were my dearest friend. Do you suppose it's wrong for us to think so much about our clothes? Marilla says it is very sinful. But it *is* such an interesting subject, isn't it?"

Marilla agreed to let Anne go to town, and it was arranged that Mr. Barry should take the girls in on the following Tuesday. As Charlottetown was thirty miles away and Mr. Barry wished to go and return the same day, it was necessary to make a very early start. But Anne counted it all joy, and was up before sunrise on Tuesday morning. A glance from her window assured her that the day would be fine, for the eastern sky behind the firs of the Haunted Wood was all silvery and cloudless. Through the gap in the trees a light was

---

5. A dense woolen cloth, more than a yard wide, used in suits and coats.

shining in the western gable of Orchard Slope, a token that Diana was also up.

Anne was dressed by the time Matthew had the fire on and had the breakfast ready when Marilla came down, but for her own part was much too excited to eat. After breakfast the jaunty new cap and jacket were donned, and Anne hastened over the brook and up through the firs to Orchard Slope. Mr. Barry and Diana were waiting for her, and they were soon on the road.

It was a long drive, but Anne and Diana enjoyed every minute of it. It was delightful to rattle along over the moist roads in the early red sunlight that was creeping across the shorn harvest fields. The air was fresh and crisp, and little smoke-blue mists curled through the valleys and floated off from the hills. Sometimes the road went through woods where maples were beginning to hang out scarlet banners; sometimes it crossed rivers on bridges that made Anne's flesh cringe with the old, half-delightful fear; sometimes it wound along a harbour shore and passed by a little cluster of weather-gray fishing huts; again it mounted to hills whence a far sweep of curving upland or misty blue sky could be seen; but wherever it went there was much of interest to discuss. It was almost noon when they reached town and found their way to "Beechwood."[6] It was quite a fine old mansion, set back from the street in a seclusion of green elms and branching beeches. Miss Barry met them at the door with a twinkle in her sharp black eyes.

"So you've come to see me at last, you Anne-girl," she said. "Mercy, child, how you have grown! You're taller than I am, I declare. And you're ever so much better-looking than you used to be, too. But I dare say you know that without being told."

"Indeed I didn't," said Anne radiantly. "I know I'm not so freckled as I used to be, so I've much to be thankful for, but I really hadn't dared to hope there was any other improvement. I'm so glad you think there is, Miss Barry."

Miss Barry's house was furnished with "great magnificence," as Anne told Marilla afterwards. The two little country girls were rather abashed by the splendour of the parlour where Miss Barry left them when she went to see about dinner.

"Isn't it just like a palace?" whispered Diana. "I never was in Aunt Josephine's house before, and I'd no idea it was so grand. I just wish Julia Bell could see this—she puts on such airs about her mother's parlour."

"Velvet carpet," sighed Anne luxuriously, "*and* silk curtains! I've dreamed of such things, Diana. But do you know I don't believe I

6. Like many fine Charlottetown homes, Miss Barry's has a romantic name.

feel very comfortable with them after all. There are so many things in this room and all so splendid that there is no scope for imagination. That is one consolation when you are poor—there are so many more things you can imagine about."

Their sojourn in town was something that Anne and Diana dated from for years. From first to last it was crowded with delights.

On Wednesday Miss Barry took them to the Exhibition grounds and kept them there all day.

"It was splendid," Anne related to Marilla later on. "I never imagined anything so interesting. I don't really know which department was the most interesting. I think I liked the horses and the flowers and the fancy work[7] best. Josie Pye took first prize for knitted lace. I was real glad she did. And I was glad that I felt glad, for it shows I'm improving, don't you think, Marilla, when I can rejoice in Josie's success? Mr. Harmon Andrews took second prize for Gravenstein apples[8] and Mr. Bell took first prize for a pig. Diana said she thought it was ridiculous for a Sunday-school superintendent to take a prize in pigs, but I don't see why. Do you? She said she would always think of it after this when he was praying so solemnly. Clara Louise MacPherson took a prize for painting, and Mrs. Lynde got first prize for home-made butter and cheese. So Avonlea was pretty well represented, wasn't it? Mrs. Lynde was there that day, and I never knew how much I really liked her until I saw her familiar face among all those strangers. There were thousands of people there, Marilla. It made me feel dreadfully insignificant. And Miss Barry took us up to the grand stand to see the horse-races.[9] Mrs. Lynde wouldn't go; she said horse-racing was an abomination,[1] and she being a church-member, thought it her bounden duty to set a good example by staying away. But there were so many there I don't believe Mrs. Lynde's absence would ever be noticed. I don't think, though, that I ought to go very often to horse-races, because they *are* awfully fascinating. Diana got so excited that she offered to bet me ten cents that the red horse would win. I didn't believe he would, but I refused to bet, because I wanted to tell Mrs. Allan all about everything, and I felt sure it wouldn't do to tell her that. It's always wrong to do anything you can't tell the minister's wife. It's as good as an extra conscience to have a minister's wife for your friend. And I was very glad I didn't bet, because the red horse *did* win, and I would have lost ten cents. So you see that virtue was its own reward.[2] We saw a man go up in

---

7. Women's handiwork: crochet, lace, knitted garments, and quilts.
8. An autumn apple, orange-red, striped; a favorite cooking apple.
9. Harness racing with pacers and trotters. The Charlottetown Driving Park with its grandstand opened in 1890: Anne must have gone to an earlier venue.
1. Biblical term for evil: many references, including Isaiah 66.3.
2. A proverb cited from Plato to Dryden (and onward), including in one of LMM's favorite plays, *Douglas* (1756), a play by Scottish author John Home.

a balloon. I'd love to go up in a balloon, Marilla; it would be simply thrilling; and we saw a man selling fortunes. You paid him ten cents and a little bird picked out your fortune for you. Miss Barry gave Diana and me ten cents each to have our fortunes told. Mine was that I would marry a dark-complected man who was very wealthy, and I would go across water to live. I looked carefully at all the dark men I saw after that, but I didn't care much for any of them, and anyhow I suppose it's too early to be looking out for him yet. Oh, it was a never-to-be-forgotten day, Marilla. I was so tired I couldn't sleep at night. Miss Barry put us in the spare room, according to promise. It was an elegant room, Marilla, but somehow sleeping in a spare room isn't what I used to think it was. That's the worst of growing up, and I'm beginning to realize it. The things you wanted so much when you were a child don't seem half so wonderful to you when you get them."

Thursday the girls had a drive in the park, and in the evening Miss Barry took them to a concert in the Academy of Music,[3] where a noted prima donna[4] was to sing. To Anne the evening was a glittering vision of delight.

"Oh, Marilla, it was beyond description. I was so excited I couldn't even talk, so you may know what it was like. I just sat in enraptured silence. Madame Selitsky[5] was perfectly beautiful, and wore white satin and diamonds. But when she began to sing I never thought about anything else. Oh, I can't tell you how I felt. But it seemed to me that it could never be hard to be good any more. I felt like I do when I look up to the stars. Tears came into my eyes, but, oh, they were such happy tears. I was so sorry when it was all over, and I told Miss Barry I didn't see how I was ever to return to common life again. She said she thought if we went over to the restaurant across the street and had an ice-cream it might help me. That sounded so prosaic; but to my surprise I found it true. The ice-cream was delicious, Marilla, and it was so lovely and dissipated to be sitting there eating it at eleven o'clock at night. Diana said she believed she was born for city life. Miss Barry asked me what my opinion was, but I said I would have to think it over very seriously before I could tell her what I really thought. So I thought it over after I went to bed. That is the best time to think things out. And I came to the conclusion, Marilla, that I wasn't born for city life and that I was glad of it. It's nice to

---

3. Charlottetown's Opera House was a noted venue for world-famous performers, but this reference is probably to the Academy of Music, located in 1867 on Kent Street, where students could also study calisthenics and French conversation. By 1882, the Academy of Music was under the patronage of the Lieutenant Governor of PEI.
4. Leading singer.
5. Perhaps an allusion the Canadian prima donna Madame Albani (Emma Lajeunesse) who appeared in Charlottetown in 1906.

be eating ice-cream at brilliant[6] restaurants at eleven o'clock at night once in awhile; but as a regular thing I'd rather be in the east gable at eleven, sound asleep, but kind of knowing even in my sleep that the stars were shining outside and that the wind was blowing in the firs across the brook. I told Miss Barry so at breakfast the next morning and she laughed. Miss Barry generally laughed at anything I said, even when I said the most solemn things. I don't think I liked it, Marilla, because I wasn't trying to be funny. But she is a most hospitable lady and treated us royally."

Friday brought going-home time, and Mr. Barry drove in for the girls.

"Well, I hope you've enjoyed yourselves," said Miss Barry, as she bade them good-bye.

"Indeed we have," said Diana.

"And you, Anne-girl?"

"I've enjoyed every minute of the time," said Anne, throwing her arms impulsively about the old woman's neck and kissing her wrinkled cheek. Diana would never have dared to do such a thing, and felt rather aghast at Anne's freedom. But Miss Barry was pleased, and she stood on her veranda and watched the buggy out of sight. Then she went back into her big house with a sigh. It seemed very lonely, lacking those fresh young lives. Miss Barry was a rather selfish old lady, if the truth must be told, and had never cared much for anybody but herself. She valued people only as they were of service to her or amused her. Anne had amused her, and consequently stood high in the old lady's good graces. But Miss Barry found herself thinking less about Anne's quaint speeches than of her fresh enthusiasms, her transparent emotions, her little winning ways, and the sweetness of her eyes and lips.

"I thought Marilla Cuthbert was an old fool when I heard she'd adopted a girl out of an orphan asylum," she said to herself, "but I guess she didn't make much of a mistake after all. If I'd a child like Anne in the house all the time I'd be a better and happier woman."

Anne and Diana found the drive home as pleasant as the drive in—pleasanter, indeed, since there was the delightful consciousness of home waiting at the end of it. It was sunset when they passed through White Sands and turned into the shore road. Beyond, the Avonlea hills came out darkly against the saffron sky. Behind them the moon was rising out of the sea that grew all radiant and transfigured in her light. Every little cove along the curving road was a marvel of dancing ripples. The waves broke with a soft swish on the rocks below them, and the tang of the sea was in the strong, fresh air.

6. Lit by gaslight, more bright than oil lamps and candles in Avonlea homes.

"Oh, but it's good to be alive and to be going home," breathed Anne.

When she crossed the log bridge over the brook the kitchen light of Green Gables winked her a friendly welcome back, and through the open door shone the hearth fire, sending out its warm red glow athwart the chilly autumn night. Anne ran blithely up the hill and into the kitchen, where a hot supper was waiting on the table.

"So you've got back?" said Marilla, folding up her knitting.

"Yes, and, oh, it's so good to be back," said Anne joyously. "I could kiss everything, even to the clock. Marilla, a broiled chicken! You don't mean to say you cooked that for me!"

"Yes, I did," said Marilla. "I thought you'd be hungry after such a drive and need something real appetizing. Hurry and take off your things, and we'll have supper as soon as Matthew comes in. I'm glad you've got back, I must say. It's been fearful lonesome here without you, and I never put in four longer days."

After supper Anne sat before the fire between Matthew and Marilla, and gave them a full account of her visit.

"I've had a splendid time," she concluded happily, "and I feel that it marks an epoch in my life. But the best of it all was the coming home."

# Chapter XXX

## THE QUEEN'S CLASS IS ORGANIZED

MARILLA laid her knitting on her lap and leaned back in her chair. Her eyes were tired, and she thought vaguely that she must see about having her glasses changed the next time she went to town, for her eyes had grown tired very often of late.

It was nearly dark, for the dull November twilight had fallen around Green Gables, and the only light in the kitchen came from the dancing red flames in the stove.

Anne was curled up Turk-fashion[1] on the hearth-rug, gazing into that joyous glow where the sunshine of a hundred summers was being distilled from the maple cord-wood.[2] She had been reading, but her book had slipped to the floor, and now she was dreaming, with a smile on her parted lips. Glittering castles in Spain[3] were

---

1. Sitting cross-legged, like nomads in a tent.
2. Wood cut for indoor fires; stacks of wood were measured in cords (usually 128 cubic feet, in a pile 8 × 4 × 4 feet).
3. An exotic dream place. This traditional phrase appears in LMM's journals: "I was very sorry the orchard existed only on the estates of my castle in Spain" (January 12, 1908). In her 1896 Longfellow ("The Golden Mile-Stone") she underlined "By the fireside there are youthful dreamers, / Building castles fair." LMM's dreams of such castles were fostered

shaping themselves out of the mists and rainbows of her lively fancy; adventures wonderful and enthralling were happening to her in cloudland—adventures that always turned out triumphantly and never involved her in scrapes like those of actual life.

Marilla looked at her with a tenderness that would never have been suffered to reveal itself in any clearer light than that soft mingling of fireshine and shadow. The lesson of a love that should display itself easily in spoken word and open look was one Marilla could never learn. But she had learned to love this slim, gray-eyed girl with an affection all the deeper and stronger from its very undemonstrativeness. Her love made her afraid of being unduly indulgent, indeed. She had an uneasy feeling that it was rather sinful to set one's heart so intensely on any human creature as she had set hers on Anne, and perhaps she performed a sort of unconscious penance for this by being stricter and more critical than if the girl had been less dear to her. Certainly Anne herself had no idea how Marilla loved her. She sometimes thought wistfully that Marilla was very hard to please and distinctly lacking in sympathy and understanding. But she always checked the thought reproachfully, remembering what she owed to Marilla.

"Anne," said Marilla abruptly, "Miss Stacy was here this afternoon when you were out with Diana."

Anne came back from her other world with a start and a sigh.

"Was she? Oh, I'm so sorry I wasn't in. Why didn't you call me, Marilla? Diana and I were only over in the Haunted Wood. It's lovely in the woods now. All the little wood things—the ferns and the satin leaves and the crackerberries[4]—have gone to sleep, just as if somebody had tucked them away until spring under a blanket of leaves. I think it was a little gray fairy with a rainbow scarf[5] that came tiptoeing along the last moonlight night and did it. Diana wouldn't say much about that, though. Diana has never forgotten the scolding her mother gave her about imagining ghosts into the Haunted Wood. It had a very bad effect on Diana's imagination. It blighted it. Mrs. Lynde says Myrtle Bell is a blighted being. I asked Ruby Gillis why Myrtle was blighted, and Ruby said she guessed it was because her young man had gone back on her. Ruby Gillis thinks of nothing but young men, and the older she gets the worse she is. Young men are all very well in their place, but it doesn't do to drag them into everything, does it? Diana and I are thinking seriously of promising each other that we will never marry but be nice old maids and live together for ever. Diana hasn't quite made up her mind though, because she

---

by Washington Irving's descriptions in *The Alhambra* (1832), a favorite book. Her 1926 novel is called *The Blue Castle*.

4. Bunchberry, a hardy northern creeping perennial plant with red berries.
5. A favorite motif in illustrations of late Victorian fairy-tale books. See n. 4, chap. 21.

thinks perhaps it would be nobler to marry some wild, dashing, wicked young man and reform him. Diana and I talk a great deal about serious subjects now, you know. We feel that we are so much older than we used to be that it isn't becoming to talk of childish matters. It's such a solemn thing to be almost fourteen, Marilla. Miss Stacy took all us girls who are in our teens down to the brook last Wednesday, and talked to us about it. She said we couldn't be too careful what habits we formed and what ideals we acquired in our teens, because by the time we were twenty our characters would be developed and the foundation laid for our whole future life. And she said if the foundation was shaky we could never build anything really worth while on it. Diana and I talked the matter over coming home from school. We felt extremely solemn, Marilla. And we decided that we would try to be very careful indeed and form respectable habits and learn all we could and be as sensible as possible, so that by the time we were twenty our characters would be properly developed. It's perfectly appalling to think of being twenty, Marilla. It sounds so fearfully old and grown up. But why was Miss Stacy here this afternoon?"

"That is what I want to tell you, Anne, if you'll ever give me a chance to get a word in edgewise. She was talking about you."

"About me?" Anne looked rather scared. Then she flushed and exclaimed:

"Oh, I know what she was saying. I meant to tell you, Marilla, honestly I did, but I forgot. Miss Stacy caught me reading *Ben Hur*[6] in school yesterday afternoon when I should have been studying my Canadian history.[7] Jane Andrews lent it to me. I was reading it at dinner-hour, and I had just got to the chariot-race when school went in. I was simply wild to know how it turned out—although I felt sure *Ben Hur* must win, because it wouldn't be poetical justice[8] if he didn't—so I spread the history open on my desk-lid and then tucked *Ben Hur* between the desk and my knee.[9] It just looked as if I were studying Canadian history, you know, while all the while I was revelling in *Ben Hur*. I was so interested in it that I never noticed Miss Stacy coming down the aisle until all at once I just looked up and there she was looking down at me, so reproachful like. I can't tell you how ashamed I felt, Marilla, especially when I heard Josie Pye

---

6. American bestseller (1880) by Lew Wallace subtitled *A Tale of the Christ*, a cherished text LMM associated with her childhood.

7. School texts used in PEI in the 1880s covered the Acadian settlements, the exploration of the North-West, the War of 1812–14, the Rebellion of 1837, and the story of Canadian Confederation, when the old Maritime colonies joined Upper Canada (Ontario) and Lower Canada (Quebec) to form a single nation. The historic meeting of the "Fathers of Confederation" was held in Charlottetown in 1867.

8. A literary term in use since the 1700s, based on Aristotle's theory that in art the good should prevail.

9. LMM's journal recounts similar hidden pleasures. *SJ1* 253.

giggling. Miss Stacy took *Ben Hur* away, but she never said a word then. She kept me in at recess and talked to me. She said I had done very wrong in two respects. First, I was wasting the time I ought to have put on my studies; and secondly I was deceiving my teacher in trying to make it appear I was reading a history when it was a story-book instead. I had never realized until that moment, Marilla, that what I was doing was deceitful. I was shocked. I cried bitterly, and asked Miss Stacy to forgive me and I'd never do such a thing again; and I offered to do penance by never so much as looking at *Ben Hur* for a whole week, not even to see how the chariot-race turned out. But Miss Stacy said she wouldn't require that, and she forgave me freely. So I think it wasn't very kind of her to come up here to you about it after all."

"Miss Stacy never mentioned such a thing to me, Anne, and it's only your guilty conscience that's the matter with you. You have no business to be taking story-books to school. You read too many novels anyhow. When I was a girl I wasn't so much as allowed to look at a novel."

"Oh, how can you call *Ben Hur* a novel when it's really such a religious book?" protested Anne. "Of course it's a little too exciting to be proper reading for Sunday, and I only read it on week-days. And I never read *any* book now unless either Miss Stacy or Mrs. Allan thinks it is a proper book for a girl thirteen and three-quarters to read. Miss Stacy made me promise that. She found me reading a book one day called *The Lurid Mystery of the Haunted Hall*.[1] It was one Ruby Gillis had lent me, and, oh, Marilla, it was so fascinating and creepy. It just curdled the blood in my veins. But Miss Stacy said it was a very silly, unwholesome book, and she asked me not to read any more of it or any like it. I didn't mind promising not to read any more like it, but it was *agonizing* to give back that book without knowing how it turned out. But my love for Miss Stacy stood the test and I did. It's really wonderful, Marilla, what you can do when you're truly anxious to please a certain person."

"Well, I guess I'll light the lamp and get to work," said Marilla. "I see plainly that you don't want to hear what Miss Stacy had to say. You're more interested in the sound of your own tongue than in anything else."

"Oh, indeed, Marilla, I do want to hear it," cried Anne contritely. "I won't say another word—not one. I know I talk too much, but I am really trying to overcome it, and although I say far too much, yet if you only knew how many things I want to say and don't, you'd give me some credit for it. Please tell me, Marilla."

---

1. An imaginary title; in LMM's manuscript of *AGG*, this title originally read *The Mystery of the Haunted Hall*.

"Well, Miss Stacy wants to organize a class among her advanced students who mean to study for the entrance examination into Queen's.[2] She intends to give them extra lessons for an hour after school. And she came to ask Matthew and me if we would like to have you join it. What do you think about it yourself, Anne? Would you like to go to Queen's and pass for a teacher?"

"Oh, Marilla!" Anne straightened to her knees and clasped her hands. "It's been the dream of my life—that is, for the last six months, ever since Ruby and Jane began to talk of studying for the entrance. But I didn't say anything about it, because I supposed it would be perfectly useless. I'd love to be a teacher. But won't it be dreadfully expensive? Mr. Andrews says it cost him one hundred and fifty dollars[3] to put Prissy through, and Prissy wasn't a dunce in geometry."

"I guess you needn't worry about that part of it. When Matthew and I took you to bring up we resolved we would do the best we could for you and give you a good education. I believe in a girl being fitted to earn her own living[4] whether she ever has to or not. You'll always have a home at Green Gables as long as Matthew and I are here, but nobody knows what is going to happen in this uncertain world, and it's just as well to be prepared. So you can join the Queen's class if you like, Anne."

"Oh, Marilla, thank you." Anne flung her arms about Marilla's waist and looked up earnestly into her face. "I'm extremely grateful to you and Matthew. And I'll study as hard as I can and do my very best to be a credit to you. I warn you not to expect much in geometry, but I think I can hold my own in anything else if I work hard."

"I dare say you'll get along well enough. Miss Stacy says you are bright and diligent." Not for worlds would Marilla have told Anne just what Miss Stacy had said about her; that would have been to pamper vanity. "You needn't rush to any extreme of killing yourself over your books. There is no hurry. You won't be ready to try the entrance for a year and a half yet. But it's well to begin in time and be thoroughly grounded, Miss Stacy says."

"I shall take more interest than ever in my studies now," said Anne blissfully, "because I have a purpose in life. Mr. Allan says everybody should have a purpose in life and pursue it faithfully. Only he says we must first make sure that it is a worthy purpose. I would call it a

---

2. Exams set by the provincial Department of Education leading to admission to the college in Charlottetown.
3. The actual tuition fees were $5 for a rural student, $10 for a city one. Other costs would include books, room, and board.
4. LMM introduces into *AGG* the public debate about educating women. Marilla takes a stand contrary to accepted Avonlea convention that education is not necessary for women. See NCE 231, 241–42. See NCE 272–75.

worthy purpose to want to be a teacher like Miss Stacy, wouldn't you, Marilla? I think it's a very noble profession."

The Queen's class was organized in due time. Gilbert Blythe, Anne Shirley, Ruby Gillis, Jane Andrews, Josie Pye, Charlie Sloane, and Moody Spurgeon MacPherson joined it. Diana Barry did not, as her parents did not intend to send her to Queen's. This seemed nothing short of a calamity to Anne. Never, since the night on which Minnie May had had the croup, had she and Diana been separated in anything. On the evening when the Queen's class first remained in school for the extra lessons and Anne saw Diana go slowly out with the others, to walk home alone through the Birch Path and Violet Vale, it was all the former could do to keep her seat and refrain from rushing impulsively after her chum. A lump came into her throat, and she hastily retired behind the pages of her uplifted Latin grammar to hide the tears in her eyes. Not for worlds would Anne have had Gilbert Blythe or Josie Pye see those tears.

"But, oh, Marilla, I really felt that I had tasted the bitterness of death,[5] as Mr. Allan said in his sermon last Sunday, when I saw Diana go out alone," she said mournfully that night. "I thought how splendid it would have been if Diana had only been going to study for the Entrance, too. But we can't have things perfect in this imperfect world, as Mrs. Lynde says. Mrs. Lynde isn't exactly a comforting person sometimes, but there's no doubt she says a great many very true things. And I think the Queen's class is going to be extremely interesting. Jane and Ruby are just going to study to be teachers.[6] That is the height of their ambition. Ruby says she will only teach for two years after she gets through, and then she intends to be married. Jane says she will devote her whole life to teaching, and never, never marry, because you are paid a salary for teaching, but a husband won't pay you anything, and growls if you ask for a share in the egg and butter money. I expect Jane speaks from mournful experience, for Mrs. Lynde says that her father is a perfect old crank, and meaner than second skimmings.[7] Josie Pye says she is just going to college for education's sake, because she won't have to earn her own living; she says of course it is different with orphans who are living on charity—*they* have to hustle. Moody Spurgeon is going to be a minister. Mrs. Lynde says he couldn't be anything else with a

---

5. "Surely, the bitterness of death is past . . ." *Holy Bible*, I Samuel 15.32.
6. Before WWI, teaching and nursing were the only paying professions normally open to young women, and they were expected to quit work if they married. Teachers' training would have been in PEI at Queen's (Prince of Wales College). In the 1880s a girl might hope to go to university, as LMM eventually did for one year at Dalhousie in Halifax, Nova Scotia.
7. A miserly person. Cream was skimmed off milk and sold for cash. Twice-skimmed milk was less tasty for his family.

name like that to live up to.[8] I hope it isn't wicked of me, Marilla, but really the thought of Moody Spurgeon being a minister makes me laugh. He's such a funny-looking boy with that big fat face, and his little blue eyes, and his ears sticking out like flaps. But perhaps he will be more intellectual-looking when he grows up. Charlie Sloane says he's going to go into politics and be a member of Parliament, but Mrs. Lynde says he'll never succeed at that, because the Sloanes are all honest people, and it's only rascals that get on in politics nowadays."

"What is Gilbert Blythe going to be?" queried Marilla, seeing that Anne was opening her Cæsar.[9]

"I don't happen to know what Gilbert Blythe's ambition in life is— if he has any," said Anne scornfully.

There was open rivalry between Gilbert and Anne now. Previously the rivalry had been rather one-sided, but there was no longer any doubt that Gilbert was as determined to be first in class as Anne was. He was a foeman worthy of her steel.[1] The other members of the class tacitly acknowledged their superiority, and never dreamed of trying to compete with them.

Since the day by the pond when she had refused to listen to his plea for forgiveness, Gilbert, save for the aforesaid determined rivalry, had evinced no recognition whatever of the existence of Anne Shirley. He talked and jested with the other girls, exchanged books and puzzles with them, discussed lessons and plans, sometimes walked home with one or the other of them from prayer-meeting or Debating Club. But Anne Shirley he simply ignored, and Anne found out that it is not pleasant to be ignored. It was in vain that she told herself with a toss of her head that she did not care. Deep down in her wayward, feminine little heart she knew that she did care, and that if she had that chance of the Lake of Shining Waters again she would answer very differently. All at once, as it seemed, and to her secret dismay, she found that the old resentment she had cherished against him was gone—gone just when she most needed its sustaining power. It was in vain that she recalled every incident and emotion of that memorable occasion and tried to feel the old satisfying anger. That day by the pond had witnessed its last spasmodic flicker. Anne

---

8. This youth is named for both Dwight Lyman Moody (1837–1899), a revivalist evangelical who, with David Sankey, preached and sang the hymns they wrote together to vast crowds in mid-Victorian England and America, and Charles Haddon Spurgeon, an English revivalist Baptist minister, famous for preaching to 6,000 people in the Tabernacle that had been built for him in London, England.

9. Julius Caesar's *Conquest of Gaul* was for years a standard entrance-year Latin text.

1. Someone worth using your weapon against. "The stern joy which warriors feel—in foeman worthy of his steel." Adaptation of Sir Walter Scott, *The Lady of the Lake* 5.10, referring to Scottish warriors' weapons.

realized that she had forgiven and forgotten without knowing it. But it was too late.

And at least neither Gilbert nor anybody else, not even Diana, should ever suspect how sorry she was and how much she wished she hadn't been so proud and horrid! She determined to "shroud her feelings in deepest oblivion,"[2] and it may be stated here and now that she did it, so successfully that Gilbert, who possibly was not quite so indifferent as he seemed, could not console himself with any belief that Anne felt his retaliatory scorn. The only poor comfort he had was that she snubbed Charlie Sloane, unmercifully, continually and undeservedly.

Otherwise the winter passed away in a round of pleasant duties and studies. For Anne the days slipped by like golden beads on the necklace of the year. She was happy, eager, interested; there were lessons to be learned and honours to be won; delightful books to read; new pieces to be practised for the Sunday-school choir; pleasant Saturday afternoons at the manse with Mrs. Allan; and then, almost before Anne realized it, spring had come again to Green Gables and all the world was abloom once more.

Studies palled just a wee bit then; the Queen's class, left behind in school while the others scattered to green lanes and leafy woodcuts and meadow by-ways, looked wistfully out of the windows and discovered that Latin verbs and French exercises had somehow lost the tang and zest they had possessed in the crisp winter months. Even Anne and Gilbert lagged and grew indifferent. Teacher and taught were alike glad when the term was ended and the glad vacation days stretched rosily before them.

"But you've done good work this past year," Miss Stacy told them on the last evening, "and you deserve a good, jolly vacation. Have the best time you can in the out-of-door world and lay in a good stock of health and vitality and ambition to carry you through next year. It will be the tug of war,[3] you know—the last year before the Entrance."

"Are you going to be back next year, Miss Stacy?" asked Josie Pye.

Josie Pye never scrupled to ask questions; in this instance the rest of the class felt grateful to her; none of them would have dared to ask it of Miss Stacy, but all wanted to, for there had been alarming rumours running at large through the school for some time that Miss Stacy was not coming back the next year—that she had been offered

---

2. Hide her feelings. Perhaps adapted from "I must speak what I would have buried in the deepest oblivion." Walter Scott, *Kenilworth* (1821) chap. 36.

3. Rival teams pulling on a sturdy rope against each other. In Scottish Highland games, this is one of the major events (and, less gloriously, a standard contest at Sunday School picnics).

a position in the graded school[4] of her own home district and meant to accept. The Queen's class listened in breathless suspense for her answer.

"Yes, I think I will," said Miss Stacy. "I thought of taking another school, but I have decided to come back to Avonlea. To tell the truth, I've grown so interested in my pupils here that I found I couldn't leave them. So I'll stay and see you through."

"Hurrah!" said Moody Spurgeon. Moody Spurgeon had never been so carried away by his feelings before, and he blushed uncomfortably every time he thought about it for a week.

"Oh, I'm so glad," said Anne with shining eyes. "Dear Miss Stacy, it would be perfectly dreadful if you didn't come back. I don't believe I could have the heart to go on with my studies at all if another teacher came here."

When Anne got home that night she stacked all her text-books away in an old trunk in the attic, locked it, and threw the key into the blanket box.

"I'm not even going to look at a school book in vacation," she told Marilla. "I've studied as hard all the term as I possibly could and I've pored over that geometry until I know every proposition in the first book off by heart, even when the letters *are* changed. I just feel tired of everything sensible and I'm going to let my imagination run riot for the summer. Oh, you needn't be alarmed, Marilla. I'll only let it run riot within reasonable limits. But I want to have a real good jolly time this summer, for maybe it's the last summer I'll be a little girl. Mrs. Lynde says that if I keep stretching out next year as I've done this I'll have to put on longer skirts.[5] She says I'm all running to legs and eyes. And when I put on longer skirts I shall feel that I have to live up to them and be very dignified. It won't even do to believe in fairies then, I'm afraid; so I'm going to believe in them with all my whole heart this summer. I think we're going to have a very gay vacation. Ruby Gillis is going to have a birthday party soon and there's the Sunday-school picnic and the missionary concert next month. And Mr. Barry says that some evening he'll take Diana and me over to the White Sands Hotel and have dinner there. They have dinner there in the evening, you know. Jane Andrews was over once last summer and she says it was a dazzling sight to see the electric lights[6] and the flowers and all the lady guests in such beautiful

---

4. Instead of a one-room schoolhouse where a teacher taught all grades, Miss Stacy would teach in a larger school where the grades are separated.

5. Young ladies, as opposed to little girls, wore floor-length skirts. Anne is in the in-between stage now. At Queen's she will wear full-length skirts.

6. *AGG* shows the shift in technology from candles to gaslights to the use of electricity. Thomas Edison produced the first electric lights in 1879, and electric power became

dresses. Jane says it was her first glimpse into high life and she'll never forget it to her dying day."

Mrs. Lynde came up the next afternoon to find out why Marilla had not been at the Aid meeting on Thursday. When Marilla was not at Aid meeting people knew there was something wrong at Green Gables.

"Matthew had a bad spell with his heart Thursday," Marilla explained, "and I didn't feel like leaving him. Oh, yes, he's all right again now, but he takes them spells oftener than he used to and I'm anxious about him. The doctor says he must be careful to avoid excitement. That's easy enough, for Matthew doesn't go about looking for excitement by any means and never did, but he's not to do any very heavy work either and you might as well tell Matthew not to breathe as not to work. Come and lay off your things, Rachel. You'll stay to tea?"

"Well, seeing *you're* so pressing, perhaps I might as well stay," said Mrs. Rachel, who had not the slightest intention of doing anything else.

Mrs. Rachel and Marilla sat comfortably in the parlour while Anne got the tea and made hot biscuits[7] that were light and white enough to defy even Mrs. Rachel's criticism.

"I must say Anne has turned out a real smart girl," admitted Mrs. Rachel, as Marilla accompanied her to the end of the lane at sunset. "She must be a great help to you."

"She is," said Marilla, "and she's real steady and reliable now. I used to be afraid she'd never get over her feather-brained ways, but she has and I wouldn't be afraid to trust her in anything now."

"I never would have thought she'd have turned out so well that first day I was here three years ago," said Mrs. Rachel. "Lawful heart, shall I ever forget that tantrum of hers! When I went home that night I says to Thomas, says I, 'Mark my words, Thomas, Marilla Cuthbert'll live to rue the step she's took.' But I was mistaken and I'm real glad of it. I ain't one of those kind of people, Marilla, as can never be brought to own up that they've made a mistake. No, that never was my way, thank goodness. I did make a mistake in judging Anne, but it weren't no wonder, for an odder, unexpecteder witch of a child there never was in this world, that's what. There was no ciphering her out by the rules that worked with other children. It's nothing short of wonderful how she's improved these three years, but especially in looks. She's a real pretty girl got to be, though I

---

available in 1885 in some parts of PEI. Avonlea, like Cavendish, was slow to hook into the electric system: LMM did most of her early writing by the light of oil lamps or candles.

7. Unsweetened tea biscuits (not cookies, as in British usage), but leavened with baking powder to make them light. They were often served with jams at tea-time. Two recipes for these are in *Aunt Maud's Recipe Book*, ed. Crawford, 12, 42.

can't say I'm overly partial to that pale, big-eyed style myself. I like more snap and colour, like Diana Barry has or Ruby Gillis. Ruby Gillis' looks are real showy. But somehow—I don't know how it is but when Anne and them are together, though she ain't half as handsome, she makes them look kind of common and overdone—something like them white June lilies she calls narcissus alongside of the big, red peonies, that's what."

# Chapter XXXI

### WHERE THE BROOK AND RIVER MEET[1]

ANNE had her "good" summer and enjoyed it whole-heartedly. She and Diana fairly lived outdoors, revelling in all the delights that Lovers' Lane and the Dryad's Bubble and Willowmere and Victoria Island afforded. Marilla offered no objections to Anne's gipsyings. The Spencervale doctor who had come the night Minnie May had the croup met Anne at the house of a patient one afternoon early in vacation, looked her over sharply, screwed up his mouth, shook his head, and sent a message to Marilla Cuthbert by another person. It was:

"Keep that red-headed girl of yours in the open air all summer and don't let her read books until she gets more spring into her step."

This message frightened Marilla wholesomely. She read Anne's death warrant by consumption in it unless it was scrupulously obeyed. As a result, Anne had the golden summer of her life as far as freedom and frolic went. She walked, rowed, berried and dreamed to her heart's content; and when September came she was bright-eyed and alert, with a step that would have satisfied the Spencervale doctor and a heart full of ambition and zest once more.

"I feel just like studying with might and main," she declared as she brought her books down from the attic. "Oh, you good old friends, I'm glad to see your honest faces once more—yes, even you, geometry. I've had a perfectly beautiful summer, Marilla, and now I'm rejoicing as a strong man to run a race,[2] as Mr. Allan said last Sunday. Doesn't Mr. Allan preach magnificent sermons? Mrs. Lynde says he is improving every day and the first thing we know some city church will gobble him up and then we'll be left and have to turn to and break in another green preacher.[3] But I don't see the use of

1. A transition point. "Standing, with reluctant feet / Where the brook and river meet / Womanhood and childhood fleet!" Henry Wadsworth Longfellow, "Maidenhood" (1842). Also a story by Augusta De Bubna in *Demorest's Monthly Magazine* (April 1882): 351–56.
2. Ready for action. "[R]ejoiceth as a strong man to run a race." *Holy Bible*, Psalms 19.5.
3. Untrained, fresh from theological college.

meeting trouble half-way, do you, Marilla? I think it would be better just to enjoy Mr. Allan while we have him. If I were a man I think I'd be a minister. They can have such an influence for good, if their theology is sound; and it must be thrilling to preach splendid sermons and stir your hearers' hearts. Why can't women be ministers, Marilla? I asked Mrs. Lynde that and she was shocked and said it would be a scandalous thing. She said there might be female ministers[4] in the States and she believed there was, but thank goodness we hadn't got to that stage in Canada yet and she hoped we never would.[5] But I don't see why. I think women would make splendid ministers. When there is a social to be got up or a church tea or anything else to raise money the women have to turn to and do the work. I'm sure Mrs. Lynde can pray every bit as well as Superintendent Bell and I've no doubt she could preach too with a little practice."

"Yes, I believe she could," said Marilla drily. "She does plenty of unofficial preaching as it is. Nobody has much of a chance to go wrong in Avonlea with Rachel to oversee them."

"Marilla," said Anne in a burst of confidence, "I want to tell you something and ask you what you think about it. It has worried me terribly—on Sunday afternoons, that is, when I think specially about such matters. I do really want to be good; and when I'm with you or Mrs. Allan or Miss Stacy I want it more than ever and I want to do just what would please you and what you would approve of. But mostly when I'm with Mrs. Lynde I feel desperately wicked and as if I wanted to go and do the very thing she tells me I oughtn't to do. I feel irresistibly tempted to do it. Now, what do you think is the reason I feel like that? Do you think it's because I'm really bad and unregenerate?"

Marilla looked dubious for a moment. Then she laughed.

"If you are I guess I am too, Anne, for Rachel often has that very effect on me. I sometimes think she'd have more of an influence for good, as you say yourself, if she didn't keep nagging people to do right. There should have been a special commandment against nagging. But there, I shouldn't talk so. Rachel is a good Christian woman and she means well. There isn't a kinder soul in Avonlea and she never shirks her share of work."

"I'm very glad you feel the same," said Anne decidedly. "It's so encouraging. I sha'n't worry so much over that after this. But I dare say there'll be other things to worry me. They keep coming up new

4. In 1853, Antoinette Louisa Brown, a Congregationalist, became the first woman to be ordained in the United States. In George Eliot's *Adam Bede* (1859), Dinah Morris is a female Methodist preacher in England. In 1903 LMM listed this as one of her "four old favorite books." *SJ1* 286.
5. Women were first ordained as Presbyterian ministers in the United States in 1956, in Canada in 1967.

all the time—things to perplex you, you know. You settle one question and there's another right after. There are so many things to be thought over and decided when you're beginning to grow up. It keeps me busy all the time thinking them over and deciding what is right. It's a serious thing to grow up, isn't it, Marilla? But when I have such good friends as you and Matthew and Mrs. Allan and Miss Stacy I ought to grow up successfully, and I'm sure it will be my own fault if I don't. I feel it's a great responsibility because I have only the one chance. If I don't grow up right I can't go back and begin over again. I've grown two inches this summer, Marilla. Mr. Gillis measured me at Ruby's party. I'm so glad you made my new dresses longer. That dark green one is so pretty and it was sweet of you to put on the flounce. Of course I know it wasn't really necessary, but flounces are so stylish this fall and Josie Pye has flounces on all her dresses. I know I'll be able to study better because of mine. I shall have such a comfortable feeling deep down in my mind about that flounce."

"It's worth something to have that," admitted Marilla.

Miss Stacy came back to Avonlea school and found all her pupils eager for work once more. Especially did the Queen's class gird up their loins[6] for the fray, for at the end of the coming year, dimly shadowing their pathway already, loomed up that fateful thing known as "the Entrance," at the thought of which one and all felt their hearts sink into their very shoes. Suppose they did not pass! That thought was doomed to haunt Anne through the waking hours of that winter, Sunday afternoons inclusive, to the almost entire exclusion of moral and theological problems. When Anne had bad dreams she found herself staring miserably at pass lists of the Entrance exams, where Gilbert Blythe's name was blazoned at the top and in which hers did not appear at all.

But it was a jolly, busy, happy swift-flying winter. School work was as interesting, class rivalry as absorbing, as of yore. New worlds of thought, feeling, and ambition, fresh, fascinating fields of unexplored knowledge seemed to be opening out before Anne's eager eyes.

"Hills peeped o'er hills and Alps on Alps arose."[7]

Much of all this was due to Miss Stacy's tactful, careful, broad-minded guidance. She led her class to think and explore and discover for themselves and encouraged straying from the old beaten paths to a degree that quite shocked Mrs. Lynde and the school trustees, who viewed all innovations on established methods rather dubiously.

Apart from her studies Anne expanded socially, for Marilla, mind-

6. Dress for battle. "Gird up now thy loins like a man." *Holy Bible*, Job 38.3; 40.7.
7. New vistas appeared. "Hills peep o'er Hills, and Alps on Alps arise!" Alexander Pope, "An Essay on Criticism" (1711) 1. 232.

ful of the Spencervale doctor's dictum, no longer vetoed occasional outings. The Debating Club flourished and gave several concerts; there were one or two parties almost verging on grown-up affairs; there were sleigh drives and skating frolics galore.

Between times Anne grew, shooting up so rapidly that Marilla was astonished one day, when they were standing side by side, to find the girl was taller than herself.

"Why, Anne, how you've grown!" she said, almost unbelievingly. A sigh followed on the words. Marilla felt a queer regret over Anne's inches. The child she had learned to love had vanished somehow and here was this tall, serious-eyed girl of fifteen, with the thoughtful brows and the proudly poised little head, in her place. Marilla loved the girl as much as she had loved the child, but she was conscious of a queer sorrowful sense of loss. And that night when Anne had gone to prayer-meeting with Diana Marilla sat alone in the wintry twilight and indulged in the weakness of a cry. Matthew, coming in with a lantern, caught her at it and gazed at her in such consternation that Marilla had to laugh through her tears.

"I was thinking about Anne," she explained. "She's got to be such a big girl—and she'll probably be away from us next winter. I'll miss her terrible."

"She'll be able to come home often," comforted Matthew, to whom Anne was as yet and always would be the little, eager girl he had brought home from Bright River on that June evening four years before. "The branch railroad[8] will be built to Carmody by that time."

"It won't be the same thing as having her here all the time," sighed Marilla gloomily, determined to enjoy her luxury of grief uncomforted. "But there—men can't understand these things!"

There were other changes in Anne no less real than the physical change. For one thing, she became much quieter. Perhaps she thought all the more and dreamed as much as ever, but she certainly talked less.[9] Marilla noticed and commented on this also.

"You don't chatter half as much as you used to, Anne, nor use half as many big words. What has come over you?"

Anne coloured and laughed a little, as she dropped her book and looked dreamily out of the window, where big fat red buds were bursting out on the creeper in response to the lure of the spring sunshine.

"I don't know—I don't want to talk as much," she said, denting

8. In the 1880s PEI, like the rest of Canada, enjoyed a second railroad building boom. (An early boom and bust in railroad building had brought PEI into Canadian confederation in the 1860s.) In 1890, LMM as a girl had enjoyed a transcontinental trip when a branch railroad was being extended to Prince Albert, Saskatchewan, her father's home.

9. Mark of conformity to social norms for a young lady.

her chin thoughtfully with her forefinger. "It's nicer to think dear, pretty thoughts and keep them in one's heart, like treasures. I don't like to have them laughed at or wondered over. And somehow I don't want to use big words any more. It's almost a pity, isn't it, now that I'm really growing big enough to say them if I did want to. It's fun to be almost grown up in some ways, but it's not the kind of fun I expected, Marilla. There's so much to learn and do and think that there isn't time for big words. Besides, Miss Stacy says the short ones are much stronger and better. She makes us write all our essays as simply as possible. It was hard at first. I was so used to crowding in all the fine big words I could think of—and I thought of any number of them. But I've got used to it now and I see it's so much better."

"What has become of your story club? I haven't heard you speak of it for a long time."

"The story club isn't in existence any longer. We hadn't time for it—and anyhow I think we had got tired of it. It was silly to be writing about love and murder and elopements and mysteries. Miss Stacy sometimes has us write a story for training in composition, but she won't let us write anything but what might happen in Avonlea in our own lives, and she criticizes it very sharply and makes us criticize our own too. I never thought my compositions had so many faults until I began to look for them myself. I felt so ashamed I wanted to give up altogether, but Miss Stacy said I could learn to write well if I only trained myself to be my own severest critic. And so I am trying to."

"You've only two more months before the Entrance," said Marilla. "Do you think you'll be able to get through?"

Anne shivered.

"I don't know. Sometimes I think I'll be all right—and then I get horribly afraid. We've studied hard and Miss Stacy has drilled us thoroughly, but we mayn't get through for all that. We've each got a stumbling-block.[1] Mine is geometry of course, and Jane's is Latin and Ruby's and Charlie's is algebra and Josie's is arithmetic. Moody Spurgeon says he feels it in his bones that he is going to fail in English history. Miss Stacy is going to give us examinations in June just as hard as we'll have at the Entrance and mark us just as strictly, so we'll have some idea. I wish it was all over, Marilla. It haunts me. Sometimes I wake up in the night and wonder what I'll do if I don't pass."

"Why, go to school next year and try again," said Marilla unconcernedly.

"Oh, I don't believe I'd have the heart for it. It would be such a

---

1. An obstacle: "But we preach Christ crucified, unto the Jews a stumbling block, and unto the Greeks foolishness." *Holy Bible*, I Corinthians 1.23.

disgrace to fail, especially if Gil—if the others passed. And I get so nervous in an examination that I'm likely to make a mess of it. I wish I had nerves like Jane Andrews. Nothing rattles her."

Anne sighed and, dragging her eyes from the witcheries of the spring world, the beckoning day of breeze and blue, and the green things upspringing in the garden, buried herself resolutely in her book. There would be other springs, but if she did not succeed in passing the Entrance Anne felt convinced that she would' never recover sufficiently to enjoy them.

## Chapter XXXII

### THE PASS LIST IS OUT

WITH the end of June came the close of the term and the close of Miss Stacy's rule in Avonlea school. Anne and Diana walked home that evening feeling very sober indeed. Red eyes and damp handkerchiefs bore convincing testimony to the fact that Miss Stacy's farewell words must have been quite as touching as Mr. Phillips' had been under similar circumstances three years before. Diana looked back at the school-house from the foot of the spruce hill and sighed deeply.

"It does seem as if it was the end of everything, doesn't it?" she said dismally.

"You oughtn't to feel half as badly as I do," said Anne, hunting vainly for a dry spot on her handkerchief. "You'll be back again next winter, but I suppose I've left the dear old school for ever—if I have good luck, that is."

"It won't be a bit the same. Miss Stacy won't be there, nor you nor Jane nor Ruby probably. I shall have to sit all alone, for I couldn't bear to have another deskmate after you. Oh, we have had jolly times, haven't we, Anne? It's dreadful to think they're all over."

Two big tears rolled down by Diana's nose.

"If you would stop crying I could," said Anne imploringly. "Just as soon as I put away my hanky I see you brimming up and that starts me off again. As Mrs. Lynde says, 'If you can't be cheerful, be as cheerful as you can.' After all, I dare say I'll be back next year. This is one of the times I *know* I'm not going to pass. They're getting alarmingly frequent."

"Why, you came out splendidly in the exams Miss Stacy gave."

"Yes, but those exams didn't make me nervous. When I think of the real thing you can't imagine what a horrid cold fluttery feeling comes round my heart. And then my number is thirteen and Josie

Pye says it's so unlucky. I am *not* superstitious and I know it can make no difference. But still I wish it wasn't thirteen."

"I do wish I were going in with you," said Diana. "Wouldn't we have a perfectly elegant time? But I suppose you'll have to cram in the evenings."

"No; Miss Stacy has made us promise not to open a book at all. She says it would only tire and confuse us and we are to go out walking and not think about the exams at all and go to bed early. It's good advice, but I expect it will be hard to follow; good advice is apt to be, I think. Prissy Andrews told me that she sat up half the night every night of her Entrance week and crammed for dear life: and I had determined to sit up *at least* as long as she did. It was so kind of your Aunt Josephine to ask me to stay at Beechwood while I'm in town."

"You'll write to me while you're in, won't you?"

"I'll write Tuesday night and tell you how the first day goes," promised Anne.

"I'll be haunting the post-office Wednesday," vowed Diana.

Anne went to town the following Monday and on Wednesday Diana haunted the post-office, as agreed, and got her letter.

"Dearest Diana," wrote Anne, "here it is Tuesday night and I'm writing this in the library at Beechwood. Last night I was horribly lonesome all alone in my room and wished so much you were with me. I couldn't 'cram' because I'd promised Miss Stacy not to, but it was as hard to keep from opening my history as it used to be to keep from reading a story before my lessons were learned.

"This morning Miss Stacy came for me and we went to the Academy, calling for Jane and Ruby and Josie on our way. Ruby asked me to feel her hands and they were as cold as ice. Josie said I looked as if I hadn't slept a wink and she didn't believe I was strong enough to stand the grind of the teacher's course even if I did get through. There are times and seasons even yet when I don't feel that I've made any great headway in learning to like Josie Pye!

"When we reached the Academy there were scores of students there from all over the Island. The first person we saw was Moody Spurgeon sitting on the steps and muttering away to himself. Jane asked him what on earth he was doing and he said he was repeating the multiplication table over and over to steady his nerves and for pity's sake not to interrupt him, because if he stopped for a moment he got frightened and forgot everything he ever knew, but the multiplication table kept all his facts firmly in their proper place!

"When we were assigned to our rooms Miss Stacy had to leave us. Jane and I sat together and Jane was so composed that I envied her. No need of the multiplication table for good steady, sensible Jane! I wondered if I looked as I felt and if they could hear my heart thumping clear across the room. Then a man came in and began distributing the English examination sheets. My hands grew cold then and my head fairly whirled around as I picked it up. Just one awful moment,—Diana, I felt exactly as I did four years ago when I asked Marilla if I might stay at Green Gables—and then everything cleared up in my mind and my heart began beating again—I forgot to say that it had stopped altogether!—for I knew I could do something with *that* paper anyhow.

"At noon we went home for dinner and then back again for history in the afternoon. The history was a pretty hard paper and I got dreadfully mixed up in the dates. Still, I think I did fairly well to-day. But oh, Diana, to-morrow the geometry exam comes off and when I think of it it takes every bit of determination I possess to keep from opening my Euclid.[1] If I thought the multiplication table would help me any I would recite it from now till to-morrow morning.

"I went down to see the other girls this evening. On my way I met Moody Spurgeon wandering distractedly around. He said he knew he had failed in history and he was born to be a disappointment to his parents and he was going home on the morning train; and it would be easier to be a carpenter than a minister, anyhow. I cheered him up and persuaded him to stay to the end because it would be unfair to Miss Stacy if he didn't. Sometimes I have wished I was born a boy, but when I see Moody Spurgeon I'm always glad I'm a girl and not his sister.

"Ruby was in hysterics when I reached their boarding-house; she had just discovered a fearful mistake she had made in her English paper. When she recovered we went up-town and had an ice-cream. How we wished you had been with us.

"Oh, Diana, if only the geometry examination were over! But there, as Mrs. Lynde would say, the sun will go on rising and setting whether I fail in geometry or not. That is true but not especially comforting. I think I'd rather it *didn't* go on if I failed!

"Yours devotedly,
"ANNE."

The geometry examination and all the others were over in due time and Anne arrived home on Friday evening, rather tired but with an air of chastened triumph about her. Diana was over at Green Gables when she arrived and they met as if they had been parted for years.

"You old darling, it's perfectly splendid to see you back again. It seems like an age since you went to town and oh, Anne, how did you get along?"

"Pretty well, I think, in everything but the geometry. I don't know

---

1. Geometry text, named for Greek mathematician of the fourth century B.C.E.

whether I passed in it or not and I have a creepy, crawly presentiment that I didn't. Oh, how good it is to be back! Green Gables is the dearest, loveliest spot in the world."

"How did the others do?"

"The girls say they know they didn't pass, but I think they did pretty well. Josie says the geometry was so easy a child of ten could do it! Moody Spurgeon still thinks he failed in history and Charlie says he failed in algebra. But we don't really know anything about it and won't until the pass list is out. That won't be for a fortnight. Fancy living a fortnight in such suspense! I wish I could go to sleep and never wake up until it is over."

Diana knew it would be useless to ask how Gilbert Blythe had fared, so she merely said:

"Oh, you'll pass all right. Don't worry."

"I'd rather not pass at all than not come out pretty well up on the list," flashed Anne, by which she meant—and Diana knew she meant—that success would be incomplete and bitter if she did not come out ahead of Gilbert Blythe.

With this end in view Anne had strained every nerve during the examinations. So had Gilbert. They had met and passed each other on the street a dozen times without any sign of recognition and every time Anne had held her head a little higher and wished a little more earnestly that she had made friends with Gilbert when he asked her, and vowed a little more determinedly to surpass him in the examination. She knew that all Avonlea junior was wondering which would come out first; she even knew that Jimmy Glover and Ned Wright had a bet on the question and that Josie Pye had said there was no doubt in the world that Gilbert would be first; and she felt that her humiliation would be unbearable if she failed.

But she had another and nobler motive for wishing to do well. She wanted to "pass high" for the sake of Matthew and Marilla—especially Matthew. Matthew had declared to her his conviction that she "would beat the whole Island." That, Anne felt, was something it would be foolish to hope for even in the wildest dreams. But she did hope fervently that she would be among the first ten at least, so that she might see Matthew's kindly brown eyes gleam with pride in her achievement. That, she felt, would be a sweet reward indeed for all her hard work and patient grubbing among unimaginative equations and conjugations.

At the end of the fortnight Anne took to "haunting" the post-office also, in the distracted company of Jane, Ruby and Josie, opening the Charlottetown dailies[2] with shaking hands and cold, sinkaway feel-

---

2. Both the Charlottetown *Examiner* and the *Daily Patriot* carried full lists of PEI students' test results. LMM was listed as coming fifth (not first) in the province in her entrance exams.

ings as bad as any experienced during the Entrance week. Charlie and Gilbert were not above doing this too, but Moody Spurgeon stayed resolutely away.

"I haven't got the grit to go there and look at a paper in cold blood," he told Anne. "I'm just going to wait until somebody comes and tells me suddenly whether I've passed or not."

When three weeks had gone by without the pass list appearing Anne began to feel that she really couldn't stand the strain much longer. Her appetite failed and her interest in Avonlea doings languished. Mrs. Lynde wanted to know what else you could expect with a Tory superintendent of education at the head of affairs, and Matthew, noting Anne's paleness and indifference and the lagging steps that bore her home from the post-office every afternoon, began seriously to wonder if he hadn't better vote Grit at the next election.

But one evening the news came. Anne was sitting at her open window, for the time forgetful of the woes of examinations and the cares of the world, as she drank in the beauty of the summer dusk, sweet-scented with flower-breaths from the garden below and sibilant and rustling from the stir of poplars. The eastern sky above the firs was flushed faintly pink from the reflection of the west, and Anne was wondering dreamily if the spirit of colour looked like that, when she saw Diana come flying down through the firs, over the log bridge, and up the slope, with a fluttering newspaper in her hand.

Anne sprang to her feet, knowing at once what that paper contained. The pass list was out! Her head whirled and her heart beat until it hurt her. She could not move a step. It seemed an hour to her before Diana came rushing along the hall and burst into the room without even knocking, so great was her excitement.

"Anne, you've passed," she cried, "passed the *very first*—you and Gilbert both—you're ties—but your name is first. Oh, I'm so proud!"

Diana flung the paper on the table and herself on Anne's bed, utterly breathless and incapable of further speech. Anne lighted the lamp, oversetting the match-safe[3] and using up half a dozen matches before her shaking hands could accomplish the task. Then she snatched up the paper. Yes, she had passed—there was her name at the very top of a list of two hundred! That moment was worth living for.

"You did just splendidly, Anne," puffed Diana, recovering sufficiently to sit up and speak, for Anne, starry-eyed and rapt, had not uttered a word. "Father brought the paper home from Bright River

---

3. Receptacle for matches ("lucifers") to light the lamp.

not ten minutes ago—it came out on the afternoon train, you know, and won't be here till to-morrow by mail—and when I saw the pass list I just rushed over like a wild thing. You've all passed, every one of you, Moody Spurgeon and all, although he's conditioned in history.[4] Jane and Ruby did pretty well—they're half-way up—and so did Charlie. Josie just scraped through with three marks to spare, but you'll see she'll put on as many airs as if she'd led. Won't Miss Stacy be delighted? Oh, Anne, what does it feel like to see your name at the head of a pass list like that? If it were me I know I'd go crazy with joy. I am pretty near crazy as it is, but you're as calm and cool as a spring evening."

"I'm just dazzled inside," said Anne. "I want to say a hundred things, and I can't find words to say them in. I never dreamed of this—yes, I did, too, just once! I let myself think *once*, 'What if I should come out first?' quakingly, you know, for it seemed so vain and presumptuous to think I could lead the Island. Excuse me a minute, Diana. I must run right out to the field to tell Matthew. Then we'll go up the road and tell the good news to the others."

They hurried to the hayfield below the barn where Matthew was coiling hay,[5] and, as luck would have it, Mrs. Lynde was talking to Marilla at the lane fence.

"Oh, Matthew," exclaimed Anne. "I've passed and I'm first—or one of the first! I'm not vain, but I'm thankful."

"Well now, I always said it," said Matthew, gazing at the pass list delightedly. "I knew you could beat them all easy."

"You've done pretty well, I must say, Anne," said Marilla, trying to hide her extreme pride in Anne from Mrs. Rachel's critical eye. But that good soul said heartily:

"I just guess she has done well, and far be it from me to be backward in saying it. You're a credit to your friends, Anne, that's what, and we're all proud of you."

That night Anne, who had wound up a delightful evening by a serious little talk with Mrs. Allan at the manse, knelt sweetly by her open window in a great sheen of moonshine and murmured a prayer of gratitude and aspiration that came straight from her heart. There was in it thankfulness for the past and reverent petition for the future; and when she slept on her white pillow her dreams were as fair and bright and beautiful as maidenhood might desire.

---

4. Given a chance to write a supplemental examination in the summer.
5. Forming the raked hay into small cones or haycocks.

# Chapter XXXIII

## THE HOTEL CONCERT

"PUT on your white organdy, by all means, Anne," advised Diana decidedly.

They were together in the east gable chamber; outside it was only twilight—a lovely yellowish-green twilight with a clear blue cloudless sky. A big round moon, slowly deepening from her pallid lustre into burnished silver, hung over the Haunted Wood; the air was full of sweet summer sounds—sleepy birds twittering, freakish breezes, far-away voices and laughter. But in Anne's room the blind was drawn and the lamp lighted, for an important toilet[1] was being made.

The east gable was a very different place from what it had been on that night four years before, when Anne had felt its bareness penetrate to the marrow of her spirit with its inhospitable chill. Changes had crept in, Marilla conniving at them resignedly, until it was as sweet and dainty a nest as a young girl could desire.

The velvet carpet with the pink roses and the pink silk curtains of Anne's early visions had certainly never materialized; but her dreams had kept pace with her growth, and it is not probable she lamented them. The floor was covered with a pretty matting,[2] and the curtains that softened the high window and fluttered in the vagrant breezes were of pale green art muslin. The walls, hung not with gold and silver brocade tapestry, but with a dainty apple-blossom paper, were adorned with a few good pictures given Anne by Mrs. Allan. Miss Stacy's photograph occupied the place of honour, and Anne made a sentimental point of keeping fresh flowers on the bracket under it. To-night a spike of white lilies faintly perfumed the room like the dream of a fragrance. There was no "mahogany furniture," but there was a white-painted bookcase filled with books, a cushioned wicker rocker, a toilet-table befrilled with white muslin, a quaint, gilt-framed mirror with chubby pink cupids and purple grapes painted over its arched top, that used to hang in the spare room, and a low white bed.

Anne was dressing for a concert at the White Sands Hotel. The guests had got it up in aid of the Charlottetown hospital, and had hunted out all the available amateur talent in the surrounding districts to help it along. Bertha Sampson and Pearl Clay of the White Sands Baptist choir had been asked to sing a duet; Milton Clark of Newbridge was to give a violin solo; Winnie Adella Blair of Carmody

---

1. Preparation for public appearance, dressing, arranging the hair.
2. A floor mat made of hemp or other fibers.

was to sing a Scotch ballad;[3] and Laura Spencer of Spencervale and Anne Shirley of Avonlea were to recite.

As Anne would have said at one time, it was "an epoch in her life," and she was deliciously athrill with the excitement of it. Matthew was in the seventh heaven of gratified pride over the honour conferred on his Anne, and Marilla was not far behind, although she would have died rather than admit it, and said she didn't think it was very proper for a lot of young folks to be gadding over to the hotel without any responsible person with them.

Anne and Diana were to drive over with Jane Andrews and her brother Billy in their double-seated buggy; and several other Avonlea girls and boys were going, too. There was a party of visitors expected out from town, and after the concert a supper was to be given to the performers.

"Do you really think the organdy will be best?" queried Anne anxiously. "I don't think it's as pretty as my blue-flowered muslin—and it certainly isn't so fashionable."

"But it suits you ever so much better," said Diana. "It's so soft and frilly and clinging. The muslin is stiff, and makes you look too dressed up. But the organdy seems as if it grew on you."

Anne sighed and yielded. Diana was beginning to have a reputation for notable taste in dressing, and her advice on such subjects was much sought after. She was looking very pretty herself on this particular night in a dress of the lovely wild-rose pink, from which Anne was for ever debarred; but she was not to take any part in the concert, so her appearance was of minor importance. All her pains were bestowed upon Anne, who, she vowed, must, for the credit of Avonlea, be dressed and combed and adorned to the queen's taste.

"Pull out that frill a little more—so, here, let me tie your sash; now for your slippers. I'm going to braid your hair in two thick braids, and tie them half-way up with big white bows—no, don't pull out a single curl over your forehead—just have the soft part. There is no way you do your hair suits you so well, Anne, and Mrs. Allan says you look like a Madonna[4] when you part it so. I shall fasten this little white house rose[5] just behind your ear. There was just one on my bush, and I saved it for you."

"Shall I put my pearl beads on?" asked Anne. "Matthew brought me a string from town last week, and I know he'd like to see them on me."

Diana pursed up her lips, put her black head on one side critically,

---

3. Traditional song, appropriate for a Scottish-Canadian community. LMM grew up immersed in the Scottish oral tradition of storytelling, recitation, and song.
4. As in traditional paintings of Mary, mother of Christ.
5. From a miniature rose-bush, kept indoors in a pot.

and finally pronounced in favour of the beads, which were thereupon tied around Anne's slim milk-white throat.

"There's something so stylish about you, Anne," said Diana, with unenvious admiration. "You hold your head with such an air. I suppose it's your figure. I am just a dumpling. I've always been afraid of it, and now I know it is so. Well, I suppose I shall just have to resign myself to it."

"But you have such dimples," said Anne, smiling affectionately into the pretty, vivacious face so near her own. "Lovely dimples, like little dents in cream. I have given up all hope of dimples. My dimple-dream will never come true; but so many of my dreams have that I mustn't complain. Am I all ready now?"

"All ready," assured Diana, as Marilla appeared in the doorway, a gaunt figure with grayer hair than of yore and no fewer angles, but with a much softer face. "Come right in and look at our elocutionist,[6] Marilla. Doesn't she look lovely?"

Marilla emitted a sound between a sniff and a grunt.

"She looks neat and proper. I like that way of fixing her hair. But I expect she'll ruin that dress driving over there in the dust and dew with it, and it looks most too thin for these damp nights. Organdy's the most unserviceable stuff in the world anyhow, and I told Matthew so when he got it. But there is no use in saying anything to Matthew nowadays. Time was when he would take my advice, but now he just buys things for Anne regardless, and the clerks at Carmody know they can palm anything off on him. Just let them tell him a thing is pretty and fashionable, and Matthew plunks his money down for it. Mind you keep your skirt clear of the wheel, Anne, and put your warm jacket on."

Then Marilla stalked down-stairs, thinking proudly how sweet Anne looked, with that

"One moonbeam from the forehead to the crown"[7]

and regretting that she could not go to the concert herself to hear her girl recite.

"I wonder if it *is* too damp for my dress," said Anne anxiously.

"Not a bit of it," said Diana, pulling up the window blind. "It's a perfect night, and there won't be any dew. Look at the moonlight."

"I'm so glad my window looks east into the sun-rising," said Anne, going over to Diana. "It's so splendid to see the morning coming up over those long hills and glowing through those sharp fir tops. It's

---

6. A person professionally trained to entertain audiences with dramatized solo recitations. In 1890, in Prince Albert, Saskatchewan, sixteen-year-old LMM thrilled to the performance of Toronto elocutionist Agnes Knox. *SJ1* 34.

7. The "silver line" where a beautiful young woman parts her hair, as described in Elizabeth Barrett Browning's *Aurora Leigh* (1859) book. 4: "No one parts / Her hair with such a silver line as you, / One moonbeam from the forehead to the crown!"

new every morning, and I feel as if I washed my very soul in that bath of earliest sunshine. Oh, Diana, I love this little room so dearly. I don't know how I'll get along without it when I go to town next month."

"Don't speak of your going away to-night," begged Diana. "I don't want to think of it, it makes me so miserable, and I do want to have a good time this evening. What are you going to recite, Anne? And are you nervous?"

"Not a bit. I've recited so often in public I don't mind at all now. I've decided to give 'The Maiden's Vow.'[8] It's so pathetic. Laura Spencer is going to give a comic recitation, but I'd rather make people cry than laugh."

"What will you recite if they encore you?"

"They won't dream of encoring me," scoffed Anne, who was not without her own secret hopes that they would, and already visioned herself telling Matthew all about it at the next morning's breakfast-table. "There are Billy and Jane now—I hear the wheels. Come on."

Billy Andrews insisted that Anne should ride on the front seat with him, so she unwillingly climbed up. She would have much preferred to sit back with the girls, where she could have laughed and chattered to her heart's content. There was not much of either laughter or chatter in Billy. He was a big, fat, stolid youth of twenty, with a round, expressionless face, and a painful lack of conversational gifts. But he admired Anne immensely, and was puffed up with pride over the prospect of driving to White Sands with that slim, upright figure beside him.

Anne, by dint of talking over her shoulder to the girls and occasionally passing a sop of civility to Billy—who grinned and chuckled and never could think of any reply until it was too late—contrived to enjoy the drive in spite of all. It was a night for enjoyment. The road was full of buggies, all bound for the hotel, and laughter, silver-clear, echoed and re-echoed along it. When they reached the hotel it was a blaze of light from top to bottom. They were met by the ladies of the concert committee, one of whom took Anne off to the performers' dressing-room, which was filled with the members of a Charlottetown Symphony Club,[9] among whom Anne felt suddenly shy and frightened and countrified. Her dress, which, in the east gable, had seemed so dainty and pretty, now seemed simple and

---

8. A number of nineteenth-century poems were published under this name, including a three-verse ballad (1869) by Caroline Oliphant, Baroness Nairne, creator of pseudo-Jacobite songs such as "Charlie is my darling" and "Will ye no come back again?" and the long privately published poem, "Mars la tour, or the Maiden's Vow" (1883), by Stafford MacGregor. See also Walter Scott's "Nora's Vow" and William Cullen Bryant's "Song of the Greek Amazon." (Anne did not recite "The Highwayman," as depicted in the 1985 movie.) See NCE 297–98.

9. A group of amateur musical performers.

plain—too simple and plain, she thought, among all the silks and laces that glistened and rustled around her. What were her pearl beads compared to the diamonds of the big, handsome lady near her? And how poor her one wee white rose must look beside all the hot-house flowers the others wore! Anne laid her hat and jacket away, and shrank miserably into a corner. She wished herself back in the white room at Green Gables.

It was still worse on the platform of the big concert hall of the hotel, where she presently found herself. The electric lights dazzled her eyes, the perfume and hum bewildered her. She wished she were sitting down in the audience with Diana and Jane, who seemed to be having a splendid time away at the back. She was wedged in between a stout lady in pink silk and a tall, scornful looking girl in a white lace dress. The stout lady occasionally turned her head squarely around and surveyed Anne through her eyeglasses until Anne, acutely sensitive of being so scrutinized, felt that she must scream aloud; and the white lace girl kept talking audibly to her next neighbour about the "country bumpkins" and "rustic belles" in the audience, languidly anticipating "such fun" from the displays of local talent on the programme.[1] Anne believed that she would hate that white lace girl to the end of life.

Unfortunately for Anne, a professional elocutionist was staying at the hotel and had consented to recite. She was a lithe, dark-eyed woman in a wonderful gown of shimmering gray stuff like woven moonbeams, with gems on her neck and in her dark hair. She had a marvellously flexible voice and wonderful power of expression; the audience went wild over her selection. Anne, forgetting all about herself and her troubles for the time, listened with rapt and shining eyes; but when the recitation ended she suddenly put her hands over her face. She could never get up and recite after that—never. Had she ever thought she could recite? Oh, if she were only back at Green Gables!

At this unpropitious moment her name was called. Somehow, Anne—who did not notice the rather guilty little start of surprise the white lace girl gave, and would not have understood the subtle compliment implied therein if she had—got on her feet, and moved dizzily out to the front. She was so pale that Diana and Jane, down in the audience, clasped each other's hands in nervous sympathy.

Anne was the victim of an overwhelming attack of stage fright. Often as she had recited in public, she had never before faced such an audience as this, and the sight of it paralyzed her energies completely. Everything was so strange, so brilliant, so bewildering—the

---

1. Unsophisticated rural people (from Dutch "boomkin," a little tree or bush). "Belles" is an old-fashioned term for beauties, from the French.

rows of ladies in evening dress, the critical faces, the whole atmosphere of wealth and culture about her. Very different this from the
plain benches at the Debating Club, filled with the homely, sympathetic faces of friends and neighbours. These people, she thought,
would be merciless critics. Perhaps, like the white lace girl, they
anticipated amusement from her "rustic" efforts. She felt hopelessly,
helplessly ashamed and miserable. Her knees trembled, her heart
fluttered, a horrible faintness came over her; not a word could she
utter, and the next moment she would have fled from the platform
despite the humiliation which, she felt, must ever after be her portion if she did so.

But suddenly, as her dilated, frightened eyes gazed out over the
audience, she saw Gilbert Blythe away at the back of the room, bending forward with a smile on his face—a smile which seemed to Anne
at once triumphant and taunting. In reality it was nothing of the
kind. Gilbert was merely smiling with appreciation of the whole affair
in general and of the effect produced by Anne's slender white form
and spiritual face against a background of palms in particular. Josie
Pye, whom he had driven over, sat beside him, and her face certainly
was both triumphant and taunting. But Anne did not see Josie, and
would not have cared if she had. She drew a long breath and flung
her head up proudly, courage and determination tingling over her
like an electric shock. She *would not* fail before Gilbert Blythe—he
should never be able to laugh at her, never, never! Her fright and
nervousness vanished; and she began her recitation, her clear, sweet
voice reaching to the farthest corner of the room without a tremor
or a break. Self-possession was fully restored to her, and in the reaction from that horrible moment of powerlessness she recited as she
had never done before. When she finished there were bursts of honest applause. Anne, stepping back to her seat, blushing with shyness
and delight, found her hand vigorously clasped and shaken by the
stout lady in pink silk.

"My dear, you did splendidly," she puffed. "I've been crying like a
baby, actually I have. There, they're encoring you—they're bound to
have you back!"

"Oh, I can't go," said Anne confusedly. "But yet—I must, or Matthew will be disappointed. He said they would encore me."

"Then don't disappoint Matthew," said the pink lady, laughing.

Smiling, blushing, limpid-eyed, Anne tripped back and gave a
quaint, funny little selection that captivated her audience still further. The rest of the evening was quite a little triumph for her.

When the concert was over, the stout, pink lady—who was the
wife of an American millionaire—took her under her wing, and introduced her to everybody; and everybody was very nice to her. The
professional elocutionist, Mrs. Evans, came and chatted with her,

telling her that she had a charming voice and "interpreted" her selections beautifully. Even the white lace girl paid her a languid little compliment. They had supper in the big, beautifully decorated dining-room: Diana and Jane were invited to partake of this, also, since they had come with Anne, but Billy was nowhere to be found, having decamped in mortal fear of some such invitation. He was in waiting for them, with the team, however, when it was all over, and the three girls came merrily out into the calm, white moonshine radiance. Anne breathed deeply, and looked into the clear sky beyond the dark boughs of the firs.

Oh, it was good to be out again in the purity and silence of the night! How great and still and wonderful everything was, with the murmur of the sea sounding through it and the darkling cliffs beyond like grim giants guarding enchanted coasts.

"Hasn't it been a perfectly splendid time?" sighed Jane, as they drove away. "I just wish I was a rich American[2] and could spend my summer at a hotel and wear jewels and low-necked dresses and have ice-cream and chicken salad every blessed day. I'm sure it would be ever so much more fun than teaching school. Anne, your recitation was simply great, although I thought at first you were never going to begin. I think it was better than Mrs. Evans'."

"Oh, no, don't say things like that, Jane," said Anne quickly, "because it sounds silly. It couldn't be better than Mrs. Evans', you know, for she is a professional, and I'm only a schoolgirl, with a little knack of reciting. I'm quite satisfied if the people just liked mine pretty well."

"I've a compliment for you, Anne," said Diana. "At least I think it must be a compliment because of the tone he said it in. Part of it was anyhow. There was an American sitting behind Jane and me—such a romantic-looking man, with coal-black hair and eyes. Josie Pye says he is a distinguished artist, and that her mother's cousin in Boston is married to a man that used to go to school with him. Well, we heard him say—didn't we, Jane?—'Who is that girl on the platform with the splendid Titian hair?[3] She has a face I should like to paint.' There now, Anne. But what does Titian hair mean?"

"Being interpreted it means plain red, I guess," laughed Anne. "Titian was a very famous artist who liked to paint red-haired women."

"*Did* you see all the diamonds those ladies wore?" sighed Jane. "They were simply dazzling. Wouldn't you just love to be rich, girls?"

"We *are* rich," said Anne stanchly. "Why, we have sixteen years to

2. Most of the Americans the Island knew were wealthy vacationers.
3. As in the sixteenth-century paintings by Titian (Tiziano Vecellio). The exact meaning of the term became an issue in LMM's lawsuit against her publisher, L. C. Page. *SJ2* 382, 386.

our credit, and we're happy as queens, and we've all got imaginations, more or less. Look at that sea, girls—all silver and shadow and vision of things not seen.[4] We couldn't enjoy its loveliness any more if we had millions of dollars and ropes of diamonds. You wouldn't change into any of those women if you could. Would you want to be that white lace girl and wear a sour look all your life, as if you'd been born turning up your nose at the world? Or the pink lady, kind and nice as she is, so stout and short that you'd really no figure at all? Or even Mrs. Evans, with that sad, sad look in her eyes? She must have been dreadfully unhappy sometime to have such a look. You *know* you wouldn't, Jane Andrews!"

"I *don't* know—exactly," said Jane unconvinced. "I think diamonds would comfort a person for a good deal."

"Well, I don't want to be any one but myself, even if I go uncomforted by diamonds all my life," declared Anne. "I'm quite content to be Anne of Green Gables, with my string of pearl beads. I know Matthew gave me as much love with them as ever went with Madame the Pink Lady's jewels."

# Chapter XXXIV

### A QUEEN'S GIRL

THE next three weeks were busy ones at Green Gables, for Anne was getting ready to go to Queen's, and there was much sewing to be done, and many things to be talked over and arranged. Anne's outfit was ample and pretty, for Matthew saw to that, and Marilla for once made no objections whatever to anything he purchased or suggested. More—one evening she went up to the east gable with her arms full of a delicate pale green material.

"Anne, here's something for a nice light dress for you. I don't suppose you really need it; you've plenty of pretty waists; but I thought maybe you'd like something real dressy to wear if you were asked out anywhere of an evening in town, to a party or anything like that. I hear that Jane and Ruby and Josie have got 'evening dresses,' as they call them, and I don't mean you shall be behind them. I got Mrs. Allan to help me pick it in town last week, and we'll get Emily Gillis to make it for you. Emily has got taste, and her fits aren't to be equalled."

"Oh, Marilla, it's just lovely," said Anne. "Thank you so much. I don't believe you ought to be so kind to me—it's making it harder every day for me to go away."

4. Suggestion of beauty. "Now faith is the substance of things hoped for, the evidence of things not seen." *Holy Bible*, Hebrews 11.1.

The green dress was made up with as many tucks and frills and shirrings as Emily's taste permitted. Anne put it on one evening for Matthew's and Marilla's benefit, and recited "The Maiden's Vow" for them in the kitchen. As Marilla watched the bright, animated face and graceful motions her thoughts went back to the evening Anne had arrived at Green Gables, and memory recalled a vivid picture of the odd, frightened child in her preposterous yellowish-brown wincey dress, the heartbreak looking out of her tearful eyes. Something in the memory brought tears to Marilla's own eyes.

"I declare, my recitation has made you cry, Marilla," said Anne gaily, stooping over Marilla's chair to drop a butterfly kiss on that lady's cheek. "Now, I call that a positive triumph."

"No, I wasn't crying over your piece," said Marilla, who would have scorned to be betrayed into such weakness by any "poetry stuff." "I just couldn't help thinking of the little girl you used to be, Anne. And I was wishing you could have stayed a little girl, even with all your queer ways. You're grown up now and you're going away; and you look so tall and stylish and so—so—different altogether in that dress—as if you didn't belong in Avonlea at all—and I just got lonesome thinking it all over."

"Marilla!" Anne sat down on Marilla's gingham lap, took Marilla's lined face between her hands, and looked gravely and tenderly into Marilla's eyes. "I'm not a bit changed—not really. I'm only just pruned down and branched out.[1] The real *me*—back here—is just the same. It won't make a bit of difference where I go or how much I change outwardly; at heart I shall always be your little Anne, who will love you and Matthew and dear Green Gables more and better every day of her life."

Anne laid her fresh young cheek against Marilla's faded one, and reached out a hand to pat Matthew's shoulder. Marilla would have given much just then to have possessed Anne's power of putting her feelings into words; but nature and habit had willed it otherwise, and she could only put her arms close about her girl and hold her tenderly to her heart, wishing that she need never let her go.

Matthew, with a suspicious moisture in his eyes, got up and went out-of-doors. Under the stars of the blue summer night he walked agitatedly across the yard to the gate under the poplars.

"Well now, I guess she ain't been much spoiled," he muttered, proudly. "I guess my putting in my oar occasional never did much harm after all. She's smart and pretty, and loving, too, which is better than all the rest. She's been a blessing to us, and there never was a luckier mistake than what Mrs. Spencer made—if it *was* luck. I don't

---

1. Tree-management simile appropriate for the orchard-rich PEI.

believe it was any such thing. It was Providence, because the Almighty saw we needed her, I reckon."

The day finally came when Anne must go to town. She and Matthew drove in one fine September morning, after a tearful parting with Diana and an untearful, practical one—on Marilla's side at least—with Marilla. But when Anne had gone Diana dried her tears and went to a beach picnic at White Sands with some of her Carmody cousins, where she contrived to enjoy herself tolerably well; while Marilla plunged fiercely into unnecessary work and kept at it all day long with the bitterest kind of a heartache—the ache that burns and gnaws and cannot wash itself away in ready tears. But that night, when Marilla went to bed, acutely and miserably conscious that the little gable room at the end of the hall was untenanted by any vivid young life and unstirred by any soft breathing, she buried her face in her pillow, and wept for her girl in a passion of sobs that appalled her when she grew calm enough to reflect how very wicked it must be to take on so about a sinful fellow creature.

Anne and the rest of the Avonlea scholars reached town just in time to hurry off to the Academy. That first day passed pleasantly enough in a whirl of excitement, meeting all the new students, learning to know the professors by sight and being assorted and organized into classes. Anne intended taking up the Second Year work,[2] being advised to do so by Miss Stacy; Gilbert Blythe elected to do the same. This meant getting a First Class teacher's license in one year instead of two, if they were successful; but it also meant much more and harder work. Jane, Ruby, Josie, Charlie, and Moody Spurgeon, not being troubled with the stirrings of ambition, were content to take up the Second Class work. Anne was conscious of a pang of loneliness when she found herself in a room with fifty other students, not one of whom she knew, except the tall, brown-haired boy across the room; and knowing him in the fashion she did, did not help her much, as she reflected pessimistically. Yet she was undeniably glad that they were in the same class; the old rivalry could still be carried on, and Anne would hardly have known what to do if it had been lacking.

"I wouldn't feel comfortable without it," she thought. "Gilbert looks awfully determined. I supposed he's making up his mind, here and now, to win the medal. What a splendid chin he has! I never noticed it before. I do wish Jane and Ruby had gone in for First Class, too. I suppose I won't feel so much like a cat in a strange garret when I get acquainted, though. I wonder which of the girls here are going

2. Anne and Gilbert will do two years' work in a single year, so as to get a First Class teaching certificate quickly; the others will get a Second Class certificate.

to be my friends. It's really an interesting speculation. Of course I promised Diana that no Queen's girl, no matter how much I liked her, should ever be as dear to me as she is; but I've lots of second-best affections to bestow. I like the look of that girl with the brown eyes and the crimson waist. She looks vivid and red-rosy; and there's that pale, fair one gazing out of the window. She has lovely hair, and looks as if she knew a thing or two about dreams. I'd like to know them both—know them well—well enough to walk with my arm about their waists, and call them nicknames. But just now I don't know them and they don't know me, and probably don't want to know me particularly. Oh, it's lonesome!"

It was lonesomer still when Anne found herself alone in her hall bedroom that night at twilight. She was not to board with the other girls, who all had relatives in town to take pity on them. Miss Josephine Barry would have liked to board her, but Beechwood was so far from the Academy that it was out of the question; so Miss Barry hunted up a boarding-house, assuring Matthew and Marilla that it was the very place for Anne.

"The lady who keeps it is a reduced gentle-woman,"[3] explained Miss Barry. "Her husband was a British officer, and she is very careful what sort of boarders she takes. Anne will not meet with any objectionable persons under her roof. The table is good, and the house is near the Academy, in a quiet neighbourhood."

All this might be quite true, and, indeed, proved to be so, but it did not materially help Anne in the first agony of homesickness that seized upon her. She looked dismally about her narrow little room, with its dull-papered, pictureless walls, its small iron bedstead and empty bookcase; and a horrible choke came into her throat as she thought of her own white room at Green Gables, where she would have the pleasant consciousness of a great green still out doors, of sweet peas growing in the garden, and moonlight falling on the orchard, of the brook below the slope and the spruce boughs tossing in the night wind beyond it, of a vast starry sky, and the light from Diana's window shining out through the gap in the trees. Here there was nothing of this; Anne knew that outside of her window was a hard street, with a network of telephone wires[4] shutting out the sky, the tramp of alien feet,[5] and a thousand lights gleaming on stranger faces. She knew that she was going to cry, and fought against it.

"I *won't* cry. It's silly—and weak—there's the third tear splashing

---

3. Someone of genteel family, financially straitened. The phrase reflects traces of aristocratic class system, still strong in a garrisoned capital city, with a regal representative of the queen in the Lieutenant Governor at Government House in Charlottetown.
4. Telephones had been in use in Charlottetown since the mid-1880s.
5. "And thou couldst bear / To see her trampled under alien feet!" Lewis Morris's "An Ode to Free Rome" (1870) 2.223–24.

down by my nose. There are more coming! I must think of something funny to stop them. But there's nothing funny except what is connected with Avonlea, and that only makes things worse—four— five—I'm going home next Friday, but that seems a hundred years away. Oh, Matthew is nearly home by now—and Marilla is at the gate, looking down the lane for him—six—seven—eight—oh, there's no use in counting them! They're coming in a flood presently. I can't cheer up—I don't *want* to cheer up. It's nicer to be miserable!"

The flood of tears would have come, no doubt, had not Josie Pye appeared at that moment. In the joy of seeing a familiar face Anne forgot that there had never been much love lost between her and Josie. As a part of Avonlea life even a Pye was welcome.

"I'm so glad you came up," Anne said sincerely.

"You've been crying," remarked Josie, with aggravating pity. "I suppose you're homesick—some people have so little self-control in that respect. I've no intention of being homesick, I can tell you. Town's too jolly after that poky old Avonlea. I wonder how I ever existed there so long. You shouldn't cry, Anne; it isn't becoming, for your nose and eyes get red, and then you seem *all* red. I'd a perfectly scrumptious time in the Academy to-day. Our French professor is simply a duck.[6] His moustache would give you kerwollops of the heart.[7] Have you anything eatable around, Anne? I'm literally starving. Ah, I guessed likely Marilla'd load you up with cake. That's why I called round. Otherwise I'd have gone to the park to hear the band play with Frank Stockley. He boards same place as I do, and he's a sport. He noticed you in class to-day, and asked me who the red-headed girl was. I told him you were an orphan that the Cuthberts had adopted, and nobody knew very much about what you'd been before that."

Anne was wondering if, after all, solitude and tears were not more satisfactory than Josie Pye's companionship when Jane and Ruby appeared, each with an inch of Queen's colour ribbon—purple and scarlet—pinned proudly to her coat. As Josie was not "speaking" to Jane just then she had to subside into comparative harmlessness.

"Well," said Jane with a sigh, "I feel as if I'd lived many moons since the morning. I ought to be home studying my Virgil[8]—that horrid old professor gave us twenty lines to start in on to-morrow. But I simply couldn't settle down to study to-night. Anne, methinks I see the traces of tears. If you've been crying *do* own up. It will restore my self-respect, for I was shedding tears freely before Ruby

6. Darling (slang), a person, as in "a queer duck."
7. Palpitations (of the heart). A made-up word. Not listed in English, American, or PEI (dialect) dictionaries.
8. Text for Latin class by Publius Virgilius Maro (70–19 B.C.E.).

came along. I don't mind being a goose so much if somebody else is goosey, too. Cake? You'll give me a teeny piece, won't you? Thank you. It has the real Avonlea flavour."

Ruby, perceiving the Queen's calendar lying on the table, wanted to know if Anne meant to try for the gold medal.

Anne blushed and admitted she was thinking of it.

"Oh, that reminds me," said Josie. "Queen's is to get one of the Avery scholarships[9] after all. The word came to-day. Frank Stockley told me—his uncle is one of the board of governors, you know. It will be announced in the Academy to-morrow."

An Avery scholarship! Anne felt her heart beat more quickly, and the horizons of her ambition shifted and broadened as if by magic. Before Josie had told the news Anne's highest pinnacle of aspiration had been a teacher's provincial license, Class First, at the end of the year, and perhaps the medal! But now in one moment Anne saw herself winning the Avery scholarship, taking an Arts course at Redmond College,[1] and graduating in a gown and mortar-board, all before the echo of Josie's words had died away. For the Avery scholarship was in English, and Anne felt that here her foot was on her native heath.[2]

A wealthy manufacturer of New Brunswick had died and left part of his fortune to endow a large number of scholarships to be distributed among the various high schools and academies of the Maritime Provinces,[3] according to their respective standings. There had been much doubt whether one would be allotted to Queen's, but the matter was settled at last, and at the end of the year the graduate who made the highest mark in English and English Literature would win the scholarship—two hundred and fifty dollars a year for four years at Redmond College. No wonder that Anne went to bed that night with tingling cheeks!

"I'll win that scholarship if hard work can do it," she resolved. "Wouldn't Matthew be proud if I got to be a B. A.? Oh, it's delightful to have ambitions. I'm so glad I have such a lot. And there never seems to be any end to them—that's the best of it. Just as soon as you attain to one ambition you see another one glittering higher up still. It does make life so interesting."

9. Financial support named in honor of a wealthy donor. Dalhousie University actually had an Avery scholarship. In 1998, an Avery Scholarship was established in PEI in tribute to the "spirit of Anne."
1. Modeled on Dalhousie University in Halifax where LMM studied for one year.
2. A proud announcement. "My foot is on my native heath . . ." Walter Scott, *Rob Roy* (1817) chap. 34.
3. A term for PEI, Nova Scotia, and New Brunswick; with Newfoundland they are now officially referred to as "Atlantic Provinces."

# Chapter XXXV

ANNE's homesickness wore off, greatly helped in the wearing by her week-end visits home. As long as the open weather lasted the Avonlea students went out to Carmody on the new branch railway every Friday night. Diana and several other Avonlea young folks were generally on hand to meet them and they all walked over to Avonlea in a merry party. Anne thought those Friday evening gipsyings over the autumnal hills in the crisp golden air, with the homelights of Avonlea twinkling beyond, were the best and dearest hours in the whole week.

Gilbert Blythe nearly always walked with Ruby Gillis and carried her satchel for her. Ruby was a very handsome young lady, now thinking herself quite as grown up as she really was; she wore her skirts as long as her mother would let her and did her hair up in town, though she had to take it down when she went home. She had large, bright-blue eyes, a brilliant complexion, and a plump showy figure. She laughed a great deal, was cheerful and good-tempered, and enjoyed the pleasant things of life frankly.

"But I shouldn't think she was the sort of girl Gilbert would like," whispered Jane to Anne. Anne did not think so either, but she would not have said so for the Avery scholarship. She could not help thinking, too, that it would be very pleasant to have such a friend as Gilbert to jest and chatter with and exchange ideas about books and studies and ambitions. Gilbert had ambitions, she knew, and Ruby Gillis did not seem the sort of person with whom such could be profitably discussed.

There was no silly sentiment in Anne's ideas concerning Gilbert. Boys were to her, when she thought about them at all, merely possible good comrades.[1] If she and Gilbert had been friends she would not have cared how many other friends he had nor with whom he walked. She had a genius for friendship; girl friends she had in plenty; but she had a vague consciousness that masculine friendship might also be a good thing to round out one's conceptions of companionship and furnish broader standpoints of judgment and comparison. Not that Anne could have put her feelings on the matter into just such clear definition. But she thought that if Gilbert had ever walked home with her from the train, over the crisp fields and along the ferny byways, they might have had many and merry and interesting conversations about the new world that was opening around them and their hopes and ambitions therein. Gilbert was a

1. LMM reports a similar feeling when young. *SJ1* 16.

clever young fellow, with his own thoughts about things and a determination to get the best out of life and put the best into it. Ruby Gillis told Jane Andrews that she didn't understand half the things Gilbert Blythe said; he talked just like Anne Shirley did when she had a thoughtful fit on and for her part she didn't think it any fun to be bothering about books and that sort of thing when you didn't have to. Frank Stockley had lots more dash and go, but then he wasn't half as good-looking as Gilbert and she really couldn't decide which she liked best!

In the Academy Anne gradually drew a little circle of friends about her, thoughtful, imaginative, ambitious students like herself. With the "rose-red" girl, Stella Maynard, and the "dream girl," Priscilla Grant, she soon became intimate, finding the latter pale spiritual-looking maiden to be full to the brim of mischief and pranks and fun, while the vivid, black-eyed Stella had a heartful of wistful dreams and fancies, as aerial and rainbow-like as Anne's own.

After the Christmas holidays the Avonlea students gave up going home on Fridays and settled down to hard work. By this time all the Queen's scholars had gravitated into their own places in the ranks and the various classes had assumed distinct and settled shadings of individuality. Certain facts had become generally accepted. It was admitted that the medal contestants had practically narrowed down to three—Gilbert Blythe, Anne Shirley, and Lewis Wilson; the Avery scholarship was more doubtful, any one of a certain six being a possible winner. The bronze medal for mathematics was considered as good as won by a fat, funny little up-country boy with a bumpy forehead and a patched coat.

Ruby Gillis was the handsomest girl of the year at the Academy; in the Second Year classes Stella Maynard carried off the palm for beauty, with a small but critical minority in favour of Anne Shirley. Ethel Marr was admitted by all competent judges to have the most stylish modes of hair-dressing, and Jane Andrews—plain, plodding, conscientious Jane—carried off the honours in the domestic science course. Even Josie Pye attained a certain preeminence as the sharpest-tongued young lady in attendance at Queen's. So it may be fairly stated that Miss Stacy's old pupils held their own in the wider arena of the academical course.

Anne worked hard and steadily. Her rivalry with Gilbert was as intense as it had ever been in Avonlea school, although it was not known in the class at large, but somehow the bitterness had gone out of it. Anne no longer wished to win for the sake of defeating Gilbert; rather, for the proud consciousness of a well-won victory over a worthy foeman. It would be worth while to win, but she no longer thought life would be insupportable if she did not.

In spite of lessons the students found opportunities for pleasant times. Anne spent many of her spare hours at Beechwood and generally ate her Sunday dinners there and went to church with Miss Barry. The latter was, as she admitted, growing old, but her black eyes were not dim nor the vigour of her tongue in the least abated. But she never sharpened the latter on Anne, who continued to be a prime favourite with the critical old lady.

"That Anne-girl improves all the time," she said. "I get tired of other girls—there is such a provoking and eternal sameness about them. Anne has as many shades as a rainbow and every shade is the prettiest while it lasts. I don't know that she is as amusing as she was when she was a child, but she makes me love her and I like people who make me love them. It saves me so much trouble in making myself love them."

Then, almost before anybody realized it, spring had come; out in Avonlea the Mayflowers were peeping pinkly out on the sere barrens where snow-wreaths lingered; and the "mist of green"[2] was on the woods and in the valleys. But in Charlottetown harassed Queen's students thought and talked only of examinations.

"It doesn't seem possible that the term is nearly over," said Anne. "Why, last fall it seemed so long to look forward to—a whole winter of studies and classes. And here we are, with the exams looming up next week. Girls, sometimes I feel as if those exams meant everything, but when I look at the big buds swelling on those chestnut trees and the misty blue air at the end of the streets they don't seem half so important."

Jane and Ruby and Josie, who had dropped in, did not take this view of it. To them the coming examinations were constantly very important indeed—far more important than chestnut buds or Maytime hazes. It was all very well for Anne, who was sure of passing at least, to have her moments of belittling them, but when your whole future depended on them—as the girls truly thought theirs did—you could not regard them philosophically.

"I've lost seven pounds in the last two weeks," sighed Jane. "It's no use to say don't worry. I *will* worry. Worrying helps you some—it seems as if you were doing something when you're worrying. It would be dreadful if I failed to get my license after going to Queen's all winter and spending so much money."

"I don't care," said Josie Pye. "If I don't pass this year I'm coming back next. My father can afford to send me. Anne, Frank Stockley says that Professor Tremaine said Gilbert Blythe was sure to get the medal and that Emily Clay would likely win the Avery scholarship."

"That may make me feel badly to-morrow, Josie," laughed Anne,

2. "On such a time as goes before the leaf / When all the wood stands in a mist of green." Alfred Tennyson, *Maud, and Other Poems* (1855), "The Brook," 2.13–14.

"but just now I honestly feel that as long as I know the violets are coming out all purple down in the hollow below Green Gables and that little ferns are poking their heads up in Lovers' Lane, it's not a great deal of difference whether I win the Avery or not. I've done my best and I begin to understand what is meant by the 'joy of the strife.'[3] Next to trying and winning, the best thing is trying and failing. Girls, don't talk about exams! Look at that arch of pale green sky over those houses and picture to yourselves what it must look like over the purply-dark beechwoods back of Avonlea."

"What are you going to wear for commencement,[4] Jane?" asked Ruby practically.

Jane and Josie both answered at once and the chatter drifted into a side eddy of fashions. But Anne, with her elbows on the window sill, her soft cheek laid against her clasped hands, and her eyes filled with visions, looked out unheedingly across city roof and spire to that glorious dome of sunset sky and wove her dreams of a possible future from the golden tissue of youth's own optimism. All the Beyond was hers with its possibilities lurking rosily in the oncoming years—each year a rose of promise to be woven into an immortal chaplet.[5]

# Chapter XXXVI

### THE GLORY AND THE DREAM[1]

On the morning when the final results of all the examinations were to be posted on the bulletin board at Queen's, Anne and Jane walked down the street together. Jane was smiling and happy; examinations were over and she was comfortably sure she had made a pass at least; further considerations troubled Jane not at all; she had no soaring ambitions and consequently was not affected with the unrest attendant thereon. For we pay a price for everything we get or take in this world; and although ambitions are well worth having, they are not to be cheaply won, but exact their dues of work and self-denial, anx-

---

3. "Some for stormy play and joy of strife:— / And some to fling away / A weary life." Mrs. Hemans, "Woman on the Field of Battle" (1827) st. 12.
4. Graduation ceremony when diplomas were conferred and prizes awarded. At her PWC graduation ceremony in the Charlottetown Opera House, LMM read her essay on "Portia." SJ1 111.
5. Wreath implying unending fame, like the classic laurel wreath.
1. "There was a time when meadow, grove and stream, / The earth, and every common sight, / To me did seem / Apparelled in celestial light, / The glory and the freshness of a dream. . . ." William Wordsworth, "Ode: Intimations on Immortality from Recollections of Early Childhood" (1807) 4.21.22. This is one of the few poems that LMM underlined in her copy of Wordsworth, purchased 1897.

iety and discouragement.[2] Anne was pale and quiet; in ten more minutes she would know who had won the medal and who the Avery. Beyond those ten minutes there did not seem, just then, to be anything worth being called Time.

"Of course you'll win one of them anyhow," said Jane, who couldn't understand how the faculty could be so unfair as to order it otherwise.

"I have no hope of the Avery," said Anne. "Everybody says Emily Clay will win it. And I'm not going to march up to that bulletin board and look at it before everybody. I haven't the moral courage. I'm going straight to the girls' dressing-room. You must read the announcements and then come and tell me, Jane. And I implore you in the name of our old friendship to do it as quickly as possible. If I have failed just say so, without trying to break it gently; and whatever you do *don't* sympathize with me. Promise me this, Jane."

Jane promised solemnly; but, as it happened, there was no necessity for such a promise. When they went up the entrance steps of Queen's they found the hall full of boys who were carrying Gilbert Blythe around on their shoulders and yelling at the tops of their voices, "Hurrah for Blythe, Medallist!"

For a moment Anne felt one sickening pang of defeat and disappointment. So she had failed and Gilbert had won! Well, Matthew would be sorry—he had been so sure she would win.

And then!

Somebody called out:

"Three cheers for Miss Shirley, winner of the Avery!"

"Oh, Anne," gasped Jane, as they fled to the girls' dressing-room amid hearty cheers. "Oh, Anne, I'm so proud! Isn't it splendid?"

And then the girls were around them and Anne was the centre of a laughing, congratulating group. Her shoulders were thumped and her hands shaken vigorously. She was pushed and pulled and hugged and among it all she managed to whisper to Jane:

"Oh, won't Matthew and Marilla be pleased! I must write the news home right away."

Commencement was the next important happening. The exercises were held in the big assembly hall of the Academy. Addresses were given, essays read, songs sung, the public award of diplomas, prizes and medals made.

Matthew and Marilla were there, with eyes and ears for only one student on the platform—a tall girl in pale green, with faintly flushed cheeks and starry eyes, who read the best essay and was pointed out and whispered about as the Avery winner.

2. Reflects LMM's experience as a would-be writer in the years before *AGG*.

"Reckon you're glad we kept her, Marilla?" whispered Matthew, speaking for the first time since he had entered the hall, when Anne had finished her essay.

"It's not the first time I've been glad," retorted Marilla. "You do like to rub things in, Matthew Cuthbert."

Miss Barry, who was sitting behind them, leaned forward and poked Marilla in the back with her parasol.

"Aren't you proud of that Anne-girl? I am," she said.

Anne went home to Avonlea with Matthew and Marilla that evening. She had not been home since April and she felt that she could not wait another day. The apple-blossoms were out and the world was fresh and young. Diana was at Green Gables to meet her. In her own white room, where Marilla had set a flowering house rose on the window sill, Anne looked about her and drew a long breath of happiness.

"Oh, Diana, it's so good to be back again. It's so good to see those pointed firs[3] coming out against the pink sky—and that white orchard and the old Snow Queen. Isn't the breath of the mint delicious? And that tea rose—why, it's a song and a hope and a prayer all in one. And it's *good* to see you again, Diana!"

"I thought you liked that Stella Maynard better than me," said Diana reproachfully. "Josie Pye told me you did. Josie said you were *infatuated* with her."

Anne laughed and pelted Diana with the faded "June lilies" of her bouquet.

"Stella Maynard is the dearest girl in the world except one and you are that one, Diana," she said. "I love you more than ever—and I've so many things to tell you. But just now I feel as if it were joy enough to sit here and look at you. I'm tired, I think—tired of being studious and ambitious. I mean to spend at least two hours to-morrow lying out in the orchard grass, thinking of absolutely nothing."

"You've done splendidly, Anne. I suppose you won't be teaching now that you've won the Avery?"

"No. I'm going to Redmond in September. Doesn't it seem wonderful? I'll have a brand-new stock of ambition laid in by that time after three glorious, golden months of vacation. Jane and Ruby are going to teach. Isn't it splendid to think we all got through even to Moody Spurgeon and Josie Pye?"

"The Newbridge trustees[4] have offered Jane their school already," said Diana. "Gilbert Blythe is going to teach, too. He has to. His

---

3. Echoes the title of New England novelist Sarah Orne Jewett's *The Country of the Pointed Firs* (1896). LMM comments that critics had seen a likeness to Jewett in her work. *SJ4* 40.
4. Local school boards consisted of three elected trustees who controlled hiring, set the salaries of teachers, and supervised their work.

father can't afford to send him to college next year, after all, so he means to earn his own way through. I expect he'll get the school here if Miss Ames decides to leave."

Anne felt a queer little sensation of dismayed surprise. She had not known this; she had expected that Gilbert would be going to Redmond also. What would she do without their inspiring rivalry? Would not work, even at a co-educational college with a real degree in prospect, be rather flat without her friend the enemy?

The next morning at breakfast it suddenly struck Anne that Matthew was not looking well. Surely he was much grayer than he had been a year before.

"Marilla," she said hesitatingly when he had gone out, "is Matthew quite well?"

"No, he isn't," said Marilla in a troubled tone. "He's had some real bad spells with his heart this spring and he won't spare himself a mite. I've been real worried about him, but he's some better this while back and we've got a good hired man, so I'm hoping he'll kind of rest and pick up. Maybe he will now you're home. You always cheer him up."

Anne leaned across the table and took Marilla's face in her hands.

"You are not looking as well yourself as I'd like to see you, Marilla. You look tired. I'm afraid you've been working too hard. You must take a rest, now that I'm home. I'm just going to take this one day off to visit all the dear old spots and hunt up my old dreams, and then it will be your turn to be lazy while I do the work."

Marilla smiled affectionately at her girl.

"It's not the work—it's my head. I've a pain so often now—behind my eyes. Doctor Spencer's been fussing with glasses, but they don't do me any good. There is a distinguished oculist[5] coming to the Island the last of June and the doctor says I must see him. I guess I'll have to. I can't read or sew with any comfort now. Well, Anne, you've done real well at Queen's I must say. To take First Class License[6] in one year and win the Avery scholarship—well, well, Mrs. Lynde says pride goes before a fall[7] and she doesn't believe in the higher education of women at all; she says it unfits them for woman's true sphere.[8] I don't believe a word of it. Speaking of Rachel reminds

---

5. An eye doctor. Few specialists were available on PEI, but a visiting oculist from Boston advertised in the issue of the Charlottetown *Patriot* that carried the names of LMM and others who had passed the entrance exam to PWC.

6. Qualified to teach in a certain range of schools, thanks to having taken second year courses at PWC.

7. "Pride goeth before destruction and an haughty spirit before a fall." *Holy Bible*, Proverbs 16.18.

8. Traditional nineteenth-century view that woman should be "an angel in the house," derived from a famous and influential poem by Coventry Patmore, "The Angel in the House" (1854/1862). In 1931, Virginia Woolf would famously declare in a lecture that "killing the Angel in the House was part of the occupation of a woman writer" in her generation.

me—did you hear anything about the Abbey Bank[9] lately, Anne?"

"I heard that it was shaky," answered Anne. "Why?"

"That is what Rachel said. She was up here one day last week and said there was some talk about it. Matthew felt real worried. All we have saved is in that bank—every penny. I wanted Matthew to put it in the Savings Bank[1] in the first place, but old Mr. Abbey was a great friend of father's and he'd always banked with him. Matthew said any bank with him at the head of it was good enough for anybody."

"I think he has only been its nominal head for many years," said Anne. "He is a very old man; his nephews are really at the head of the institution."

"Well, when Rachel told us that, I wanted Matthew to draw our money right out and he said he'd think of it. But Mr. Russell told him yesterday that the bank was all right."

Anne had her good day in the companionship of the outdoor world. She never forgot that day; it was so bright and golden and fair, so free from shadow and so lavish of blossom. Anne spent some of its rich hours in the orchard; she went to the Dryad's Bubble and Willowmere and Violet Vale; she called at the manse and had a satisfying talk with Mrs. Allan; and finally in the evening she went with Matthew for the cows, through Lovers' Lane to the back pasture. The woods were all gloried through with sunset and the warm splendour of it streamed down through the hill gaps in the west. Matthew walked slowly with bent head; Anne, tall and erect, suited her springing step to his.

"You've been working too hard to-day, Matthew," she said reproachfully. "Why won't you take things easier?"

"Well now, I can't seem to," said Matthew, as he opened the yard gate to let the cows through. "It's only that I'm getting old, Anne, and keep forgetting it. Well, well, I've always worked pretty hard and I'd rather drop in harness."

"If I had been the boy you sent for," said Anne wistfully, "I'd be able to help you so much now and spare you in a hundred ways. I could find it in my heart to wish I had been, just for that."

"Well now, I'd rather have you than a dozen boys, Anne," said Matthew patting her hand. "Just mind you that—rather than a dozen boys. Well now, I guess it wasn't a boy that took the Avery scholarship, was it? It was a girl—my girl—my girl that I'm proud of."

---

9. Canadian banking law was reformed in 1890 because of failures of several private banks between 1880 and 1890. Canadian bank law now favors a few large chartered banks, rather than the USA's unit banking system.

1. Bank underwritten by the government of PEI under the revised banking act.

He smiled his shy smile at her as he went into the yard. Anne took the memory of it with her when she went to her room that night and sat for a long while at her open window, thinking of the past and dreaming of the future. Outside the Snow Queen was mistily white in the moonshine; the frogs were singing in the marsh beyond Orchard Slope. Anne always remembered the silvery, peaceful beauty and fragrant calm of that night. It was the last night before sorrow touched her life; and no life is ever quite the same again when once that cold, sanctifying touch has been laid upon it.

# Chapter XXXVII

### THE REAPER WHOSE NAME IS DEATH[1]

"MATTHEW—Matthew—what is the matter? Matthew, are you sick?"

It was Marilla who spoke, alarm in every jerky word. Anne came through the hall, her hands full of white narcissus,—it was long before Anne could love the sight or odour of white narcissus again,— in time to hear her and to see Matthew standing in the porch door-way, a folded paper in his hand, and his face strangely drawn and gray. Anne dropped her flowers and sprang across the kitchen to him at the same moment as Marilla. They were both too late; before they could reach him Matthew had fallen across the threshold.

"He's fainted," gasped Marilla. "Anne, run for Martin—quick, quick! He's at the barn."

Martin, the hired man, who had just driven home from the post-office, started at once for the doctor, calling at Orchard Slope on his way to send Mr. and Mrs. Barry over. Mrs. Lynde, who was there on an errand, came too. They found Anne and Marilla distractedly try-ing to restore Matthew to consciousness.

Mrs. Lynde pushed them gently aside, tried his pulse, and then laid her ear over his heart. She looked at their anxious faces sorrow-fully and the tears came into her eyes.

"Oh, Marilla," she said gravely. "I don't think—we can do anything for him."

"Mrs. Lynde, you don't think—you can't think Matthew is—is—" Anne could not say the dreadful word; she turned sick and pallid.

"Child, yes, I'm afraid of it. Look at his face. When you've seen that look as often as I have you'll know what it means."

---

1. "There is a Reaper, whose name is Death / And, with his sickle keen, / He reaps the bearded grain at a breath / And the flowers that grow between." Henry Wadsworth Long-fellow, "The Reaper and the Flowers" (1839) st. 1. Montgomery's copy of Longfellow, purchased in 1896, is heavily underlined.

Anne looked at the still face and there beheld the seal of the Great Presence.[2]

When the doctor came he said that death had been instantaneous and probably painless, caused in all likelihood by some sudden shock. The secret of the shock was discovered to be in the paper Matthew had held and which Martin had brought from the office that morning. It contained an account of the failure of the Abbey Bank.

The news spread quickly through Avonlea, and all day friends and neighbours thronged Green Gables and came and went on errands of kindness for the dead and living. For the first time shy, quiet Matthew Cuthbert was a person of central importance; the white majesty of death had fallen on him and set him apart as one crowned.

When the calm night came softly down over Green Gables the old house was hushed and tranquil. In the parlour lay Matthew Cuthbert in his coffin, his long gray hair framing his placid face on which there was a little kindly smile as if he but slept, dreaming pleasant dreams. There were flowers about him—sweet old-fashioned flowers which his mother had planted in the homestead garden in her bridal days and for which Matthew had always had a secret, wordless love. Anne had gathered them and brought them to him, her anguished, tearless eyes burning in her white face. It was the last thing she could do for him.

The Barrys and Mrs. Lynde stayed with them that night. Diana, going to the east gable, where Anne was standing at her window, said gently:

"Anne dear, would you like to have me sleep with you to-night?"

"Thank you, Diana." Anne looked earnestly into her friend's face. "I think you won't misunderstand me when I say that I want to be alone. I'm not afraid. I haven't been alone one minute since it happened—and I want to be. I want to be quite silent and quiet and try to realize it. I *can't* realize it. Half the time it seems to me that Matthew can't be dead; and the other half it seems as if he must have been dead for a long time and I've had this horrible dull ache ever since."

Diana did not quite understand. Marilla's impassioned grief, breaking all the bounds of natural reserve and lifelong habit in its stormy rush, she could comprehend better than Anne's tearless agony. But she went away kindly, leaving Anne alone to keep her first vigil with sorrow.

Anne hoped that tears would come in solitude. It seemed to her a terrible thing that she could not shed a tear for Matthew, whom she

2. Mark of God—*i.e.*, death. Compare "Ten minutes later Rebecca came out from the Great Presence looking white and spent." Kate Douglas Wiggin, *Rebecca of Sunnybrook Farm* (1903) chap. 31.

had loved so much and who had been so kind to her, Matthew, who had walked with her last evening at sunset and was now lying in the dim room below with that awful peace on his brow. But no tears came at first, even when she knelt by her window in the darkness and prayed, looking up to the stars beyond the hills—no tears, only the same horrible dull ache of misery that kept on aching until she fell asleep, worn out with the day's pain and excitement.

In the night she awakened, with the stillness and the darkness about her, and the recollection of the day came over her like a wave of sorrow. She could see Matthew's face smiling at her as he had smiled when they parted at the gate that last evening—she could hear his voice saying, "My girl—my girl that I'm proud of." Then the tears came and Anne wept her heart out. Marilla heard her and crept in to comfort her.

"There—there—don't cry so, dearie. It can't bring him back. It—it—isn't right to cry so. I knew that to-day, but I couldn't help it then. He'd always been such a good, kind brother to me—but God knows best."

"Oh, just let me cry, Marilla," sobbed Anne. "The tears don't hurt me like that ache did. Stay here for a little while with me and keep your arm round me—so. I couldn't have Diana stay, she's good and kind and sweet—but it's not her sorrow—she's outside of it and she couldn't come close enough to my heart to help me. It's our sorrow—yours and mine. Oh, Marilla, what will we do without him?"

"We've got each other, Anne. I don't know what I'd do if you weren't here—if you'd never come. Oh, Anne, I know I've been kind of strict and harsh with you maybe—but you mustn't think I didn't love you as well as Matthew did, for all that. I want to tell you now when I can. It's never been easy for me to say things out of my heart, but at times like this it's easier. I love you as dear as if you were my own flesh and blood and you've been my joy and comfort ever since you came to Green Gables."

Two days afterwards they carried Matthew Cuthbert over his homestead threshold and away from the fields he had tilled and the orchards he had loved and the trees he had planted; and then Avonlea settled back to its usual placidity and even at Green Gables affairs slipped into their old groove and work was done and duties fulfilled with regularity as before, although always with the aching sense of "loss in all familiar things."[3] Anne, new to grief, thought it almost sad that it could be so—that they *could* go on in the old way without Matthew. She felt something like shame and remorse when she discovered that the sunrises behind the firs and the pale pink buds

3. "But still I wait with ear and eye / For something gone which should be nigh, / A loss in all familiar things. . . ." Of "Snow-bound" LMM writes in her copy of Whittier, "one of my favorite poems." John Greenleaf Whittier, "*Snow-bound: A Winter Idyl*" (1865) l. 421.

opening in the garden gave her the old inrush of gladness when she saw them—that Diana's visits were pleasant to her and that Diana's merry words and ways moved her to laughter and smiles—that, in brief, the beautiful world of blossom and love and friendship had lost none of its power to please her fancy and thrill her heart, that life still called to her with many insistent voices.

"It seems like disloyalty to Matthew, somehow, to find pleasure in these things now that he has gone," she said wistfully to Mrs. Allan one evening when they were together in the manse garden. "I miss him so much—all the time—and yet, Mrs. Allan, the world and life seem very beautiful and interesting to me for all. To-day Diana said something funny and I found myself laughing. I thought when it happened I could never laugh again. And it somehow seems as if I oughtn't to."

"When Matthew was here he liked to hear you laugh and he liked to know that you found pleasure in the pleasant things around you," said Mrs. Allan gently. "He is just away[4] now; and he likes to know it just the same. I am sure we should not shut our hearts against the healing influences that nature offers us. But I understand your feeling. I think we all experience the same thing. We resent the thought that anything can please us when some one we love is no longer here to share the pleasure with us, and we almost feel as if we were unfaithful to our sorrow when we find our interest in life returning to us."

"I was down to the graveyard to plant a rosebush on Matthew's grave this afternoon," said Anne dreamily. "I took a slip of the little white Scotch rose-bush his mother brought out from Scotland long ago;[5] Matthew always liked those roses the best—they were so small and sweet on their thorny stems. It made me feel glad that I could plant it by his grave—as if I were doing something that must please him in taking it there to be near him. I hope he has roses like them in heaven. Perhaps the souls of all those little white roses that he has loved so many summers were all there to meet him. I must go home now. Marilla is all alone and she gets lonely at twilight."

"She will be lonelier still, I fear, when you go away again to college," said Mrs. Allan.

Anne did not reply; she said good night and went slowly back to Green Gables. Marilla was sitting on the front door-steps and Anne sat down beside her. The door was open behind them, held back by

4. "I can not say, and I will not say / That he is dead.—He is just away!" James Whitcomb Riley. "Away" (1884) ll. 1–2.
5. In Ian MacLaren's novel, *Beside the Bonnie Brier Bush* (1895), admired by LMM in her youth, a white rose-bush grows in the Scottish kailyard. The white rose in Scotland was also a symbol of Bonnie Prince Charlie, implying sentimental loyalty and chivalry.

a big pink conch shell[6] with hints of sea sunsets in its smooth inner convolutions.

Anne gathered some sprays of pale yellow honey-suckle[7] and put them in her hair. She liked the delicious hint of fragrance, as of some aerial benediction, above her every time she moved.

"Doctor Spencer was here while you were away," Marilla said. "He says that the specialist will be in town to-morrow and he insists that I must go in and have my eyes examined. I suppose I'd better go and have it over. I'll be more than thankful if the man can give me the right kind of glasses to suit my eyes. You won't mind staying here alone while I'm away, will you? Martin will have to drive me in and there's ironing and baking to do."

"I shall be all right. Diana will come over for company for me. I shall attend to the ironing and baking beautifully—you needn't fear that I'll starch the handkerchiefs or flavour the cake with liniment."

Marilla laughed.

"What a girl you were for making mistakes in them days, Anne. You were always getting into scrapes. I did use to think you were possessed. Do you mind the time[8] you dyed your hair?"

"Yes, indeed. I shall never forget it," smiled Anne, touching the heavy braid of hair that was wound about her shapely head. "I laugh a little now sometimes when I think what a worry my hair used to be to me—but I don't laugh *much*, because it was a very real trouble then. I did suffer terribly over my hair and my freckles. My freckles are really gone; and people are nice enough to tell me my hair is auburn now—all but Josie Pye. She informed me yesterday that she really thought it was redder than ever, or at least my black dress made it look redder, and she asked me if people who had red hair ever got used to having it. Marilla, I've almost decided to give up trying to like Josie Pye. I've made what I would once have called a heroic effort to like her, but Josie Pye won't *be* liked."

"Josie is a Pye," said Marilla sharply, "so she can't help being disagreeable. I suppose people of that kind serve some useful purpose in society, but I must say I don't know what it is any more than I know the use of thistles.[9] Is Josie going to teach?"

"No, she is going back to Queen's next year. So are Moody Spurgeon and Charlie Sloane. Jane and Ruby are going to teach and they have both got schools—Jane at Newbridge and Ruby at some place up west."

---

6. A large trumpet-shaped shell, probably the souvenir of early voyages of Maritime sailors to the south seas.
7. Woodbine: a vine with clusters of small fragrant trumpet-shaped flowers, yellow or pink.
8. Remember when (dialect).
9. A pun on Josie's name as the Joe-Pye weed is useless. As weeds, thistles (with their strong root systems) are a nuisance to farmers, but the Scotch thistle is a national symbol standing for endurance in adversity.

"Gilbert Blythe is going to teach too, isn't he?"

"Yes"—briefly.

"What a nice-looking young fellow he is," said Marilla absently. "I saw him in church last Sunday and he seemed so tall and manly. He looks a lot like his father did at the same age. John Blythe was a nice boy. We used to be real good friends, he and I. People called him my beau."

Anne looked up with swift interest.

"Oh, Marilla—and what happened?—why didn't you—"

"We had a quarrel. I wouldn't forgive him when he asked me to. I meant to, after awhile—but I was sulky and angry and I wanted to punish him first. He never came back—the Blythes were all mighty independent. But I always felt—rather sorry. I've always kind of wished I'd forgiven him when I had the chance."

"So you've had a bit of romance in your life, too," said Anne softly.

"Yes, I suppose you might call it that. You wouldn't think so to look at me, would you? But you never can tell about people from their outsides. Everybody has forgot about me and John. I'd forgotten myself. But it all came back to me when I saw Gilbert last Sunday."

# Chapter XXXVIII

### THE BEND IN THE ROAD

MARILLA went to town the next day and returned in the evening. Anne had gone over to Orchard Slope with Diana and came back to find Marilla in the kitchen, sitting by the table with her head leaning on her hand. Something in her dejected attitude struck a chill to Anne's heart. She had never seen Marilla sit limply inert like that.

"Are you very tired, Marilla?"

"Yes—no—I don't know," said Marilla wearily, looking up. "I suppose I am tired but I haven't thought about it. It's not that."

"Did you see the oculist? What did he say?" asked Anne anxiously.

"Yes, I saw him. He examined my eyes. He says that if I give up all reading and sewing entirely and any kind of work that strains the eyes, and if I'm careful not to cry, and if I wear the glasses he's given me he thinks my eyes may not get any worse and my headaches will be cured. But if I don't he says I'll certainly be stone blind in six months. Blind! Anne, just think of it!"

For a minute Anne, after her first quick exclamation of dismay, was silent. It seemed to her that she could *not* speak. Then she said bravely, but with a catch in her voice:

"Marilla, *don't* think of it. You know he has given you hope. If you are careful you won't lose your sight altogether; and if his glasses cure your headaches it will be a great thing."

"I don't call it much hope," said Marilla bitterly. "What am I to live for if I can't read or sew or do anything like that? I might as well be blind—or dead. And as for crying, I can't help that when I get lonesome. But there, it's no good talking about it. If you'll get me a cup of tea I'll be thankful. I'm about done out. Don't say anything about this to any one for a spell yet, anyway. I can't bear that folks should come here to question and sympathize and talk about it."

When Marilla had eaten her lunch Anne persuaded her to go to bed. Then Anne went herself to the east gable and sat down by her window in the darkness alone with her tears and her heaviness of heart. How sadly things had changed since she had sat there the night after coming home! Then she had been full of hope and joy and the future had looked rosy with promise. Anne felt as if she had lived years since then, but before she went to bed there was a smile on her lips and peace in her heart. She had looked her duty courageously in the face and found it a friend—as duty ever is when we meet it frankly.

One afternoon a few days later Marilla came slowly in from the yard where she had been talking to a caller—a man whom Anne knew by sight as John Sadler from Carmody. Anne wondered what he could have been saying to bring that look to Marilla's face.

"What did Mr. Sadler want, Marilla?"

Marilla sat down by the window and looked at Anne. There were tears in her eyes in defiance of the oculist's prohibition and her voice broke as she said:

"He heard that I was going to sell Green Gables and he wants to buy it."

"Buy it! Buy Green Gables?" Anne wondered if she had heard aright. "Oh, Marilla, you don't mean to sell Green Gables!"

"Anne, I don't know what else is to be done. I've thought it all over. If my eyes were strong I could stay here and make out to look after things and manage, with a good hired man. But as it is I can't. I may lose my sight altogether; and anyway I'll not be fit to run things. Oh, I never thought I'd live to see the day when I'd have to sell my home. But things would only go behind worse and worse all the time, till nobody would want to buy it. Every cent of our money went in that bank; and there's some notes[1] Matthew gave last fall to pay. Mrs. Lynde advises me to sell the farm and board somewhere—with her I suppose. It won't bring much—it's small and the buildings are old. But it'll be enough for me to live on I reckon. I'm thankful you're

1. I.O.U.'s, acknowledging debt.

provided for with that scholarship, Anne. I'm sorry you won't have a home to come to in your vacations, that's all, but I suppose you'll manage somehow."

Marilla broke down and wept bitterly.

"You mustn't sell Green Gables," said Anne resolutely.

"Oh, Anne, I wish I didn't have to. But you can see for yourself. I can't stay here alone. I'd go crazy with trouble and loneliness. And my sight would go—I know it would."

"You won't have to stay here alone, Marilla. I'll be with you. I'm not going to Redmond."

"Not going to Redmond!" Marilla lifted her worn face from her hands and looked at Anne. "Why, what do you mean?"

"Just what I say. I'm not going to take the scholarship. I decided so the night after you came home from town. You surely don't think I could leave you alone in your trouble, Marilla, after all you've done for me. I've been thinking and planning. Let me tell you my plans. Mr. Barry wants to rent the farm[2] for next year. So you won't have any bother over that. And I'm going to teach. I've applied for the school here—but I don't expect to get it for I understand the trustees have promised it to Gilbert Blythe. But I can have the Carmody school—Mr. Blair told me so last night at the store. Of course that won't be quite as nice or convenient as if I had the Avonlea school. But I can board home[3] and drive myself over to Carmody and back, in the warm weather at least. And even in winter I can come home Fridays. We'll keep a horse for that. Oh, I have it all planned out, Marilla. And I'll read to you and keep you cheered up. You sha'n't be dull or lonesome. And we'll be real cosy and happy here together, you and I."

Marilla had listened like a woman in a dream.

"Oh, Anne, I could get on real well if you were here, I know. But I can't let you sacrifice yourself so for me. It would be terrible."

"Nonsense!" Anne laughed merrily. "There is no sacrifice. Nothing could be worse than giving up Green Gables—nothing could hurt me more. We must keep the dear old place. My mind is quite made up, Marilla. I'm *not* going to Redmond; and I *am* going to stay here and teach. Don't you worry about me a bit."

"But your ambitions—and—"

"I'm just as ambitious as ever. Only, I've changed the object of my ambitions. I'm going to be a good teacher—and I'm going to save your eyesight. Besides, I mean to study at home[4] here and take a

2. Mr. Barry wants to rent the use of farm fields, not the farmhouse.
3. Teachers in rural communities usually boarded with one of the farm families, but Anne can stay at "Green Gables" and drive to the Carmody school.
4. As a young teacher in Bideford, LMM kept up a course of study in preparation for going to university, meanwhile creating and publishing short stories and poems.

little college course all by myself. Oh, I've dozens of plans, Marilla. I've been thinking them out for a week. I shall give life here my best, and I believe it will give its best to me in return. When I left Queen's my future seemed to stretch out before me like a straight road. I thought I could see along it for many a milestone. Now there is a bend in it. I don't know what lies around the bend, but I'm going to believe that the best does. It has a fascination of its own, that bend, Marilla. I wonder how the road beyond it goes—what there is of green glory and soft, checkered light and shadows—what new land-scapes—what new beauties—what curves and hills and valleys fur-ther on."

"I don't feel as if I ought to let you give it up," said Marilla, refer-ring to the scholarship.

"But you can't prevent me. I'm sixteen and a half, 'obstinate as a mule,'[5] as Mrs. Lynde once told me," laughed Anne. "Oh, Marilla, don't you go pitying me. I don't like to be pitied, and there is no need for it. I'm heart glad over the very thought of staying at dear Green Gables. Nobody could love it as you and I do—so we must keep it."

"You blessed girl!" said Marilla, yielding. "I feel as if you'd given me new life. I guess I ought to stick out and make you go to college—but I know I can't, so I ain't going to try. I'll make it up to you though, Anne."

When it became noised abroad in Avonlea that Anne Shirley had given up the idea of going to college and intended to stay home and teach there was a good deal of discussion over it. Most of the good folks, not knowing about Marilla's eyes, thought she was foolish. Mrs. Allan did not. She told Anne so in approving words that brought tears of pleasure to the girl's eyes. Neither did good Mrs. Lynde. She came up one evening and found Anne and Marilla sitting at the front door in the warm, scented summer dusk. They liked to sit there when the twilight came down and the white moths flew about in the garden and the odour of mint filled the dewy air.

Mrs. Rachel deposited her substantial person upon the stone bench by the door, behind which grew a row of tall pink and yellow hollyhocks,[6] with a long breath of mingled weariness and relief.

"I declare I'm glad to sit down. I've been on my feet all day, and two hundred pounds is a good bit for two feet to carry round. It's a great blessing not to be fat, Marilla. I hope you appreciate it. Well, Anne, I hear you've given up your notion of going to college. I was real glad to hear it. You've got as much education now as a woman

---

5. Stubborn (a cliché, based on the observable nature of a mule). A mule is a sterile cross between a horse and a donkey, and mules were sometimes used in PEI, as well as horses, for farm work.
6. Tall plants with single or ruffled blossoms, usually planted beside hedges or walls in rural settings.

can be comfortable with. I don't believe in girls going to college with the men and cramming their heads full of Latin and Greek and all that nonsense."[7]

"But I'm going to study Latin and Greek just the same, Mrs. Lynde," said Anne laughing. "I'm going to take my Arts course right here at Green Gables, and study everything that I would at college."

Mrs. Lynde lifted her hands in holy horror.

"Anne Shirley, you'll kill yourself."

"Not a bit of it. I shall thrive on it. Oh, I'm not going to overdo things. As 'Josiah Allen's wife' says, I shall be 'mejum.'[8] But I'll have lots of spare time in the long winter evenings, and I've no vocation for fancy work. I'm going to teach over at Carmody, you know."

"I don't know it. I guess you're going to teach right here in Avonlea. The trustees have decided to give you the school."

"Mrs. Lynde!" cried Anne, springing to her feet in her surprise. "Why, I thought they had promised it to Gilbert Blythe!"

"So they did. But as soon as Gilbert heard that you had applied for it he went to them—they had a business meeting at the school last night, you know—and told them that he withdrew his application, and suggested that they accept yours. He said he was going to teach at White Sands. Of course he gave up the school just to oblige you, because he knew how much you wanted to stay with Marilla, and I must say I think it was real kind and thoughtful in him, that's what. Real self-sacrificing, too, for he'll have his board to pay at White Sands, and everybody knows he's got to earn his own way through college. So the trustees decided to take you. I was tickled to death when Thomas came home and told me."

"I don't feel that I ought to take it," murmured Anne. "I mean—I don't think I ought to let Gilbert make such a sacrifice for—for me."

"I guess you can't prevent him now. He's signed papers with the White Sands trustees. So it wouldn't do him any good now if you were to refuse. Of course you'll take the school. You'll get along all right, now that there are no Pyes going. Josie was the last of them, and a good thing she was, that's what. There's been some Pye or other going to Avonlea school for the last twenty years, and I guess their mission in life was to keep school-teachers reminded that earth isn't their home. Bless my heart! What does all that winking and blinking at the Barry gable mean?"

"Diana is signalling for me to go over," laughed Anne. "You know we keep up the old custom. Excuse me while I run over and see what she wants."

---

7. Traditional response to higher learning for women. See NCE 272–75.
8. Marietta Holley, writing as "Josiah Allen's Wife," published comic dialect books such as *Samantha at Saratoga, or Flirtin' with Fashion* (1887). In later books, she "rastles with the woman question." "Mejum" is comic dialect for "moderate."

Anne ran down the clover slope like a deer, and disappeared in the firry shadows of the Haunted Wood. Mrs. Lynde looked after her indulgently.

"There's a good deal of the child about her yet in some ways."

"There's a good deal more of the woman about her in others," retorted Marilla, with a momentary return of her old crispness.

But crispness was no longer Marilla's distinguishing characteristic. As Mrs. Lynde told her Thomas that night.

"Marilla Cuthbert has got *mellow*. That's what."

Anne went to the little Avonlea graveyard the next evening to put fresh flowers on Matthew's grave and water the Scotch rose-bush. She lingered there until dusk, liking the peace and calm of the little place, with its poplars whose rustle was like low, friendly speech, and its whispering grasses growing at will among the graves. When she finally left it and walked down the long hill that sloped to the Lake of Shining Waters it was past sunset and all Avonlea lay before her in a dreamlike afterlight—"a haunt of ancient peace."[9] There was a freshness in the air as of a wind that had blown over honey-sweet fields of clover. Home lights twinkled out here and there among the homestead trees. Beyond lay the sea, misty and purple, with its haunting, unceasing murmur. The west was a glory of soft mingled hues, and the pond reflected them all in still softer shadings. The beauty of it all thrilled Anne's heart, and she gratefully opened the gates of her soul to it.

"Dear old world," she murmured, "you are very lovely, and I am glad to be alive in you."

Half-way down the hill a tall lad came whistling out of a gate before the Blythe homestead. It was Gilbert, and the whistle died on his lips as he recognized Anne. He lifted his cap courteously, but he would have passed on in silence, if Anne had not stopped and held out her hand.

"Gilbert," she said, with scarlet cheeks, "I want to thank you for giving up the school for me. It was very good of you—and I want you to know that I appreciate it."

Gilbert took the offered hand eagerly.

"It wasn't particularly good of me at all, Anne. I was pleased to be able to do you some small service. Are we going to be friends after this? Have you really forgiven me my old fault?"

Anne laughed and tried unsuccessfully to withdraw her hand.

"I forgave you that day by the pond landing although I didn't know it. What a stubborn little goose I was. I've been—I may as well make a complete confession—I've been sorry ever since."

---

9. "[G]ray twilight pour'd / On dewy pastures, dewy trees, / Softer than sleep—all things in order stored, / A haunt of ancient peace." Alfred Tennyson, "The Palace of Art" (1832) 2.85–88.

"Come, I'm going to walk home with you"

"We are going to be the best of friends," said Gilbert, jubilantly. "We were born to be good friends, Anne. You've thwarted destiny long enough. I know we can help each other in many ways. You are going to keep up your studies, aren't you? So am I. Come, I'm going to walk home with you."

Marilla looked curiously at Anne when the latter entered the kitchen.

"Who was that came up the lane with you, Anne?"

"Gilbert Blythe," answered Anne, vexed to find herself blushing. "I met him on Barry's hill."

"I didn't think you and Gilbert Blythe were such good friends that you'd stand for half an hour at the gate talking to him," said Marilla, with a dry smile.

"We haven't been—we've been good enemies. But we have decided that it will be much more sensible to be good friends in future. Were we really there half an hour? It seemed just a few minutes. But, you see, we have five years' lost conversations to catch up with, Marilla."

Anne sat long at her window that night companioned by a glad content. The wind purred softly in the cherry boughs, and the mint breaths came up to her. The stars twinkled over the pointed firs in the hollow and Diana's light gleamed through the old gap.

Anne's horizons had closed in since the night she had sat there after coming home from Queen's; but if the path set before her feet was to be narrow she knew that flowers of quiet happiness would bloom along it. The joys of sincere work and worthy aspiration and congenial friendship were to be hers; nothing could rob her of her birthright of fancy or her ideal world of dreams. And there was always the bend in the road!

" 'God's in his heaven, all's right with the world,' "[1] whispered Anne softly.

**THE END**

---

1. "God's in his Heaven— / All's right with the world." Robert Browning, Song from *Pippa Passes* (1841) 2.7–8.

Cover of the first edition (Boston: L. C. Page & Company, 1908).

# A Note on the Text

The copy-text for this Norton Critical Edition is the first printing of the L. C. Page 1908 edition of *Anne of Green Gables*. Its copyright page reads "First Impression, April, 1908," and it is illustrated by W. A. and M. A. J. Claus. The 1908 Page text was set from L. M. Montgomery's own typescript (now lost). In 1907, Montgomery read through the page proofs, correcting and approving them. Although L. C. Page sent out some advance proofs to reviewers, the April impression was not officially released until June 13, 1908, the day after its copyright registration became effective.

Montgomery received her personal copy from the publisher on June 20, 1908. A few noticeable errors were quickly corrected in the subsequent impressions of 1908 and 1909, probably at Montgomery's own behest: it was her practice to read her novels through after she received her own copy. Most of the serious substantive errors were discovered and corrections were stripped in either by the second impression in July 1908 or the fifth impression in October 1908: errors like "pail the barge" for "pall the barge" and "resent the license" for "repent the license."

The 1908 Page edition has another claim to acceptance as the one Montgomery approved. In 1916, when she inscribed and gave copies of *Anne of Green Gables* to her sons Chester and Stuart, she made no further corrections in either of their books, as she was accustomed to doing if she noticed errors. The copyright page in Stuart's book shows that it was the fortieth impression (i.e., printing) of the 1908 edition, printed in February 1916. No other copy-text can claim to represent her final intentions as much as this 1908 edition.

Because the typescript which she gave the Page Company is now missing, we have no way of knowing what changes Montgomery might have introduced into it from her manuscript, but we do know that some entire sentences in the published version are not in the handwritten pen-and-ink manuscript (technically called a "holograph") which is preserved in the Confederation Centre in Prince Edward Island. We also do not know what editorial changes might have been made to her typescript in the L. C. Page Company offices. All that we know for sure is that Montgomery corrected and approved the L. C. Page proofs and the subsequent 1908 book.

*Anne of Green Gables* was an instantaneous bestseller. The 1908
edition went through seven printings (impressions) in 1908 alone,
for a total of about 20,000 copies, another nine printings in 1909,
nine in 1910, six in 1911, two in 1912, and four in 1913. Each time
Page reprinted it, he used the same plates. (A "new edition" technically occurs when there is either a new resetting of type, the use
of new illustrations, design, or presentation features, or a new publisher. An "impression" is only a new printing of an "edition.")

As the book went into multiple printings, he merely listed (somewhat disingenuously) "First Impression, June, 1908," "Second
Impression, July, 1908," "Third Impression, August, 1908," etc., in
sequence on the copyright page. According to Bernard Katz, an
authority on Montgomery editions, there appears in fact to have been
no printing in June—the first impression had actually been in April,
and the second was in July.

The same plates were also used for a first British edition, published
in 1908 by Sir Isaac Pitman, and for a much cheaper 1914 "Popular
Edition" issued by Grosset and Dunlap, as arranged with Page, using
Page's plates, but on cheaper paper for a different market. We do
not know the total figures for the Grosset and Dunlap reprints, but
their May 1914 "Popular Edition" states that it was "limited to
150,000 copies." The first 1908 Page edition had gone through 49
"impressions" (printings from the same 1908 plates) by 1920 when
a special "Mary Miles Minter" edition, illustrated with stills from the
1919 silent movie, brought the total number of books he had printed
to 349,000, according to L. C. Page's figures.

*Anne of Green Gables* had been appearing steadily in foreign translations: Swedish (1909), Dutch (1910), Polish (1912), Danish
(1918), Norwegian (1918), Finnish (1920). In 1924, the Cornstalk
Publishing Company of Sydney brought out the first Australian edition. Later foreign translations would include French (1925), Icelandic (1933), Hebrew (1951), Japanese (1952), Slovak (1959),
Spanish (1962), Korean (1963), Portuguese (1972), Turkish (1979),
Italian (1980), and Chinese (1987).

According to Montgomery's journal entry of April 4, 1925, L. C.
Page had to make new plates for *Anne of Green Gables* because the
old plates were worn out. He would update his new edition with fresh
illustrations by Elizabeth R. Withington, and reset the type, introducing changes (such as "Home boy" for "Barnado [sic] boy" in chapter 1).

In the same year, the George G. Harrap Company prepared
another new edition in London, England. These two editions, edited
and typeset independently in America and Britain, have many small
differences. Most of the changes in the Harrap edition were made

to adapt the book to a British audience, but there are also other small substantive changes.

The 1925 Harrap editors caught certain errors that the Page editors had missed. Other changes were made, probably in ignorance, to "correct" the grammar of Montgomery's rural Islanders, or to change an idiom.

Montgomery gave no personal input into either of these completely new 1925 editions. In 1919, after her first bitter lawsuit with the L. C. Page Company—which had ended in her signing over all her rights to *Anne* and the other six books they had published—she had no more contact with L. C. Page except through her lawyers. Likewise, she would have had no contact with the British publisher (Harrap) over the books they had acquired the rights to through the Page Company. Montgomery had no financial interest in these books, and by 1925 she was so enraged at the Page Company that she would not have participated willingly in the creation or the proof-reading of either of the new editions.

Yet some of the small changes made by editors in the 1925 Page and Harrap editions seem to harken back to Montgomery's own handwritten manuscript. This observation might lead one to wonder if Harrap had access to the handwritten manuscript. Given the bad blood between the Page Company and Montgomery, and the fact that Montgomery's manuscript of *Anne of Green Gables* was her most prized piece of memorabilia—one she retained all her life—this is all but impossible. However, a careful comparison of the newly set Harrap and L. C. Page texts (which are very different in themselves) reveals a common line of descent—not from the manuscript but from the lost typescript.

The L. C. Page Company of Boston accepted the book for publication in April 1907, and they would have retained the typescript in their company vaults. In 1925, when preparing the novel for resetting of the type, the Page editors appear to have consulted that typescript (and possibly the corrected proof copy which is another intermediate stage where changes can occur). This process would have allowed them to restore small elements that had been altered when the novel was first set to type in 1908. When Harrap in turn prepared their own edition for a British audience in 1925, they likely used both the old 1908 Page (Pitman) edition as well as the new 1925 Page page proofs. And L. C. Page may have sent them copies of uncorrected page proofs (not the valuable corrected page proofs) left over from the 1908 edition—all of which would explain why the Harrap edition appears at times to return to the holograph.

The original typescript most likely went back into L. C. Page's vaults and remained there over the years. The late Roger W. Straus, who co-founded Farrar and Straus in 1946 (later Farrar, Straus & Giroux), purchased the rudderless and faltering L. C. Page Company following Lewis C. Page's death in 1956. In 1991, in an interview with Mary Henley Rubio, he stated that he bought the company primarily to acquire the copyright to *Anne of Green Gables*, still a best-selling novel producing steady income. The original contract for *Anne* was removed from the Page vault, along with a few other less important contracts, and everything else in the house was discarded. This was an era before archives generally were seen as valuable by many publishers, and the now-missing typescript of *Anne of Green Gables* undoubtedly disappeared into the dumpster—along with more than fifty years of other publishing history.

Whatever happened to Montgomery's original typescript, her manuscript fortunately remains in existence. By 1926, there were three print versions of the text of *Anne of Green Gables*: the 1908 Page edition (which had LMM's full approval and is our copy-text), the 1925 Page edition (which follows the 1908 edition closely, but appears to consult LMM's typescript or corrected proofs), and the 1925 Harrap edition (which is based on the 1908 Page edition, but appears to consult the uncorrected proofs of the 1908 edition, and possibly the 1925 Page edition).

In creating this new Norton Critical Edition, we have proofread the Norton text against the April 1908 L. C. Page edition, and also against Montgomery's son Stuart Macdonald's 1916 copy ("40th impression").

Corrections and variants discovered in this process were then checked against the holograph and against a number of later printed versions: the April 1920 "Mary Miles Minter Movie Edition," the 1925 L. C. Page edition (consulted in the 1927 impression), the 1925 Harrap British edition, the 1942 Ryerson Press edition (the first Canadian edition, printed from the new 1925 Page plates), the 1964 illustrated Ryerson edition (consulted mostly in its 1965 impression), the 1997 Oxford *The Annotated Anne of Green Gables* (which creates a new text that draws heavily on the holograph and the 1925 Harrap text, but not on the newly reset 1925 Page edition), and the 2004 Broadview edition (which makes a "1908 Page first edition" the copy-text, checking it against other editions). There have been, of course, a host of non-scholarly editions of *Anne*, especially after the copyright expired in 1992, as well as others authorized by or published by Farrar, Straus & Giroux after 1956.

In preparing a critical edition, modern editors face a new challenge: ensuring that word processors and typesetting programs do not make silent "corrections" at some stage of production, destroying distinctions between variants or introducing inaccuracies.

We here present a selection of the variants we examined, and we also offer possible reasons for some of the similarities and differences between particular editions. We have retained the spelling of Montgomery's original text—which is a mixture of British and American spelling—noting in the list of variants where Canadian, British, and American spelling differ. In Montgomery's time, the Canadian Maritime provinces were strongly connected to the culture of the Eastern seaboard in the United States.

We refer in the notes to *Webster's New International Dictionary of the English Language* (1909 edition), originated by Noah Webster in 1828, and developed in the United States to establish the standard for American usage (and to differentiate American and British usage), which became a standard reference work in the American publishing industry. We also cite the *Canadian Oxford Dictionary* (2004 edition) as the standard reference work for current Canadian spelling and usage. We have departed from the 1908 copy-text only a few times, when there is a clear spelling or punctuation error which could mislead readers. Additional variants and textual history are available on the University of Guelph "L. M. Montgomery Research Center" website: <LMMRC.ca>.

## Selected Examples of Variants

**Code: HM** = handwritten manuscript (c.1905–6); **1908 LCP** = L. C. Page's first illustrated edition, Boston 1908 (Apr); **1908 PIT** = Sir Isaac Pitman's British edition, London 1908; **1914 G&D** = Grosset and Dunlap edition, New York 1914; **1916 LCP** = the fortieth impression of the 1908 Page edition, given by LMM to her son Stuart; **1920 LCP** = Page's movie edition (April) from the 1908 plates; **1924 Cornstalk** = Cornstalk edition, Sydney, Australia, 1924; **1925 LCP** = Page's new 1925 USA edition (examined in the 1927 impression), Boston 1925; **1925 GGH** = George G. Harrap's new 1925 British edition, London 1925; **1942 RP** = Ryerson Press, first Canadian edition, Toronto 1942; **1965 RP** = Ryerson Press, newly illustrated Canadian edition (examined in the seventeenth impression) Toronto 1965; **1997 OUP** = Oxford (NY) Press annotated edition, New York 1997; **2004 BP** = Canadian Broadview Press critical edition, Peterborough, ON, 2004; **2007 NCE** = Norton Critical Edition, New York 2007.

**WID** = *Webster's New International Dictionary* (1909 edition); **COD** = *Canadian Oxford Dictionary* (2004 edition).

**CHAPTER 1: MRS. LYNDE IS SURPRISED**

**Paragraph begins:** She was sitting there one afternoon . . .
■ **HM** (Note E in handwritten manuscript): Rachel Lynde's husband"— ■ **1908 LCP** *1st impression Apr* (2–3), **1908 LCP** *5th imp Oct* (2–3), **1908 PIT** (2–3): husband— ■ **1909 LCP** *12th imp Sept* (2–3): husband"— ■ [*This typo—a dropped quotation mark after "husband" and before the dash—was corrected sometime between the 5th and the 12th impression in September 1909.*]

**Paragraph begins:** Accordingly after tea Mrs. Rachel set out . . .
■ **HM** (6): made it a good deal further . . . was built at the furthest edge ■ **1908 LCP** *1st imp Apr* (4); **1908 LCP** *Oct 1909* (4), **1916 LCP** (4), **1920 LCP** *Apr* (4): further . . . furthest ■ **1925 GGH** (11): farther . . . farthest ■ **1925** [**1927** *imp*] **LCP** (4), **1942 RP** (4); **1965 RP** (4), **1997 OUP** (41), **2004 BP** (55), **2007 NCE** (9): further . . . furthest. ■ [*British editors changed LMM's "further" and "furthest" to "farther" and "farthest" to conform to usage in the UK. The 1909 WID comments: Syn.—FARTHER, FURTHER are often used without distinction. But in modern usage FARTHER commonly conveys a more or less explicit reference to the actual idea of far; FURTHER is more frequently employed in secondary or figurative senses, esp. with the implication of something additional (cf. its use in furthermore).*]

**Paragraph begins:** "Well, we've been thinking about it . . ."
■ **HM** (13): Barnardo boy ■ **1908 LCP** *Apr* (8); **1916 LCP** (8): **1920 LCP** (8): Barnado boy ■ **1924 Cornstalk** *Australia* (9): Barnardo boy ■ **1925 GGH** (15): Barnado boy ■ **1927 GGH** (15): 'Home' boy ■ **1925** [**1927** *imp*] **LCP** (8): Home boy ■ **1935 GGH** (15): 'Home' boy ■ **1942 RP** (8); **1965 RP** (7): Home boy ■ **1997 OUP** (45); **2004 BP** (58); **2007 NCE** (11): Barnardo boy. ■ [*LMM's holograph clearly has "Barnardo," but the 1908 Page edition misspells "Barnardo" as "Barnado," an error still appearing in the 1920 edition, and in much later Grosset & Dunlap and Farrar, Straus & Giroux editions; in 1925, when Page re-keyed the text, the term was changed to "Home boy," a more widely known term for children who lived in orphanage "homes." The 1925 Harrap edition replicated the Page misspelling "Barnado" into their edition, but by 1927, they have changed the term to " 'Home' boy" like the Page edition. The 1942 Ryerson Press edition (identical to the Page resetting in 1925) was reset in 1964, so the page numbering is different.*]

**Paragraph begins:** (Chapter 1) "Well, we've been thinking about it . . ." (See also: Chapter 2) "Why, a bride, of course—a bride. . . ." (See also: Chapter 5) "I lived up river with Mrs. Hammond . . ."

■ **HM** (12, 31): Hopetown, Hopetown, Hopetown ■ **1908 LCP** *Apr* (8, 19, 57); **1909 LCP** *12th imp, Sept* (8, 19, 57); **1916 LCP** (8, 19, 57), **1920 LCP** (8, 19, 57): Hopetown, Hopeton, Hopeton ■ **1925 GGH** (14, 23, 53): Hopetown, Hopetown, Hopeton ■ **1925** [**1927** *imp*] **LCP** (8, 18, 52), **1942 RP** (8, 18, 52), **1964** and **1965 RP** (6, 15, 43): Hopeton, Hopeton, Hopeton ■ **1997 OUP** (45, 54, 87); **2004 BP** (58, 66, 90); **2007 NCE** (11, 18, 39): Hopetown, Hopetown, Hopetown. ■ [*LMM uses this imaginary name three times in the text of AGG (in Chapters 1, 2, and 5), always spelling it "Hopetown" in the HM, but the 1908 Page errs in spelling it "Hopetown" in Chapter 1 and "Hopeton" in Chapter 2 and 5. The 1925 UK edition reversed this inconsistency, spelling it Hopetown, Hopetown, and Hopeton, which suggests that they consulted the 1908 Page/Pitman edition for typesetting. In the 1927 Page, the name is "Hopeton" all three times, as with the identical Ryerson edition. In 1997, 2004, and 2007, editors have corrected it to the consistent holograph spelling of "Hopetown."*]

**CHAPTER 2:** MATTHEW CUTHBERT IS SURPRISED

**Paragraph begins:** "A child of about eleven, garbed in a very . . . ugly dress of yellowish gray wincey."
■ **HM**: yellowish gray wincey (25) ■ **1908 LCP** *Apr* (16), **1916 LCP** (16), **1920 LCP** (16): yellowish gray wincey ■ **1925 GGH** (20): yellowish white [*sic*] wincey ■ **1925** [**1927** *imp*] **LCP** (14), **1942 RP** (14), **1965 RP** (12): yellowish gray wincey ■ **1997 OUP** (51): yellowish-gray wincey ■ **2004 BP** (63), **2007 NCE** (15): yellowish gray wincey. ■ [*The British change to "yellowish white" in 1925 is an inexplicable substantive alteration. LMM corrected it to "yellowish gray" in her personal copy. See also: Chapter 34 (LCP 384; NCE 220), where the same dress is called "yellowish-brown wincey," an inconsistency in color and word hyphenation that has remained in subsequent editions.*]

**Paragraph begins:** "Oh, I can carry it," the child responded . . .
■ **HM** (4, F1): I *am* dreadfully thin, ain't I? ■ **1908 LCP** *Apr* (18), **1908 LCP** *Oct. 1909* (18), **1916 LCP** (18), **1920 LCP** (18): dreadful thin ■ **1925 GGH** (22): dreadfully thin ■ **1925** [**1927** *imp*] **LCP** (17), **1942 RP** (17), **1965 RP** (14): dreadful thin ■ **1997 OUP** (53): dreadfully thin ■ **2004 BP** (65), **2007 NCE** (17): dreadful thin. ■ [*LMM probably removed the "ly" when preparing the typescript to make Anne's speech more authentic. Anne had been living with rather coarse people whose grammar would have been imperfect, and dropping the "ly" would have been a marker of their educational level. The 1925 UK editors likely added the "ly" to correct Anne's grammar with-*]

*out realizing they were altering LMM's idiomatic use of language. LMM walked a careful line between maintaining reasonably correct grammar and striving for authenticity with rural folk. Mrs. Lynde, Matthew, and occasionally Marilla use the word "ain't" which marks their use of rural idiom.*]

**Paragraph begins:** "She came out of her reverie . . ."
■ **HM** (41): a soul that had been wandering afar, star-led ■ **1908 LCP** *Apr* (26), **1916 LCP** (26), **1920 LCP** (26): wondering afar ■ **1925 GGH** (28): wandering afar ■ **1925** [**1927** *imp*] **LCP** (24), **1940 LCP** (24), **1942 RP** (24), **1965 RP** (20), **1997 OUP** (59): wondering afar ■ **2004 BP** (70): wondering afar [*with a note saying it should be "wandering"*] ■ **2007 NCE** (21): wandering afar. ■ [*LMM's holograph clearly has "wandering." This error appeared in all early Page editions, and it continued when Page re-keyed the novel in 1925. The misspelling was corrected by the British editors, but the error has been replicated in the 1942 and 1965 Canadian editions, as well as in the 1997 Oxford edition. The phrase "wandering afar" echoes language in the poem in Chapter 17: "When twilight drops her curtain down / And pins it with a star / Remember that you have a friend / Though she may wander far."*]

## CHAPTER 5: ANNE'S HISTORY

**Paragraph begins:** "Mr. and Mrs. Thomas moved away . . ."
■ **HM** (83): if I hadn't an imagination ■ **1908 LCP** *Apr* (57), **1909 LCP** (57), **1916 LCP** (57), **1920 LCP** (57): if I hadn't had an imagination ■ **1925 GGH** (53): if I hadn't an imagination ■ **1925** [**1927** *imp*] **LCP** (52), **1942 RP** (52): if I hadn't had an imagination ■ **1965 RP** (43): if I hadn't had any [*sic*] imagination: ■ **1997 OUP** (87): if I hadn't an imagination ■ **2004 BP** (90), **2007 NCE** (39): if I hadn't had an imagination. ■ [*We do not know if LMM's typescript followed her HM, and the extra "had" was added by the Page editors in 1908, or if she added it herself. Nor is it clear why the Harrap editors dropped this word. The clause is more informal and colloquial without the "had." The change to "any" in 1965 RP appears to be an error.*]

**Paragraph begins:** "Not a great deal. I went . . ."
■ **HM** (85): James Thompson ■ **1908 LCP** *Apr* (58): **1916 LCP** (58), **1920 LCP** (58): Thompson ■ **1925 GGH** (54): Thomson ■ **1925** [**1927** *imp*] **LCP** (53), **1942 & 1954 RP** (53): Thompson ■ **1964 & 1965 RP** (44), **1997 OUP**: Thomson (88) ■ **2004 BP** (91): Thompson [*with a note that it should be Thomson*] ■ **2007 NCE** (39): Thomson. ■ [*LMM misspells the eighteenth-century Scottish poet's name "Thomson" as "Thompson" in her HM, and undoubtedly did so*

*in her typescript; neither she nor the Page editors caught the error. The alert British editor corrected the error in 1925, but the 1925 (1927 imp) Page editor perpetuates the error. It is corrected in the 1964 Ryerson Canadian edition, in 1997 OUP, and in 2007 NCE.]*

## CHAPTER 6: MARILLA MAKES UP HER MIND

**Paragraph begins:** "I'm dreadful sorry," said Mrs. Spencer.
■ HM (92): dreadfully sorry ■ **1908 LCP** *Apr* (63), **1916 LCP** (63), **1920 LCP** (63): dreadful sorry ■ **1925 GGH** (57), **1925** [**1927** *imp*] **LCP** (57), **1942 RP** (57), **1965 RP** (48), **1997 OUP** (92): dreadfully sorry ■ **2004 BP** (94), **2007 NCE** (42): dreadful sorry. ■ [*"Dreadful sorry" is idiomatically (but not grammatically) correct for LMM's rural Islanders. It is likely that LMM, whose own written grammar was impeccable, instinctively wrote "dreadfully sorry" in her holograph, but changed it in the now-missing typescript to represent local dialect. The editors overseeing the new 1925 editions in Britain and America may not have recognized that the missing "ly" was idiomatic, and a marker of Mrs. Spencer's social class.*]

## CHAPTER 9: MRS. RACHEL LYNDE IS PROPERLY HORRIFIED

**Paragraph begins:** Leaving this Parthian shaft . . .
■ HM (145): dumbfounded ■ **1908 LCP** *Apr* (97), **1916 LCP** (97), **1920 LCP** (97): dumfounded ■ **1925 GGH** (85): dumbfounded ■ **1925** [**1927** *imp*] **LCP** (89), **1942 RP** (89), **1965 RP** (73): dumfounded ■ **1997 OUP** (118): dumbfounded ■ **2004 BP** (117), **2007 NCE** (61): dumfounded. ■ [*The 1909 WID lists both spellings as acceptable: "dumfounded" comes first and "dumbfounded" second. The 2004 COD prefers "dumbfounded," but "dumfounded" is an acceptable variant.*]

## CHAPTER 11: ANNE'S IMPRESSIONS OF SUNDAY-SCHOOL

**Paragraph begins:** "I don't know what 'squadrons' means . . ."
■ HM (156b): I'll practise it all the week. ■ **1908 LCP** *Apr* (115), **1916 LCP** (115), **1920 LCP** (115): practise ■ **1925 GGH** (99): practice ■ **1925** [**1927** *imp*] **LCP** (106), **1942 RP** (106), **1965 RP** (87), **1997 OUP** (132), **2004 BP** (129), **2007 NCE** (72): practise. ■ [*We have retained the 1908 spelling, which in this case reflects older North American usage. In the 1909 WID, the words "practise" and "practice" were interchangeable. In the 2004 COD, the noun is spelled as "practice" and the verb as "practise." The 1925 British editors changed the spelling to "practice" when used as a verb here.*]

**CHAPTER 15:** A TEMPEST IN THE SCHOOL TEAPOT

**Paragraph begins:** Lovers' Lane opened out below . . .
■ **HM** (228): Lovers Lane [*no apostrophe*] ■ **1908 LCP** (148), **1909 LCP** (148), **1916 LCP** (148), **1920 LCP** (148): Lover's Lane ■ **1925 GGH** (123, 124): Lover's Lane . . . Lovers' Lane [*multiple usages and different spellings on these pages*] ■ **1927 GGH** (123, 124): Lovers' Lane . . . Lovers' Lane ■ **1925** [**1927** *imp*] **LCP** (134, 135), **1942 RP** (134, 135): Lover's Lane ■ **1965 RP** (112): Lovers' Lane ■ **1997 OUP** (160): Lover's Lane ■ **2004 BP** (149), **2007 NCE** (88, 89): Lovers' Lane. ■ [*LMM was inconsistent in her spelling of "Lover's Lane/Lovers' Lane" throughout this novel and in others, and editors of various editions have been vexed by which spelling to use. In her manuscripts, written with great speed, it is often impossible to tell where she wanted her apostrophes to settle, and on page 228 in her HM of AGG, she uses no apostrophe at all in one instance. By contrast, in another instance, she puts an apostrophe both before and after the "s." The Harrap editors actually changed the spelling between 1925 and 1927, moving from both "Lover's Lane" and "Lovers' Lane" in 1925 to exclusively "Lovers' Lane" in 1927 and later editions. Both choices have merits: in her journals, this lane was a place where LMM often went for solitary contemplation; but in AGG it is solely a place where Anne and Diana go to talk about friendship and dream of lovers, whether alone or with each other. We have therefore standardized the spelling as "Lovers' Lane," given LMM's indeterminate spelling.*]

**CHAPTER 16:** DIANA IS INVITED TO TEA WITH TRAGIC RESULTS

**Paragraph begins:** "No, indeed! The rosebud tea-set! . . ."
■ **HM** (265): it's beginning to go ■ **1908 LCP** *Apr* (170), **1916 LCP** (170), **1920 LCP** (170): it's beginning to work ■ **1925 GGH** (141): it's beginning to go ■ **1925** [**1927** *imp*] **LCP** (156), **1942 RP** (156), **1965 RP** (129): it's beginning to work ■ **1997 OUP** (178): it's beginning to go ■ **2004 BP** (164), **2007 NCE** (102): it's beginning to work. ■ [*Both phrases mean that the jam was beginning to spoil (e.g., to mold or to lose proper consistency). However, the British editors may have felt that "go" would be more easily understood. This variant reinforces the theory that Harrap consulted uncorrected proofs from the 1908 edition.*]

**Paragraph begins:** "I should think Marilla's raspberry cordial . . ."
■ **HM** (56, note Z8): such a pathetic little tale ■ **1908 LCP** *Apr* (174), **1916 LCP** (174), **1920 LCP** (174): such a pathetic tale ■ **1925 GGH** (145): such a pathetic little tale ■ **1925** [**1927** *imp*]

LCP (160), **1942 RP** (160), **1965 RP** (132): such a pathetic tale ■ **1997 OUP** (182): such a pathetic little tale ■ **2004 BP** (167), **2007 NCE** (105): such a pathetic tale. ■ [*In the HM, LMM crossed out "sad" and wrote "pathetic little tale." It is unclear whether she or the Page editor struck out "little" in the editing process, or if a compositor dropped it by error. It does seem appropriate for it to be there, and that may be why the British editor added it. Or, alternatively, the word "little" may have been in uncorrected proof sheets, pulled from the Page vault and sent to Harrap in 1925.*]

## CHAPTER 17: A NEW INTEREST IN LIFE

**Paragraph begins:** "I love you devotedly, Anne," . . .
■ **HM** (285): said Diana stanchly ■ **1908 LCP** *Apr* (185), **1916 LCP** (185), **1920 LCP** *Apr* (185), **1925 GGH** (154), **1925** [**1927** *imp*] **LCP** (170), **1942 RP** (170): stanchly ■ **1965 RP** (141): staunchly ■ **1997 OUP** (192): stanchly ■ **2004 BP** (174): staunchly ■ **2007 NCE** (110): stanchly. ■ [*The 1909 WID considers both "stanchly" and "staunchly" acceptable. In the 2004 COD, the adverbial form (like the adjectival form) is only spelled with the "u," and prefers "staunch" as a verb, but gives "stanch" as a variant. Some current word-processing programs automatically "correct" the spelling of words when they are being transcribed which complicates any transcription process.*]

## CHAPTER 20: A GOOD IMAGINATION GONE WRONG

**Paragraph begins:** "One June evening, when the orchards . . ."
■ **HM** (354, C12): silvery sweet ■ **1908 LCP** *Apr* (226), **1916 LCP** (226), **1920 LCP** (226): silverly sweet ■ **1925 GGH** (185): silverly-sweet ■ **1925** [**1927** *imp*] **LCP** (206), **1942 RP** (206), **1965 RP** (171): silverly sweet ■ **1997 OUP** (226): silvery-sweet ■ **2004 BP** (200), **2007 NCE** (133): silverly sweet. ■ [*Either spelling is acceptable, but "silverly" is more unusual and poetic; LMM's manuscript spells this phrase "silvery sweet" without a hyphen, and her low loops for the "e" and "r" are squashed, looking like the loop of an "l," but there are not enough loops for a second "l." It is possible that in 1907 LMM changed the word to "silverly" in her now-missing typescript or in the proof copy, and that in 1925 the British editors simply amended it to "silvery," thinking there was an error. Or the phrase could have been "silvery sweet" in an uncorrected 1908 proof copy.*]

**Paragraph begins:** Anne marched.
■ **HM** (363): repent the license she had given to her imagination ■ **1908 LCP** *Apr* (231), **1908 PIT** (231), resent [*sic*] the license ■ **1909 LCP** *12th imp, Sept* (231), **1916 LCP** (231), **1920 LCP**

(231), **1925 GGH** (190): repent the licence ■ **1925** [**1927** *imp*]
**LCP** (211), **1942 RP** (211), **1997 OUP** (231), **2004 BP** (204),
**2007 NCE** (136): repent the license. ■ [*This substantive typo
("resent" for "repent") was caught early and the correction was stripped
in by the 5th impression of October 1908. The British edition alters
the spelling of the noun "license" to "licence" to conform to British
usage.*]

## CHAPTER 21: A NEW DEPARTURE IN FLAVOURINGS

**Paragraph begins:** "I suppose we must have Mr. and Mrs. Allan . . ."
■ **HM** (380): He's got so used to ■ **1908 LCP** *Apr* (239), **1916 LCP**
(239), **1920 LCP** (239): He'd got ■ **1925 GGH** (197): He's got ■
**1925** [**1927** *imp*] **LCP** (219), **1942 RP** (219), **1965 RP** (182): He'd
got ■ **1997 OUP** (237): He's got ■ **2004 BP** (209), **2007 NCE**
(140): He'd got. ■ [*This change in the British edition lends credence
to the theory that their editors had access to an uncorrected proof copy.*]

**Paragraph begins**: Monday and Tuesday great preparations . . .
■ **HM** (390): She talked it all over with Diana on Tuesday night ■
**1908 LCP** *Apr* (240), **1916 LCP** (240), **1920 LCP** *Apr* (240): with
Diana Tuesday night ■ **1925 GGH** (197): with Diana on Tuesday
night ■ **1925** [**1927** *imp*] **LCP** (219), **1942 RP** (219), **1965 RP**
(182): with Diana Tuesday night ■ **1997 OUP** (238): with Diana on
Tuesday night ■ **2004 BP** (209), **2007 NCE** (140): with Diana Tuesday night. ■ [*In rural and colloquial North American speech, the preposition is typically omitted before the day of the week in constructions
like this, and LMM herself omits it in her journals. She probably
instinctively wrote "correct" written English in her HM, but made the
shift to colloquial language when she prepared the typescript. The British editor likely re-inserted the preposition "on" thinking that this
would "correct" the English.*]

## CHAPTER 25: MATTHEW INSISTS ON PUFFED SLEEVES

**Paragraph begins:** He had recourse to his pipe . . .
■ **HM** (440): at the solution of his problem ■ **1908 LCP** *Apr* (272),
**1916 LCP** (272), **1920 LCP** (272): at a solution ■ **1925 GGH**
(223): at the solution ■ **1925** [**1927** *imp*] **LCP** (249), **1942 RP**
(249): at a solution ■ **1997 OUP** (266): at the solution ■ **2004 BP**
(231), **2007 NCE** (158): at a solution. ■ [*This change also supports
the theory that Harrap might have been given an uncorrected proof
copy of the 1908 edition. It is possible that "a" was substituted for "the"
in the corrected proof copy by the 1908 Page editors.*]

**Paragraph begins:** The more Matthew thought about the matter . . .
■ HM (103, S14): it is as much as he did ■ 1908 LCP *Apr* (272), **1908 PIT** (272): it is much as he did ■ **1909 LCP** *12th imp, Sept* (272): it is as [*sic*] much as he did ■ **1916 LCP** (272), **1920 LCP** (272), **1924 Cornstalk** (273), **1925 GGH** (223), **1925** [**1927** *imp*] **LCP** (249), **1942 RP** (249), **1965 RP** (208), **1997 OUP** (266), **2004 BP** (231), **2007 NCE** (158): it is as much as he did. ■ [*This typo was caught by 1909 and corrected in all future editions.*]

**CHAPTER 28:** AN UNFORTUNATE LILY MAID

**Paragraph begins:** "Well, I'll be Elaine," said Anne.
■ HM (503): pall the barge ■ **1908 LCP** *Apr* (310): pail [*sic*] the barge ■ **1908 LCP** *Sept* (310), **1908 PIT** (310), **1909 LCP** *Oct* (310), **1916 LCP** (310), **1920 LCP** (310), **1925 GGH** (253), **1925** [**1927** *imp*] **LCP** (283), **1965 RP** (236), **1997 OUP** (295), **2004 BP** (255), **2007 NCE** (178): pall the barge. ■ [*This typo probably resulted from the compositor's lack of familiarity with the verb "to pall" which means "to place a shrouding cloth over a funeral bier." It was corrected in Page's subsequent editions, including the Pitman edition. It is unclear whether Page sent Pitman duplicate plates or loose sheets for the first British edition.*]

**CHAPTER 31:** WHERE THE BROOK AND RIVER MEET

**Paragraph begins:** "I feel just like studying with might and main . . ."
■ HM (573): If I was a man I think I'd be a minister ■ **1908 LCP** *Apr* (350), **1909 LCP** *Oct* (350), **1916 LCP** (350), **1920 LCP** (350), **1925 GGH** (286), **1925** [**1927** *imp*] **LCP** (320), **1965 RP** (267): If I were a man ■ **1997 OUP** (328): If I was a man ■ **2004 BP** (282), **2007 NCE** (202): If I were a man. ■ [*It is likely that LMM changed "was" in the holograph to "were" in the typescript to show Anne speaking proper English now that she is older (that is, using the subjunctive because the statement is contrary to fact: she is not a man). The local idiom would have been "was." This is yet another indication that the publishing firms did not have LMM's holograph, only her typescript.*]

**Paragraph begins:** "Hills peeped o'er hills and Alps on Alps arose."
■ HM (578): "Hills peeped o'er hills and Alps on Alps arose." ■ **1908 LCP** *Apr* (353), **1916 LCP** (353), **1920 LCP** (353): "Hills peeped o'er hill and Alps on Alps arose." ■ **1925 GGH** (288), **1925** [**1927** *imp*] **LCP** (323), **1965 RP** (269): "Hills peeped o'er hill and Alps

on Alps arose." ■ **1997 OUP** (330): "Hills peeped o'er hills and Alps on Alps arose." ■ **2004 BP** (284): "Hills peeped o'er hill and Alps on Alps arose." [*with a note that this should be "hills"*] ■ **2007 NCE** (203): "Hills peeped o'er hills and Alps on Alps arose." ■ [*LMM creates a variation on Alexander Pope's "An Essay on Criticism": "Hills peep o'er hills, and Alps on Alps arise!" Many later editions have followed the error in Page's 1908 edition, showing a clear line of transmission until it is corrected to "hills" in the 1997 Oxford edition. It is possible that LMM made an error typing her manuscript, or the Page compositors may have made the error on the proof copy, missing her correction, or she may have missed it in proofing altogether. It was correct in her HM.*]

**CHAPTER 33:** THE HOTEL CONCERT

**Paragraph begins:** "We *are* rich," said Anne stanchly.
■ **HM** (629): all silver and shadow and visions of things not seen [*with "s" on visions*] ■ **1908 LCP** *Apr* (381), **1920 LCP** (381): all silver and shadow and vision [*no "s" on vision*] ■ **1925 GGH** (312): all silver and shallow [*sic*] and vision ■ **1925** [**1927** *imp*] **LCP** (351), **1965 RP** (290), **1997 OUP** (356), **2004 BP** (302), **2007 NCE** (219): all silver and shadow and vision. ■ [*"Shallow" is clearly a typographical error, but it still appears in the 1937 Harrap edition. LMM crossed out "shallow" and substituted "shadow" in ink in her own personal copy of the Harrap text, now in the University of Prince Edward Island archival holdings. The "shallow" error still appears in the 1937 Harrap edition. Our principle is to follow the 1908 Page edition unless there is evidence of clear error. However, since LMM did not add the missing "s" to "visions" in her personal copy when she corrected the word "shadow," we have not added the "s" here, despite believing that "visions" (as in her HM) is more appropriate.*]

**CHAPTER 34:** A QUEEN'S GIRL

**Paragraph begins:** Anne and the rest of the Avonlea scholars . . .
■ **HM** (638): a First Class teacher's license ■ **1908 LCP** *Apr* (386), **1916 LCP** (386), **1920 LCP** (386): teacher's license ■ **1925 GGH** (316): teacher's licence ■ **1925** [**1927** *imp*] **LCP** (355), **1942 & 1954 RP** 9th *imp* (355): teacher's license ■ **1965 RP** (295): teacher's licence ■ **1997 OUP** (361), **2004 BP** (305), **2007 NCE** (221): teacher's license. ■ [*The 1909 WID did not distinguish between "license" and "licence" used either as nouns or as verbs. Today, "licence" is a noun and "license" is a verb. Note that the 1942 Canadian edition set from Page plates had the "s" in license, but when it was reset by Ryerson in 1964 the spelling was changed.*]

# Manuscript Additions

The changes that L. M. Montgomery wrought when revising the manuscript of *Anne of Green Gables* offer an unusual visit backstage to an author's workshop, as she added to and subtilized her novel. Montgomery first wrote out her story in a clear round hand, jotting in a few insertions and corrections as she went. Then, as second thoughts occurred to her, she resorted to a system of revision that she had devised in her apprentice years as a writer. She kept her revisions on separate sheets, coded to show where they fitted into the original manuscript.

Dr. Elizabeth Epperly, who has done pioneer work on all the Montgomery manuscripts, explains the system. "Rather than make long additions on the original pages of the story she was writing, she simply marked a place for the addition with the word 'Note' and a letter of the alphabet. She dropped the word 'Note' somewhere along in the first run of the alphabet, and then used only a letter and its corresponding sequence number. After completing the alphabet the first time, she would follow through with A1 through Z1 and then A2 through Z2 and so on, going through the alphabet as many as twenty-five times in one novel. The additions were written on separate sheets and kept at the end of the manuscript * * *. The alphabet notations are clear and orderly."[1] Later, when Montgomery was typing out her story, she would cross out the additions as she worked them into the manuscript.

For the first part of the story (up to "A Tempest in the School Teapot") she wrote on the blank back pages of old manuscripts—poems, short stories—but for the later part of the book she used new 8 × 11 inch paper. The revisions are written in a less careful hand, on fresh 8 × 11 inch sheets. The manuscript, with its accompanying revision sheets, is held at the Confederation Centre, Charlottetown, PEI.

We here reproduce samples of the additional materials, chosen from the complete list of revisions we have compiled. They show

---

1. Elizabeth Epperly, "L. M. Montgomery's Manuscript Revisions," *Atlantis* 20.1 (1995): 150. See also Epperly, "Approaching the Montgomery Manuscripts," *Harvesting Thistles: The Textual Garden of L. M. Montgomery*, ed. Mary Henley Rubio (Guelph: Canadian Children's P, 1994) 74–83.

some of the changes in method developed as LMM's work progressed. In the first chapter she added many small details to sharpen the sense of the natural setting, of Mrs. Lynde's character, of the past history of Matthew and Marilla and their father, of the sound of farm and village voices—all specific parts of the community that Anne will come into. Such tiny tweakings gradually diminish in subsequent chapters. The author begins to insert longer passages to intensify (for instance) awareness of Anne's romantic imagination and to clarify her relations with Marilla. Fewer revisions appear as LMM warms to her work. Yet we are amazed to find that even in the final chapter such an essential phrase as "the bend in the road" occurred as an afterthought.

## Sample Revisions

Phrases set in bold (*e.g.,* **fringed**) are those that appear on Montgomery's add-on revision pages. The strike-throughs (*e.g.,* ~~jewel-weed~~) and insertions (*e.g.,* ^**below the house**^) indicated in the added phrases are hers. We give the page of the NCE text where each phrase can be found, and add a word or two in regular type before and after the added phrase, to help readers locate the spot where Montgomery inserted her additional material.

### CHAPTER 1: MRS. RACHEL LYNDE IS SURPRISED

■ (7) hollow, **fringed with alders and** ~~jewel-weed~~ **ladies' eardrops and** traversed
■ (7) passed, **from brooks and children up,** and
■ (7) quilts—**she had knitted** ~~twenty~~ **sixteen of them, as Avonlea housekeepers were wont to tell in awed voices**—and keeping
■ (8) bright; **the orchard on the slope** ^**below the house**^ **was in a bridal flush of pinky-white bloom, hummed over by a myriad of bees.** Thomas
■ (8) Lynde—**a meek little man whom Avonlea people called "Rachel Lynde's husband"**—was sowing
■ (8) Cuthbert, **at half-past three on the afternoon of a busy day,** placidly
■ (8) Rachel, **deftly putting this and that together,** might
■ (9) doctor. **Yet something must have happened since last night to start him off.** I'm clean
■ (9) for more; **he wasn't driving fast enough to be going for a doctor.** Yet
■ (9) father, **as shy and silent as his son after him,** had got

■ (9) of them. **I'd ruther look at people.** To be sure
■ (9) **be seen, for Mrs. Rachel would have seen it if there had been.** Privately she
■ (10) **dishes and there was only crab-apple preserves and one kind of cake**, so that
■ (10) sorrel mare? **Mrs. Rachel was getting fairly dizzy with this unusual mystery about quiet, ^unmysterious^ Green Gables.** "Good
■ (10) all your folks? **Something that for lack of any other name might be called friendship existed and always had existed between Marilla Cuthbert and Mrs. Rachel, in spite of^—or perhaps because of—^their dissimilarity.** Marilla was a tall, thin
■ (11) more astonished. **She was actually stricken dumb for five seconds.** It was unsupposable
■ (11) said Marilla, **as if getting boys from orphan asylums in Nova Scotia were part of the usual spring work on any well-regulated Avonlea farm instead of being an unheard of innovation.** Mrs. Rachel
■ (11) disapprovingly. **This had been done without her advice being asked, and must perforce be disapproved.** "Well, we've
■ (12) to-day—**the mail-man brought it from the station**—saying
■ (12) beds. **And I know another case where an adopted boy used to suck the eggs—they couldn't break him of it.** If you
■ (13) this world. **There's risks in people's having children of their own if it comes to that—they don't always turn out well.** And then
■ (13) getting a girl," said Marilla, **as if poisoning wells were a purely feminine accomplishment and not to be dreaded in the case of a boy.** "I'd never
■ (13) grandfather, **if so be's he ever had a grandfather, which is doubtful.** It seems
■ (13) was built—**if they ever were children, which is hard to believe when one looks at them.** I wouldn't

**CHAPTER 10:** ANNE'S APOLOGY

■ (62) obdurate. **After each meal Marilla carried a well-filled tray to the east gable and brought it down later on not noticeably depleted. Matthew eyed its last descent with a troubled eye. Had Anne eaten anything at all?** When Marilla
■ (62) before her. **Matthew recollected that he must say what he had come to say without loss of time, lest Marilla return prematurely.** "Well now
■ (63) all night. **I know I did because I woke up three times and I was just furious every time.** But this
■ (63) well." **Marilla's crispness gave no sign of her relief. She**

had been wondering what under the canopy she should do if Anne did not give in. "I'll take

- ▪ (63) along, her eyes fixed on the sunset sky and an air

- ▪ (64) to you—and I've disgraced the dear friends, Matthew and Marilla, who have let me stay at Green Gables although I'm not a boy. I'm a

- ▪ (65) grew up. It would be so much easier to be good if one's hair was ^a handsome^ auburn, don't you think? And now

- ▪ (65) thing. Take this chair, Marilla; it's easier than the one you've got; I just keep that for the hired boy to sit on. Yes, she certainly is an odd child, but

- ▪ (66) comment. Marilla was dismayed at finding herself inclined to laugh over the recollection. She had also an uneasy feeling that she ought to scold Anne for apologizing so well but then that was ridiculous! She compromised with her conscience by saying severely, "I hope

- ▪ (66) to-night? If you could live in a star, which one would you pick? I'd like that lovely clear big one away over there above that dark hill." "Anne

- ▪ (66) own lane. A little gypsy wind came down it to meet them, laden with the ^spicy^ perfume of young dew-wet ferns. Far up in the shadows a cheerful light gleamed out through the trees from the kitchen at Green Gables. Anne

- ▪ (67) in the ferns—and then I'll fly over to Mrs. Lynde's garden and set the flowers dancing—and then I'll ~~blow~~ go with one great swoop over the clover field—and when

## CHAPTER 20: A GOOD IMAGINATION GONE WRONG

- ▪ (132) them, coming home in the clear, echoing twilight with arms and baskets full of flowery spoil. "I'm so

- ▪ (132) <u>romantic</u> spot. Charlie Sloane dared Arty Gillis to jump over it, and Arty did because he wouldn't take a dare. Nobody would in school. It is very <u>fashionable</u> to dare. Mr. Phillips

- ▪ (132) them with scorn. I can't tell you the person's name because I have vowed never to let it cross my lips. We made

- ▪ (133) evening, when the orchards were pink-blossomed again, when the frogs were singing silvery sweet in the marshes about the head of the Lake of Shining Waters, and the air

- ▪ (133) evidently." Headaches always left Marilla somewhat sarcastic. "Oh, I'm

- ▪ (133–34) dinner table. I was firmly resolved, when you left me in charge this morning, not to imagine anything but keep my thoughts on facts. I did pretty well until I put the pie in, and then an ~~irris~~ irresistaible temptation came to me to imagine I was an enchanted princess shut up in a lonely tower with a handsome night riding to my rescue on a ~~cold~~ coal-black steed. So that is how I came to forget the pie. I didn't

- (135) amusement. We began it in April. A haunted wood is so very romantic, Marilla. We chose the spruce grove because it's so gloomy. Oh, we

- (135) religious woman. And Mrs. Thomas' father was pursued home one night by a lamb of fire with its head cut off hanging by a strip of skin. He said he knew it was the spirit of his brother and that it was a warning he would die within nine days. He didn't, but he died two years after, so you see it was really true. And Ruby

- (136) spectres beyond. "Oh, Marilla, how can you be so cruel?" sobbed Anne. "What would you feel like if a white thing did snatch me up and carry me off?" "I'll risk it," said Marilla unfeelingly. "You know I always mean what I say. I'll cure you of imagining ghosts into places. March, now." Anne marched

- (136) into being. A white strip of birch bark blowing up from the hollow over the brown floor of the grove made her heart stand still. The long-drawn wail of two old boughs rubbing against each other brought out the perspiration in beads on her forehead. The swoop of bats in the darkness over her was as the wings of unearthly creatures. When she

- (136) a white thing. When she finally stumbled over the log bridge she drew one long shivering breath of relief. "Well, so nothing

## CHAPTER 30: THE QUEEN'S CLASS IS ORGANIZED

- (191) hearth-rug, gazing into that joyous glow where the sunshine of a hundred summers was being distilled from the maple cord-wood. She had

- (192) Diana." Anne came back from her other world with a start and a sigh. "Was she

- (192) wood things—the ferns and the satin leaves and the crackerberries—have gone

- (192) she is. Young men are all very well in their place, but it doesn't do to drag them into everything, does it? Diana and I

- (193) developed. It's perfectly appalling to think of being twenty, Marilla. It sounds so fearfully old and grown up. But why

- (195) my life—that is, for the last six months, ever since Ruby and Jane began to talk of studying for the entrance. But I

- (195) diligent." Not for worlds would Marilla have told Anne just what Miss Stacy had said about her; that would have been to pamper vanity. "You needn't

■ (196) Lynde says. **Mrs. Lynde isn't exactly a comforting person sometimes, but there's no doubt she says a great many very true things.** And I

■ (196) ambition. **Ruby says she will only teach for two years after she gets through and then she intends to be married. Jane says she will devote her whole life to teaching, and never, never marry because you are paid a salary for teaching, but a husband won't pay you anything,** ~~I expect Jane~~ **and growls if you ask for a share in the egg and butter money. I expect Jane speaks from** ^mournful^ **experience, for Mrs. Lynde says that her father is a perfect old crank and meaner than** ~~poison~~ **second skimmings.** Josie Pye

■ (197) was gone—**gone just when she most needed its sustaining power.** It was

■ (198) to read; **new pieces to be practised for the Sunday-school choir;** pleasant

■ (198) next year. **It will be the tug of war, you know—the last year before the Entrance."** "Are you

■ (198–99) next year—**that she had been offered a position in the graded school of her own home district and meant to accept.** The Queen's

■ (199–200) you know. **Jane Andrews was over once last summer and she says it was a dazzling sight to see the electric lights and the flowers and all the lady guests in such beautiful dresses. Jane says it was her first glimpse into high life and she'll never forget it to her dying day."** Mrs. Lynde

**CHAPTER 38: THE BEND IN THE ROAD**

■ (239) done out. **Don't say anything about this to any one for a spell yet, anyway. I can't bear that folks should come here to question and sympathize and talk about it."** When Marilla

■ (241) for a week. **I shall give life here my best, and I believe it will give its best to me in return. When I left Queen's my future seemed to stretch out before me like a straight road. I thought I could see along it for many a milestone. Now there is a bend in it. I don't know what lies around** ~~it~~ **the bend but I'm going to believe that the best does. It has a fascination of its own,** ~~Marilla~~ **that bend, Marilla. I wonder how the road beyond it goes—what there is of green glory and soft, checkered light and shadows—what new landscapes—what new beauties—what curves and hills and valleys further on."** "I don't feel

■ (241) summer dusk. **They liked to sit there when the twilight came down and the white moths flew about in the garden and the odour of mint filled the dewy air.** Mrs. Rachel

■ (242) overdo things. **As 'Josiah Allen's wife' says, I shall be 'mejum.'** But

■ (242) the school. **You'll get along all right, now that there are no Pyes going. Josie was the last of them, and a good thing she was, that's what. There's been some Pye or other going to Avonlea school for the last twenty years, and I guess their mission in life was to keep school-teachers reminded that earth isn't their home.** Bless my

■ (243) poplars **whose rustle was like low, friendly speech**, and its

■ (243) ancient peace." **There was a freshness in the air as of a wind that had blown over honey-sweet fields of clover.** Home

# BACKGROUNDS

# Journals, Juvenilia, and Related Writings

## Journal Entry (1889)†

Cavendish, P.E. Island
Sept. 21, 1889

I am going to begin a new kind of diary. I have kept one of a kind for years—ever since I was a tot of nine. But I burned it to-day. It was so silly I was ashamed of it. And it was also very dull. I wrote in it religiously every day and told what kind of weather it was. Most of the time I hadn't much else to tell but I would have thought it a kind of crime not to write daily in it—nearly as bad as not saying my prayers or washing my face.

But I'm going to start out all over new and write only when I have something worth writing about. Life is beginning to get interesting for me—I will soon be fifteen—the last day of November. And in this journal I am never going to tell what kind of a day it is—unless the weather has something to do worth while. And—last but not least—I am going to keep this book locked up!!

To be sure, there isn't much to write about to-day. There wasn't any school, so I amused myself repotting all my geraniums. Dear things, how I love them! The "mother" of them all is a matronly old geranium called "Bonny." I got Bonny ages ago—it must be as much as two or three years—when I was up spending the winter with Aunt Emily in Malpeque. Maggie Abbott, a girl who lived there, had a little geranium slip in a can and when I came home she gave it to me. I called it Bonny—I like things to have handles even if they are only geraniums—and I've loved it next to my cats. It has grown to be a great big plant with the cunningest little leaves with a curly brown stripe around them. And it blooms as if it meant it. I believe that old geranium has a soul!

† From *The Selected Journals of L. M. Montgomery: Volume I*, ed. Mary Rubio and Elizabeth Waterston, 1. Copyright © 1985 University of Guelph and published by Oxford University Press. This is the first entry in LMM's Journal, kept from 1889 to 1942; it is also the first entry published in *SJ*. Reprinted by permission of Mary Rubio, Elizabeth Waterston, the University of Guelph, and the publisher.

# A Girl's Place at Dalhousie College (1896)†

\* \* \*

"Pretty were the sight,
If our old halls could change their sex and flaunt
With prudes for proctors, dowagers for deans,
And sweet girl graduates in their golden hair."
Tennyson—"THE PRINCESS"

It is not a very long time, as time goes in the world's history, since the idea of educating a girl beyond her "three r's" would have been greeted with up lifted hands and shocked countenances. What! Could any girl, in her right and proper senses, ask for any higher, more advanced education than that accorded her by tradition and custom? Could any girl presume to think that the attainments of her mother and grandmother before her, insufficient for her? Above all, could the dream of opposing her weak feminine mind to the mighty masculine intellect which had been dominating the world of knowledge from a date long preceding the time when Hypatia was torn to pieces by a mob of Alexandria?

"Never," was the approved answer to all such questions. Girls were "educated" according to the standard of the time. That is they were taught reading and writing and a small smattering of foreign languages; they "took" music and were trained to warble pretty little songs and instructed in the mysteries of embroidery and drawing. The larger proportion of them, of course, married, and we are quite ready to admit that they made none the poorer wives and mothers because they could not conjugate a Greek verb or demonstrate a proposition in Euclid. It is not the purpose of this article to discuss whether, with a broader education, they might not have fulfilled the duties of wifehood and motherhood equally well and with much more of ease to themselves and others.

Old Traditions die hard and we will step very gently around their death bed. But there was always a certain number of unfortunates— let us call them so since the world would persist in using the term— who, for no fault of their own probably, were left to braid St. Catherine's tresses for the term of their natural lives; and a hard lot truly was theirs in the past. If they did not live in meek dependence with some compassionate relative, eating the bitter bread of unappreciated drudgery, it was because they could earn a meagre and precarious subsistence in the few and underpaid occupations then open to women. They could do nothing else! Their education had not fitted

† From "A Girl's Place at Dalhousie College," Halifax *Herald*, April, 1896. Preserved in L. M. Montgomery's scrapbook, 1890–1898. An uncut version of this article is available in Bolger, *The Years Before 'Anne'* and in Devereux's Critical Edition of *Anne of Green Gables*.

them to cope with any and every destiny; they were helpless straws, swept along the merciless current of existence.

If some woman, with the courage of her convictions, dared to make a stand against the popular prejudice, she was sneered at as a "blue-stocking," and prudent mothers held her up as a warning example to their pretty, frivolous daughters, and looked askance at her as a not altogether desirable curiosity.

But, nowadays, all this is so changed that we are inclined to wonder if it has not taken longer than a generation to effect the change. The "higher education of women" has passed into a common place phrase.

A girl is no longer shut out from the temple of knowledge simply because she is a girl; she can compete, and has competed, successfully with her brother in all his classes. The way is made easy before her feet; there is no struggle to render her less sweet and womanly, and the society of to-day is proud of its "sweet girl-graduates."

If they marry, their husbands find in their wives an increased capacity for assistance and sympathy; their children can look up to their mothers for the clear-cut judgment and the wisest guidance. If they do not marry, their lives are still full and happy and useful they have something to do and can do it well, and the world is better off from their having been born in it.

In England there have been two particularly brilliant examples of what a girl can do when she is given an equal chance with her brother; these are so widely known that it is hardly necessary to name them. Every one has read and heard of Miss Fawcett, the brilliant mathematician, who came out ahead of the senior wrangles at Cambridge, and of Miss Ramsay, who led the classical tripos at the same university.

In the new world, too, many girl students have made for themselves a brilliant record. Here, every opportunity and aid is offered to the girl who longs for the best education the age can yield her. There are splendidly equipped colleges for women, equal in every respect to those for men; or, if a girl prefers co-education and wishes to match her intellect with man's on a common footing, the doors of many universities are open to her.

\*   \*   \*

\* \* \*This year there is a larger number of girls in attendance at Dalhousie than there has been in any previous year. In all, there are about fifty-eight, including the lady medical students. Of course, out of these fifty-eight a large proportion are not undergraduates. They are merely general students taking classes in some favorite subject, usually languages and history.

\* \* \*

Dalhousie is strictly co-educational. The girls enter on exactly the same footing as the men and are admitted to an equal share in all the privileges of the institution. The only places from which they are barred are the gymnasium and reading room. They are really excluded from the former, but there is nothing to keep them out of the reading room save custom and tradition. It is the domain sacred to masculine scrimmages and gossips and the girls religiously avoid it, never doing more than cast speculative glances at its door as they scurry past into the library. We have not been able to discover what the penalty would be if a girl should venture into the reading room. It may be death or it may be only banishment for life.

The library, however, is free to all. The girls can prowl around there in peace, bury themselves in encyclopedias, pore over biographies and exercise their wits on logic, or else they can get into a group and carry on whispered discussions which may have reference to their work or may not.

\* \* \*

\* \* \*The question of the higher education of girls involves a great many interesting problems which are frequently discussed but which time alone can solve satisfactorily. Woman has asserted her claim to an equal educational standing with man and that claim has been conceded to her. What use then, will she make of her privileges? Will she take full advantage of them or will she merely play with them until, tired of the novelty, she drops them for some mere fad? Every year since girls first entered Dalhousie, has witnessed a steady increase in the number of them in attendance; and it is to be expected that, in the years to come, the number will be very much larger. But beyond a certain point we do not think it will go. It is not likely that the day will ever come when the number of girl students at Dalhousie, or at any other co-educational university, will be equal to the number of men. There will always be a certain number of clever ambitious girls who, feeling that their best life work can be accomplished only when backed up by a broad and thorough education, will take a university course, will work conscientiously and earnestly and will share all the honors and successes of their brothers. There will, however, always be a limit to the number of such girls.

Again, we have frequently heard this question asked: "Is it, in the end, worth while for a girl to take a university course with all its attendant expense, hard work, and risk of health?" How many girls, out of those who graduate from the universities, are ever heard of prominently again, many of them marrying or teaching school? Would not an ordinarily good education have benefited them quite as much? Is it then worth while, from this standpoint, for any girl who is not exceptionally brilliant, to take a university course?

The individual question of "worth while" or "not worth while" is one which every girl must scramble for herself. It is only in its general aspect that we must look at the subject. In the first place, as far as distinguishing themselves in after life goes, take the number of girls who have graduated from Dalhousie—say thirty, most of whom are yet in their twenties and have their whole lives before them. Out of that thirty, eight or nine at the very least have not stood still but have gone forward successfully and are known to the public as brilliant, efficient workers. Out of any thirty men who graduate, how many in the same time do better or even as well? This, however, is looking at the question from the standpoint that the main object of a girl in taking a university course is to keep herself before the public as a distinguished worker. But is it? No! At least it should not be. Such an ambition is not the end and aim of a true education.

A girl does not—or, at least, should not—go to university merely to shine as clever students take honors, "get through and then do something very brilliant." Nay; she goes—or should go—to prepare herself for living, not alone in the finite but in the infinite. She goes to have her mind broadened and her powers of observation culti- vated. She goes to study her own race in all the bewildering per- plexities of its being. In short, she goes to find out the best, easiest and most effective way of living the life that God and nature planned out for her to live.

If a girl gets this out of her college course, it is of little conse- quence whether her after "career" be brilliant, as the world defines brilliancy, or not. She has obtained that from her studies which will stand by her all her life, and future generations will rise up and call her blessed, who handed down to them the clear insight, the broad sympathy with their fellow creatures, the energy of purpose and the self-control that such a woman must transmit those who come after her.

## Journal Entry (1901)†

Cavendish, P.E.I.
Aug. 28, 1901
* * *There are certain essentials to an old-fashioned garden. Without them it would not be itself. Like the poet it must be born not made—

† From The Selected Journals of L. M. Montgomery: Volume I, ed. Mary Rubio and Elizabeth Waterston, 263–64. Copyright © 1985 University of Guelph and published by Oxford University Press. Reprinted by permission of Mary Rubio, Elizabeth Waterston, the Uni- versity of Guelph, and the publisher.

the outgrowth and flowering of long years of dedication and care. The least flavor of newness or modernity spoils it.

For one thing, it must be secluded and shut away from the world— a "garden enclosed"—preferably by willows—or apple trees—or firs. It must have some trim walks bordered by clam-shells, or edged with "ribbon grass," and there must be in it the flowers that belong to old-fashioned gardens and are seldom found in the catalogues of to-day—perennials planted there by grandmotherly hands when the century was young. There should be poppies, like fine ladies in full-skirted silken gowns, "cabbage" roses, heavy and pink and luscious, tiger-lilies like gorgeously bedight sentinels, "Sweet-William" in striped attire, bleeding heart, that favorite of my childhood, south-ernwood, feathery and pungent, butter-and-eggs—that is now known as "narcissus"—"bride's bouquet," as white as a bride's bouquet should be, holly hocks like flaunting overbold maiden's, purple spikes of "Adam and Eve," pink and white "musk" "Sweet Balm" and "Sweet May," "Bouncing Bets" in her ruffled, lilac-tinted skirts, pure white "June lilies," crimson peonies—"pinies"—velvety-eyed "Irish Prim-roses," which were neither primroses nor Irish, scarlet lightning and Prince's feather—all growing in orderly confusion.

Dear old gardens! The very breath of them is a benediction.

# The Strike at Putney (1903)†

The church at Putney was one that gladdened the hearts of all the ministers in the Presbytery whenever they thought about it. It was such a satisfactory church. While other churches here and there were continually giving trouble in one way or another, the Putneyites were never guilty of brewing up internal or presbyterial strife.

The Exeter church people were always quarrelling among them-selves and carrying their quarrels to the courts of the church. The very name of Exeter gave the members of presbytery the cold creeps. But the Putney church people never quarreled.

Danbridge church was in a chronic state of ministerlessness. No minister ever stayed in Danbridge longer than he could help. The people were too critical and they were also noted heresy hunters. Good ministers fought shy of Danbridge and poor ones met with a chill welcome. The harassed presbytery, worn out with "supplying," were disposed to think that the millennium would come if ever the Danbridgians got a minister whom they liked.

† From *Western Christian Advocate*, 16 Sept. 1903, 14–15. This story was republished in the *National Magazine*, May 1909, 193–96, and again in *Westminister* May 1914, 467–72.

At Putney they had the same minister for fifteen years and hoped and expected to have him for fifteen more. They looked with horror-stricken eyes on the Danbridge theological coquetries.

Bloom Valley church was over head and heels in debt and had no visible prospect of ever getting out. The moderator said under his breath that they did over much praying and too little hoeing. He did not believe in faith without works. Tarrytown Road kept its head above water but never had a cent to spare for missions or the schemes of the church.

In bright and shining contradistinction to these the Putney church had always paid its way and gave liberally to all departments of church work. If other springs of supply ran dry the Putneyites enthusiastically got up a "tea" or a "social," and so raised the money. Naturally the "heft" of this work fell on the women, but they did not mind—in very truth, they enjoyed it. The Putney women had the reputation of being "great church workers," and they plumed themselves on it, putting on airs at conventions among the less energetic women of the other churches.

They were especially strong on societies. There was the Church Aid Society, the Girl's Flower Band, and the Sewing Circle. There were a Mission Band and a Helping Hand among the children. And finally there was the Women's Foreign Auxiliary, out of which the whole trouble grew which convulsed the church at Putney for a brief time and furnished a standing joke in Presbyterial circles for years afterwards. To this day ministers and elders tell the story of the Putney church strike with sparkling eyes and subdued chuckles. It never grows old or stale. But the Putney elders are an exception. They never laugh at it. They never refer to it. It is not in the wicked, unregenerate heart of man to make a jest of his own bitter defeat.

It was in June that the secretary of the Putney W.F.M. Auxiliary wrote to a noted returned missionary who was touring the country, asking her to give an address on mission work before their society. Mrs. Cotterell wrote back saying that her brief time was so taken up already that she found it hard to make any further engagements, but she could not refuse the Putney people who were so well and favorably known in mission circles for their perennial interest and liberality. So, although she could not come on the date requested, she would, if acceptable, come the following Sunday.

This suited the Putney Auxiliary very well. On the Sunday referred to there was to be no evening service in the church owing to Mr. Sinclair's absence. They therefore appointed the missionary meeting for that night, and made arrangements to hold it in the church itself, as the classroom was too small for the expected audience.

Then the thunderbolt descended on the W.F.M.A. of Putney from a clear sky. The elders of the church rose up to a man and declared that no woman should occupy the pulpit of the Putney church. It was in direct contravention to the teachings of St. Paul.

To make matters worse, Mr. Sinclair declared himself on the elders' side. He said that he could not conscientiously give his consent to a woman occupying his pulpit, even when that woman was Mrs. Cotterell and her subject foreign missions.

The members of the Auxiliary were aghast. They called a meeting extraordinary in the classroom and, discarding all forms and ceremonies in their wrath, talked their indignation out.

Out of doors the world basked in June sunshine and preened itself in blossom. The birds sang and chirped in the lichened maples that cupped the little church in, and peace was over all the Putney valley. Inside the classroom disgusted women buzzed like angry bees.

"What on earth are we to do?" sighed the secretary plaintively. Mary Kilburn was always plaintive. She sat on the steps of the platform, being too wrought up in her mind to sit in her chair at the desk, and her thin, faded little face was twisted with anxiety. "All the arrangements are made and Mrs. Cotterell is coming on the tenth. How can we tell her that the men won't let her speak?"

"There was never anything like this in Putney church before," groaned Mrs. Elder Knox. "It was Andrew McKittrick put them up to it. I always said that man would make trouble here yet, ever since he moved to Putney from Danbridge. I've talked and argued with Thomas until I'm dumb, but he is as set as a rock."

"I don't see what business the men have to interfere with us anyhow," said her daughter Lucy, who was sitting on one of the window sills. "We don't meddle with them, I'm sure. As if Mrs. Cotterell would contaminate the pulpit!"

"One would think we were still in the dark ages," said Frances Spenslow sharply. Frances was the Putney school teacher. Her father was one of the recalcitrant elders and Frances felt it bitterly— all the more that she tried to argue with him and had been sat upon as a "child who couldn't understand."

"I'm more surprised at Mr. Sinclair than at the elders," said Mrs. Abner Keech, fanning herself vigorously. "Elders are subject to queer spells periodically. They think they assert their authority that way. But Mr. Sinclair has always seemed so liberal and broad-minded."

"You never can tell what crochet an old bachelor will take into his head," said Alethea Craig bitingly.

The others nodded in agreement. Mr. Sinclair's inveterate celibacy was a standing grievance with the Putney women.

"If he had a wife who could be our president this would never have happened, I warrant you," said Mrs. King sagely.

"But what are we going to do, ladies?" said Mrs. Robbins briskly. Mrs. Robbins was the president. She was a big, bustling woman with clear blue eyes and crisp, incisive ways. Hitherto she had held her peace.

"They must talk themselves out before they can get down to business," she had reflected sagely. But she thought the time had now come to speak.

"You know," she went on, "we can talk and rage against the men all day if we like. They are not trying to prevent us. But that will do no good. Here's Mrs. Cotterell invited, and all the neighboring auxiliaries notified—and the men won't let us have the church. The point is, how are we going to get out of the scrape?"

A helpless silence descended upon the classroom. The eyes of every woman present turned to Myra Wilson. Every one could talk; but when it came to action they had a fashion of turning to Myra.

She had a reputation for cleverness and originality. She never talked much. So far to-day she had not said a word. She was sitting on the sill of the window across from Lucy Knox. She swung her hat on her knee, and loose, moist rings of dark hair curled around her dark, alert face. There was a sparkle in her gray eyes that boded ill to the men who were peaceably pursuing their avocations, rashly indifferent to what the women might be saying in the maple-shaded classroom.

"Have you any suggestion to make, Miss Wilson?" said Mrs. Robbins, with a return to her official voice and manner.

Myra put her long, slender index finger to her chin.

"I think," she said decidedly, "that we must strike."

When Elder Knox went in to tea that evening he glanced somewhat apprehensively at his wife. They had had an altercation before she went to the meeting and he supposed she had talked herself into another rage while there. But Mrs. Knox was placid and smiling. She had made his favorite soda biscuits for him and inquired amiably after his progress in hoeing turnips in the southeast meadow.

She made, however, no reference to the Auxiliary meeting, and, when the biscuits and maple syrup and two cups of matchless tea had nerved the elder up, his curiosity got the better of his prudence—for even elders are human and curiosity knows no gender—and he asked what they had done at the meeting.

"We poor men have been shaking in our shoes," he said facetiously.

"Were you?" Mrs. Knox's voice was calm and faintly amused. "Well, you didn't need to. We talked the matter over very quietly and came to the conclusion that the session knew best and that women hadn't any right to interfere in church business at all."

Lucy Knox turned her head away to hide a smile. The elder beamed. He was a peace loving man and disliked "runctions" of any sort and domestic ones in particular. Since the decision of the session Mrs. Knox had made his life a burden to him. He did not understand her sudden change of base, but he accepted it very thankfully.

"That's right—that's right," he said heartily. "I'm glad to hear you coming out so sensible, Maria. I was afraid you'd work yourselves up at the meeting and let Myra Wilson or Alethea Craig put you up to some foolishness or other. Well, I guess I'll jog down to the Corner this evening and order that barrel of pastry flour you want."

"Oh, you needn't," said Mrs. Knox indifferently. "We won't be needing it now."

"Not needing it! But I thought you said you had to have some to bake for the social week after next."

"There isn't going to be any social."

"Not any social?"

Elder Knox stared perplexedly at his wife. A month previously the Putney church had been recarpeted, and they still owed fifty dollars for it. This, the women declared, they would speedily pay off by a big cake and ice-cream social in the hall. Mrs. Knox had been one of the foremost promoters of the enterprise.

"Not any social?" repeated the elder again. "Then how is the money for the carpet to be got? And *why* isn't there going to be a social?"

"The men can get the money somehow, I suppose," said Mrs. Knox. "As for the social why, of course, if women aren't good enough to speak in church they are not good enough to work for it either. Lucy, dear, will you pass me the cookies?"

"Lucy dear" passed the cookies and then rose abruptly and left the table. Her father's face was too much for her.

"What confounded nonsense is this?" demanded the elder explosively.

Mrs. Knox opened her mellow brown eyes widely, as if in amazement at her husband's tone.

"I don't understand you," she said. "Our position is perfectly logical."

She had borrowed that phrase from Myra Wilson and it floored the elder. He got up, seized his hat, and strode from the room.

That night, at Jacob Wherrison's store at the Corner, the Putney men talked over the new development. The social was certainly off—for a time, anyway.

"Best let 'em alone, I say," said Wherrison. "They're mad at us now and doing this to pay us out. But they'll cool down later on and we'll have the social all right."

"But if they don't," said Andrew McKittrick gloomily, "who is going to pay for that carpet?"

This was an unpleasant question. The others shirked it.

"I was always opposed to this action of the session," said Alec

Craig. "It wouldn't have hurt to have let the woman speak. 'Tisn't as if it was a regular sermon."

"The session knew best," said Andrew sharply. "And the minister—you're not going to set your opinion up against his, are you, Craig?"

"Didn't know they taught such reverence for ministers in Danbridge," retorted Craig with a laugh.

"Best let 'em alone, as Wherrison says," said Abner Keech.

"Don't see what else we can do," said John Wilson shortly.

On Sunday morning the men were conscious of a bare, deserted appearance in the church. Mr. Sinclair perceived it himself. After some inward wondering he concluded that it was because there were no flowers anywhere. The table before the pulpit was bare. On the organ a vase held a sorry, faded bouquet left over from the previous week. The floor was unswept. Dust lay thickly on the pulpit Bible, the choir chairs, and the pew backs.

"This church looks disgraceful," said John Robbins in an angry undertone to his daughter Polly, who was president of the Flower Band. "What in the name of common sense is the good of your Flower Banders if you can't keep the place looking decent?"

"There is no Flower Band now, father," whispered Polly in return. "We've disbanded. Women haven't any business to meddle in church matters. You know the session said so."

It was well for Polly that she was too big to have her ears boxed. Even so, it might have not saved her if they had been anywhere else than in church.

Meanwhile the men who were sitting in the choir—three basses and two tenors—were beginning to dimly suspect that there was something amiss here, too. Where were the sopranos and the altos? Myra Wilson and Alethea Craig and several other members of the choir were sitting in their pews with perfectly unconscious faces. Myra was looking out of the window into the tangled sunlight and shadow of the great maples. Alethea Craig was reading her Bible.

Presently Frances Spenslow came in. Frances was organist, but to-day, instead of walking up to the platform, she slipped demurely into her father's pew at one side of the pulpit. Eben Craig, who was the Putney singing master and felt himself responsible for the choir, fidgeted uneasily. He tried to catch Frances' eye, but she was absorbed in reading the mission report she had found in the rack, and Eben was finally forced to tiptoe to the Spenslow pew and whisper, "Miss Spenslow, the minister is waiting for the doxology. Aren't you going to take the organ?"

Frances looked up calmly. Her clear, placid voice was audible not only to those in the nearby pews, but to the minister.

"No, Mr. Craig. You know if a woman isn't fit to speak in the church she can't be fit to sing in it either."

Eben Craig looked exceedingly foolish. He tiptoed gingerly back to this place. The minister, with an unusual flush on his thin, ascetic face, rose suddenly and gave out the opening hymn.

Nobody who heard the singing in Putney Church that day ever forgot it. Untrained basses and tenors, unrelieved by a single female voice, are not inspiring.

There were no announcements of society meetings for the forthcoming week. On the way home from church that day irate husbands and fathers scolded, argued or pleaded, according to their several dispositions. One and all met with the same calm statement that if a noble, self-sacrificing woman like Mrs. Cotterell were not good enough to speak in the Putney church, ordinary, every-day women could not be fit to take any part whatever in its work.

Sunday School that afternoon was a harrowing failure. Out of all the corps of teachers only one was a man, and he alone was at his post. In the Christian Endeavor meeting on Tuesday night the feminine element sat dumb and unresponsive. The Putney women never did things by halves.

The men held out for two weeks. At the end of that time they "happened" to meet at the manse and talked the matter over with the harassed minister. Elder Knox said gloomily:

"It's this way. Nothing can move them women. I know, for I've tried. My authority has been set at naught in my own household. And I'm laughed at if I show my face in any of the other settlements."

The Sunday School superintendent said the Sunday School was going to wreck and ruin, also the Christmas Endeavor. The condition of the church for dust was something scandalous and strangers were making a mockery of the singing. And the carpet had to be paid for. He supposed they would have to let the women have their own way.

The next Sunday evening after service Mr. Sinclair arose hesitatingly. His face was flushed, and Alethea Craig always declared that he looked "just plain every-day cross."

He announced briefly that the session after due deliberation had concluded that Mrs. Cotterell might occupy the pulpit on the evening appointed for her address.

The women all over the church smiled broadly. Frances Spenslow got up and went to the organ stool. The singing in the last hymn was good and hearty. Going down the steps after dismissal Mrs. Elder Knox caught the secretary of the Church Aid by the arm.

"I guess," she whispered anxiously, "you'd better call a special meeting of the Aids at my house to-morrow afternoon. If we're to get that social over before haying begins we've got to do some smart scurrying."

The strike in the Putney church was over.

# Journal Entry (1905) †

Sunday, Mar. 26, 1905
Cavendish, P.E.I.
* * *In our sitting room there has always been a big bookcase used as a china cabinet. In each door is a large, oval glass, dimly reflecting the room. When I was very small each of my reflections in these glass doors were "real folks" to my imagination. The one in the left-hand door was *Katie Maurice,* the one in the right-hand *Lucy Gray.* Why I named them thus I cannot say. Wordsworth's ballad had no connection with the latter, because at that time I had never read it or heard of it. Indeed, I have no recollection of deliberately naming them at all. As far back as consciousness runs *Katie Maurice* and *Lucy Gray,* lived in the fairy room behind the bookcase. *Katie* was a little girl like myself and I loved her dearly. I would stand before that door and prattle to her for hours, giving and receiving confidences. In especial, I liked to do this at twilight when the fire had been lighted for the evening, and the room and its reflections were a glamour of light and shadow.

# Journal Entry (1907)‡

Friday, Aug. 16, 1907
Cavendish, P.E.I.
Here is a gap with a vengeance! But there has not been much to write about and I've been very busy and contented. Since spring came I haven't been dismal and life has been endurable and—by spells—pleasant.

One really important thing *has* come my way since my last entry. On April 15th I received a letter from the L. C. Page Co. of Boston accepting the MS of a book I had sent them and offering to publish it on a royalty basis!

All my life it has been my aim to write a book—a "real live" book. Of late years I have been thinking of it seriously but somehow it seemed such a big task I hadn't the courage to begin it. I have always hated *beginning* a story. When I get the first paragraph written I feel

† From *The Selected Journals of L. M. Montgomery: Volume I*, ed. Mary Rubio and Elizabeth Waterston, 306. Copyright © 1985 University of Guelph and published by Oxford University Press. Reprinted by permission of Mary Rubio, Elizabeth Waterston, the University of Guelph, and the publisher.

‡ From *The Selected Journals of L. M. Montgomery: Volume I*, ed. Mary Rubio and Elizabeth Waterston, 330–31. Copyright © 1985 University of Guelph and published by Oxford University Press. Reprinted by permission of Mary Rubio, Elizabeth Waterston, the University of Guelph, and the publisher.

as though it were half done. To begin a *book* therefore seemed a quite enormous undertaking. Besides, I did not see just how I could get time for it. I could not afford to take time from my regular work to write it.

I have always kept a notebook in which I jotted down, as they occurred to me ideas for plots, incidents, characters and descriptions. Two years ago in the spring of 1905 I was looking over this notebook in search of some suitable idea for a short serial I wanted to write for a certain Sunday School paper and I found a faded entry, written ten years before:—"Elderly couple apply to orphan asylum for a boy. By mistake a girl is sent them." I thought this would do. I began to block out chapters, devise incidents and "brood up" my heroine. Somehow or other she seemed very real to me and took possession of me to an unusual extent. Her personality appealed to me and I thought it rather a shame to waste her on an ephemeral little serial. Then the thought came, "Write a book about her. You have the central idea and character. All you have to do is to spread it out over enough chapters to amount to a book."

The result of this was "Anne of Green Gables".

I began the actual writing of it one evening in May and wrote most of it in the evenings after my regular work was done, through that summer and autumn, finishing it, I think, sometime in January 1906. It was a labor of love. Nothing I have ever written gave me so much pleasure to write. I cast "moral" and "Sunday School" ideals to the winds and made my "Anne" a real human girl. Many of my own childhood experiences and dreams were worked up into its chapters. Cavendish scenery supplied the background and *Lover's Lane* figures very prominently. There is plenty of incident in it but after all it must stand or fall by "Anne". *She* is the book.

I typewrote it out on my old second-hand typewriter that never makes the capitals plain and won't print "w" at all. The next thing was to find a publisher. I sent it to the Bobbs-Merrill firm of Indianapolis. This was a new firm that had recently come to the front with several "best sellers". I thought I might stand a better chance with a new firm than with an old established one which had already a preferred list of writers. Bobbs-Merrill very promptly sent it back with a formal printed slip of rejection. I had a cry of disappointment. Then I went to the other extreme and sent it to the MacMillan Co. of New York, arguing that perhaps an "old established firm" might be more inclined to take a chance with a new writer. The MacMillan Co. likewise sent it back. I did not cry this time but sent it to Lothrop, Lee and Shepard of Boston, a sort of "betwixt and between" firm. They sent it back. Then I sent it to the Henry Holt Co. of New York. *They* rejected it, but not with the formal printed slip of the others. They sent a typewritten screed stating that their readers had found "some merit" in the story but "not enough to warrant its acceptance". This "damning with faint praise" flattened me out as not even the printed slips could do. I put "Anne" away in an old hat box in the clothes room, resolving that some day when I had time I would cut her down to the seven chapters of my original idea and send her to the aforesaid Sunday School paper.

The MS lay in the hat box until one day last winter when I came across it during a rummage. I began turning over the sheets, reading a page here and there. Somehow, I found it rather interesting. Why shouldn't other people find it so? "Ill try once more," I said and I sent it to the L. C. Page Co.

They took it and asked me to write a sequel to it. The book may or may not sell well. I wrote it for love, not money—but very often such books are the most successful—just as everything in life that is born of true love is better than something constructed for mercenary ends.

I don't know what kind of a publisher I've got. I know absolutely nothing of the Page Co. They have given me a royalty of ten percent on the *wholesale* price, which is not generous even for a new writer, and they have bound me to give them all my books on the same terms for five years. I didn't altogether like this but I was afraid to protest, lest they might not take the book.* * *

## Journal Entry (1910)†

January 7, 1910
Cavendish, P.E.I.
* * *I do not think that the majority of grown people have any real idea of the tortures sensitive children suffer over any marked difference between themselves and the other denizens of their small world. I remember one winter when I was sent to school wearing a new style of apron. I think still it was very ugly. Then I thought it hideous. It was a long, sack-like garment *with sleeves.* Those sleeves were the crowning indignity. Nobody in school had ever worn aprons with sleeves before. When I went to school one of the girls sneeringly remarked that they were "baby aprons." This capped all! I could not bear to wear them—but wear them I had to, until they were worn out. But the humiliation never grew less. To the end of their exis-

† From *The Selected Journals of L. M. Montgomery: Volume I*, ed. Mary Rubio and Elizabeth Waterston, 377–78. Copyright © 1985 University of Guelph and published by Oxford University Press. Reprinted by permission of Mary Rubio, Elizabeth Waterston, the University of Guelph, and the publisher.

tence—and they *did* wear horribly well, never getting any fortunate rents or tears—those "baby" aprons marked for me the extreme limit of human endurance.

I had nothing else to complain of in regard to my clothes. I was always kept nicely dressed and my clothes were generally pretty and becoming, though occasionally a little old fashioned owing to grandmother's inability to adapt herself to changing modes. *Materially,* I was well cared for. *Mentally* I had the power of foraging for myself to a certain extent. It was *emotionally* and *socially* that my nature was starved and restricted.

\* \* \*

I was not fortunate in my Sunday School teachers. They were three old maids in succession and their personality was neither lovable nor helpful to a child. One of them, I remember, became insane a few years later and drowned herself. Yet she was a kind, gentle woman and I liked her the best of the three. One of them was the homeliest woman I ever saw with a face spotted with moles and a pendulous lower lip. None of them did anything to make Christianity beautiful or appealing or even clear to me. Indeed, they rather prejudiced me against it, since they were "Christians" and I somehow had the idea that to be a Christian meant to be as ugly and stupid and—and—well, as *unromantic* as those "good" women were. They made me feel—and I believe that this feeling is still firmly embedded in my subconscious mind—that *religion* and *beauty* were antagonists and as far as the poles asunder. They gave me the same feeling towards it as they did towards matters of sex—that it was something necessary but ugly—something you were really ashamed of, although you had to have it—or go to hell! As for "heaven," I don't remember that they ever discussed it but I thought it was a rather dull though gorgeous place where we did nothing but stand around and sing. Not even my dearly beloved "What must it be to be there" could counteract this impression. As for the personality and teachings of Christ, I had as little idea of their real meaning as the young heathen for whom I occasionally gave my "five cent pieces" or went around collecting with a "Mission Card."

# Journal Entry (1911)†

January 27, 1911
Cavendish, P.E.I.

\* \* \*

I have *never* drawn any of the characters in my books "from life," although I may have taken a quality here and an incident there. I have used real places and speeches freely but I have never put any person I knew into my books. I may do so some day but hitherto I have depended wholly on the creative power of my own imagination for my book folk.

Nevertheless I have woven a good deal of reality into my books. Cavendish is to a large extent *Avonlea*. Mrs. *Rachel Lynde's* house, with the brook below, was drawn from Pierce Macneill's house. I also gave Mrs. Pierce's name to *Mrs. Lynde* but beyond that there was no connection whatever between them. *Green Gables* was drawn from David Macneill's house, now Mr. Webb's—though not so much the house itself as the situation and scenery, and the truth of my description of it is attested by the fact that everybody has recognized it. Had they stopped there it would be well, but they went further and insist that David and Margaret Macneill figure as *Matthew* and *Marilla*. They do not. The *Matthew* and *Marilla* I had in mind were entirely different people from David and Margaret. I suppose the fact that David is a notoriously shy and silent man makes people think I drew Matthew from him. But I made Matthew shy and silent simply because I wished to have all the people around *Anne* as pointedly in contrast with her as possible.

In connection with this there was one odd coincidence which probably helped to establish the conviction that David was *Matthew*. *Green Gables* was illustrated by an artist unknown to me and to whom Cavendish and David were alike unknown. Nevertheless, it cannot be denied that the picture of Matthew when he brings *Anne* home, has a very strong resemblance to David Macneill.

The brook that runs below the *Cuthbert* place and through *Lynde's Hollow* is, of course, my own dear brook of the woods which runs below Webb's and through "Pierce's Hollow."

Although I had the Webb place in mind I did not confine myself to facts at all. There are, I think, willows in the yard but there are

† From *The Selected Journals of L. M. Montgomery: Volume II*, ed. Mary Rubio and Elizabeth Waterston, 38–44. Copyright © 1987 University of Guelph and published by Oxford University Press. Reprinted by permission of Mary Rubio, Elizabeth Waterston, the University of Guelph, and the publisher. Omitted from this excerpt are details about the original of Diana's vow of friendship, the "play house," the teacher who resembled Miss Stacy, the Story Club, the liniment cake, and other *AGG* matters.

no "Lombardies," such as *Anne* heard talking in their sleep. Those were transplanted from the estates of my castle in Spain. And it was by no means as tidy as I pictured *Green Gables*—at least, before the Webbs came there. Quite the reverse in fact, David's yard was notoriously *untidy*. It was a local saying that if you wanted to see what the world looked like on the morning after the flood you should go into David's barnyard on a rainy day!

They had a good cherry orchard but no apple orchard. However, I can easily create an apple orchard when I need one!

*Marilla* is generally accredited to Margaret. This is absurd. Whatever accidental resemblance there may be between David and *Matthew* there is none whatever between Margaret and *Marilla*. The former is a very intelligent, broad-minded woman, which poor *Marilla* certainly was not. Others imagine *Marilla* was drawn from grandmother. This is also false. There are certain qualities common to Marilla and grandmother—and to many others—but those qualities I put into *Marilla* for the same reason I made *Matthew* silent and shy—to furnish a background for *Anne*.

When I am asked if *Anne* herself is a "real person" I always answer "no" with an odd reluctance and an uncomfortable feeling of not telling the truth. For she is and always has been, from the moment I first thought of her, so real to me that I feel I am doing violence to something when I deny her an existence anywhere save in Dreamland. Does she not stand at my elbow even now—if I turned my head quickly should I not see her—with her eager, starry eyes and her long braids of red hair and her little pointed chin? To tell that haunting elf that she is not *real*, because, forsooth, I never met her in the flesh! No, I cannot do it! She *is* so real that, although I've never met her, I feel quite sure I shall do so some day—perhaps in a stroll through Lover's Lane in the twilight—or in the moonlit Birch Path—I shall lift my eyes and find her, child or maiden, by my side. And I shall not be in the least surprised because I have always known she was *somewhere*.

\*   \*   \*

*Bright River* is Hunter River. *Anne's* dislike of being laughed at because she used big words is a bitter remembrance of my own childhood. *The White Way of Delight* is practically pure imagination. Yet the idea was suggested to me by a short stretch of road between Kensington and Clinton, which I always thought very beautiful. The trees meet overhead for a short distance but they are beech trees, not apple trees.

*Anne's* habit of naming places was an old one of my own. The *Lake of Shining* Waters is generally supposed to be the Cavendish Pond. This is not so. The pond at Park Corner is the one I had in mind.

But I suppose that a good many of the effects of light and shadow I have seen on the Cavendish pond figured unconsciously in my descriptions; and certainly the hill from which *Anne* caught her first glimpse of it was "Laird's Hill," where I have often stood at sunset, enraptured with the beautiful view of shining pond and crimson-brimmed harbor and dark blue sea.

\* \* \*

*Anne's* tribulations over puffed sleeves were an echo of my old childish longing after "bangs." "Bangs" came in when I was about ten. In the beginning they figured as a straight, heavy fringe of hair cut squarely across the forehead. A picture of "banged" hair of course looks absurd enough now; but, like all fashions, "bangs" looked all right when they were "in." And to anybody with a high forehead they were very becoming.

Well, bangs were "all the rage." All the girls in school had them. I wanted a "bang" terribly. But grandfather and grandmother would never hear of it. This was unwise and unjust on their part. Whatever the present day taste may think of "bangs" it would not have done me or anyone any harm to have allowed me to have one and it would have saved me many a bitter pang. How I did long for "bangs"! Father wanted me to have them—he always wanted me to have any innocent thing I desired. Oh, how well he understood a child's heart! I often pleaded with him when he came to see me (that was the winter he was home from the west) to cut a "bang" for me, but he never would because he knew it would offend grandmother. I was often tempted to cut one myself but I dreaded their anger too much. I knew that if I did I would be railed at as if I had disgraced myself forever and that I would never set down to the table that grandfather would not sneer at them.

"Bangs" remained in a long time—nearly twenty years. When I was fifteen and went out west I got my long-wished for "bang" at last. Grandfather sneered at it when I went home, of course, but the thing was done and he had to reconcile himself to it. Besides, the "bang" had changed a good deal in that time. The heavy straight bang was gone and the accepted fashion was an upward curling fluff, not unlike the pompadour of today in general effect, with only a loose curl or two downwards. How I did envy girls with naturally curly hair! My hair was very straight. I had to curl my poor fringe constantly and even then the least dampness would reduce it to stringy dismalness. It is only about six years since bangs went hopelessly out. It is not likely they will ever come in again—in my time at least. But I shall never forget them. I longed for them and how humiliated I felt when I could not have them.

I had beautiful hair when I was a child—very long, thick, and a golden brown. It turned very dark when I grew up—much to my disappointment. I love fair hair.

The *Spectator,* in reviewing *Green Gables*—*very* favorably, I might say—said that possibly *Anne's* precocity was slightly overdrawn in the statement that a child of eleven would appreciate the dramatic effect of the lines,

> "Quick as the slaughtered squadrons fell
> In Midian's evil day."

But I was only nine years old when those lines thrilled my very soul as I recited them in Sunday School. All through the following sermon I kept repeating them to myself. To this day they give me a mysterious pleasure.

\*   \*   \*

\* \* \*The dialogues which the girls had in their concerts "The Society for The Suppression of Gossip" and "The Fairy Queen" were old stand-bys of schooldays. We had the former at our first school concert in which I personated the amiable "Miss Wise," and the latter at a school examination. I was the *Fairy Queen*, being thought fitted for the part by reason of my long hair which I wore crimped and floating over my shoulders from a wreath of pink tissue roses. I "appeared" suddenly through the school door, in answer to an incantation, in all the glory of white dress, roses, hair, kid slippers and wand—and I enjoyed my own dramatic appearance quite as much as anybody! That really was one of the most satisfying moments of my life.

\*   \*   \*

The entrance examination of *Queen's* was "drawn from life" as well as the weeks of suspense that followed. *Matthew's* death was not, as some have supposed, suggested by grandfather's. Poor Matthew must die so that there might arise the necessity for self-sacrifice on Anne's part. So he joined the long procession of ghosts that haunt my literary past.

# Journal Entry (1914)†

Saturday, April 18, 1914
The Manse, Leaskdale, Ont.

\* \* \*

I remember well the very evening I wrote the opening paragraph of *Green Gables.* It was a moist, showery, sweet-scented evening in June ten years ago. I was sitting *on the end of the table,* in the old kitchen, my feet on the sofa, beside the west window, because I wanted to get the last gleams of daylight on my portfolio. I did not for a moment dream that the book I had just begun was to bring me the fame and success I had long dreamed of. So I wrote, the opening paragraphs quite easily, not feeling obliged to "write up" to any particular reputation or style. Just as I had finished my description of *Mrs. Lynde* and her home, *Ewan* walked in. He had just moved to Cavendish from Stanley, where he had previously been boarding and this was his first call since moving. He stayed and chatted most of the evening, so no more of *Green Gables* was written that night. And now today I began my seventh book, a thousand miles from that twilight window looking out into the rain-wet apple trees of the front orchard. The window by which I wrote today looked out on several unlovely, spring-naked back yards—for the only chance I have to write is to shut myself in my room.\* \* \*

# I Dwell Among My Own People (c. 1920–21)‡

\* \* \*

I never "try my hand" at a problem novel for four reasons. The first is that a problem novel never yet solved any problem. The second is that most folks have problems enough in their own lives and want something different when they seek a little rest and relaxation in a book; and the third and fourth reasons are—I don't want to.

---

† From *The Selected Journals of L. M. Montgomery: Volume II*, ed. Mary Rubio and Elizabeth Waterston, 47. Copyright © 1987 University of Guelph and published by Oxford University Press. Reprinted by permission of Mary Rubio, Elizabeth Waterston, the University of Guelph, and the publisher.

‡ Text of an article preserved in LMM's "Scrapbook of Reviews From Around the World Which L. M. Montgomery's Clipping Service Sent to Her, 1910–1935" 195. L. M. Montgomery Collection, U of Guelph Library Archives, Guelph, Ontario. Reproduced in Douglas Daymond and Leslie Monkman, eds., *Canadian Novelists on Canadian Fiction* (Ottawa: Borealis Press, 1981) 113–14. See also LMM, "The Way to Make a Book," *Everywoman's World* April 1915, 24–27 (also in "Scrapbook of Reviews . . ." 193), reproduced in *Anne of Green Gables,* by L. M. Montgomery, ed. Cecily Devereux (Peterborough: Broadview, 2004) 365–70.

The people I know best and love best, having lived among them and been one of them all my life, are not very deeply concerned with what are known as "present-day problems." Their problems are simple and belong to yesterday and to-morrow as well as to-day. They live in a land where nature is neither grudging nor lavish; where faithful work is rewarded by competence and nobody is very rich and nobody very poor; where everybody knows about everybody else, so there are few mysteries; where there is always someone to keep tab on you and so prevent you from running amuck with the Decalogue; where the wonderful loveliness of circling sea and misty river and green, fairy-haunted woods is all around you; where the Shorter Catechism is not out of date; where there are still to be found real grandmothers and genuine old maid aunts; where the sane, simple, wholesome pleasures of life have not lost their tang; where you are born into a certain political party and live and die in it; where it is still thought a great feather in a family's cap if it has a minister among its boys; where it is safer to commit murder than to be caught without three kinds of cake when company comes to tea; where loyalty and upright dealing and kindness of heart and a sense of responsibility and a glint of humor and a little decent reserve—great solvents of any and all problems if given a fair trial—still flower freely.* * *

* * *

# Journal Entry (1930)†

[The Manse, Norval, Ontario]
March 1, 1930
* * *One evening recently I got out my scrapbooks of reviews and skimmed through them. They are amusing reading. The great majority are laudatory but an occasional one is contemptuous or venomous. But the amusing thing was their contradictoriness—if there be such a word. One critic makes a statement. Another flatly says the opposite. They cannot possibly be reconciled. Here are some bracketed specimens I culled in my hurried ramble through those dusty old scrapbooks.* * *

"Anne is one of the most delightful girls that has appeared for many a day." / "Anne is altogether too queer."

† From *The Selected Journals of L. M. Montgomery: Volume IV*, ed. Mary Rubio and Elizabeth Waterston, 36–41. Copyright © 1998 University of Guelph and published by Oxford University Press. Reprinted by permission of Mary Rubio, Elizabeth Waterston, the University of Guelph, and the publisher.

"One of the most charming girls in modern fiction." / "Anne is overdrawn and something of a bore."

"An altogether fascinating child." / "We would leave the house if Anne lived with us."

"Anne is unconvincing." / "Anne is absolutely convincing."

"Quite too precocious." / "No more charming child was ever conceived by an author."

"The book is not without interest." (Oh, what damnable faint praise!) / "A charming story told in a charming way."

\*　\*　\*

"It will find more favor with maids under 14 than with their elders." / "Old and young alike will fall beneath its charm."

"The first half of the book is the best." (I agree with this completely.) / "The poorest chapter is the first one."

"There is no maudlin sentiment about the book." / "A book of sugary sentimentality."

\*　\*　\*

I did not write *Green Gables* for children.

# Literary Context

## THE HOLY BIBLE

### *From* Daniel†

Then the king commanded, and they brought Daniel, and cast *him* into the den of lions. *Now* the king spake and said unto Daniel, Thy God whom thou servest continually, he will deliver thee.

And a stone was brought, and laid upon the mouth of the den; and the king sealed it with his own signet, and with the signet of his lords; that the purpose might not be changed concerning Daniel.

Then the king went to his palace, and passed the night fasting: neither were instruments of music brought before him: and his sleep went from him.

Then the king arose very early in the morning, and went in haste unto the den of lions. And when he came to the den, he cried with a lamentable voice unto Daniel: *and* the king spake and said to Daniel, O Daniel, servant of the living God, is thy God, whom thou servest continually, able to deliver thee from the lions?

Then said Daniel unto the king, O king, live for ever.

My God hath sent his angel, and hath shut the lions' mouths, that they have not hurt me: forasmuch as before him innocency was found in me; and also before thee, O king, have I done no hurt.

Then was the king exceeding glad for him, and commanded that they should take Daniel up out of the den. So Daniel was taken up out of the den, and no manner of hurt was found upon him, because he believed in his God.

And the king commanded, and they brought those men which had accused Daniel, and they cast them into the den of lions, them, their children, and their wives; and the lions had the mastery of *them*, and brake all their bones in pieces or ever they came at the bottom of the den.

† From *Holy Bible* (King James Version) 6.16–24.

# JOHN MORISON

## *From* The Race That Long in Darkness Pined†

The race that long in darkness pined,
Have seen a glorious Light;
The people dwell in day, who dwelt
In death's surrounding night.

5 To hail Thy rise, Thou better Sun,
The gathering nations come,
Joyous as when the reapers bear
The harvest treasures home.

For Thou our burden hast removed,
10 And quelled the oppressor's sway,
Quick as the slaughtered squadrons fell
In Midian's evil day.

\* \* \*

# SIR WALTER SCOTT

## *From* Marmion‡

\* \* \*

The English shafts in volleys hail'd,
In headlong charge their horse assail'd;
5 Front, flank, and rear, the squadrons sweep
To break the Scottish circle deep,
    That fought around their King.
But yet, though thick the shafts as snow,
Though charging knights like whirlwinds go,
10 Though hill-men ply the ghastly blow,
    Unbroken was the ring;
The stubborn spearmen still made good
Their dark impenetrable wood,
Each stepping where his comrade stood,

---

† From *Scottish Paraphrases* (Edinburgh: Church of Scotland, 1781) 1–12.
‡ From *Marmion: A Tale of Flodden Field* (Edinburgh: Constable, and London: Murray, 1808) 6.34.3–19.

15     The instant that he fell.
     No thought was there of dastard flight;
     Link'd in that serried phalanx tight,
     Groom fought like noble, squire like knight,
       As fearlessly and well;

\*   \*   \*

# LORD BYRON

## *From* Childe Harold's Pilgrimage†

\*   \*   \*

There was a sound of revelry by night,
And Belgium's capital had gathered then
Her Beauty and her Chivalry, and bright
The lamps shone o'er fair women and brave men;
185    A thousand hearts beat happily; and when
Music arose with its voluptuous swell,
Soft eyes looked love to eyes which spoke again,
And all went merry as a marriage bell;
But hush! hark! a deep sound strikes like a rising knell!

\*   \*   \*

# CAROLINE OLIPHANT, BARONESS NAIRNE

## *From* The Maiden's Vow‡

I've made a vow, I'll keep it true,
   I'll never married be;
For the only ane that I think on
   Will never think o' me.

\*   \*   \*

† From *Childe Harold's Pilgrimage* (London: John Murray, 1816) 3.21.
‡ From "The Maiden's Vow" (ca 1821) 1–4. Reprinted in *The Life and Songs of Baroness Nairne* (London: Griffin, 1872).

# WILLIAM CULLEN BRYANT

## Song of the Greek Amazon†

\* \* \*

I buckle to my slender side
   The pistol and the scimitar,
And in my maiden flower and pride
   Am come to share the tasks of war.
5  And yonder stands my fiery steed,
   That paws the ground and neighs to go,
My charger of the Arab breed—
   I took him from the routed foe.

My mirror is the mountain-spring,
10    At which I dress my ruffled hair;
My dimmed and dusty arms I bring,
   And wash away the blood-stain there.
Why should I guard from wind and sun
   This cheek, whose virgin rose is fled?
15 It was for one—oh, only one—
   I kept its bloom, and he is dead.

But they who slew him—unaware
   Of coward murderers lurking nigh—
And left him to the fowls of air,
20    Are yet alive—and they must die!
They slew him—and my virgin years
   Are vowed to Greece and vengeance now,
And many an Othman dame, in tears,
   Shall rue the Grecian maiden's vow.

25 I touched the lute in better days,
   I led in dance the joyous band;
Ah! they may move to mirthful lays
   Whose hands can touch a lover's hand.
The march of hosts that haste to meet
30    Seems gayer than the dance to me;
The lute's sweet tones are not so sweet
   As the fierce shout of victory.

† From *Poems by William Cullen Bryant. An American* (London: J. Andrews, 1832) 66. This poem may have appeared in school readers as "The Maiden's Vow."

# HENRY WADSWORTH LONGFELLOW

## Hymn to Night†

Ασπαίη, τρίλλιστος [Aspasie, trillistos]

I heard the trailing garments of the Night
　　Sweep through her marble halls!
I saw her sable skirts all fringed with light
　　From the celestial walls!

5　I felt her presence, by its spell of might,
　　Stoop o'er me from above;
The calm, majestic presence of the Night,
　　As of the one I love.

I heard the sounds of sorrow and delight,
10　　The manifold, soft chimes,
That fill the haunted chambers of the Night,
　　Like some old poet's rhymes.

From the cool cisterns of the midnight air
　　My spirit drank repose;
15　The fountain of perpetual peace flows there,—
　　From those deep cisterns flows.

O holy Night! from thee I learn to bear
　　What man has borne before!
Thou layest thy finger on the lips of Care,
20　　And they complain no more.

Peace! Peace! Orestes-like I breathe this prayer![1]
　　Descend with broad-winged flight,
The welcome, the thrice-prayed-for, the most fair,
　　The best-beloved Night!

---

† "Hymn to Night" (1839), *Poetical Works of Henry Wadsworth Longfellow* (Boston and NY: Houghton, Miflin, 1890) 19–20.
1. Orestes, who has murdered his mother to avenge the killing of his father, wants to find peace. [Longfellow's note]

# CAROLINE NORTON

## *From* Bingen on the Rhine†

A soldier of the Legion lay dying in Algiers,<br>
There was a lack of woman's nursing, there was dearth of woman's tears;<br>
But a comrade stood beside him, while his lifeblood ebbed away,<br>
And bent with pitying glances, to hear what he might say.<br>
5   The dying soldier faltered, and he took that comrade's hand,<br>
And he said, "I nevermore shall see my own, my native land:<br>
Take a message, and a token, to some distant friends of mine,<br>
For I was born at Bingen,—at Bingen on the Rhine.

\* \* \*

"There's another,—not a sister: in the happy days gone by<br>
You'd have known her by the merriment that sparkled in her eye;<br>
35   Too innocent for coquetry,—too fond for idle scorning,—<br>
O friend! I fear the lightest heart makes sometimes heaviest mourning!<br>
Tell her the last night of my life (for, ere the moon be risen,<br>
My body will be out of pain, my soul be out of prison),—<br>
I dreamed I stood with her, and saw the yellow sunlight shine<br>
40   On the vine-clad hills of Bingen,—fair Bingen on the Rhine.

\* \* \*

# ALFRED, LORD TENNYSON

## *From* Tears, Idle Tears‡

Tears, idle tears, I know not what they mean,<br>
Tears from the depths of some divine despair<br>
Rise in the heart, and gather in the eyes,<br>
In looking on the happy Autumn-fields,<br>
5   And thinking of the days that are no more.

\* \* \*

† From "Bingen on the Rhine" (ca 1840), reprinted in *A Library of Poetry and Song*, ed. William Cullen Bryant (NY: Ford, 1874) 383; *Songs of Three Centuries*, ed. John Greenleaf Whittier (Boston: Osgood, 1875); and many other anthologies.
‡ From "Maid's Song," *The Princess: A Medley* (London: Edward, Moxon, 1847) 1–5.

# ALFRED, LORD TENNYSON

## *From* Lancelot and Elaine†

Elaine the fair, Elaine the loveable,
Elaine, the lily maid of Astolat,
High in her chamber up a tower to the east
Guarded the sacred shield of Lancelot;

\* \* \*

Marred as he was, he seemed the goodliest man
That ever among ladies ate in hall,
255 And noblest, when she lifted up her eyes.
However marred, of more than twice her years,
Seamed with an ancient swordcut on the cheek,
And bruised and bronzed, she lifted up her eyes
And loved him, with that love which was her doom.

\* \* \*

Death, like a friend's voice from a distant field
Approaching through the darkness, called;\* \* \*

\* \* \*"O sweet father, tender and true,
Deny me not," she said—"ye never yet
1105 Denied my fancies—this, however strange,
My latest: lay the letter in my hand
A little ere I die, and close the hand
Upon it; I shall guard it even in death.
And when the heat is gone from out my heart,
1110 Then take the little bed on which I died
For Lancelot's love, and deck it like the Queen's

\* \* \*

1120 And therefore let our dumb old man alone
Go with me, he can steer and row, and he
Will guide me to that palace, to the doors."

\* \* \*

But ten slow mornings past, and on the eleventh
Her father laid the letter in her hand,

† From *Idylls of the King* (London: Edward Moxon, 1847) 1–5.

And closed the hand upon it, and she died.
So that day there was dole in Astolat.

1130 But when the next sun brake from underground,
Then, those two brethren slowly with bent brows
Accompanying, the sad chariot-bier
Past like a shadow through the field, that shone
Full-summer, to that stream whereon the barge,
1135 Palled all its length in blackest samite, lay.
There sat the lifelong creature of the house,
Loyal, the dumb old servitor, on deck,
Winking his eyes, and twisted all his face.
So those two brethren from the chariot took
1140 And on the black decks laid her in her bed,
Set in her hand a lily, o'er her hung
The silken case with braided blazonings,
And kissed her quiet brows, and saying to her
"Sister, farewell for ever," and again
1145 "Farewell, sweet sister," parted all in tears.
Then rose the dumb old servitor, and the dead,
Oared by the dumb, went upward with the flood—
In her right hand the lily, in her left
The letter—all her bright hair streaming down—
1150 And all the coverlid was cloth of gold
Drawn to her waist, and she herself in white
All but her face, and that clear-featured face
Was lovely, for she did not seem as dead,
But fast asleep, and lay as though she smiled.

\*    \*    \*

# LOUISA MAY ALCOTT

## *From* Little Women†

\*    \*    \*

As she spoke, Jo took off her bonnet, and a general outcry arose,
for all her abundant hair was cut short.

"Your hair! Your beautiful hair!"

"Oh, Jo, how could you? Your one beauty."

---

† From *Little Women* (Boston: Roberts, 1868; New York: W. W. Norton and Company, 2004), 132 [Chapter 15].

"My dear girl, there was no need of this."

"She don't look like my Jo any more, but I love her dearly for it!"

As everyone exclaimed, and Beth hugged the cropped head tenderly, Jo assumed an indifferent air, which did not deceive anyone a particle, and said, rumpling up the brown bush, and trying to look as if she liked it, "It doesn't affect the fate of the nation, so don't wail, Beth. It will be good for my vanity: I was getting too proud of my wig. It will do my brains good to have that mop taken off; my head feels deliciously light and cool, and the barber said I could soon have a curly crop, which will be boyish, becoming, and easy to keep in order. I'm satisfied; so please take the money, and let's have supper."

\* \* \*

# KATE DOUGLAS WIGGIN

## *From* Rebecca of Sunnybrook Farm†

\* \* \*

"I think it would be all right to let Rebecca have one pink and one blue gingham," said Jane. "A child gets tired of sewing on one color. It's only natural she should long for a change; besides she'd look like a charity child always wearing the same brown with a white apron. And it's dreadful unbecoming to her!"

" 'Handsome is as handsome does,' say I. Rebecca'll never come to grief along of her beauty, that's certain, and there's no use humoring her to think about her looks. I believe she's vain as a peacock now, without anything to be vain of."

"She's young and attracted to bright things—that's all. I remember well enough how I felt at her age."

"You was considerable of a fool at her age, Jane."

"Yes I was, thank the Lord! I only wish I'd known how to take a little of my foolishness along with me, as some folks do, to brighten my declining years."

There finally was a pink gingham.\* \* \*

---

† From *Rebecca of Sunnybrook Farm* (Boston: Houghton, Mifflin, 1903) 67–68.

# CLARENCE KARR

## Addicted to Books†

\* \* \*

"I am simply a 'book drunkard,' " 24-year-old Montgomery wrote in her journal in 1899.[1] "*Books* have the same irresistible temptation for me that liquor has for its devotees. I *cannot* withstand them." Less than a year later, reading Anthony Hope's *Rupert of Hentzau* (1898) in one sitting rendered her "*mentally drunk*. I was as thoroughly intoxicated in brain as the most confirmed drunkard ever was in body" (*SJ1* 235, 247). In 1905, after a two-week spree in which she read herself "stupid and soggy" with books such as Jack London's *The Sea-Wolf* (1904), she confessed to her correspondent Ephraim Weber: "I must sober up from book-saturation, get work done, and take up my pen again."[2] In 1901, after lugging heavy encyclopedias home two or three volumes at a time from the Cavendish Literary Society's library, she noted that, "When I get book hungry, even the whole of an encyclopedia is better than no loaf" (*SJ1* 263). Once the demands of marriage, motherhood, and being a clergyman's wife changed Montgomery's life in her mid-thirties, she no longer had the luxury of indulging in week-long sprees. Yet she remained a compulsive reader throughout her life, and there were still certain types of adventure and mystery novels that demanded to be read in one sitting.[3] Simply put, reading was something she could not do without.

Most addictions involve cravings, some loss of control over behavior, and feelings of pleasure, euphoria, being transported into an altered state of consciousness or another dimension. "The reading habit," writes Victor Nell in his study of reading entrancement, *Lost in a Book: The Psychology of Reading for Pleasure*, "has often been branded as a form of drug habit," and people who read at least one

† From "Addicted to Books: L. M. Montgomery and the Value of Reading," *CCL: Canadian Children's Literature* 113–114 (2004): 17–33. Copyright © Clarence Karr 2004. Reprinted by permission of the author. Footnotes have been renumbered and edited with permission of the author [*Editors*].

1. The author records finding 1800 references—located in L. M. Montgomery's journals, letters, and periodical pieces as well as in her fiction—to her reading experiences from the age of eight until her death in her late sixties [*Editors*].
2. *Green Gables Letters* 31.
3. The one-sitting readings were most frequently of adventure novels. A wider list includes S. R. Crockett's *The Black Douglas* (1899), Anthony Hope's *Phroso* (1897), Edward Bulwer-Lytton's *Devereux* (1829), George du Maurier's *Trilby* (1894), Anthony Trollope's *Framley Parsonage* (1861), and Edward Lester Pearson's non-fiction *Studies in Murder* (1924).

book a week often define themselves as "reading addicts."[4] For people willing to abandon self-control and rationality, these are wonderful sensations that William James, in *The Varieties of Religious Experience* (1902), ties to positive spiritual-like experiences. Reading addicts commonly enter these non-rational spiritual realms.

\* \* \*

\* \* \*[F]or compulsive readers like Montgomery, books replace people as friends to a certain degree. After an intense period of working, visiting, teaching Sunday School, and other activities in late summer 1901, a tired, lonely Montgomery concluded in her journal that she needed a fix, a "fairy-land" that only the right kind of novel could supply (*SJ1* 262). This fairyland was \* \* \* the product of being lost in a book, which, as Nell reminds us and as Montgomery illustrates, can be the product of all types of books, not just adventure novels. Although not restricted to compulsive readers, experiences of becoming lost are normal for them. In the same journal entry of 1901, Montgomery goes on to describe her engagement and disengagement with this fairyland: "Novels—some delightful ones, so delightful that I could not sleep until I had . . . read until the hero had reached the end of his adventures and I came back with a mental jolt to the real world, to discover that my oil had almost burned out, that my back and eyes were aching and that I was very sleepy" (*SJ1* 262). Inevitably, she was transported into the world being read, whether that be the fifteenth-century England of Pepys's *Diary*; the ancient Greece of 2,400 years ago in Grote's *History,* where she was present at the death of Socrates; Washington Irving's enchanted Moorish palace, Alhambra, in Spain; or Anthony Hope's 1897 adventure novel *Phroso* (*SJ2* 210, 141; *SJ4* 247; *SJ1* 286, 235).

Of these, Irving's *Alhambra* (1832) is the most significant and prompted more out-of-body experiences for Montgomery than any other recorded source. Irving had lived in this Granada palace and combines in his sketch its Turkish past and mythology with his own observations. "It was a volume of pure delight and I burned the heart out of a dismal day with it," Montgomery noted on her first reading (*SJ1* 286). \* \* \* She felt that it was some combination of style and content which made this book special, since other Irving stories, such as "The Legend of Sleepy Hollow" or "Rip Van Winkle," did not have the same effect on her. Although she would have liked to visit this real palace, she feared that it might prevent her from visiting the imagined castle of Irving's text in the same way: "I should be so much the poorer by reason of a lost ideal," she explained (*SJ1* 75).

4. Victor Nell, *Lost in a Book: The Psychology of Reading for Pleasure* (New Haven: Yale UP, 1988) 29, 2.

One of Montgomery's other favorites was Rudyard Kipling, whose virile strength she adored. Her experience of reading his *Barrack-Room Ballads* (1892), which she received as a Christmas present in 1898, provides one of her best descriptions of being lost in a book. Kipling's stories, she recorded in her journal,

> thrill and pulsate and burn, they carry you along in their rush and swing, till you forget your own petty interests and cares and burst out into a broader soul-world and gain a much clearer realization of all the myriad forms of life that are beating around your own little one. (*SJ1* 230)

\*     \*     \*

Her reading of two works, Ralph Waldo Emerson's *Essays* (1841) and Edward Gibbon's *The Decline and Fall of the Roman Empire* (1776/1778), does fit into a more serious scale, however. At age seventeen, she commented that "To be interested in Emerson," whom she did not always understand, "you must get right into the grooves of his thought and keep steadily in it. Then you can enjoy him. There can be no skipping or culling if you want to get at his meaning." She found Gibbon "so big and massive that he seems to suck one's individuality clean out of one—swallow one up like a huge, placid, slow-moving river" (*SJ1* 75; *SJ2* 356). The necessary antidote to such an experience was usually to then plunge into the most frivolous novel as a way of returning to a normal state of consciousness.\* \* \*

\*     \*     \*

One aspect of Rolf Engelsing's delineation of intensive, pre-modern reading involves multiple readings, supposedly necessitated by the scarcity of texts.[5] While Nell found that his modern compulsive readers rarely read books more than once, Montgomery and numerous other historical compulsive readers did. "How I do love books! Not merely to read once but over and over again," gushed an eighteen-year-old Montgomery in 1893. "I enjoy the tenth reading of a book as much as the first. Books are a delightful world in themselves. Their characters seem as real to me as my friends in central life" (*SJ1* 88). In "My Favourite Bookshelf," she revealed that her favorite books, the books she loved as friends as opposed to other books which were mere acquaintances, had their own special shelf and had acquired "an aroma and personality all their own, quite irrespective of their contents."[6] For Montgomery, then, reading a

5. See Barbara Sicherman, "Sense and Sensibility: A Case Study of Women's Reading in Late-Victorian America," *Reading in America: Literature and Social History*, ed. Cathy N. Davidson (Baltimore: Johns Hopkins UP, 1989) 216, 221n29 for further context.
6. "My Favourite Bookshelf," in Scrapbook of Reviews, unpaginated, L. M. Montgomery Collection, U of Guelph archives.

book again was similar to inviting a dear friend over for another visit. As with friends, just being in the company of books had its own special rewards. There are, however, other dimensions to the phenomenon. Montgomery claimed that this habit began in childhood when there were too few volumes available to satisfy her voracious appetite. In an article titled "The Gay Days of Old" and published in *Farmer's Magazine*, Montgomery recalled that "I read and reread what we did have until I knew whole pages and even chapters by heart."[7] While this reading and memorization included such standard poetry as Milton's *Paradise Lost* and Scott's *Lady of the Lake*, it also included such diverse items as Hans Christian Andersen's *Fairy Tales*, Edward Bulwer-Lytton's *Zanoni* and *Last Days of Pompeii*, and John Bunyan's *Pilgrim's Progress*. This memorization occurred outside the usual classroom and Sunday School venues where memory work was a part of the curriculum. It also continued into adulthood and was, at times, a deliberate act. In 1905, a 30-year-old Montgomery was learning Byron's "Prisoner of Chillon" by heart because she wanted to "remember it in the next world."[8]

Of the favorite books kept in a separate bookshelf during her childhood, these included a variety of genres, including poetry, fiction, and non-fiction. Later in life, there continued to be no class or genre restrictions in Montgomery's bookshelf of favorites, which she spoke of in the article "My Favourite Bookshelf" as "belonging to the household of faith," implying deeper, more complex psychological and intellectual dimensions to the ownership and reading of these volumes. There were books for every mood and need in this "motley collection:" a little book of modern verse for when the mind "feels dusty and commonplace and longs for a pleasant bit of starfaring" and the "Great Poet to whom I turn when I need consolation for some deep grief or expression for some mighty emotion." She fled into travel books when she was "desperately weary of well-trodden ways." When life became too exciting or too strenuous, she yearned for the "quiet meandering book." From childhood, there were "girl's books which I love most when I feel old and sophisticated and too worldly-wise and want to stray back to the fairy realm of sweet sixteen" as well as a "boy's book of adventure which is to me manna in the wilderness when I grow tired of ordering my household with a due regard for calories and desire wildly to . . . go hunting for buried treasure or shooting grizzly bears." There were "garden books . . . which I love best when a snowstorm is howling" and historical novels for "the hours I yearn for the society of kings and queens, garrulous and intimate and savory." History was "for the serious hour of deter-

7. "Gay Days of Old," Scrapbook of Reviews.
8. Mollie Gillen, *The Wheel of Things: A Biography of L. M. Montgomery* (1975; Halifax: Goodread, 1983) 161.

mined self-culture and essays for the literary bookish mood." Finally, there were "delicious ghost stories which I must read when midnight is near and the wind is keening round the eves and the stairs are creaking and anything might be true."[9] Some might think such a list to be eclectic, but each of these genres sustained multiple readings and each genre fulfilled a different psychological need for her.

Montgomery spoke frequently of the books in her special bookcase as not only friends to visit often but as books she *lived* as opposed to simply read. They had magical powers; magic is a frequent key-word in her description of the effect of these books. In her journals and letters she always underlined *lived* to doubly emphasize the importance of both the books and the phenomenon itself. This is noteworthy because she did very little underlining in her writing. * * * [C]ertain types of texts, intersecting with her personality and the circumstances of her life, had the power to alter her conscious-ness whether she willed it or not. After the first reading, however, subsequent visits to the same book involved a deliberate decision to reproduce the sensation. The phenomenon is not necessarily linked, as some might imagine, to sentiment, pathos, and empathy, which Montgomery did not value highly in her reading. She persistently sought such sensations because she enjoyed them. As a person for whom the imagination was one of the greatest human attributes, these experiences of a compulsive reader opened the door to limitless flights of imagination.[1]

\* \* \*

Of all the windows into Montgomery's soul, none is as important as the record of her reading experiences. Her interactions with texts as recorded in her journals and letters reveal many of her innermost thoughts and reflections more fully and more deeply than any other evidence that she bestows on researchers. * * *

\* \* \*

9. "My favourite Bookshelf," Scrapbook of Reviews.
1. See Clarence Karr, *Authors and Audiences: Popular Canadian Fiction in the Early Twen-tieth Century* (Montreal: McGill-Queen's UP, 2000) 132–33. For general background on the theory of reading experience, Karr recommends Elizabeth Freund, *The Return of the Reader: Reader-Response Criticism* (London: Methuen, 1987); Janice Radway, *A Feeling for Books: The Book-of-the-Month Club, Literary Taste, and Middle-Class Desire* (Chapel Hill: U of North Carolina P, 1997); Jane P. Tompkins, ed., *Reader-Response: From For-malism to Post-Structuralism* (Baltimore: Johns Hopkins UP, 1980); Martyn Lyons, "New Readers in the Nineteenth Century: Women, Children, Workers," *A History of Reading in the West*, ed. Guglielmo Cavallo and Roger Chartier (Boston: U of Massachusetts P, 1999) 313–44 [*Editors*].

# Cultural Context

## CAROLE GERSON

### Author, Publisher, and Fictional Character†

"Elderly couple apply to orphan asylum for a boy. By mistake a girl is sent them" (*SJ1* 330). As later recounted in L. M. Montgomery's revised journals, an 1895 notebook jotting eventually resulted in a 1906 manuscript that was rejected by four major American fiction publishers before being accepted by the Boston firm of L. C. Page in 1907. Issued the following year as *Anne of Green Gables*, the book soon achieved worldwide recognition as a classic novel of girlhood and adolescence. "They took it and asked me to write a sequel to it," Montgomery wrote in her journal: "I don't know what kind of a publisher I've got. I know absolutely nothing of the Page Co. They have given me a royalty of ten percent on the wholesale price, which is not generous even for a new writer, and they have bound me to give them all my books on the same terms for five years. I don't altogether like this but I was afraid to protest, lest they might not take the book, and I am so anxious to get it before the public. It will be a start, even if it is no great success" (*SJ1* 331). Success indeed it was. Classed as an "overall bestseller" by Frank Mott, who states that *Anne of Green Gables* had sold between 800,000 and 900,000 copies by 1947, the book had earned Montgomery over $22,000 for more than 300,000 copies by the time a bitter lawsuit resulted in the sale of her copyright to Page in 1919.[1]

Before recounting Montgomery's long and troubled connection with her publisher, and her equally problematic relationship with her most famous character, I would like to explore the implications and expectations of Page's terms by situating Montgomery at the

† From " 'Dragged at Anne's Chariot Wheels': The Triangle of Author, Publisher, and Fictional Character," *L. M. Montgomery and Canadian Culture*, ed. Irene Gammel and Elizabeth R. Epperly. Copyright © 1999 University of Toronto Press Inc. Reprinted by permission of the publisher. Footnotes have been renumbered and edited with permission of the author [*Editors*].

1. Mott, *Golden Multitudes: The Story of Best Sellers in the United States* (NY: Bowker, 1947) 312; Mary Rubio, "*Anne of Green Gables*: The Architect of Adolescence," *Such a Simple Little Tale: Critical Responses to L. M. Montgomery's Anne of Green Gables*, ed. Mavis Reimer (Metuchen, NJ: Children's Language Association and Scarecrow P, 1992) 67.

intersection of several specific issues. These are the contested literary and cultural value of the sequel; the publication of Canadian-authored books at the turn of the century, in particular series and sequels, and writing for children (two formulations that sometimes coincide); and the international commodification of children's literature in children's periodicals and series.

Positing that the sequel originates in a "charismatic text" that has had an unusually powerful effect on a large reading public, Terry Castle opens her discussion of *Pamela Part 2* with the "commonplace" assertion that "sequels are always disappointing." The same generalization is applied more specifically to *Anne of Green Gables* in an article by Gillian Thomas that begins, "It is a cliché of popular literature that sequels tend to be disappointing, and students of children's literature are all too sadly familiar with the decline of writers who turn themselves into human factories on the basis of a successful first book."[2] Disappointing for whom, one might ask. For the general reading public, the audience and consumers of sequels, who have always been eager to buy not only additional Anne books, but more recently have been gobbling up associated texts such as the edited volumes of Montgomery's journals and newly issued collections of her scattered magazine stories?[3] * * * For the province of Prince Edward Island, and especially the residents of Charlottetown and Cavendish, whose economy benefits enormously from the tourist industry generated by the popularity of Anne in North America and Japan?[4]

* * *Clearly, the charisma of *Anne of Green Gables* spills far beyond the notions of value constructed by the traditional literary critic, into a dense web of cultural activity that includes romance and popular culture, national identity, provincial and international economics, and social history. Full analysis of these concerns would constitute an intriguing cultural studies project requiring a collaborative team of interdisciplinary experts; the intention of this essay is to discuss some of the earlier historical events and contexts that

2. Terry Castle, *Masquerade and Civilization: The Carnivalesque in Eighteenth-Century Culture and Fiction* (Stanford: Stanford UP, 1986) 133–35; Thomas, "The Decline of Anne: Matron vs. Child," *CCL: Canadian Children's Literature* 3 (1975): 23.

3. These are (to date) *The Road to Yesterday* (Toronto: McGraw-Hill Ryerson, 1974); *The Doctor's Sweetheart and Other Stories*, ed. Catherine McLay (Toronto: McGraw, 1979); and a series of books edited by Rea Wilmshurst and published by McClelland and Stewart: *Akin to Anne: Tales of Other Orphans* (1988); *Along the Shore: Tales by the Sea* (1989); *Among the Shadows: Tales from the Darker Side* (1990); *After Many Days: Tales of Time Passed* (1991); *Against the Odds: Tales of Achievement* (1993); *At the Altar: Matrimonial Tales* (1994); *Across the Miles: Tales of Correspondence* (1995); and *Christmas With Anne and Other Holiday Stories* (1995).

4. See Calvin Trillin, "Anne of Red Hair: What do the Japanese see in *Anne of Green Gables?*" *The New Yorker* (5 Aug. 1996): 56–61; Douglas Baldwin, "L. M. Montgomery's *Anne of Green Gables*: The Japanese Connection," *Journal of Canadian Studies* 28.3 (1993): 123–33; and Diane Tye, "Multiple Meanings Called Cavendish: The Interaction of Tourism with Traditional Culture," *Journal of Canadian Studies* 29.1 (1994): 122–34.

underpin the later commodification of L. M. Montgomery and her works.

### L. M. Montgomery and the American Market

At the turn of the century, Maud Montgomery was an unmarried woman in her late twenties, single-mindedly forging a commercially viable literary career by working her way upward from occasional newspaper poems and stories to larger commissions and serials in popular American periodicals such as *Outing* and *The Boy's World*. Trapped in the rural community of Cavendish, Prince Edward Island, [Canada], as the sole caretaker of her aging grandmother, even if she had so desired she could not have followed the route taken by Janet Royal, a secondary character in her 1925 novel, *Emily Climbs*, who moves to New York to pursue a successful career as a literary journalist.* * *

A canny businesswoman, Montgomery recorded in her letters her preference to sell her work to American publications as they could pay substantially better than Canadian magazines. Regardless of her personal patriotism and her subsequent difficulties with Page, she declared she "wouldn't give [an] MS. to a Canadian firm. It is much better financially to have it published in the United States."[5] Her comments on the selection of publishers to whom she first sent the manuscript of *Anne of Green Gables* demonstrate her pragmatic assessment of the publishing industry. She began with Bobbs-Merrill as a new firm just establishing its list, then "went to the other extreme and sent it to the MacMillan Co. of New York," then tried Lothrop, Lee and Shepard, "a sort of 'betwixt and between' firm" specializing in juvenile series (including the series of boys' books written three decades earlier by fellow Maritimer James De Mille), then Henry Holt and finally, L. C. Page (*SJ1* 331).

* * *For Montgomery, one of Page's initial attractions was the firm's recent publication of books by Charles G. D. Roberts and Bliss Carman, two major Canadian literary figures of Maritime origin like herself, who successfully established visible identities in the United States[6]—although they both had to move there in order to do so, and both subsequently experienced considerable difficulty with Page.

If the primary market was the United States, how appealing was fiction set in Canada? On the one hand, a number of American publishers successfully promoted Canadian-authored popular and juvenile fiction series (sometimes comprised of sequels) with distinctively Canadian settings. These include James De Mille's Brethren of the

5. *Green Gables Letters* 46, 59, 80.
6. *Green Gables Letters* 52.

White Cross series, set in the Grand Pré area of Nova Scotia (first published 1869–73 and still in print with the Boston firm of Lee and Shepard in the early 1900s); Norman Duncan's Billy Topsail books (1906–16), set in a Newfoundland not yet part of Canada; Ralph Connor's Glengarry series, set in rural Ontario and the West (1901–33). * * * On the other hand, it is known that several Canadian authors working in the market area of juvenile and popular fiction were required to change their Canadian settings to American locations in order to secure publication, such as Marshall Saunders for *Beautiful Joe* (1894).* * *

## Enter Lewis Page, Boston Publisher

While it is always necessary to keep in mind the often precarious position of identifiably Canadian texts within the larger world of British and American publishing, more significant with regard to the development of Montgomery's career was the late-nineteenth-century explosion in commercial publishing aimed at children, particularly through the production of series. Series production, according to Norman Feltes, developed as the capitalist system's mode of controlling and profiting from commodity-texts by producing both the audience (i.e., the market) and the wares purchased and consumed by that market.[7] In the realm of juvenile literature, this occurred in conjunction with the rapid expansion of children's periodicals in the second half of the nineteenth century, in both Britain and the United States, many originating as Sunday school publications. For example, series issued under the name of the American Tract Society gave the imprimatur of respectability to the often suspect genre of fiction. Faye Kensinger, whose *Children of the Series* documents the production of juvenile serial literature in the United States, reports two specific findings important for our understanding of the atmosphere into which Montgomery launched herself as an author: series aimed specifically at girls were especially likely to follow the maturation of the main character—to be sequels rather than a chronologically static sequence of vacation adventures—and series production peaked during the second decade of the twentieth century,[8] the decade when Montgomery produced most of the Anne books.

* * *

Available evidence suggests that Lewis Page was an exploitive publisher who grew increasingly difficult over the years due to his volatile

7. Feltes, *Modes of Production in Victorian Fiction* (Chicago: U of Chicago P, 1986) 9–12.
8. Kensinger, *Children of the Series and How They Grew* (Bowling Green: Bowling Green State U Popular P, 1987) 19.

temperament and his costly recreations of gambling and philandering, neither of which endeared him to an author who in 1911 became the wife of a Presbyterian clergyman.[9] Intersecting with this personal level of antagonism were conflicts stemming from the changes in practices and attitudes analyzed by Norman Feltes in his two books on the evolving structure of publishing in the nineteenth and earlier twentieth centuries. Although Montgomery wanted to make money, like most authors she also aspired to literary respectability and thought of herself as an artist who should control the terms of her work. Page, however, as a commercial entrepreneur, regarded her as the producer of raw material for the process of book production over which he had absolute control.[1] From the time he established his company in 1896, his staple was juvenile series, beginning with Annie Fellows Johnston's twelve-volume Little Colonel series, which eventually sold over a million copies.

In Feltes's terms, Page was a "speculative" publisher whose acceptance of *Anne of Green Gables* was a gamble on the value of "future texts" to be produced by Montgomery. Hence, while Montgomery seemed surprised and pleased that Page requested a sequel upon his acceptance of *Anne of Green Gables*, to Page, who inevitably viewed the first Anne book as the beginning of a series, there was nothing unusual about requesting a "second story dealing with the same character"[2] long before the originating text had been produced and tested in the market. In other words, the second Anne book, *Anne of Avonlea*, was generated not by the clamor of enchanted readers, but by the current practices of market publishing; the charismatic quality of *Anne of Green Gables* was not substantive to the production of its initial sequels, but rather an incidental surprise.

In fact, in the spring of 1909 Page decided to delay the appearance of *Anne of Avonlea* until the following autumn to avoid competition with the unexpectedly brisk sales of *Anne of Green Gables*. Moreover, Page's contracts did not distinguish between sequels and series; his reiterated demand for Montgomery's books for the next five years, whatever they happened to be, indicates that he saw his product as commodity-texts whose selling point was Montgomery's name, rather than as the on-going story of a character named Anne. This interpretation is borne out by the uniform appearance of all Montgom-

9. There is very little information available about Page, other than the entry by Margaret Becket and Theodora Mills in volume 49 of the *Dictionary of Literary Biography* (1986), 349–51. I would like to thank Sid Huttner at the University of Tulsa for his assistance with references to Page. Montgomery's published journals refer many times to Page's gambling and philandering (SJ2 117, 226).

1. Feltes, *Literary Capital and the Late Victorian Novel* (Madison: U of Wisconsin P, 1993) 15.

2. L. C. Page & Company to Miss L. M. Montgomery, 8 April 1907. This is the only letter from Page in the Montgomery papers at the University of Guelph.

ery's books issued by Page (*SJ2* 134), and by his insistence on symmetrical titles.[3]

\* \* \*Moreover, many earlier and contemporary authors turned the novel of adolescence into a narrative sequence on family life, beginning with Louisa May Alcott and continuing with sequential series like Coolidge's What Katy Did books and Lothrop's stories of the Five Little Peppers. In other words, while Montgomery might not have openly acknowledged (even to herself) the possibility of writing a sequel, she had nonetheless prepared the way. Once she got started, sequels and sequences proved her natural mode.\* \* \*

\*    \*    \*

When Montgomery commenced her second Anne book, her journals describe how her initial pleasure in returning to her fictional character—"Anne is as real to me as if I had given her birth—as real and as dear" (*SJ1* 332)—soon yielded to frustration: "My publishers are hurrying me now for the sequel. I'm working at it but will not be as good as Green Gables. It doesn't come as easily. I have to force it" (*SJ1* 335–36). In Montgomery's case, the disappointment generated by sequels includes the plight of the author, now fearing she is "to be dragged at Anne's chariot wheels the rest of my life."[4] Trapped in Lewis Page's ongoing binding contracts, she produced *Anne of Avonlea* (1909), *Chronicles of Avonlea* (1912), and *Anne of the Island* (1915) (as well as three other unrelated books: *Kilmeny of the Orchard*, 1910; *The Story Girl*, 1911; *The Golden Road*, 1912). Her journal records that in September 1913, "I began work on a third 'Anne' book. I did not want to do it—I have fought against it. But Page gave me no peace and every week brought a letter from some reader pleading for 'another Anne book.' So I have yielded for peace sake. It's like marrying a man to get rid of him" (*SJ2* 133). This troubling, ironic image (suggesting a dynamic that we now associate with battered wife syndrome) adumbrates the gendered subtext of Montgomery's narrated relationship with Page, in which her gratitude to him for having launched her career conflicts with her anger at the knowledge that his royalty arrangements have paid her less than half of what she should have received (*SJ2* 171). After signing two contracts promising him all her books for the next five years, she

3. Montgomery wanted the second book to be *The Later Adventures of Anne*, not *Anne of Avonlea* and disliked the title *Anne of the Island* (*SJ2* 163). The titles of *Kilmeny of the Orchard* (*SJ1* 362) and *Chronicles of Avonlea* were also Page's creation, the latter, in Montgomery's view, a "somewhat delusive title" (*SJ2* 94). *Further Chronicles of Avonlea* (1920), the unauthorized collection issued by Page, was presented as an Anne book (*SJ2* 376). In addition, the maturity of the red-headed young woman appearing as the cover portrait on all the Anne books predicts the direction of the series.
4. *Green Gables Letters* 74.

determined to break what threatened to become an eternal commitment. But in November 1910 Page cunningly invited her to Boston for a fortnight, during which visit he wined and dined her so graciously that as his guest, despite her "disgust" with the "binding clause" she once again signed away her books for the next five years (*SJ2* 25). This would, however, be the last such contract.

## Montgomery's War with Lewis Page

Montgomery does not seem to have considered seeking professional assistance until 1916, when she joined the Author's League of America.[5] That year she gained some control over her lucrative series of Anne sequels by selecting John McClelland as her Canadian publisher and literary agent, to whom she assigned the task of negotiating a better deal with an American firm.* * *

Further complicating the picture was her view that "The Page firm are the best bookmakers in America. Everybody admits that"—a detail that would explain why Page seemed to thrive despite the complaints of booksellers, authors, and former employees. Montgomery's suit against Page for unpaid royalties ended with his firm buying out the rights to her earlier books for $18,000—"nothing like the value of my books," she fumed. But with a pair of scoundrels like the Pages, "a bird in the hand is worth half a dozen in the bush" (*SJ2* 285). Page then countered with the unauthorized publication of the only known text that could be described as a "false sequel" to Anne. *Further Chronicles of Avonlea*, cobbled together in Page's office from discards from *Chronicles of Avonlea* that were still in his possession, was manufactured uniformly with the earlier Anne books. Montgomery sued again; he threatened counter-suits, and then dealt the greatest blow of all by selling the film rights to *Anne of Green Gables* for $40,000.[6]

\* \* \*

For Montgomery, extricating herself from Page did not, however, mean extricating herself from Anne. * * * [S]he complained: "I want to do something different. But my publishers keep me at this sort of

5. In a section omitted from this excerpt, Gerson quotes a 1916 letter from LMM: "Three months ago, I had no real distrust of Mr. Page in any way. Since then I have heard so much against him and his methods from different quarters that I am distrustful; but the fact of his threatening me with 'the courts' is the one thing that has really turned my former loyalty into suspicion." From George Parker's notes on Montgomery's files with McClelland and Stewart, McMaster University, quotation from letter of 29 April 1916.

6. Louisa May Alcott encountered similar difficulties when she attempted to change her publisher. See Martha Saxton, *Louisa May: A Modern Biography of Louisa May Alcott* (Boston: Houghton Mifflin, 1977).

stuff because it sells and because they claim the public, having become used to this from my pen, would not tolerate a change" (*SJ2* 278).* * *

                                    *   *   *

Sequels were a determining factor in Montgomery's literary and personal life, producing the launch of her first book and her financial well-being, as well as decades of bitter dispute with her publisher and a problematic relationship with an intrusive, adoring readership. In her last years, they provided a refuge from an increasingly troubled world. By the end of Montgomery's life, sequels had ceased to be disappointing. For her publishers and other beneficiaries of the Anne industry, the sequels and spinoffs of *Anne of Green Gables* continue to produce tremendous profits. And for her public, who today still eagerly welcome every new text written by or associated with Montgomery, there can never be enough of Anne.


# KATE WOOD

## In the News†

We can better understand L. M. Montgomery's significance as an icon in * * * popular culture today if we recover her relationship with the popular culture of her own time. In this article, I examine the author's most famous novel, *Anne of Green Gables*, from within Montgomery's own print culture by placing the text alongside the most powerful and pervasive medium of its time—the newspaper.[1] * * * I examine the discourses surrounding community, education, and gender, illustrating how these are expressed both in the news and in *Anne of Green Gables*.[2]* * *

---

† From "In the News: Anne of Green Gables and PEI's Turn-of-the-Century Press," *CCL: Canadian Children's Literature* 99 (2000): 23–42. Copyright © Kate Wood. Reprinted with permission of the author. Footnotes have been renumbered and edited with the author's permission.

1. PEI's news production increased dramatically at the end of the nineteenth century. In 1885, PEI had a population of almost 108,891 and produced only 12 papers in total. While the population between 1885 and 1895 rose by only 109 to 109,000, newspaper production almost doubled, to 20 papers. London, England, in 1896 boasted a population of 4.8 million and was producing 22 newspapers. See Marion T. Marzolf, "American 'New Journalism' Takes Root in Europe at the End of the Nineteenth Century," *Journalism Quarterly* 61 (1984): 535. Elsewhere in the original article Kate Wood cites Aled Jones, *Powers of the Press Newspapers, Power and the Public in Nineteenth Century England* (Brookfield, VT: Ashgate, 1996), and Herbert Altschull, *From Milton to McLuhan: The Ideas Behind American Journalism* (White Plains, NY: Longmans, 1990).

2. The *Examiner* Charlottetown, PEI (January 1, 1903–December 31, 1911) Archival Resource, University of Guelph; the *Daily Patriot* Charlottetown, PEI (January 1, 1880–

My primary archives are two Charlottetown papers: the *Daily Patriot* and the *Examiner* \* \* \* from 1880 to 1911 (the year Montgomery married Ewan Macdonald and left her Island for good).

\*   \*   \*

Community notes appear in both the *Daily Patriot* and the *Examiner* daily. Signed in pseudonym, notes range from detailing the weather, to noting the comings and goings of various villagers, to offering sarcastic reflections on rural life. Such notes appear to be submitted without solicitation and they appear sporadically, suggesting that they were penned in leisure hours. Some towns, like Earnscliffe and Donaldston, are represented almost weekly; others, like Montgomery's Cavendish, are represented only once or twice a year. Correspondents from any town or settlement, however small, qualify for publication; neither wit nor regularity are key requirements. One must simply write and submit to enjoy the glory of one's name in print.\* \* \*

\* \* \*Men like the pseudonymed "Rex" of Earnscliffe and "Starlight" of Donaldston interact on the pages of the *Examiner* throughout the first decade of the twentieth century, but with most energy and enthusiasm in the years directly surrounding Montgomery's writing of *Anne*, suggesting that Montgomery's creative impulses did not flourish in isolation.

As Montgomery wove her community discourses into her fiction, country correspondents were engaged in a similar process in the newspaper. "Starlight" of Donaldston writes:

> What is going to be done for the winter's amusement? It is high time to be evolving a programme. Intellectual culture is needed for young and old. A community without it is not in a progressive state. Our young men are desirous to have some intellectual exercise. Let us have a debating society, to meet every Thursday night in Glendale school during the winter months, or some such interesting and instructive amusement. (December 8, 1904, 7)

"Starlight's" discussion affirms that community, in isolated rural PEI, was providing its members with intellectual and social stimulation, an idea that is reinforced throughout *Anne of Green Gables* with concert recitations (125), Sunday school picnics (77), the formation of the story club (165), and Ladies Aid meetings (86). Montgomery even makes an explicit link between community events and

---

December 31, 1911) Archival Resource, University of Guelph. The author also studied the *Guardian* Charlottetown, PEI (August–December 1903) Archival Resource, University of Guelph.

community notes. Diana says to Anne, " 'Mind you, Mr. Allan is going to send an account of it to the Charlottetown papers.' " And Anne replies, " 'Oh Diana, will we really see our names in print? It makes me thrill to think of it . . . ' " (164).[3] * *

*    *    *

* * *Avonlea is not drawn as uniformly harmonious, but instead mimics the Island communities shown in the newspapers: community is figured as problematic, powerful, and pertinent to the lives of its members.

*    *    *

* * *Dominant discourses on the Island well into the twentieth century reinforce PEI's continuing commitment to education. One cannot read more than a few days of the *Patriot* or the *Examiner* before stumbling on extensive articles titled, for example, "Public Schools Report for 1895" (*Daily Patriot* March 31,1896, 2) or "Our Education" (*Daily Patriot* March 1, 1909, 2). Exam scores and final grades are reported and published for every single student from each school—from local rural one-room schoolhouses to the Prince of Wales College, from kindergarten to university. Education is rivaled only by election news as the hottest topic in the Island newspaper.[4] Similarly, in *Anne of Green Gables*, school achieves a central position in the novel.* * *

* * *At the turn of the century, the *Daily Patriot* publishes an ongoing series of articles by a Judge Warburton. Entitled "Education As It Is," the articles assert that Islanders must remain vigilant in their pursuit of academic excellence. Warburton exposes and suggests solutions to a variety of educational problems on the Island. * * * [A] character like Montgomery's ineffectual Mr. Phillips would have been all too familiar in the domain of the real on Prince Edward Island; teaching was a choice often made for reasons of survival, accompanied by fairly pitiable compensation.[5] Montgomery writes:

> Mr. Phillips was back in the corner explaining a problem in algebra to Prissy Andrews and the rest of the scholars were doing pretty much as they pleased, eating green apples, whispering, drawing pictures on their slates, and driving crickets, harnessed to strings, up and down the aisle. (93)

3. Page references to *AGG* correspond with the NCE text.
4. Similarly, one can identify room for growth and some dissension in discussions of religion, despite the fact that the Island (and Island newspapers) are often overwhelmingly religious in focus and tone.
5. See Erol Sharpe, *A People's History of Prince Edward Island* (Toronto: Steel Rail, 1976) 132.

The impression such a criticism leaves suggests there was a grey area separating PEI's lofty ideas about education from practical application. Appearing in the *Daily Patriot* on June 28, 1901, the following article reinforces this idea:

> To reach the maximum results our schools must be supplied with properly qualified teachers. This can be effected only by making remuneration for work faithfully performed. . . . Till this is done the present undesirable condition of things must remain, and the irreparable loss is the parents' and the children's. ("Education and Teachers" 4)

Contradictorily, on an island where education was highly prized, remuneration for teachers was barely livable. An article on the Teacher's Convention in September 1901, appearing in the *Daily Patriot*, affirms the idea that teaching was compensated inadequately: "The fact is only too evident that teachers are too poorly paid and therefore too poorly qualified" (September 12, 1901, 4). The *Daily Patriot* and Montgomery are not exclusively negative, however, in their presentations of education on the Island. * * * Montgomery eventually dismisses the lamentable Mr. Phillips and replaces him with the infinitely more-qualified Miss Stacey, who is eventually replaced herself by Anne (242). One receives a picture of education on the Island in a state of hopeful progress; the newspaper's unrelenting goal is undoubtedly to better educational practice on PEI.:

> [T]here is one thing upon which every man can congratulate himself and his generation—the fact that we have progressed far enough to give education free to every child born in Canada. (*Daily Patriot* July 3, 1908, 4)

* * * But the ideological flexibility identifiable in Island education (which educated both males and females) had its limits when extended outside of the classroom and into the home. An examination of gender in the novel and the news illustrates that discourses concerned with the public sphere were infinitely more expansive than those concerned with the private.

Both the *Daily Patriot* and the *Examiner* abound with poetry, anecdotes, and stories offering women up as the model of domestic purity and morality. Passivity and generosity are presented as the most integral characteristics of womanhood. The notion that women are inherently suited to life in a domestic sphere reinforces the idea of the differences between men and women widely circulating in British culture of that era.[6] * * * [M]en are viewed as separate, active

---

6. See Mary Poovey, *Uneven Developments: The Ideological World of Gender in Mid-Victorian England* (Chicago: U of Chicago P, 1988).

entities, while women are only represented in regard to their relationship with men, as lesser counterparts, never partners.

*   *   *

* * *Examining the *Daily Patriot*'s relationship with the column
entitled "Woman and Home," for example, one can see that representations of women undergo seismic shifts in the newspaper. Often
appearing on the front page throughout the 1890s, this column is
pushed to the fourth page in the final years of the decade, and then,
by the end of 1900, disappears altogether.* * *

"Woman and Home," while certainly reinforcing popular notions
of a woman's place in Victorian society and planting her firmly in
the home, also transgresses nineteenth-century perceptions of
domesticity. Publicizing the achievements of women in the public
sphere, the column does not limit itself to Victorian ideals and
instead promotes the image of woman as capable, dynamic, and competent both inside and outside of the home. A typical column,
appearing on the third page on February 16, 1900, contains a small
article celebrating Julia Holmes Smith, a woman who broke out of
a traditional role and "pursued the study of medicine in the Boston
University School of Medicine for three years." The article details
Dr. Smith's path to fame with approval. But discourses applauding
female successes are at least partially neutralized by more traditional
perceptions of a woman's place. The article directly following the
piece on Dr. Smith reads:

> Girls Men Want to Marry
> Men who are looking for wives are growing more cautious daily.
> The up to date maiden of society must be careful if she would
> wear orange blossoms. . . . Remember, girls, men are born hunt-
> ers. They value the girl who is not to be had for the first asking.
> . . . Odious mannerisms are fatal to a girl. Giggling simply mad-
> dens some men. One girl missed becoming the wife of a nabob
> because she 'sniffed.' (*Daily Patriot* February 16, 1900, 3)

Such discourse affirms the idea that marriage was still considered as
of primary importance to even progressive women, and that passivity
and repression were helpful in winning a husband. The title of
"Woman and Home" itself implies that dominant discourses about
domesticity are the ones most affirmed by the publication, but it
would be unfair to suggest that this column, like the *Daily Patriot* or
*Anne of Green Gables* itself, was predictable in its messages.
Women's voices in the *Daily Patriot*, *after* the disappearance of
"Woman and Home" at the turn of the century, are heard directly
only in advertising testimonials and in the poetry section, repre-

sented most notably by L. M. Montgomery. While women's voices are not regularly given space within the newspaper, references to their presence and their potential power abound. Representations of women appearing in the newspapers, within community notes, advertising, and on the front page, firmly place women in the home. Subsequently, concerns about the potential ramifications of entrenching such public discourses into daily, private life surface within the pages of the newspapers.* * *

\* \* \*

* * *Anxiety about the power of women, located specifically in their ability to shape community perceptions, is a theme that recurs in community correspondence in Island news, as well as in *Anne of Green Gables*. There is a distinction made, in the *Daily Patriot* and the *Examiner*, between the local news described in published country correspondence and that whispered in country kitchens; it is a distinction based upon categories distinguishing the legitimate from the frivolous, skill from weakness, patriarchy from matriarchy, male from female. Despite the fact that male country correspondents are often circulating information culled directly from the private sphere, they never consider naming themselves gossips. Such a moniker, it seems, falls securely on the female sex.[7]

Male commentary on the power of the female gossip subculture can range from tolerant and mocking to vaguely threatening and definitively patronizing. On October 14, 1903, the following appears in the *Examiner*: "Some of our correspondents are sending the latest news by the *new telewoman system*, which they find much better and faster than by mail" (7; my emphasis). "Starlight" of Donaldston writes, more maliciously, on December 5, 1904:

> Our local gossip announces that they have been talking too much of late and says that they are going to keep quiet awhile. We fear, however, that the good gossips' control over their speaking apparatus is nominal rather than real, and that they are overestimating their power of self representation. (*Examiner* 3)

\* \* \*

In *Anne of Green Gables*, however, Montgomery offers the possibility that female gossip can in fact be associated with a kind of community power and greatness, providing a counter to the narrow,

---

7. A general discussion on gossip (omitted here) includes references to Patricia Meyer Spacks, *Gossip* (New York: Alfred A Knopf, 1985), and to Mary Rubio, "Subverting the Trite," *CCL: Canadian Children's Literature* 65 (1992): 6–39.

patriarchally voiced disparagement presented in the newspapers.
Montgomery presents an illustration of the power derived from
female gossip that is only hinted at, filtered through male voices, in
the newspapers.

Mrs. Lynde, strong, domineering, controlling and militantly
domestic, challenges the simplistic image of the passive, idealized
lady by giving shape and voice to the rural "telewoman." * * * The
pragmatic and verbal Mrs. Lynde is certainly never fully supported
by Montgomery or her core characters, but she is conveyed as a social
inevitability. Her seemingly unchallengeable power is felt by all she
comes in contact with, as Anne learns in her first explosive meeting
with her. Marilla is horror-stricken at Anne's initial treatment of Mrs.
Lynde, not because she recognizes it as unwarranted or unjust, but
because she recognizes the extent of this woman's community power:

> How unfortunate that Anne should have displayed such temper
> before Mrs. Rachel Lynde, of all people! Then Marilla suddenly
> became aware of an uncomfortable and rebuking consciousness
> that she felt more humiliation over this than sorrow over the
> discovery of such a serious defect in Anne's disposition. (59)

Marilla later tells Anne, " 'Well, you made a fine exhibition of yourself I must say. Mrs. Lynde will have a nice story to tell about you
everywhere—and she'll tell it, too . . . ' " (60). Mrs. Lynde's power as
a gossip is recognized as potentially destructive within the small rural
community; she, like the *Daily Patriot*'s "resourceful woman," has
the power to create people and destroy futures with her network of
talk.

* * *

* * *Fitting Matthew in with the world constructed in the newspapers studied, a world that only truly legitimizes and authorizes the
male voice, one can see that * * * Montgomery's inclusion of Matthew is at least partially manipulative. She is responding to the
demands of her culture by inserting a male voice into her narrative,
but she is subverting those same demands by allowing her representative of patriarchy to be supportive of progressive gender ideologies.

* * *

Matthew is * * * Montgomery's version of a different kind of man,
a different kind of patriarch. Shaped by dominant discourses that
privileged the male voice and imbued only it with authority, * * *
Matthew is ultimately less symbolic of traditional, status-quo–

enforcing patriarchy (and subsequently less long-lived) than the story's supposed matriarch—Mrs. Rachel Lynde. * * * [S]ignificantly, it is Mrs. Lynde who pronounces Matthew dead in the final pages of the novel (233). I suggest that this narrative choice is symbolic of the book's shift, from Matthew's kind of progressive patriarchy into Mrs. Lynde's narrower one. Mrs. Lynde's presence within the text at this precise moment is reflective of the book's losing battle with patriarchy; her presence reflects a narrative choice precipitated by the cultural ideals that were so pervasive in the news. From the point of Matthew's death onwards, a reversal occurs in the text, and Anne, up until the moment of Matthew's death in pursuit of a higher education, takes up her position, with Mrs. Lynde's full approval (241), as the self-sacrificing feminine woman of Green Gables.

\* \* \*

So why does Montgomery work backwards in her construction of gender? Why does she allow her progressive vision of education to stand unchallenged but feel compelled to kill off Matthew and keep Anne at home?

It is clear, upon close examination of the oppressive dominant discourses manifested in the Island newspaper, that Montgomery had little alternative for her novel, culturally and personally. * * * Surrounded by a popular culture that defined itself according to patriarchal notions of female inequality, Montgomery wrote a text that frequently affirmed social conventions and, in so doing, further inscribed them into the discourses of her time.

Produced daily and with vigor, turn-of-the-century Island newspapers provide readers with an opportunity to reconstruct a culture, to identify the preoccupations, values, and ideologies specific to a time and a place. * * * The *Daily Patriot* and the *Examiner* work to illustrate the cultural context out of which *Anne of Green Gables* was born.* * *

No less powerful for its concessions to dominant discourse, *Anne of Green Gables* works to affirm, dismantle, and rewrite the master narratives of its own time and place.* * *

# MARY HENLEY RUBIO

## Scottish-Presbyterian Agency†

Culture is a force that spreads as much through stories as it does through political revolution. L. M. Montgomery was a storyteller supreme, and her worldwide impact is only now being charted. The cultural impact of Montgomery is part and parcel of the enormous influence wielded by the Scottish immigrants to Canada (and other countries). This impact is deeply rooted in the religious and cultural ethos of the Scottish-Canadian society in which she was raised; that ethos, in turn, is a continuation of unique ideas about education, egalitarianism, and agency that her ancestors brought from Scotland. Montgomery is inescapably a descendant of ancestors who came out of Scotland's Presbyterian culture in the late eighteenth century. Her cultural and intellectual heritage is already evident in her very first novel, *Anne of Green Gables* (1908).[1]

The principles of Scottish Presbyterianism—specifically those placing emphasis on empowerment of *all* classes of people through education, on participatory democracy in church and civic govern-ment, on constant self-examination through one's reasoning facul-ties, on "plain speaking" and accessibility in rhetorical style and public discourse, on valuing intellectuality, book-learning, and achievement—were deeply held beliefs that the Scottish emigrants took with them wherever they settled. They were ideals that gave them a sense of agency. Also, the Scots have had great impact in creating imaginative literature, coming as they did from a culture that valued *both* the oral tradition and the written word. They rec-ognized the power of story in the transmission and critiquing of cul-tural values.

Montgomery's genius was to embed in narrative, and particularly in narrative about women and ordinary people, many of the basic ideas and energies that fuelled the rest of the Scottish diaspora and subsequent colonial enterprise. Montgomery is vigorously against cant, hypocrisy, and authoritarianism. She has a strong sense of social class, but she sees status as maintained through people's behavior and social responsibility. She admires moral seriousness,

---

† From "L. M. Montgomery: Scottish-Presbyterian Agency in Canadian Culture," *L. M. Montgomery and Canadian Culture*, ed. Irene Gammel and Elizabeth R. Epperly, 89–105. Copyright © 1999 Mary Henley Rubio. This article has been slightly revised and shortened by the author. Reprinted by permission of the author. Page references to *AGG* are to this NCE.

1. The Presbyterian Church was institutionalized as the National Church of Scotland, but Scotland retained a large Roman Catholic population, and animosity lingered. * * * The Presbyterian distrust of Catholics is registered various places in Montgomery's novels, but in other places she depicts Catholics kindly.

but she shows how it often is misguided in a strict religion that has become somewhat calcified. She grows up in a society that values reason and the intellect above all, but she uses her fiction to show that the intellect is often driven by the emotions. And, very important, she values education—for women as well as for men—which undercuts the exclusion of women (in her era and earlier) from official positions of power, although Scottish-Presbyterian women were not excluded from getting a basic education in itself.

In short, she continues in the tradition of her Presbyterian ancestors from Scotland who used "common sense" and learning to renew their evolving society. She did not accept the status quo without critiquing it. Hers is essentially a subtle and subversive approach—one that challenges authoritarianism and that creates a space for elevating women within a society *supposedly* built on egalitarian principles. Narrative is her chosen medium, and it has been uniquely effective. Her books have been uniquely empowering for women, as well as for those living under authoritarian regimes.

L. M. Montgomery grew up on the north shore of Prince Edward Island in an enclave of Scottish Presbyterians who were militantly proud of their ancestry, their literacy, their educational system, and their cultural heritage in general.[2] Her ancestors on both sides had been in the first wave of emigrants who came to PEI, and were from a higher socioeconomic class than many later Scots, especially the impoverished Scots who came as the result of the Highland Clearances in the early nineteenth century. Her Montgomery and Macneill forebears did well after they left Scotland, obtaining land (through land grants or purchase) in Prince Edward Island in the late eighteenth century. Their clannishness, their moral seriousness, their belief in the Protestant work ethic, their faith in the possibility of human improvement, and their insistence on setting up the best possible school systems for all their children without the prejudice of social class—all this contributed to their success and their subsequent pride in this success. The educational system in Scotland had long allowed exceptionally able "lads o' pairts" to rise out of humble beginnings.* * *

The early Presbyterians in sixteenth-century Scotland—a backward country compared to England—had been religious fanatics. * * * It is highly ironic that early Scotland—where the Presbyterian faith was exceedingly militant and rigid, and where religion and state education were *not* separated—nevertheless, by virtue of promoting education for the common man, created the instrument that eventually fostered the seeds of democratic egalitarianism.* * *

---

2. The Montgomeries are believed to have arrived in PEI between 1769 and 1772, and the Macneills around 1775. Her English grandmother Woolner's ancestors came in 1836.

In early Scotland, the first Education Act of 1496 had consolidated power in the hands of the literate elite, namely the Catholic clergy and the landowners. In 1560, after much religious unrest, Presbyterianism was established as the national religion of Scotland by an Act of Parliament, and this strongly affected Scottish education from then on. The Presbyterians, rejecting the idea that education was only for the elite, legislated a second Education Act in 1696 which proclaimed that a school was to be established in every church parish, and that all children, rich and poor, male and female, should at least have access to education, though they were not forced to attend school. (This system was far more deliberately egalitarian than England's, which did not nationalize education for the lower classes until the Education Act of 1870.)[3]

* * *The Scots, with their deeply ingrained respect for education from a very early era, had a great advantage as colonizers. * * * The Scots were particularly adept at conceptualizing because in their educational system the study of philosophy was a base for further specializations. From their understanding of first principles, students then proceeded to the study of specialized subjects like mathematics, science, medicine, and law. * * * The Scots felt their educational system—as well as much else about their culture—was markedly superior to England's.[4]* * *

* * *A further skill that the Scots admired and honed was that of fluency and force in oral argument. Arguing fine points of theology, philosophy, and law had long been a national pastime in Scotland, and the effects had been both good and bad: over the centuries, the disputatious and polemical Scots had carried many of their arguments to the battlefield, and their early history is full of bloody encounters. But they eventually carried their arguments into the halls of learning, producing an extraordinary flowering of knowledge

3. North Americans frequently treat England and Scotland as a single country when they are discussing the two countries. However, when Scotland united with England and Wales to become Great Britain in 1707, the Scots kept control of three institutions: the religious, educational, and legal systems. * * * Thus, although the two countries are geographically attached, and although they shared a government structure in England (from 1707 until the Scottish vote for devolution in 1997), they remained two somewhat different cultures.

4. England was much slower than Scotland in instituting education. * * * It was only in the last quarter of the eighteenth century that the English began to seriously debate the question of whether mass elementary education should be offered to the lower classes. In England there was widespread resistance to mass education, and even to church and charity schools that were local initiatives, partly because of the fear that education might upset the class system by making "members of the working class discontented with their lot." See David Wardle, *English Popular Education, 1780–1970* (London: Cambridge UP, 1970) 7. * * * Thus, England's late start in national education for all classes put the English working class at a disadvantage when competing in the colonies with the better-educated Scots. The Presbyterian habit of starting schools and then universities wherever the Scots dispersed to sustained their success as colonizers. PEI is believed to have had the earliest public education system in the British Commonwealth.

during the eighteenth-century Scottish Enlightenment, starting around 1740.

The radical new ideas which flowed out of the Scottish Enlightenment are now widely regarded as underpinning much of Western culture—the belief in egalitarianism, in separating church and state for greater social harmony, and in creating government mechanisms to help achieve a civil society (all ideas which were accepted or reinforced by other political philosophers, and which subsequently found a place in the American Constitution). L. M. Montgomery's educated ancestors emigrated to Canada toward the end of the Scottish Enlightenment, and they brought with them the belief in the importance of good education, book-learning, oral fluency, and public service. On both her mother's and father's side of the family, Montgomery's ancestors had been influential leaders and political figures on the Island. "Anne of Green Gables" belongs to this word-bound society, and a part of the humor in the book comes from little Anne's following in the tradition of the highly literate and articulate Scotsman—but in her case, one who is writ comically *small* and *female*.

The Presbyterians held that basic education should be offered to anyone of ability, even women. For Montgomery, this meant not only that she had access to good schools, but also that she learned in those schools to respect the prime Scottish educational ideals of reasoning and rhetoric. Montgomery's novels take a strong stand for the higher education of women, something believed a waste of money in her day in rural communities.

* * *Montgomery's novels and stories gave agency to the women of her era, showing that they could have considerable power if they exercised it. They could talk, joke, harass their husbands, and gossip (a very powerful form of social control in small communities); in her own case, they could write humorous accounts of patriarchal structures in church and society that oppressed women.* * *

Montgomery also retained from her Scottish heritage a belief that telling stories was a slow but effective way to change public attitudes. In addition to being a nation that particularly esteemed written texts and book-learning, the Scots also cherished the oral tradition. Their storytelling is often located in a vague "Celtic legacy," or the Highland culture, which was primarily an oral culture, but it had widely spread roots. Family and community history were passed down through stories, children were taught by stories, and storytellers provided local entertainment before the world became wired in the twentieth century. Good storytellers had especial status in their communities, and a sense of ironic humor was particularly valued.

Having access to the stories of the *Bible*, which their education allowed them to read in the vernacular, was another site of cultural

enrichment—again a point where religion and education intersected. The *Bible* was, of course, more than a source of theological
points to argue about—it was full of good stories, as well as examples
of teaching through stories and parables. And it was read daily in the
homes of the Presbyterians of Cavendish, where Montgomery grew
up. Montgomery's fiction draws on the storytelling of her cultural
milieu, too, as well as on the general ethos of her religious background.

In the narratives of L. M. Montgomery, we see a community that
is always examining itself. This too is part of the intellectual, emotional, and social heritage of Presbyterianism. Presbyterians were
taught by their religion—a particularly demanding and fervent one—
to constantly examine their own lives for signs of slackness. Since
they believed that humanity's responsibility was to enact God's
teachings (as laid out in the *Bible*), constant self-examination was in
order. Intense self-examination became a habit of mind with them.

More amusing, perhaps, was the way that Presbyterians enthusiastically extended this process of self-examination to an examination
of the lives of their relatives and neighbors. The Scottish Presbyterians in Cavendish could be very hard on themselves, but they could
be harder on their neighbors, for it is human nature to look for faults
in others to mitigate a sense of one's own imperfections. Montgomery's stories are laced with ironic judgments about people's morality,
theology, behavior, and general rectitude. This constant judging of
others is a religious exercise in the purest sense, for it shows up the
people who are mean-spirited, selfish, and otherwise unworthy of
God's grace.

Montgomery's cast of fictional characters always includes those
yeasty souls like Mrs. Rachel Lynde who take it as their "Christian
duty" to gratuitously detail others' faults to them. * * * Her well-
meaning but judgmental people take aim at others, delivering hurtful
remarks, all in the service of being good Christians. They justify their
"plain speaking" easily: since barbs keep others humble, and since
humility is a prerequisite for getting into Heaven, it follows that the
induction of humility can only be good. Besides presenting sharp-
tongued characters, Montgomery revels in examining the foibles of
men and women, grown-ups and children, the pious and the repro-
bates.

However, ultimately Montgomery's fiction presents communities
like Avonlea as safe places to be: however much people prick their
neighbors, they also care deeply about each other. Their society is
run by law and order. They intend to be fair-minded even when they
are not. Thus, the ever-present Scotch thistles are ultimately contained and neutralized by the coddling wool of community caring.
* * * They constitute a society that has high standards of personal

moral earnestness, a reverence for rational individual thought based on careful discernment, and a deep commitment to civic good. * * * They believe everyone has the right to respect unless he or she forfeits that right by unacceptable behavior. The Scots who emigrated to Canada, and elsewhere, came with these ideas of duty, of personal responsibility, and of agency. Matthew and Marilla exhibit their sense of "duty" by keeping Anne because they might be "some good to her."

As a private person, L. M. Montgomery felt that the Presbyterians were a special breed apart from the other Protestant sects—to say nothing of Catholics. * * * However, when she is writing fiction, Montgomery can be objective and satirize her own prejudices, which were those of her beloved Cavendish, a very typical tightly knit nineteenth-century Scottish community, with life organized around its churches.[5]

It is remarkable that Montgomery was able to have such sport with religion in her novels—in an era that still took church doctrine and denominational rivalry very seriously—and yet not offend her readers. Her techniques are subtle: like Mark Twain, she puts the most partisan remarks (which are often offensive, if not blasphemous) in the voices of the people who are already flagged as comical characters, either as opinionated adults or as engaging children who can be scolded for their statements. These comical characters, like the young Anne (and adults like Miss Cornelia and Susan Baker, in later novels), can say anything and get away with it because the reader sees that even if their statements are sometimes true, they are unacceptable. * * *

In *Anne of Green Gables*, Montgomery creates a little girl whose first foray into the Avonlea Presbyterian church results in her shocking report to Marilla that she spent her time there looking out the window and dreaming, rather than listening to the boring minister. Montgomery is * * * touching on a theme that comes up repeatedly in her novels: long prayers and tedious sermons that a captive child—and captive adults—must endure. * * *

However, there is more to her dissatisfaction than mere childhood memory of churchly incarceration on beautiful Sunday mornings. One needs to read Montgomery's characterizations of ministerial style in light of the ideas of Hugh Blair's widely circulated and immensely influential 1783 *Lectures on Rhetoric and Belles Lettres*, the best-known of the many books that he wrote in Scotland during

---

5. Elsewhere I have compared how Mark Twain and L. M. Montgomery recreate and satirize the nineteenth-century Presbyterian communities that they were raised in. See also John Kenneth Galbraith's *The Scotch* (Toronto: Macmillan, 1967) for an account of the author's formative years growing up in a Scottish-Presbyterian community. Like Montgomery, Galbraith regards his strict childhood upbringing with a comic eye.

the eighteenth century. These lectures were originally given at the University of Edinburgh and heard by thousands of young men going into the ministry, commerce, law, or education. They were also printed and widely distributed throughout the English-speaking world.* * *

[S]ermons were *not* to be read, as was the custom in England; they were to be delivered extemporaneously. A good sermon was a persuasive sermon, one designed to persuade hearers to be good. To achieve this, ministers had to be interesting, show both "gravity and warmth," and be free of abstruse "doctrinal discourse." The Scots rated oratorical skills very highly, and "ostentatious swells of words or a pointed ornamented foppery of style" were regarded as the nadir of pulpit oratory.[6] They valued fluency and "plain speaking" and hated pomposity in the pulpit or elsewhere. They regarded the purpose of language as communication and persuasion, not obfuscation.* * *

Montgomery often expresses the opinion in her books and journals that dullness is a cardinal sin. Even little Anne condemns dullness: "It was a very long text. . . . The sermon was awfully long, too. I suppose the minister had to match it to the text. I didn't think he was a bit interesting. The trouble with him seems to be that he hasn't enough imagination" (*AGG* NCE 72).* * *

There was another kind of sermon that Montgomery also satirized: the thunderous "old-style" sermon that stressed hellfire and brimstone. Before the Scottish Enlightenment, there had been a stereotype of Scottish Presbyterian ministers as being bigoted, fanatical, and narrow-minded. This type of minister, trained in the older theology (which included the outmoded doctrine of Predestination), * * * was still occasionally found in the rural areas, preaching the terrors of Hell.[7]* * *

L. M. Montgomery's view is not necessarily that of her characters, of course. She stands enough outside them that she knows when their viewpoint will sound quite comical, not only to the Presbyterians who will read her novels, but also to millions of other people with different religious beliefs who are equally convinced that their

6. See Richard Sher's *Church and University in the Scottish Enlightenment: The Moderate Literati of Edinburgh* (Princeton: Princeton UP, 1985), which discusses the impact of Hugh Blair's ideas.
7. Predestination was that austere doctrine that held that before each child's birth God had determined whether a person was of the "Elect" (chosen for salvation in the afterlife) or the "damned" (consigned to Hell in the afterlife). Many old-timers in Montgomery's era believed in the doctrine. See, for instance, the *Charlottetown Examiner* for 27 February 1890, in which the Archbishop of Halifax attacks "Predestination." On 15 June 1893, there is another letter complaining that some Presbyterian ministers teach old dogma they don't believe in, just to keep the older parishioners happy (especially the "elders" who might dismiss them). In Mark Twain's *Tom Sawyer*, chapter 5 refers to "the predestined elect."

own religious view is superior to every other. In many cases, she takes aim at those whose practice of religion misses its spirit.

However, Montgomery's point of view is very complex and sometimes unstable. * * * The Montgomery who writes the novels is often not the Montgomery who writes her personal journals. As a writer, Montgomery can take the ironic perspective, but as a human being she is often heir to those prejudices learned in childhood that she satirizes in others. This is clear in her fiction when she satirizes the view of Presbyterians that they are superior to others, while in her own journals she often speaks disapprovingly of other religious denominations.

* * *The Presbyterian Church structure played a large role in creating a sense of agency in ordinary people, and in making them resistant to any authoritarian structures imposed from above. The Presbyterian Church structure was built on the "presbyteral system," a type of government that vested power in ordinary people at the grassroots level. Much of the political and religious strife in Scotland from the sixteenth century onward had been centered around the question of whether authority should be organized around the "presbyteral" or the "episcopal" system (where power was vested at the top, as in the Episcopal and the Catholic churches). Scotland favored the former, England the latter.

The presbyteral system of the Church of Scotland held that authority should begin at the most local level: a community would designate its own lay leaders (called the "church elders") and select their own minister. This minister was ordained in the church, but was subject to the "call of the people." * * * The church elders and the local minister constituted the "local Kirk [church] session." A gathering of local sessions constituted the next level, called the "presbytery." A subsequent gathering of "presbyteries" made up the "regional synod," and the top level was the "General Assembly," which had supreme authority. But it did not have the power to impose a minister on any local group—each Presbyterian community "called" its own minister, and could dismiss him at will.

* * *Conversely, in the Church of England, power was vested at the top, in the hands of the bishops, *under* whom were priests, with deacons below. This system also created a hierarchy of power, but its organizational structure was inverted, with the episcopal system locating greater authority at the top, whereas the presbyteral system placed more at the local level.* * *

Montgomery describes in her books deeply principled and religious people whose communities are evolving.* * *

* * *[Montgomery] takes us where the real action comes from, someplace in the unfathomable mysteries of the human heart and mind. Here, evil merely shifts its manifestations in human society.

Montgomery registers the massive shift in the early twentieth century away from a teleological world to a secular one: theology is losing its position as the site for human discussion of evil.

This social change was noted by two "old-timers" on Prince Edward Island in a book of social history by Island historian David Weale. He asked these men what the biggest change in their lifetime had been. Both comment on the decentering of religion. The first says, "There have been many great changes in my lifetime, but I do believe that the greatest change of all is the change that has come over God . . . when I was growin' up, God was something to be feared. Oh yes! The fear of God was drilled into us every chance they got." Another notes: "I can tell you right now I didn't like Him [God] much. Who would? He seemed to disapprove of the very appetites He had put in us. Not only that, He watched all the time, every little misstep. And if you stumbled, He was right there, on the spot, to wag his big finger."[8] Montgomery's books catch this era of change, and considering the force wielded by popular literature that is widely circulated and repeatedly reread, they undoubtedly also contributed to it. They are social criticism writ large into comedy, but she laces her morality with humor, rather than thundering away like John Knox, the early Scottish-Presbyterian theologian. As Montgomery wrote in a letter to a friend, George Boyd MacMillan in March 19, 1906, right after finishing *Anne of Green Gables*, and before she knew she had written an international best-seller, "Often times a truth can be taught by a jest better than by earnest."

* * *In Montgomery's fiction, the Scottish-Presbyterian ethos was the core to almost all of her central characters' identity. Like her forebears, Montgomery remains a thinking and judging Presbyterian who contemplates how individuals and wider human society might be improved. In her writing endeavor, she knows the powers of "story"—a lesson learned as a captive little Presbyterian lass listening to Sunday school lessons and *Bible* stories, as well as to ministerial sermons, which were all designed in the most practical and immediate sense to alter human behavior for the better. The idea of "personal agency" is encoded in Montgomery's texts (such as *Anne of Green Gables*), which have traveled all over the world, wielding their own quiet influence.[9]

8. See David Weale, *Them Times* (Charlottetown: Institute of Island Studies, 1992) 108; 109.
9. See Barbara Wachowicz, "L. M. Montgomery at Home in Poland," *CCL: Canadian Children's Literature* 46 (1987): 7–36, for the reception of Montgomery's novels in Poland. This article, written before Communist rule was relaxed in Poland, could not say anything controversial about Montgomery's real impact, part of which came through Montgomery's challenges to authoritarianism and her affirmation of values of trust, love, and family. After World War II, the communist government in Poland tried to ban Montgomery's books.

# CRITICISM

# Early Reviews and Responses

## *NEW YORK TIMES*

### A Heroine from an Asylum (1908)†

A farmer in Prince Edward's Island ordered a boy from a Nova Scotia asylum, but the order got twisted and the result was that a girl was sent the farmer instead of a boy. That girl is the heroine of L. M. Montgomery's story, "Anne of Green Gables" (L. C. Page & Co.), and it is no exaggeration to say that she is one of the most extraordinary girls that ever came out of an ink pot.

The author undoubtedly meant her to be queer, but she is altogether too queer. She was only 11 years old when she reached the house in Prince Edward's Island that was to be her home, but, in spite of her tender years, and in spite of the fact that, excepting for four months spent in the asylum, she had passed all her life with illiterate folks, and had had almost no schooling, she talked to the farmer and his sister as though she had borrowed Bernard Shaw's vocabulary, Alfred Austin's sentimentality, and the reasoning powers of a Justice of the Supreme Court. She knew so much that she spoiled the author's plan at the very outset and greatly marred a story that had in it quaint and charming possibilities.

The author's probable intention was to exhibit a unique development in this little asylum waif, but there is no real difference between the girl at the end of the story and the one at the beginning of it. All the other characters in the book are human enough.

---

† From *New York Times Book Review* 18 July 1908: 404. In its 150th anniversary number, the *New York Times Book Review* included an excerpt from this review in a column headed "Oops!" The column listed several major reviews that were later proved wrong.

# *GLOBE*

## [Sunshine and Shadow] (1908)†

The craze for problem novels has at present seized a large section of the reading public, and it must be confessed that several recent stories have not been healthy reading, and can serve no useful purpose that we can see. In these days of unhealthy literature it is, however, a real pleasure to come across a story so pure and sweet as "Anne of Green Gables," by L. M. Montgomery, from the press of Messrs. L. C. Page & Co., of Boston, Mass. There are no pretensions to a great plot in the story, but from the first line to the last the reader is fascinated by the sayings and doings of the girl child taken from a Nova Scotia home, adopted by the old Scotch maid and bachelor, brother and sister, who owned Green Gables, a Prince Edward Island farm, situated in one of the garden spots of the beautiful Island Province in the St. Lawrence Gulf.

The quaintness of the child, the funny scene when the old bachelor brother finds a girl waiting at the station for him, and not a boy, as ordered from the home, are pictured in irresistible drollery. Then the reader's interest is evoked as the author pictures how the poorly-trained and often hitherto harshly-treated little maiden develops into womanhood, under the strict yet kindly training of the strange couple who loved her so dearly, and who, Scotch like, could not find words to give utterance to that love. * * * "Anne of Green Gables" is worth a thousand of the problem stories with which the bookshelves are crowded today, and we venture the opinion that this simple story of rural life in Canada will be read and re-read when many of the more pretentious stories are all forgotten. There is not a dull page in the whole volume, and the comedy and tragedy are so deftly woven together that it is at times difficult to divide them. The story is told by an author who knows the Island of Prince Edward thoroughly, and who has carefully observed the human tide which flows through that Island, as it does over all places where human beings live. With the pen of an artiste she has painted that tide so that its deep tragedies are just lightly revealed, for she evidently prefers to show us the placid flow, with its steadiness, its sweetness, and witchery, until

† "Anne of Green Gables, by L. M. Montgomery," *The Globe* (Toronto) 15 Aug. 1908: F7. In a letter to Ephraim Weber, LMM also cited the following journals as having published reviews in 1908: "Phila. *Inquirer*, Montreal *Herald*, Boston *Transcript*, St. John *Globe*, Pittsburgh *Chronicle*, Boston *Herald*, Detroit *Saturday Night*, Montreal *Star*, Chicago *Record Herald*, Milwaukee *Free Press*, N.Y. *American*, Phila. *North American*, Brooklyn *Times*, N.Y. *Times*, N.Y. *World*, *The Outlook*, Buffalo *News*, Boston *Budget*, Chicago *Inter-Ocean*." (*Green Gables Letters*, 114–16). Other 1908 reviews appeared, among other places, in *American Library Association Booklist*, *The Bookman: A Magazine of Literature and Life*, *The Canadian Magazine*, and *The Nation*.

the reader stands still to watch the play of sunshine and shadow as it is deftly pictured by the hand of the author of "Anne of Green Gables".

# SPECTATOR

## [Winning Our Sympathies] (1908)†

We can pay the author of *Anne of Green Gables* no higher compliment than to say she has given us a perfect Canadian companion picture to *Rebecca of Sunnybrook Farm*. There is no question of imitation or borrowing; it is merely that the scheme is similar and the spirit akin. To all novel-readers weary of problems, the duel of sex, broken Commandments, and gratuitous suicides, Miss Montgomery provides an alternative entertainment, all the more welcome because what we get in place of those hackneyed features is at once wholesome and attractive. As for Prince Edward Island, in which the scene is laid, no better advertisement of the charm of its landscape could be devised than the admirable descriptions of its sylvan glories which lend decorative relief to the narrative. Miss Montgomery has not merely succeeded in winning our sympathies for her *dramatis personae*; she makes us fall in love with their surroundings, and long to visit the Lake of Shining Waters, the White Way of Delight, Idlewild, and other favourite resorts of 'the Anne-girl.'

The mechanism of the plot is simple enough. An elderly farmer and his unmarried sister decide to adopt an orphan boy and bring him up to assist them on the farm; but owing to a blunder on the part of an intermediary, a girl, and not a boy, is sent from the asylum in Nova Scotia. Anne Shirley, an 'outspoken morsel of neglected humanity,' with a riotous imagination, a genius for 'pretending,' a passionate love of beauty, and a boundless flow of words, bursts like a bombshell on the inarticulate farmer and his dour, honest, undemonstrative sister. But the law of extremes prevails. Matthew succumbs on the spot, and after a short space Anne casts her spell over Marilla as well, for in three weeks that excellent dragon admitted to her brother that it seemed as if Anne had always been with them.* * *

The process of Anne's education both at home and at school is chequered and dramatic, and the way in which this little lump of human quicksilver and her grim but just mistress act and react on

---

† From "Anne of Green Gables, by L. M. Montgomery," *The Spectator* (London) 13 March 1909: 426–27.

each other is brought out by scores of happy touches and diverting incidents. Anne is a creature of irresistable loquacity when we first meet her, and meeting with kindness and consideration for the first time after years of poverty and neglect, she expands in a way that is at once ludicrous and touching. Perhaps her literary instinct is a little overdone, but otherwise Miss Montgomery shows no disposition to idealise her child heroine.* * *

Miss Montgomery has given us a most enjoyable and delightful book, which, when allowance is made for altered conditions, is in direct lineal descent from the works of Miss Alcott. It needed considerable restraint on her part to leave off where she did without developing the romantic interest hinted at in the last chapter, but the result is so excellent that we trust she will refrain from running the greater risk of writing a sequel. Having sown her wild oats, 'the Anne-girl' could never be so attractive as the little witch, half imp, half angel, whose mental and spiritual growth is vividly set forth in these genial pages.

## DAILY PATRIOT

## [Favourably Received in the Old World] (1909)†

The English *Press* is now reviewing "Anne of Green Gables," by Miss Lucy M. Montgomery, and the reviews, so far as we can note, are without exception, greatly in favour of the story and highly complimentary to the writer. Among the newspapers in which the different reviews appear are the *Publishers' Circulation*, London; the London *Observer*, the Nottingham (England) *Guardian*, the Aberdeen (Scotland) *Press*, the London *Daily News*, the *Western Mail* (London), and the *London World*. The latter says: "It is given to so very few writers to be able to tell so simple a tale as this history of an imaginative, precocious, but lovable little Anne, in such a thoroughly human and interesting fashion. It is a book full of laughter and tears. . . . It speaks well for the genius of the writer that the book has been so favourably received in the Old World."

† From *Daily Patriot* (Charlottetown), 9 March, 1909: 8. In Montgomery Scrapbook, the Red Album, at Confederation Centre, Charlottetown.

## ENGLISH-CANADIAN LITERATURE

## [Sudden Spring to Fame] (1913)†

In the little fertile island province washed by the waters of the Atlantic and inhabited by a people of simple manners and customs, a novelist appeared in the closing years of the nineteenth century who was to make Prince Edward Island, its inhabitants and external nature, known to the world as they never had been before. Lucy Maud Montgomery, at that time a school-teacher in the province, sprang suddenly into fame by her first book, *Anne of Green Gables*. In 1911 Miss Montgomery married the Rev. Ewen McDonald [*sic*], and has since resided in Ontario. *Anne of Green Gables*, published in 1908, took the reading public by storm.* * *

* * *Sympathy with child life and humble life, delight in nature, a penetrating, buoyant imagination, unusual power in handling the simple romantic material that lies about every one, and a style direct and pleasing, make these books delightful reading for children, and, indeed, for readers of all ages.

## HEAD-WATERS OF CANADIAN LITERATURE

## [Just Missed] (1924)‡

* * *Miss Lucy M. Montgomery * * * had strong literary ambitions, and worked long and hard with little or no recognition before she was rewarded with an immense popular success. This was *Anne of Green Gables* (1908). More than three hundred thousand copies were sold within eight years. Mark Twain wrote to a friend: "In Anne Shirley you will find the dearest and most moving and delightful child of fiction since the immortal Alice." The heroine so praised is a little waif adopted by a childless couple in "The Island." Unlike the central figure of the usual child's story, she is not pathetic, or misunderstood, or neglected; nor does she immediately blossom into a genius, with love affairs. She is a good-natured, affectionate, garrulous, imaginative tomboy, who, with the best will in the world, is always getting into innocent scrapes, and ruing the consequences. One

---

† From Thomas Guthrie Marquis, *English-Canadian Literature* (Toronto and Glasgow: Brook, 1913) 564.

‡ From Archibald MacMechan, *Head-Waters of Canadian Literature* (Toronto: McClelland and Stewart, 1924) 209–12. LMM took English courses from Professor MacMechan at Dalhousie University in 1895–96.

striking physical feature is her red hair, an unappreciated beauty, indeed a source of mortification, which aroused the sympathy of "every red-haired girl in the world." Anne would be at home in the household of *Little Women*; Jo March would have understood and appreciated her; but the mention of that classic is rather dangerous.

The Canadian book just misses the kind of success which convinces the critic while it captivates the unreflecting general reader. The story is pervaded with a sense of reality; the pitfalls of the sentimental are deftly avoided; Anne and her friends are healthy human beings; their pranks are engaging; but the "little more" in truth of representation, or deftness of touch, is lacking; and that makes the difference between a clever book and a masterpiece.* * *

# POTEEN

## [Sugary Stories] (1926)†

Lucy M. Montgomery of Prince Edward Island shared the quick popularity of Connor in a series of girls' sugary stories begun with "Anne of Green Gables" (1908). Canadian fiction was to go no lower; and she is only mentioned to show the dearth of mature novels at the time. We have to-day twenty other producers of highly saleable fiction, little of which would get even passing notice in a history of the country's literature.

# PETERBOROUGH EXAMINER

## [Happiness of an Inoffensive Sort] (1942)‡

Nations grow in the eyes of the world less by the work of their statesmen than their artists. Thousands of people all over the globe are hazy about the exact nature of Canada's government and our relation to the British Empire, but they have clear recollections of *Anne of Green Gables*. The simple story, written when the Dominion was much younger than it is now, and much less troubled, was enormously popular in its day and it may still be read with enjoyment.

Stern critics may be dismayed that what is probably the best-known book to come out of Canada should be such a simple and

---

† From William Arthur Deacon, *Poteen: A Pot-Pourri of Canadian Essays* (Ottawa: Graphic, 1926) 169.
‡ From Robertson Davies, obituary comment in *Peterborough Examiner* 2 May 1942: 4.

sentimental work. Admittedly it would have been better if we had produced a *Don Quixote* or a *War and Peace*, but in the world of art we have to be content with what we can get; Canada produced *Anne of Green Gables* and that must suffice us for a while. The book has great charm, and is somewhat reminiscent of the work of Louisa Alcott. *Anne* never set the world on fire, and launched no crusade, but she gave a great deal of happiness of an inoffensive sort.

Because of the happiness which her book gave[,] Canadians will be sorry to hear of the death of its author, L. M. Montgomery, who in private life was Mrs. Ewan Macdonald, on the 24th of last month, in Toronto. Apart from her writing, she performed the many duties of a clergyman's wife with dignity and true kindness, and by her death Canada loses a most valuable and beloved citizen.

# Modern Critical Views

## NORTHROP FRYE

### The Pastoral Myth[†]

At the heart of all social mythology lies what may be called, because it usually is called, a pastoral myth, the vision of a social ideal. The pastoral myth in its most common form is associated with childhood, or with some earlier social condition—pioneer life, the small town, the *habitant* rooted to his land—that can be identified with childhood. The nostalgia for a world of peace and protection, with a spontaneous response to the nature around it, with a leisure and composure not to be found today, is particularly strong in Canada. It is overpowering in our popular literature, from *Anne of Green Gables* to Leacock's Mariposa.[1]* * *

## ELIZABETH R. EPPERLY

### Romancing the Voice: *Anne of Green Gables*[‡]

*     *     *

The delightful, young Anne Shirley is a self with a most distinctive voice; in fact, the whole of *Anne of Green Gables* is charged with the rhythm and energy of Anne's voice and personality. Anne's determined romanticism enriches her own spoken language and informs/

---

[†] From "Conclusion," *Literary History of Canada: Canadian Literature in English*, ed. C. F. Klinck, 840. Copyright © 1965 University of Toronto Press Inc.

[1.] The "little town" in Stephen Leacock, *Sunshine Sketches of a Little Town* (London: John Lane, The Bodley Head, 1912; New York: W. W. Norton and Company, 2006).

[‡] From *The Fragrance of Sweet-Grass: L. M. Montgomery's Heroines and the Pursuit of Romance*. Copyright © 1992 University of Toronto Press Inc. Reprinted by permission of the publisher. Footnotes have been renumbered and edited with permission of the author [*Editors*].

complements the narrator's nature descriptions. Appropriately, important events in beauty-loving Anne's life are marked by nature descriptions that reflect her own rapture over her surroundings. We become a part of the world of Avonlea as the powerfully imaginative Anne sees and loves it. Seeing with Anne's eyes and hearing her voice, we too are heroines as we read the novel.

But before we hear Anne, we hear the narrator, and the narrator prepares us for Anne's energy and also for the quality of world Anne will herself intensify, explore, and join. In the very first sentence of the novel, the narrator, supposedly describing Mrs. Lynde and the course of a brook in Avonlea, invites us to engage with Avonlea life. The brook has personality and conscious will—and knows how to regulate its rushing and murmuring to evade the community busy-body, Rachel Lynde. Montgomery pairs up nature and human emotions so that we take sides: it's the brook against Rachel Lynde, just as it will soon be Anne Shirley against unimaginativeness. Even before we meet Anne, we too have experienced how the guardians of Avonlea expect conformity and quiet from Avonlea inhabitants—be they brooks or people—and we suspect that defying such vigilance will be great fun. As we accept the restraint and the secrets of the brook, we are really entering into a complex arrangement between reading about and participating in Anne's story. Look at how Montgomery encourages the reader to respond to (at least) four different positions in reading the first sentence of *Anne of Green Gables*.[1]

The energetic one-hundred-and-forty-eight-word-long sentence, divided by three semi-colons, involves several viewpoints and sets of values: (1) Rachel Lynde and her demand for propriety and knowledge, (2) the brook's secret, free, and then regulated movements and its consciousness of Mrs. Rachel's vigilance, (3) the narrator's view of Mrs. Rachel's demands on the brook and inhabitants of Avonlea and the brook's and inhabitants' apparent conformity, (4) the reader's invited understanding of Mrs. Rachel's vigilance, the brook's apparent conformity, and the narrator's amusement over Mrs. Rachel, the brook, and the inhabitants who conform with or defy Mrs. Rachel Lynde. Thus in one loaded, laughing sentence Montgomery's narrator introduces the expectations of the Avonlea establishment and at the same time suggests both the delight of rebelling against such conformity and the satisfaction of living in a community where conformity and independence have places and seasons.

This very first sentence, with its introduction of different points of view, is itself a lengthy imitation of the twists of the road and stream it describes and also a mimicry of Rachel Lynde's relentless

---

1. Elizabeth Epperly here quotes the long first sentence of *AGG* in full. Since the present volume contains the full text of the novel, page references to this Norton Critical Edition of *AGG* are used here and throughout the article to replace such direct quotations.

questionings and vigilance. More than half the sentence pretends to be about the brook that runs by Mrs. Lynde's place, but is also a comic imitation of Mrs. Lynde's projected self-image: she believes that all in Avonlea should behave—in front of her at least—with "decency and decorum," whatever they may do beyond her ken. Much of the first chapter of the novel plays with Mrs. Lynde's way of thinking. The narrator and Mrs. Lynde even use some of the same words, as though the narrator's imitation of Mrs. Lynde's mental rhythms is almost identical with Mrs. Lynde's own speech. Notice, for example, how the phrase "to be sure" is used in a summary of Mrs. Lynde's thoughts (given by the narrator) and then repeated in Mrs. Lynde's own words (9). This kind of echoing between the narrator and a character invites the reader to hear in the narrator's words an extension of the character's thoughts.

A blurring of the borders between imitation and commentary here in chapter one with Mrs. Lynde encourages the reader, in chapter two, to recognize Anne's perspective in the narrator's poetic interpretations of sky and landscape. The narrator continues throughout the novel to use playful echoes between commentary and speech with characters other than Anne. With Anne, the fun is of a different kind, and the imitations of Anne's thinking are the serious, poetic descriptions of nature. Any fun the narrator wants to have with Anne is done with direct comment, ironic interjection, or comic chronicle—any imitation of Anne's tone of mind is offered as seriously as Anne would want herself to be taken (and, by obvious extension, as Anne's participant-readers would also want to be taken). In other words, every role the narrator plays in the novel enhances the focus on Anne and appreciation of her; other characters may be mimicked comically, but Anne belongs either with serious poetry or with straightforward comedy where she is an actor.

Apart from the comic tension the narrator establishes between vigilance and rebellion in the initial sentence of the novel, we also know from the opening descriptive phrases that the "eye" of the story is an appreciator of beauty. The road "dipped" into a "hollow, fringed with alders and ladies' eardrops"; back in the woods we imagine the brook's "dark secrets of pool and cascade." Clearly the narrator of the story will note the beauties of nature while sharing with the reader the comic struggles between those who would regulate behavior and those who would be free.

Before Anne is introduced, in chapter two, the narrator treats us to two apparently fanciful descriptions of nature. In both, the narrator is describing the pleasures of the June day, [i]n Mrs. Lynde's kitchen [and o]n Matthew's trip to Bright River (8, 14). The "bridal flush" of the orchard, the "snug" farms, the hollows where wild plums shyly "hung out their filmy bloom" all suggest the welcoming personality of the countryside and the season; Anne is due to arrive in a world that is more than ready for her. We will shortly find out that she belongs here—she belongs (as does the reader) because she can see and feel the loveliness around her.

With Anne, the narrator is frequently a careful stage director. It is easiest to appreciate this directing by looking closely at Anne's five confession/apology scenes, ranging from the early fury with Mrs. Lynde, to the last embarrassed thank-you to Gilbert Blythe. In each, the narrator quietly bolsters sympathy with Anne and Anne's voice. When Anne apologizes to Mrs. Lynde, the narrator concentrates on Marilla's dismay and Anne's obvious sincerity. When Anne makes up a story about the amethyst brooch, since Marilla told her she must confess, the narrator does not tell us Anne is innocent—we should have learned to trust Anne already—but the narrator tells us that Anne confesses "as if repeating a lesson she had learned" (84). Anne's apology to Mrs. Barry about accidentally giving Diana currant wine instead of raspberry cordial is a failure, and we judge Mrs. Barry by the narrator's cue: "* * *her anger was of the cold, sullen sort which is hardest to overcome" (108). Miss Josephine Barry capitulates to Anne's charm when Anne apologizes to her, and the narrator describes the change in Miss Barry's eyes. The scene focuses on Anne's speech, but the narrator tells us that Miss Barry's eyes were initially "snapping through her gold-rimmed glasses" (129); then Anne talks, and "Much of the snap had gone" (130). When Anne finishes explaining, "All the snap had gone by this time" (130). The narrator's small touches complement Anne's energetic speeches.

At the very end of the novel, we find the fifth confession. When Anne thanks Gilbert for giving up the Avonlea school for her so that she can board at home with Marilla, she also has to confess that she has long ago forgiven him and was sorry for her earlier stubbornness. The narrator's role here is to suggest Gilbert's delight and Anne's pleasure in becoming friends. The narrator tells us that with "scarlet cheeks" Anne thanks him and extends her hand; "Gilbert took the offered hand eagerly" (243). After Gilbert speaks, "Anne laughed and tried unsuccessfully to withdraw her hand," and the reader sees that instead of being offended by Gilbert's warmth, it prompts Anne to confess: "I've been—I may as well make a complete confession—I've been sorry ever since" (243). The small scene is meant to tie together the last of the novel's threads and prepare the way for a romance between Anne and Gilbert. As the expected culmination of the novel's preoccupation with romance, the scene will work only if the comic rejection of romance used throughout the book is here displaced by the narrator's gentle but insistent revelation of Anne's discomfort and pleasure.

In each of the five confession scenes the narrator describes others' motivations or changes, but Anne's own words are the primary stimulators of reader sympathy. We will probably remember Anne's—not the narrator's—own persuasive, colorful language (64, 82, 109, 130, 243). In the first four of these, when Anne is still a young girl, we hear her self-dramatization in the confession. She pictures herself as the heroine of a glamorized story of her own orphanhood—or as willing to be led to the block for honor and truth. Anne creates herself as the romantic heroine of her own adventures, and the narrator provides the setting and reinforcement for her self-drama.

The narrator helps to orchestrate a book-length, comic deconstruction and reconstruction of romance. While Anne's own notion of romance is carefully deflated or inverted, another form of romance is created from the substance of what is supposed to be real life. The story of Gilbert's interest in Anne and hers in him is the conventional plot-line version of romance. In the book itself this one kind of romance is a far less prominent feature of Anne's discovery of self, and of her sense of home, than is Anne's own exploration of beauty and harmony and her consequent rejection of exaggeration and impossible intensity.

Catherine Sheldrick Ross says that the whole of *Anne of Green Gables* plays with romance and that Montgomery turns Anne's notion of romance on its head while at the same time creating in Avonlea a place every bit as romantic as anything Anne has imagined. Thus while readers laugh at Anne's unreal concept of the romantic and the ideal, they are encouraged to accept the beauties of Avonlea with all the breathlessness and wonder that romance invites. Further, Anne is encouraged to reject the unreal romantic stories she reads, while all the while her own attachment to Gilbert is developing for the reader into a species of romance. Ross sees Montgomery's novel as a very sophisticated handling of genre and an inversion and restoration of genre.[2]

Certainly what Ross describes can be heard in Anne's own voice and seen in the nature descriptions that we are encouraged to believe are often offered from Anne's perspective. Anne creates herself the heroine of a romance she discovers to be false, while the reader sees Anne as a genuine heroine of a romantic world that the book conspires to make us believe is real. Anne's imagination may need curbing, but Anne's perception of and joy in her surroundings is romantic enough for any of Anne's readers. Prince Edward Island itself is a part of Anne's identity, the bedrock of her love of home, and the romance surrounding its beauties is powerful enough to make the passages describing them stand apart from and yet related to Anne's

2. Catherine Sheldrick Ross, "Calling Back the Ghost of the Old-Time Heroine: Duncan, Montgomery, Atwood, Laurence, and Munro," *Studies in Canadian Literature* 4.1 (1979): 43–58.

most ingenious and delightful speeches. Montgomery's/Anne's/the narrator's love affair with Prince Edward Island is what counterbalances Anne's self-conscious speeches and what offers us hope that even a mature Anne, who has dropped the endearing verbal eccentricities of her childhood, will have a loving vitality great enough to sustain continued reading about her.

Anne's own words show us how thoroughly romantic she is, how she has been shaped by early reading of sentimental and chivalric poems and stories. Her very first words to Matthew, on the Bright River platform, show how she has learned to imagine herself as the heroine of her own continuing private fiction, created to counteract the dullness or harshness of the real world around (16). * * * [T]he image and the picturing of herself in a romantic setting is clearly what has sustained the orphan Anne Shirley in her neglected eleven years. She tells Matthew that she spent time in the orphanage creating stories for her otherwise dismal life: "It *was* pretty interesting to imagine things about them—to imagine that perhaps the girl who sat next to you was really the daughter of a belted earl, who had been stolen away from her parents in her infancy by a cruel nurse who died before she could confess" (17). We recognize in this hackneyed plot a host of popular (and often inferior) romances and Gothic tales of the kind Henry Fielding parodies with such zest in *Joseph Andrews*. Anne has been reading romances and has learned their addictive appeal: creating yourself the heroine makes all the adventures your own.[3]

Anne continues to tell herself stories about her surroundings, even insisting on giving human names to plants and places since they, too, have personalities and parts in her ceaseless internal drama. (Certainly the personification in Montgomery's opening sentence and in the nature descriptions seems a ready-made part of Anne's drama.) Though she is enraptured with the real surroundings of Avonlea, Anne feels that the predictability of life in general could still use help from her romantic story-telling and retelling. She acknowledges on her first morning at Green Gables, when she thinks she will have to return to the orphanage, that romances don't exactly square with life and are not really preferable to it.

Nevertheless, once established at Green Gables, she continues to embroider life with romance, and usually comes to grief in the process. She imagines herself a raven-haired beauty, and dyes her hair—green, by accident; she pictures herself a nun, romantically renouncing life and taking the veil, and forgets to cover the pudding sauce so that a mouse drowns in it; she imagines herself dishonored in

---

3. See Rachel M. Brownstein, *Becoming a Heroine: Reading about Women in Novels* (London: Penguin, 1984).

front of Josie Pye, accepts a dare to walk the ridge-pole of the Barry kitchen, falls, and breaks her ankle. Even her separation from Diana, whom Mrs. Barry believes Anne has made drunk deliberately, is turned into a romantic and "tragical" beauty: " 'Fare thee well, my beloved friend. Henceforth we must be as strangers though living side by side* * *' " (111). When a distraught Diana comes to Anne to rescue her baby sister from an attack of croup, Anne, who shows great practicality in remembering to take the ipecac with her, is actually transported by excitement (118). A sense of chivalric bravery uplifts her when she faces Miss Barry and begs her to forgive her for jumping on her in the spare-room bed. And, as we have seen, it is this bravery and Anne's quaint phraseology that win Miss Barry's heart, just as sincere melodrama had won Mrs. Lynde's earlier when Anne apologized to her for losing her temper.

Anne's imagination seriously betrays her twice, and as a result of these two incidents, she recognizes a need to change her attitude to romance, though she is not sure until later what such a change will mean. Anne gets carried away imagining gruesome creatures, and the innocent spruce grove becomes the sinister Haunted Wood with a vengeance. When an unsympathetic Marilla makes Anne walk through the wood in the dark, Anne learns that she must constrain her imagination. Nevertheless, we find that Anne's reading continues to feed her morbid fancies, until Miss Stacy makes her promise to give up Gothic horror. Nearly eighty pages after the Haunted Wood episode, Anne confesses to Marilla: "She found me reading a book one day called, 'The Lurid Mystery of the Haunted Hall.' It was one Ruby Gillis had lent me, and, oh, Marilla, it was so fascinating and creepy. It just curdled the blood in my veins. But Miss Stacy said it was a very silly, unwholesome book, and she asked me not to read any more of it or any like it" (194). Obviously Anne has not made the connection between reading material and development of imagination that the reader of Montgomery's book is encouraged to make at every turn in the understanding of Anne.

The second episode in which Anne's imagination betrays her—indeed, threatens her very life—is with the game based on Tennyson's "Lancelot and Elaine," a book in the epic-length Arthurian poem *Idylls of the King*.[4] Anne and her friends have studied Tennyson's romantic poem in school, and it is certainly a perfect example of the blighted-love and pure-sacrifice story Anne's childhood reading and imagining have prepared her to embrace. Montgomery's use of the poem is a brilliant stroke in the novel. When Elaine/Anne's barge/dory springs a leak, Anne is truly in need of rescue, and, as life

---

4. Montgomery used Tennyson's poem "Lancelot and Elaine" as a central device in a 1901 short story about a suicide, "The Waking of Helen," *Along the Shore* (Toronto: McClelland & Stewart, 1989) 243–53.

would have it, the boy to do this knightly deed is none other than Gilbert Blythe for whom Anne has sworn eternal enmity. In this one comic inversion of romance, Tennyson's idealized story is overthrown and the prosaic Gilbert rescues Anne in his father's dory.[5] Quick to see romance almost anywhere but in Avonlea, and certainly not with Gilbert as the hero, Anne scorns Gilbert's attempt at reconciliation. With truly queenly dignity she rejects him—and thus Montgomery brings into clash the imagined romance of the story with the real-life romance of Gilbert's timely rescue and eager appeal. A sucker for book romance (and natural beauty), Anne cannot recognize a new kind of romance behind school rivalry or even behind friendship and camaraderie. (Interestingly, Anne dotes on the pathetic Elaine, who can only choose to die when Lancelot will not love her, and yet finds satisfaction in her own powers to reject a potential suitor.)

The nearly fatal imitation of Tennyson reminds us how thoroughly Anne has been indoctrinated by literary romances. The scanty catalogue of her early childhood reading suggests the quality of contrivance, exaggeration, and idealization Anne has revered. She has been tutored in heroic battle and in (hopeless) loves. * * * Anne early tells Marilla, "I read in a book once that a rose by any other name would smell as sweet" (38) and does not realize she is quoting from Shakespeare, evidently lumping *Romeo and Juliet* together with many other tragic love stories. Anne's early speeches especially are liberally sprinkled with archaisms, romantic clichés, or quaint turns of phrase ("depths of despair" [28], "My life is a perfect graveyard of buried hopes" [37]), and we learn to recognize in her outlandish sentences ("I am well in body although considerably rumpled up in spirit, thank you, ma'am" [74]) products of a romance-fed imagination and an instinctive ear for poetry. It is this instinct for the grand or beautiful turn of phrase, after all, that makes so effective the combination of Anne's perspective and the narrator's words.

But Anne gradually outgrows the odd language and self-dramatization, even if she has more trouble reconciling herself to a world shorn of its earlier romantic glory. Anne grows to value the beauty around her and understands better than Diana why Avonlea is preferable to Charlottetown, or why an artificial romance is inferior to consciousness of belonging to a world of solid values and lasting but humble pleasures. When Miss Barry asks Anne which place she would prefer, the city or the country, Anne thoughtfully replies: "It's nice to be eating ice-cream at brilliant restaurants at eleven o'clock at night once in awhile; but as a regular thing I'd rather be in the east gable at eleven, sound asleep, but kind of knowing

5. See Ross 46–48.

even in my sleep that the stars were shining outside and that the wind was blowing in the firs across the brook" (189–90). Having learned the true romance of nature and belonging, Anne is almost ready to give up the artificial speech that before separated her from an uncaring environment. Miss Barry herself notices a change in her own response to Anne's spirit (190).

Everything in the novel conspires to make us hear Anne's voice and to understand her point of view. We watch her as she has "pruned down and branched out" (220), and we come to identify her with the broader, thoughtful view of the narrator's descriptions, just as we hear in their poetry her rapture with beauty. Anne's self-deluding reliance on romantic stories may have to give way, but Anne's love of beauty will be a lifelong romance Montgomery constantly supports.[6]

Montgomery's nature descriptions are full of poetry. She uses the conventions of poetry—appeal to the senses, personification, simile, metaphor—and chooses her words with the intention of transporting the reader both into and beyond the elements she describes. As in her poems, in the prose-poetry Montgomery favors flowers both as subjects and for comparison (skies of crocus or saffron or rose or marigold or violet); she delights in precious stones, metals, or wood largely for their color and shine (crystal, pearl, diamond, emerald, sapphire, amethyst, ruby, gold, silver, ebony); she loves brilliant colors of all kinds (particularly scarlet and yellow) and especially enjoys the qualifiers "misty" "filmy" "ethereal" in front of colors (notably purple and green); she has a passion for sunsets and twilight just after sunset. Despite the obvious preoccupation with color, Montgomery's descriptions also appeal to touch and hearing and taste and smell—the "satin-smooth roads with the snow crisping under the runners" (126), the spicy scent of ferns, the fragrance of trampled mint, and the tang of the sea are never far away. Montgomery celebrates the four seasons, the wind in the leaves and boughs of trees, sunshine, shadow, starlight, moonlight. The sea does not play a prominent part in the descriptions, and there is probably more emphasis on sky than on earth; on flowers and trees than on fields.

What characterizes all the descriptions is their humanness, their invitation to participate in a kind of communion. The descriptive passages are not just vivid ornaments to the narrative, but are instead expressions of attitude, indexes of the observers' ability to join the spirit of love and the pursuit of beauty that characterize Anne's quest for identity and home. The humanness of the descriptions is evident not only in personification (as we saw in the opening sentence of the

6. Note that, in explaining the appeal of the "green-world archetype," Annis Pratt says, "nature for the young hero remains a refuge throughout life." *Archetypal Patterns in Women's Fiction* (Bloomington: Indiana UP, 1981) 17.

novel), but in the tenderness of appreciation (young ferns are not just young ferns, but are "little curly ferns" [132] struggling to grow). Enjoying the descriptions involves accepting or at least entertaining a way of being in relationship to the world around. And when we realize that three-quarters of the novel's nature descriptions (by my count, twenty-six out of thirty-five descriptions) are offered as though through Anne's eyes, we see that Montgomery was using poetry as a means to initiate the reader into a way of seeing the world, to express Anne's delight in beauty, to suggest the hidden possibilities for seeing and feeling in the most commonplace of things, to celebrate the feeling of "coming home" that a communion with beauty offers to all who share in it, and to punctuate Anne's story with appropriate reminders of her spirit's capabilities and growth.

Shortly after Anne is introduced and we hear her nimble imagination startling the shy Matthew with insight and story, we find the narrator's words and Anne's point of view joined together. Anne is staggered by the blossom-embowered lane she later names the White Way of Delight, and the narrator provides a description of what Anne's otherwise undaunted tongue cannot utter. Mid-sentence Anne breaks off and the narrator takes over: " '—oh, Mr. Cuthbert! Oh, Mr. Cuthbert!! Oh, Mr. Cuthbert!!!' . . . Overhead was one long canopy of snowy fragrant bloom. Below the boughs the air was full of a purple twilight and far ahead a glimpse of painted sunset sky shone like a great rose window at the end of a cathedral aisle. Its beauty seemed to strike the child dumb" (20–21). We find that for the rest of the book, when the narrator describes the beauty of nature, Anne is usually looking at it, and we are thus encouraged to read the words as though they capture her feelings. In those few times when Anne is not present, we still hear (or are free to hear) Anne's quality of mind, for the narrator and Anne share the same spirit.

Within four pages of Anne's rapture over the White Way of Delight, the narrator reinforces this identification between Anne's mind and narrative words. She has just confessed to Matthew a "pleasant ache . . . just to think of coming to a really truly home" (22) when she looks out over Barry's Pond. Anne calls it "pretty," and then the narrator launches into a description that is quintessential Montgomery—full of color, personification, metaphor, and simile (22). This rhapsody of light, color, and sound is the poetic wish-fulfillment of the beauty-starved, love-starved orphan. It is also an invitation to the reader to "come home," as well. In responding to the images, as Anne responds to the scene itself, we participate in the lush beauty of "home," a place where the commonplace is revealed to be compounded of the richest colors and the miracle of sentient trees and houses. The elements of the place belong together, interact in harmony with each other, and the charm Montgomery offers her readers—through the narrator and Anne—is that we, too, belong whenever we can see and feel the power of this beauty.

In the narrator's description of Barry's Pond, we feel the human-ness of the landscape (wild plums "tip-toeing" to their own reflec-tions; a house "peering around a white apple orchard'), and on the very next page, Anne says to Matthew about the Lake of Shining Waters: "I always say good night to the things I love, just as I would to people. I think they like it. That water looks as if it was smiling at me" (23). We are encouraged to believe that the girl who considers the feelings of water would be the one to imagine wild plum trees looking at their own reflections. The joining of Anne's fancy and the narrator's fanciful descriptions is completed within a few pages of our introduction to Anne.

Interestingly, the narrator's romanticizing of the general landscape translates into very specific appreciations of Anne Shirley and Prince Edward Island. Montgomery's generic elements—sand, trees, water, lights—seem to be special because they are on Prince Edward Island, not simply because they are beautiful in themselves and can be appreciated elsewhere in the world. After all, Anne herself has come "from away" (as local P.E.I. dialect dubs it) to this place; she was starved for beauty when she was not on P.E.I. Evidently, the whole novel conspires to convey, Prince Edward Island is an enchanted place where orphans suddenly find the home they have longed for and beauty and magic fairly leap from the sky and earth and sea. Children of all ages have long loved islands, and Montgomery gives us an island that is geographically undeniable and is at the same time almost incredibly, exquisitely lovely. The mixture of magic and fact is personified in Anne herself—we can believe in Anne the girl with the vivid imagination and heightened awareness because Anne is also prone to mishap and full of temper. In other words, Mont-gomery's use of a real place, P.E.I., helps us to believe in the beauty of it, just as Anne's normal problems and conflicts help us to believe in the powers of her imagination. Eventually, with the constant rein-forcement of the identification of narrator and Anne, we identify Anne herself with Prince Edward Island and with all the enchant-ment of its moods and features.

The novel's thirty-odd other descriptive passages broaden our view of Prince Edward Island and enrich our understanding of Anne. And even when the narrator speaks about Anne and not as though (partly) through her eyes, the scene described merely confirms our faith in what Anne sees. For example, when the narrator describes the Birch Path that Diana and Anne use to walk to school, we know that though Anne is not looking at it at this particular moment, she has seen all of what the narrator is describing (89). The humanness, the metaphor using emerald and diamond, the joyous luxuriance of the very plants and trees, all work together to affirm our view of Anne as the incarnation of and the interpreter within a fecund and benign natural world. Anne's energy is reflected in and is charged by nature even when Anne is not there.

Montgomery also uses the nature descriptions to mark events in Anne's life. Montgomery's favorite image in the novel is sunset; splendid sunsets celebrate or herald changes. Elizabeth Waterston and Mary Rubio draw our attention to the first sunset passage (quoted above), where Anne is struck dumb by the beauty of the White Way of Delight; in their analysis, sunsets and roses are bound together in the novel to suggest Anne's transformation and maturity.[7] In all, there are some eleven sunset or just post-sunset descriptions in the novel, and each of these punctuates some important event: the recognition of beauty almost beyond words (mentioned above 21); the first sight of Barry's Pond and the setting for Green Gables (22, 24); after Anne rescues Minnie May and Mrs. Barry relents (121); the celebration of Diana's birthday before the catastrophic jumping on Miss Josephine Barry (126); Anne's triumphant tea with Mrs. Allan, the new minister's wife who is both role model and kindred spirit (146); after Anne's sobering lily-maid episode with Gilbert Blythe and just before Diana tells her they have been invited by Miss Barry to come to Charlottetown for the Exhibition (184); relishing the thought of home after the dissipations of the Exhibition (190); the pass list is out for the examinations (210); just before her recitation at the White Sands Hotel (212); preparing for the final examinations at Queen's (228); at the very end of the novel, just before Anne apologizes to Gilbert (243). In many of Anne's key moments, we are invited to share the intensity of nature with her and to equate beauty with the multiple experiences of being, discovering, and reading.

In each of the sunset-marked experiences Anne learns something about herself and grows. Anne and the descriptions themselves change as Anne's story develops. The quality of poetic images is consistent throughout the novel, but the quality of perspective changes as Anne becomes more mature. Two-thirds of the way through the novel, in the chapter entitled "Where the Brook and River Meet," when Anne is fifteen, we see that the girl Anne has become the young woman. Marilla notices that "You don't chatter half as much as you used to, Anne, nor use half as many big words. What has come over you?" (204). Anne's reply marks the end of the child's most spontaneous and whimsical speeches, and suggests a new conformity and consciousness of restraint (205). After this there is a subtle change in the narrator and an obvious change in Anne. Anne goes off to

---

7. Mary Rubio and Elizabeth Waterston, eds., Afterword to *Anne of Green Gables*, by L. M. Montgomery (New York: Signet Classics, 1987) 312.

Charlottetown to get a teacher's license, and the narrator makes room for more of Anne's own comments on her surroundings. The childhood exuberance is now replaced by more mature (and, alas, far less interesting) comments made to her friends or even to herself. For example, in the sunset scene that includes the penultimate quotation given above, where Anne and her friends are preparing for examinations at Queen's, Anne makes the first observations about the sunset sky and then the narrator kicks in and completes the description, the commentary, and the chapter. Anne says, rather sententiously, to Josie and Jane and Ruby: "Next to trying and winning, the best thing is trying and failing. Girls, don't talk about exams! Look at that arch of pale green sky over those houses and picture to yourselves what it must look like over the purply-dark beechwoods back of Avonlea" (228). The three other girls, understandably, ignore Anne's sky and her abjuration and begin to talk about fashions; but Anne herself, with clasped hands, gazes out the window and the narrator offers the "glorious dome of sunset sky" (228) as what she sees. We have only to think back to the first sunset description to realize how different Anne is now. There the narrator offered the rose window of the cathedral and shortly after described Barry's Pond and the setting for Green Gables; here Anne characterizes the scene in her own words, and the narrator offers a brief, somewhat philosophical postscript. As with the earlier passages, we recognize in the narrator's description Anne's own vision, but now Anne's words are actually echoed by the narrator.

Because of the blurring between Anne's consciousness and the narrator's and also because of this newer development of the echoing of Anne's words by the narrator, it is hard to say who is responsible for a quotation from Tennyson's poem, "The Palace of Art" in the last sunset scene in the novel. Since Anne has been an avid reader of Tennyson, as the lily-maid episode illustrates, she could herself be thinking of Tennyson's phrase when she is admiring the tranquil beauty of the countryside just before she meets up with Gilbert Blythe. But the Tennyson quotation is ironically appropriate to the situation, too, in a way Anne could not possibly have realized—since she did not know she was going to meet Gilbert—and so the irony of the words seems also to be a product of the omniscient narrator's broader view of the significance of Anne's determination to be friends with Gilbert. * * * "[A]ll Avonlea lay before her in a dreamlike afterlight—'a haunt of ancient peace'"* * *(243).

In the context of the passage, and to anyone not familiar with Tennyson's poem, the phrase "a haunt of ancient peace" seems innocently descriptive, and could belong to either Anne or the narrator; troubling to make the distinction between the two points of view would seem like hair-splitting. And, indeed, perhaps Anne and/or the narrator merely liked the phrase out of its context and thought of it where its words, not irony, suited. But to ignore the original context of Tennyson's phrase makes no more sense here than it does in Anne's final quotation of the novel (only one page later) "God's in his heaven, all's right with the world" (245). This final line is from Browning's verse drama *Pippa Passes*, which Anne would surely have read in its entirety. In it the young factory girl Pippa, unaware that there is a plot afoot to abduct her on this one day's holiday and sell her into prostitution in Rome, passes through the streets of the village of Asolo, singing about love and kindness and, ironically, working against evil simply by being so cheerful and innocent herself. The line is often quoted as though it is a purely ecstatic expression of well-being—and it is—but it is meant to be appreciated in the context of the danger around the unsuspecting Pippa. The line is a reminder to readers and to those who hear Pippa within the poem that good may be powerful, but it is constantly threatened by evil. To those who know Browning's poem (as Montgomery did) and his complex suggestions, Anne's quotation expresses Anne's determination as well as her happiness. Anne is choosing to believe in harmony and joy, not just chirruping over a pretty evening. A knowledge of the original work enriches our understanding of Anne's spirit.[8] And so it is here, too, with Tennyson's phrase from the allegorical debate "The Palace of Art." In this early poem, Tennyson shows the futility of art's trying to live separate from people, from human life. At the outset of the poem the artist determines to build a palace high on a crag, to be the dwelling place of his soul (called "she"). Each room is furnished for a different mood, and each mood suggests some place on the earth—among others, a rock-bound coast with violent waves, a broad moonlit sandshore where a solitary figure walks, "And one, an English home—gray twilight poured / On dewy pastures, dewy trees, / Softer than sleep—all things in order stored, / A haunt of ancient Peace."[9]

Tennyson's lines suggest the quality of peace and tranquillity Anne has just been experiencing by Matthew's grave and in the mellow afterglow of the sunset. But Anne is not meant to live forever in appreciation of scenery and tranquillity alone; she is destined to interact with many others, and most intimately with Gilbert Blythe. In the poem, the palace of art becomes a prison, and the soul eventually is horrified by the isolation and self-centeredness she before thought to be contented seclusion. The soul "shrieked" in her agony and later fled down to a "cottage in the vale" where she could learn

8. For helpful insight into the powers of literary allusion, see Ziva Ben-Porat, "The Poetics of Literary Allusion," *PTL: A Journal for Descriptive Poetics and Theory of Literature* 1 (1976): 105–28 and also Carmela Perri, "On Alluding," *Poetics* 7 (1978): 289–307.
9. "The Palace of Art," *Poems, Chiefly Lyrical* (1830) 85–88.

to live with others. Similarly, Anne decides that enmity against Gilbert Blythe has separated her from a richer, fuller life. When, a few moments later, she meets him on the hill, she extends her hand in friendship and puts behind her forever a mistaken loftiness and self-sufficiency.

Knowing the context for Tennyson's line, as Montgomery did, suggests a subtle and ironic depth to the choice of it in this description of twilight. Whether it is the narrator's or Anne's there is irony involved—though not quite the same irony—and either way Montgomery's choice of the phrase offers a wonderful subtextual commentary on the pastoral serenity of Avonlea life and on Anne's preference for a peopled rather than a peopleless landscape. Sadly, of course, there is the further (unconscious?) suggestion that Anne has indeed forsaken the palace of art when she accepts Gilbert's friendship. Perhaps the covert suggestion is that in deciding to explore a friendship with Gilbert, Anne has chosen to live in a conventional emotional and intellectual "cottage" when her nature has fitted her for variety and experiment on a far more splendid scale. Tennyson's soul's dilemma is very like the dilemma of the intelligent and artistic woman of Montgomery's own time (his choice of female gender for the soul has never seemed accidental). But, of course, this subversive subtext is well below the surface, and what most obviously greets the reader with the choice of Tennyson's phrase is a pleasant consciousness of a lovely line used to grace a lovely scene.

The Tennyson quotation and the Browning one are, at least superficially, consistent with Anne's language throughout the novel. Their unexamined use might also be consistent with Anne's earlier love of romance and could suggest that the narrator and Montgomery are using Anne's uncritical identification with the poems to comment ironically on the incompleteness of Anne's self-knowledge. In any case, as with the sunset passages, these late allusions remind us to reconsider the novel's revaluing of romance.

Romanticized nature and romantic allusions are parts of Anne's identity, self-discovery, and love of home and of the novel's overall preoccupation with romance. Anne's own language, after all, is shown from the first to be saturated with romance. Free though the young Anne's imagination seems to be, it is actually constrained by the expectations of romance, honor, and chivalry. And yet the older, supposedly wiser Anne is probably equally constrained by a different kind of romance. In giving up ecstatic identification with Tennyson's Elaine and the other romantic poems and stories of her childhood and adapting to "real" male-female relations, Anne may merely be conforming to a romanticized stereotype of her times. Anne's quieting down, two-thirds of the way through the book, suggests her tentative leanings towards the stereotypical image of womanhood that favors reserve, tolerance, self-sacrifice, domesticity, and dreamy-eyed abstraction. A reader of [today] may well wonder if Anne puts aside her early love of romance fiction only to take on a fiction her culture creates, one that includes rigid gender roles and the promise of happily-ever-after family life.[1] In thinking about Anne's early self-dramatizations and Montgomery's later imposition of a conventionally romantic ending on Anne's story, we may uncover in the text and in ourselves startling assumptions about love and roles and alternatives. We may come to recognize Anne's dilemma as a useful warning against any form of romance that sentimentalizes, restrains, diminishes, or subordinates.

The conventional, audience-pleasing end of *Anne of Green Gables* suggests that the way has now been cleared for Anne to get on with the real romance—the loving of Gilbert. Yet while Montgomery may even have believed such a union to be good, she did not let Anne succumb to all the conventions and stereotypes at once. We read through two more novels—six years of Anne's life—before Anne recognizes her love for Gilbert. Anne goes to college and graduates and then, faced with Gilbert's possible death, realizes her love for him. Anne does not instantly swap the old tortured, chivalric romance ideal for the equally prescriptive romance of love and marriage, nor does she immediately bury her identity in Gilbert's. That immolation comes, but Montgomery delays it for as long as she can.

And perhaps the love story was inevitable, as was the eventual marriage and possibly the disappearance of Anne, considering the time in which and the audience for whom Montgomery wrote.[2] But providing the expected conclusion does not mean Montgomery erased Anne's possibilities at the end of this novel. What Gilbert and perhaps the reader see as romance, Anne still chooses to interpret as friendship. Readers truly "akin to Anne" can choose to imagine that a continuing independence and self-knowledge will take Anne to a happy self-sufficiency.[3] That is, until they read *Anne of Avonlea*.

No matter how we are tempted to read beyond the ending of *Anne of Green Gables*, what we do find in the book itself is an undeniably

---

1. Annis Pratt says of women: "Our quests for being are thwarted on every side by what we are told to be and to do, which is different from what men are told to be and to do: when we seek an identity based on human personhood rather than on gender, we stumble about in a landscape whose signposts indicate retreats from, rather than ways to, adulthood" (6).

2. For a comparison of Montgomery with some other leading writers from whom she learned, see T. D. MacLulich, "L. M. Montgomery and the Literary Heroine: Jo, Rebecca, Anne, and Emily," *CCL: Canadian Children's Literature* 37 (1985): 5–17.

3. See chapter six of Janice Radway's *Reading the Romance: Women, Patriarchy and Popular Literature* (Chapel Hill: U of North Carolina P, 1984) 186–208. At the end of the chapter we find this chilling reminder of closure: "even as the narrative conveys its overt message that all women are different and their destinies fundamentally open, the romance also reveals that such differences are illusory and short-lived because they are submerged or sacrificed inevitably to the demands of that necessary and always identical romantic ending" (208).

"real" girl and young woman whose speech and thoughts encourage us to reexamine, even yet, our public and private voices and values, and our complex involvements with romance.

## MARAH GUBAR

### The Pleasures of Postponement†

\*   \*   \*

\*  \* \*In *Anne of Green Gables* and its sequels, L. M. Montgomery dramatizes how difficult it is for her female characters to conform their unruly desires to the dictates of the conventional marriage plot. Through her portrayal of numerous "dilatory courtships"[1]— including the romance that finally flowers between Anne and Gilbert—and her ingenious manipulation of the series format, Montgomery demonstrates the enormous expenditure of time and effort necessary to bring about "The End" embodied by heterosexual union. At the same time, she indicates that these lengthy delays make room for passionate relationships between women that prove far more romantic than traditional marriages.

\*   \*   \*

Indeed, the flying leap that lands Anne and Diana in the bed of the crotchety spinster Miss Josephine Barry in *Anne of Green Gables* can be viewed as a metaphor for Anne's whole career; as the series opens, she catapults herself into the quiet life of Marilla Cuthbert (and her retiring brother Matthew) and then proceeds to adopt a slew of female mentors, such as Miss Stacy, her sympathetic schoolteacher, and the equally kind Mrs. Allen, the minister's wife. An impassioned Anne confides to Marilla, " 'I love Miss Stacy with my whole heart,' " and the narrator echoes her enthusiasm in lines like, "With Mrs. Allen Anne fell promptly and whole-heartedly in love" (139).[2] Nevertheless, the ecstatic language employed to describe Anne's adoration for these women pales in comparison to the intensity of affection she bestows on her "bosom friend" and "kindred spirit," Diana Barry. And unlike the halting start that characterizes

---

† From " 'Where Is the Boy?' The Pleasures of Postponement in the *Anne of Green Gables* Series," *The Lion and the Unicorn* 25.1 (2001): 47–69. Copyright © The Johns Hopkins University Press. Reprinted with permission of the Johns Hopkins University Press. Footnotes have been renumbered and edited with the author's permission [*Editors*].

1. *Chronicles of Avonlea* (1912; NY: Bantam Books, 1993) 2.

2. Gubar quotes *AGG* throughout her essay. All page references have been reassigned to match the NCE text [*Editors*].

Anne's rocky acquaintanceship with Gilbert, the first encounter
between Anne and Diana constitutes a case of love at first sight.

With equal force, Anne excludes Gilbert from her circle of friends
and launches herself into Diana's life. Montgomery explains that
"[a]s much as she hated Gilbert, however, did she love Diana, with
all the love of her passionate little heart, equally intense in her likes
and dislikes" (100). At odds with each other before they are even
introduced, Anne and Gilbert quarrel on her first day at school; eager
to initiate contact, he picks up a braid of her hair and whispers,
" 'Carrots! Carrots!,' " leading Anne to break her slate over his head.
In contrast, Anne and Diana share a rapturous first meeting in the
idyllic space of the Barry garden, a "bowery wilderness of flowers.
. . . There were rosy bleeding-hearts and great splendid crimson peonies; white fragrant narcissi and thorny, sweet Scotch roses . . . scarlet lightning that shot its fiery lances over prim, white musk-flowers"
(74–75). While Anne obstinately refuses to sample the "strawberry
apple" Gilbert leaves on her desk as a peace offering, she eagerly
initiates a lover's compact with Diana in this Edenic garden: after
"gazing bashfully at one another," Anne entreats Diana to swear to
be her "bosom friend . . . for ever and ever" (75). The two join hands
and repeat vows in a kind of mock wedding service, in which Anne
functions as both minister and participant, vowing, " 'I solemnly
swear to be faithful to my bosom friend, Diana Barry, as long as the
sun and moon shall endure. Now you say it and put my name in' "
(75). Diana acquiesces to this rather abrupt initiation into intimacy,
following up her "solemn vow and promise" with the words, " 'You're
a queer girl, Anne. I heard before that you were queer. But I believe
I'm going to like you real well' " (75).

In *Odd Girls and Twilight Lovers: A History of Lesbian Life in
Twentieth-Century America*, Lillian Faderman describes the preva-
lence and passion of what she terms "romantic friendships," intimate
relationships between women that remained socially acceptable
throughout the nineteenth and early twentieth century, despite their
potentially subversive nature.[3] In many ways, the love that blossoms
between Anne and Diana resembles the actual affairs Faderman
describes, and their friendship continues to evolve along romantic
lines, even living up to Shakespeare's saying that the course of true
love never did run smooth. Diana's mother quickly assumes the role
of the stern parent who stands in the way of the lovers, attempting
to separate them, and the grounds of her objection metaphorically
indicate the strength of the infatuation shared by Diana and Anne.
Mrs. Barry calls Anne "a thoroughly bad, wicked little girl" and

---

3. Lillian Faderman, *Odd Girls and Twilight Lovers: A History of Lesbian Life in Twentieth-Century America* (NY: Columbia UP, 1991).

refuses to allow Diana to play with her after Anne *intoxicates* Diana, mistakenly serving her currant wine rather than raspberry cordial (107). In keeping with romantic tradition, Mrs. Barry's decree only intensifies the bond between the two girls; as they bid each other farewell, Diana sobs, " 'I couldn't love anybody as I love you.' " Her use of the word "love" thrills Anne and prolongs the scene into a lengthy "romantic parting":

> "Oh, Diana," cried Anne, clasping her hands, "do you *love* me?" . . . "I love you devotedly, Anne," said Diana stanchly, "and I always will, you may be sure of that."
> "And I will always love thee, Diana," said Anne solemnly extending her hand. "In the years that come thy memory will shine like a star over my lonely life, as that last story we read together says. Diana, wilt thou give me a lock of thy jet-black tresses in parting to treasure forever more?" (110)

As Anne's high-flown language and her reference to a shared reading experience demonstrate, she delights in copying the expressive parlance and romantic conventions popular in the sentimental fiction she has read. In general, Montgomery comically deflates her heroine's reliance on such exalted standards. * * * Yet Anne's fantasies about female friendship largely escape this authorial pruning. Where women are concerned, Anne's dreams are almost inevitably fulfilled, attesting to Montgomery's sympathy with her heroine's desire to find sustenance and excitement in relationships with other girls and women.

To begin with, Anne's meeting and subsequent friendship with Diana more than live up to her hopes of finding " 'A bosom friend— an intimate friend, you know—a really kindred spirit to whom I can confide my innermost soul. I've dreamed of meeting her all my life' " (52). Although Diana occasionally disappoints her fanciful friend by responding to various situations with more common sense than imagination, Anne constantly avers that they have loyally and lovingly kept their early vow. In fact, two of the sequels feature a scene in which Anne and Diana explicitly recall " 'the evening we first met . . . and "swore" eternal friendship in [the] garden.' "[4] Each time, Anne affirms that, " 'We've kept that "oath" . . . we've never had a quarrel nor even a coolness.' "[5] The fulfillment of this fantasy of

4. *Anne of Avonlea* (1909; NY: Bantam Books, 1992) 237.
5. *Anne of Ingleside* (1939; NY: Bantam Books, 1992) 12. Temma F. Berg, in "Sisterhood is Fearful: Female Friendship in L. M. Montgomery," 41, brings up the possibility that "the friendship between Anne and Diana might not be as perfect as it seem[s]," an idea she attributes to Mary Rubio, a Montgomery scholar and biographer. However, Berg ultimately concludes that the series presents an extremely idealistic, optimistic picture of female/female friendship. And she goes on to argue that Montgomery's fellow Canadian Margaret Atwood revises and undermines this idyllic vision of girlhood bonding in her disturbing novel *Cat's Eye*.

perfect companionship at an early age leads Anne to imagine many more scenarios starring herself and Diana. For example, as her friend imbibes the infamous currant wine, Anne describes how she has recently composed

> "the loveliest story about you and me, Diana. I thought you were desperately ill with smallpox and everybody deserted you, but I went boldly to your bedside and nursed you back to life; and then I took the smallpox and died and I was buried under those poplar-trees in the graveyard and you planted a rose-bush by my grave and watered it with your tears; and you never, never forgot the friend of your youth who sacrificed her life for you." (104–05)

Minutes after Anne relates this woeful fancy, Diana does indeed become ill, causing her credulous friend to exclaim, " 'Oh, Diana, do you suppose that it's possible you're really taking the smallpox? If you are I'll go and nurse you, you can depend on that' " (106). Of course, Diana is simply drunk, but a few weeks later Anne's dream comes true; Diana's sister Minnie May falls desperately ill with the croup, and "everyone," including her parents and the local doctors, has in fact "deserted" her, by going to a big political meeting thirty miles away just before the onset of her illness. In their absence, Anne does indeed "go boldly to [her] bedside and nurse [her] back to health." As the doctor tells Mrs. Barry afterward, "[t]hat little red-headed girl . . . saved that baby's life," thanks to her experience caring for croupy twins in her previous home (119). Anne does not fall ill herself after this incident, but her heroism leads to the fulfillment of a happier hope: Mrs. Barry relents and allows the girls to resume intimate relations.

Similarly, although Marilla is highly amused when she discovers Anne sobbing as she envisions Diana's eventual wedding day, this schoolgirl fantasy comes to pass. On the day of Diana's marriage, Anne remarks, " 'It's all pretty much as I used to imagine it long ago, when I wept over your inevitable marriage and our consequent parting. . . . You are the bride of my dreams, Diana.' " As the wording of this final line suggests, Anne clings to her cherished fancy for Diana rather than embracing the idea of becoming Gilbert's bride. Shedding a few more "big painful tears" before the wedding, Anne ponders, " 'how horrible it is that people have to grow up—and marry—and change!' "[6] * *

\* \* \*

\* \* \*Indeed, rather than portraying Anne's love for Gilbert as an unforced, natural flowering of feeling, Montgomery characterizes

6. *Anne of the Island* (1915; NY: Bantam Books, 1992) 179.

their relationship as the hard-won product of an extremely painful process. Even their engagement does not complete the job: at the end of *Anne of the Island*, Gilbert informs Anne that their wedding must be delayed until he finishes a three year medical course. By concentrating on the fact that "many years of work must be completed before [Anne and Gilbert] can marry," the final moments of *Anne of the Island* hint at the sheer effort involved in bringing about this kind of union.[7]

\* \* \*Perhaps Montgomery's own unhappy marriage, which she entered into relatively late in life, partly explains her reluctance to dilate on the joys of matrimony. In any case, the scene of heterosexual romance is invariably relegated to and associated with the finales of these novels. Each of the first four books delays a reunion between Anne and Gilbert until the last few pages of the narrative. In *Anne of Green Gables*, for example, Anne refuses to accept Gilbert's apologies and friendship until the very last scene. Incapable of holding a grudge in general, Anne hardens her heart against Gilbert for an inordinate amount of time, given the fact that his sole offense—the schoolroom taunt mentioned above—occurred at a tender age, in a single mischievous moment. Montgomery thus links Anne's love for Gilbert to the cessation of the pleasures of narrative, while simultaneously connecting her relationship with Diana with openings, the realm of endless possibility. No less than three of the sequels—including the two that most closely chronicle Anne's married life—begin with scenes in which Anne and Diana meet and renew the "old unforgotten love burning in their hearts." For example, although *Anne of Ingleside* (1939) focuses on Anne's role as a matronly mother of six, the narrative opens with Anne and Diana alone together, sharing "a perfect ramble" through their "old haunts" in the woods.[8]\* \* \*

\*     \*     \*

\* \* \*[E]ach successive *Anne* book highlights the fact that finality is never truly final since the series as a genre invites almost endless additions. Even as the multiple volume format stresses continuity, it invariably creates gaps, interstices between installments, and Montgomery dramatizes this empty space internally via postponements and delays, as well as by incorporating—and returning to fill in—

---

7. K. L. Poe, "The Whole of the Moon: L. M. Montgomery's Anne of Green Gables Series," *Nancy Drew and Company: Culture, Gender, and Girls' Series*, ed. Sherrie A. Inness (Bowling Green: Bowling Green State U Popular P, 1997) 26.

8. *Anne of Ingleside*, 13, 4, 7. Jennie Rubio, in "Strewn with Dead Bodies: Women and Gossip in *Anne of Ingleside*," \* \* \* argues that while "*Anne of Ingleside* is loosely structured as a domestic romance with a sentimental ending . . . its central metaphors and internal logic deny the possibility of women's experience ever being contained in this kind of fiction" (171). In her influential work on Montgomery, Mary Henley Rubio also elaborates on the ingenious way in which Montgomery's fiction subverts the conventions and institutions that it appears to condone.

actual gaps in the narrative. Although marriage inevitably caps the halting progress of Montgomery's heroines,[9] it stands revealed as a desultory move, a tacked-on storybook convention that cannot adequately conclude the life stories of these singular characters, many of whom are repeatedly described as "queer."[1]

As this choice of expression indicates, characters in the *Anne* books find romance not in the process of heterosexual courtship, but in other, odder places. Indeed, it could be argued that the real romance in this series develops between young people and grownups who are not their parents, since the Sleeping Beauty metaphor enters the text explicitly in reference to Anne's relationship with her elderly guardians, an "old maid" (Marilla) and an "old bachelor" (Matthew). Commenting on the latter's transformation after the advent of Anne, Mrs. Lynde remarks, " '[t]hat man is waking up after being asleep for over sixty years' " (161). Similarly, although Marilla chides her brother for becoming "bewitched" and "infatuated" by their new ward, she herself is transfigured by the girl's presence; at the touch of Anne's kiss, a "sudden sensation of startling sweetness thrill[s] her," and magical moments like this one gradually mellow her into a new and more affectionate person (31, 78). This application of the Sleeping Beauty plot aids Montgomery in her project of eroticizing (and feminizing) the unmarried; at the same time, as Margaret Doody points out, it places a female child in the role of prince.[2] Then, in what could be called the primal scene of the series, Prince

9. Anne is not the only Montgomery heroine who proves "annoyingly slow in realizing what Montgomery makes glaringly obvious to the reader." T. D. MacLulich in "L. M. Montgomery's Portraits of the Artist" uses these words to describe how the eponymous heroine of Montgomery's *Emily* trilogy refuses to recognize that her childhood companion Teddy Kent "is her destined soul-mate" (97). Like Anne, Emily postpones romantic involvement as long as possible, preferring to keep her relationships with men platonic. Furthermore, as Marie Campbell points out in "Wedding Bells and Death Knells: The Writer as Bride in the *Emily* Trilogy," *Harvesting Thistles: The Textual Garden of L. M. Montgomery*, the *Emily* series refuses to bathe "the institution of marriage . . . in the traditional glow of romance and idealism"; like the *Anne* books, the trilogy is "peopled by virgin spinsters, bachelors, and the widowed," and Emily's engagement to Teddy comes about only after a string of improbable and traumatic episodes (138). Indeed, as Campbell notes, Montgomery "must resort to a supernatural event in order to bring Teddy and Emily together" (143).

1. Muriel A. Whitaker, in " 'Queer Children': L. M. Montgomery's Heroines," highlights Montgomery's use of this expression, noting that it is the queerness of Anne Shirley, both in physical appearance (bright red hair, with flowers in her hat) and character (garrulity, imagination) that catches the eye and ear of Avonlea and of the reader. The orphaned Emily Starr [in Montgomery's *Emily* trilogy] is told that her Murray relatives won't like her because "you're queer, and folks don't care for queer children" (12–13). Whitaker attaches no unusual importance to the choice of the word "queer"; she simply argues that Montgomery portrays the oddness of these children in a positive light, thus offering an implicit criticism of the concept of the Puritan child, whose inability to adhere to adult belief systems and conventions requires stern punishment and guidance.

2. In her introduction to *The Annotated Anne of Green Gables*, ed. Wendy E. Barry, Margaret Anne Doody, and Mary E. Doody Jones (NY: Oxford UP, 1997), Margaret Doody offers a less general version of this idea when she points out that "the real 'love story' of the novel as a whole remains the difficult, evolving love between Anne and Marilla" (21). Later in her argument, she contends that Avonlea itself represents the Sleeping Beauty that Anne must awaken (22).

Charming almost gets turned away at the door because he is the wrong sex. Seeing Anne for the first time, Marilla demands,

> "Where is the boy?"
> "There wasn't any boy," said Matthew wretchedly. "There was only *her*."
> . . . "No boy! But there must have been a boy," insisted Marilla. . . .
> "You don't want me!" [Anne] cried. "You don't want me because I'm not a boy!" (25)

\* \* \*[T]his "queer mistake" ultimately results in a great deal of unexpected pleasure (41). Just as inappropriate ambivalence and equally inappropriate desires draw out, and in some sense generate, the serial gratification of the *Anne* saga, this gender confusion proves extremely productive. Whatever the endings of the *Anne* novels tell us—and they invariably refuse to offer anything conclusive—the beginning of the series asserts in no uncertain terms that only a misguided fool would dismiss a potential prince simply because he's a girl.


# CECILY DEVEREUX

## The Culture of Imperial Motherhood†

\*    \*    \*

Readers of the "Anne" novels \* \* \* know that the heroine's "ambition" is not to be a teacher or a principal or a writer—at least, a writer of more than what she herself describes as "pretty, fanciful little sketches that children love and editors send welcome cheques for."[1] \* \* \* In what Gillian Thomas has described as the "[d]ecline of Anne" through five "progressively unsatisfactory . . . sequels,"[2] we see that the "dreams" of the heroine of Green Gables lead not to the literary fame for which Anne's celebrated imagination and her experiments with writing in the first three novels seem to establish a foundation, but to motherhood.\* \* \*

† From " 'Not one of those dreadful new women': Anne Shirley and the Culture of Imperial Motherhood," *Windows and Words: A Look at Canadian Children's Literature in English*, ed. Aïda Hudson and Susan-Ann Cooper, 119–30. Copyright © 2003 University of Ottawa Press. Reprinted by permission of the publisher. Footnotes have been renumbered and edited with permission of the author. Page references to *AGG* correspond with the NCE text [*Editors*].

1. *Anne's House of Dreams* (New York: Frederick A. Stokes, 1917) 17.
2. Gillian Thomas, "The Decline of Anne: Matron vs. Child," *Such a Simple Little Tale: Critical Responses to L. M. Montgomery's Anne of Green Gables*, ed. Mavis Reimer (Metuchen, NJ: Children's Literature Association and Scarecrow P, 1992) 23.

*    *    *

* * *Anne's "self-sacrifice" is a specifically "feminine" one: she chooses home and domestic duty over education and independence.

Although, as [Eve] Kornfeld and [Susan] Jackson note, this conclusion is described in the novel as a much more limited one than Anne had anticipated while at school,[3] the point is also made that, "if the path set before her feet was to be narrow she knew that flowers of quiet happiness would bloom along it. The joys of sincere work and worthy aspiration and congenial friendship were to be hers" (245). In fact, we are to see that her decision was the *right* one: "[B]efore she went to bed," we are told, "there was a smile on her lips and peace in her heart. She had looked her duty courageously in the face and found it a friend—as duty ever is when we meet it frankly" (239). Anne's first story ends happily—if quietly—precisely *because*, when she is confronted by a choice between "new womanhood"—education and independence—and domestic duty, she chooses the latter. * * * [S]he has come to believe that her primary vocation is domestic, and that "happiness" is to be found at home, within what are represented as the already determined boundaries of "womanly" duty.

Despite there being little explicit indication in the conclusion of *Anne of Green Gables* that the "domestic" path which Anne has chosen leads to motherhood—as the subsequent seven novels demonstrate it does—we are nonetheless already alerted to this trajectory for Anne's "progress" by the extent to which the narrative is shaped by a discourse of maternalism. *Anne of Green Gables* begins with the bringing together of an older woman characterized by childlessness and a girl who immediately draws our attention to her own motherlessness: telling Marilla the few details she knows of the mother who had died of typhoid when she was three months old, Anne says, "I do wish she'd lived long enough for me to remember calling her mother. I think it would be so sweet to say 'mother,' don't you?" (38). While Marilla resists any relational reconfiguration, and insists that Anne address her by her first name, she nonetheless does enter into a relationship with her adopted child that becomes progressively motherly.

It is Anne's desire to find her mother—the counterpart of her desire for children in the later novels, and the crucial element in Anne's "quest" throughout the first three novels—that sets in motion Marilla's "progress," or the story in which she discovers what is significantly represented as her own innate maternalism. * * * Indeed, Anne's sacrifice at the end of the story indicates that Marilla is

3. Eve Kornfeld and Susan Jackson, "The Female *Bildungsroman* in Nineteenth-Century America," in Reimer 151.

rewarded for taking in a child whom she initially regarded as "a sort of duty" and came to see as "if [she] were [her] own flesh and blood," "dearer to her than anything on earth" (42, 235, 151).

\* \* \*Marilla's conversion is Anne's work, and it is she who awakens in the older woman what we see the novel implying is an essential female instinct, a "natural" desire to have children, and to care for them. Anne can "teach" the older woman to tap into this "instinct" because, as we see from her first appearance, she has it in abundance. From the beginning, Anne is configured as a child whose salient characteristic is not only her motherlessness, but her motherliness. At the age of eleven, she has been caring for children younger than herself for several years: she is, we are told, "handy with children." This "natural" ability with children is dramatically foregrounded in the narrative when she saves Minnie May Barry from an attack of croup (118). Anne, who first appears to Matthew Cuthbert as a "stray woman-child" (16), is represented as simultaneously maternal and in need of the kind of mothering which Marilla can offer once what is represented as her "natural" desire for a child is awakened.

If, on the one hand, Anne's work has been to awaken "mother-love" in Marilla Cuthbert, we might see Marilla's work, on the other, as the protection and cultivation of Anne's instinctive maternalism. Her "duty," that is, is to preserve Anne's best instincts for her own future domestic and, it is implicit, reproductive work: she is, after all, watching over a child who is described in this novel as a "Madonna" (213). Noted by Marilla as "a nice, teachable little thing" (40), Anne, we see, is already being primed for the motherhood which will so insistently be foregrounded throughout the series. There are, thus, two mutually reinforcing narratives of maternal identification in *Anne of Green Gables*: this first novel is not only about the conversion of an older woman from spinsterhood to a kind of spiritual motherhood, it is also about a young girl who is establishing, as the teacher Miss Stacy puts it to all the girls in their "teens," "the foundation for [her] whole future life" (193) in what the remaining novels confirm is a maternal ideal.

It is, of course, the representation of motherhood as the "highest" aspiration for a woman that has problematized feminist readings of the "Anne" series. Gillian Thomas has not been alone in seeing Anne's rejection of a literary career in favor of domesticity as an indication of the heroine's "decline," and her seeming failure to overcome what are seen to be conventional notions of late nineteenth-century femininity [as] a sign of what T. D. MacLulich has suggested is Montgomery's "never dar[ing] to let her protagonists put themselves deeply and permanently at odds with their society" and "[i]n her life and her art . . . always adhering to the conventional pattern."[4] But the series' foregrounding of maternalism and its construction of a narrative which deliberately leads its heroine to a conclusion in motherhood indicates that, in fact, Anne's whole story is rooted in an early twentieth-century imperial notion of progress, achieved through the advancement of women—or, at least, white Anglo-Saxon and, in English Canada, Anglo-Celtic women—as mothers. It is this notion that suggests that the Anne books—and even *Anne of Green Gables*—ought to be positioned in relation to early twentieth-century feminist discourse.

If Anne is not generally regarded as a "feminist" heroine because she chooses a path of domestic "duty" and not of "new womanhood," this can only be because the series' politics of representation have usually been discussed when they are treated historically—in relation to Montgomery's own well-known lack of interest in the cause of woman suffrage, rather than to the discursive basis of so-called "first-wave" feminism itself. Indeed, the Anne books serve to remind us that what is still rather inaccurately called "first-wave" feminism is characterized in English Canada not necessarily by suffragism, and, after the 1890s, not by the "new woman," but by the idea of woman as imperial "mother of the race," something Anne Shirley arguably realizes more fully than any of her fictional contemporaries.

\* \* \*The primary characteristic of the new woman of the '90s— and the basis for "the tremendous amount of polemic which," as [Ann] Ardis points out, "was wielded against her"—was her "choosing not to pursue the conventional bourgeois woman's career of marriage and motherhood." "Indeed," Ardis suggests, "for her transgressions against the sex, gender, and class distinctions of Victorian England, she was accused of instigating the second fall of man."[5] But anxiety about the new woman's resistance to her reproductive "duty" focused on the possibility of another "fall": it was the British Empire itself that was threatened by her "transgressions."

Concerns about the continued dominance of what had come to be called the imperial Anglo-Saxon "race" were rampant by the turn of the century, as the British Empire undertook what John Strachey has noted was an unprecedentedly large and rapid territorial expansion.[6] Every census after 1881 had shown, Anna Davin points out, a decline in the British birth rate. The Boer War had been disastrous,

4. T. D. MacLulich, "L. M. Montgomery's Portraits of the Artist: Realism, Idealism, and the Domestic Imagination," *English Studies in Canada* 11.4 (1985): 471–72. Also see Laura M. Robinson's " 'Pruned down and branched out': Embracing Contradiction in *Anne of Green Gables*," *Children's Voices in Atlantic Literature and Culture: Essays on Childhood*, ed. Hilary Thompson (Guelph: Canadian Children's P, 1995) 35–44, for her discussion of what she sees as Montgomery's feminist "negotiations" in *Anne of Green Gables*.
5. Ann Ardis, *New Women, New Novels: Feminism and Early Modernism* (New Brunswick, NJ, and London: Rutgers UP, 1990) 10, 1.
6. John Strachey, *The End of Empire* (1959; New York: Frederick A. Praeger, 1960) 79–81.

not only in terms of the loss of South Africa, but in its revelation of the poor physical condition of so many young male recruits.[7] Anxieties were increasing about the spread of what came to be called "racial diseases," infectious and incurable diseases such as tuberculosis, which acted through the individual upon the race by affecting reproduction and depleting the population. Venereal disease and alcohol, which eugenist Caleb Saleeby had argued in early twentieth century were affecting the quality of the imperial race, continued to be seen as a threat to future generations of Britons.[8] Since so many of these "problems" had to do with reproduction and with the perceived effect of a woman's influence upon the home, "those dreadful new women"—and, by extension, all feminists—were easy targets for blame. If the race was in decline, as it seemed to be, then one explanation was to be found, as Anna Davin has shown, in the argument that women were not doing their duty.

It is no doubt because of the burden of responsibility for imperial social decline laid upon the new woman that, early in the new century, Anglo-imperial feminist discourse struggled to distance itself from most of the ideas associated with what middle-class British women had appeared to want in the 1890s. In the years between the Boer War and World War One, the new woman as the standard-bearer in the pursuit of women's rights was displaced by a figure who was profoundly maternal. Lucy Bland has noted that

> [t]he idea of "Woman as Mother" was mobilized by many feminists. It both empowered women, giving them a vantage point of superiority from which to speak, while simultaneously locating that vantage point within a discourse of racial superiority. For women were superior not as mothers in general, but as mothers of "the nation" and of "the race." Such constructions were inevitably placed within an Imperialist framework of which the vast majority of feminists were blithely uncritical.[9]

The promotion of motherhood for the purposes of populating the Empire had not always been concerned with the advancement of women, and eugenists such as Francis Galton, writing in the 1880s, did not necessarily endorse the notion that women had any duty beyond reproduction and the raising of children. Feminism, when it "appropriated" as Bland puts it, the idea of woman as "mother of the race" effectively undermined the position taken by such opponents as Galton, by affirming that the "advancement" of women and the race—and, of course, the Empire—were necessarily linked. Suffrage

7. Anna Davin, "Imperialism and Motherhood," *History Workshop Journal* 5 (1978): 10, 11.
8. Caleb Williams Saleeby, *Parenthood and Race Culture: An Outline of Eugenics* (London: Cassell, 1909) 205–53.
9. Lucy Bland, *Banishing the Beast: Sexuality and the Early Feminists* (NY: New Press, 1995) 70.

was to be one "advance," but it was arguably less important to most women than the empowerment, social validation, and professionalization of maternal work.* * *

If the new woman of the 1890s was represented as a sign and an index of imperial decline, the newer woman popularized as the "mother of the race" was positioned in feminist rhetoric as the Empire's last hope. Anglo-imperial feminists increasingly capitalized on the appeal of the idea of woman as mother.[1]* * *

Anne Shirley epitomizes this imperial "hope:" the first novel in her series is, after all, the story of the adoption of a girl ("native born" [12], and of Anglo-Celtic stock) who was supposed to be a boy. Indeed, her gender, far from being represented as a handicap or an explanation of what Kornfeld and Jackson have described as her "limited" destiny, is foregrounded and insistently valorized. * * * Montgomery, in other words, when she aims her heroine toward maternity, is not capitulating to "limited" late nineteenth-century ideas of womanhood, but, rather, is effectively engaging with first-wave feminism's discourse of imperial motherhood.

*    *    *

# GABRIELLA ÅHMANSSON

## Lying and the Imagination†

*    *    *

At the time when Montgomery wrote *Anne of Green Gables*, the gravest sin a child could commit was telling lies. In her book *Childhood's Pattern* Gillian Avery says that the connection between children, lies, and damnation probably originates with the Evangelical movement and Wesley. Presbyterians also held similar beliefs; a liar was predestined for hell. At the end of the nineteenth century lying had become a cardinal sin for a child to commit in the eyes of people in general. Avery writes:

> Indeed lying came to evoke such emotions, such horror, that the later Victorians could not bring themselves to create a central child character who lied. It was so obviously a mortal sin that there was no point in constructing a moral tale round it;

---

1. See Nellie McClung, *In Times Like These* (Toronto: McLeod and Allen, 1915) 100–01.
† From "Anne Shirley," *A Life and Its Mirrors: A Feminist Reading of L. M. Montgomery's Fiction, Volume 1* (Stockholm: Almquist and Wiksell International, 1991) 102–14. Copyright © 1991 Gabriella Åhmansson. Reprinted by permission of the author. Footnotes have been renumbered and edited with permission of the author [*Editors*].

one did not moralise to children about murder. The very word "lie" became an obscenity; "untruth", "story", "fib", "whopper", "crammer" were substituted for it. It became a crime that only foreigners or the lower classes could commit, parents might worry that their children showed "want of openness," but never that they were liars.[1]

Truthfulness then became the ultimate test of a child's breeding and prospects in general. Lying was vulgar; a propensity for lying branded the perpetrator as socially and morally inferior: "It was something that no English gentleman could possibly contemplate, since he acquired a love of truth as a birthright."[2] Hand in hand with these concepts of innate truthfulness was the "openness" that Avery mentions above, which meant that a child was supposed to confess her/his faults promptly and in fact tell her/his parents everything. For a child to be secretive was a kind of lying in reverse.

The first really serious clash between Marilla's values and Anne's behavior occurs when Anne has been at Green Gables a month. Anne is wrongly accused of losing Marilla's brooch and, as a consequence, of lying to cover up her crime. The basic plot behind this episode is a common one. To quote Avery again:

> The hero might not lie, but he could be falsely accused of lying, and this was to become a popular plot. In story after story the child who has been wild, disobedient, even insolent, the despair of the authorities, faces up to the charge of lying with brave fearless eyes.[3]

Montgomery, however, has added her own twist to the story. It does not simply serve as proof of Anne's innate gentility, it is also one of the episodes in the book which works towards humanizing Marilla. Montgomery is clearly on Anne's side here, and every young reader can feel the childish indignation of being wrongfully accused surge up as she reads of Marilla's unfair treatment of Anne. The only fault that Anne has committed is "meddling"; she has entered Marilla's room and tried on her amethyst brooch. When the brooch subsequently is missing, Marilla accuses Anne of taking it, not paying any attention to her denials. Therefore the serious offender all through this episode is Marilla, who accuses Anne of stealing and lying, forces a false confession out of her and then punishes her accordingly. The event is crucial because to Marilla a lying child is not only "wicked" and "crazy," she is also "utterly bad" (86, 85),[4] which is

1. Avery, *Childhood's Pattern* (London: Hodder and Stoughton, 1965) 30.
2. Avery 141.
3. Avery 31–2.
4. Here and elsewhere, Åhmansson quotes from *AGG* at length. Since the full text is included in the present volume, we have shortened or omitted some quotations and simply given page references to the NCE text [*Editors*].

irrevocable proof of an inferior character and faulty parentage. That the crime is serious also according to Avonlea standards is made clear by the fact that Marilla "could not even go to Mrs. Lynde for advice" (83). If Anne was found to be a liar, Marilla has made a terrible mistake in taking her in, since the myths surrounding lying also implied that lying was an incurable vice. From Marilla's inner monologue * * * one can deduce her anxiety and her moral dilemma, which is sharpened by her growing fondness for Anne (82–83).

This episode is not only built up around child/adult interaction and the wrongful accusation of lying. Equally important is the question whether having an imagination should be considered as part and parcel of having a tendency to tell falsehoods. At the end of the previous chapter which deals with an eagerly awaited picnic (it is Anne's overpowering wish to attend this picnic which is the prime motive behind her "confession" in the next chapter) Anne describes a playhouse she has set up with Diana. She illustrates how she uses her imagination to transform everyday things into romantic objects, creating a world full of poetical imagery by renaming the prosaic. She also mentions a romance that she has borrowed from Diana, which is the major source of material she uses to fantasize around. Marilla is very distrustful of novels, which she considers equal to lies, albeit in print. When Anne first is accosted with the alleged crime she makes things worse by resorting to a stock phrase borrowed from the world of historical romance: "I never took the brooch out of your room and that is the truth, if I was to be led to the block for it—although I'm not very certain what a block is" (82).

Anne, who has concluded that owning up would eradicate the offence, however grave, fabricates a false confession with the help of her imagination, incidentally making the same imagination the scapegoat in her story, exactly according to Marilla's earlier conjectures. Unwittingly Anne therefore confirms Marilla's suspicion that it is her imaginative nature that is to blame: Anne has taken the brooch to "help along that imagination of hers* * *" (82). When the lost brooch is found, Marilla has to admit that she made a mistake and that she learnt something by it. It is doubtful if that lesson goes deep enough for her to realize the severity of her accusation. Anne's character and her future at Green Gables are not saved by Marilla seeing her initial mistake and rectifying it. On the contrary, had the brooch never been found, it is unlikely that Marilla would have changed her mind about Anne, and Anne, in no position to exonerate herself, would have been branded as a liar. Two ends have been met with this important episode; Anne's character has been established and Marilla's initial distrust of her active imagination has been somewhat dispelled, although not entirely, as future episodes in the book will show.

## Lady Anne Cordelia Elaine Shirley and the
## Elusive World of Romance

Before we even meet Anne Shirley in person we are told that the girl on the deserted platform is sitting there because she prefers "scope of imagination" to the comfort of the "ladies waiting-room" (15). The lonely girl is prompted by a desire not to be hemmed in; she is fighting against the restrictive walls of adult conformity with her imagination as prime weapon. And imagination used in this way gives power, something that children are not supposed to have and which adults regard as disturbing. A child who can slip through authoritative fingers by means of power of the mind is in possession of an explosive which can shatter the walls and upset the accepted distribution of authority: "* * *[W]hile this odd child's body might be there at the table, her spirit was far away in some remote airy cloudland, borne aloft on the wings of imagination. Who would want such a child about the place?" (33–34).

Anne's imagination is a magic lens through which the commonplace is transformed and this is also true about the book. Without "scope of imagination" (and the comic situations that Montgomery creates out of it) *Anne of Green Gables* could have been as easily forgotten as scores of other books with similar themes. To Montgomery imagination was the most powerful mental tool in the world and her definition of the concept was borrowed mainly from the romantic poets. The term in itself has been used and misused during the centuries, until it is easy to lose track of the connotations that the now so diluted word once carried. [Mary] Rubio gives the following definition, inspired mainly by William Blake:

> The term "imagination" was a prominent one in the 18th and 19th centuries. By the time Montgomery used the term, it had become quite ambiguous through application to many contexts. At its worst it had come to mean pure escapism; at its best, it was a faculty by which man ordered the world into a complex set of symbols, both verbal and spatial, and determined his own relationship to them. To have an imagination (then and now) designated an ability to create dimensions to one's internal landscape into which one could go, alone or with companions, to explore fully the meaning of being human.[5]

Anne's imagination spans the entire spectrum from one extreme to the other. Initially she used her imagination as a means of escape, borrowing freely from her reading of romantic material to cover up

---

5. Rubio, "Satire, Realism and Imagination in *Anne of Green Gables*," CCL: *Canadian Children's Literature* 3 (1975): 33.

the drab and colorless life she was forced to lead.[6] Here she is telling Matthew about her experiences in the Hopetown asylum: "But there is so little scope for the imagination in an asylum—only just in the other orphans. It was pretty interesting to imagine things about them* * *" (17). Later the same imagination helps her to transform the real world into something that she can accept and thus her imagination becomes a powerful tool when she shapes her own future.[7]

The Romantic movement also saw in imagination an ability to create visions through works of art such as poetry or romance, and this "divine" imagination almost amounted to a sixth sense, a medium by which sensory perceptions could be interpreted and thus made visible. Gillian Beer explains the Romantic poets' preoccupation with romance thus: "For the poets of the high Romantic period romance was essentially an introspective mode: its pleasure domes and faerie lands were within the mind."[8] The visionary eye was a very special gift that set you apart from ordinary people. Montgomery herself was fond of the definition of a poet as a visionary with a special gift, and used it freely in her production. Thus any character in Montgomery's texts who has an imagination is a potential poet or writer, very much in accordance with the famous description from A Midsummer Night's Dream:

> The poet's eye, in a fine frenzy rolling,
> Doth glance from heaven to earth, from earth to heaven;
> And as imagination bodies forth
> The forms of things unknown, the poet's pen
> Turns them to shapes, and gives to airy nothing
> A local habitation and a name.[9]

Naming and renaming is important to a poet. Naming, as Rubio points out in an interesting comparison of Anne to Adam, was the first act mankind was asked to perform after creation.[1] A young female Adam is a daring leap of the mind, a concept which adds new dimensions to the received hierarchy with God at the top, whose words are taken to embody the creative impulse, and women and children at the bottom. When Anne names and renames objects in

---

6. Discussing Anne's imaginative powers in "Anne of Green Gables and the Regional Idyll," *Dalhousie Review* 63 (1983): 488–501, T. D. MacLulich says: "To escape from a consciousness of her drab existence, Anne has developed a rich fantasy life, based largely on the inflated clichés of phrase and action that she finds in popular sentimental fiction" (496).

7. Note the following statement by Northrop Frye, taken from *The Educated Imagination* (Toronto: Canadian Broadcasting Corporation, 1963): "The fundamental job of the imagination in ordinary life, then, is to produce, out of the society we have to live in, a vision of the society we want to live in" (140).

8. Gillian Beer, *The Romance* (London: Methuen & Co. Ltd, 1970) 60.

9. William Shakespeare, *A Midsummer Night's Dream* 5.1.12–17.

1. Rubio 34.

her new surroundings she starts a process by which Avonlea is gradually transformed. The names that Anne chooses originate either
from her reading, such as "The Snow Queen,"[2] or they spring from
her own imagination, colored by romantic diction, such as "Dryad's
Bubble" or "Violet Vale."

The danger of immersing yourself in romantic literature is in itself
a popular fictional theme. Emma Bovary, for instance, let her reading
impair her judgement and in effect ruined her own life by reading
exactly the same kind of books that Montgomery had read and made
use of:

> They were all about love and lovers, damsels in distress swoon-
> ing in lonely lodges, postillions slaughtered all along the road,
> horses ridden to death on every page, gloomy forests, troubles
> of the heart, vows, sobs, tears, kisses, rowing-boats in the moon-
> light, nightingales in the grove, gentlemen brave as lions and
> gentle as lambs, too virtuous to be true, invariably well-dressed,
> and weeping like fountains. And so for six months of her six-
> teenth year, Emma soiled her hands with this refuse of old
> lending libraries. Coming later to Sir Walter Scott, she con-
> ceived a passion for the historical, and dreamed about oak
> chests, guardrooms, minstrels.[3]

Young innocent females, especially motherless ones, were considered especially vulnerable in this respect, since their lack of proper
guidance as well as their lack of experience of the real world (something which in itself was considered a virtue) made them ready vic-
tims of romantic plots, unable as they were to distinguish between
reality and fiction. The tendency common in adolescent girls to
inscribe themselves as romantic heroines in imaginary worlds was
also seen as a consequence of novel reading, which, since it
"inflamed the senses," was considered highly improper for young
girls.[4] The ban on novels as being wicked was also deeply ingrained
in Presbyterian ethics.[5] The fictional character Marilla had, for

2. "The Snow Queen" is the title of a fairy tale by Hans Christian Andersen, a writer whom
Montgomery herself appreciated. See *SJ1* 350, 375.
3. Gustave Flaubert, *Madame Bovary*, trans. Alan Russel (Harmondsworth: Penguin Classics,
1950) 1150. Quoted in Beer 15.
4. In their study *The Physician and Sexuality in Victorian America* (Urbana: University of
Illinois Press, 1974) John S. Haller and Robin Haller have scrutinized sex manuals from
the nineteenth century and found that a majority of writers "condemned the romantic
novel as responsible for the increase in sexual neurasthenia, hysteria, and generally poor
health among American women. . . . Whatever stimulated emotions in the young girl
caused a corresponding development in her sexual organs. Over-indulgence in romantic
stories produced a flow of blood to certain body organs causing 'excessive excitement' and
finally disease. . . . Thus, the writers cautioned parents to examine carefully every piece of
literature placed in their daughters' hands, even to the extent of editing prurient Sunday-
school books" (102–104).
5. * * *Sir Andrew Macphail, a prominent Island politician, describes in a book of remem-

instance, in all probability never opened a novel or romance in her
life. Romance, because of its decidedly unrealistic content, was
branded as especially dangerous. Beer writes:

> The fear that romance would seduce the imagination, as well as
> mislead, may have been based on a half-acknowledged recog-
> nition that women's lives were very circumscribed in their actual
> possibilities. The "marvelous" is mistrusted, partly because it
> tallies so ill with experience, but, perhaps, even more because
> coincidence and magic create a kind of pagan freedom far
> removed from the world of duty.[6]

One of the places that Anne can escape to from duty-ridden Green
Gables is a playhouse which she has named "Idlewild." This playhouse, where Anne presumably can be both idle and wild, represents
exactly the "pagan freedom" mentioned by Beer above, and Marilla
is disapproving from the beginning: "You'll have to learn to resist the
fascination of Idle-whatever-you call-it" (78).

To some extent Marilla's distrust of Anne's imagination is well
founded. Anne has to learn not to confuse what is real and what is
imaginary and to understand when to use her imagination and when
to curb it.[7] * * * The most momentous "disciplining" episode is the
story of the Haunted Wood. The chapter is in itself a small masterpiece, describing childish terror and adult insensitivity. For Anne's
terror is real in a way that Marilla is unable to understand and the
punishment that she forces Anne to undergo is therefore nothing
short of mental child abuse. The shock treatment works, however,
and Anne is never again to give her imagination such loose reins.
Later episodes illustrating the same theme are no more than humorous reminders of Anne's first serious offence and Marilla's prompt
action.* * *

To my mind, the theme of self-dramatization is more interesting
from a psychological point of view than the ghostly excesses of * * *
imagination. Anne's different alter egos illustrate her development
and since real life has so far failed to provide her with any attractive
role models, Anne has borrowed hers from the imaginary world that
attracts her most, the world of romance. The fantasy world that Anne
wants to recreate in Avonlea is inspired by her reading, which is
conveniently listed inside the text (39). Anne's fictional world is a
legendary Scotland, a world peopled by heroes and heroines created
by Sir Walter Scott especially in his poems "The Lady of the Lake"

---

brances his mother's distrust of anything fictional. She maintained the position that "reading was mere idle curiosity. One could not understand another way of life unless one lived
it." This attitude, Macphail comments, "restricted or destroyed, the value of reading." *The
Master's Wife* (1939; Toronto: McClelland and Stewart Ltd., 1977) 79.

6. Beer 53.
7. See MacLulich 498.

and "Marmion."[8] As Anne grows up and her reading expands, her fantasy world also includes the age of chivalry in the form of Camelot. * * * [T]he "realistic" world of Avonlea resists any attempt of Anne's to turn it into a second Camelot. Anne's retreat into fantasy is part of her defence against a world that has so far treated her cruelly. Everything from neglectful guardians to ugly dresses and the common frustrations of daily life are changed by the help of a magic formula in which the key word is romantic (178).

Inside her fantasy worlds, Anne herself has different guises, the oldest being a blond guileless creature with an "alabaster brow" called Geraldine (20). At the time when Anne arrives at Green Gables she has abandoned the innocuous Geraldine for another fantasy heroine, Lady Cordelia Fitzgerald (27). Following the traditional juxtaposition of fair and dark heroine Montgomery has given Cordelia hair "of midnight darkness" and a character to match (54, 168). Her appearance seems to be modelled largely on Scott's heroine Ellen Douglas from "The Lady of the Lake." Her hair is "black as the raven's wing" (20) which is directly taken from Scott. The dark Cordelia represents a step in Anne's development. If the fair maiden Geraldine embodies total childlike innocence, Cordelia with her "duskly flashing eyes" presumably harbors dark feelings such as resentment or rebellion against an unjust fate. When Anne enters adolescence Lady Cordelia is supplanted by a heroine who is a mixture of [Tennyson's] Lady of Shalott and Elaine, the Lily Maid from [his] poem "Lancelot and Elaine." The unlucky Elaine, who pines away and dies because of her unrequited love for Lancelot the Brave, is a suitable heroine for a pubescent girl with her growing awareness of incipient womanhood as well as the other sex. The discarding of Cordelia is marked by her appearance as one of the heroines in a short story that Anne has written herself called "The Jealous Rival: or In Death not Divided." * * * In this story Cordelia goes mad from jealousy and drowns both Geraldine and her suitor, poetically named Bertram de Vere. Anne herself describes Cordelia's fate thus: "As for Cordelia, she went insane with remorse and was shut up in a lunatic asylum. I thought that was a poetical retribution for her crime" (169).

The technique of contrasting what is supposedly realistic (red hair and freckles) with unrealistic features (hair of raven black or pure gold and an alabaster brow) and thus lending verisimilitude as well as humor to the realistic alternative is used frequently in *Anne of Green Gables*. Anne's attempts at acting the part of a romantic heroine always precipitate head on collisions with so called reality. As

---

8. In her diary Montgomery mentions her own fascination with *The Lady of the Lake*: "How I always gloried in that poem—its spirited descriptions, its atmosphere of romance, the dramatic situations with which it abounded! What food it was for my eager young mind and fancy!" *SJ1* 247.

Anne writes out her tale of tragic love in "The Jealous Rival" she has problems about how to phrase a properly romantic proposal. As she casts around in Avonlea for a suitable model she comes up against prosaic reality with a vengeance (168). Nothing daunted, Anne has to fall back on her romantic readings again and produce her "masterpiece" entirely with the help of her imagination: "I made it very flowery and poetical and Bertram went on his knees, although Ruby Gillis says it isn't done nowadays" (168–69).

Very early Anne makes an attempt to install her romantic alter ego in her new setting, the east gable room at Green Gables. She does this by trying to "imagine things into this room so that they'll always stay imagined" (54). * * * On an imaginary couch "all heaped with gorgeous silken cushions" Anne as Lady Cordelia Fitzgerald is "reclining gracefully": "I am tall and regal, clad in a gown of trailing white lace. . . . My hair is of midnight darkness, and my skin is a clear ivory pallor" (54). This strategy, however, does not work. Reality intervenes and the "realistic" persona Anne of Green Gables takes over. The same thing happens when Anne tries to turn Marilla into her imaginary aunt. Anne comes up against Marilla's innate distrust of imagination as such: " 'I don't believe in imagining things different from what they really are,' retorted Marilla. 'When the Lord puts us in certain circumstances He doesn't mean for us to imagine them away' " (50).

In the chapter "The Unfortunate Lily Maid" Montgomery tells the story of how Anne and her schoolmates decide to dramatize "Lancelot and Elaine." * * * For a few minutes the fake Elaine is allowed to revel in the true romance of her situation, before reality catches up with her: "The flat began to leak* * *" (179).

Reality is literally pouring in and threatening to submerge the romantic heroine in cold water facing the fake Elaine with a very real death by drowning. After this parody of romantic elegy Montgomery switches into the mock-heroic. Finding herself in real danger Anne has to take action if she is not going to follow the ghost of the doomed lily maid into "a watery grave." She saves herself temporarily by climbing up unto a bridge pile, where she can do nothing except wait for someone to find her. Staging a mock-heroic rescue Montgomery lets Gilbert Blythe come along in Harmon Andrews' dory. (Harmon Andrews, his wife Mrs. Harmon Andrews, and their daughter Jane are just about the most prosaic and unimaginative inhabitants that Avonlea can muster.)

The violent clash between the romantic model and the realistic present is very comic to the reader, but not to Anne/Elaine herself. The humiliation of her situation makes Anne reject Gilbert's offer of reconciliation yet again. She is not ready to cast him in the role of "a handsome knight riding to [her] rescue on a coal-black steed"

(134). [Catherine Sheldrick] Ross writes: "This ending undercuts the romantic formulas by asserting the superior claims of reality that, with its sharp stakes, tears bottoms out of barges."[9] With the Lily Maid episode Anne's attempts to evoke Camelot in Avonlea come to a climactic close and her harrowing experience has finally brought home to her that the elusive world of romance cannot be re-enacted in real life, nor can models borrowed from romantic fiction be applied to real live persons or in this case fictional realistic characters: "I have come to the conclusion that it is no use trying to be romantic in Avonlea. It was probably easy enough in towered Camelot hundreds of years ago, but romance is not appreciated now" (184).

When Anne symbolically has been forced to drown the image of Elaine in cold water, she also outgrows the need for personae borrowed from romance. From that point on the tone of the book changes and Anne is depicted as a young woman and her world expands accordingly. The change is marked by the chapter headed "Where the Brook and River Meet," a phrase borrowed from Longfellow's poem "Maidenhood."[1] What really remains then of Anne's imaginative powers is her ability to discern beauty in the commonplace in order to make her world a better place.[2]

Because people with a visionary eye like the fictional character Anne (as well as her creator Montgomery) supposedly are rather scarce, Anne's ability in this respect is described as almost magical to ordinary people. * * * Anne's talkative nature is really an aspect of her imaginative faculties and part of her role as an interpreter and changer of reality. Anne is always eager to communicate her feelings, her impressions, her point of view and Marilla's initial distrust of her is literally drowned in a torrent of words. * * * To Anne the ideal world would be a place peopled with "kindred spirits," the kind of people who would be able to understand what she is talking about, who can respond to the beauty of nature the way she does. The idea of intellectual soul mates is described thus by Keats in his poem "O Solitude":

> Yet the sweet converse of an innocent mind,
> Whose words are images of thought refin'd,
>     Is my soul's pleasure; and it sure must be
>     Almost the highest bliss of human kind,
> When to thy haunts two kindred spirits flee.[3]

9. See Catherine Sheldrick Ross, "Calling Back the Ghost of the Old-Time Heroine: Duncan, Montgomery, Atwood, Laurence, and Munro," *Studies in Canadian Literature* 4.1 (1979): 48.
1. *The Poetical Works of Henry Wadsworth Longfellow* (London: Oxford UP, 1934), 66.
2. See Rubio 34.
3. John Keats, "O Solitude!", *Poetical Works*, ed. H. W. Garrod (London: Oxford UP, 1973) 36.

To ordinary people the chosen ones would look very much like fools, which is the price you pay for your gift. As Anne grows older and becomes aware of the fact that "kindred spirits" are few and far between she also grows quieter (204). * * * Instead her volubility is channeled into creating literature, which is simply the same ability to create word magic, but in a different medium.

\* \* \*

"[A] magic web of colours gay," [a phrase in "The Lady of Shalott," is] a very good description of Anne's gift.[4] This famous poem is also an excellent caption of the elusive world of Romance. The most common interpretation is that the poem illustrates the plight of the poet, who has to turn his back on life in order to render a true picture of it. Reality, having to earn a living for instance, would be the curse that cracks the mirror and destroys "divine" imagination.[5] This interpretation sees the traditionally female craft of weaving as a symbol for the traditionally male art of creating poetry, which is an entirely plausible interpretation considering that the poem was written by a man. If instead one retains the image of the Lady of Shalott as a woman, it is possible to find new and interesting aspects of the dilemma voiced in the poem. To begin with, the Lady is a proper fairy tale princess, "an enchanted princess shut up in a lonely tower." Her dilemma is that the "handsome knight riding to [her] rescue on a coal-black steed" can only bring death, not release.[6] She is performing a seemingly endless task (a female prerogative) albeit a creative one. The curse laid upon her is never to return to a life outside her prison. Confined forever within the fictional world of romance, a hall of mirrors with no escape except death, and trapped inside the image of women in the male-oriented world of chivalry, she is also denied release from that role in a creative act, simply because there are no available models for her to adopt except those that are suggested by that world.[7] Anne fails to find a suitable female model inside the rigidly set world of romance because "[t]his world can be preserved only by being kept from contact with the real world, which sinks the barge, cracks the mirror, explodes the illusion."[8] In order to build a future in the real world you need to look for more appropriate models, models that do not elevate womanhood in general

4. Alfred Lord Tennyson, *Poems* (Boston, 1842), 1.38.
5. See for instance A. Dwight Culler, *The Poetry of Tennyson* (New Haven: Yale UP, 1977) 45–46.
6. The romantic phrases are Anne's, taken from an account of a daydream she offers as an excuse to Marilla when she has forgotten to take a pie out of the oven in time (134).
7. This alternative reading of "The Lady of Shalott" could very well be incorporated into the arguments found in the introductory chapter of Sandra Gilbert and Susan Gubar, *The Madwoman in the Attic: The Woman Writer and the Nineteenth-Century Literary Imagination* (New Haven: Yale UP, 1979).
8. Ross 49.

while they dwarf individual women into so many Alices trying to find
what they want on the other side of a mirror. For women the elusive
world of romance is truly nothing but a dead end.

# FRANK DAVEY

## Ambiguity and Anxiety in *Anne of Green Gables*†

L. M. Montgomery's *Anne of Green Gables* played an ambiguously
progressive role in various turn-of-the century ideological conflicts
concerning religion, child rearing, and opportunities for women.* * *

\* \* \*

\* \* \*[D]espite the clarity with which Montgomery delineates * * *
gender issues and suggests progressive and perhaps—in her time—
"scandalous" positions on them, the extent of her novel's progres-
siveness is arguably ambiguous. The novel risks asking "scandalous"
questions such as why women cannot occupy a church minister's
position of authority, but carefully qualifies and contains them. This
particular question concerning female clergy is placed by Montgomery in the context of Anne's childish garrulousness—a characteristic
that can elsewhere produce quite a mixture of naive, mundane, and
penetrating observations. Here Anne's simplicity becomes immediately apparent when she follows her question with the suggestion
that the dogmatic Rachel Lynde could have been a minister—that
Mrs. Lynde can pray as well as the school superintendent, Mr. Bell,
and could likely learn to preach as well.[1]

Moreover, although the novel allows Anne some years of education, and qualification as a public school teacher by the time she is
sixteen, in the overall structure of the novel this attainment is not
exactly progress. She has done no more than attain the position that

---

† From "The Hard-Won Power of Canadian Womanhood: Reading *Anne of Green Gables*
Today," *L. M. Montgomery and Canadian Culture*, ed. Irene Gammel and Elizabeth R.
Epperly; 163–82. Copyright © 1999 University of Toronto Press Inc. Reprinted by permission of the publisher. Footnotes have been renumbered and edited with the permission
of the author.

1. Perhaps not yet knowing how well the job of minister can be done (Mr. Allan has only
recently been hired), Anne unwittingly produces a double-edged praise of Mrs. Lynde.
Her example of a woman who might do the job appropriately is also an example of one
who might do so only because her talents resemble those of Mr. Bell, someone whom
Anne has already appraised as long-winded and uninteresting (71). The irony of this is
evident to Marilla, who then undercuts Anne's suggestion by remarking "drily" that Mrs.
Lynde could indeed learn to preach. "She does plenty of unofficial preaching as it is.
Nobody has much of a chance to go wrong in Avonlea with Rachel to oversee them" (202).
(Here, and in the body of the essay, page references to *AGG* correspond with the NCE
text.)

her mother had held some twenty years before. If she should eventually marry her suitor, Gilbert Blythe, who has also qualified as a school teacher, she will have replicated her mother and father's status as school teachers, and in a sense returned her family to the occupational standing it had far in the past. The Anne that the novel develops is not someone who necessarily wishes to lead a life greatly different from that enjoyed briefly by her parents, or lived by Marilla. Although she speaks often about her imagination, what she seems to desire most deeply is a home, and people who will want and care for her.* * *

Another sign of the novel's ambivalence about women's capabilities is its handling of the competition between Anne and Gilbert Blythe for top academic honors at the village school and later at Queen's school in Charlottetown. In the early stages of this competition the novel repeatedly emphasizes the key role that Gilbert's teasing of Anne (his calling her "Carrots"), and the rage and bitterness she feels toward him in response, is playing in motivating her to compete. Here Gilbert is often portrayed as not especially motivated, and as earning the high grades he would have earned no matter what the circumstance, while Anne is portrayed as driven by her anger toward him to perform at a level higher than she would have otherwise attained (114). Yet despite this tenacity, Gilbert appears to top the class at least as often as Anne.

Later, as public school graduation nears, the narrator tells us that Anne's anger toward Gilbert has faded, but not her determination to defeat him, and that Gilbert's competitiveness has increased (197). Throughout their final exams "Anne had strained every nerve . . . So had Gilbert" (209). This is the period in which Anne has the greatest success, tying Gilbert for the highest grades in the province. Toward the novel's end, during their last competition for grades at Queen's, Montgomery suggests that another change has occurred in Anne (226). Without the bitterness, however, Anne apparently cannot win. Gilbert earns the medal for first place in the class, while Anne wins only the Avery Scholarship for top standing in English.[2]

There are a number of implications here. One is that Anne may have been performing above her abilities when motivated by bitterness. Another is that her talents may be concentrated mostly around "imagination"—something associated in the novel elsewhere with women and the arts—and may not range, as Gilbert's seem to do, across the more "useful" areas of history and mathematics. A third—

2. While Montgomery *seems* to have arranged events here once again to balance Anne and Gilbert's accomplishments, as she did before when arranging for them to tie for the highest public school grades in the province, and indeed presents Anne and the Cuthberts as being as pleased by the scholarship as they would have been by the medal, the suggestion of equivalent performance is illusory. Gilbert has received the higher honor, for grades across the curriculum, while Anne has excelled only in English.

latent in the ease with which Anne and others accept Gilbert's victory—is that it is normal or natural for a male to win. This imbalance between Gilbert and Anne is reinforced by Montgomery when they look for employment. Gilbert is the Avonlea board's first choice to teach at their school. Anne gets this board's position only because Gilbert, conscious that the power he thereby has over her is also a power to be generous, declines its offer and signs a contract with a nearby district.* * *

\* \* \*

\* \* \*One of the strongest features of *Anne of Green Gables*—and this despite its numerous heart-warming scenes—is the high level of anxiety that permeates Anne's speech. It is as if only Anne knows how uncertain life can be, and what unpleasant surprises change can bring. From her recurrent fears during her first years in Avonlea that Marilla may send her back to the orphanage, to her fear that she will fail her examinations and disgrace her adoptive family, Anne is plagued by uncertainty. Her anxiety is signaled in part by the numerous invocations of authority in her speech: phrases like "as Mrs. Lynde says," "as Mrs. Allan says," "as Miss Stacy says" at times punctuate every second of her sentences. It is signaled by her terror of not getting things "right"—her fear that she will break rules of etiquette when she is invited to visit Mrs. Allan, or that she will fail to be a "model student" at school.

The notion of rules and methods and models both terrifies and fascinates Anne—as it does lower-middle-class Avonlea—because it promises both the disaster of failure and the security of getting things punctiliously correct. Her anxiety is signaled most visibly by her garrulousness, her nervous habit of talking on about a matter by covering all its possibilities, and all views of it, as if terrified of omitting the single "right" one. This anxiety signals the undoubted power of convention and conformity in Avonlea, and the limits these impose on the power of Anne's energy and so-called imagination.[3] It signals also the extent to which Anne's desire for the security of "home" recurrently overpowers any desire she has for independence and creativity.

\* \* \*

\* \* \*[I]mplicit, but difficult to notice, in the novel is the role that the rigidity of society plays in Anne's early difficulties, and the extent

3. Even Anne's "imagination," however, as a possible ground of her independence and creativity, is suspect in the novel. Almost all of its images are taken from the clichés of gothic romance. The conflict that Montgomery appears to characterize initially as one between Anne's imagination and Rachel Lynde's orthodoxy is textually a conflict between two sets of conventions—those of popular romantic literature and those of a nineteenth-century Prince Edward Island village.

to which she must adjust to its expectations and hypocrisies in order to receive its approbation. The extent of this adjustment, and Anne's awareness of it, is signaled by the prominence the novel gives to the theme of performance. Very early on, Anne learns the usefulness of melodrama, and of people's willingness to accept its fulfillment of social norms. She masters the genres of confession and apology, impressing even Marilla with her invented confession of having lost the amethyst brooch, and triumphing in her apologies to Rachel Lynde and Miss Barry, largely through her grasp of what the genres require. She experiences the same challenge with praying, having to learn the genre in order to avoid scandalizing Marilla and, presumably, God. Her early schooling, done largely on her own, has consisted mostly of memorizing poems, including most of Thomson's *The Seasons*. This learning of other people's scripts continues at school, where she must eventually master the genre conventions of final examinations and produce acceptable answers. Her major triumph at Avonlea before leaving for college is a recitation, "The Maiden's Vow," that she gives at the hotel concert. The genre of recitation—so important to the culture of this time—can be read as a metaphor for what has been demanded of Anne since her arrival in Avonlea: the mastery of scripts and roles, including apologizing, confessing, praying, cooking, studying, and entertaining. Far from resisting the mastery of these and other genres, Anne eagerly acquires them, as part of the bargain she wishes to make for acceptance in a home.* * *

In nineteenth-century Avonlea society, of course, someone like Anne would indeed be unlikely to survive unless she had the ability to learn, recite, and mimic such scripts. In our own time women have numerous scripts to master in order to produce identities acceptable to the various parts of society they encounter. * * * Anne's growing success at performing a variety of scripts—and the way in which the novel, through Marilla's, Matthew's, Mrs. Lynde's, and Anne's own expressions of pleasure at these accomplishments, leads a reader to interpret this success as a good thing—masks the extent to which the scripts are coming to control her disruptive and "imaginative" aspects.[4] Anne may claim that her identity is unchanged, but by the end of the novel she has become a trusted agent of the society that her red hair and passions once disrupted. In effect,

---

4. In this regard it is noteworthy that the several crises of the novel, in which a reader is led to fear that Anne may be rejected by the community she so wishes to belong to, all involve incidents in which the community may come to believe that Anne has not truly exchanged her impetuousness for the community's conventions of honesty, politeness, and thoughtfulness. On each occasion—Anne's talking back to Rachel Lynde, Marilla's loss of her brooch, Diana's accidental drunkenness, and Anne and Diana's disturbing of Miss Barry's sleep—Anne must demonstrate that she indeed has accepted the community's conventions.

the novel that appeared to have been endorsing the "headlong" brook of its opening paragraph concludes by implying that the brook could survive only in the decorous channels of the Lynde farm.

In the final chapters Anne makes two decisions that further clarify the novel's ideological emphases and further modify the meaning of the image of the headlong brook. One is to give up her scholarship to Redmond College in order to stay at Green Gables with the rapidly aging Marilla. * * * The narrator's comment that "Anne's horizons have closed in" and that "the path set before her" was now "to be narrow" but bordered by "flowers of quiet happiness" (245) suggests that the once headlong brook may be better off in narrower and more decorous channels.

Her second decision is to make peace with Gilbert, extending her hand to him, thanking him for having given up the Avonlea school position, and offering a "complete confession" of her regret that she had not made peace with him long ago. As well as re-invoking the genres of apology and confession, ones Anne has learned well, this scene, with its distant echoes of Austen's *Pride and Prejudice*, reverses the relationship between passion and decorum offered at the novel's beginning. It is by giving up her passion—her passionate indignation toward Gilbert—and by approaching him with the conventions of good manners that Anne opens the way to a relationship with him.

Anne's last words in the novel reassert the security and stability her recent actions have moved her toward. "God's in his heaven, all's right with the world," she cites Browning's song from *Pippa Passes* "softly" (245). Perhaps all is right, from her sixteen-year-old perspective, and on this particular night, with her world—although I suspect that few contemporary teenage readers, in this time of shrinking employment and ecological decay, would be as sanguine about theirs. Anne is again safely in the home she has wanted since first seeing Green Gables from beside Matthew in his buggy, and with reasonable expectation of being able to continue living in it. Oh that the rest of us should be similarly fortunate. The narrator clearly intends some irony here, as Browning did in *Pippa*, but one that appears directed more against a young woman's continuing optimism than against the stability for which she yearns.

# T. D. MacLULICH

## L. M. Montgomery and the Literary Heroine: Jo, Rebecca, Anne, and Emily†

L. M. Montgomery has reported how, shortly after *Anne of Green Gables* (1908) was first published, she was pleased to receive a congratulatory note from Mark Twain, who described Anne as "the dearest, and most lovable child in fiction since the immortal Alice."[1] Twain, of course, was himself renowned as a creator of memorable fictional children. In fact, it seems possible that Twain had recognized some points of affinity between Montgomery's novel and his own famous boys' book, *The Adventures of Tom Sawyer*. One particularly striking similarity between the two books is the protagonist's fondness for playacting and self-dramatization. Tom's imaginative life is shaped by his reading of lurid adventure stories. Anne, for her part, is infatuated with sentimental ladies' fiction. Anne's penchant for casting herself as an actor in romantic adventures—which leads, for example, to her disastrous impersonation of the Lady Elaine—is a feminine analogue of Tom's compulsion to play out scenarios based on the adventure stories that are his favorite reading. We should not press this comparison too far, however. Montgomery's story, in which Anne eventually puts aside her personal ambitions in order to take care of the failing Marilla, differs significantly from the fantasy of irresponsible adventures and unearned rewards that Twain creates.

The link between Montgomery and Twain may be tenuous, but it does provide a convenient way of introducing the main argument of my paper. I want to suggest that relatively little attention has been paid to the literary context within which Montgomery's books took shape. Montgomery inherited a tradition of juvenile fiction that had become prominent in the later years of the nineteenth century, and was well established by the time she began to write. It is quite natural that Montgomery's novels should bear a closer resemblance to nineteenth-century girls' books than they do to the boys' books written by Twain and other male authors. In fact, Montgomery's two best books, *Anne of Green Gables* and *Emily of New Moon* (1923), belong to a tradition that descends from one the most important

---

† From "L. M. Montgomery and the Literary Heroine: Jo, Rebecca, Anne, and Emily" *CCL: Canadian Children's Literature* 37 (1985): 5–17. Copyright © 1985 by T. D. MacLulich. Reprinted by permission of Orleen MacLulich. Footnotes have been renumbered and edited with permission of the author's literary executor.

1. Quoted by Montgomery in a letter to Ephraim Weber, 22 December 1908, in *The Green Gables Letters: From L. M. Montgomery to Ephraim Weber, 1905–1909* (Toronto: Ryerson, 1960) 80.

books in nineteenth-century children's literature, Louisa May Alcott's *Little Women* (1868). The heroines of Montgomery's two books are examples of a particularly interesting character who was first introduced into children's fiction in Alcott's story, the aspiring young writer or literary heroine.

In a general way, the emergence of children's fiction during the nineteenth century can be traced to an important shift in the prevailing view of children and of childhood itself. Philippe Aries in *Centuries of Childhood* has described the process whereby childhood was recognized as a distinct phase in the cycle of human development, and children ceased to be regarded simply as small adults.[2] This acceptance of childhood and adolescence as distinct phases in the human life cycle eventually affected the literature that was written specially for children. Throughout much of the nineteenth century, ordinary fiction—the novels of Dickens are a leading example—often showed sympathy for the child's viewpoint, and a recognition that children could not be expected to conform to impossibly perfect standards of behavior. By the latter half of the century, however, authors of children's books even started to judge society by how well it treated the children in its midst, rather than judging children by how well they adapted themselves to society's expectations.

The nineteenth century, then, virtually created the idea of a "literature" that was specially written with children's needs in mind. Before that, children had been forced to borrow occasional books from adult literature (outstanding examples are *Pilgrim's Progress*, *Robinson Crusoe*, and *Gulliver's Travels*), or sustain their imaginations on the meager fare contained in the didactic tales and moral verses that their elders considered suitable for young readers. This overtly didactic literature was written without regard for the real imaginative needs of its proposed readers. As a result, very few of the early works written for children are still read today. Indeed, out of all the books written specifically for children and published prior to 1800, Lillian H. Smith can find only one work, Oliver Goldsmith's *Goody Two Shoes*, that has survived to become a children's classic.[3]

During the nineteenth century, however, a significant change took place. In the latter half of the century, an increasing number of authors of children's books began to depict their juvenile heroes and heroines as neither paragons of virtue nor examples of vice incarnate. The authors of these books must have shared the attitudes Alcott attributes to Jo March in *Good Wives* (1869), the continuation of *Little Women*. Alcott tells us that Jo could not bring herself to use

2. Philippe Aries, *Centuries of Childhood: A Social History of Family Life*, trans. Robert Baldick (New York: Vintage, 1962).

3. Lillian H. Smith, *The Unreluctant Years: a Critical Approach to Children's Literature* (Harmondsworth, Eng.: Penguin, 1976) 24.

the simple didactic patterns expected in stories for young readers: "much as she liked to write for children, Jo could not consent to depict all her naughty boys as being eaten by bears or tossed by mad bulls, because they did not go to a particular Sabbath-school, nor all the good infants, who did go, as rewarded by every kind of bliss, from gilded gingerbread to escorts of angels, when they departed this life with psalms or sermons on their lisping tongues."[4]

*Little Women* was a landmark in the development of fiction for children. The four March sisters have been described as "unique in the children's literature of their time, for they are not perfect, but neither are they wholly depraved. . . . The March sisters are the first 'naughty' children allowed to survive and prosper in American children's literature. After them comes a long line of literary children who are accepted and loved in spite of their faults: Katy Carr in *What Katy Did* by Susan Coolidge (1872); Tom Bailey in *The Story of a Bad Boy* by Thomas Bailey Aldrich (1870); and most important, Mark Twain's *Tom Sawyer* (1876) and *Huckleberry Finn* (1884)."[5] That is, along with boys' books such as *The Story of a Bad Boy* and *The Adventures of Tom Sawyer*, girls' books such as *Little Women* and *What Katy Did* helped to pioneer the creation of a children's literature that was realistic rather than moralistic.

Despite Alcott's very real understanding of children's psychological makeup, her book ultimately judges human conduct by a standard that is moral rather than psychological. Indeed, *Little Women* is structured as an illustration of the moral allegory contained in Bunyan's *Pilgrim's Progress*. Each of the March sisters has a "burden" which she must learn to overcome before she can become worthy of happiness. That is, Jo and her sisters are presented as "little women" with exactly the same moral responsibilities as adults. Their immature years do not entitle them to special consideration when they err.

On the other hand, Alcott's male contemporaries allow their heroes a much greater degree of freedom than Alcott and other woman writers grant to their heroines. In other words, the attitudes that shaped girls' fiction remained more conservative than did the attitudes that shaped boys' fiction. For every story like Susan M. Coolidge's *What Katy Did*, whose heroine "tore her dress every day, hated sewing, and didn't care a button about being called 'good,' "[6] there was a book like Martha Finley's *Elsie Dinsmore* (1868), whose heroine remains an insufferable prig in the old-fashioned manner.

4. Louisa May Alcott, *Little Women*, ed. Anne K. Phillips and Gregory Eiselein (1868; New York: W. W. Norton and Company, 2004) 281.
5. Ruth K. MacDonald, *Louisa May Alcott* (Boston: Twayne, 1983) 19.
6. Susan M. Coolidge, *"What Katy Did" and "What Katy Did at School"* (London: Collins, 1955) 23.

And even the rambunctious Katy Carr rather quickly turns into the proud and capable chatelaine of her father's home. The heroines of girls' books, then, could not enact the dreams of adventure and temporary escape from society that were permitted to the heroes of boys' books as a matter of course.

Tom Sawyer, for example, is able to evade his Aunt Polly's supervision virtually at will, and whenever he desires he joins the happily irresponsible Huck Finn. Of course, Tom's rebellion against society (unlike Huck's) is not deep seated or lasting. In fact, although Tom often joins the disreputable Huck Finn, he is drawn to the daughter of a member of the town's social elite. And Twain eventually rewards Tom for his youthful adventures by providing him with money, the key to Tom's acceptance into middle-class respectable society. In girls' fiction, however, the heroine seldom leaves the domestic setting, and she earns the greatest adult approval by acting as a homemaker. In other words, there exists in children's fiction a counterpart of the gender gap that has often been pointed out in conventional fiction.

* * *

* * *Alcott's heroine is not a typical representative of her sex. As a child, she is more enterprising and active, as well as more outspoken and spontaneous, than the common run of girls. Moreover, she gets into far more mischief than girls normally create for themselves. In short, she is a tomboy. In effect, Jo's conduct expresses a rebellion against the restrictive conception of proper feminine conduct that prevailed in Alcott's society. Yet in the end, as Patricia Meyer Spacks points out, *Little Women* endorses a viewpoint that equates femininity with submission, self-restraint, and service to others.[7] As a result, Jo eventually learns to restrain precisely those traits that make her character so distinctive and interesting. Yet Jo does retain one trait that distinguishes her from most of the other juvenile heroines of her day: in late adolescence she earns money and at the same time asserts her independence by embarking on a literary career. Jo March is thus the earliest example in nineteenth-century girls' fiction of that character I have already labeled the literary heroine.

Jo March's literary aspirations are undoubtedly in part a response to the enormous popularity attained by woman authors in nineteenth-century America. [Nina] Baym points out that the woman's fiction of mid century "was by far the most popular literature of its time, and on the strength of that popularity, authorship in America was established as a woman's profession, and reading as a woman's avocation." Although later in the century woman's fiction gave way to

7. Patricia Meyer Spacks, *The Female Imagination* (New York: Avon, 1975) 120–28.

other "more androgynous" forms of the novel, the link between women and authorship remained strong, for literature offered women of the middle classes one of their very few respectable alternatives to a career as wife and mother.[8]

The writers of girls' books often used literary ambition as a clear sign of a heroine's reluctance to submit to all the restrictions imposed by her society. In consequence, the literary heroine usually experiences a conflict between her desire for personal autonomy and her reluctance to upset her family by opposing the conventional social proprieties. The literary heroine is therefore a potential rebel, for the logical outcome of her youthful protests would be a systematic rejection of the values and attitudes that prevail in the heroine's male-dominated society. But the literary heroine's rebellion is never carried through into adult life. Instead, she resolves her inner conflict in favor of submission to social convention. That is, although the creators of literary heroines attach considerable importance to the right of children to follow their own bent without undue restraint, they cannot allow adult women the same freedom to express themselves in socially unconventional ways.

Even Jo March, the most original of all literary heroines, moves towards conventionality as she ages. The lapse into propriety is even more striking in the stories of subsequent literary heroines. The most conspicuous of Jo's successors are probably Rebecca Rowena Randall in Kate Douglas Wiggin's *Rebecca of Sunnybrook Farm* (1903) and Anne Shirley in Montgomery's *Anne of Green Gables*. Like Jo March, these heroines are also given to impulsive behavior and occasional acts of rebellion. But as they grow older, Rebecca and Anne increasingly yield to social pressures. Above all, they start to take care of other people, as respectable women are supposed to do. In later life, then, the unconventionality of these literary heroines narrows to a single trait, a penchant for literary self-expression. And in the end, like most other fictional heroines, even Rebecca and Anne must be married off—although this conventional denouement is postponed to the sequels of the stories in which these literary heroines make their debuts.[9]

It seems likely that the popularity of Wiggin's book provided the stimulus that prompted Montgomery to tell the story of her vivacious orphan child. There are even a few phrases in *Anne of Green Gables* that may be verbal echoes of Wiggin's book. For example, both Rebecca's Aunt Miranda and Anne's guardian Marilla Cuthbert use

8. Nina Baym, *Woman's Fiction: A Guide to Novels by and about Women in America, 1820–1870* (Ithaca and London: Cornell UP, 1978) 11, 198.
9. There is no sequel, properly speaking, to *Rebecca of Sunnybrook Farm*, but Wiggin did publish additional stories about her heroine's childhood in *New Chronicles of Rebecca* (1907). In both books Rebecca's eventual marriage to Adam Ladd is strongly implied.

the distinctive phrase "what under the canopy."[1] At one point, when Rebecca's aunts are debating whether to return Rebecca to her family, Aunt Miranda remarks grimly: "We have put our hand to the plough, and we can't turn back" (*RSF* 244). Marilla remarks at one crisis in Anne's upbringing, "I've put my hand to the plough and I won't look back" (85). Perhaps these verbal echoes may simply result from the imitation of regional speech patterns. But it seems less likely that the numerous and striking parallels between Anne's story and Rebecca's story are purely coincidental. Rebecca and Anne are both poetic spirits set down in a pragmatic community; they are about the same age when the reader first meets them: they both come to live with elderly, unmarried guardians, whose emotions have practically atrophied, and both girls reawaken their guardians' interest in life; both girls attend a one-room local school, where they encounter an unsympathetic teacher; later they both move on to a collegiate in a nearby town, where they prove their intellectual mettle in a wider arena. Most importantly, both girls become embroiled in a series of scrapes that exasperate their staid and conventional guardians; and eventually the guardians of both girls suffer from illness, and must be looked after by their wards, now grown almost to adulthood. Many of these details have a basis in the events of Montgomery's own life; but not until Wiggin's novel had appeared did she feel emboldened to make them the basis of her own fiction.

Wiggin and Montgomery do not make their fiction illustrate a systematic feminist theory, as Alcott did. Wiggin does make her youthful heroine complain: "Boys always do the nice splendid things, and girls can only do the nasty dull ones that get left over. They can't climb so high, or go so far, or stay out so late, or run so fast, or anything" (*RSF* 13). But Rebecca, and Anne as well, soon abandon their incipient feminism as they approach maturity. Yet Wiggin and Montgomery are not entirely innocent of ideas. Examined carefully, their fiction embodies a view of human nature that differs markedly from Alcott's view. I mean that Montgomery and Wiggin understand their heroines primarily from a psychological perspective, whereas Alcott understood her characters primarily in moral terms. In other words, Rebecca and Anne are not presented as "little women" but as children: they are part of a separate class of humanity, with special emotional and intellectual needs that adults have a duty to meet. However, Rebecca and Anne lose their privileged status as they approach maturity; Wiggin and Montgomery could never allow an adult the latitude that they permit to their juvenile protagonists.

When *Anne of Green Gables* was first published, one American

---

1. Kate Douglas Wiggin, *Rebecca of Sunnybrook Farm* (Boston: Houghton, Mifflin & Co., 1903) 149. Subsequent page references are identified by the abbreviation *RSF*. References to *AGG*—p. 63, in this case—are to pages in the present Norton Critical Edition [*Editors*].

reviewer astutely described it as "a sort of Canadian 'Rebecca of Sunnybrook Farm.' "[2] But Montgomery has done more than imitate Wiggin's successful formula. She has improved on her model. Montgomery takes a more penetrating look than Wiggin does at the feelings of rejection and the longing for approval and love that childhood insecurities can create. Montgomery also displays greater literary skills, particularly in her use of irony, than Wiggin does. For example, Wiggin's book includes a great deal of effusive emotional posturing, of the sort Montgomery makes into an object of humor when she satirizes the stereotyped language and idealized emotions that Anne has learned from her reading of sentimental popular fiction. The divergence in tone between the two books can be readily illustrated. Wiggin describes Rebecca's offering of a public prayer as "an epoch in her life" (*RSF* 209). Montgomery allows Anne to describe her visit to Diana's Aunt Josephine in Charlottetown as "an epoch in my life" (191), but Montgomery clearly intends her readers to recognize that Anne's phrasing is naively borrowed from her reading.

Montgomery also shows a greater sociological acuity than Wiggin does in depicting the sometimes oppressive nature of life in a small rural community. Consider just the novel's opening scene, in which Mrs. Rachel Lynde is described as the self-appointed watchdog of Avonlea society. Mrs. Rachel is effectively portrayed as a busybody and a gossip; and she is self-righteous and offensive into the bargain. The narrator later tells us: "Mrs. Rachel was one of those delightful and popular people who pride themselves on speaking their mind without fear or favor" (51). We meet this Avonlea avatar of Mrs. Grundy even before we meet Marilla, Matthew, or Anne. That is, we are immediately introduced to the restrictive nature of Avonlea society, where convention and custom rule all conduct. Marilla and Matthew have never left their family home; their inhibited natures are the natural product of this convention-bound society. The effervescent Anne supplies what Marilla and Matthew—and Avonlea in general—have been missing. Like Rebecca, Anne has a salutary impact on many of the adults she meets—think of her enlivening effect not only on Marilla and Matthew but also on other adults, such as Diana's imperious Aunt Josephine.

One of the great strengths of Montgomery's book is her ability to present events from Anne's point of view. In the scenes in which Anne confronts adult authority, we invariably side with Anne rather than with her older opponent. Even Anne's most childish enthusiasms are accorded a dignified treatment, for Montgomery wants her readers to remember the overwhelming importance that children can

2. *The Outlook* 22 Aug. 1908: 956.

attach to trifles such as wearing puffed sleeves, attending a community concert, eating ice cream, or sleeping in a spare room bed. If these things are important to any child, they are doubly significant to Anne, who has never done any of them before.

Anne's sufferings are treated very lightly. She was three months old when she was orphaned, and she tells Marilla "nobody wanted me even then" (38). We are told: "Evidently she did not like talking about her experiences in a world that had not wanted her" (39). But we can infer the urgency of her need for a home of her own when she tells Matthew: "Oh, it seems too wonderful that I'm going to live with you and belong to you. I've never belonged to anybody—not really" (17). Marilla and Matthew, as well, quickly find that Anne fills a void in their lives. Matthew starts to accept Anne from the moment he first sees her (19). He soon finds her lively conversation enchanting, and Marilla is not far behind (35). It is clear that Montgomery approves of her heroine's wide-eyed approach to life. In fact, Anne's exuberant outlook is held out by Montgomery as a fruitful way for adults to meet the world—or at least as a healthy corrective to the overly somber outlook adopted by most adults in Avonlea.

Despite its attractiveness for adult readers, *Anne of Green Gables* is fundamentally a children's book. In *Emily of New Moon*, on the other hand, Montgomery may have aspired to higher things. * * * But in *Emily of New Moon* Montgomery has not managed to work the sort of transformation on children's fiction that Twain achieved in *Adventures of Huckleberry Finn*. Like Twain's book, Montgomery's novel often reveals the shortcomings of the adult world seen by her young protagonist; however, Montgomery's book avoids the satire and the social criticism that Twain injects into his story. Moreover, Huck's adventures lead to his estrangement from society, but the first volume of the Emily series culminates in Emily's heart-warming reconciliation with her previously unsympathetic guardian. Both of Montgomery's best novels, then, remain children's books, whereas Twain's best novel crosses over into the category of "adult" fiction.

In the shape of its plot, *Emily of New Moon* resembles *Anne of Green Gables*. Like Anne Shirley, Emily Byrd Starr eventually finds a secure and affectionate home, and Emily displays a contagious vitality that enables her to enrich the lives of the emotionally reticent adults who reluctantly take her in. But the two novels differ considerably in tone. *Anne of Green Gables* is a far sunnier book than is *Emily of New Moon*.* * *

* * *

In Emily Byrd Starr, the heroine of *Emily of New Moon*, Montgomery has created a literary heroine who is a worthy successor of

Alcott's Jo March.[3] All of Emily's most striking assertions of her individuality revolve around her determined pursuit of her literary ambitions. When Emily insists that she simply must write—the need to express herself is part of her very being—she is defending herself against those who view her as little more than another piece of family property. Like Anne, Emily is given to imagining romantic fantasies, which she projects into her youthful literary efforts. But Emily's literary ambitions are central to her being in a way that Anne's are not. Anne's writing is not meant to be taken very seriously. Anne has learned to spin romantic stories as compensation for the bleakness of her life before she arrived at Green Gables, and once she begins to feel secure in the emotional support of her new home she feels less need for a private fantasy world. Emily's emotional scars are less easily healed, and she can only express her feelings of isolation and loss by projecting them into her writing so that the progress of her various literary efforts becomes an integral part of her story.

*  *  *

Montgomery wrote most effectively when she dealt with juvenile heroines, whose difficulties appeared to be associated with a special phase of life. Privately, in her journals and letters, she sometimes chafed against the restrictions that both publishers and readers imposed on the writer of children's fiction. However, she never attempted to break free from the conventions that hedged the form in which she cast the great majority of her work. As a result, Montgomery never made her fiction a vehicle for expressing a mature criticism of society. Social criticism entered her work principally when she protested against the overly strict and repressive way that adults sometime treated children. Her stories of literary heroines contain her strongest assertions of an individual's right to pursue her own course in life. But in her fiction she seldom expressed her awareness that grown women, too, could be subjected to constraints that were very similar to those she criticized when they were inflicted upon children.

3. *Emily of New Moon* (Toronto: McClelland and Stewart, 1923). It may be more than coincidence that Jo and Emily both have youthful male companions named Teddy. It is a measure of Alcott's originality, however, that she resisted having Jo marry Teddy Laurence. Montgomery, on the other hand, makes it clear at an early stage in the Emily series that Emily and Teddy Kent are destined to be united.

# VIRGINIA CARELESS

## L. M. Montgomery and Everybody Else†

Scholars have compared L. M. Montgomery's books, and in partic-
ular *Anne of Green Gables*, to many others, including *The House of
the Seven Gables*, *Uncle Tom's Cabin*, *The Five Little Peppers and
How They Grew*, *Little Women*, *The Adventures of Tom Sawyer*,
*Alice's Adventures in Wonderland*, *Adventures of Huckleberry Finn*,
*A Little Princess*, *The Country of the Pointed Firs*, *Heidi*, *Treasure
Island*, *Pride and Prejudice*, *Elizabeth and Her German Garden*, *The
Story of an African Farm*, and *Rebecca of Sunnybrook Farm*. L. M.
Montgomery was compared (and still continues to be compared) to
a number of different authors in her own time: in 1930, she herself
listed twenty-two others to whom she had been likened.[1]

\* \* \*

\* \* \*[M]any of these comparisons do more than just compare, that
is, note similarities and differences. They go on to explain the similarities by positing a historical link between those works compared:
that the first in date had a causal effect upon the second one. This
link may only be hinted at, by suggesting that apparently coincidental
similarities may not be so; or it may be actually stated, and the claim
made that the later one was somehow the result of the earlier. The
terms used in such studies show the different degrees of definiteness
with which such a claim is made, and the different degrees of inten-
tional derivation attributed to Montgomery.

Ordering some of these claims from the mildest to the strongest,
we find, for example: "may have been influenced by," "inherited a

---

† From "L. M. Montgomery and Everybody Else: A Look at the Books," *Windows and Words:
A Look at Canadian Children's Literature in English*, ed. Aïda Hudson and Susan-Ann
Cooper, 143–74. Copyright © 2003 U of Ottawa P. Reprinted by permission of the publisher. Footnotes have been renumbered and edited with the permission of the author
[*Editors*].
1. In the original version of this article, Virginia Careless mentions the authors (all listed in
the bibliography at the end of this volume) who made these comparisons: to *The House
of the Seven Gables*: Selkowitz; to *Uncle Tom's Cabin*: Smith; to *The Five Little Peppers
and How They Grew*: Kornfeld and Jackson; to *Little Women*: Berg, Kornfeld and Jackson,
Litster, MacLulich; to *The Adventures of Tom Sawyer*: MacLulich, Rubio; to *Alice's Adven-
tures in Wonderland*: Litster; to *Adventures of Huckleberry Finn*: Rubio; to *A Little Princess*:
McCabe; to *The Country of the Pointed Firs*: Gay, Santlemann; to *Heidi*: McCabe,
Nodelman; to *Treasure Island*: Weiss-Townsend; to *Pride and Prejudice*: Santlemann; to
*Elizabeth and Her German Garden*: Epperly, Waterston; to *The Story of an African Farm*:
Epperly, Waterston; *Rebecca of Sunnybrook Farm*: Cadogan and Craig, Classen, Epperly,
Kornfeld and Jackson, MacLulich, McCabe, Nodelman, Townsend. In subsequent para-
graphs, omitted here, Careless adds to this list the names of other scholars who made
specific comparisons: on structure: adds McGrath; on social background: adds Gates,
Drew, Mills; on individual features and character: adds Eggleston, Mott, Whitaker, Pike.
For LMM's own list of comparisons see *SJ4* 40 [*Editors*].

tradition of juvenile fiction," "belongs to a tradition that descends from," "recalls," "Montgomery's parallels and echoes," "likely . . . provided the stimulus," "drew associative force," "having offered inspiration," "there is a connection with," "tipping her hat to," "had a few classic models," "modeled [sic]," "admired and was influenced by," "a formative text," "very probably patterned after," "borrowed liberally from," "resemblance . . . too close to be merely circumstantial," "leaves very little doubt that the former was strongly influenced by," "draws heavily on," and "has openly appropriated, or modified only slightly."[2]

These latter kinds of comparisons are more charged, for their implications are serious. Some acceptance of literary borrowing has been discussed in the *Canadian Children's Literature* journal's editorial of 1989. This editorial makes reference to a historical literary tradition of derivation, conscious or unconscious, which has resulted in a rich web of interrelated books. Further, this practice has been recognized and sanctioned in the world of literature by the concept of "intertextuality."[3]

However, there are implications in a claim of derivation that can quickly go beyond the limits of acceptance. Even claiming that an author "echoes" another somewhat reduces the first's creativity and value. To go to the furthest extreme and claim actual copying is to accuse an author of plagiarism, the ultimate literary crime and degradation. To take the issue into the unconscious or subconscious realm in effect condemns accused—however lightly—authors to no defence, for the action is now beyond their conscious awareness and control.

*    *    *

Besides the particular issue of L. M. Montgomery's works possibly being derivative from other authors, there is also the larger question to consider of why a claim like this is made: why are similarities noted in literary works explained in terms of some historical link between them? Is this the only answer possible, or are there other sorts of explanations that can be offered, which may be as, or more, valid than a causal one?

Drawing upon my own background, I would say that there are other explanations, and some may indeed be more valid. Much of my training has been in the discipline of anthropology, which deals with the study of culture in its various aspects, including literary expression. In the course of examining different societies, anthro-

2. Authors cited by Careless as using these quoted phrases are: Whitaker; MacLulich; Epperly; Waterston; Smith; Selkowitz; Litster; Classen; McGrath; Cadogan and Craig [*Editors*].

3. "On Literary Debt," editorial, *CCL: Canadian Children's Literature* 55 (1989) 2–3.

pologists regularly deal with cultural similarities and differences—
so much so that the "comparative method" is regarded as a fundamental anthropological approach.[4]* * *

* * *

In discussing the context of Montgomery's writing, we are moving
from the general, or macro, level of the anthropological theories to
the specific, or micro, level of a particular culture at a particular
time. This culture * * * can be, for ease of identity, labelled "Victorian"—allowing, of course, for the fact that it was not only also found
in places where Victoria was not queen, but also continued into the
early twentieth century, when she no longer reigned. But the term
is apt in applying to the period Montgomery, and many of those to
whom she was compared, lived in, worked in, and wrote about.

In discussing aspects of this Victorian culture, I bring my work
experience in the field of history to my training in anthropology.* * *
* * *I do not find many of the apparent similarities in the comparisons between books as significant as do some of the literary
scholars. Take, for instance, the question of physical appearance
* * * [in] the descriptions of both Rebecca and Anne, first quoting
Kate Douglas Wiggin's description of Rebecca:

> The buff calico was faded, but scrupulously clean and starched
> within an inch of its life . . . the head looked small to bear the
> weight of dark hair that hung in a thick braid to her waist. She
> wore an odd little vizored cap . . . Her face was without color
> and sharp in outline. [*Rebecca of Sunnybrook Farm* (1903)
> 9]* * *

> . . . garbed in a very short, very tight, very ugly dress of yellowish
> gray wincey . . . She wore a faded brown sailor hat and beneath
> the hat, extending down her back, were two braids of very thick,
> decidedly red hair. Her face was small, white and thin. [*AGG*
> 15]

* * *[T]he similarity between these two examples is among the proofs
that Anne "had as its model an American import."[5] However, to a
historian, there are other and more obvious, cultural reasons for the
similarity.

What is being described in both cases is more telling about the

---

4. In the original article the author reviews several anthropological theories: diffusionism,
independent invention, cultural ecology, and structuralism. See also A. R. Radcliffe-
Brown, "The Comparative Method in Social Anthropology," *Journal of the Royal Anthropological Institute* 81 (1952): 108–29; Stanley R. Barrett, *Anthropology: a Students' Guide
to Theory and Method* (Toronto: U of Toronto P, 1996) 76.
5. Constance Classen, "Is *Anne of Green Gables* an American Import?" *Canadian Children's
Literature* 55 (1989): 49.

fabrics, dyes, and laundry techniques of the books' periods. Many dyes were fugitive, even the synthetic aniline dyes that came into being in the mid-nineteenth century. Fabrics made completely or partially of cotton, as were calico and wincey, did not hold aniline dyes well. Buff, a dye made from iron, was not a bright color to begin with. Washable clothes, including ones made of cotton, were generally boiled with harsh soaps to clean them, and this treatment faded dyes, wore fibers, and shrunk clothing.[6]

What the historian further sees in these passages is that the two girls had clothes that had been washed a great deal, with the common detrimental results for both garment and wearer. But the important question is why the girls were wearing such clothes. And the answer is that the girls were poor. The 1887 *Dictionary of Needlework* described wincey as being "used by the poorer class of people." Barrie's *Sentimental Tommy* illustrates this point well: his working class characters in Thrums wear wincey, in contrast to Tommy's mother's aspiration to silk as a sign of socio-economic success in London.[7] The issue in the descriptions of Rebecca's and Anne's clothing, therefore, is not about whether or not Montgomery copied Wiggin. Both authors depicted the physical evidence of poverty.

The fact that each girl is wearing a hat is also of little significance to the historian. In fact, apart from some curiosity about the different hat styles the two girls are wearing, the historian would find much more of note if both of them were not wearing hats. As Gwen Raverat pointed out in her reminiscences of Victorian Cambridge, wearing hats then was as normal as wearing shoes today.[8] In future, when perhaps human beings are born with some space-age surface on their feet that obviates the need for any added footwear, literary scholars may find two books from our period that have characters wearing shoes, and perhaps they will postulate that the later book was a copy of the first.

The similarity of the girls' hairstyles is also not of much significance for one who knows the period being described. There was not much choice of style available: long hair was common, unless a girl had a mother or guardian who went against the prevailing style per-

6. On wincey, the author cites F. A. Caulfield, *The Dictionary of Needlework* (1887; New York: Dover, 1972) 521; Carolyn A. Farnfield and P. J. Alvey, *Textile Terms and Definitions* (Manchester: The Textile Institute, 1975) 219; on dyes: *Cassell's Household Guide, Being a Complete Encyclopaedia of Domestic and Social Economy, and Forming a Guide to Every Department of Practical Life* (London, 1878) vol. 1: 360–61, vol. 2: 22; on color: Rita Adrosko, *Natural Dyes and Home Dyeing* (1968; New York: Dover, 1971) 49; on clothing: *Cassell's* vol. 1: 299, vol. 2: 51. These references and similar lists in following footnotes are drawn from citations within the original text of this article [*Editors*].

7. On poverty, the author cites: Caulfield 521; J. M. Barrie, *Sentimental Tommy: The Story of his Boyhood* (London, 1896) 35.

8. Gwen Raverat, *Period Piece: a Cambridge Childhood* (London: Faber & Faber, 1952) 259–60.

haps for medical reasons. As she has recorded, Montgomery's own hair in childhood was very long.[9]

Furthermore, with long hair, there were not many style options: loose, in one braid, or in two. The first of these tended to be found if it was in style in a particular period—apart from being a popular style for portrait photographs. Rebecca's one braid and Anne's two would not alert a historian to some possible causal link between the two books. They both depict styles that existed in the periods in which the books are set.* * *

* * *

* * *[T]he orphan tale was obviously a very popular genre.[1] Explanations for this popularity take into consideration the freedom and power that, in some ways, an orphan has, divorced from family ties and restrictions. Florence Nightingale talked about the advantages for the Victorian female who was free of family expectations and controls, saying that "the family uses people, not for what they are . . . but for what it wants them for. . . ."[2] Then too, explanations for the pervasiveness of orphan stories consider the difficulties that orphans face, having been neglected, abandoned, and deserted through their parents' death: these very difficulties elicit the interest that readers have in such lives.

Yet, it is also a fact that there were a great many orphans in Victorian times; and this fact documents both the good and the bad sides of that period's health conditions. Many more children were surviving infancy in this than in previous centuries. Life expectancy was rising as was the size of families. Where the typically large family between 1800 and 1850 had 4.5 children, couples married in the mid-Victorian period would have an average family of 5.5 to 6 live children. G. Kitson Clark has attributed this reduction in mortality to improvements in sanitation and hygiene, as well as a good supply of food and the lack of a killing agent, such as any serious epidemic.[3]

However, many adults were still dying, whether mothers in child-

---

9. *SJ2* 42; photograph in F. W. P. Bolger, *The Years Before "Anne"* (Charlottetown: P.E.I. Heritage Foundation, 1974) 45.

1. On this popularity, the author cites Nina Auerbach, *Romantic Imprisonment: Women and Other Glorified Outcasts* (New York: Columbia UP, 1985) 17–18, 57–58; Claudia Mills, "Children in Search of a Family: Orphan Novels through the Century," *Children's Literature in Education* 18.4 (1987): 228.

2. Quoted in Elaine Showalter, "Family Secrets and Domestic Subversion: Rebellion in the Novels of the 1860s," *The Victorian Family: Structure and Stresses*, ed. Anthony S. Wohl (London: Croom Helm, 1978) 105–06.

3. On life expectancy, the author cites: J. A. Banks and Olive Banks, *Feminism and Family Planning in Victorian England* (New York: Schocken, 1964) 28; on size of families: David Roberts, "The Paterfamilias of the Victorian Governing Classes," in Wohl 60; J. A. Banks, *Prosperity and Parenthood: a Study of Family Planning among the Victorian Middle Classes* (London: Routledge and Kegan Paul, 1954) 3; on sanitation and hygiene: Kitson Clark, *The Making of Victorian England* (London: Methuen, 1962) 71–72.

birth—even in 1882, women were cautioned that preparing for birth might also mean preparing for death—or mothers and fathers as a result of other disease or injury. Because more children were surviving, potentially more might become orphans. Then too, larger families meant additional stress on often very limited family finances. As a result, many children, even with living parents, were sent to orphanages, or to relatives, for foster care.[4] This happened in the fictional Rebecca's case—she was not in fact an orphan—and, under slightly different circumstances, in the real Montgomery's case also.[5]

Another theme discussed by those who have compared Montgomery to other authors is Nature. A strong response to the natural world in L. M. Montgomery's books, and in others to which they are compared, has also been seen as indicative of links between Montgomery and those books' authors. In some of the examples that have been discussed in scholarly literature, the explanation is given that Montgomery and these authors were all influenced by Romanticism, in which Nature figures so strongly.[6] But, again, there were other and more recent cultural influences in these authors' lives that could make them, and their fictional characters, so attuned to Nature.

Popular literature from the mid-nineteenth to late-nineteenth century in Canada and abroad reflects a concern with the natural world. * * * This concern came about partly as a reaction to the damage created by the Industrial Revolution, and it is against this background that the English Victorian nature poetry and the popularity of Wordsworth in particular is to be understood.[7]

The geological and archaeological discoveries of the time, as well as the development of evolutionary theory, carried with them the implication that Man had now to be seen as a part of Nature, and not as something distinct from it. The view of an immanent God in Nature, as expressed by Wordsworth, Kingsley, and others, was one way of accepting this new view of the whole natural world without abandoning religious belief. Also, on a more practical level, there was concern about the loss of the connection with the earth through the continuing rural depopulation in many countries at the turn of

4. On childbirth: John Hawkins Miller, " 'Temple and Sewer': Childbirth, Prudery, and Victoria Regina," in Wohl 25–26; disease or injury: Wendy E. Barry, Margaret Anne Doody, and Mary E. Doody Jones, eds., *The Annotated Anne of Green Gables* (New York: Oxford UP, 1997) 424; Roberts 59.

5. Kate Douglas Wiggin, *Rebecca of Sunnybrook Farm* (Boston and New York: Houghton Mifflin, 1903) 12; Mary Rubio, "*Anne of Green Gables*: The Architect of Adolescence," *Such a Simple Little Tale: Critical Responses to L. M. Montgomery's Anne of Green Gables*, ed. Mavis Reimer (Metuchen, NJ: Children's Literature Association and Scarecrow P, 1992) 71–72.

6. The author cites these critics as noting links to romanticism: Cadogan and Craig; Drew; McCabe; Nodelman; Waterston; Weiss-Townsend.

7. Walter E. Houghton, *The Victorian Frame of Mind 1830–1870* (New Haven: Yale UP, 1957) 79–80.

the century. Sir Andrew Macphail, in L. M. Montgomery's own home province, was one of those trying to halt this process.[8]

There were many other instances of a broad and active interest in Nature in its varied aspects. For example, there was a Conservation movement, as exemplified by the establishment of the National Trust in England in late-Victorian England, the concern with the preservation of wilderness in the United States from the 1870s on, and the efforts to establish national parks systems in North America. There was the growth of vegetarianism, the establishment of societies for the protection of animals, anti-vivisection campaigns, a widespread interest in gardening, with a related expression in the genre of flower garden paintings, and so forth.[9] Readers * * * today may know only the examples of Anne, Rebecca, and Heidi, among others in literature, and their response to Nature, but these characters, and their authors, all existed within a context in which such concerns were not at all unusual.

*   *   *

One cannot, of course, go so far as to argue for cultural determinism in the creation of literature. Still, to the extent that an author draws upon her own culture, and to the extent that that culture is similar to another author's, it is not so surprising to find similarities in their works. Certainly, as we know from the examples of literary comparisons given at the beginning of this paper, a great many similarities have been found between the work of L. M. Montgomery and other authors. As the detailed examination of some of those similarities has shown here, reference to the authors' shared cultural

8. On belief the author cites: C. E. Raven, "Men and Nature," *Ideas and Beliefs of the Victorians: an Historic Revaluation of the Victorian Age* (New York: E. P. Dutton, 1949) 173–79; on Macphail: Ian Ross Robertson, "Sir Andrew Macphail and Orwell," *Kindred Spirits* (Winter 1997–98): 16–17.

9. On conservation the author cites: Margaret Lane, *The Tale of Beatrix Potter* (1968; London: Collins, 1972) 46; Judy Taylor, *Beatrix Potter: Artist, Storyteller, and Countrywoman* (Harmondworth, MX: Frederick Warne, 1986) 39; on wilderness: Ray Stannard Baker, "John Muir." *The Outlook* 74 (1903): 365; Monte Hummel, ed., *Protecting Canada's Endangered Species: an Owner's Manual* (Toronto: Key Porter, 1995) 19, 21; on national parks: Ric Careless, *To Save the Wild Earth: Field Notes from the Environmental Frontline* (Vancouver: Raincoast, 1997) 23; on vegetarianism: Sarah Freeman, *Mutton and Oysters: the Victorians and their Food* (London: Victor Gollancz, 1989) 94–95, 250–70; on protection of animals: Barry et al. 423; Richard D. French, *Antivivisection and Medical Science in Victorian Society* (Princeton: Princeton UP, 1975) 27–35; Adrian Desmond, *Huxley: from Devil's Disciple to Evolution's High Priest* (Reading, MA: Addison-Wesley, 1994) 457–59; Nicolas A. Rupke, *Vivisection in Historical Perspective* (London: Croom Helm, 1987) 2–3; Society for the Abolition of Vivisection, London, England, advertisement, *The Spectator* 30 May 1903: 873; on gardening: John Highstone, *Victorian Gardens* (San Francisco: Harper & Row, 1982) 1–10; Cyril Hume, "The Point Ellice House Garden: Recovery and Restoration," *APT Bulletin: the Journal of Preservation Technology* 29.2 (1989): 30–31; on paintings: Andrew Clayton-Payne and Brent Elliott, *Victorian Flower Gardens* (London: Weidenfeld and Nicolson, 1988) 711.

context does yield useful explanations. Satisfactory explanations do result from this approach, without our needing any * * * interpretation in terms of possible causal links between works of literature. It helps to return the text to its context.

# JULIET McMASTER

## Hair Red, Black, Gold, and Nut-Brown†

"It can't be denied your hair is terrible red," Rachel Lynde tells Anne Shirley (65).[1] If we remember nothing else about *Anne of Green Gables*, we remember that this garrulous orphan girl has red hair, that the red hair troubles her sorely, and that it also gets her into trouble. Anne's flaming red hair is her visible and identifying sign: it is what gives her her mythopoetic power and makes the helpless orphan denizen of a small Canadian island a heroine for all seasons and all climes, "popular" in the widest sense. Her red hair is her Achilles' heel, her Waterloo, her fatal flaw, her touch of nature that "makes the whole world kin." We all know what it is like to think we have a "defective" body part. Anne of Green Gables focuses that anxiety for us and articulates the uneasy relation between the body and culture.

Anne's intense sensitivity about her hair and its color is part of her developed awareness of the multitudinous social codes and taboos, popular and otherwise, with which her culture surrounds her. What she reads and is taught, what people say and imply, the whole apparatus of social approval that is distinct from moral and religious systems though coexisting with them: all this Anne absorbs and reflects with a vividness beyond the reach of more prosaic souls like Marilla and Diana. And her accessibility to influence from her surrounding society realizes it for us, and moreover feeds back into the culture of which she has become a beloved icon.

Hair, like fingernails, eyebrows, and the outer layer of skin, is dead tissue that is still attached to the body, and growing out of it. At the growing end, it is physiological and deeply personal. At its extremities, it is available for many kinds of social structuring—cutting, trimming, dyeing, curling, straightening. Hair is the body substance that mediates between the individual and the culture. No wonder it

---

† From "Taking Control: Hair Red, Black, Gold, and Nut-Brown," *Making Avonlea: L. M. Montgomery and Popular Culture*, ed. Irene Gammel. Copyright © 2002 University of Toronto Press Inc. Reprinted by permission of the publisher. Footnotes have been renumbered and edited with the permission of the author.
1. Here and throughout her essay, McMaster quotes from *AGG*. Page references correspond with the NCE text [*Editors*].

is a site of intense conflict: external authorities—parents, church, peer groups, schools, gangs, fashion gurus—seek to impose their conventions on the individual, while the individual may want her hair to declare allegiance to a different authority altogether. In the long history of women's war to win control over their bodies, the subject of hair would deserve a substantial chapter. And in that putative chapter, *Anne of Green Gables* could furnish [an] eloquent example.

*   *   *

Anne Shirley is alert and dedicated to the conventions of popular culture of her day, both oral and literary. And to demonstrate her allegiance to the literary, I begin my study of *Anne of Green Gables* by a consideration of the story Anne writes for her Story Club, with its intertexts. "It's a sad, sweet story," Anne tells Diana of her own composition:

> It's about two beautiful maidens called Cordelia Montmorency and Geraldine Seymour who lived in the same village and were devotedly attached to each other. Cordelia was a regal brunette with a coronet of midnight hair and duskly flashing eyes. Geraldine was a queenly blonde with hair like spun gold and velvety purple eyes. (168)

Anne's usual artistic mode is oral rather than literary; her best creations, like the flowery, fictional "confession" about taking the amethyst brooch, come in speech; and even here, where the subject is a written story, we hear of it as described to Diana. But written or spoken, Anne's compositions show a developed awareness of literary precedent. When she invents her blonde and brunette heroines, she has the authority of Walter Scott and Tennyson and James Fenimore Cooper behind her, as well as many other writers, popular and otherwise.

On this important matter of hair color, many of her precedents are familiar, not to say clichéd. The fair-dark contrast goes back at least as far as Shakespeare's "Two loves . . . of comfort and despair" (sonnet 144), the fair Mr. W. H. and the Dark Lady of the sonnets—and probably much farther. John Caspar Lavater, in his immensely influential *Essays on Physiognomy* of the late eighteenth century, also lurks behind Scott, because he claimed some scientific authority for moral judgments based on physical appearance. He associated tenderness and weakness with flaxen hair, the opposite with dark.[2]

Most famous for the contrast of blonde and brunette, of course,

2. John Caspar Lavater, *Essays on Physiognomy: Calculated to Extend the Knowledge and Love of Mankind*, trans. Rev. C. Moore (London: Symonds, 1797) 299.

is Scott, for whom it is virtually a trademark. In *Waverley* (1814) the hero is placed between Rose Bradwardine, who has "a profusion of hair of paley gold, and a skin like the snow of her own [Scottish] mountains in whiteness," and Flora Mac-Ivor with "dark eyes" and hair that "fell in jetty ringlets on her neck." Together, we hear, they "would have afforded an artist two admirable subjects for the gay and the melancholy muse." *The Pirate* (1821) presents the Troil sisters, Minna of the "raven locks," and Brenda, whose hair "receives from the passing sunbeam a tinge of gold." And perhaps most famously, in *Ivanhoe* (1819) we have the Anglo-Saxon Rowena, with "clear blue eyes" and "profuse hair, of a colour betwixt brown and flaxen," over against the Jewess Rebecca with her "profusion of sable tresses."[3] By the time of James Fenimore Cooper's *The Last of the Mohicans* (1826) the contrast is routine. Again we have sisters, Alice the fair, with "golden hair," and Cora the dark, with tresses "shining and black, like the plumage of the raven."[4] And again the fate of the blonde is happy, that of the dark beauty tragic. "Profuse . . . dark . . . raven"; "clear . . . bright . . . golden:" the terms recur with the persistence of ritual.

The Victorians often reacted from this set of stereotypes. Thackeray, for instance, though he also presents contrasting women, tends to reverse the Scott pattern: he makes *his* Rebecca, named after Scott's, a blonde, while milky Amelia is the brunette. And George Eliot's Maggie Tulliver, unapproved for her shaggy dark hair, refuses to finish reading *The Pirate* and *Corinne* because she's tired of books, she says, "where the blond-haired women carry away all the happiness . . . I want to avenge Rebecca and Flora Mac-Ivor, and Minna and all the rest of the dark unhappy ones."[5] But Scott's paradigm asserts itself none the less, and Maggie goes to the bottom of the river, like Anne's heroine. The story Anne writes, then, would not be one that Maggie would rejoice in, because Anne, too, still thoroughly conventional, awards the guy to "the fair Geraldine" rather than to the raven-haired Cordelia (168).[6]

The novel *about* Anne, though, carries on the reaction to the stereotypes. Replacing the tall, dark, tragic beauties, we have plump,

3. References to Scott's novels are to *Waverley* (1814) chap.10: 70; chap. 21: 146; and chap. 21: 148; *The Pirate* (1821) chap. 3: 148; *Ivanhoe* (1819) chap. 4: 54, and chap. 7: 86.
4. *The Last of the Mohicans* (1826) chap. 1: 10.
5. *The Mill on the Floss* (1860) book. 5, chap. 1: 401, and chap. 4: 433.
6. The Scott heroine who does lurk behind *Anne of Green Gables*, I think, is *Anne of Geierstein*, in the 1829 novel of that name. It's not only that Montgomery's title echoes Scott's, but Scott's Anne is also a child of nature, spiritual and ethereal. When she emerges out of the mists of her native Swiss mountains, she shows "rather the undefined lineaments of a spirit than a mortal maiden," as Montgomery's Anne seems a creature of "rainbow and moonshine" (133). Anne Shirley makes her conventional heroine Geraldine passive: the hero Bertram De Vere saves her life and she dies in his arms (169). But Anne herself is more unconventional and more active, like Scott's Anne, who actually rescues the hero instead of being rescued by him. And Scott's hero, like Anne's, is called De Vere.

imperturbable Diana Barry, with "black hair and eyes and rosy cheeks" (74), a habit of laughing before she talks (75), and a tendency to be "just a dumpling" (214). And instead of the stately golden-haired beauty, we have Anne Shirley, with hair not blonde, not golden, but "red as carrots," in Rachel Lynde's words (57).

In fashion, different conventions obtain for hair color. When Jo of [Louisa May Alcott's] *Little Women* sells her "chestnut" locks, she gets only twenty-five dollars because her hair "wasn't the fashionable color." "One black tail" in the hairdresser's window, though not as thick as hers, is priced at forty dollars;[7] so unless the mark-up on hair is considerable, it seems that for that time and place black hair is the fashionable color. Somewhat later, though, in the rural England of [Thomas] Hardy's *The Woodlanders*, Marty South's profuse locks, of "a rare and beautiful approximation to chestnut," are considered highly desirable.[8]

Anne identifies with both her blonde and her dark heroines, Geraldine and Cordelia—both names she covets for herself. But she most likes to imagine that her hair "is a glorious black—black as the raven's wing" (20). More realistically, she hopes for her hair to turn "auburn," the more fashionable variation on red. Auburn is the *de rigueur* color for Jane Austen's personnel in her youthful parody *Love and Freindship* [*sic*]: From the fact that a certain young man's hair "bore not the least resemblance to Auburn," the narrator instantly concludes that he can have "no soul."[9] A triumphant moment from late in *Anne of Green Gables* arrives when Anne is called the girl "with the splendid Titian hair" (218). "Being interpreted, ["Titian"] means just plain red, I guess," she laughs (218). Now it's all in a word. But when she was eleven, her red hair was no laughing matter.

The popular associations of red hair that she inherits are unpropitious both aesthetically and morally. Early in the novel, Anne puts the question to Matthew: "Which would you rather be if you had the choice—divinely beautiful or dazzlingly clever or angelically good?" (20). Not surprisingly, the question is puzzling to shy old male Matthew. But girls have to ponder such things. They are forever bombarded with such maxims as "Be good, sweet maid, and let who will be clever." The three categories of brains, beauty, and morality are recalled in the forfeit of party games, which requires the boy to "Bow to the wittiest, kneel to the prettiest, and kiss the one you love best." And by the end, Matthew echoes these categories when he rejoices, "She's smart and pretty, and loving, too, which is better than all the rest" (416).

7. *Little Women*, ed. Anne K. Phillips and Gregory Eiselein (1868; New York: W. W. Norton and Company, 2004) 132.
8. *The Woodlanders* (1887) 48.
9. Austen letter 12.19.

For the young Anne, however, the priorities are different. Her first prayer goes "Please let me stay at Green Gables; and please let me be good-looking when I grow up" (47). Diana tries to convince Anne that she is "the smartest girl in school. That's better than being good-looking." But Anne, "feminine to the core," firmly responds, "No, it isn't . . . I'd rather be pretty than clever" (92).

In the world-view she inherits from the popular culture of her own day, "pretty" is incompatible with having red hair. For Rachel Lynde, the oracle of Avonlea, being skinny and freckled and red-haired is the same as being "homely" (57). Indeed, in certain contexts in the nineteenth century, "red hair" was virtually synonymous with "ugly," as "dark" was for Shakespeare. When the hero of Thackeray's *The Rose and the Ring* awakens from his magically induced love for the Princess Angelica, he instantly recognizes she is ugly—that is, marked by smallpox, squinting, and red-haired.[1]

If literary precedent suggests that you can't be beautiful with red hair, it also determines that you can't be good. Long tradition declares that the devil and Judas both have red hair. Novels provide a string of red-haired villains: Dickens's Fagin, Samson Brass, Sally Brass, and Uriah Heep, and the devilish Peter Quint in James's *The Turn of the Screw*. No wonder Anne laments, "You'd find it easier to be bad than good if you had red hair" (46). Her hot temper is another attribute linked to her red hair. Her most furious outbursts—verbally attacking Rachel Lynde and physically attacking Gilbert Blythe—are both immediate responses to their drawing attention to her carroty hair. "Her temper matches her hair, I guess," says Rachel Lynde sagely (59). Even as far back as Elizabethan times, red hair was associated with the choleric temperament.

What Anne overlooks, in her agony over her red hair as ugly, is its association with that other attribute of doubtful value in a female, intelligence. After her prompt and effective action with the colicky baby, the doctor says, "That little red-headed girl they have over at Cuthbert's is as smart as they make 'em" (119). But Anne's maxim continues to be "Be pretty, sweet maid, and let who will be smart."

For Anne—and for thousands of readers since—her hair color is almost as closely bound up with her identity as her gender. Although she tries to, she "*cannot* imagine that red hair away" (20). She knows she is a reject from Green Gables for being a girl rather than a boy. She also wistfully wonders, "If I was very beautiful and had nut-brown hair, would you keep me?" (28). In fact, her red hair connects her deeply with the island of her adoption. "What *does* make the roads red?" she asks Matthew on that first journey to Green Gables, as well as drawing attention to the color of her glowing braids. We

1. *The Rose and the Ring* (1858) chap. 7: 255–56.

are meant to recognize a propitious kinship between Anne's red braids and Prince Edward Island's red roads. (Better to match the roads than the gables, she learns later.) As other critics have noted, Anne's body is indeed mythologized, though not always in the ways she supposes. "Her hair is a sign that she belongs to her tribe—she just bears its standard more vividly than others do."[2] Her hair color connects her not only with the earth but with blood, passion, and creativity.

The nineteenth century fetishized hair: because it is a body part relatively easy to detach and preserve, it regularly served as a relic to be mounted in jewellery, and a synecdoche for the whole person. One can't read far in nineteenth-century novels, for instance, without coming across a ring with Lucy Steele's hair in it, or a locket in which Cathy's hair is braided with Edgar's and Heathcliff's.[3] Anne, too, is steeped in this culture. She covets Marilla's amethyst brooch with the hair in it; and when she is parted from her bosom friend, she begs poetically, "Diana, wilt thou give me a lock of thy jet-black tresses in parting to treasure forever more?" (110).

When Jo March of *Little Women* saw her "dear old hair laid out on the table," she explains, "It almost seemed as though I'd an arm or a leg off."[4] Likewise, Anne's hair is irreducibly a part of her self; and one she must come to terms with. In a sense, Anne is already healthily at home in her body. There is a moment when she renounces her fantasy identity of Lady Cordelia Fitzgerald and reminds herself, as she looks in the mirror,

> "You're only Anne of Green Gables," she said earnestly . . .
> "But it's a million times nicer to be Anne of Green Gables than Anne of nowhere in particular, isn't it?"
> She bent forward, [and] kissed her reflection affectionately. (54)

This genuine and innate self-satisfaction is not viewed as transgressive vanity but as part of Anne's value, and as part of the reason that the Cuthberts and so many of the rest of us *need* her, for her delight in the world and its beauties and pleasures, and in her own place among them. Her problem is her cultural inheritance, and the dour moral, religious, and social influences that teach her to want to renounce her red hair.

Deprived of love as she has been for the first eleven years of her lonely, starved childhood (40), Anne desperately craves approval.

2. See Introduction, *The Annotated Anne of Green Gables*, ed. Wendy E. Barry, Margaret Anne Doody, and Mary E. Doody Jones (NY: Oxford UP, 1997) 29.
3. Lucy Steele appears in Jane Austen's *Sense and Sensibility*; Cathy, Edgar, and Heathcliff are from Emily Brontë's *Wuthering Heights* [*Editors*].
4. *Little Women* 132.

Like the battered wife who is cowed into believing *she* must be the
one at fault, Anne instinctively seeks a reason for the world's rejection, and locates it in her hair color. The books she reads and the
people around her give her sufficient reason to believe this stigma
of hers marks her out as an inferior brand of humanity. In real life,
her orphan's experience of alternating exploitation and rejection
would be apt to produce a child crushed, withdrawn, resentful. But
it is part of Anne's generous spirit that she doesn't blame people for
her painful lot in life. They can be *expected* to disapprove of her for
her red hair, as she does herself. Blaming God for purposely visiting
her red hair on her is as far as she ever goes in resentment, and even
that is a temporary attitude.

If thy hand offend thee, cut it off. And likewise, if thy hair color
offend thee, dye it. Anne can hardly be blamed for the radical action
she takes, at least not by us readers.* * *

                          *    *    *

* * *[S]he takes her bold resolution to choose her own hair color
and buys the package "warranted to dye any hair a beautiful raven
black" (174). The historical placement of *Anne of Green Gables* is
significant here. Set in about 1890,[5] but published in 1908, the narrative allows Montgomery to endow Anne and surrounding personnel with Victorian attitudes, while herself bringing twentieth-century
views to bear on them.

Marilla is scandalized by Anne's action: "Dyed it! Dyed your hair!
Anne Shirley, didn't you know it was a wicked thing to do?" (174).
Anne's response is in a different register altogether: it belongs to a
new generation and a meliorated world view. "Yes, I knew it was a
little wicked," she admits. "But I thought it was worth while to be a
little wicked to get rid of red hair. I counted the cost, Marilla.
Besides, I meant to be extra good in other ways to make up for it"
(174). Anne is practical and pragmatic. Where for Marilla wickedness is generic and monolithic, for Anne it is subject to qualification:
there are degrees of wickedness, and one can choose among them.
Unlike the copiously haired Pre-Raphaelite beauties whose main
function is merely to *be*, Anne takes steps and *acts*—though not without counting the cost. Her hair is her own, like Jo's, and she takes
responsibility not just for having it but for doing something about it.
The moral and existential issues are not so portentous for her as for
Marilla.

The fact that her hair turns green instead of the beautiful raven

---

5. The datable historical event of the visit of the Canadian "Premier" (115) with the notable
nose—evidently Sir John A. Macdonald (Doody et al. 207n)—brings the action to about
1890.

black she aspired to is for her a failure in technology rather than morality. But for Marilla, the green affords a heaven-sent opportunity to moralize: "Well, I hope you'll repent to good purpose," she says severely, "and that you've got your eyes opened to where your vanity has led you" (175). But the lesson Anne actually does learn is somewhat different. On seeing her cropped hair in the mirror, she resolves: "I won't try to imagine [my hair] away, either. I never thought I was vain about my hair, of all things, but now I know I was, in spite of its being red, because it was long and thick and curly" (176). In *doing* something about her hair, even though the act was not an immediate success, she has learned to claim her own appearance and her own identity, and to be proud of both. It won't be long until she is ready to kiss her own reflection again.

\* \* \*

# ROSEMARY ROSS JOHNSTON

## L. M. Montgomery's Interior/Exterior Landscapes†

Landscape—place, space—is a provocative literary and artistic idea. Cognitive scientists, discussing perception, refer to a concept of "the embodied, embedded mind;" landscape is the background and foreground in which humans are embodied (given body in, given life in), and in which they are embedded (given shape and space). It is a liminal and subliminal presence which commits identity, as well as social and, by extension national, attachment.[1]

Literary landscape is not only spatial; it is temporal. The Russian theorist Mikhail Bakhtin's idea of the *chronotope* (*chronos* = time, *topos*=place) provides an apt way of describing how space is always tuned by time; for Bakhtin, the chronotope (time-space) is "the organizing center for the fundamental narrative events of a novel."[2]

---

† From "L. M. Montgomery's Interior/Exterior Landscapes: Landscape as Palimpsest, Pentimento, Epiphany: Lucy Maud Montgomery's Interiorisation of the Exterior, Exteriorisation of the Interior." Keynote address presented at Montgomery Conference, Charlottetown, 23 June, 2004. Copyright © 2004 Rosemary Ross Johnston. A revised version of this address appears in *CREArTA: Journal of the Centre for Research and Education in the Arts* 5 (2005): 13–31. Copyright © 2005 CREA Publications. Reprinted with permission of the author and CREA Publications. Footnotes have been renumbered and edited with the permission of the author.
 1. Andy Clark, *Being There: Putting Brain, Body and World Together Again* (Cambridge: MITP, 1997).
 2. Bahktin, *The Dialogic Imagination*, ed. Michael Holquist, trans. Caryl Emerson and Michael Holquist (Austin: U of Texas P, 1981) 250. The word "chronotope" (*xronotop*) was not invented by Mikhail Mikhailovitch Bakhtin; it was a mathematical term relating to Einstein's theory of relativity which redescribed time not as the objective absolute of

In simple terms, the chronotope describes relationships between people and events on the one hand and time and space on the other. Time and space are dynamic co-existing elements of landscape; they are ideologically encoded, culturally threaded. Pieced together in many different ways, they tell stories—stories of the present that may unravel into past, stories not only of *now* but *then,* not only of *here* but *there.* Imagine landscape as a canvas, freshly painted, but with bits of other older paintings showing through, like a pentimento, and with the colors of the world outside the frame seeping in around the edges.

Lucy Maud Montgomery's representations of landscape (which somehow continue to captivate and enchant despite twentieth century modernism and postmodernism, and twenty-first century focus on the quick grab of action) overtly describe a real-life geography and topography; in Bakhtin's words, "a definite and absolutely concrete locality serves as the starting point for the creative imagination."[3] This locality is in the obvious sense exterior—the condition of land ("scape" is derived from the Middle Dutch suffix *schap* = "condition"). Landscape is always landscape perceived, just as, in Bal's words, space is place perceived.[4] Indeed, the cognitive scientists argue that place can only exist in human consciousness through human perception of it. This argument activates the significance of the perceiving subject—the character who is situated in it (or outside it), perceiving and reacting—and shifts emphasis from traditional ideas of "setting" to more profound, metaphorical tropes, as "external forms [are] filtered back through the conscious and unconscious mind."[5] In literary narrative, landscape—the condition of the land— is represented to readers (to be assimilated by their own perceptions) through the narrator or focalizer, as well as, of course, through the subjective perceptions of the author. Thus at both textual and supratextual levels, for both literary character and writer-creator, space or *schap* becomes part of an "internalization of external processes" that helps to construct the view of individual self theorized as "subjectivity."[6]

Subjectivity pertains to the construction of the self as someone in relation to other someones, as an 'I' in a world of other 'I's, and as a

---

Newtonian physics, but rather as subjective, changeable, multiple, and dependent on the position of the observer. In the words of Holquist, it gives "an optic for reading texts as x-rays of the forces at work in the culture system from which they spring" (425–27).

3. Bahktin, *Speech Genres and Other Late Essays,* trans. V. W. McGee (Austin: U of Texas P, 1986) 49.

4. Mieke Bal, *Narratology: Introduction to the Theory of Narrative* (Toronto: U of Toronto P, 1985) 93.

5. R. Stow, "Raw Material: Some Ideas for a New Epic Art in an Australian Setting," *Westerly* 6 (1961): 4.

6. G. Turner, *National Fictions: Literature, Film, and the Construction of Australia Narrative* (North Sydney: Allen and Unwin, 1986) 88.

performativity of identity, community, and belonging. Any subjective internalization of external processes and conditions is densely colored by prevailing socio-cultural ideologies, as well as by the prevailing inner condition of the personal. In this way landscape is not only the way the condition of land is seen and perceived, and the philosophical lens through which this is portrayed; it may also, in a sort of mirroring and replicating, become a reflection of the interiority of the perceiver. A version of this relates to the familiar Shakespearean device of macrocosmic events such as wild storms reflecting what is happening in the microcosm.

\* \* \*7

What does this mean in relation to L. M. Montgomery?

There are four points I want to make here. First, for Montgomery landscape is always *relational,* an intimate part of the subjectivity of her protagonists, and an intimate part of her own writerly subjectivity. Anne interiorizes the beauty of the natural exterior world, dances with it, and reproduces it as she moves through the often less-beautiful world of people.\* \* \*

The second point is this: Montgomery's landscapes, cosmic as they are, have as their central locus the idea of home, and the powerful associations of coming home, finding home, making home, are part of her ideology of home as ontological beingness. Home is the center from which the perceiving subject connects or is connected to, in varying degrees, a wider context; it is a concept of space and relationship. At the core of the idea of "home" is a moral expectation of personal significance and care, a reinforcement of the integrity of subjectivity. And at the rim of home is nation—not just a geography but a history, shared views of the world, shared codes of relationships, shared values and concerns.\* \* \*

Third, landscape is deeply, profoundly, spiritual, imbricated with what Montgomery often refers to as "soul", and this spirituality becomes part of what Bal calls the "deep structure" of the text; as, in her words, place is "thematized . . . [it] becomes an acting place rather than a place of action."[8] This thematizing is inherently Bible-based, particularly in the earlier books where the language is full of biblical phrases and metaphors and snippets of these; despite the doubts and disappointments recorded in her journals, Montgomery's own interior world is God-oriented.

The fourth point relates to landscape as an organization and representation of time and space that braids landscape with inner space,

7. A paragraph in the original, omitted here, develops and intertwines the theories of Bakhtin, Maurice Merleau-Ponty, Andy Clark, Dave Hilditch, and F. Varela to examine the "cohesive artistic interconnectivity" in books like *Anne of Green Gables* [Editors].
8. Bal 95.

and in particular with female space. Thus the first description of Green Gables serves as an introduction to Marilla's, pre-Anne, barren and cloistered life—it is "built at the farthest edge of [the] cleared land," "barely visible from the main road," with a yard that is "very green and neat and precise," where "not a stray stick nor stone was to be seen" (9).[9]

These are four distinct ideas but in applying various critical hermeneutics to the *poetics of Montgomery's landscapes,* it becomes apparent that between them there is a coherent and cohesive artistic interconnectivity. This network of connections begins with the postmodern notion of *everydayness* and the related concept of what Bakhtin calls *"the inserted novellas of everyday life"*[1]—little day-by-day, what Montgomery would call "commonplace," stories, complete in themselves, such as, in *Anne of Green Gables,* Anne's going out for tea, or visiting the Island's capital. The critic Mike Featherstone notes that everydayness has an emphasis on the common, taken-for-granted, "seen but unnoticed" aspects of everyday life that modernism excluded as unimportant or as other. Thus it is often concerned with "the sphere of reproduction and maintenance . . . in which the basic activities which sustain other worlds are performed, largely by women."[2] Featherstone contrasts the postmodern celebration of everydayness to the literary tradition of the "Heroic Life," which among other things is characterized by action, risk and danger, but finds that everydayness is often heroic.

\*   \*   \*

Montgomery's houses are always figuratively significant. Houses have thresholds and doors that keep out and keep in, but Montgomery's houses spill over the thresholds into a phenomenology of landscape where home and place become one. Marilla has kept life and the messiness of flowers outside, but from the moment on that first morning when Anne pushes up the window—which "went up stiffly and creakily, as if it hadn't been opened for a long time" (31)—Anne begins to break down any barrier between outside and inside. Anne at her window is Anne in the security of home; in the famous example at the end of the first book there is a looking outwards that constitutes a deep looking inwards, and a deep peace related to a decision about home.\* \* \*

\*   \*   \*

9. Page references to *AGG* correspond with the NCE text.
1. Bahktin, *Dialogic Imagination* 128.
2. Featherstone, "The Heroic Life and Everyday Life," *Cultural Theory and Social Change,* ed. Mike Featherstone (London: Sage, 1992) 159; 160–61.

Landscape is *read* by Montgomery, and then *written* by her, as being interior and exterior; relational; a powerful dimension of home; the representation and consolation and edification of inner secret space; and profoundly spiritual. If we abide by postmodern injunctions *re* the death of the author, and simply focus on the texts themselves, this is all that needs to be said. But the publication of the journals (and letters) presents other texts that surely must also be considered as part of the *oeuvre*. The journals were carefully edited and revised by their author and left by her to be read; long letters to various others have been painstakingly transcribed into them; photographs have been inserted. Her expressed urge to use the journals as a place to "write it out" and for "grumbles" does not really explain the need to prepare it for posterity. Whatever her reasons, the Journals increasingly constitute a sometimes dark and disturbing palimpsest to her novels.\* \* \*

\*    \*    \*

We can only speculate about the ambiguities in texts and journals, and what they tell us and why, but their correlations and disjunctions indicate a multi-faceted, complex artistic personality who, I think, above all craved the disposition of her own space.\* \* \*

\*    \*    \*

Montgomery's landscapes \* \* \* demonstrate, on the one hand, the precision and excellence with which she melds perception and subjectivity to create absolutely specific time-spaces that are physical, emotional, and spiritual; and on the other hand, how she does so with a gaze that is infinite-focussed. Montgomery is a wonderful storyteller, and a wonderful creator of character, but stories and characters cannot with integrity be divorced from their symbiotic relationships with landscape.\* \* \*

# ELIZABETH WATERSTON

## To the World of Story†

\*    \*    \*

When L. M. Montgomery wrote *Anne of Green Gables* she was already an accomplished story teller, skilled in delivery of dialogue,

† From *Kindling Spirit: L. M. Montgomery's Anne of Green Gables*, 27–37. Copyright © 1993 ECW Press. Reprinted by permission of ECW Press.

description, and narrative bridging. By the time she was sixteen—a time when most of us settle for the more humdrum narratings of jokes or gossip—she had written and published short stories, drawing on her heritage as a member of a community which still treasured the skills of anecdote. A bibliography of her early short stories, compiled by Toronto researcher Rea Wilmshurst, lists titles suggesting the kind of little incident she was working up into short stories in the years before she composed *Anne of Green Gables*; for example "A New-Fashioned Flavoring," "The Way of the Winning of Anne," "What Came of a Dare," and "Diana's Wedding-Dress."[1]

In her long apprenticeship period from 1889 to 1904 when she was sending short stories successively to the Sunday school papers, the women's journals, the agricultural magazines, and the glossier magazines, she had learned the tricks of the trade: creating a swift and suggestive opening, moving toward a moment of dramatic conflict quickly succeeded by another related but intensified clash, devising an ingenious unraveling. When she carried her story-telling into the more ample scope of a full-length novel, Montgomery maintained the narrative skills she had already developed and added new ones. She worked carefully over each chapter as a unit, a mini-story, and then repeated the narrative strategies on a grander scale. One way to appreciate her narrative art is to notice the structure, sequence, and grouping of chapters.

In *Anne of Green Gables* a clever manipulation of suspense and surprise pulls us into the fictional world of Avonlea. The first eight chapters set up three puzzles: in a predictable community something unexpected is observed; into the home of a self-controlled and aging man and woman something alien, young, and exuberant erupts; and the unexpected, alien girl child who comes into the home and the community, wanting desperately to be accepted, is herself invaded by inexplicable rushes of impulse, aspiration, and sensibility. The opening draws readers into the puzzle-solving pleasure of unraveling these mysteries, finding out what happens to the child, the older people, and the community.

\* \* \*L. M. Montgomery's opening eight chapters use realistic detail to facilitate \* \* \* gentle entry into imagined experience. She begins with the ordinary world of Mrs. Rachel Lynde: a world of knitting and turnips, gossip and routine; then she lifts imperceptibly into a world of surprise, a world of story.

Repetitive titles suggest that the eight opening chapters function like stanzas in a poem, discrete in content but connected in form. The three opening chapters signal "surprise . . . surprise . . . sur-

---

1. Ruth Weber Russell, D. W. Russell, and Rea Wilmshurst, *Lucy Maud Montgomery: A Preliminary Bibliography* (Waterloo: U of Waterloo Library, 1986) 67–70.

prise." That Marilla and Matthew Cuthbert would think of adopting an orphan surprises Mrs. Lynde, the community's monitor; that the orphan should turn out to be a small scrawny girl surprises Matthew and Marilla in turn. Anne herself is more than surprised to discover she is unwanted: yet, even when devastated by this "most tragical thing," she can still answer Marilla's question, "What's your name?" by surprising Marilla—and us—with a request to be called Cordelia, or if that queenly name is withheld, at least "please call me Anne spelled with an *e*" (27).[2]

By the end of chapter 8, Anne has settled into Green Gables, the Cuthbert homestead. Her imagination, her honesty, her pathos have breached the accepted patterns of adult life on the farm. Green Gables has begun to accept Anne, and we too, as readers, have accepted her and her world—the cherry-tree in full bloom outside the window, the big barns, the blue glimpse of the sea, the sound of Matthew's voice—"She's such an interesting little thing"—and of Marilla's—"It'd be more to the point if you could say she was a useful little thing" (45). Montgomery has whisked us neatly into a realm which has its own brand of "usefulness," the world of fiction. She is ready to carry us forward into the community of Avonlea, and to show us how imagination can lead us into and out of a series of adventures, in a sequence of growth.

Like a traditional story-teller she is ready to say, "And then . . ." ready to follow the balloon ascent with a series of engaging incidents in an imagined realm. We will be enticed into the next major section, the narration of Anne's adventures in Avonlea, with a related sign-post: "Mrs. Rachel Lynde is properly horrified" (55).

In heroic stories, as critic Joseph Campbell says in *The Hero with a Thousand Faces*, the protagonist in this active part of the story will fight the elders, meet a rival, find an ally.[3] In her early short stories, Montgomery usually created just such conflicts between heroes and thwarting antagonists. A sample title, chosen from many confrontational stories written just before *Anne of Green Gables*, is "The Strike at Putney" (1903), the story of women pitting themselves against the men who run a local church. The conflicts presented when Anne faces Avonlea, however, fit neither the patterns perceived by Campbell and other commentators on traditional initiation stories, nor those established in Montgomery's own earlier fiction. Anne, a small hero, goes not into a lion's den or a fiery furnace, but into Mrs. Lynde's kitchen, or into Sunday school.

Anne is memorable not only because her adventures are like those in all the folk tales of questing heroes, but also because they are

---

2. Page references to *AGG* correspond with the NCE text [*Editors*].
3. Joseph Campbell, *The Hero with a Thousand Faces* (Princeton: Princeton UP, 1949). A seminal book on archetypal narrative.

different. Like every hero, Anne finds a troublesome tempter in each of her adventures, and is rescued by an ingenious ally. But in her first conflicts her foe is neither a parental power figure nor a politically repressive force. The tempter, the trickster, each time is something in Anne's own nature: her impetuosity, or her moral pragmatism, or her carelessness, or her blindness to conventions. And in each of her early adventures, her rescuer is also a part of her own nature: her openness, her humility, her ingenuity, or her common sense. Anne's early scrapes are always the result not of an external challenge but of her own over-active imagination; the exits are always gloriously achieved by revving up that imagination in order to find an appropriate way to back out of trouble.

The story of Anne in Avonlea fills the next twenty chapters (9 to 28). As Anne develops, Montgomery varies the formula slightly. Scrape and escape still follow each other, but Anne will increasingly find salvation not from her own resources, but from adults in Avonlea enlisted as her helpers.

At first Anne's surprising troubles and their equally surprising and amusing solutions come in neatly paired chapters. Mrs. Lynde's horror in chapter 9 at Anne's outburst of insults is allayed in chapter 10 by Anne's outburst of abasement. Anne giving offense to the godly in chapter 11 by the outlandish act of wreathing her Sunday school hat in wild flowers is balanced by the moment in Diana's garden in chapter 12, when Anne's outlandish quality charms Diana into friendship. The "delights of anticipation" of a picnic, connected with the delighted admiration of Marilla's brooch in chapter 13, are countered by the loss-confession-discovery-picnic events in chapter 14. In this last case the glib tongue that has served to placate Mrs. Lynde by putting a real truth into a rhetorically effective form is wrongly used. Anne considers that the end (going to a picnic) justifies the means (misapplying her powers of confession). This time the intensity of her disappointment becomes her ally. And this time Matthew points out another part of Anne's armor as she faces her own nature—she is "such a little thing," so young. Her childish sense of right and wrong got her into this scrape, and the sheer fact of her being a child gets her out of it.

After these three pairs of chapters (9–10, 11–12, 13–14) the pattern of scrape-and-solution threatens to become predictable. Montgomery breaks the rhythm with the climactic chapter 15 ("A Tempest in the School Tea-pot"), unmatched in two senses. Nothing in the book matches the power of this tempest chapter, in which Gilbert first appears as admirer, antagonist, would-be friend, academic rival, and source of excruciating humiliation. And no following chapter matches Anne's dilemma with a pat solution. For a resolution of the drama set up in this chapter, when Anne thwacks him over the head with her slate, we will have to wait until chapter 28 ("An Unfortunate Lily Maid"); and then again, since the "Lily Maid" chapter resolves nothing, till the end of the book, and indeed beyond it.

Gilbert's first appearance in the story thus offers an aesthetic surprise as well as a freshening of plot interest by the suggestion of boy-and-girl romance. The interruption of the two-chapter units is a welcome break in the predictable pattern; and when, after chapter 15, Montgomery resumes the pattern of problem and quick solution, she delicately varies the units.

Three chapters (16–18) link Anne's October loss of her bosom friend Diana through the cordial wine mix-up with her January regaining of Diana by saving the life of little sister Minnie May. This three-chapter group reiterates the motif established in earlier two-chapter units: a memorable misadventure is linked with an apt reversal. Anne gets Diana drunk by overplaying the part of mannerly hostess; she atones for this by acting on memories of early days in an unmannerly foster-home.

Next, two single chapters (19 and 20) each create both suspense and release. In chapter 19 Anne leaps into bed on top of "thin, prim and rigid" Miss Barry because she is filled with high spirits and pride at being a guest; by the end of the chapter she has charmed the cross old lady by her genuine humility and her rich volubility. In chapter 20, her rejection of the commonplace leads to the terror of the Haunted Wood; her response to Marilla's commonsense order lets her outface that terror.

Montgomery restores the paired-chapter structure in chapters 21–22, and 23–24. But now the solutions come not from Anne working through her own turbulence, but from the efforts of others. The comic humiliation of the liniment cake caused by over-intense desire to impress Mrs. Allan is salved by Mrs. Allan's kindness. The fall from the ridge pole thanks to Josie Pye's taunts is balanced by Anne's rise to competent performance on stage, thanks to Miss Stacy's encouragement. The two adult women who have recently come into Avonlea thus change the essential pattern of Anne's growing up.

Variations in the reiterated pattern of scrape and escape are like the change in tone and pace of an oral story-teller. They signal the ending of Anne's childish storms and stresses. In chapter 25 as if to emphasize the shift to maturity, Montgomery briefly moves away from Anne and focuses on Matthew's thoughts and actions. It is Matthew who enables Anne to achieve stylish beauty and the rounded shape of maturing womanhood. Marilla has her turn in chapter 27 to help Anne find a rational escape from her most theatrical misadventure in search of beauty—the green-dyed hair.

In chapter 26 the Story Club daringly turns us inward toward contemplation of the very art form we are in the process of enjoying. I will return in a moment to the question of where that wheel within the fictional wheel carries us.

The "Lily Maid" chapter ends the Avonlea epoch and the story of Anne as a child. This time it is Gilbert who saves Anne from a dilemma brought on by literary romancing. Anne ends the chapter and the confrontational phase of her life by renouncing not only Gilbert but also imagination, vanity, meddling, and "being too romantic" (184).

The adventure on the pond notably does not solve the Anne-Gilbert tension, but its events mark a surprising twist in traditional story motifs. In the traditional tale of any young person's quest for a position in society, the hero usually strains to achieve a fortune, a mate, sovereignty, or a combination of these desirables. In Montgomery's early stories the object of desire was usually a mate: for example the list of short stories published in 1908, the same year as *Anne*, includes these revealing titles: "Anna's Love Letters," "The Winning of Frances," "The Twins and a Wedding," "A Will, a Way, and a Woman."[4] In *Anne of Green Gables* Montgomery reverses the formula: Anne renounces the mating game.

Thus far, the novel as a whole has moved toward its conclusion with a steady, lightly varied, yet firmly recurring beat. Now the expected rhythm of recurring scrapes and escapes, maintained through twenty chapters, ends. Anne experiences unmitigated success throughout the next eight chapters.

The archetypal story would have followed the accounts of heroic conflict first with a traumatic descent into an underworld of terror and grief, a plunge beneath dark waters; then it would have moved to a triumphant period of power and reign. Montgomery reverses this order. She gives her protagonist the glory first, and then the descent into sorrow.

Aesthetically, the eight triumphant chapters (29 to 36) appear to round off the story with a formal unit symmetrically concording with the opening. Like the opening eight chapters, they are tied together by the device of reiterative titles. "Queen's" . . . "Queen's" . . . "Queen's" echoes, in those titles, suggesting female glory and power; and the chapter that ends this movement is titled "The Glory and the Dream." Part of the glory eventuates at White Sands—one of many plot devices that link the closing movement with the opening one. At White Sands, in chapter six, Anne, "a helpless little creature," was menaced by scrawny Mrs. Blewett; now, six chapters from the end of the book, Anne is acclaimed and admired at White Sands by the stout and wealthy Pink Lady. The symmetrical framing effect is

4. Russell *et al.* 83–84.

all the more effective because the symmetry will in the end be broken by the addition of the two final chapters, on death and change.

These eight chapters have been criticized for sentimentality. Something saccharine, detractors say, surfaces in chapters 29 to 36. Here, say the critics, Montgomery loses the bite and snap of the early chapters. Anne loses her amusing rhetoric; Marilla loses her gaunt common sense. There are no more confrontations, no more ridiculous enterprises or aspirations. Anne acts with grace during a visit to Miss Josephine Barry in Charlottetown. Anne is encouraged by Marilla to join the "Queen's Class" and prepare for college. Anne learns to use short strong words and to keep her imaginative thoughts to herself. She ties with Gilbert for first place in the Provincial matriculation exams, and stars alone on the concert stage at White Sands. As a Queen's girl she wins a scholarship and makes Matthew and Marilla proud of her. All social problems seem solved; Anne and Avonlea subside into mutual respect for each other.

Too much sweetness and light? One could argue for the realism of these eight chapters in psychological terms. Overactive little girls do grow up and learn to redirect their energies. Sharp-tongued sixty-year-old women soften. Teenagers learn to talk a little less and to work a little harder. Shy and inhibited people learn to express their pride and love. Surely Montgomery was working from her own memory of a stage in life when the early stresses were over and later ones not yet felt.

\* \* \*

Anne's unmitigated success makes a good story, even if "story" is taken in the sense of meaning "false." Reading this penultimate part of the book we soar with Anne in a waking dream, out-riding earlier storms of misapplied energies.

The flight ends, of course, with a shock. The death of Matthew, dearest of the older generation, as a point of plotting, caps all the earlier surprises. Montgomery has dropped clues about Marilla's impending troubles, with references to her headaches, the eye doctor, the vision blurs. But Matthew's death comes with less warning.

The story began with Matthew and the surprising change that came into his life with Anne; it moves toward its ending with the surprise of his death.\* \* \*

Aesthetically, the death of Matthew is the perfect denouement. In relation to the eight chapters that preceded it, the ending is surprising not only for its placement (tragic trauma would normally precede glorious rewards) but also for its proportion: the descent to the shadows is very brief. At first reading, one is not conscious of the slightly asymmetric structure of the chapter organization (an eight-chapter entry, a twenty-chapter unfolding, an eight-chapter apparent denouement, and a surprising two-chapter reversal). Yet Montgomery's care in shaping the book as a whole contributes subliminally to the pleasure of simply progressing from page to page. The shock of the tragic ending may be partly counterbalanced by the pleasure of the subtle imbalance in form.

The last chapter also packs in final plot surprises. Having suffered the shock of Matthew's death in one chapter, in the next and final one Anne grieves, suffers a second and third shock (Marilla's blindness and her financial ruin), renounces college, laughs at Mrs. Lynde, exchanges signals with Diana (left behind during the Queen's days), finds a job, makes up with Gilbert. Then this flurrying dynamic chapter ends with a curiously static scene with Anne alone. She is seated, as we first saw her, but no longer rigid with expectation as she was at Bright River station. The story offers its last surprise in the concluding frame. Anne sits, as worthy Mrs. Rachel Lynde once sat, looking out her window. Anne dreams of a bend in the road; but *she* is now, we realize with a final shock, the new monitor, teacher in Avonlea, proponent of work and of worthy aspiration and community service. Mrs. Lynde has joined her, and she in effect has joined Mrs. Lynde.

We shut the book; we are back in our own world, a world very much like Avonlea. The fictional balloon has set us down on ordinary earth, though we still see its trailing ribbons of fancy and idealism. Idealism—and maybe sentimentality?* * *

\* \* \*

* * *L. M. Montgomery defended herself against these charges by embedding two other kinds of stories within the novel. With the first mini-story she seems to say, "I could write about the darker side if I chose to." With the second, she mocks, "You think this is sentimental? Let me show you what sentimental romance can really be like."

The first mini-story appears early, in "Anne's History," chapter 5. Drunkenness, meanness, unimaginative life, and undignified death have been part of Anne's experience before she came to the island. Anne flushes with embarrassment when Marilla brusquely asks for the truth about that early life; she swings the talk instead to "happy dreams" (41). * * * The little exchange also says in effect, "I know about these aspects of life, but that's not the kind of story I want to tell."

The second mini-story appears in chapter 26, "The Story Club Is Formed." Cultivating her imagination, Anne grows a crop of wild seedlings. The passions of Cordelia Montmorency, Geraldine Seymour, and Bertram de Vere should satisfy any reader intent on tragedy. But the reader, like Mr. and Mrs. Allan, is likely to laugh in the wrong places. Assigning to Anne the nom-de-plume of Rosamond Montmorency, Montgomery laughingly plays with the criticism of her own earliest writing as high-falutin' and overly dependent on hectic plotting.* * *

The introduction of the Story Club is the mark of Montgomery's assurance as creator of fiction. * * * Continuing skill in manipulating surprise and suspense, chapter by chapter, and section by section, thus provides effective access not only to the joy of a story, but also to a relishing of the story-teller's art. And then *Anne of Green Gables* lifts to a third level of story-pleasure. It turns in on its own genre, with the two embedded mini-fictions, stories within the story, stories essentially about story-telling.

\* \* \*

## CATHERINE SHELDRICK ROSS

## Readers Reading L. M. Montgomery†

Within a few years of each other at the beginning of the twentieth century, two very different writers succeeded in transforming their own psychic distress into bestsellers. These two books, Owen Wister's *The Virginian* (1902) and L. M. Montgomery's *Anne of Green Gables* (1908), have continued to be popular because the stories their authors needed to tell happened to coincide with stories that a great many readers have needed to hear.[1] But popularity aside, the books are opposites in almost every possible way, offering their readers contrasting textual elements: the western frontier vs. the eastern garden; danger vs. safety; traveling vs. rootedness; the cowboy vs. the child. * * *

\* \* \*

* * * Readers are offered clear choices about worlds to enter. Do they want to crawl on their hands and knees across a burning desert with buzzards circling overhead? Or do they want to be in the snug, enclosed space of the house in an apple orchard on an island? Do they respond to the solitary horseman who lives in the saddle with death on his trail? Or do they respond to the solitary orphan who transforms the hostile world into a place of belonging? Do readers want to be the Western hero, who is as bleak, silent, and long-

† From *Harvesting Thistles: The Textual Garden of L. M. Montgomery*, ed. Mary Henley Rubio, 23–35. Copyright © 2002 Catherine Sheldrick Ross. Reprinted by permission of the author. Footnotes have been renumbered and edited with the permission of the author.
1. See John Cawelti, *Adventure, Mystery, and Romance: Formula Stories as Art and Popular Culture* (Chicago: U of Chicago P, 1976).

suffering as the rockhewn land that formed him? Or do they want to be a "kindred spirit," finding "scope for the imagination" in spruce groves and sunsets?

* * * [One] way to discover the responses of readers is to ask the readers themselves about their reading experiences. I have done this as part of a larger ongoing study of readers based on more than 100 open-ended interviews with readers chosen because they said that reading for pleasure was an important part of their lives. To check the representativeness of the interviews, I also posted a question about reading Montgomery on a user group for leisure reading enthusiasts, available over the Internet, and I heard from fifteen more readers.[2]

In the interviews, readers were encouraged to talk about what was important to them about their reading experience, starting with the earliest thing they could remember and moving chronologically through their reading history. When asked, "Can you remember the books that were important to you growing up?" about a quarter of the female readers spontaneously mentioned the Montgomery books. The Internet readers, responding to my question about reading Montgomery, said that above all that they were fans of Anne: "AofGG is still special . . . so moving, both funny and sad"; "I LOVED *Anne of Green Gables*"; "Wow, kindred spirits! . . . Emily is fascinating, and her growth is wonderful to watch, but Anne makes me laugh and cry much more." One Internet reader offered the detail that "during the height of my Anne craze . . . I wrote out the Blythe-Meredith family trees," while a Finnish reader said, "I put *The Blue Castle* on my 'ten books I won't part with' list without any doubt." Internet readers variously praised "the freshness with which [Montgomery] writes about children," her ability to "make you feel like you are seeing it through the eyes of a child," and her success at "taking you back into the time period"; they criticized the decline in quality of the last four Anne books and "the dated *Kilmeny of the Orchard*, which even as a child I found nauseating"; and they asked, "Between Gilbert Blythe and Teddy Kent who would you choose?"

What was remarkable about the responses from both interviewed readers and Internet readers was their consistency. With variations, the same points were made again and again, suggesting that readers are in fact responding to a common set of satisfying elements in Montgomery's books.

* * *

2. People who communicate through user groups on the Internet are, admittedly, a select group of articulate and bookish readers. When I posted a message on the Rec.arts.books user group asking for responses from L. M. Montgomery readers, the fifteen readers who responded were all women. All but one Finnish reader were North Americans, and most had access to the Internet because they were either university students or faculty members.

In these accounts of readers reading Montgomery, there is a common core of shared experience. These readers place *Anne of Green Gables* within a larger category of books that includes the rest of the Montgomery books, *Little Women*, *The Five Little Peppers*, *The Secret Garden*, *Heidi* and *Rebecca of Sunnybrook Farm*.[3] A 64-year-old woman said, "Of course I read all of the *Anne of Green Gables* books and *Little Women* and all those books." Readers don't have a name for this category of books, but they expect a shorthand explanation such as "things worked out" will be understood to mean that a hostile, imprisoning world is transformed into a safe place for the female character. Jean Little, Governor-General's Award–winning children's author, has described the shape of these books in terms of "the finding of friends and the change from an unhappy lonely child to a happier child. The change must be credible. Books like *Anne of Green Gables* gave me hope. In one way or another, the characters all transformed their worlds from an initially unhappy place to a much happier one."[4]

Secondly, these books provide a link with the generation of the reader's parents or grandparents. Some said that the books had been special in the first instance because they had belonged to a collection in the attic or basement from their parents' childhood or had been a gift from a favorite uncle, grandmother or much-beloved great-aunt. For example, a 29-year-old social worker said, "I was turned on to *Anne* by being given it as a gift by grandparents and then I went on to read others like *Kilmeny of the Orchard*." A 35-year-old Ph.D. candidate commented that "the books I read as a child that were nearest to my own experience were certainly L. M. Montgomery's . . . The children seemed to be recognizable as me and my classmates, and the experiences were recognizable as those which my grandparents would have had as children." Other readers said that Anne had been read aloud to them by their mother and that they, in turn, were reading the Anne books to their own children. Some said that they were rereading Montgomery to get back in touch with their own childhoods. Said one Internet reader who is a college teacher, "I have been going through a phase recently of rereading many of my childhood favorites . . . I found that Anne was just as wonderful as I remembered . . . I don't like Emily quite as much as Anne. Anne is my friend, but I'm not sure that Emily would be."

Third, a big part of the pleasure of reading Montgomery is the knowledge that the experience can be repeated. * * * [R]eaders can

3. For an explanation of the popularity of a similar grouping (*Rebecca of Sunnybrook Farm*, *Pollyanna*, *Anne of Green Gables*, *The Secret Garden*, and *Heidi*), see Perry Nodelman, "Progressive Utopia: Or, How to Grow Up Without Growing Up," in Reimer 29–38.
4. Little, "An Interview with Jean Little," *CCL: Canadian Children's Literature* 34 (1984): 7–8.

recover the same satisfying experience by rereading. Many readers in my study resembled the scores of fans who reported to Mary Rubio that "they reread their favorite Montgomery books every year."[5] An Internet reader who works in a Chicago bookstore said, "Montgomery, like Alcott . . . is comfort reading for me. I go back through parts or all of the series every other year or so, renew my fantasies (I'm Gilbert's sister, or Laura Ingalls' second cousin, or . . . you get the picture)."

Unfortunately for Montgomery's reputation, literary critics in this century have had little use for books that help readers to feel secure.[6] Texts offering us more of what we already have and love are not nearly so good, we are told, as texts that challenge our expectations, dislodge us from the security of cherished beliefs, shatter our complacencies, split open the congealed surfaces of things, and propel us into new adventures of transgression and defamiliarization. Despite this expert opinion, readers obstinately persist in valuing what they call "safe books" where, as a 38-year-old medical doctor put it, "you know what to expect and what [the book] will expect of you." Especially during a period when the rest of life is stressful, readers said they want a "safe book" by a "trusted author" that can be counted on not to give any nasty surprises. Readers talked about the need for "a place to stand and feel secure," the desire for "reassurance" or "a sense of comfort." To illustrate this point, one reader contrasted herself with a character in Italo Calvino's *If on a Winter's Night a Traveller,* who says she likes books that make her feel uncomfortable from the very first page:

> I don't like those kinds of books. I don't like feeling uncomfortable from the very first page . . . [The books I like to reread provide reassurance] that things do work out . . . It reassures you that, even if you're not getting the rewards you think you've earned, you can keep on going, because eventually things will work out, eventually life will get better. It just helps you cope because of increasing your faith that things are really going to end up right. I think that's how it works for me.

At such times when they needed reassurance, many female readers reported that they read and reread Anne.* * *

---

5. Rubio, "Subverting the Trite: L. M. Montgomery's 'Room of Her Own,' " *CCL: Canadian Children's Literature* 65 (1992): 12.
6. See, for example, two critics as different as Q. D. Leavis and H. R. Jauss. Leavis describes the best literature as that which invites critical distance and detachment, keeps the reader at arm's length and disappoints expectations and contrasts this with inferior literature that encourages the reader to "live at the novelist's expense" by inviting easy identification. Leavis, *Fiction and the Reading Public* (1931; Harmondsworth, England: Penguin, 1979) 188–89. Jauss argues that the quality of a work can be measured by the degree to which there is distance between the new work and the reader's already existing "horizon of expectation." Jauss, *Toward an Aesthetic of Reception*, trans. Timothy Bahti (Minneapolis: U of Minnesota P, 1982) 25.

\* \* \*

However, since time spent with Anne as a friend is time *not* spent with flesh-and-blood friends, some readers acknowledged that reading was partly a guilty pleasure. To express their ambivalence, they used terms such as "escape," "compulsion," and "addiction" and sometimes reported parental disapproval of their childhood reading—e.g. "My parents actually tried to discourage me from reading because I spent a lot of time reading—time that, according to them, I should have spent doing other things like socializing." Behind these comments lies a conflicted sense of a split between active participation in the world and retreat to an imagined world, between social engagement and anti-social immersion in reading.[7] A 44-year-old teacher-librarian admitted,

> Sometimes I think books are more important to me than people and I don't think that's very good. . . . I think sometimes that reading is my way out of relationships or interactions. Books are lovely companions. They don't talk back. They're very accessible. They give you what you want out of it. And if you don't want it, you can close it and hand it back. If it's uncomfortable, you don't have to read it; you can stop.

But having admitted the justice of non-readers' complaints that reading involves the withdrawal of attention and regard from other people, readers immediately qualify their sense of the relationship they feel exists between their own world and the world of the book. It's not exactly retreat, they say; the movement isn't all in one direction, away from the social world. One reader tried to find the right term to describe movement in the other direction, incorporating the reality of the book into her own life:

> I think translation is the nearest image I can think of. Some things are easier to translate than others. Perhaps that's why I say I can't read a book that pushes me too far away from the central characters. If the author is continuously expecting me to dislike or feel alienated from the characters, then I can't satisfactorily read the book, because the experience of reading that I like is to get soaked in the material. There is kind of a translation, and that may be why I always responded well to books about little girls growing up. The translation was very easy there.

7. Over the past thirty years, study after study has confirmed the finding that individuals who are the most committed book readers are also the most active participants in almost every other activity except sleeping. According to the *1983 Consumer Research on Reading and Book Purchasing* (New York: Book Industry Study Group, 1984), "Far from being introverted or social outcasts, book readers emerge as well rounded individuals active in a wide range of social and cultural activities. . . . Book readers as a group are simply more likely to participate in a whole range of activities than are non-book readers and nonreaders" (71–73).

Whereas adventure stories like *Treasure Island* I never took to very much . . .

I think as a child anyway—perhaps it's not true of me as an adult—that I translated from my reading into my real life rather than the other way around. To take L. M. Montgomery, for example. My friend Eleanor had read L. M. Montgomery too. I think our friendship was partly shaped by the way in which Anne and Diana were friends, the way in which Emily and Ilse were friends. (35-year-old Ph.D. candidate)

Much of the discussion so far has emphasized Montgomery's achievement in creating an intensely realized world that is more comforting and more secure than the reader's everyday world. But the last quotation suggests that reading Montgomery can also offer readers a way of engaging the world in a more creative and imaginative way. There is translation and double translation. In childhood, Montgomery herself tried to model her own friendships on ideas about "bosom friends," "kindred spirits," and ten-year letters[8] that appear to have come from books. Later the friendships represented in her own books—the relationships between Anne and Diana, Emily and Ilse, Pat and Jingles—helped to shape her readers' experience of friendship. Similarly, Montgomery's own responses to nature may have been heightened by her reading of Wordsworth, Longfellow, and Emerson, but Anne has taught several generations of readers how to see nature with the eye of the imagination. Shorthand expressions such as "kindred spirits," "scope for the imagination," and "of the tribe of Joseph" turn readers into an insider group of special initiates who, it is implied, would also weep over cut-down trees, rejoice over a birch grove, and feel their souls filled with a nameless exhilaration over the beauty of a sunset.

\*   \*   \*

This is presumably what all readers desire from fiction reading—an experience more intense or more real than their everyday life. Readers of Westerns satisfy their hunger for meaning by immersing themselves directly in physical sensation, mediated as little as possible by language: they experience the glare of the sun, the smell of stale sweat and old leather, the pounding of hooves, the heat of the horse's straining body, the searing pain of a bullet hole through flesh, the salt taste of blood, the warmth of a swallow of whiskey in the throat. Western readers want to feel an ache in their own muscles as they experience with the cowboy the brute physical reality of life

8. A journal entry for July 31, 1891, records a plan made with Will Prichard that they should write each other a "ten year letter" not to be opened or read for ten years (*SJ1* 59).

stripped down to its essentials. But Montgomery readers want to be with the dreaming child, protected in the safe dormer room of an attic but catching a glimpse of something beyond.

# CALVIN TRILLIN

## What Do the Japanese See in *Anne of Green Gables?*†

I can't say that when I heard about the Japanese infatuation with *Anne of Green Gables* a simple explanation came to mind. It was not immediately clear to me why, for instance, some Japanese couples would travel to Prince Edward Island, the bucolic Canadian province that was the setting for the Anne stories, in order to have a wedding ceremony in the parlor where Lucy Maud Montgomery, the creator of Anne, herself got married, in 1911.* * *

\* \* \*

\* \* \*[A] survey taken by a Japanese travel magazine in 1992 listed the places its readers most wanted to visit as New York, Paris, London, and Prince Edward Island.* * *

\* \* \*

But why? Douglas Baldwin, in his article on the Anne phenomenon in Japan, lists any number of theories propounded by experts on Japanese culture to explain Anne's appeal: the Japanese devotion to innocence, their traditional love of nature, the admiration that people in a repressed society have for someone who can be frank and spontaneous, the Japanese sympathy for a poor protagonist who triumphs over long odds.* * *

\* \* \*

\* \* \*Lee Miller, who works in tourism marketing for Prince Edward Island, \* \* \* said that the feeling the Japanese have for Anne is of a different order from the feeling that my daughters had when they were ten or twelve. "I've seen people get off the bus at Green Gables and cry," he said. He paused, and shook his head. Then he said, "We don't fully understand this phenomenon."

† From "Anne of Red Hair: What Do the Japanese See in Anne of Green Gables?" *The New Yorker* 5 August, 1996: 56–61. Copyright © 1996 *The New Yorker.*

428

# CAROL SHIELDS

## Exuberant Vision†

It is easy enough to see what [my mother] found in *Anne of Green Gables*. She found what millions of others have found, a consciousness attuned to nature, a female model of courage, goodness, and candor, possessed of emotional capacity that triumphs and converts. Unlike Tom Sawyer who capitulates to society, Anne transforms her community with her exuberant vision. She enters the story disentitled and emerges as cherished daughter, with loving friends and a future ahead of her, and she has done it all without help: captured Gilbert Blythe, sealed her happiness, and reshuffled the values of society by a primary act of re-imagination.

# MARGARET ATWOOD

## Revisiting *Anne*†

*Anne of Green Gables* is one of those books you almost feel guilty liking, because so many other people seem to like it as well. If it's that popular, you feel, it can't possibly be good, or good for you.

Like many others, I read this book as a child, and absorbed it so thoroughly that I can't even remember when. I read it to my own daughter when she was eight, and she read it to herself later, and acquired all the sequels.* * *

\* \* \*

It may be the ludicrous escapades of Anne that render the book so attractive to children, but it is the struggles of Marilla that give resonance for adults. Anne may be the orphan in all of us, but then, so is Marilla. Anne is the fairy-tale wish-fulfillment version, what Montgomery longed for. Marilla is, more likely, what she feared she might become: joyless, bereft, trapped, hopeless, unloved. Each of them saves the other. It is the neatness of their psychological fit—as well as the invention, humor, and fidelity of the writing—that makes *Anne* such a satisfying and enduring fable.

† From "Thinking Back through our Mothers," *Re/Discovering Our Foremothers*, ed. Lorraine McMullen, 10. Copyright © 1990 University of Ottawa Press.
† From Afterword, *Anne of Green Gables*, by L. M. Montgomery (Toronto: McClelland & Stewart, 1992) 331–36. Afterword Copyright © 1992 by O. W. Toad Ltd. Reprinted with permission of the author.

# Lucy Maud Montgomery: A Chronology

1874        Lucy Maud Montgomery born 30 November into a family of Scots-English farmers, long established on the north shore of Prince Edward Island, Canada. Grandfathers on both sides had been prominent politicians.

1876        Death of her mother, Clara Macneill Montgomery; left by her father Hugh John Montgomery (a storekeeper) to be raised by maternal grandparents Alexander and Lucy Woolner Macneill within a large extended family in Cavendish and Park Corner, PEI.

1880–90    Spends winters in Cavendish school, summers at the seashore and in Park Corner, PEI, with her young Campbell cousins. Listens to family story-tellers, writes poetry and keeps a diary from the age of nine. Her father moves to Saskatchewan, remarries in western Canada, and starts a new family.

1890        Travels by rail with her paternal grandfather, Senator Donald Montgomery, to join her father, stepmother and year-old half-sister and to attend high school in Prince Albert, Sask. Forms strong friendships with Laura and Will Pritchard. First publication: a poem in the *Daily Patriot* (Charlottetown), 1890.

1891        Half-brother Bruce born February. Essay "The Wreck of the Marco Polo" published in the Montreal *Witness*. In March, taken out of school to help with housework. Publishes article "A Western Eden" in the Prince Albert *Times*. Returns home to PEI in August.

1891–93    In Cavendish and Park Corner; out of school for the better part of a year; in the Prince of Wales College entrance exams, she attains fifth highest marks in the Province.

1893–94    Enrolls in the teacher's course at Prince of Wales College in Charlottetown, PEI, taking a two-year course in one year. Publishes in College *Record* and Charlottetown *Guardian*.

429

1894–95     Teaches at one-room village school at Bideford, PEI. Publishes short stories and poems in Sunday School papers and *Ladies' Journal*, some under pseudonyms including "Maud Cavendish" and "Maud Eglinton."

1895–96     Studies at Dalhousie University, Halifax, Nova Scotia. First earnings from her writing, from Philadelphia *Golden Days* and Boston *Youth's Companion*.

1896–97     Teaches in Belmont, PEI, a rural area. Becomes secretly engaged to Edwin Simpson, a theological student and a distant cousin, preparing for Baptist ministry. Poems and stories published in *American Agriculturist*, *Ladies' World*, *Philadelphia Times*, etc., signed "L. M. Montgomery."

1897–98     Teaches at Lower Bedeque, PEI. Falls in love with Herman Leard, a young Bedeque farmer, and breaks off engagement to Simpson. Grandfather Macneill's death in March brings her back to Cavendish, to help her seventy-six-year-old grandmother. Publishes nineteen light romantic short stories and fourteen poems.

1899     Death of Herman Leard. Stories published this year include one republished in *Anne of Avonlea*.

1900     Death of her father in Prince Albert. In magazines including *Good Housekeeping*, *Waverley*, and *Family Herald*, publishes eleven short stories, including "The Winning of Anne."

1901–02     Works as copyeditor in Halifax, NS, on the *Daily Echo*; after seven months returns to Cavendish. Begins correspondence with Ephraim Weber, school teacher in Alberta, western Canada.

1902–04     Keeps house for her grandmother, reading, writing, gardening, and acting as assistant postmistress. Settling into work as a professional writer, sells 103 stories in this period and 92 poems. A new teacher, Nora Lefurgey, boards at the Macneill farm and joins LMM in writing a frivolous diary. Begins a long-lasting correspondence with George B. Macmillan, journalist in Scotland. Stories from this period will reappear in *Chronicles of Avonlea*, *The Story Girl*, and *Further Chronicles of Avonlea*.

1905     Friendship with cousin Frederica Campbell and with Cavendish's new Presbyterian minister, the Rev. Ewan Macdonald. Works on *Anne of Green Gables*.

1906     Engaged to marry Ewan Macdonald. He leaves for a year's study in Scotland. Writes "Una of the Garden," later revised as *Kilmeny of the Orchard*. Publishes forty-three stories, many of them republished in other magazines and in her later collections.

1907    *Anne of Green Gables* accepted by L. C. Page Co. of Boston. At Page's urging, begins work on a sequel, *Anne of Avonlea*. LMM writes her friend Ephraim Weber in May that the L. C. Page Company accepted *AGG* in April 1907. Her assertion that the book is "merely a juvenilish story, ostensibly for girls" sounds like false modesty in light of her comments later in life that it was not written just for children.

1908    *Anne of Green Gables* printed in April, but officially published in June; goes through seven printings between release and December 1908, selling 19,000 copies in first five months; evokes praise from reviewers and letters from admirers including Mark Twain.

1909    *Anne of Avonlea* (about Anne as a young teacher) published as well as over fifty stories and poems. *Anne of Green Gables* translated into Swedish.

1910    The Rev. Ewan Macdonald moves to the Presbyterian church in the small rural village of Leaskdale, Ontario, Canada. *Kilmeny of the Orchard* (a romance set in PEI) is published. Canada's Governor General Earl Grey asks to meet Montgomery in Charlottetown, PEI. Travels to Boston to visit publisher L. C. Page. *Anne of Green Gables* is translated into Dutch.

1911    Grandmother dies, aged eighty-seven, in March. Publishes *The Story Girl* (a group of PEI cousins welcomes two boys from Toronto; all relish stories told by Sara Stanley) in May. July 5 LMM marries Ewan Macdonald in Park Corner. After two months' honeymoon (paid for from her royalties) in Scotland and England, where LMM meets George B. Macmillan, the Macdonalds settle into Presbyterian manse at Leaskdale, sixty miles northeast of Toronto.

1912    Publishes *Chronicles of Avonlea* (older stories revised to include references to Anne). First child Chester Cameron Macdonald born 7 July. *Anne of Green Gables* translated into Polish.

1913    Finishes *The Golden Road*, (sequel to *The Story Girl*) first of her novels composed in Ontario. Summer visit to PEI. Begins work on her third "Anne" book.

1914    Second son Hugh Alexander born and dies 13 August. Canada joins World War I on 5 August. Celebrates her fortieth birthday in November. L. C. Page sells cheap reprint rights to Grosset and Dunlap, angering LMM.

1915          Publishes *Anne of the Island* (about Anne's college days).
              Gives birth to youngest son Ewan Stuart Macdonald 7
              October. Experiences pressures as a minister's wife in a
              parish devastated by wartime casualties.

1916          Publishes *The Watchman, and Other Poems* (thirteen
              new poems plus fifty others published since 1899).
              Events lead LMM to change publishers, from L. C. Page
              of Boston to McClelland, Goodchild & Stewart of
              Toronto.

1917          Publishes *Anne's House of Dreams* (about Anne's early
              days of marriage and motherhood) and "The Alpine
              Path," an autobiographical essay, in Toronto *Every-
              woman's World*.

1918          Lawsuit against L. C. Page Company over their short-
              changing in royalties, unauthorized selling of reprint
              rights, and proposal to publish *Further Chronicles of
              Avonlea* without her permission. *Anne of Green Gables*
              translated into Norwegian.

1919          Her dear cousin Frederica Campbell dies of influenza.
              Wins first case against Page in Boston; assigns right to
              her seven early works to him in return for a cash settle-
              ment of $17,880, not knowing he is negotiating film
              rights. *Anne of Green Gables* made into a Hollywood
              film: the $40,000 from the sale of rights all goes to Page.
              Ewan Macdonald suffers nervous breakdown. Publishes
              *Rainbow Valley* (Anne's children befriend the motherless
              children of a minister).

1920          *Further Chronicles of Avonlea* is published, with unau-
              thorized revisions of her stories; LMM sues Page, who
              brings a countersuit for malicious litigation. *Anne of
              Green Gables* translated into Finnish. Mary Miles Min-
              ter silent movie edition of *Anne* published (49th impres-
              sion, April 1920, 349th thousand).

1921          *Rilla of Ingleside* (Anne's children as young adults in
              World War I) published. The Macdonalds travel to PEI
              with Ewan's longtime friend Edwin Smith and his wife
              and cousins.

1921–22       Involved in a car accident that results in acrimonious
              lawsuit in Toronto, brought by a man in a nearby village.
              The Macdonalds enjoy a brief holiday in Muskoka cot-
              tage country. They lose lawsuit in Toronto court.

1923          Wins her case against Page in American courts, but Page
              retains rights to early books. Publishes *Emily of New
              Moon* (a new heroine, again in a PEI setting). Becomes

first Canadian woman to be elected member of British
Royal Society of Arts.

1925      Publishes *Emily Climbs* (Emily strives to become a
writer). Elder son Chester leaves for boarding school
north of Toronto. The Macdonalds work to prevent
Church Union (Presbyterians, Methodists, and Congre-
gationalists), but the United Church of Canada is established by vote in June. *Anne of Green Gables* translated
into French. The original 1908 plates for *Anne* are worn
out, and two separate (and different) new editions are
reset and published: the 1925 Page edition, with new
illustrations by Elizabeth Withington, and the 1925 British Harrap edition.

1926      Ewan Macdonald accepts a call to a continuing Presbyterian Church in Norval, Ontario, thirty miles west of
Toronto; the Macdonalds move into the Norval manse.
Publishes *The Blue Castle* (adult romance set in Mus-
koka area of Northern Ontario, a lake district). In February 1926, Page's 59th printing of *Anne* reads "403rd
Thousand."

1927      Publishes *Emily's Quest*. Invited to meet Prince of Wales
(later King Edward VIII) in Toronto. British Prime Minister Stanley Baldwin writes a fan letter from 10 Down-
ing Street. Summer trip to PEI. Wins another round of
lawsuits against Page.

1928–29   Publishes *Magic for Marigold* in 1929 (focused on a pre-
school child). Meets longtime correspondent Ephraim
Weber. Autumn visit to PEI. Younger son Stuart leaves
for boarding school. Reunion with Nora Lefurgey Campbell, now living in Toronto. Lawsuit against publisher
Page brought to successful conclusion.

1930      On a speaking tour through the Canadian West, renews
friendship with Laura Pritchard Agnew and meets
Ephraim Weber.

1931      Publishes *A Tangled Web* (adult novel set in PEI). Elder
son Chester enters University of Toronto as an engineering student.

1932      Directs play for Norval amateur group. Chester, having
failed his year, repeats his first-year courses.

1933      Publishes *Pat of Silver Bush* (focused on a home like the
Campbell farmhouse in Park Corner). *Anne of Green
Gables* translated into Icelandic. Second son Stuart
enters University of Toronto to study medicine. Chester
fails his second year, withdraws from engineering;

reveals his secret marriage to a young Norval woman, Luella Reid. L. C. Page brings out a "Silver Anniversary Edition" of *AGG* with colored illustrations by Sybil Tawse: it is the "Sixty-eighth Impression (553rd Thousand)."

1934    In company with two other Canadian novelists, publishes *Courageous Women* (biographies of notable women). Second Hollywood film version of *Anne of Green Gables*; as in 1919, her legal settlement with L. C. Page means that the profits from the film go to him. Chester begins study of law. First grandchild, Luella Macdonald, born. Ewan spends four months in Guelph's Homewood sanatorium for private mental patients. Stock market reverses contribute to LMM's six-week breakdown of nerves and general health.

1935    Publishes *Mistress Pat* (a lonely woman loses her home but finds romance). Ewan Macdonald retires from the ministry under pressure of some members of the congregation. Macdonald family buys a house in west-end Toronto on Riverside Drive and moves there. Awarded the Order of the British Empire as part of King George V's Jubilee Honours list. Elected to the Literary and Artistic Institute of France.

1936    Publishes *Anne of Windy Poplars* (Anne as a young school principal). Birth of second grandchild, Cameron Macdonald. Distress over Chester's infatuation with Ida Birrell (later his second wife, and mother of two more children, David and Catherine). Part of Cavendish designated by Canadian government as a national "Green Gables" park.

1937    Publishes *Jane of Lantern Hill* (a young girl leaves Toronto for happiness in PEI). LMM's mental health breaks down under stress of worry over Ewan, loss of her beloved cat "Good Luck," Chester's extramarital affairs and his failure to attend to his study in law, and Stuart's affection for a young woman in Norval.

1938    Nervous collapse brought on by worry over her finances, Chester's behavior, her husband's mental health, attacks on her reputation as a writer, and her own health. She remakes her will in an attempt to sober Chester. Continues work on her final "Anne" book.

1939    Last visit to PEI. Island scenes reappear in *Anne of Ingleside* (Anne's early days of marriage and motherhood), the last work published in LMM's lifetime. Chester called to the bar in June. She stakes him in a law practice and he reconciles with his wife. Stuart finishes final year of medicine and begins interning. LMM sells film rights to RKO Studios for *Anne of Windy Poplars*. Depression deepens with outbreak of World War II in September. Discontinues regular entries in the journal kept since 1889.

1940    Chester's marriage and law practice fail. Chester turned down for military service; Stuart put on deferred list until the end of his medical internship. Damaged arm resulting from a fall contributes to another bout of nervous depression. Work proceeds on a final collection of Anne stories (published 1974 as *The Road to Yesterday*).

1941    Continues to send postcards to George B. Macmillan in Scotland: the final note in December reveals worry over the war, Ewan's mental illness, her own health, and the future of her sons.

1942    First Canadian edition of *Anne of Green Gables* published by Ryerson of Toronto. Lucy Maud Montgomery Macdonald dies in her Toronto home, 24 April. Buried in Cavendish, PEI. Ewan dies the following year.

# Selected Bibliography

• Indicates works included or excerpted in this Norton Critical Edition

## BIBLIOGRAPHIES

"Bibliography of Materials on L. M. Montgomery Published in *Canadian Children's Literature* 1975–2004." *CCL: Canadian Children's Literature* (Spring-Summer 2004): 117–20. [This is also available on-line, with summaries of the articles, through the "Canadian Children's Literature Database": <http://www2.lib.uoguelph.ca/resources/ccl/>.]

Garner, Barbara Carman, and Mary Harker. "*Anne of Green Gables*: An Annotated Bibliography." *CCL: Canadian Children's Literature* 55 (1989): 18–41.

Lefebvre, Benjamin. "L. M. Montgomery: An Annotated Filmography." *CCL: Canadian Children's Literature* 99 (2000): 43–73.

Russell, Ruth Weber, D. W. Russell, and Rea Wilmshurst. *Lucy Maud Montgomery: A Preliminary Bibliography*. Waterloo: University of Waterloo Library, 1986.

## BIOGRAPHIES, JOURNALS, AND CORRESPONDENCE

Bolger, Francis W. P. *The Years Before 'Anne.'* Charlottetown: Prince Edward Island Heritage Foundation, 1974.

• Bolger, Francis W. P., and Elizabeth R. Epperly, eds. *My Dear Mr. M.: Letters to G. B. MacMillan*. Toronto: McGraw-Hill Ryerson, 1980. [Republished with a new Preface by Oxford UP in 1992.]

• Eggleston, Wilfrid, ed. *The Green Gables Letters from L. M. Montgomery to Ephraim Weber*. Toronto: Ryerson, 1960.

Gillen, Mollie. *The Wheel of Things: A Biography of L. M. Montgomery*. Markham: Fitzhenry and Whiteside, 1975.

Montgomery, L. M. *The Alpine Path: The Story of My Career*. 1917. Markham: Fitzhenry and Whiteside, 1997.

———. *Akin to Anne: Tales of Other Orphans*. Ed. Rea Wilmshurst. Toronto: McClelland & Stewart, 1989.

———. "The Way to Make a Book." In "Scrapbook of Reviews from Around the World Which L. M. Montgomery's Clipping Service Sent to Her, 1910–1935." 86. L. M. Montgomery Collection, U of Guelph Library Archives, Guelph, Ontario. [XZ5 MS A003]. Reprinted in: Cecily Devereux, ed. *Anne of Green Gables*. By L. M. Montgomery. Peterborough: Broadview, 2004. 365–70.

• ———. "I Dwell Among My Own People." In "Scrapbook of Reviews From Around the World Which L. M. Montgomery's Clipping Service Sent to Her, 1910–1935." 195. L. M. Montgomery Collection, U of Guelph Library Archives, Guelph, Ontario. [XZ5 MS A003]. Reprinted in: *Canadian Novelists and the Novel*. Ed. Douglas Daymond and Leslie Monkman. Ottawa: Borealis, 1981. 113–14.

• ———. *The Selected Journals of L. M. Montgomery, 1: 1889–1910*. Ed. Mary Rubio and Elizabeth Waterston. Toronto: Oxford UP, 1985.

• ———. *The Selected Journals of L. M. Montgomery, 2: 1910–1921*. Ed. Mary Rubio and Elizabeth Waterston. Toronto: Oxford UP, 1987.

———. *The Selected Journals of L. M. Montgomery, 3: 1921–1929*. Ed. Mary Rubio and Elizabeth Waterston. Toronto: Oxford UP, 1992.

• ———. *The Selected Journals of L. M. Montgomery, 4: 1929–1935*. Ed. Mary Rubio and Elizabeth Waterston. Toronto: Oxford UP, 1998.

————. *The Selected Journals of L. M. Montgomery, 5: 1935–1942.* Ed. Mary Rubio and Elizabeth Waterston. Toronto: Oxford UP, 2004.

————. *Unpublished Sections of the Holograph Journals, 1889–1942.* L. M. Montgomery Collection, U of Guelph Archives.

Ridley, Hilda M. *The Story of L. M. Montgomery.* London: George G. Harrap, 1956.

Rubio, Mary, and Elizabeth Waterston. *Writing a Life: L. M. Montgomery.* Toronto: ECW Press, 1995.

Tiessen, Hildi Froese, and Paul Gerard Tiessen, eds. *After Green Gables: L. M. Montgomery's Letters to Ephraim Weber, 1916–1941.* Toronto: U of Toronto P, 2006.

Waterston, Elizabeth. "Lucy Maud Montgomery 1874–1942." *The Clear Spirit: Twenty Canadian Women and Their Times.* Ed. Mary Quayle Innis. Toronto: U of Toronto P, 1966. 198–220.

Wiggins, Genevieve. *L. M. Montgomery.* Twayne's World Authors Ser. 834. New York: Twayne, 1992.

## CRITICAL STUDIES OF L. M. MONTGOMERY AND CONTEXT

•Åhmansson, Gabriella. *A Life and Its Mirrors: A Feminist Reading of L. M. Montgomery's Fiction, Volume 1: An Introduction to Lucy Maud Montgomery and Anne Shirley.* Uppsala: Almqvist and Wiksell International, 1991.

————. "Mayflowers Grow in Sweden too: L. M. Montgomery, Astrid Lindgren, and the Swedish Literary Consciousness." *Harvesting Thistles: The Textual Garden of L. M. Montgomery.* Ed. Mary Henley Rubio. Guelph: Canadian Children's P, 1994. 14–22.

Alexander, Joy. " 'I hear what you say': Soundings in L. M. Montgomery's Life Writings." *The Intimate Life of L. M. Montgomery.* Ed. Irene Gammel. Toronto: U of Toronto P, 2005. 210–21.

Buss, Helen M. "Decoding L. M. Montgomery's Journals/Encoding a Critical Practice for Women's Private Literature." *Essays on Canadian Writing* 54 (Winter 1994): 80–100.

Cavert, Mary Beth. "L. M. Montgomery and Friendship." *The Lucy Maud Montgomery Album.* Comp. Kevin McCabe and ed. Alexandra Heilbron. Markham: Fitzhenry and Whiteside, 1999. 281–85.

Collins, Carolyn Strom, and Christina Wyss Eriksson. *The Anne of Green Gables Treasury.* Toronto: Viking Penguin, 1991.

Crawford, Elaine, and Kelly Crawford. *Aunt Maud's Recipe Book.* Norval, ON: Moulin Press, 1996.

•Epperly, Elizabeth R. *The Fragrance of Sweet-Grass: L. M. Montgomery's Heroines and the Pursuit of Romance.* Toronto: U of Toronto P, 1992.

Drew, Lorna. "The Emily Connection: Ann Radcliffe, L. M. Montgomery and 'The Female Gothic.' " *Canadian Children's Literature* 77 (1995): 19–32.

Gammel, Irene. "Making Avonlea: An Introduction;" *Making Avonlea: L. M. Montgomery and Popular Culture.* Ed. Irene Gammel. Toronto: U of Toronto P, 2002. 3–13.

————. "Safe Pleasures for Girls: L. M. Montgomery's Erotic Landscapes." *Making Avonlea: L. M. Montgomery and Popular Culture.* Ed. Irene Gammel. Toronto: U of Toronto P, 2002. 114–27.

Gammel, Irene, and Ann Dutton. "Disciplining Development: L. M. Montgomery and Early Schooling." *L. M. Montgomery and Canadian Culture.* Ed. Irene Gammel and Elizabeth R. Epperly. Toronto: U of Toronto P, 1999. 106–119.

Gammel, Irene, and Elizabeth R. Epperly. "Introduction: L. M. Montgomery and the Shaping of Canadian Culture." *L. M. Montgomery and Canadian Culture.* Ed. Irene Gammel and Elizabeth R. Epperly. Toronto: U of Toronto P, 1999. 3–13.

Gerson, Carole. "Canadian Women Writers and American Markets, 1880–1940." *Context North America: Canadian/US Literary Relations.* Ed. Camille La Bossiere. Ottawa: U of Ottawa P, 1994. 106–18.

•————. " 'Dragged at Anne's Chariot Wheels': The Triangle of Author, Publisher, and Fictional Character." *L. M. Montgomery and Canadian Culture.* Ed. Irene Gammel and Elizabeth R. Epperly. Toronto: U of Toronto P. 1999. 49–63.

————. " 'Fitted to Earn Her Own Living': Figures of the New Woman in the Writing of L. M. Montgomery." *Children's Voices in Atlantic Literature and Culture: Essays on Childhood.* Ed. Hilary Thompson. Guelph: Canadian Children's P, 1995. 24–35.

Hammill, Faye. *Literary Culture and Female Authorship in Canada 1760–2000.* Cross/Cultures 63. New York and Amsterdam: Rodopi, 2003: 81–113.

Katz, Bernard, "The Bend in the Road: L. M. Montgomery and Her English Language Publishers, a Case Study." Fifty-ninth annual meeting of the Bibliographical Society of Canada. McMaster University, Hamilton, Ontario. 28 June 2004. [unpublished paper]

•Johnston, Rosemary Ross. "L. M. Montgomery's Interior/Exterior Landscapes: Landscape as

Palimpsest, Pentimento, Epiphany: Lucy Maud Montgomery's Interiorisation of the Exterior, Exteriorisation of the Interior." Montgomery Conference, Charlottetown. 23 June 2004. Now available as: Johnston, Rosemary Ross. "Landscape as Palimpsest, Pentimento, Epiphany: Lucy Maud Montgomery's Interiorisation of the Exterior, Exteriorisation of the Interior." *CREArTA. Journal of the Centre for Research and Education in the Arts* 5 (2005): 13–31.

———. " 'Reaching Beyond the Word:' Religious Themes as 'Deep Structure' in the 'Anne' Books of L. M. Montgomery." *CCL: Canadian Children's Literature* 88 (1997): 7–18.

Litster, Jennifer H. " 'The Golden Road of Youth': L. M. Montgomery and British Children's Books." *CCL: Canadian Children's Literature* 113–14 (2004): 56–72.

———. "The Scottish Context of L. M. Montgomery." PhD Diss., U of Edinburgh. 1998.

McCabe, Kevin. "Maud's Early Schooldays." *The Lucy Maud Montgomery Album.* Comp. Kevin McCabe and ed. Alexandra Heilbron. Markham: Fitzhenry and Whiteside, 1999. 49–54.

———. " 'The Happiest Year of My Life': Prince of Wales College, Charlottetown, 1893–94." *The Lucy Maud Montgomery Album.* Comp. Kevin McCabe and ed. Alexandra Heilbron. Markham: Fitzhenry and Whiteside, 1999. 94–99.

• MacMechan, Archibald. *Head-Waters of Canadian Literature.* Toronto: McClelland & Stewart, 1924. 209–13.

Mount, Nick. *When Canadian Literature Moved to New York.* Toronto: U of Toronto P, 2005.

• Rubio, Mary Henley. "L. M. Montgomery: Scottish-Presbyterian Agency in Canadian Culture." *L. M. Montgomery and Canadian Culture.* Ed. Irene Gammel and Elizabeth Epperly. Toronto: UTP, 1999. 89–105.

———, ed. *Harvesting Thistles: The Textual Garden of L. M. Montgomery.* Guelph: Canadian Children's P, 1994.

———. "L. M. Montgomery." *Profiles in Canadian Literature* 7. Ed. Jeffrey M. Heath. Toronto: Dundurn P, 1991. 37–45.

———. " 'A Dusting Off': An Anecdotal Account of Editing the L. M. Montgomery Journals." Working in Women's Archives: Researching Women's Private Literature and Archival Documents. Ed. Helen M. Buss and Marlene Kadar. Waterloo, ON: Wilfrid Laurier Press. 51–78.

Tausky, Thomas E. "L. M. Montgomery and 'The Alpine Path, So Hard, So Steep.' " *CCL: Canadian Children's Literature* 30 (1983): 5–20.

Tye, Diane. "Women's Oral Narrative Traditions as Depicted in Lucy Maud Montgomery's Fiction, 1918–1939." *Myth and Milieu: Atlantic Literature and Culture, 1918–1939.* Ed. Gwendolyn Davies. Fredericton: *Acadiensis,* 1993. 123–35.

Wachowicz, Barbara. "L. M. Montgomery: At Home in Poland." *CCL: Canadian Children's Literature* 46 (1987): 7–36.

Waterston, Elizabeth. "Barrie, Montgomery, and the Mists of Sentiment." *Rapt in Plaid: Canadian Literature and Scottish Tradition.* Toronto: U of Toronto P, 2001. 175–91.

———. *Children's Literature in Canada.* New York: Macmillan, 1992. [Twayne World Author Series.]

———. "Flowers and L. M. Montgomery." *The Lucy Maud Montgomery Album.* Comp. Kevin McCabe and ed. Alexandra Heilbron. Markham: Fitzhenry and Whiteside, 1999. 301–04.

———. "Orphans, Twins, and L. M. Montgomery." *Family Fictions in Canadian Literature.* Ed. Peter Hinchcliffe. Waterloo: U of Waterloo P, 1987. 68–76.

Whitaker, Muriel A. "Missing Fathers: A Development Motif in Some Atlantic Fiction." *Children's Voices in Atlantic Literature and Culture: Essays on Childhood.* Ed. Hilary Thompson. Guelph: Canadian Children's P, 1995.

———. " 'Queer Children' L. M. Montgomery Heroines." *L. M. Montgomery: An Assessment.* Ed. John Sorfleet. Guelph: Canadian Children's P, 1975. 50–59.

White, Gavin. "Falling out of the Haystack: L. M. Montgomery and Lesbian Desire." *CCL: Canadian Children's Literature* 102 (2001): 43–59.

———. "L. M. Montgomery and the French." *CCL: Canadian Children's Literature* 78 (1995): 65–68.

Wilmshurst, Rea. "L. M. Montgomery's Use of Quotations and Allusions in the 'Anne' Books." *CCL: Canadian Children's Literature* 56 (1989): 15–45.

Yeast, Denyse. "Negotiating Friendships: The Reading and Writing of L. M. Montgomery." *Harvesting Thistles: The Textual Garden of L. M. Montgomery.* Ed. Mary Henley Rubio. Guelph: Canadian Children's P, 1994. 113–25.

York, Lorraine. " 'I Knew I Would "Arrive" Some Day': L. M. Montgomery and the Strategies of Literary Celebrity." *CCL: Canadian Children's Literature* 113–14 (2004): 98–116.

## CRITICAL STUDIES OF *ANNE OF GREEN GABLES*

Akamatsu, Yoshiko. "Japanese Readings of *Anne of Green Gables*." *L. M. Montgomery and Canadian Culture*. Ed. Irene Gammel and Elizabeth R. Epperly. Toronto: U of Toronto P, 1999. 201–12.

Allard, Danièle. "The Popularity of *Anne of Green Gables* in Japan—A Study of Hanako Muraoka's Translation of L. M. Montgomery's Novel and Its Reception." PhD Diss. Université de Sherbrooke, 2002.

•Atwood, Margaret. Afterword. *Anne of Green Gables*. By L. M. Montgomery. Toronto: McClelland & Stewart, 1992. 331–36. See also: "Introduction: *Anne of Green Gables*. By L. M. Montgomery. London: The Folio Society, 2004. ix–xiv.

Baldwin, Douglas. "L. M. Montgomery's *Anne of Green Gables*: The Japanese Connection." *Journal of Canadian Studies* 28.3 (1993): 123–33.

Barry, Wendy E. "The Geography of *Anne of Green Gables*." *The Annotated Anne of Green Gables*. By L. M. Montgomery. Ed. Wendy E. Barry, Margaret Anne Doody, and Mary E. Doody Jones. New York: Oxford UP, 1997. 418–21.

———. "The Settlers of P.E.I.: The Celtic Influence in *Anne*." *The Annotated Anne of Green Gables*. By L. M. Montgomery. Ed. Wendy E. Barry, Margaret Anne Doody, and Mary E. Doody Jones. New York: Oxford UP, 1997. 415–18.

Barry, Wendy E., Margaret Anne Doody, and Mary E. Doody Jones, eds. *The Annotated Anne of Green Gables*. New York: Oxford UP, 1997.

Berg, Temma F. "*Anne of Green Gables*: A Girl's Reading." *Children's Literature Association Quarterly* 13.3 (1988): 124–28.

———. "Sisterhood is Fearful: Female Friendships in L. M. Montgomery." *Harvesting Thistles: The Textual Garden of L. M. Montgomery*. Ed. Mary Henley Rubio. Guelph, ON: Canadian Children's P, 1994. 36–49.

Berke, Jacqueline. "Mother I Can Do It Myself: The Self-Sufficient Heroine in Popular Girls' Fiction." *Women's Studies* 6.1 (1978): 187–203.

Brennan, Joseph Gerard. "The Story of a Classic: Anne and After." *American Scholar* 64.2 (1995): 247–56.

Burns, Jane. "Anne and Emily: L. M. Montgomery's Children." *Room of One's Own* 3.3 (1977): 37–48.

Cadogan, Mary, and Patricia Craig. *You're a Brick, Angela! A New Look at Girls' Fiction from 1839 to 1975*. London: Victor Gollancz, 1976.

Cameron, Silver Donald. "Anne, with an 'E.' " *Sniffing the Coast: An Acadian Voyage*. Toronto: Macmillan, 1993. 109–20.

Careless, Virginia. "The Hijacking of Anne." *CCL: Canadian Children's Literature* 67 (1992): 48–56.

•———. "L. M. Montgomery and Everybody Else: A Look at the Books." *Windows and Words: A Look at Canadian Children's Literature in English*. Ed. Aïda Hudson and Susan-Ann Cooper. Ottawa: U of Ottawa P, 2003. 143–74.

Clarkson, Adrienne. Foreword. *L. M. Montgomery and Canadian Culture*. Ed. Irene Gammel and Elizabeth R. Epperly. Toronto: U of Toronto P, 1999. ix–xii.

Classen, Constance. "Is 'Anne of Green Gables' An American Import?" *CCL: Canadian Children's Literature* 55 (1989): 42–50.

•Davey, Frank. "The Hard-Won Power of Canadian Womanhood: Reading *Anne of Green Gables* Today." *L. M. Montgomery and Canadian Culture*. Ed. Irene Gammel and Elizabeth R. Epperly. Toronto: U of Toronto P, 1999. 163–82.

•Davies, Robertson. Obituary: L. M. Montgomery. *Peterborough Examiner* 2 May 1942: 4.

Dawson, Janise. "Literary Relations: Anne Shirley and Her American Cousins." *Children's Literature in Education* 33.1 (2002): 29–51.

Devereux, Cecily. "Anatomy of a 'National Icon': *Anne of Green Gables* and the 'Bosom Friends' Affair." *Making Avonlea: L. M. Montgomery and Popular Culture*. Ed. Irene Gammel. Toronto: U of Toronto P, 2002. 32–42.

———. " 'Canadian Classic' and 'Commodity Export': The Nationalism of 'Our' Anne of Green Gables." *Journal of Canadian Studies* 36.1 (2001): 11–28.

•———. " 'Not one of those dreadful new women': Anne Shirley and the Culture of Imperial Motherhood." *Windows and Words: A Look at Canadian Children's Literature in English*. Ed. Aïda Hudson and Susan-Ann Cooper. Ottawa: U of Ottawa P, 2003. 119–30.

———. " 'See my Journal for the full story': Fictions of Truth in *Anne of Green Gables* and L. M. Montgomery's Journals." *The Intimate Life of L. M. Montgomery*. Ed. Irene Gammel. Toronto: U of Toronto P, 2005. 241–57.

———. "The 'Anne' in 'Canadianness.' " *Canadian Literature* (2002): 166–67.

———, ed. *Anne of Green Gables*. By L. M. Montgomery. Peterborough: Broadview, 2004.

Doody, Margaret Anne. "Food Preparation, Cookery, and Home Decoration." *The Annotated Anne of Green Gables.* By L. M. Montgomery. Ed. Wendy E. Barry, Margaret Anne Doody, and Mary E. Doody Jones. New York: Oxford UP, 1997. 443–52.

———. "Gardens and Plants." *The Annotated Anne of Green Gables.* By L. M. Montgomery. Ed. Wendy E. Barry, Margaret Anne Doody, and Mary E. Doody Jones. New York: Oxford UP, 1997. 434–38.

———. "Homemade Artifacts and Home Life." *The Annotated Anne of Green Gables.* By L. M. Montgomery. Ed. Wendy E. Barry, Margaret Anne Doody, and Mary E. Doody Jones. New York: Oxford UP, 1997. 438–43.

———. Introduction. *The Annotated Anne of Green Gables.* By L. M. Montgomery. Ed. Wendy E. Barry, Margaret Anne Doody, and Mary E. Doody Jones. New York: Oxford UP, 1997. 9–34.

Drain, Susan. "Community and the Individual in *Anne of Green Gables*: The Meaning of Belonging." *Children's Literature Association Quarterly* 11.1 (1986): 15–19.

———. "Feminine Convention and Female Identity: The Persistent Challenge of *Anne of Green Gables.*" *CCL: Canadian Children's Literature* 65 (1992): 40–47.

———. " 'Too Much Love-Making': *Anne of Green Gables* on Television." *The Lion and the Unicorn* 2.2 (1987): 63–72.

Epperly, Elizabeth. "Approaching the Montgomery Manuscripts." *Harvesting Thistles: The Textual Garden of L. M. Montgomery.* Ed. Mary Henley Rubio. Guelph. ON: Canadian Children's P, 1994. 74–83.

———. "L. M. Montgomery and the Changing Times." *Acadiensis* 17.2 (1988): 177–85.

———. "L. M. Montgomery's Manuscript Revisions." *Atlantis* 20.1 (1995): 149–55.

———. "The Restraints of Romance: L. M. Montgomery's Limiting and Liberating Fictions." *The More We Get Together: Women and Disability.* Ed. Houston Stewart, Beth Percival, and Elizabeth R. Epperly. Charlottetown: Gynergy Books, 1992. 215–22.

Fenwick, Julie. "The Silence of the Mermaid: *Lady Oracle* and *Anne of Green Gables.*" *Essays on Canadian Writing* 47 (1992): 51–64.

Foster, Shirley, and Judy Simons. *What Katy Read: Feminist Re-Readings of 'Classic' Stories for Girls.* Iowa City. U of Iowa P, 1995. 149–71.

Frever, Trinna S. "Adaptive Interplay: L. M. Montgomery, William Shakespeare, and Virginia Woolf's Shakespearean Sister." Ed. Daniel Fischlin / Canadian Adaptations of Shakespeare Project / 2004. University of Guelph. 30 Mar. 2006. <www.canadianshakespeares.ca/multimedia/pdf/l_m_montgomery.pdf>.

•Frye, Northrop. Conclusion. *Literary History of Canada.* Ed. C. F. Klinck. Toronto: U of Toronto P, 1965. 840.

Gates, Charlene E. "Image, Imagination and Initiation: Teaching as a Rite of Passage in the Novels of L. M. Montgomery and Laura Ingalls Wilder." *Children's Literature in Education* 20.3 (1989): 165–73.

Gay, Carol. " 'Kindred Spirits' All: Green Gables Revisited." *Children's Literature Association Quarterly* 11.1 (1986): 9–12.

•Gubar, Marah. " 'Where Is the Boy?' The Pleasures of Postponement in the *Anne of Green Gables* Series." *The Lion and the Unicorn* 25.1 (2001): 47–69.

Heilbron, Alexandra. "Was Anne a Real Girl?" *The Lucy Maud Montgomery Album.* Comp. Kevin McCabe and ed. Alexandra Heilbron. Toronto: Fitzhenry and Whiteside, 1999. 195–99.

Hilder, Monika B. " 'That Unholy Tendency to Laughter': L. M. Montgomery's Iconoclastic Affirmation of Faith in *Anne of Green Gables.*" *CCL: Canadian Children's Literature* 113–14 (2004): 34–55.

Hubler, Angela E. "Can Anne Shirley Help 'Revive Ophelia'? Listening to Girl Readers." *Delinquents and Debutantes.* Ed. Sherrie A. Inness. New York and London: New York UP, 1998. 266–84.

Jones, Mary E. Doody. "Breaking the Silence: Music and Elocution," *The Annotated Anne of Green Gables.* By L. M. Montgomery. Ed. Wendy E. Barry, Margaret Anne Doody, and Mary E. Doody Jones. New York: Oxford UP, 1997. 452–57.

———. "Education on P.E.I." *The Annotated Anne of Green Gables.* By L. M. Montgomery. Ed. Wendy E. Barry, Margaret Anne Doody, and Mary E. Doody Jones. New York: Oxford UP, 1997. 430–34.

———. "The Exceptional Anne: Child Care, Orphan Asylums, Farming Out, Indenturing, and Adoption." *The Annotated Anne of Green Gables.* By L. M. Montgomery. Ed. Wendy E. Barry, Margaret Anne Doody, and Mary E. Doody Jones. New York: Oxford UP, 1997. 422–29.

———. "Literary Allusion and Quotation in *Anne of Green Gables.*" *The Annotated Anne of Green Gables.* By L. M. Montgomery. Ed. Wendy E. Barry, Margaret Anne Doody, and Mary E. Doody Jones. New York: Oxford UP, 1997. 457–62.

Kajihara, Yuka. "An Influential Anne in Japan." *The Lucy Maud Montgomery Album.* Comp.

Kevin McCabe and ed. Alexandra Heilbron. Toronto: Fitzhenry and Whiteside, 1999. 432–38.

•Karr, Clarence. "Addicted to Books: L. M. Montgomery and the Value of Reading." *CCL: Canadian Children's Literature* 113–14 (2004): 17–33.

———. *Authors and Audiences: Popular Canadian Fiction in the Early Twentieth Century.* Montreal: McGill-Queen's UP, 2000.

Katsura, Yuko. "The Reception of *Anne of Green Gables* and Its Popularity in Japan." *Okayama Prefectural College: Design Department Kiyo* 2.1 (1995): 39–44.

———. "Red-haired Anne in Japan." *CCL: Canadian Children's Literature* 34 (1984): 57–60.

Keefer, Janice Kulyk. *Under Eastern Eyes: A Critical Reading of Maritime Fiction.* Toronto: U of Toronto P, 1987.

Kornfeld, Eve, and Susan Jackson. "The Female Bildungsroman in Nineteenth Century America: Parameters of a Vision." *Journal of American Culture* 10.4 (1987): 69–75.

Huse, Nancy. "Journeys of the Mother in the World of Green Gables. *Proceedings of the Thirteenth Annual Conference of the Children's Literature Association held at the University of Missouri-Kansas City, May 16–18, 1986.* Ed. Susan R. Gannon and Ruth Anne Thompson. Children's Literature Association, 1988. 60–63.

Kotsopoulos, Patsy Aspasia. "Our Avonlea: Imagining Community in an Imaginary Past." *Pop Can: Popular Culture in Canada.* Ed. Lynne van Luven and Priscilla L. Walton. Toronto: Prentice-Hall Canada, 1999. 98–105.

Kruk, Laurie. "Settling for 'the bend in the road': The Rehabilitation of the Artist in *Anne of Green Gables*." *Western Journal of Graduate Research* 1.1 (1989): 58–63.

Lefebvre, Benjamin. "Assessments and Reassessments." Editorial. *CCL: Canadian Children's Literature* 113–14 (2004): 6–13.

———. "Stand By Your Man: Adapting L. M. Montgomery's *Anne of Green Gables*." *Essays on Canadian Writing* 76 (2002): 149–69.

Lynes, Jeanette. "Consumable Avonlea: The Commodification of the Green Gables Mythology." *CCL: Canadian Children's Literature* 91–92 (1998): 7–21.

MacLeod, Anne Scott. "The Caddie Woodlawn Syndrome: American Girlhood in the Nineteenth Century." *A Century of Childhood, 1820–1920.* Ed. Mary Lynn Stevens. Heininger. Rochester, NY: Margaret Woodbury Strong Museum, 1984. 97–119.

MacLulich, T. D. "*Anne of Green Gables* and the Regional Idyll." *Dalhousie Review* 63 (1983): 488–501.

•———. "L. M. Montgomery and the Literary Heroine: Jo, Rebecca, Anne, and Emily." *CCL: Canadian Children's Literature* 37 (1985): 5–17.

———. "L. M. Montgomery's Portraits of the Artist: Realism, Idealism, and the Domestic Imagination." *English Studies in Canada* 11.4 (1985): 459–73.

McCabe, Kevin, compiler, and Alexandra Heilbron, ed. *The Lucy Maud Montgomery Album.* Markham, ON: Fitzhenry & Whiteside, 1999.

•McMaster, Juliet. "Taking Control: Hair Red, Black, Gold, and Nut-Brown." *Making Avonlea: L. M. Montgomery and Popular Culture.* Ed. Irene Gammel. Toronto: U of Toronto P, 2002. 58–71.

McQuillan, Julia, and Julie Pfeiffer. "Why Anne Makes Us Dizzy: Reading *Anne of Green Gables* from a Gender Perspective." *Mosaic* 34.2 (2001): 17–32.

Mills, Claudia. "Children in Search of a Family: Orphan Novels Through the Century." *Children's Literature in Education* 18.4 (1987): 227–39.

Mott, Frank L. *Golden Multitudes: The Story of Best Sellers in the United States.* New York: Bowker, 1947.

Nodelman, Perry. "Progressive Utopia: Or How to Grow Up Without Growing Up." *Proceedings of the Sixth Annual Conference of the Children's Literature Association 1979.* Ed. Priscilla A. Ord. Villanova Pennsylvania: Villanova University, 1980. 146–54.

———. "Some Heroes Have Freckles." *Children and Their Literature: A Readings Book.* Ed. Jill P. May. West Lafayette: Children's Literature Association of America, 1983. 41–54.

Pike, Holly E. "The Heroine Who Writes and Her Creator." *Harvesting Thistles: The Textual Garden of L. M. Montgomery.* Ed. Mary Henley Rubio. Guelph. ON: Canadian Children's P, 1994. 50–57.

Poe, K. L. "The Whole of the Moon: L. M. Montgomery's *Anne of Green Gables* Series." *Nancy Drew and Company: Culture, Gender, and Girls' Series.* Ed. Sherrie A. Inness. Bowling Green: Bowling Green State U Popular P, 1997. 15–35.

Reid, Verna. "From Anne of G. G. to Jacob Two-Two: A Response to Canadian Children's Fiction." *English Quarterly* 9.4 (1976/1977): 11–23.

Reimer, Mavis. "Introduction: The Anne Girl and the Anne Book." *Such a Simple Little Tale: Critical Responses to L. M. Montgomery's* Anne of Green Gables. Ed. Mavis Reimer. Metuchen, New Jersey: The Children's Literature Association and Scarecrow P, 1992. 1–10.

• Rev. of *Anne of Green Gables*, by L. M. Montgomery. *New York Times Book Review* 18 July 1908: 404.

• Rev. of *Anne of Green Gables*, by L. M. Montgomery. *Globe* [Toronto] 15 August 1908: 7.

• Rev. of *Anne of Green Gables*, by L. M. Montgomery. *Spectator* 13 March 1909: 426–27.

Robinson, Laura M. " 'A Born Canadian': The Bonds of Communal Identity in *Anne of Green Gables* and *A Tangled Web*." *L. M. Montgomery and Canadian Culture*. Ed. Irene Gammel and Elizabeth R. Epperly. Toronto: U of Toronto P, 1999. 19–30.

———. "Bosom Friends: Lesbian Desire in Montgomery's *Anne* Books." *Canadian Literature* 180 (2004): 12–28.

———. " 'Pruned Down and Branched Out': Embracing Contradiction in *Anne of Green Gables*." *Children's Voices in Atlantic Literature and Culture: Essays on Childhood*. Ed. Hilary Thompson. Guelph. ON: Canadian Children's P, 1995. 35–44.

———. "Remodeling An Old-Fashioned Girl: Troubling Girlhood in Ann-Marie MacDonald's *Fall on Your Knees*." *Canadian Literature* 186 (2005): 30–45.

Ross, Catherine Sheldrick. "Calling Back the Ghost of the Old-Time Heroine: Duncan, Montgomery, Atwood, Laurence, and Munro." *Studies in Canadian Literature* 4.1 (1979): 43–58.

• ———. "Readers Reading L. M. Montgomery." *Harvesting Thistles: The Textual Garden of L. M. Montgomery*. Ed. Mary Henley Rubio. Guelph. ON: Canadian Children's P, 1994. 23–38.

Rubio, Mary Henley. "*Anne of Green Gables*: The Architect of Adolescence." *Touchstones: Reflections of the Best in Children's Literature*. Ed. Perry Nodelman. West Lafayette: Children's Literature Association of America, 1985. 173–87. Reprinted in *Such A Simple Little Tale*, ed. Mavis Reimer. The ChLA & Scarecrow P: Metuchen, N. J., & London, 1992. 65–82.

———. "Introduction: Harvesting Thistles in Montgomery's Textual Garden." *Harvesting Thistles: The Textual Garden of L. M. Montgomery*. Ed. Mary Henley Rubio. Guelph. ON: Canadian Children's P, 1994.

———. "L. M. Montgomery: Where Does the Voice Come From?" *Canadiana: Studies in Canadian Literature/Etudes de Littérature Canadienne (Proceedings of the Canadian Studies Conference)*. Ed. Jørn Carlsen and Knud Larsen. Aarhus, Denmark: Department of English, 1984. 109–19.

———. "Satire, Realism, and Imagination in *Anne of Green Gables*." *L. M. Montgomery: An Assessment*. Ed. John Sorfleet. Guelph. ON: Canadian Children's P, 1975. 27–36.

———. "Subverting the Trite: L. M. Montgomery's 'Room of Her Own.' " *CCL: Canadian Children's Literature* 65 (1992): 6–39.

Rubio, Mary, and Elizabeth Waterston. Afterword. *Anne of Green Gables*. By L. M. Montgomery. New York: Signet Classics, 1987. 307–17.

Sabatini, Sandra. *Making Babies: Infants in Canadian Fiction*. Waterloo, ON: Wilfrid Laurier UP, 2003. 36–45.

Santelmann, Patricia Kelly. "Written as Women Write: *Anne of Green Gables* Within the Female Literary Tradition." *Harvesting Thistles: The Textual Garden of L. M. Montgomery*. Ed. Mary Henley Rubio. Guelph. ON: Canadian Children's P, 1994. 64–73.

Seeyle, John. *Jane Eyre's American Daughters: From the Wide, Wide World to Anne of Green Gables: A Study of Marginalized Maidens*. Newark: U Delaware P, 2005.

Selkowitz, Robert. "*Anne of Green Gables* Meets *The House of the Seven Gables*." *Kindred Spirits* (Summer) 1993: 12–13.

Sheckels, Theodore F. "Anne in Hollywood: The Americanization of a Canadian Icon." *L. M. Montgomery and Canadian Culture*. Ed. Irene Gammel and Elizabeth R. Epperly. Toronto: U of Toronto P, 1999. 183–91.

———. "In Search of Structures for the Stories of Girls and Women: L. M. Montgomery's Life-Long Struggle." *The American Review of Canadian Studies* 23.4 (1993): 523–38.

———. *Studies on Themes and Motifs in Literature: The Island Motif in the Fiction of L. M. Montgomery, Margaret Laurence, Margaret Atwood, and Other Canadian Women Novelists*. New York: Peter Lang, 2003: ix–43.

Smith, Edith K. "Adoption in Shades of Black and Red: the Taming of Topsy and Adoption of Anne." *Kindred Spirits* (Autumn 1996): 20–21.

Solt, Marilyn. "The Uses of Setting in *Anne of Green Gables*." *Children's Literature Association Quarterly* 9.4 (Winter 1985): 179–80.

Sorfleet, John R. "From Pagan to Christian: The Symbolic Journey of *Anne of Green Gables*." *Windows and Words: A Look at Canadian Children's Literature in English*. Ed. Aïda Hudson and Susan-Ann Cooper. Ottawa: U of Ottawa P, 2003. 175–83.

Squire, Shelagh J. "Literary Tourism and Sustainable Tourism: Promoting 'Anne of Green Gables' in Prince Edward Island." *The Journal of Sustainable Tourism* 4.3 (1996): 119–34.

Stallcup, Jackie E. " 'She Knew She Wanted to Kiss Him': Expert Advice and Women's

Authority in L. M. Montgomery's Works." *Children's Literature Association Quarterly* 26.3 (2001): 121–32.

Steffler, Margaret. "The Canadian Romantic Child: Travelling in the Border Country, Exploring the 'Edge.' " *CCL: Canadian Children's Literature* 89 (1998): 5–17.

Stoffman, Judy. "Anne in Japanese Popular Culture." *CCL: Canadian Children's Literature* 91–92 (1998): 53–63.

Thomas, Gillian. "The Decline of Anne: Matron vs. Child." *L. M. Montgomery: An Assessment.* Ed. John Sorfleet. Guelph. ON: Canadian Children's P, 1975. 37–41.

Trillin, Calvin. "Anne of Red Hair: What Do the Japanese See in *Anne of Green Gables?*" *The New Yorker* 5 Aug. 1996: 56–61.

Tye, Diane. "Multiple Meanings Called Cavendish: The Interaction of Tourism with Traditional Culture." *Journal of Canadian Studies* 29.1 (1994): 122–34.

———. "Women's Oral Narrative Traditions as Depicted in Lucy Maud Montgomery's Fiction, 1918–1939." *Myth and Milieu: Atlantic Literature and Culture, 1918–1939.* Ed. Gwendolyn Davies. Fredericton: Acadiensis, 1993. 123–35.

van Herk, Aritha. "How I Found *Anne of Green Gables*: An Appreciation." *Editions & Impressions: Collectors and Their Love of the Work of L. M. Montgomery.* Exhibition curated by Mary McConnell et al. Library and Archives Canada Cataloguing in Publication, 2005. Unpaginated.

•Waterston, Elizabeth. *Kindling Spirit: L. M. Montgomery's* Anne of Green Gables. Toronto: ECW Press, 1993.

Weale, David. " 'No Scope for Imagination': Another Side of Green Gables." *Island Magazine* 20 (1986): 3–8.

Weaver, Laura. " 'Plain' and 'Fancy' Laura: A Mennonite Reader of Girls' Books." *Children's Literature* 16 (1988): 185–90.

Weber, E. "L. M. Montgomery's 'Anne.' " *Dalhousie Review* 24.1 (1944): 64–73.

Weiss-Townsend, Janet. "Sexism Down on the Farm? *Anne of Green Gables.*" *Children's Literature Association Quarterly* 11.1 (1986): 12–15.

Whitaker, Muriel. " 'Queer Children': L. M. Montgomery's Heroines." *Such a Simple Little Tale: Critical Responses to L. M. Montgomery's* Anne of Green Gables. Ed. Mavis Reimer. Metuchen, NJ: The Children's Literature Association and The Scarecrow P, 1992. 11–22.

Willis, Lesley. "The Bogus Ugly Duckling: Anne Shirley Unmasked." *Dalhousie Review* 56.2 (1976): 247–51.

•Wood, Kate. "In the News: *Anne of Green Gables* and PEI's Turn-of-the-Century Press." *CCL: Canadian Children's Literature* 99 (2000): 23–42. See Kate Wood, "Patriotic Discourse: Historicizing Anne of Green Gables and PEI's Turn-of-the-Century Newspapers" (MA Thesis). U of Guelph, 1999.

Yokokawa, Sumiko. "The Forty Years of *Anne of Green Gables* in Japan." *Teaching and Learning Literature with Children and Young Adults* (Mar./Apr. 1996): 39–43.

## WEBSITES

Bala Museum: www.bala.net/museum/
[The museum website features material about Montgomery and her family's vacations in Bala (in the lake district of Ontario) which led to her novel *The Blue Castle* being set there.]

Canadian Children's Literature Database: www2.lib.uoguelph.ca/resources/ccl/
[Search for "L. M. Montgomery" to obtain a list of all the articles and reviews published on her in *CCL: Canadian Children's Literature* between 1975 and 2005. Click on the title for a summary of each.]

Confederation Centre (PEI): www.confederationcentre.com/lmm
[The Confederation Centre houses extensive LMM archival items and manuscripts, including the holograph of *Anne of Green Gables*, as well as an online Virtual Museum about LMM called "Picturing a Canadian Life: L. M. Montgomery's Personal Scrapbooks and Book Covers."]

L. M. Montgomery Institute (PEI): www.upei.ca/lmmi/
[The Institute hosts biennial conferences on LMM, fosters research, and houses a growing collection of books and memorabilia.]

Lucy Maud Montgomery Research Center, University of Guelph: www.lmmrc.ca
[This site features research materials, including fuller versions of the texts of many articles in the Norton Critical Edition of *Anne of Green Gables*, as well as materials from Guelph's extensive L. M. Montgomery Collection.]

National Library/Archives of Canada (ON): www.nlc-bnc.ca
    [Has extensive LMM archival holdings, including the originals of the G. B. MacMillan
    letters.]
Parks Canada (ON): www.parkscanada.gc.ca/
    [This site furnishes information about the Prince Edward Island National Park at Cav-
    endish, PEI, where LMM lived the first half of her life (1874–1911).]
Prince Edward Island Public Archives: www.gov.pe.ca/educ/archive/
Silver Bush Museum/Kindred Spirits Society (PEI): www.annesociety.org/
    [The website of the "Silver Bush Museum," formerly the home of LMM's beloved "Camp-
    bell cousins" where she was married in 1911.]
University of Guelph Library, Special Collections (ON): www.lib.uoguelph.ca
    [This links to other special archival holdings like the Scottish Collection that contextualize
    LMM's Scottish heritage and her life in Canada.]
University of Guelph Library, L. M. Montgomery Collection: www.lib.uoguelph.ca/
    resources/archives/special_collections/lmmontgomery_collection.htm
    [A direct link that gives information about the extensive collection of LMM documents
    and memorabilia.]
University of Prince Edward Island Library [Robertston Library]: www.upei.ca/library/
    [Holds an extensive collection of LMM books, articles, and memorabilia.]
Uxbridge-Scott Museum (ON): uxlib.com/museum/
    [LMM lived in Uxbridge from 1911–26, and this museum contains memorabilia from that
    period.]